Maggie Furey was born in north-east England. She is a qualified teacher, but has also reviewed books on BBC Radio Newcastle, been an advisor in the Durham Reading Resources Centre and organized children's book fairs. She lives in County Wicklow, Ireland.

Find out more about Maggie Furey and other Orbit authors by registering for the free monthly newsletter at www.orbitbooks.co.uk

AURIAN

Book One of the Artefacts of Power

Maggie Furey

www.orbitbooks.co.uk

An *Orbit* Book

First published in Great Britain by Legend 1994
Reprinted by Orbit 1999, 2000, 2002

© Maggie Furey 1994

The moral right of the author has been asserted.

ISBN 1 85723 973 3

Printed and bound in Great Britain by
Mackays of Chatham plc, Chatham, Kent

Orbit
An imprint of
Time Warner Books UK
Brettenham House
Lancaster Place
London WC2E 7EN

To Eric, for his unflagging support throughout a long, long
project, this book is dedicated with love.

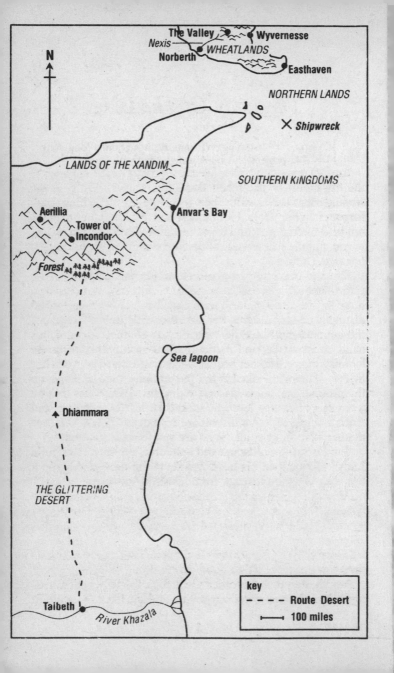

1
The Lady Of The Lake

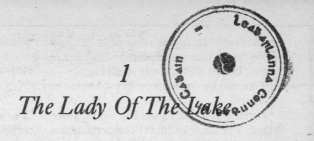

'Ho, little girl!'

Aurian jumped, the blue fireball dropping from her hands to the dry mould of the forest floor. She scuffed hastily at the smouldering leaves with her foot, the extinguishing spell forgotten in her panic. Her mother had forbidden her to come out here on her own, and it was too late to hide. Aurian turned to run, but the strangeness of the intruder in the glade stopped her in her tracks.

She had never seen a man before. He was tall and broad; clad all in brown leather beneath his heavy cloak, and bearing a huge sword at his side. The brown hair on his face looked distinctly odd, reminding her, together with his brown eyes, of the animals that were her friends. He stepped forward, his hand outstretched, and Aurian backed hastily away from the looming figure, another fireball beginning to form between her fingers. The man looked at her thoughtfully, then sat down on the ground, his hands clasped round his knees. Now that he was nearer her own level, he looked far less threatening, and Aurian began to feel a little more confident. These were her mother's lands, after all. 'Who are you?' she demanded.

'I'm Forral – swordsman and wanderer, at your service, little Lady.' He inclined his head gravely in the nearest thing to a bow that he could manage from his sitting position.

'Yes, but who *are* you?' Aurian insisted, still keeping a safe distance between them. 'What do you want? You're not supposed to be here, you know. The animals were supposed to keep you out.'

Forral smiled. 'They didn't bother me. I don't hurt animals – they don't hurt me. It's a good way to live.'

Aurian, despite her mother's warnings, found herself warming to him. It *was* a good way to live, and she liked his smile. It

1

seemed only fair to warn him what her mother would do to him if she found him wandering around her lands. 'Look . . .' she began, but he was already speaking.

'Can you by any chance direct me to the Lady of the Lake?'

'Who?'

Forral waved his hands in a vague gesture. 'You know – the Mage. The Lady Eilin. If I'm not mistaken, you must be young Aurian, her daughter. You're the image of Geraint.'

Aurian's mouth fell open. 'You knew my father?'

Forral's face was shadowed with sadness. 'Indeed I did,' he said softly. 'Your father and mother both. Geraint gave me my start in life. I was an orphan, only about your age, when he found me. He got me into the swordsman's school at the garrison in Nexis, and was a friend to me in all the years that followed.' He sighed. 'I was away soldiering in foreign parts, across the sea, when your father died. News of – the accident – never spread that far. I've only just returned, and when I heard –' For a moment, he struggled to find his voice. 'Well, I came at once. I'm here to offer my services to your mother.'

'She won't want you.' The words were out of her mouth before Aurian realized her tactlessness. It seemed an awful thing to say, when he had come so far. And she liked him already. In all her nine years, Aurian could remember no other human company save that of her mother, and Eilin had little time to spare for her daughter. She was too preoccupied with her Great Task. With only the animals for companionship, Aurian's life was a lonely one. Desperately she cast around for a way to explain, so as not to hurt her new friend's feelings. 'You see,' she said, 'My mother never has visitors. She's so busy that she hardly ever sees me.'

Forral looked her up and down. Had Aurian had a normal upbringing she might have been embarrassed by the torn grey shift she was wearing, the tangles in her red curls, the smears on her face and the dirt ingrained into her bare knees. As it was she returned his gaze unselfconsciously. 'Who looks after you, then?' he asked at last.

Aurian shrugged. 'Nobody.'

The big man frowned. 'Then it's high time somebody did. Speaking of which, are you supposed to be doing that?' He

2

pointed at the forgotten fireball that still danced over the palm of her hand. Aurian snuffed it hastily and hid her hands behind her back, wishing that she could hide her guilty expression so easily.

'Well . . . not exactly,' she confessed. 'But it was an emergency.' She bit her lip. 'You won't tell on me, will you?'

Forral seemed to be thinking it over. 'All right. I won't tell – this time,' he added sternly. 'But don't do it again, do you hear me? It's very dangerous. And don't think I didn't notice what you were up to when I arrived. It wasn't an emergency then, was it?' Aurian felt her face turn crimson, and Forral grinned. 'Come on, youngster, let's go and see your mother.'

'She won't be very pleased,' Aurian warned him, but she could tell he didn't believe her.

They set off up the tree-covered slope; Forral leading his tired horse and the skinny, gangling child mounted bareback on her shaggy brown pony. Cool autumn sunlight filtered through the naked branches, gilding the deeply drifted leaves that crackled underfoot. At the top of the long rise, the woods came to an abrupt end. The child halted, her expression closed and grim.

'Gods preserve us!' Forral gazed at the devastation below him, hardly able to believe his eyes. The news of Geraint's accident had come as a shock, but he had never expected anything on this scale. The vast, barren crater stretched beyond the ridge, as far as the eyes could see. It was almost more than the swordsman could bear, to witness such proof of his friend's violent end. Geraint, the most brilliant and impetuous of the Magefolk, favourite candidate to be the next Archmage. Arrogant and stubborn, as were all his kind. Tall, red-headed Geraint of the explosive temper, the expansive laugh, the endless joy of life, and the kindness of heart to befriend a ragged young boy who dared to dream, had killed himself down there.

Geraint had dared to dream, too, Forral thought sadly. Eight years ago he had tried, using the ancient, half-comprehended magic of the lost Dragonfolk, to harness vast amounts of magical energy in order to pass instantly from world to world, with disastrous results. It was said that Geraint had come perilously close to destroying the earth, and it was already clear that his name would be cursed through generations of Mage and Mortal alike. Forral preferred to believe that his friend, recognizing the danger too late, had given his life to confine the damage to as small an area as possible. Even so, the deep crater below was at least five leagues across; its sides a cracked and twisted mess of melted rock, its sloping floor like rippled black glass. In the centre of the lifeless waste, the swordsman's eyes caught the gleam of sunlight on water.

Forral had no idea how long he stood there, dismayed by the destruction Geraint had wrought. At last he became aware of the child gazing up at him.

'My mother hasn't got this far,' she said in a small, flat voice. 'I told you she was busy. There's a lot to do.'

The swordsman was filled with pity for the girl, growing up neglected and friendless in this bleak wasteland. Were the rumours true, that Eilin had lost her sanity with the death of her beloved soulmate? An adept in Earth-magic, it was said that she had buried her grief in her obsession to restore to fruitfulness the devastation caused by Geraint's tragic mistake. For the child's sake, he pulled himself together and tried to look cheerful, but his heart was sinking as they went on their way.

They had some difficulty getting Forral's horse down to the floor of the crater, but Aurian's sure-footed pony had few problems. The girl could ride like a centaur, and was accustomed, no doubt, to negotiating the slippery, folded terrain in the bottom of the massive bowl. It must be terrible here in summer, Forral thought as they rode along. Even now, the glass-like rock was throwing up heat and shimmering reflections from the pallid autumn sun. Water had gathered in the bottoms of some of the deeper folds, but the only sign of life was the occasional bird flying overhead.

Aurian finally broke the long silence between them. 'What was my father like?'

The question took Forral by surprise, and he was aware of the plea that lay behind the words. 'Hasn't your mother told you?'

'No,' she replied. 'She won't talk about him. She said that

4

this was all his fault.' She gestured around her, her voice quavering. 'She said he'd done a bad thing, and that it was our duty to make up for it.'

Forral shuddered. What had happened to Eilin? That was far too terrible a burden to lay on a child! 'Nonsense,' he said firmly. 'Geraint was a good, kind man, and a true friend to me. What happened was an accident. He didn't do this on purpose, pet. He made a mistake, that's all – and don't let anybody tell you otherwise.'

Aurian's face brightened. 'I wish I could remember him,' she said softly. 'Will you tell me about him as we ride?'

'Gladly.'

About two leagues from the centre of the bowl, the ground began to level off to a smooth surface with a slight downward slope. Soon the rock was covered with a thin layer of soil, and tiny, struggling plants began to appear. By the time the lake came into view again they were riding on wiry turf starred with daisies, and passing thickets of hawthorn, blackberry and elder that were bowed down beneath a rich harvest of fruit and alive with birds. Groves of shapely trees stood along the green shore, some still bearing apples and pears. Forral could not help but be impressed by the scale of Eilin's accomplishments in eight short years. A pity she couldn't have lavished the same attention on the child.

The lake was large and round, formed by water draining into the bottom of the crater. In the centre stood an island, obviously man- or Mage-made, that was connected to the shore by a slender wooden bridge. On the island a tower rose above the lake like a spear of light. Forral caught his breath. The ground floor was surrounded by gardens and built of black stone, but above it was an airy, glittering structure of crystal that soared high above the gleaming water. The ethereal building was topped by a slender glass spire on which a single point of light glowed like a fallen star. 'Dear gods, it's lovely!' he gasped.

Aurian looked at it dourly. 'It's where we live.' She shrugged and dismounted, setting her pony free with a farewell pat. Forral did likewise, on her assurance that his horse would stay nearby where there was grazing. Leaving his saddle under a tree, he followed the girl across the bridge.

A white-sanded path led through Eilin's gardens, past neat rows of late-season vegetables, herb-beds laid out in a precise, intricate mosaic of varied greens, and banks of fiery autumn flowers in which sat a cluster of beehives, their occupants humming busily among the copper-gold blooms as they made the most of this last, rare warm spell before winter. As he followed the child into the tower, Forral reflected that the Mage had managed to support herself and her daughter very well in their isolation, though he wondered how Eilin obtained grain, cloth, and other necessities that could not be won from the valley's soil.

The outer door of the tower led straight into the kitchen, which was obviously the main living area. Its walls were hewn out of the dark stone of the tower's base, giving it a cave-like appearance made cosy by the glow of the pot-bellied metal stove in the corner. Coloured rugs of woven wool brightened the floor, and there was a scrubbed wooden table with benches tucked beneath. Two chairs with padded seats were pulled up near the stove, and shelves and cupboards lined the walls, making the most of the cramped space. Two doors hid other rooms, and Aurian gestured to the one on the right. 'That's my room,' she informed the swordsman. '*She* sleeps upstairs, to be near her plants.'

A delicate, twisting metal staircase led to the upper storeys. Aurian hesitated at the bottom, gesturing for Forral to precede her. His boots striking bell-like notes on the vibrating metal treads, Forral climbed the stairs, wondering at the look of trepidation on the child's face.

Looking into the glass rooms of the tower as they led off the staircase, Forral saw the practical purpose behind the building's exuberant design. The chambers were filled with benches, on which stood trays of earth planted with young seedlings that basked in the warmth of the afternoon sunlight trapped by the crystal walls. A fine spray, seemingly appearing from nowhere, filled the air with moisture, and Forral's skin prickled with the thick build-up of magic. He was sure that the plants were actually growing before his eyes. When he finally found the Mage in one of the upper rooms, she was too preoccupied to notice him. 'Go away, Aurian,' she muttered,

6

without looking up. 'I've told you not to bother me when I'm working.'

Eilin had aged, the swordsman thought. It surprised him. Magefolk, like Mortals, could be killed by illness or accident, but otherwise they lived as long as they wanted, dying only when they chose to leave the world and preserving their physical forms at whatever age they wished. Forral remembered Eilin as a vibrant young woman, but now her dark hair was streaked with grey and her forehead was furrowed. Deep, bitter lines tugged at the corners of her mouth, and she looked pale and pitifully thin in her patched and faded robes.

'Eilin, it's me – Forral,' he said, stifling his dismay. He stepped forward, holding out his arms to hug her, and recoiled as her face twisted with rage at the sight of him.

'Get out!' Eilin snapped. She bore down on the child, and hit her across the face. 'How dare you bring him here!'

Aurian dodged behind Forral. 'It wasn't my fault,' she wailed.

Forral, anger boiling inside him, turned to put an arm around her. 'Are you all right?'

Aurian nodded, biting her lip, her pale face branded with an ugly red mark. Forral saw tears in her eyes, and gave her a quick hug.

'Go downstairs and wait for me by the bridge,' he told her softly.

When the girl had gone, the swordsman turned back to Eilin. 'That wasn't very fair,' he said coldly.

'There's no such thing as fair, Forral – I found that out when Geraint died. The wretched child should have told you that I never see anyone!'

'She did. And I ignored it. Do you want to hit me now?' He was fighting hard to keep his anger in check.

Eilin turned away, avoiding his eyes. 'I want you to go away. Why did you come here?'

'I came as soon as I could, when I heard what had happened to Geraint. I wish it had been sooner. It might have saved you from turning into a bitter old woman.'

'How dare you!'

'It's the plain truth, Eilin. But I came to offer you my service for Geraint's sake, and that still stands.'

7

Eilin stalked away to the far side of the room, her movements jerky with anger. 'Curse you, Mortal! Fickle and faithless, like all your kind! What use is your service now? Where were you and your service eight years ago, when I needed you? You were Geraint's friend – he listened to you! With your help I might have dissuaded him from his insanity! But no – you had an itch to wander – to see the world. Well, I hope the experience was enough to recompense you for the death of a friend! Your service comes far too late, Forral! Get out of here, and don't come back!'

Hardened warrior though he was, Forral flinched from Eilin's bitter words. His grief at Geraint's death was still raw, and her accusations contained just enough truth to hurt. Perhaps it would be as well if he did go ... Then Forral remembered the child. 'No.' He squared his shoulders. 'I'm not leaving, Eilin. It's obviously been bad for you to be alone like this, and the child needs someone to care for her. Get used to the fact that I'm staying, because there's nothing you can do about it.'

'Oh, isn't there?' She whirled, and Forral saw too late that she held her staff in her hand. The floor seemed to drop away beneath him, and a loud roaring filled his ears. His vision exploded in a burst of coloured lights and he gasped with pain as a brief wrenching sensation tore through his body. Then the ground came up to hit him, hard.

He opened his eyes gingerly. He was lying on a smooth carpet of turf on the other side of the bridge. He stared across the calm waters at the island with its tower and gave himself up to some serious swearing. The girl came running across the bridge, her bare feet echoing on the planks. She skidded to a halt beside him. 'She threw you out, then.' She didn't sound in the least surprised, but he read anxiety in her face. He sat up and groaned.

'What the blazes was that?'

'An apport spell.' Aurian sounded proud of knowing the right word. 'She's good at those – it's how she moved all the soil into the Valley. She's had a lot of practice.'

'An apport spell, eh?' Forral frowned, running his fingers distractedly through his curling brown hair. 'Aurian, how far could she move me with that spell?'

The child shrugged. 'About as far as she did, I think. You're heavier than the loads she usually moves. Why?'

'I want to be sure she can't hurl me right out of the Valley. It's an unpleasant way to travel!'

'I think she expects you to ride the rest of the way,' Aurian said seriously, and Forral burst out laughing.

'I just bet she does! Well, she's in for a surprise. Aurian, how would you like to help me set up camp?'

The girl's face lit up with incredulous delight. 'You mean you're staying?'

'It'll take more than a few wizardly shenanigans to chase me off, lass. Of course I'm staying!'

It was the happiest afternoon of Aurian's life. She and Forral set up his camp in a copse of sturdy young beeches that grew to the left of the bridge. She worried about his choice of spot, knowing he'd be safer out of her mother's sight, but Forral simply laughed. 'This is exactly what I want, youngster. Whenever Eilin looks out of her windows she's going to see me right here. I intend to be a thorn in your mother's side until she gives up this nonsense!'

The camp looked very good, Aurian thought. She wished she could live there. Forral had slung a rope between two sturdy trees and untied a rolled sheet of oiled canvas from behind his saddle. He hung this over the rope so that both sides reached the ground, then pulled the two sides apart and weighed them with stones to form a rough tent.

'But the wind will blow through,' Aurian objected.

Forral shrugged. 'I've put up with worse.' He was cross, though, when she told him that he couldn't burn any of the wood in the Valley. Her mother had set spells to protect it, and brought her own fuel in from outside. Aurian had a hard time convincing him, but to her relief he finally gave in, though with ill grace. 'I can live without a fire for now, but Eilin had better hurry up and come to her senses before winter,' he growled.

When her mother called her in at dusk there was trouble, of course. Eilin, gazing tight-lipped out of the window at Forral's camp, forbade Aurian to speak to him, or go anywhere near him. But the swordsman's cheerful defiance had filled her with new-found courage. 'I will talk to him, and you can't stop me!' she blurted.

Eilin stared at her in amazement, her face darkening with anger. Aurian's rebellion earned her a thrashing, but it only increased her determination. When it was over she turned on her mother. 'I hate you!' she sobbed, 'and you won't stop me seeing Forral no matter what you do to me!'

Eilin's eyes blazed. 'Don't count on it. He won't be here for long.'

'He will! He promised!'

'We'll see about that,' Eilin said grimly.

Early next morning, Aurian let herself out of the tower and crept across the bridge. She had bread tied up in a cloth for Forral's breakfast, and cheese from her mother's goats that grazed the lake shore. When she reached the copse, she stopped dead. The swordsman's camp had vanished beneath a dense cluster of bristling vines that had sprung up overnight. Her mother's work, of course.

'Forral,' Aurian called frantically, tugging at the unyielding creepers, 'Forral!'

After a moment, there came a rustling from within the thicket, followed by copious swearing. It took the swordsman the better part of the morning to hack his way out. When he finally emerged, green and grimy, the vines began to collapse in on themselves, and within minutes they had withered away to dust. Forral looked at Aurian. 'This is going to be tougher than I thought,' he said.

The following morning the vines were back. Aurian stole Forral an axe from her mother's storeroom. The next day it was a blackberry thicket with long sharp thorns. Forral suggested that Aurian gather the berries before they vanished, and when he had hacked himself free, they had them for breakfast. It began to turn into a game between them, and Aurian's loneliness vanished in her new friend's company. In those few days she found herself laughing and smiling more than she had done in her life. She introduced him to her animal friends. Shy birds, elusive deer or fierce wildcats from the forest – they all flocked happily to Aurian and she reached out to them with her mind, relaying their simple emotions to Forral. She was

10

disappointed that he couldn't communicate with them himself, though. She thought everybody could do that.

The swordsman could do many other things, however. He was a genius at inventing games, and had a fund of stories about his life as a soldier, or about princesses and dragons and heroes. Forral was Aurian's hero, and she adored him. She never told him how her mother had beaten her, in case it made more trouble, but to her relief she was no longer forbidden to see him. Instead, Eilin found many long and onerous tasks in the garden to occupy her daughter's time, but they were completed twice as fast with Forral helping. Aurian knew better than to broach the subject with her mother, and contented herself with stealing food for him whenever Eilin's back was turned.

The Mage, however, had not given up. On the fourth day, Forral's shelter was surrounded by a forest of stinging nettles. Forral looked very grim when he emerged, and Aurian, handing him dock leaves for his stings, was afraid he would decide to leave after all. But as he rubbed the soothing herb over his blotched hands and face, the swordsman glared at the tower. 'We'll see who gives up first,' he muttered through clenched teeth. 'She's bound to run out of ideas sooner or later.'

As autumn gave way to the first frosts of winter, matters continued in a similar vein. Eilin's speciality was Earth-magic, and she tried to dislodge her unwelcome guest with all the powers at her command. One night the level of the lake rose mysteriously, and Forral's camp was flooded. Another afternoon he and Aurian returned from a walk to find goats eating his blankets and gear. Eilin set the birds that roosted in the grove to attack him, but Aurian scolded them firmly and put a stop to that. She had less success with the ants, however. The day they struck, it took hours to get them out of Forral's clothes and bedding.

One grey, chilly morning, Aurian went out with Forral's stolen breakfast and a flask of her mother's blackberry wine. It would cheer him up, she thought. As she reached the other side of the bridge, an anguished yell came from the camp. When Aurian arrived, panting, there was no sign of the swordsman. Trembling, she peered into his shelter.

11

Forral was sitting bolt upright, paralysed with terror and covered in hundreds of writhing snakes, which were so thickly intertwined that it was impossible to tell where one began and another ended. Aurian, wondering where her mother had found them all, felt sorry for the poor things. It was too cold for them to be out and about, and not surprising that they clustered around the one source of heat – Forral's body. But the swordsman was her friend, and he needed her help. Aurian sighed and reached out with her mind to the serpents. 'Shoo,' she said firmly, speaking out loud for Forral's benefit. One by one and with great reluctance, the snakes disentangled themselves and slunk out of the tent.

Forral's face was absolutely white, and his hand trembled as he mopped his brow. She handed him the flask of wine and he drained it without pausing for breath. Aurian, in the meantime, was busy with her own angry thoughts. 'That does it!' she said suddenly, making Forral look up in surprise. 'How dare she! All those poor snakes!'

'Poor snakes?' the swordsman echoed in a strangled voice.

'They'll die,' she replied impatiently. 'It's far too cold for them. I don't know what she's thinking of.'

He stared at her in disbelief. 'Poor *snakes*?'

Aurian peeped out of the shelter, where the snakes waited, sluggish with cold and obviously hoping to be readmitted. 'They can't stay outside,' she said.

'I hope you weren't proposing to move them back in here.'

Aurian frowned, thinking hard. Then a wonderful idea struck her. 'I know!' Reaching out with her mind, she addressed the snakes.

Forral joined her as she watched the last of the serpents making its way across the wooden bridge. 'Where are they going?'

Aurian turned to him with a broad grin. 'Where is the warmest place you can think of around here?'

A slow smile spread across Forral's face as he perceived her plan. 'You dreadful child!' He roared with laughter and swept her off her feet in a great bear hug.

They were halfway through breakfast when Eilin discovered the snakes in her plant rooms. A shriek of outrage resounded

12

across the lake. Aurian turned to Forral. 'It looks as if I'm in trouble again,' she grinned, 'but it was worth it. At least mother will have to send the poor things back where they came from.'

But Eilin had only to wait. A few days later Aurian awakened, shivering, in her little room off the kitchen. She couldn't see out of the window for the thick blooms of frost that covered the inside of the glass. 'Forral!' she gasped. Snatching the blankets from her bed she shot out of the room, not even waiting to put on her only pair of shoes. Outside, the world was sparkling white and the air so cold it took her breath away. Aurian ran.

It took her a long time to wake him. When Forral finally opened his eyes, his teeth chattered and his lips were blue. Aurian helped him to sit up and draped her blankets around him, rubbing his hands and feet. Then, cupping her palms, she concentrated to make a fireball.

'I told you not to do that!'

Aurian was stricken by the harshness of Forral's voice. The blue flame died between her fingers, and tears sprang into her eyes. 'I only wanted to help,' she quavered.

Forral put his arm around her shoulders. 'I know, love. I'm sorry. I'm worried, that's all. If your mother doesn't change her mind . . . Well, I can't survive a winter without hot food and a fire, just living on bread and honey and cheese. You can see that, can't you? It may be that I'll be forced to leave.'

Aurian couldn't bear it. She flung herself into his arms, sobbing. 'Take me with you!'

Forral sighed. 'I can't, lass. You belong with your mother, and there are laws against stealing children. You don't want me to end up in prison, do you?'

'Then I'll run away! I won't stay here without you!'

The swordsman's arms tightened around her. 'Don't do that!' he said hastily. 'Anything could happen to you. We'll give it a few more days, shall we? Maybe things will change.'

Over the next few days the frosts were less severe, to Aurian's relief. She left all her blankets with Forral, telling him that she had others of her own and easing her conscience over the barefaced lie by assuring herself that it was for his benefit. Shivering in her bed each night was a small sacrifice, if only Forral would stay. Apart from nagging her mother, which only

13

incurred Eilin's wrath, there was nothing more she could do. As winter deepened, Aurian began to despair.

Then one night the snow came. When Aurian looked out of the window at suppertime the landscape had already been obscured by the blizzard. She couldn't eat her stew, knowing that Forral was out there, freezing, with no hot supper to warm him. Once more she begged and pleaded with Eilin to relent, almost hysterical with fear for Forral. Eventually her exasperated mother locked her in her room. Aurian pounded on the door until her fists bled and yelled herself hoarse. At last, exhausted, she threw herself on the bed and cried herself to sleep.

It was still night when she awakened. Her throat was sore and her eyes felt gritty, but the blood on her hands had dried. How long had she slept? Aurian leaned on the windowsill and peered out. The blizzard had worsened, and she could see nothing but driving snow. She gulped back a sob. Forral would die out there, and she would be left here with her cruel mother who had killed him. It was more than she could bear. She wished that she were dead, too. At least she'd be with Forral. The idea frightened her, but the more she thought about it, the more it made sense. Her mother wouldn't miss her. Aurian made her decision. She would go and find Forral, and they could die together.

The window catch was frozen shut. Aurian hammered at it with her shoe, muttering Forral's favourite curses, but it refused to budge. Then it occurred to her that if she was going to die, she wouldn't need the room again. Picking up a stool, she drove it through the window with a satisfying crash. Wind and snow came howling into the room, and a piece of flying glass cut her forehead. Wiping blood out of her eyes and praying that the storm had masked the noise from her mother, she laid her pillow over the jagged shards of glass in the bottom of the frame and climbed out.

The snow had drifted deep below the window, and Aurian sank almost over her head, gasping. The cold was intense. When she floundered out of the drift the wind hit her, flaying her face with flying snow. But it wasn't so deep here, and she could struggle forward with difficulty on feet that were already numb. She struck out towards the bridge, slipping and falling and picking herself up; bending into the gale that wiped out her footprints behind her.

Aurian stopped, uncertain. Where was the copse? She should have reached it ages ago! She was sure she had been going in the right direction, but the swirling snow made it impossible to see. I'm tired from crossing the bridge, she thought. That's why it's taking so long. The memory made her shudder. She'd been forced to slide across the slender, slippery span inch by inch, clinging to the frozen rail with numb fingers, terrified that the wind would blow her into the lake. Now she could hardly keep her frozen body moving, and she couldn't feel her hands and feet. Aurian was suddenly very frightened. She wasn't sure that she wanted to die after all, but she did want Forral very much. A tear froze on her face. 'Don't be stupid,' she scolded herself. 'The sooner you get going, the quicker you'll find him.' Bracing herself, she set off into the darkness once more.

It was so cold that Forral had stopped shivering. A bad sign. His shelter had blown down in the storm, but he had managed to snatch the tarpaulin just in time. He huddled in the lee of a tree with the canvas wrapped round him, toying with the idea of breaking into the tower. But it was useless, he knew. Eilin would only throw him out again. If she hadn't let him in by now, he had to face the fact that it was hopeless. 'Forral, you're a fool,' he muttered. 'What a senseless way to die!' He felt himself drifting into sleep, and knew that it would finish him. He wished he could have said goodbye to the child. The thought of Aurian nagged at him, keeping him from the sleep that tugged so strongly. 'Got to say goodbye to Aurian,' he mumbled. Hooking an arm over a low branch, he struggled stiffly to his feet. What was that? A faint, ghostly glimmer flickered through the whirling snow. Someone was coming towards him, carrying a lantern.

As the figure drew nearer, the swordsman recognized the slender silhouette of Eilin, her hair soaked into whipping, snakelike tendrils, her cloak blown back from her shoulders, her brown robe flattened by the wind against her bony frame and whitened by a clinging plaque of snow. The glimmer that he'd mistaken for a lantern was the bluish-white glow of a pale, cool ball of Magelight that hovered over the head of her staff.

'Forral, she's gone. Aurian is gone!' Eilin tugged at his arm, distraught. The swordsman stared at her. Somehow his brain wouldn't focus on her words. Eilin cursed and fumbled beneath her cloak, bringing out a small flask which she unstoppered and forced between his lips. The liquor seared a trail of fire down Forral's throat, making him gasp for breath. He had no idea what the stuff was, but it was effective. Within minutes he felt his limbs beginning to tingle painfully as the feeling returned to them. His mind was clearing rapidly.

'What did you say? Where's Aurian?'

'I told you! She's gone! I locked her in and she broke the window! There's blood everywhere and she's out in the storm and . . .'

'This is your fault!' Forral slapped her out of her hysterics, feeling grim satisfaction at her gasp of pain. With an effort he checked the urge to throttle her. They had to find the child. 'Come on,' he shouted, plunging ahead into the blizzard, leaving Eilin floundering behind. Common sense told him that he would never find Aurian in this blinding storm – that it was already too late – but he cast the thought savagely away from him. It hurt too much.

'Forral – wait!' Eilin cried, but the swordsman took no notice. Try as she might, she could not keep up with him. Another instant, and he had vanished without trace into the storm. The Mage cursed savagely. 'Oh, you fool!' she muttered. 'You hot-headed, idiot Mortal! Now both of you are lost!' For a moment Eilin stood oblivious of the freezing gale and paralysed by guilt. Geraint would have been furious to see how she had put his daughter and his friend at risk! Forral was right to say it was all her fault. Had she only let him stay with Aurian in the tower, this tragedy would never have happened. Then she gathered her wits. She had alerted those of Aurian's animal friends who could endure the storm to search for the child, but Forral could not understand them. For the swordsman, she would need a surer guide. Such a guide could be summoned, she knew – but the risk was appalling!

Mortals had ceased long ago to believe in the Phaerie. Only the Magefolk knew the truth behind the tales of a fey and ancient race that wielded the powers of the Old Magic – for the ancient Magefolk, fearing their mischief and meddling, had exiled them outside the world, imprisoning them in a mysterious Elsewhere beyond the realms of Mortal ken. The Phaerie could not return into the world unless summoned by a Mage – and such a summoning bore a price. But it was her only chance to save the swordsman and her child. Gripping her staff with shaking fingers, Eilin spoke the words that would summon the Lord of the Phaerie.

Forral staggered blindly through the snowdrifts, fighting cold and exhaustion, feeling as though he was trapped in an endless nightmare. The effects of Eilin's potion were wearing off, and his aching limbs were stiff with cold. Each time he slipped and fell, it seemed less likely that he would ever get up again. But lost as he was, spent as he was, he refused to give in. 'What sort of feeble excuse for a warrior are you?' he goaded himself, to blot out the fear that coiled within his breast, far colder than the blizzard outside. 'Aurian needs you! No, by the gods – if this is the bloody end, you'll die on your feet, still searching!'

For a while he had left the woods, but now he was back in them, staggering like a drunken man on untrustworthy legs. The going was easier here – the trees broke the force of the wind, and Forral could use their branches for support. And thank the gods – that must be Eilin ahead of him. He could see her glimmering light dancing between the treetrunks. 'Eilin!' he bawled, with all the force that his labouring lungs could muster. Curse the stupid woman – why didn't she hear him? 'Eilin!' But she did not stop – and Forral, terrified of losing her, had no choice but to follow the eerie glow. Suddenly, the trees came to an end – and there, flickering fitfully through a whirl of snow, were *two* lights, side by side.

'Forral!'

He heard the Mage's voice. As the swordsman staggered towards her, he slipped and fell once more. When he picked himself up out of the snow, Eilin was bending over him, and the two lights had somehow become one. After a sip from Eilin's flask, Forral began to feel better. 'Thank goodness for that,' he muttered. 'I was seeing double there for a minute! Have you found her?'

'No – but I know she's close by. Can you go on?'

Forral nodded. 'Aurian,' he cried desperately, trying to pitch his voice over the keening storm. But wait – that was not the wind! Through the blizzard came the chilling howl of a wolf, eerie and triumphant. Forral stopped dead, transfixed with horror. 'No!' he whispered.

Eilin tugged at his arm, her face alight with joy. 'They've found her!' she shouted.

Forral flinched. Gods, was she truly insane? Did she really hate the child that much? Sickened beyond measure, he raised his fist to strike her down.

'Forral, no!' Eilin screamed. 'Those are Aurian's wolves – her friends! I called them to search for her!'

Stunned, Forral slowly lowered his arm. The wolf howled again. 'Hurry,' Eilin said.

Keeping a wary eye on the huge grey forms that surrounded him, Forral lifted the limp body out of the snow, feeling for a pulse with chill fingers. 'She's alive!' He could have wept with relief, but that was for later. 'We've got to hurry. Can you find your way back?'

'I can always find my way home,' the Mage retorted. She struggled along at his side with her Magelight, followed by the dozen or so lean and shaggy wolves that had been huddled round the child, keeping her alive with the warmth of their bodies. Their eyes never left Aurian's still form.

When Forral reached the tower the wolves followed him determinedly inside. Keeping out of the way, they watched as he and Eilin stripped off Aurian's wet clothes and laid her on a makeshift bed near the stove, wrapped in every quilt and blanket they could find. As Eilin set water to boil, Forral sat with the child, stroking the damp curls away from her bluish face with a trembling hand. 'Can't you do something?' he snapped.

'I am!' Eilin banged the pan down on the top of the stove, and water hissed as it slopped over on to the hot surface. Covering her face with her hands, the Mage burst into tears.

'It's too late for that now,' Forral said brutally. 'As soon as she's well – if she gets well – I'm taking her out of here, and you can do what you like about it.'

'No!' Eilin lowered her hands to stare at him. 'You cannot! I forbid it! Aurian is my child!'

'And what does that signify, when you do nothing but neglect her? The child needs love, Eilin!'

'I do love her, you dolt!'

The swordsman shook his head. 'I don't believe you, Eilin. If you did, you would show it.'

Eilin was stung by his words. 'And what would you know about it?' she retorted. She thought of her meeting with the awesome Lord of the Phaerie, who had agreed to find Forral and lead her to her child – for a price.

'Remember,' he had said, 'that this matter is not resolved between us. We will meet again, Lady – and when we do, I will claim my debt.' What he might ask of her Eilin shuddered to think, but it would be worth it. The Phaerie had saved her, in her folly, from causing Aurian's death. Believe what you like, Forral, she thought, but there are many ways to love – and more ways than one of showing it!

Forral looked on as with shaking hands the Mage concocted a stimulating tea from the dried herbs, berries and blossoms that hung in bunches in the kitchen. Once they had trickled some of the brew down Aurian's throat, the child breathed more easily and her colour began to return. Forral let out a deep breath, only now aware of his own soaked and frozen state. 'We could use some of that stuff,' he suggested.

Eilin filled two mugs and sat down beside him, handing him his steaming brew. At first she simply sat, still and abstracted, watching her sleeping child. Then at last she spoke. 'Forral, I owe you an apology. I've been a selfish fool.'

'A complete ass,' the swordsman agreed gently. He took her hand. 'It's been terrible for you, hasn't it?'

'You have no idea.' She shook her head. 'I warned him, you know – I begged him not to do it. I'm an Earth-Mage – I knew it was folly. But Geraint was always stubborn . . .'

19

'Not an uncommon trait among the Mageborn, is it?' Forral pointed out.

Eilin flinched. 'How dare you judge me, Mortal!' she flared, and he knew his words had struck home. 'Afterwards,' she went on, still glaring at him, 'people sought revenge. There were Mortals here, you know, before . . .' She shuddered. 'Aurian and I were in Nexis – she was only a baby – and we barely escaped with our lives. I wanted to undo the damage Geraint had done; to erase his memory. But as Aurian grew, she came to resemble him – do you know, the poor child will even inherit that hawk-profile of his when she's older? And her eyes change from green to grey when she's angry, just as his did. I can't look at her without seeing his face . . . Oh, gods, Forral, I hate him!'

'You think you hate him because he left you,' Forral said softly. 'You still love him, Eilin.'

'If he had loved me, would he have left me alone like this?' Her voice broke. 'I miss him so much!'

'Then let yourself mourn him. It's high time.'

Forral held her while she wept. 'You know,' he said at last, 'Geraint hasn't gone completely. He left part of himself here.' He indicated the sleeping child.

'I'm aware of that!' Eilin snapped.

'And that's the problem, isn't it? Don't take it out on her, Eilin. She's not responsible.'

Eilin sighed. 'When you came, you made me feel so guilty – that was why I wanted to be rid of you. You, a mere Mortal, forcing me to realize how I had failed my own child! But how can I help it, when . . .' She took a deep breath. 'Forral, will you stay and look after her? Aurian deserves more than I can give her. And she loves you.'

'And I love her. Of course I'll stay! That was the idea from the start, remember? It just took a long time to get it into that stubborn Mage head of yours. But that doesn't absolve you of responsibility, Eilin. You're still her mother, and I'll expect you to make an effort.'

Eilin nodded. 'I'll try, I promise. Thank you, Forral.' She leapt to her feet. 'Perhaps I should make some broth, for when she wakes. She had no supper . . .'

Forral gave her an encouraging smile. 'See how easy it is to care, Eilin, when you try?'

Aurian thought she must still be dreaming. There had been a terrible nightmare about being lost in the snow – and then there were her wolves – and now Forral, sitting in the kitchen with her mother. And Eilin never smiled at her like that.

'How are you feeling, love?' Forral's face cracked in a delighted grin.

'Forral?' Her voice came out as a feeble croak.

'It's all right – I'm here. Drink some of this.' Putting his arm around her, he propped her while he held a cup of warm broth to her lips. 'Better?' he asked.

'Everything hurts. And I'm cold.'

'I'm not surprised. Running off into the snow like that. You daft child!' His voice was gruff.

'I'm sorry.' Aurian glanced nervously at her mother. 'But it was an emergency.'

'Now where have I heard that excuse before?' Forral grinned. 'Well, I have news for you, young lady. I'm going to be looking after you from now on, so you'd better start behaving yourself!'

Aurian's eyes widened slowly. She looked at her mother. 'Is it true?' she whispered.

Eilin nodded. 'I asked Forral to stay. He can take better care of you than I have ever done.'

'Oh, thank you!' Beaming, Aurian reached up to hug her mother. Eilin froze, looking startled, then returned her daughter's embrace.

Forral smiled.

2

The Swordswoman

Forral had never guessed that taking care of a child would prove to be such hard work. He moved into the storeroom that led off the kitchen, and two or three happy days passed while Aurian helped him clear a living space amidst tools, seeds, sacks of grain and garden produce, round white cheeses, wrinkled apples, pots of honey and bottled fruit that Eilin had laid aside for winter. The resulting accommodation was cramped and spartan, but it was enough for a soldier's needs, and Forral had no objection to the mixed aromas of good food in his bedroom. The swordsman also took the time to board up Aurian's broken window until it could be repaired properly. When she complained that it made the room too dark he looked at her sternly. 'It's your own fault. You broke it, remember?' Aurian's jaw dropped.

After that the battles of will happened almost daily. Aurian had been allowed to run wild all her life, and though it wrenched Forral's heart to be firm with her, he knew it had to be done, for her own good. They fell out first over the matter of baths. Aurian refused point blank, protesting that she bathed in the lake in summer. Wasn't that enough? Forral handed her the soap and towel. 'Very well,' he said. 'Go and bathe in the lake, then.'

Aurian stared out of the window, wide-eyed with disbelief. Thick snow covered the ground and the deep, dark waters were rimmed with a broad band of ice. 'But . . .' she protested.

'Go on, get moving. You're smelling the place up,' he added callously.

Aurian's lip trembled, then the Magefolk stubbornness took over. She set her jaw and scowled. 'Right!' she snapped and stamped out, slamming the door behind her.

The obstinate little wretch had called his bluff! Forral,

horrified, ran after her. The lake was deep around the island, and in weather this cold, he placed no trust in the old tale that it was impossible to drown a Mage. He reached the bottom of the garden just in time to see Aurian jump into the freezing water.

With a curse, the swordsman leapt forward and grabbed a handful of her hair before she could flounder away from the bank. When he fished her out, she was already blue. He wrapped her in his cloak and carried her inside, dumping her straight into the steaming tub that he had placed in front of the stove. 'There,' he said, as her shivering subsided in the hot water. 'Isn't that better than the lake?'

Aurian glared at him.

'If you don't like it, I can always take you back out there,' he suggested.

After a moment the child dropped her eyes. 'Perhaps it's not so bad after all,' she said. Forral smiled, and produced a little wooden boat that he had made for her to play with.

Fortunately, once she got used to the idea, Aurian became so addicted to hot baths that his chief problem lay in getting her out of them. Persuading her to comb her hair was less easy, however. Her long, thick, glowing red curls were snarled with years' worth of tangles. The first time, it took Forral a terrible hour to get the mess sorted out while he held the struggling, shrieking child down. At last he threw down the comb, filled with guilt. Gods, I'd rather fight a dozen warriors, he thought, taking the sobbing little girl into his arms.

'You hurt me!' she accused him.

'I'm sorry, love. I know I did. But that was only because it had been left for so long. When you do it every day . . .'

'I'd rather die!'

'What a pity,' Forral sighed. 'You look so beautiful now.'

Aurian's head came up sharply. 'Me? Beautiful? Like the princess in your story?'

Forral looked into her face. The childish roundness was already going, and Eilin had been right. She would have her father's hawkish looks; angular and high-cheekboned, with the same fierce aquiline nose. 'You're the most beautiful girl I've ever seen,' he told her sincerely. 'It would be a shame if a

23

handsome prince came by and didn't like you because you hadn't combed your hair.'

'I don't want a stupid prince,' Aurian declared firmly. 'I'm going to marry you.'

The swordsman froze. This was a complication that he hadn't considered. 'Don't you think I'm a bit old for you?' he said lamely.

'How old are you?'

'Thirty.'

'That's not old.' Aurian shrugged. 'You said my father was ninety-six when he married my mother.'

Forral was lost for a reply. She was too young to understand the fundamental difference between Mortal and Magefolk.

'Don't you want to marry me?' Aurian looked hurt. 'You just said I was beautiful.'

'You are,' he reassured her, 'and I would love to marry you. But you're not old enough yet. We'll talk about it again when you grow up.'

'Promise?'

'Promise.' Hating himself, he added, 'But only if you comb your hair. I can't marry someone who looks like a hedge.'

Aurian sighed. 'Oh, all right, then.'

To Forral's relief, Eilin taught her daughter to braid the unruly mane. That solved the problem of most of the tangles, and Aurian began to take a delight in looking after her hair, although the speculative glances she cast his way as she did so gave the swordsman some cause for alarm. He knew how stubborn she could be, once she got an idea into her head.

When Forral had been about Aurian's age, Geraint had taught him to read. It was only now that he appreciated how he must have tried the Mage's patience. Eilin unearthed Geraint's old library, and Forral tried to select the books that would appeal to a child. They were old histories mostly, filled with tales of adventures and bravado, and they proved to be the same ones with which Forral had been taught. The wound of the swordsman's grief opened anew as he recalled his old friend's face, bent over the page as Geraint struggled patiently to explain the mystery to the baffled youth that had been himself.

Aurian hated it. Not used to sitting still and concentrating, she considered the whole business a waste of time. She took to hiding at lesson-times, and Forral came to bless his skill as a tracker. He would haul her back, Aurian protesting bitterly all the way, and she fought him so vehemently that Forral became concerned that their relationship would be irrevocably damaged.

In the end the swordsman resorted to subterfuge, pretending to give in. 'All right,' he told her with a shrug. 'If it's too difficult for you we won't bother.' Aurian scowled at him suspiciously. She knew by now that Forral always got his way in the end. Pretending to ignore her, he brewed some of Eilin's rosehip tea, a perfect antidote to the wintry weather. Stirring a dollop of honey into his cup, he sat back with his feet propped on the stove, opened the book of legends and began to read.

After a while, Aurian began to drift around the room, looking for something to do. The weather was much too bad to go out. Another blizzard was howling outside, and the wind rattled the frames of the thick crystal casement. Forral watched the child out of the corner of his eye. Eventually she approached him. 'Can't we play something?'

'Not now,' Forral said absently. 'I'm busy.'

Aurian's face fell. She hung around for a while, scuffling her feet. 'Forral, I'm bored,' she whined.

'I'm not,' he replied smugly. 'This story is much too exciting.'

Aurian stamped her foot. 'I don't believe you!' she shouted. 'You're only saying that to make me read the stupid thing!'

Forral winced. The child was too quick for her own good. Thinking quickly, he assumed an injured expression. 'Would I lie? If you don't believe me I'll read it to you.' Looking relieved, Aurian sat down at his feet.

It really was an exciting story. Forral had chosen it for that very reason. He glanced down at the child's rapt expression. When they reached the climax of the tale, where the brave young heroine was trapped on a mountain by savage goblins and trolls, he put the book down and yawned.

'Don't stop,' Aurian urged him anxiously, biting her lip. 'What happens next?'

25

Forral shrugged. 'I can't be bothered to read any more. I think I'll go for a nap.' Leaving the book on the chair, he went to his room, closing the door firmly on the child's outraged protests.

The swordsman returned an hour later to find Aurian poring over the book, tears of frustration in her eyes. 'It doesn't make sense,' she wailed. 'It's just little black marks, and I'll never find out what happened!'

Forral put his arm around her. 'That's just what I said to your father when he taught me with this book.'

Aurian's eyes widened. 'You did? What did he say?'

'Tough.' Forral grinned at the stunned expression on her face. 'He said that if I wanted to find out what happened, I would have to work hard and let him teach me.'

Aurian's face grew stormy. 'You tricked me! You rotten, sneaky beast!' She threw the book against the wall and ran off to her room, slamming the door.

She sulked for two days, refusing to speak to him. Eilin raised her eyebrows at the change, but forbore to comment. Forral missed Aurian's cheerful company more than he would have thought possible, and began to blame himself for pushing the child too far. In the end he could bear her angry silence no longer. 'I'm sorry,' he told her. 'You're absolutely right. I was rotten and sneaky, and I apologize. I'll read the rest of the story if you want.'

Aurian threw her arms around him, her face alight with her smile. 'I love you, Forral.'

Forral felt his throat tighten. 'I love you too,' he said huskily. 'Why don't you go and fetch the book?'

She drew back and looked at him thoughtfully. 'You really do want me to learn to read, don't you?'

He nodded. 'It means a lot to me, Aurian. You can't imagine how important it is.'

Aurian sighed, looking like a prisoner about to be dragged to the scaffold. 'I suppose we'd better get started, then.'

It took the child a long time to grasp the rudiments of reading. Forral suspected that much of the fault lay with him, for Aurian was intelligent enough, and he knew that he lacked skill as a teacher. All he could do was substitute patience for

26

skill and keep their lessons short, stopping before Aurian became too tired or despondent. Then he would read to her, hoping that she would be encouraged to want to read the stories for herself. Eventually it worked. By the end of the long winter, Aurian was reading everything she could lay her hands on, and Eilin had to make sure that Geraint's spell books were well hidden.

Forral taught Aurian many other things that winter. He told her of Nexis, queen of cities, which lay to the southwest and contained the Academy of the Magefolk, where all magical lore was studied under the rule of the Archmage Miathan. He told her of the Nexis garrison that housed the city's crack fighting force, and was the greatest military school in the land. Aurian learned what lay beyond her Valley – the nearby northern hills, where men lived mainly by forestry, and farming cattle and sheep; the east coast, famed for fishing; the countryside south and west, where clay for pots was dug, and people grew grain, flax, and grapes for wine that was marketed by the powerful Merchants' Guild of Nexis, who coordinated trade between farmers and fishers, and the craftsmen of villages and towns.

They spent hours by the fire as Aurian listened, enthralled, to Forral's stories of mercenary life in the secretive Southern Kingdoms across the sea, with their fierce, swarthy-skinned warriors. She would sit at his feet, wide-eyed and entranced, while he spoke of ships and storms, and the mighty whales who were lords of the deep. He told her bloodcurdling tales of ancient legend about the lost Dragonfolk – powerful Mages in their own right whose eyes flashed killing fire; or the fearsome race of winged warriors who were said to inhabit the southern mountains. Though the swordsman was no scholar, he taught her what little history he knew, including the names and natures of the gods themselves: the goddesses, Iriana of the Beasts, Thara of the Fields, and Melisanda of the Healing Hands; and the gods – Chathak, god of fire, the special deity of warriors; Yinze of the sky; and Ionor the Wise, the god of Oceans who was called the Reaper of Souls in the pantheon of the Southern Kingdoms. Aurian marvelled, and learned.

Spring that year came in a single, glorious burst that quickly

27

erased the last traces of the terrible winter. Trees leapt into leaf and blossom, and flowers suddenly appeared everywhere. Once again the woods around the lake became alive with birdsong. Aurian and Forral took to spending much of their time outdoors in the sunshine, searching for early greens to supplement their limited winter diet, and helping Eilin with her work of planting and extending the fertile land beyond the lake.

Now that the woods were burgeoning with life, Forral began to think of hunting. They had eaten little meat over the winter – mostly the tough, salted meat of the male kids borne by Eilin's goats the previous year. Though the Mage had tried to disguise the strong flavour in well seasoned soups and stews, Forral was frankly sick of the stuff. Some rabbit might go down well, he thought, or perhaps a bird – anything but goat! During his mercenary career, the swordsman had learned some skill with bow and snare, and somewhat hesitantly he broached the subject with Eilin. Since the Earth-Mage lived at one with the land and its creatures, he half-expected an angry denial. He also feared that Aurian might be upset if one of her friends appeared on the supper table. So Forral was staggered by the Mage's reply to his diffident question. 'By all means, Forral. If you want to hunt, Aurian will show you how we do it in the Valley.'

On a golden evening, Aurian led Forral through the birch grove and the deeper mixed woodland beyond, until they came to a wild grassy area dotted with clusters of gorse and bramble. The spaces between their roots were laced with a multitude of runs and holes. 'This is where the rabbits live,' Aurian told him softly. 'They'll soon be coming out to feed.'

Forral nodded, wondering what she planned to do. Aurian had forbidden him to bring his bow, and had dismissed his snares as cruel.

'Stay quiet,' the child whispered. She stepped out from the trees, wrapping a thick piece of cloth around her wrist. Lifting her arm, she shrilled a piercing whistle. For a moment, nothing happened. Then, far above, a tiny dot appeared in the vault of the sky. The speck plummeted – grew – took shape. Forral heard the rushing whisper of wind through feathers and a harsh cry. A winged form swooped to Aurian's wrist and clung there, extending its short, streamlined wings for balance as it rubbed its proud head and cruel, curved beak caressingly along her face.

Aurian glowed with delight. 'This is Swiftwing,' she said. 'At least, I call him that.' The falcon gave Forral a scornful sideways glance with its great dark eye, hissed at him through open beak, and returned to nibbling at her hair. For a moment the child lingered, eye to eye in soundless communion with the fierce bird of prey; then with a swift, upward jerk of her arm, she launched him into the sky, where he climbed in spirals to hover, fluttering, above them. Aurian drew the bemused swordsman into the shelter of the trees. 'Now we wait,' she murmured.

After a time, the rabbits began to emerge from the bushes to feed, venturing timidly forth with their gentle, rocking gait. Forral felt Aurian's hand clutch his arm. 'Now,' she breathed. Above them, the falcon folded his wings and dropped like a stone. Forral gasped. It would smash into the . . .

The hawk's wings flashed open at the last second. He levelled out a bare inch from the ground, hitting the targeted rabbit in a cloud of flying fur and bowling it over and over. Skimming over the grass at fingertip height, the hawk circled back to the limp brown form that lay motionless and stunned. Talons extended, he settled on the creature and finished it with one swift blow from his beak.

Forral blinked, and remembered to breathe. The whole episode had happened almost too quickly for his brain to register. He followed Aurian as she ran out to the hawk. 'Well done,' she told the bird. 'Oh, very well done!' Swiftwing hopped off the rabbit, and settled into the grass to wait. Aurian sighed as she picked up the dead creature. 'Poor little thing,' she murmured, briefly stroking its fur before she stowed it in her bag.

'Doesn't it bother you, this killing?' the swordsman asked her curiously.

'Of course.' She turned to him, her expression serious and somehow more adult than he had seen it before. 'It's very sad, Forral, but it happens. Swiftwing needs to eat, and so do his mate and babies. Rabbits are rather big for him – that's why he often stuns them first – but he eats them, and so do we. We only take what we need, and he kills quick and clean, not like snares.' She smiled dreamily at the falcon. 'And he's so beautiful . . .' For a moment she was lost for words, but Forral understood, for the swift, fearless flight of the hawk had touched his own heart. 'He makes me feel as though I'm up there, flying with him,' Aurian finished softly, then shook herself, and whistled Swiftwing back to her wrist; all business once more. 'We'll need to beat the bushes to bring the rabbits out again – they're scared now,' she said. 'If you thought that was good, wait till you see him with a moving target. How many rabbits did you say you wanted, anyway?'

Forral shook his head in amazement. Aurian never failed to astonish him – and this time, he had learned something from her.

The warm days passed, and soon the time came for the Mage to travel round the villages and farms that lay close to the Valley. Each spring, the Mortals in the nearby countryside welcomed her help as she used her Earth-magic to 'bless' their crops and herbs, ensuring a good harvest. In return, they supplied her with grain, tools, cloth, and other items that she could not grow or manufacture for herself. This time, she particularly wanted a new glass for Aurian's window, and some poultry, for her own had all perished in the savage winter storms. The swordsman was horrified to learn that Aurian stayed alone in the Valley while Eilin was away. He was dismayed by this new evidence of the Mage's neglect; however, both she and Aurian seemed quite happy with the arrangement. 'I don't want to go,' the child insisted, 'I'd miss Swiftwing and the animals. I'm all right here.'

'Of course she is,' Eilin agreed. 'She has the wolves to guard her, and if anything should go wrong Swiftwing or one of the other birds would soon bring me a message.'

Forral sighed, and gave it up. What a foolish, stubborn, independent pair they were. Typical Magefolk! He consoled himself that this year, at least, someone responsible would be around to keep an eye on the child.

After Eilin had set out on her horse, a white mare that Forral had never seen before since the Mage rarely had time for riding, Forral found that there was enough work in the Valley to keep himself and Aurian busy. Sometimes they would go hunting with Swiftwing. The goats needed milking and the fish-traps that the Mage kept on the borders of the lake had to be regularly cleared and reset. Worse, the weeds in the garden seemed to be making the most of the Mage's absence by springing up overnight. Still awed by the magnitude of the task that Eilin had undertaken, Forral felt duty bound to offer what help he could. As well as labouring in the garden, he spent a good deal of time around the tower, working to repair the worst of winter's ravages.

Aurian soon grew bored with it all. She would start helping with the best intentions, but after a while she inevitably slipped away, supposedly to see her animals. But as time went by, the swordsman noticed that the child was disappearing more and more often, and began to wonder. When he asked her how she had spent her days, her replies were vague and evasive. Basically an honest child, she was a terrible liar. Inevitably, Forral thought of the day they met, when he had caught her playing with fireballs in the glade.

The suspicion that she might be doing it again filled him with deep concern. He already knew she had inherited Eilin's Earth-magic. She could communicate with animals, and knew the trick of making young plants thrive. That was no problem. Eilin could supervise her efforts, and there was little she could do with Earth-magic to hurt herself. But Geraint's skill had been Fire-magic, and the control of raw energy that it required made it the most perilous of disciplines. The swordsman worried. Had the child inherited that too? Was she one of those rare Mages whose powers encompassed all forms of magic? If so, then without proper teaching she would be in grave danger, as would all who came into contact with her.

Forral thought about confiding his suspicions to Eilin on her return, but found himself hesitating. Obsessed with her grief for Geraint, she would never be able to live with a child who had inherited his potentially destructive powers. It would be tragic if she rejected Aurian just when their relationship was improving. In any case, he had no proof, and there was no point in upsetting matters until he did. He would have to deal with this himself.

The next time Aurian slipped away, Forral followed her. He was afraid that the birds would give him away, but they were too busy feeding their voracious broods to think of anything else. Once she was away from the tower Aurian called her pony, and Forral, cursing, had to run back to catch his horse. Now mostly idle, the beast had grown fat and frisky, and he had a hard time restraining its exuberance. When he picked up the track again, the swordsman saw that Aurian had headed off towards the forest beyond the crater's rim, using a roundabout route. He frowned. She was definitely hiding something. Eventually her trail led to the very clearing where they had first met. Forral, peering through the screening undergrowth, gasped.

Aurian had to concentrate very hard. Six fireballs were the most she had ever juggled at once, and she was finding it hard to keep them all in the air under control without burning herself. Her face was damp with sweat, and she was tiring quickly. One of the glowing, coloured balls of flame gave a sudden swerve, heading straight for a tree, and she pulled it back under control with a wrenching effort of will, almost singeing her hair in the process. That was quite enough. With great care she snuffed the bobbing flames in mid air and sat down on a fallen treetrunk, feeling exhausted but pleased with herself.

Before her ears had time to register the crashing in the undergrowth, Aurian found herself seized by the shoulders, hauled upright and spun round to stare into Forral's face. She gulped, her own face burning with guilt. She had never seen the big man look so angry.

'What were you doing?' he shouted. 'Say it!'

Aurian opened her mouth, but nothing came out. He shook her hard enough to rattle her teeth. 'Say it!' he roared.

'P-playing with fireballs.' Aurian struggled to get the words out.

'And what did I tell you?'

'N-not to.'

'Why?'

'Because it's very dangerous,' Aurian replied in a small voice, too scared even to cry, and shocked by this transformation from kindly friend to wrathful grownup.

'Well, you're about to find out how dangerous it is!' His face grim, Forral sat down on the fallen trunk, put her across his knee, and walloped her until she howled. The spanking was painful enough, but what hurt Aurian more was the fact that she was being punished by her beloved Forral. After what seemed to her to be several lifetimes, he stopped. 'You deserved that,' he said harshly over her wails. 'You knew perfectly well that you were doing wrong, but you did it anyway. I thought I could trust you, Aurian. I see that I can't.' He dumped her on the ground. The child buried her face in the leaf mould and sobbed her heart out. When she looked up, Forral had gone.

Aurian was mortified. She couldn't believe that Forral had spanked her. He never hit her. He was supposed to be her friend. Slowly it began to dawn on her that she must truly have done a bad thing. But it was so much fun! 'I won't stop doing it,' she muttered rebelliously. 'I'll show him!' But the voice of conscience intervened. Forral never did anything without good reason, and he had always turned out to be right. Then a new thought struck her. What if he was so angry with her that he had gone away? Aurian scrambled to her feet and called her pony, suddenly desperate to get home. 'Oh, let him be there,' she prayed. 'I'll never do it again, if only he's there.'

She couldn't ride. It hurt too much. Aurian scrambled off the pony and swore, then clamped a guilty hand over her mouth. Gritting her teeth, she set off to walk, wiping away the occasional tear that rolled down her cheek. Darkness fell as she trudged along. She knew that nothing would harm her within the crater's bowl, for the wild creatures were her friends. Like all Magefolk, her night vision was superb, and if she was careful there was no danger of falling down one of the hidden folds in the land. There was no chance of getting lost, either. All she had to do was head for the twinkling light that burned like a beacon on top of the tower. But apart from the time she had been lost in the snow, Aurian had never been out alone at night in the vast, empty darkness of the wasteland. She felt overwhelmed and lonely, and Forral didn't love her any more . . . she gulped back a sob, feeling desperately sorry for herself. Her feet began to hurt, and her bottom still burned, appropriately enough. It was a sorry little girl who finally crept across the bridge towards the tower.

Forral didn't tell her until years later that he had never been far from her side; shadowing her until she was safely within reach of home, and, without her night vision, having a far worse journey than she did.

To Aurian's relief, a soft light glowed in the kitchen window. Forral hadn't left yet, then. All the same, it took the child a long time to pluck up enough courage to open the door. Forral sat at the table, his head in his hands, looking as dishevelled as she felt. She noticed that his clothes were scuffed and stained, as if he had fallen over somewhere. He had not heard her enter – or maybe he was ignoring her. Aurian crept closer. 'Forral, I'm sorry,' she said in a small voice. The swordsman slowly raised his head and held out his arms. Aurian, too relieved to speak, ran to him and climbed on to his lap. He hugged her hard, then she was crying and to her surprise he was crying too. 'Don't cry,' she begged him, puzzled. 'Nobody spanked *you*,' she added, with a touch of indignation.

Forral's mouth twitched in a smile. 'Oh, child,' he said. 'Don't you know how much it hurt me to punish you like that?'

For the first time, Forral told her exactly what had happened to her father – how Geraint had been destroyed by his own Fire-magic. By the time he had finished, Aurian was trembling. 'I didn't know,' she gasped.

'I should have told you sooner,' Forral said, 'but I'd hoped to spare you until you were older. Now do you see why I was angry? It was because you frightened me, love. What if you accidentally did the same thing? I'll do anything to stop you, even if it means hurting you. I love you too much to lose you the way your father was lost.'

'But I can't help it,' Aurian protested. 'Really and truly I can't! It's inside me, and if I have nothing to do it just sort of – pops out. What shall I do, Forral?' She was truly frightened now.

'Don't worry, love, we'll think of something.' Forral held her in silence for a while, his brow furrowed with thought. Aurian found herself growing more and more tired, but was reluctant to leave the comfort of his arms for her bed.

'Forral, will you tell me a story?' she said sleepily. 'Tell me the one about the world's greatest swordsman. It's my favourite.'

'That's it!' Forral shot bolt upright, almost spilling her from his lap. 'Aurian, how would you like to become the world's most famous swordswoman?'

Aurian's face lit up with incredulous delight. 'Could I?' she asked, awed.

'I don't see why not. I'll teach you – but I warn you, it'll be very hard work. You won't get to be the greatest swordswoman by messing about. When I started to learn I was just about battered to bits, and I was so sore and tired at the end of every day that I could hardly crawl into bed. If you want me to teach you, you'll have to endure all that – and it'll be too late then to change your mind. But at least you won't have a single spare minute of the day to get yourself into trouble. What do you say?'

Aurian thought about it. It didn't sound like fun the way he described it, but on the other hand she was sore and tired and she never wanted to go through another day like this one. If it would keep her out of that kind of trouble, she was all for it. The heroes from Forral's stories marched through her memory, firing her imagination. 'Yes,' she cried, suddenly filled with determination. 'I'll do it!'

That was the beginning of Aurian's training. The very next day, Forral made them two wooden practice swords, and they found a secluded spot for their lessons, well away from the tower. When Eilin returned, Forral swore Aurian to secrecy. 'I'm sure your mother wouldn't approve of this, and we don't want to have to explain to her why we started doing it,' he warned her. Aurian agreed wholeheartedly.

Ar first it was terrible. Forral made no allowance for her lack of size and strength, and she soon learned that she would have to become very good in a very short time if she wanted to avoid a bludgeoning. At first it was all she could do to dodge and turn his blows, without thinking about attacking. Each night she went to her bed aching and bruised all over, and the first valuable lesson she learned was how to endure. Forral also taught her other things: exercises to stay supple and build muscle; and practices of breathing and meditation to calm and sharpen the mind for battle. Aurian had no idea how lucky she was. Forral, though he was too modest to admit it, was the best. Under his tutelage she eventually learned the Is of the Warrior – the trancelike state in which all senses combine to become something far greater than the sum of their parts – a single sense that becomes an extension of the living sword – that *is* the sword, so that by the time the mind works out the next move, the blade is already there.

Aurian began to love it. She lived for her lessons, going out with Forral in summer and winter alike. She suffered and slogged and sweated and endured, and by the time she was twelve she had the skill to take on an average swordsman twice her age and size – and win. She was growing like a weed, and that helped. When her breasts began to grow she was appalled. They kept getting in the way. When she complained about it to Forral he grunted uncomfortably, but made her a tight-fitting leather vest such as female warriors favoured. It laced tightly up the front and kept the ridiculous things in check very effectively.

A few weeks before her thirteenth birthday, Forral went away on a mysterious errand of his own. Aurian pined, missing him keenly. In his absence the temptation to take up her tricks with the fireballs surfaced strongly, but she was determined to keep her promise to the swordsman. Instead, she asked her mother to teach her more about Earth-magic. 'Ah, now that Forral is away, you suddenly have time to spend with your mother,' Eilin complained, but she was smiling. Forral's presence had made a tremendous difference to her, and mother and daughter were getting along much better these days. Over those few weeks, Aurian found herself enjoying Eilin's company. As well as magic, the Mage took the opportunity to teach her daughter what would soon happen to her maturing body, and the way that Mages dealt with the matter. And of course Aurian worked hard at Forral's exercises, hoping to impress him with her improvement when he came back.

Forral's return more than made up for his absence. He had brought her a princely gift for her birthday – her own full-size sword. There was a lump in Aurian's throat as she unwrapped it and drew the long, keen blade out of its black and silver scabbard with a steely hiss. She flung her arms around Forral. 'Oh, thank you,' she gasped. The sword shone brilliant blue-white in the pale winter sunlight that ran like glittering fire down its razor-sharp edges. There was a single white gem set into the hilt. It was more slender than Forral's great broadsword; strong, elegant – and deadly. Aurian had never seen anything so beautiful.

It was like going back to the beginning. The sword had been crafted for Aurian to grow into, and she could barely lift the heavy blade, let alone swing it. She gritted her teeth, and doubled her muscle-building exercises. At the end of every lesson her back and arms ached. She found that fighting with a proper blade called for a very different technique from the one that had served her so well with the light wooden practice swords, and she was forced to start all over again. Aurian had been growing rather arrogant about her prowess, fancying herself a great swordswoman already. Now she learned otherwise. Safety became an important factor in their sessions. Now that she and Forral were using lethal steel blades there was every chance that they could inflict serious injury on one another, and Aurian had to learn that she could no longer improvise, as she had formerly done.

It seemed to take for ever, but gradually, as she worked through the following spring and summer, Aurian began to improve. Now, at last, the blade went where she wanted it to. Well balanced and finely crafted, it was a delight to use. Forral taught her how to take care of it, and she kept both blade and scabbard meticulously clean and well oiled. The sword glittered as she swung it, and as it clove the air it sang. Because of this, Aurian named it Coronach, which meant Deathsong, and Forral didn't smile at her fancy. 'A good blade deserves a good name,' he agreed gravely.

Disaster struck near the end of that year, when the first snow covered the ground with a thin sprinkling of white. Perhaps Forral had been too enthusiastic in giving her the sword so soon; or maybe Aurian had become over confident. Whatever the reason, she made a deadly mistake. She and Forral were sparring in their usual place when she decided, on her own initiative, to try a new move that she had been thinking about lately. Moving back from him she ducked and twisted, planning to bring her blade up beneath her opponent's guard to strike at his throat. It went dreadfully wrong. As she twisted, Aurian slipped on the snow. She lost her balance and her stroke went wide, leaving her open to Forral's lethal downswing. He cried out and tried to wrench the heavy blade aside, but the momentum was too great. The great sword sheared into Aurian's left shoulder with a sickening crunch of shattered bone.

Eilin came thundering down the tower staircase, alerted by Forral's frantic shouts for help. She stopped dead at the bottom of the steps, her face ashen. Forral, tears streaming down his face, bore Aurian's still body wrapped in his blood-soaked cloak. A trail of blood led out through the open door behind him, and pooled on the stone flags of the kitchen floor. He felt it seeping, warm and sticky, into his clothing. 'Oh gods,' he sobbed, his face twisting with anguish. 'Eilin, I've killed her!'

Eilin was shaking as she took Aurian from him and laid her gently on the kitchen table. He heard her gasp as she revealed the dreadful injury. The Mage felt for a pulse in Aurian's throat. 'Thank the gods, she still lives,' she murmured. Only then did Forral dare look. His sword had bitten deep into Aurian's shoulder, shattering her collarbone and almost severing her arm. Her face was grey from shock and loss of blood. Forral sagged. The room blurred around him as he swayed dizzily. On far too many occasions he had seen good friends maimed and killed, and had inflicted worse wounds on enemies in battle without flinching, but this was a young girl, and one he loved more than life itself. It was more than he could bear. 'I'm sorry. It was my fault. I –'

'Quiet!' Eilin snapped. She laid her hands on the wound, her eyes narrowing in concentration as she summoned her powers. 'I wish I'd learned more about healing,' she muttered helplessly. But as Forral watched, holding his breath, the flow of blood diminished to a trickle, then slowly died away altogether.

Eilin straightened up and turned on him, her eyes blazing. Forral dropped to his knees.

'Eilin, it was an accident . . .'

'Never mind! Ride to Nexis, Forral. Fetch the healer from the Academy! Hurry! We may lose her yet!'

Relieved to be doing something positive, Forral ran; his last glimpse of Aurian's pale, stricken face blazoned on his mind's eye. His horse plunged violently, frightened by this wild-eyed madman who flung the saddle so roughly across its back. He clouted it hard across the nose and jerked the girth tight. Springing to its back he spurred away in a welter of snow, anxious to be out of the rough terrain of the crater before dusk fell. The journey on horseback to Nexis took five days. Forral intended to do it in two.

3

The Baker's Son

'Gee up, there!' Anvar flipped the reins, urging the old horse along the rough rutted track that slanted up from the mill by the riverside. Lazy tossed his head and whinnied, protesting at having to haul the heavy cartload of flour up the steep hill. 'Never mind,' Anvar told the horse. 'At least you're warm. I'll give you a good breakfast when we get home.' He blew on his hands and slapped them against his thighs, trying to thaw the stiffness out of his fingers. The icy dawn chill had seeped into his bones, and the mill's roaring fire already seemed a million miles away. But a different sort of fire warmed Anvar's blood as he recalled the smile of the miller's pretty daughter Sara.

The wealth and power in the city of Nexis rested with the rich merchants, the high-placed warriors from the garrison, and the lofty Mageborn. Life was much harder for the common folk; the craftsmen and dressmakers, the servants, labourers, shopkeepers, bargemen and lamplighters who kept the city running with their menial but essential tasks. Children, perforce, learned to shoulder responsibility at an early age, and Anvar's father, a master-baker in the city, had given his eldest son the task of fetching the flour as soon as he was old enough to drive the cart. Though the journey was longer by road, and hard in winter, it saved the ruinous freight tolls charged by the river's bargemen.

Ever since Anvar's first visit to the mill long ago, fair-haired, elfin little Sara had been his best friend. When they were younger they would sneak away in the afternoons to play together, meeting along the narrow towpath that ran downriver to the city. Now that they had reached the grand old age of fifteen, however, their games had started to take a new and serious turn. Anvar was in love, and he had no doubt that Sara felt the same. Both sets of parents viewed this development with tolerance. Torl, Anvar's father, and Jard the miller both saw the advantage in combining the two businesses some day, and of course the mothers had no say in the matter.

Anvar smiled, still thinking of Sara, as he reached the top of the hill and turned the creaking cart on to the main highway. Nexis was hidden by the freezing mist that lay grey in the forested valley below. Only the shimmering white towers and dome of the Academy, high on their rocky promontory above the rest of the city, were visible above the fog. Anvar's smile turned to a scowl at the sight. They would still be asleep up there, he thought. Snoring on swansdown mattresses while honest folk had been up and working well before daylight! His father had no time for the Magefolk, calling them arrogant parasites and an insult to proper men. This was such a common point of view in Anvar's neighbourhood that he had never questioned it, though he noticed that the men in the taprooms kept their voices low as they said it, glancing nervously over their shoulders as they spoke.

Suddenly Anvar was wrenched out of his daydreams as the old horse shied and laid its ears back at the sound of hoofbeats. Someone was coming up behind him, galloping perilously fast on the icy road. He sighed and pulled the cart well into the side. It was probably a courier, headed for the garrison, the Academy, or the merchants' quarter, and it would be more than Anvar's hide was worth to get in the way of his betters' business.

The horse was finished. As it thundered past, Anvar could hear the wheeze of its laboured breathing above the sound of hooves. He caught a glimpse of its sweat-streaked, blood-stained flanks as it hurtled by, and heard the burly rider curse it as he lashed it with the end of the reins. The swine! Anvar raged inwardly, furious at this cruel treatment. He urged his own horse onward gently, as if by his kindness he could somehow make amends for what he had just witnessed. Then he heard the fading hoofbeats falter. There was a sick thud as the horse went down, followed by a stream of savage curses.

Anvar rounded the bend to see the dark bulk of the dead horse lying in the road. The body still steamed. The great bully who had been riding it stood over it, quite unscathed and scalding the air with oaths. Anvar was consumed with anger. Without pausing to consider the consequences, he leapt from the cart and hurled himself at the big, bearded horseman. 'You bastard!' he screamed. 'You callous bastard!' The man ignored him completely, his eye suddenly lighting on the cart. Brushing Anvar aside with casual, contemptuous strength, he ran forward and drew a dagger from his belt to cut the old horse free from the traces.

Anvar hauled himself out of the ditch, horrified at the result of his folly. 'No!' he yelled and ran forward to tug at the madman's arm. A blow sent him spinning. The big man threw the last of the harness aside, cut off the trailing ends of the long reins and leapt astride the horse's bare back. Lazy shied, rolling his eyes, and the man gave a savage jerk at the reins. Anvar picked himself up, tears in his eyes, and hauled desperately at the rider's muddy cloak. 'Please, sir,' he begged, 'he's old. You can't . . .'

The stranger turned to look at him as though noticing him for the first time, his grim expression suddenly softening to compassion and regret. 'I'm truly sorry, lad,' he said gently, 'but it's an emergency. There's a young girl's life at stake, and I must get to the healer. Try to understand. I'll leave him at the Academy. Tell them Forral sent you.' He clasped Anvar's shoulder briefly, and was gone with a clatter of hooves. Anvar stared after him for a long moment, then turned to contemplate the abandoned cart with its precious load. The flour would be late that morning and Torl would be unable to start work. They would lose money through this, for sure. Anvar sighed, and set off walking back towards the mill to borrow a horse. His father was going to be livid.

Anvar's family lived in the north of Nexis, in the thickly populated labyrinth of narrow streets that clustered within the great city wall on the upper slopes of the broad valley. Further down were the great stone thoroughfares with their magnificent, colonnaded buildings and marvellous markets and shops; and slightly apart, on a plateau where the slope levelled briefly before continuing its descent, stood the large grey fortress-like complex of the legendary garrison. Lining the northern riverbank at the bottom of the vale were the warehouses and wharves of the merchants, with their usual dockside complement of rats, beggars, cutpurses and whores. Elegant bridges leaped across the river's broad flow at various points, connecting the working areas in the north of the city to the very different environment on the south bank.

South of the river, the valley sloped upwards in a series of steep wooded terraces. Set like jewels among the trees were the opulent mansions of the merchants with their smooth lawns and lush, glowing gardens where coloured lanterns burned on balmy summer evenings when the air was thick with the scent of many flowers. At the mid-point of its journey through the city, the river made a detour, looping north in an oxbow before re-emerging to resume its path to the sea. Within this loop stood a high, rocky promontory, almost an island, connected to the southern bank by a narrow tongue of land barred with a white, arched gate. Set on top of the promontory, the highest point in the city, were the white-walled towers of the academy where the Magefolk dwelt in splendid and lofty isolaton.

The morning was wearing away when Anvar drove his borrowed horse past the guards at the northern city gate and threaded his way through the narrow streets towards home. The houses and workshops in this part of the city were simply but solidly constructed of wood, brick and plaster. Most of the homes were well cared for, and the streets were cobbled but clean. Anvar had heard that in smaller towns, people threw their waste out of the windows, turning the thoroughfares into open sewers. In Nexis, jewel among cities and home of the Magefolk, such a thing would be unthinkable. Some two hundred years previously, Bavordran, a Mage skilled in Water-magic, had designed an elaborate and effective system of underground sewers to furnish the entire city, and the Magefolk, for once (for they were not exactly famed for helping the Mortal population of Nexis), took the duty of their magical upkeep very seriously indeed.

Anvar's family lived above Torl's bakery, where bread, cakes and pies were made to sell in the little market held daily in a nearby square. Usually the fragrance of baking loaves filled the street, but not today. As he neared the house, Anvar could hear his father's voice raised in anger, and chewed his lip nervously. He'd be in trouble over this, for sure. He turned the cart carefully down the narrow alleyway that led to the little stable behind the house, and made Jard's horse comfortable in Lazy's stall. There was no point in delaying. The later he was, the more angry Torl would become. Squaring his shoulders, Anvar crossed the yard and went reluctantly into the bakery. He hoped that his father would give him a chance to explain.

Torl was in no mood for excusses. 'But it wasn't my fault!' Anvar pleaded. 'He just knocked me down and took the horse . . .'

'And you just let him! That animal is our livelihood, you stupid boy! Do you know what you've done? Do you?' Torl raised his big fist, his arm brawny from years of lifting bags of flour and kneading stiff dough. Anvar ducked and the blow caught him on the shoulder, spinning him into the corner where he knocked over a clattering stack of empty bread trays as he fell.

'Clumsy fool!' His father advanced on him like a menacing shadow, hauled him up and hit him again. 'Stay still, you!' The baker began to unbuckle his belt.

'Leave him alone, Torl. It wasn't the boy's fault.' Grandpa's voice was filled with quiet authority. Anvar, nursing his bruises, sagged with relief at the unexpected reprieve. The old man was the only person who could defy his son's temper when Torl was in this mood.

Grandpa was Anvar's confidant, teacher, protector and friend; a great hulk of a man, with a shock of white hair, a gentle expression and a bristling moustache. He'd been a carpenter by trade, and his thick-fingered hands could do miracles of intricate, delicate carving that were much in demand, and brought in welcome pennies to the household; but he gave away as many pieces as he sold, much to Torl's disgust. A countryman at heart, the old man had come to live with his son after the tragically early death of his wife, a legendary cook. It was she who had taught Torl the skills that made his baking so much in demand. For years grandpa had tried to bury his grief in his work, but now he was content to rest and enjoy his grandsons, trying to teach them the older, simpler values of his youth. In Anvar he had a willing pupil, but Bern, the younger brother, was his father's son from his dark, sturdy appearance to his love of business and the worship of profit.

Torl scowled. Letting go of Anvar, he turned on grandpa. 'You stay out of this, old man!'

'I don't think so, Torl. Not this time.' Grandpa placed himself between the wrathful baker and his victim. 'You're too hard on the lad.'

'And you spoil him, you and his mother! No wonder the boy is good for nothing!'

'He's good for a great many things, if you would give him a chance,' grandpa said firmly. 'Instead of taking it out on him, why don't you go up to the academy and see what's happened to the horse?'

'What? Trek all the way across town and up that hill? Have you lost your wits, father? Enough of today's been wasted, thanks to this idiot!'

'Nonsense, Torl. You can take Jard's horse, and the trip may well be worth your time. It won't hurt to have your name known at the academy – they eat bread there too, you know. We can start the baking while you're gone, and there's a good chance that you'll be compensated by this Forral. From what Anvar said he seemed an honourable man, and if it was an emergency what else could he do? You'd have done the same thing yourself, if anything had happened to Bern.'

Torl hesitated for a moment, still scowling. 'Those bastards could starve before I'd sell them a crumb of my bread. Besides, you old fool, they bake their own – or at least they get the bootlicking Mortal scum who serve them to do it!' Satisfied that he had had the last word he stamped out, slamming the door behind him. Grandpa shrugged, and put an arm around Anvar's shoulders. 'Come on, son, we'd better get started. We're well behind this morning, and your father's temper isn't likely to improve with the day.'

As Anvar followed his grandfather, the old man's last words to Torl echoed in his head. Bern – his father's favourite, and he never bothered to hide it. Always Bern. Anvar looked sourly at his dark-haired younger brother, who was smirking in the doorway. Why did Torl favour him so? Grandpa was right. If

Bern had been hurt, his father would move mountains to help him. For himself, on the other hand . . . Anvar sighed. He knew only too well what his father thought about him. But he wished he knew why.

At nightfall Anvar dragged himself up the ladder to the cramped little attic that he shared with Bern, having finished work at last. He had been too tired to eat the special supper that his mother had prepared to placate his father's black mood. Lacking the energy to undress, he threw himself down on his bed. Gods, what a terrible day it had been! Torl had worked them like slaves, taking Anvar's mishap out on the whole family. His mother had been pale and shaking with fatigue by the end of the day, and Anvar was consumed with guilt, knowing that her exhaustion was his fault. Ria had never been strong, but she toiled without complaint; afraid that if she faltered, Torl's wrath would fall on her son again. Anvar wondered, as he often did, how this gentle, intelligent woman had come to wed his rough and greedy father. She deserved far better. Delicate and slender, she had dark-blonde hair and blue eyes like her elder son, and had obviously once been very beautiful.

Ria's past was a mystery. Unlike anyone else in their neighbourhood, she could read and write and play music, and had taught these skills to Anvar. A waste of time, Torl had called it, and pointed out that Bern had more sense than to ape his betters. *He* was learning to follow in his father's footsteps like a proper son. But for once Ria had defied her husband, and Anvar was glad. Ever since the day his grandfather had carved him his first little wooden flute, he had fallen in love with music and practised every spare minute, driving his family, especially his father, to distraction. Soon he had mastered all the simple tunes he knew, and had begun to compose his own, stretching the limits of the simple flute until even grandpa's ingenuity was hard-pressed to construct new instruments that would give him the sounds he wanted. Anvar lived for his music. His playing and Sara were the only consolations in his hard-working life, and he blessed his mother for giving him such a priceless gift.

Anvar loved Ria. Now she was faded, fragile and careworn,

46

and too cowed to stand up to the bullying Torl. He wished he could protect her, but although he was growing up tall and broad-shouldered, his frame was still lanky and gangling. If it came to a confrontation, Torl could fell him with a single blow.

Anvar sighed. He had other troubles that night. He had arranged to meet Sara in their usual trysting place along the riverbank, but Torl's gruelling workload had put paid to that. He hoped she wouldn't be angry. He was sad too about poor Lazy. His wind had been ruined, and Torl had callously sold him to the knacker-men. Anvar mourned the loss of the old horse. Though balky and stubborn, he had great character and intelligence, which he constantly used to avoid work. Anvar was going to miss him. Torl, however, only thought of the generous sum that Forral had left for him at the Academy. He had not seen Anvar's horseman, for Forral had only stopped long enough to pick up the Lady Meiriel, the healer, and the two had set off as fast as possible for the north on fresh horses.

Anvar wondered what she was like, this child whose life was in danger. At first he felt inclined to resent the mysterious dying girl who had caused all this trouble, but when he thought about it, he found himself hoping that the healer would get there in time to save her. That way at least some good would come out of Lazy's death.

Some weeks later, Anvar's own family was in desperate need of the healer's services. All winter long, grandpa had been complaining of tiredness and aches in his bones, and after Solstice, in the bleak grey season that stretched beyond the turn of the year, the old man took to his bed, growing weaker by the day despite Ria's diligent nursing with the herbal brews and folk remedies that were the only recourse of the Mortals in the city. But when Anvar, remembering Forral, begged his father to send for the healer, Torl admonished him harshly. 'I don't know where you get your ideas from,' he said. 'A family like us send for the healer? She'd laugh in our faces! Besides, I'll have none of those Mageborn scum over my threshold! Now get back to work, boy, before I take my belt to you!'

That night, when Anvar visited grandpa, the old man was too weak even to speak to him. He simply lay back on the pillows, his face yellow and sunken. There was an odd transparency about his skin that Anvar had never seen before, and without knowing why he felt a stab of fear. 'Mother, help him,' he begged.

Ria shook her head, tears in her eyes. 'Anvar, you have to face it,' she said softly. 'Grandpa's dying.'

'No!' Anvar gasped. 'He can't die!' He came to a sudden decision. 'I'm going for the healer, if father won't.'

'You can't!' Ria went absolutely white, her eyes wide with stark terror. Even in his extremity, Anvar was stunned by her reaction. Then he looked back at his grandfather's face.

'Why not?' he demanded. 'I'm not afraid of father. Anyway, he's gone to the tavern. If I'm quick he need never know.'

'It's not that!' Ria was trembling. She caught hold of Anvar's hands. 'Anvar, you and I – we must never have any dealings with the Magefolk. I can't tell you why, but you must believe me. Stay away from them, son, for my sake – and especially for your own.'

Anvar was dumbfounded. What had his mother to do with the Magefolk, that she should be so terrified? But she wouldn't tell him, and there was no time to find out. He pulled away. 'I'm sorry, mother.' Quietly he slipped downstairs, hoping to avoid Bern, who was always on the lookout for opportunities to get him into trouble. When Anvar reached the street he started to run, heading downhill towards the river. From the open window behind him came the sound of his mother's weeping.

Anvar pounded along the quiet, lamplit streets. It was a long way to the river, and his breath was coming in gasps by the time he neared the wharves, taking a short cut to the bridge nearest the academy. Lamps were scarce in the warehouse district and Anvar hurried nervously through the dark alleys, his feet slipping on cobbles that were covered with filth. He was already regretting that he had chosen this route. The district had a bad reputation. As he passed the dark, stinking entrance to one of the smaller alleys there was a sudden scuffling noise, and several ragged figures burst out of the shadows. Anvar was forced to slide to a halt as they surrounded him. They closed in on him, and he gagged on the acrid stench of unwashed bodies. In the dim light from a rag-draped window above, he saw the flash of knives in their hands, and his mouth went dry with fear.

'Hand over your money, boy,' a voice growled in an unfamiliar accent. Anvar backed away until he was stopped by the wall.

'I – I haven't got any,' he stammered. 'Please let me go. I'm going for the healer – it's an emergency.' Irrationally, Forral's face flicked into his mind as he echoed the big man's words.

The cut-throat laughed. 'My, aren't we grand! Going for the healer, eh? And with no money? Search him, boys!'

Anvar was thrown to the ground. Rough, bony fingers rummaged through his clothing, making his flesh crawl. He had time for one enormous bellow for help before they started to hit him.

The nightmare came to an abrupt end as the clatter of hooves echoed down the alley. 'Troopers!' somebody yelled. 'Run for it!'

Anvar suddenly found himself alone, and struggled to raise his bruised and aching body. A hand grasped his collar, and he was hauled to his feet. 'Got you!' Anvar found himself staring up into the stern face of a tall soldier. 'What were you up to, eh, brat?' the man rasped.

'Please, sir,' Anvar stammered, squirming in the man's iron grip, 'they set on me. I was going to the Academy for the healer . . .'

The trooper burst out laughing. 'Come, can't you manage a better tale than that? Do you think I came up with the grass?' He hauled Anvar to the end of the alley, where a single lamp hung from the wall on an iron bracket. As he took in Anvar's appearance, his expression altered. 'You don't come from round here,' he accused him. 'What's a lad like you doing wandering alone in this district at night? Have you lost your wits?'

Haltingly, Anvar told him about his grandfather.

The trooper let go of his collar. 'Lad,' he said gently, 'the Lady Meiriel won't bother herself with the likes of your grandpa. Don't you know how the Magefolk are?'

'I've got to try,' Anvar insisted. 'Why wouldn't she help me? A while ago I met this man called Forral, and . . .'

'You know Forral?' A look of profound respect crossed the trooper's seamed face.

'We met on the road – he took my horse. He said he was going for the healer to save a little girl's life. If she would do that, why wouldn't she help grandpa?'

The soldier sighed. 'Lad, don't you know who Forral is? He's a living legend – the world's greatest swordsman – and he's friendly with some of the Magefolk. The girl was the daughter of Eilin, the Lady of the Lake. We heard about it at the garrison. Why, I don't even know if the Lady Meiriel is back yet – the Valley is a long way north of here. I'm sorry, son, but even if she has come back she won't haul herself out at this time of night for somebody's grandpa.'

'But if I could explain to her . . .' Anvar persisted.

'Well, don't say I didn't warn you.' The trooper sounded resigned. 'Come on, I'll take you on my horse. If you go up there alone, the Magefolk will likely have you flogged for your cheek before they throw you out.'

The horse's hooves sounded loud on the causeway that led across the promontory as Anvar and the trooper approached the white gate. The gatekeeper was an old man – a Mortal, as were all the servants of the Magefolk. When Anvar's new friend explained their errand, he gaped in disbelief. 'What? Are you joking? The Lady Meiriel has just returned from a long journey this very day. It's more than my hide's worth to disturb her. You should have more sense, Hargorn, than to bring the boy here.'

'I know, but this is a special case,' Hargorn insisted. 'This is the lad who gave Forral his horse. Why, if it hadn't been for that, the little Mage lass might have died before the healer could reach her. Surely that deserves some consideration.'

The old man sighed. 'Oh, very well. I'll ask her. But she's not going to be very pleased.'

He ducked back into the squat white gatehouse. On a shelf inside stood a rack of crystals, each glowing with a different coloured light. The gatekeeper picked up a stone that shone a deep violet-blue and spoke into it softly. After a moment a patch of luminescence shimmered into existence in front of him, and Anvar gasped as it resolved itself into a woman's face, with dark, cropped hair, high cheekbones and an arrogant beaked nose. Her expression was sleepy and cross. 'What is it?' she demanded brusquely. 'I trust you've a good reason for bothering me at this hour?' With many bows and apologies, the gatekeeper explained the situation. The Lady Meiriel frowned. 'How often have I told you not to bother me with such trifles? If I had to attend every sick Mortal in Nexis, I'd exhaust my power in a day! Send the brat away – and as for you, the Archmage shall hear tomorrow that I'll bear your incompetence no longer. This sort of thing is happening far too often! You're obviously not fit for your post!'

The face flickered into darkness. The gatekeeper turned to Hargorn. 'See what you've done,' he whined. But there was no one there.

The trooper caught up with Anvar before he reached the end of the causeway. 'Leave me alone!' the lad shouted, blinded with tears. Hargorn laid a kindly hand on his shoulder.

'I'm sorry, lad, but I did warn you. Come on – I'll take you home.'

Grandpa died before morning. As Anvar wept over the old man's body, his mother sought to comfort him. 'Don't grieve so,' she said softly, putting an arm around his shaking shoulders. 'Look at him.' Grandpa's expression was transfigured by a smile of pure, sublime joy. 'He's gone back to grandma,' Ria said. 'He loved her so very much, and he's been missing her terribly all these years. You can see from his face that they're together again. I know how much you'll miss him, dear, but you should be happy for him too.'

'How do you know?' Anvar demanded. 'How can you be sure he knows about anything now? He's dead! When that accursed healer could have saved him!'

Ria sighed. 'Anvar, grandpa was old and worn out. He never really liked living in the city and he'd had a hard life. He was tired, that's all. It's not likely that the Lady Meiriel could have done anything . . .'

'She could have tried!' Anvar was dimly aware that he was shouting. 'She could have cared! But he was only a Mortal. We mean less to those Magefolk than animals!'

Ria sighed again and left the room, leaving him alone for the last time with his grandfather. And as he knelt there in the cold chamber beside the empty remains of what had been a good and loving man, a deep and remorseless hatred of the Magefolk took root within his heart.

4

The Archmage

The sound of voices woke Aurian from a fitful sleep. For a panic-stricken moment she wondered where she was, until she saw lamplight glowing beyond the open door that led to Meiriel's quarters at the far end of the infirmary. 'Lady Meiriel?' she called out nervously. This place seemed very strange to her, with its stark white walls and smooth, polished marble floor reflecting the row of empty beds. The healer came in, brisk and smiling.

'Did I wake you?'

'Is something wrong?' Aurian asked.

'Nought to worry about.' Meiriel shrugged dismissively. 'Only an ignorant Mortal making a pest of himself down at the gate. Because we have powers, they think our sole purpose in life is to run around helping them!'

Aurian frowned. Any talk of Mortals reminded her painfully of Forral – but then everything seemed to remind her of the swordsman. She clenched her fists, willing the tears not to gather in her eyes. 'Aren't we supposed to help them?' she asked. 'I don't understand.'

The healer sat down on the edge of her bed. 'Here at the academy, Aurian, you'll learn that it's simply not done to waste your powers on such stupid, whining people. Now, we've had a long journey, and you need to rest. Can I get you something to help you sleep?'

'Yes please, Meiricl.' Anything was better than lying awake thinking.

Trying not to grimace, Aurian finished the potion that the healer had brought her as quickly as possible. Although it was sticky and tasted vile, she preferred it to Meiriel's sleep-magic, which was most unnerving. No time seemed to pass while she was under the spell – she only closed her eyes for a second, it seemed – but when she opened them, hours had been lost. Luckily, she thought, the healer had been understanding about her fears. Having been dragged, unwilling, away from her home to this new and frightening place, Aurian was pitifully grateful even for Meiriel's brusque, no-nonsense kindness. Fighting back her tears, she snuggled down beneath the quilt, hoping that for once she would fall asleep before her mind could start dwelling on the catastrophe that had overtaken her life.

It had taken the healer several weeks to repair Aurian's damaged shoulder, but she couldn't remember anything of those first days, when Meiriel had laboured endlessly with healing magic to save her arm; piecing together fragments of shattered bone with painstaking skill, and repairing the severed muscles. Meiriel had then used her powers to accelerate the body's natural healing, a process which sapped a great deal of the patient's own resources and left her in a deep sleep for several days while her body recovered its energies. When Aurian finally awoke, the wound had closed and was mending fast, though her arm was still stiff, feeble, and sore. Naturally, she had wanted Forral. At first her mother kept putting her off, but in the end, on Meiriel's advice, she had relented, and given Aurian the letter. By now she knew every word by heart:

'Aurian love, I'm sorry I can't be here when you awake, but if I stayed to say goodbye, I would never be able to go. I don't know if I can explain so that you'll understand, but I'll try. Don't blame your mother – she didn't send me away this time. I'm leaving because I feel so bad about what I did to you. I know it was an accident, but it happened because of me. I had no right to expose you to such risks – I can't believe how stupid I was. The Lady Meiriel says you'll be all right and have full use of your arm again, and I only thank the gods I didn't kill you outright. As it is, I can never forgive myself.

'I had to tell your mother why we started with your sword training, but don't worry – she's not angry, unless it's with me for not telling her sooner. Anyway, she and the healer want you to go away to the Academy at Nexis to be trained properly, which is only right, because you are a Mage after all. I thought about going back with you and joining the garrison again so that we could see each other, but it wouldn't be fair to you. You need to settle down with your own kind and learn to use your gifts, and I would only be in the way. So I'm going away soldiering again.

'Aurian, please forgive me for leaving you like this. It breaks my heart, but it's for the best, truly. Please don't forget me, as I'll never forget you. And never doubt that some day we'll meet again. I'll think of you always. All my love, Forral.'

The following weeks had passed in a blur of misery. Nothing mattered now that Forral had gone. Had she been wrong about the swordsman? If he had truly loved her, how could he have left her like this? Aurian, numb and aching inside, had simply done what her mother and the healer told her, and gradually her body had recovered sufficiently for her to make the journey back to Nexis with Meiriel. Even the sight of so much unfamiliar new country had failed to lift her spirits. The weather, unremittingly cold and bleak, was a perfect match for her mood as they rode: first over wild and snowy moors, and then, once they had reached the great road that led to the lower country, through tame and tended farmland and forest. All this was lost, however, on Aurian. She was barely aware of her surroundings, let alone the import of the journey she was making.

It had taken the city to bring Aurian sharply out of her self-pity. After spending almost all her life in the solitude of her mother's isolated Valley, Nexis, with its looming buildings and hordes of people, had terrified her. Everything was so big, noisy, and crowded, that she couldn't breathe. She hadn't known that there were so many people in the world! Meiriel, in her brisk way, had been sympathetic. 'Brace up, child,' she had said. 'Don't panic, they won't hurt you! Take deep breaths, and stay close to me. It's a lot more peaceful at the academy, and you'll get used to the city in time.'

Aurian doubted that she would ever get used to the city or

the Academy. Meiriel's pristine infirmary was very different from the familiar clutter of her mother's tower, and since everything was so alien to her, she lived in constant fear of doing or saying something wrong. She longed for the sanctuary of her own room, and the strong, comforting presence of Forral.

To bolster her faltering courage, Aurian clung tightly to the hard, slender shape of her sword. She slept with the sheathed blade every night, for it was all she had left of Forral. As soon as she had recovered sufficiently from her injury to walk, she had gone to the clearing where they had spent so many happy hours in practice. Her precious sword lay untouched on the ground where it had fallen, its leather scabbard already stiff and starting to discolour, its blade spotted with rust. Shaking with sobs, Aurian had gathered it up carefully and taken it home. She spent hours cleaning and oiling both blade and scabbard with the greatest care, pausing often to wipe off the tears that threatened to mar her work. And despite the objections of Meiriel and her mother, she had refused to be parted from it, reacting so violently to the very suggestion that they had relented and allowed her to keep it. Holding tightly to the sword, Aurian cried herself to sleep, as she had done every night since Forral went away.

In her quarters, Meiriel listened to the soft sounds of weeping, regretting that it had been necessary to wrench the child away from home like this. When silence fell at last, she crept to Aurian's bedside to assure herself that she was truly asleep. Then, calling a servant to watch her charge, she flung a cloak around her shoulders and set off across the frost-silvered courtyard to the Mages' Tower. A red light burning high in the crimson-draped windows of the uppermost floor showed that the Archmage was in residence.

'How goes it with the child, Meiriel?' The Archmage, like all his kind, was very tall. With his long silvery hair and beard, his bony hooked nose, his dark, burning eyes and his haughty demeanour, he looked the very epitome of the most powerful Mage in the world. His scarlet robes swept the richly carpeted floor as he crossed the room to pour Meiriel a goblet of wine.

As she took a seat, the healer saw the slim, silver-clad figure of Eliseth sitting in the shadows by the window, and frowned. She neither liked nor trusted the scheming, ice-cool Weather-Mage. 'I thought this was to be a private meeting,' she objected.

Miathan handed her a brimming crystal goblet. 'Come, Meiriel, don't be foolish,' he chided. 'Since we received your message, Eliseth has been helping me to make plans. If what you say is true, Geraint's child has talents we can use, and will need very special handling. I should hardly have to remind you that we need the utmost loyalty from all our people these days. The Magefolk have dwindled. Our powers are severely proscribed by the Mages' Code, and dissension among the wretched Mortals grows ever stronger. I still control the garrison's voice on the Council of Three, but Rioch will be retiring before long and there is no suitably accommodating successor among his warriors. And the new merchants' representative, that jumped-up ruffian Vannor, is already giving me trouble.'

The Archmage frowned, and took a sip of wine. 'Because a Magewoman loses her powers during pregnancy, our race has always been slow to breed, and no new children are being born to us. We're seriously outnumbered by the Mortals. Not counting Eilin, who refuses to return to us, that only leaves seven Magefolk: you and I, Eliseth and Bragar, the twins and Finbarr. And of those, the twins seem unable to access their full power, and Finbarr never leaves his archives – no offence, Meiriel. I know he's your soulmate, and I regret that we can't spare your healing skills long enough for you to lose them during a pregnancy. And of course we can't spare Eliseth, for the same reason. Her studies are at a critical point . . .'

'Otherwise, of course, I would be only too happy to make the sacrifice,' Eliseth interjected smoothly. Meiriel bit back a sarcastic retort. Liar, she thought. All you want is power. You'd be quick enough to bear Miathan's child, if he asked you. She turned back to the Archmage. 'What has this to do with Aurian?' she asked. 'You surely don't expect her to breed you some new Magefolk? The child is barely fourteen!'

Miathan assumed a patient expression, looking at the healer over his steepled hands. 'My dear Meiriel,' he said suavely, 'what a suggestion! Of course I don't expect such a thing! Not yet, at any rate. But we must take the long view here. She will not be fourteen for ever. And if, as you say, her powers may range over the entire spectrum, then they must be passed on for the benefit of our race. In the meantime, however, I was thinking of our precarious position among the Mortals. If word should be passed that we have a new Mage – one whose powers are, shall we say, spectacular – then they might think twice before crossing us. After all, they've already had an example of what her father could do.'

'That's appalling, Miathan! It's completely immoral,' Meiriel exploded. 'The Mages' Code expressly forbids the use of magic to gain power over others!'

'Of course it does, my dear,' Miathan's voice was melodious and smooth. 'But if you check the wording carefully, it says nothing about people *believing* that a Mage might use his powers against them. If the Mortals should happen to get hold of such an outlandish notion, then it would hardly be our fault, would it?'

'That's sophistry, and you know it! You're coming perilously close to breaking your vows under the Code, Miathan, and you'll take us all to perdition with you. Do you plan to corrupt the child, too?'

Eliseth shrugged her elegant shoulders. 'Surely you're overreacting,' she said silkily. 'After all, this is pure conjecture on the part of the Archmage. All he cares about at present is helping the child, and winning her trust. Who knows what nonsense Eilin and that uncouth Mortal have been putting into her head? You know how hard our training is, and the girl is starting late. She'll lack discipline, I dare say, so there will be some difficult times ahead of her. The last thing we want is for her to end up resenting the Magefolk – after all, we are her people. So Miathan and I have thought of a way to deal with the problem. We only have her welfare at heart – you'll see, Meiriel.'

'Indeed she will,' Miathan said heartily. 'Meiriel, tomorrow morning you will turn Aurian over to Eliseth. After that, your part in her training is over for the time being, and you'll leave the rest to us. Stay away from the child, and don't interfere.'

'But . . .'

Miathan's face grew stony. 'That is a direct order from your Archmage, Meiriel. You may go now.'

Aurian disliked Eliseth on sight. Although her face was flawlessly beautiful and her silver hair flowed right down to her feet like a shimmering waterfall, the Magewoman's smile never reached her grey eyes, which were hard and cold as steel. She led Aurian to the chamber that would be her own – a tiny whitewashed cell on the ground floor of the Mages' Tower. Furnished with the barest simplicity, it contained a narrow bed, a table and chair, and shelves and a chest for her possessions and clothes.

Aurian had no belongings to arrange. Apart from the clothes she stood up in, all she had was her sword. When Eliseth saw it, she frowned. 'You can't keep that,' she said flatly. 'It's much too dangerous for a young girl. Give it to me.' She reached for the sword.

In a flash Aurian had the blade unsheathed, as Forral had taught her. 'Don't touch my sword!'

Eliseth's eyes narrowed, and she made a peculiar twisting little gesture with her left hand. Aurian gasped as a chill, translucent blue cloud surrounded her. She couldn't move. Her body was frozen rigid. Icy cold seemed to burn into her very bones. Eliseth swooped down and plucked Coronach from her unresisting grasp, then stood looking coldly down on her. 'Listen to me, brat,' she hissed. 'While you are in this place, you'll learn discipline and obedience – especially obedience to me – or you'll suffer the consequences! Now I'm going to find the seamstress to measure you for some decent clothes, and as a punishment for your appalling behaviour you can remain like that until I return!'

She swept out, taking the sword with her and leaving Aurian still frozen, unable even to weep. Although she was seething with hatred for the cold-eyed Eliseth, the lesson had left its mark. Aurian had already learned to fear her.

Later that day, Eliseth showed her subdued and unhappy charge around the Academy. There was a good deal to see. The promontory was shaped like the broad blade of a spear, with its point cut off in a gentle curve by the high wall that guarded the drop on all sides. The main entrance gate stood at the place where the haft of the spear would be joined, with a small gatehouse on its left hand side. Below the gate, the steep road up which Aurian had climbed the previous day zigzagged down to the causeway, with its lower gatehouse.

The buildings all faced on to a central oval courtyard designed in a mosaic pattern with coloured flagstones. In the centre, an elegant fountain sang a soothing, bubbling song as it flung feathery arcs of water into a white marble basin. To the left of the gatehouse was Meiriel's small infirmary, and next to this were the kitchens and servants' quarters which adjoined the Great Hall with its soaring arched windows. Beyond, where the wall curved round to cut off the end of the promontory, stood the elegant and lofty Mages' Tower, where the Magefolk dwelt. Opposite the tower on the other side of the curve was the huge library with its complex, convoluted architecture; and beyond this, arcing back towards the gate, were the buildings designed for the study of the individual disciplines of magic, dominated by the massive white weather-dome whose outline was visible for miles around.

All the buildings, down to the gatehouse and the humble servants' quarters, were constucted of dazzling white marble that seemed to be imbued with its own internal, pearly glow. It was breathtakingly beautiful – and Aurian, scared and homesick as she was, hated it, though she marvelled at the great library with its priceless archives, the open rooftop temple on top of the Mages' Tower with its great standing stones, and the imposing Great Hall, which stood mostly unused now that the Magefolk were so few in number.

Aurian was shown the special windowless building that had metal doors and furniture in order that Fire-magic could be studied there in safety. A low white building contained a deep pool and many fountains, streams, conduits and waterfalls for the study of Water-magic. There was a large building constructed of glass that contained plants, grass, and even some small trees. It reminded Aurian, with a pang, of her mother's workroom in her tower, and was intended for the study of Earth-magic. But the grass was brown and withered,

60

and all the plants were shrivelled and dead. If any animals had dwelt within, they were long gone. Eilin was the only living Mage who practised Earth-magic, and the room had been abandoned when she left the Academy.

The place that Aurian found most wonderful of all was the massive dome whose outline dominated the Mages' complex. The curved chamber within was so high that small clouds could actually gather beneath its roof, which housed a complex series of valves and vents. This was Eliseth's room, for the study of Weather-magic, and she left Aurian in no doubt that this was the most important discipline of all. Aurian didn't dare ask why.

While they were making their tour of the Academy, Eliseth introduced Aurian to the other Magefolk. 'We tend to be a solitary people,' she said. 'Mostly we're occupied with our own projects, and we usually eat in our own rooms, unless there's a feast or a special occasion. That being the case, you might as well meet everyone now. All except the Archmage, of course. He's much too busy to bother with little girls.' Aurian was crushed.

Finbarr cheered her a little, however. They found him down in the archives; the maze of cellars that had been carved out of the living rock beneath the library. He was sitting at a table in a small cavern whose walls were lined with racks of ancient scrolls. The table was completely bare except for a stylus, two neat stacks of paper, one written on and the other awaiting use, and some half-dozen scrolls, neatly rolled and tied. Finbarr was reading from another ancient document by the light of a brightly glowing ball of luminescence that hovered dutifully and with perfect steadiness above his head.

'Still wasting your time with this old rubbish, I see,' was Eliseth's dismissive greeting. Aurian half-expected the Mage to jump, he had seemed so preoccupied when they entered. But he simply sighed and placed the scroll on the table, where the two rolled-up ends immediately tried to spring together. 'Stay!' Finbarr commanded in a sharp voice. The scroll quivered, and promptly flattened out in the correct position.

Finbarr turned to regard them with a piercing blue gaze. He was very thin, and his clean-shaven face had the typical bony angularity of the Magefolk. His long brown hair was streaked with grey, but his face was neither old nor young, and his eyes twinkled. 'Hail, O Lady of Thunder, Mistress of Storms,' he intoned mockingly. 'Have you come to blast me with a blizzard of icy contempt, or are you just going to rain on me and ruin my day?' He winked at Aurian, who tried to stifle a giggle.

'Finbarr, one of these days your so-called wit is going to get you into trouble,' Eliseth snapped. 'You're about as much use as these wretched old scrolls of yours!'

Finbarr shrugged. 'At least my scrolls are pleasant company,' he said, 'though not undemanding. I take it that the reason for your totally unprecedented visit to this sanctuary of learning and wisdom is to introduce me to this beauteous young Lady.' He gave Aurian a kindly smile.

'You know who she is, Finbarr.' Eliseth was scowling. 'That renegade Geraint's brat.'

Aurian stifled a small sound of protest, clenching her fists. With a swift movement Finbarr pushed back his chair and squatted before her, bringing his tall lanky frame down to her level. He lifted her chin with a gentle finger and looked deeply into her eyes. 'Child, you're going to hear a lot of that kind of nonsense within these venerable walls,' he said softly. 'Just let it pass. Geraint's only fault was pride, and the same applies to all the Magefolk who would blacken his name.' He shot a flinty look at Eliseth. 'I'm not saying that what he did was right, but the same disaster could have happened to any of us. Take no notice of what people say, child, but be prepared to learn from his errors – and ours, for what Geraint did was hardly unique. History is filled with similar examples – the Cataclysm, for instance, when ancient Magefolk warred amongst themselves. They came perilously close to destroying the world with the four great Artefacts of Power, and . . .'

'For goodness sake, Finbarr, spare us the lecture!'

Aurian was shocked by Eliseth's rudeness, but Finbarr seemed unsurprised. He continued to address her as though the Magewoman's ill-tempered outburst was of no importance. 'I hope, my young friend, that you will never let Eliseth teach you to scorn the knowledge that is so important to us all. If we study our history, it teaches us not to repeat mistakes. I know that Eliseth is in charge of your training just now, but when you're allowed to, come back and talk to me. I can teach you other things apart from magic, and I'll always be here to answer your questions. I always keep a welcome for civilized company. And now, I don't believe that Eliseth told me your name?'

'It's Aurian.' She managed a smile for him.

'Mine is Finbarr. I'm Meiriel's soulmate, and I hope you'll be seeing much more of us as time goes on. In the meantime, here's my advice: apply yourself diligently, keep out of trouble – and don't let the Lady of Misrule here grind you down.'

'It's time we were going, Aurian,' Eliseth interrupted icily.

Finbarr grinned. 'See what I mean? We'd better do as she says, or she'll have us neck deep in hailstones in no time!'

'Blast you, Finbarr!' Eliseth snarled. 'Don't you dare try to be funny at my expense!'

'Sorry, Eliseth.' To Aurian, the Archivist did not look at all repentant. 'Goodbye, Aurian – for the present.'

The introduction to the other Magefolk was much less satisfactory. The twins simply treated her with dismissive contempt, and Aurian felt very uneasy in their company. There was something unsettlingly strange about them that she couldn't quite place. They both had the appearance of beardless young men and were both fair, but Davorshan had a surprisingly coarse and stocky frame for one of Mage blood. His short-cropped blond hair had a distinct gingerish cast, and his colourless eyes were framed with pale lashes. Aurian found it almost impossible to look him in the eye, for the anonymous colouring seemed to automatically divert her gaze elsewhere. What was worse, he seemed to be very much aware of the fact, and she suspected that he used it deliberately to unnerve people.

Davorshan's brother D'arvan was completely different in appearance – so much so that it seemed impossible that they could be brothers, let alone twins. His pale, flaxen hair was shoulder length, and his bone structure was so finely carved and fragile-looking that he seemed ethereal in appearance. His beautiful face looked almost feminine, and his deep, luminous grey eyes had long, sweeping dark lashes that many a maid would have sold her soul for. He hung back behind his brother, saying nothing and letting Davorshan do all the talking. Had Aurian been more mature and confident herself, she might have suspected him of being painfully shy, but as it was she found him cold and fey.

'What do they do?' Aurian asked Eliseth timidly, as they left the twins' quarters.

The Magewoman shrugged. 'The gods only know. They're of Mage blood – their father was the famous Water–Mage Bavordran, and their mother was Adrina, the Earth-Mage. Miathan is certain they must have power, but whatever it is, it hasn't surfaced yet. We think that because they are twins, they're so tangled up in each other's minds that the power cannot be released. Davorshan shows some aptitude for Water-magic, but he seems fascinated with physical methods of control rather than magical ones. His mind is full of pumps and pipes and aqueducts and so on. We keep telling him that such stuff is for Mortals – we have other methods at our disposal – but we cannot break him of his nonsense. As for D'arvan, he can't spit without his brother's help. I've told the Archmage that it's a waste of time, but Miathan insists that we keep trying with him.'

Eliseth did, however, seem to think a lot of the last Mage, Bragar. His discipline was Fire-magic, as Geraint's had been, and Aurian had been looking forward to meeting him. Her enthusiasm died as soon as she saw him. Bragar was gaunt-faced and completely bald. His dark eyes, like Eliseth's, were devoid of warmth and expression, giving him a reptilian appearance. His aura was as dark as his purple robes, and Aurian, young and inexperienced though she was, could feel the cruelty of his nature shadowing him like the blackest of wings. He looked down at her over his high-bridged nose as though she were some species of insect, and his voice, when he deigned to speak to her, was sardonic and patronizing. He made Aurian's flesh creep, and she vowed to herself that she'd keep out of his way. She already knew that she possessed her father's talent of Fire-magic, and the thought of studing under Bragar filled her with fear.

*

The weeks that followed Aurian's arrival at the Academy became one long, inescapable nightmare. She was left in Eliseth's sole charge, and the Mage was unremittingly harsh with her. Aurian lacked any formal training in magic, and hitherto her use of her powers had been spontaneous and instinctive. Now she had to learn to discipline her wildfire talent into the controlled and focused power that was the true secret of the Magehood. This, according to Eliseth, could only be done by the endless repetition of drills and exercises that seemed, to Aurian, to explain nothing and accomplish very little.

Eliseth tried her with Fire-magic, using a candle flame which Aurian had to ignite, extinguish, or make larger or smaller. Aurian had no idea where to start. She also failed at mental communication – a rarity among the Magefolk in any case, though Aurian did not know this – since no sympathy existed between her and Eliseth. She had some limited success with simple levitation and Earth-magic, but Water-magic she found impossible to grasp. The magic of Air – which, as a Weather-Mage, was Eliseth's speciality – the Magewoman dismissed as being far too difficult for Aurian, given her poor performance to date.

Forral's exercises in concentration helped a little, but Aurian found that focusing her will differed greatly from disciplining her mind. Time after time, some small distraction would interfere with her attention, and she would either lose her gathered power completely or it would get out of control, with unfortunate results. Eliseth's punishments on these occasions were inventive, cruel and humiliating, and Aurian soon became afraid even to try lest she fail once more. But this only got her into more trouble with her impatient teacher. Even in the evenings her time was not her own, for Eliseth set her to learning the entire Mages' Code by heart, and tested her on it every day.

Aurian was more miserable and lonely than she had ever been in her life. Things might have been easier if she could have sent a message to her mother, or talked to Finbarr or Meiriel, but Eliseth kept her a virtual prisoner, making her work all day and locking her into her room at night. Aurian lost her appetite and couldn't sleep. Each night she lay awake tossing and fretting, and each morning the face that looked back from her mirror seemed more pale, gaunt and hollow-eyed. She became increasingly nervous and timid, and wept at the slightest provocation. As the weeks turned into months and spring came slowly round again, she became more and more convinced that she would never be a Mage. Inevitably, her hopelessness overcame even her fear of the city and the great world outside, and she became driven by a desperate need to escape.

At last an opportunity arrived. After a particularly trying day, Eliseth sent her to her room – and forgot to lock the door. Aurian waited breathlessly until well into the night, praying that the Mage would not return to imprison her once more. Then she bundled up her spare clothing in a blanket and crept out of the tower, expecting at any moment to hear an angry voice calling her back.

It seemed almost too easy. The air was mild and springlike, the full moon gave her plenty of light, and the courtyard was completely deserted. Aurian flitted silently from shadow to shadow, searching for another exit apart from the main gate, which was guarded, and would only lead her down the exposed road to the gatehouse on the causeway. As she circled the high wall of the complex, she began to despair. Surely there must be another way out. But her searching only brought her full circle, back to the Mages' Tower. Aurian could have sat down and wept, but the chance to escape might never come again, and she couldn't afford to waste it. She gritted her teeth and swore one of Forral's favourite oaths. 'Right,' she muttered. 'I'll climb out!' Searching for a better purchase on the smooth stonework, she crept into the corner where the wall joined the rounded side of the tower. And there, hidden in shadow, was a small wooden postern, set deep within the thick stones of the wall. Biting her lip, Aurian wrestled with the great iron ring that served as a handle, and pushed. The little door swung open. Aurian slipped through, and her heart sank. Before her was an enclosed garden, not a way out.

From her hiding place in the bushes that grew along the wall, Aurian scanned the garden. It was beautifully kept, with smoothly trimmed lawns, sparkling fountains and neat beds of delicate spring flowers that shimmered palely in the moonlight. Their fragrance drifted to Aurian on the warm breeze, and early moths danced above them as though some of the blossoms had taken to the air. Apart from a circular arbour in the centre, only the walls with their blanket of shrubs and vines offered cover for a fugitive. But one wall – the one furthest away from her – was only waist high. She could climb out! For a moment Aurian's heart leapt. Then she got her bearings. It was the wall bounding the edge of the steep cliff face that sheared down like the prow of a ship to the river below. She set her jaw stubbornly, and fought down her despair. I'll just have to try to climb down, that's all, she decided. Maybe it won't be too bad. I'd rather die than spend another night in this place!

Aurian slunk around the edge of the garden, staying in the shadow of the bushes and heading for the low wall. Then suddenly she saw the old man. He had been hidden by the arbour when she entered, but now he was in plain sight, kneeling over a flowerbed with a trowel in his hand. Her heart pounding, Aurian backed into the bushes, discovering too late that they were roses. The thorns stuck painfully into her back and caught in her clothes and hair, but she didn't dare make a sound or move to free herself, though the old gardener seemed to be completely engrossed in his task.

Aurian waited. And waited, praying that the old fool would hurry up and go away. Surely he wasn't planning to work all night? Evidently not. Without looking up, he said: 'Isn't it uncomfortable in there?' Aurian caught her breath, feeling the thorns drive deeper into her skin as she shrank back into the concealing foliage.

'You might as well come out, you know.' The rough old voice was not unkind. 'The Archmage's private garden is never the best place to hide, my dear. They say the very flowers whisper secrets in his ears.'

With a gasp, Aurian shot out of the rose bushes, ripping her clothes on the thorns. The old man smiled. 'That's better. This garden hasn't seen a pretty girl in more years than I could count.' From a pocket in his patched old tunic he took a small flask of wine, and a package neatly wrapped in a clean white cloth. 'I'm just about to eat,' he said. 'Do you like bread and cheese?'

He obviously wasn't right in the head. Aurian began to sidle towards the low wall. 'No, thank you,' she said. 'I'm afraid I don't have time.'

'Nonsense. It's better to run away on a full stomach than an empty one, I always say.'

'How did you know?' The words were out before she could stop them.

He shrugged. 'It's fairly obvious. I shouldn't try the cliff, though. Nobody has managed it yet, and you'll look a mess when you're just broken bones on those rocks at the bottom.'

Aurian stared at him, defeated. A single tear trickled down her cheek.

'Come along,' the old man said kindly. 'Have some supper and tell me all about it. Perhaps I can help you.'

Aurian had never drunk wine before. Somehow she ended up with the lion's share of the flask, and it loosened her tongue. Before long he had coaxed from her the whole story of her life, ending with the difficulties and misery of her time at the academy. The old man listened gravely, slipping in a question from time to time. He even gave her his handkerchief when her tears began to fall once more. When she had finished, he held out his hand. 'Come with me,' he said gently. 'It's time that matters were set to rights.'

Obediently, Aurian followed him across the garden and out through the postern door. It was only when they reached the Mages' Tower that she faltered. The old fool was insane!

'I can't!' she gasped. 'Eliseth is in there, and – and the Archmage!' She tried to pull away from him, but he held her firmly, his dark eyes burning into hers.

'My dear child, have you not guessed yet? I am the Archmage!'

Aurian almost fainted. She had been complaining bitterly about the Academy to the Archmage himself. He had caught her trying to run away and trespassing in his private garden. She couldn't speak, and she was trembling so hard that her legs threatened to give way beneath her.

Miathan put a steadying arm around her shoulders. 'Don't be afraid, child,' he said. 'If I set anyone by the ears over this business, it will certainly not be you.' Still Aurian hung back, frightened by the sudden steel in his voice. The Archmage looked down at her and sighed. 'Come along, girl. I won't turn you into a toad. But I will turn you into a first-class Mage.' And he smiled at her. It was such a dazzling, kind smile that Aurian's fears vanished like snow.

When they reached his rooms, the Archmage summoned a sleepy servant and ordered a second, far more sumptuous, supper for them. He seated Aurian in a soft chair by the fire while he changed from his patched old gardening clothes into the splendid, scarlet robes of his office. She gazed around the chamber while she waited, awed by the richness of the splendid furnishings, the deep soft carpet, and the gold-stitched tapestries that decorated the walls. Why, this place was fit for a king. It was a far, far cry from her cramped, bare little cell on the bottom floor.

The food arrived with amazing promptness, considering that the kitchen workers must have been hauled from their beds to prepare it. Aurian gazed, bewildered, at the tempting array – far too much for two people. She wondered, nervously, if she'd be expected to eat it all. And the food itself! Eilin had little time to cook, so her meals had been good but simple; and Eliseth seemed to think that bread and milk was enough for her to live on. Now she was faced with meats that were unrecognizable beneath rich sauces, and vegetables and fruits prepared in a wildly elaborate fashion. To her embarrassment, Aurian had no idea what to do with some of the exotically-shaped foodstuffs. Should she pick them up in her fingers, or would that be a breach of manners? Miathan, however, seemed aware of her predicament. He insisted on serving her himself, and explaining the complicated dishes to her whenever he saw her hesitate. Encouraged by his kindness and helped by the wine, which was beginning to make her head spin, Aurian began to relax and enjoy her food.

As they ate, Miathan explained that there had been a misunderstanding, and that from now on he would supervise her training personally. Aurian went suddenly cold. 'But – but Eliseth says I'm useless,' she confessed, shamefaced.

Miathan raised his eyebrows. 'What? Geraint and Eilin's daughter useless? I don't believe it!' Reaching out a hand, he

69

snuffed the single candle that burned in a silver holder in the centre of the table. The room was suddenly plunged into shadow; the only light coming from the roaring flames in the fireplace. 'Aurian, will you light the candle for me? I can't see to eat,' the Archmage said.

Aurian's mind went blank with panic. The more she tried to focus her scattered thoughts, the worse it became. What would he do to her if she failed? Suddenly Miathan's strong hand closed around hers, and his warm voice cut through the chaos in her mind. 'Relax, child. Think of the flame. Picture it in your mind. It's only a glowing spot at first, clinging to the wick. Then the wax on the wick starts to melt and splutter – you can smell it – and the little flame starts to blossom and grow . . .'

Aurian's eyes widened. It was happening! A soft pool of light crept towards the edges of the room as her little flame caught and expanded. 'I did it!' she cried triumphantly, then clamped her hand over her mouth in horror as a roaring column of fire, responding to her euphoria, shot up from the candle to scorch the ceiling. 'Oh!' Aurian damped the flame automatically, as she had done so often with her fireballs at home, and shrank away from Miathan. 'I'm sorry,' she whispered.

The Archmage threw back his head and roared with laughter. 'Well,' he spluttered, 'I asked for that! I see that I shall have to be very careful about my requests to you in future!'

Aurian was dumbfounded. 'You mean – it's all right? But I've just ruined your ceiling.'

'Never mind the ceiling, my dear. The servants will soon put it right,' Miathan said. 'More important, you've proved that, far from being hopeless, you have a very powerful talent at your disposal. All we need do is teach you to summon it – which you managed very well, once I explained how to do it – and control it. You failed to break your link with the flame, you see, and it was simply responding to your emotions.'

'Will you show me how?' Aurian asked eagerly.

Miathan smiled. 'Aren't you tired? It's very late.'

'Tired? No, not a bit. It's all so . . .' Aurian's voice was swallowed in a huge yawn.

The Archmage held out his hand. 'Come along,' he said. 'You can sleep in my bed tonight, and in the morning I'll arrange to have you moved. There's a set of empty rooms on the floor below – they belonged to your father, as a matter of fact – and I think they will suit you well. We'll be working very closely together in future, so I'll want you near me. How does that sound?'

'Oh, thank you, Archmage!' In an excess of gratitude, Aurian threw her arms around Miathan's neck and hugged him. For a nervous moment she wondered if she had gone too far, but then she saw that his stern old face was beaming. It was in that instant that Aurian came to love him. She fell asleep in his great canopied bed feeling happier and more secure than she had done for months, and instead of Forral, it was Miathan who filled her last drowsy thoughts.

A knock on the door interrupted the Archmage's contemplation of the sleeping young girl. Sighing, he left the bedchamber, closing the door quietly behind him. As he had expected, his visitor was Eliseth. 'Could it not wait until morning?' he said crossly.

Eliseth walked across to the fire and warmed her hands. 'I couldn't sleep. I wanted to know how it went.'

'Well, you certainly played your part successfully. The poor child was terrified almost beyond functioning. But her power, Eliseth! It was incredible in one so young.'

'Just what are your plans for her?' Eliseth's voice turned sharp. 'You're training her yourself – does that mean you have her in mind to succeed you?'

Miathan chuckled. 'So that's what this nocturnal visit is about. I might have guessed. Well, you can relax, my dear. I have no plans to appoint a successor just yet – in fact, I may never appoint one.'

'What? But – but the maximum tenure for the position is two hundred years. It always has been.'

'Traditionally, yes. But traditions may be put aside. I enjoy being Archmage, and besides, who would succeed me? You and Bragar have ambitions in that direction . . .'

'Bragar?' Eliseth gasped.

Miathan laughed. 'How naive you are! Did you think you had tamed him with the lure of your body? It failed to work on

71

me – what made you think it would succeed any better with him? It's been most entertaining to watch the two of you manoeuvring and plotting around each other, but I'm still ahead of you both in the game of power. You'd do better to remain on my side, my dear. One day I plan to rule the world, and there will be power and wealth to spare for my loyal supporters.' Miathan's face grew grim. 'Don't think of crossing me, Eliseth. I'm ten times more powerful than you alone, but now you'll have Aurian to deal with too. You've trapped yourself nicely there, with this plan of ours. Aurian already hates you – and now the child is mine.'

5

A Voice in the Dark

'So that's how you do it!' Aurian ran her fingers along the racks of scrolls, and the field of magic, marked by an aura of glittering blue Magelight, shimmered at her touch. Aurian's face was alight with enthusiasm, and Finbarr marvelled again at the change that six years had wrought in the young Mage. At twenty, she had blossomed into a tall, slender young woman. Her mane of glowing dark red hair was the same, but her face had matured into the sculpted planes and angles that reminded him so strongly of her father. With that nose, she would never be called pretty, but her features had a strong, stark, compelling beauty that was all her own. And her manner had changed radically from the cowed and nervous child he had first known. Now she was happy, confident and glowing, her powers increasing by the day, and her thirst for knowledge unquenchable. Miathan had done well with her. Almost too well, Finbarr sometimes thought.

'Finbarr, are you listening?'

'What? Yes, of course . . . What were you saying?'

Aurian gave a long-suffering sigh, but she was smiling. 'I asked you if the preserving spell you use on the old documents actually takes them out of time in some way?'

Finbarr was startled. 'Why yes, I suppose it does. I never really thought of it that way, but the idea would make sense. I found the spell in a scroll written by Barothas – you know, that ancient historian obsessed with proving the existence of the lost Dragonfolk? He talks of several earlier references – alas, now lost to us – that mention their ability to manipulate time, as well as other dimensions. Indeed, your poor father used his notes in his tragic experiment to move from world to world. Of course, to manipulate space, as opposed to time, one would . . .'

'Good gracious, Finbarr, have you never considered the implications of that?'

'What implications?' The archivist, jolted from the realms of scholarly discourse, felt the first stirrings of alarm.

Aurian frowned. 'Well, I don't know exactly. But I'm sure I could think of a few things.' Her voice took on a wheedling note. 'Finbarr, would you teach me that spell?'

Finbarr gave the young Mage a severe look. Her face was a picture of innocence, but he was not fooled – he knew Aurian too well. 'If by that you mean will I let you see the scroll, the answer is absolutely not. After what happened to Geraint, I locked it safely away, and there it stays. It may console you to know, however, that you are not the only one forbidden such knowledge – I decided long ago that Dragon-magic is too dangerous for the Magefolk to tamper with. I deeply regret not burning the scroll when I first found it – yet even now, even knowing the damage it can wreak, I cannot bring myself to destroy part of our history. No one but ourselves, and possibly your mother, knows of its existence – and Aurian, I put you on your honour not to say a word of it to a single soul, not even the Archmage.' He took her hands in his own. 'Have I your promise?'

'Of course you do!' Aurian assured him. 'On condition that you teach me the time spell!'

The archivist hesitated. 'You must check with Miathan first,' he said at last. 'He's in charge of your training, and your schedule is too crowded as it is.'

'Oh, that's all right,' Aurian said. 'I can make the extra time. In fact, if you show me this spell, I may find a way of doing exactly that.' Her eyes twinkled mischievously.

It took Finbarr a moment to grasp her meaning, and when he did his blood went cold. 'Aurian! Don't you dare even contemplate playing around with time! Have you any notion how dangerous that could be? The gods only know what damage you might do!'

Aurian patted his arm. 'It's all right, Finbarr. I was only teasing.' But her eyes remained thoughtful.

'Listen,' Finbarr said, hoping to change the subject. 'Meiriel and I would like you to come to supper with us tonight. She says she never sees you these days.'

Aurian's face fell. 'Oh, I can't tonight. I need to get busy with these books on Weather-magic you've found for me. Miathan has been a help, but Eliseth is the specialist, and since she's so reluctant to teach me I have to pick up the theory where I can. If only I could get into the dome and practise. But she always has some excuse. It's so frustrating!' She banged her fist on the table.

Finbarr blinked. 'I didn't know you had actually started on Weather-magic,' he said.

'Well, I needed something to fill my time when I stopped studying Fire-magic with Bragar.'

The archivist frowned. 'Yes, I'd heard about that. My dear child, don't you think it was unwise to quarrel with Bragar?'

'Meaning that you do, I suppose?' Aurian scowled. 'Bragar is an ass! He thinks he's such an expert, but he barely knows the first thing about Fire-magic. I had learned everything that I could possibly learn from him, and if he didn't like it when I told him so, that's his hard luck!'

'As I heard it, you were tactless in the extreme,' Finbarr admonished her, 'and I advise you to apologize. Mark my words, Bragar will make a bad enemy.'

Aurian shrugged. 'I don't have time to be soothing Bragar's sulks. He'll get over it. Finbarr, *please* will you teach me that spell?'

'Don't you think you have enough on your plate? You work all the hours the gods send. If you're not too busy to eat, you forget – and I've seen that light burning in your rooms all night. Don't you think you should make time for a little recreation? Or even sleep occasionally, for goodness sake?'

'I'm all right.' Aurian's face grew serious. 'Finbarr, I want to make Miathan proud of me. He's been so good to me – like the father I never knew. The only way I can repay him is to become the best Mage that ever lived – and I will.' Her jaw tightened in the stubborn expression that Finbarr, not to mention everyone else in the Academy, from the servants to the Archmage, knew only too well. The archivist sighed. Meiriel was right to be concerned. Aurian had become completely obsessed with her work, forgetting to eat and sleep, and putting far too much strain on the inner energies that were the source of her magical powers. The danger signs were already showing. Her face was wan and drawn, and her skin seemed to burn with an inner light. Her green eyes were vague and glowing.

Last summer, when Finbarr had taken Aurian to visit her mother, he had tried to enlist Eilin's aid in persuading her to slow down, but the Earth-Mage, used to her own gruelling labours, had dismissed his concerns. Eilin had also been pushing herself too hard – her self-imposed task was far too much for one Mage. Finbarr had been alarmed by her haggard appearance, and knew that she was missing Aurian more than she would admit; but when he begged her to return to the Academy, she had refused outright. Like mother like daughter, Finbarr thought. I can see where Aurian gets her obsessive behaviour from – and her impossible stubbornness!

None the less, he decided on one last attempt to get through to the headstrong young Mage. 'Aurian, listen. You *must* take better care of yourself. Meiriel believes you're in danger of burning yourself out. Terrible things can happen to a Mage who overstretches herself as you do. Miathan is proud of your accomplishments, but he doesn't want you to lose your powers – and your mind – through being overzealous. Believe me, it can happen. I have cases documented right here, if you want to see them.'

Aurian's face grew grave. 'Is Meiriel really worried?'

'She certainly is. If you would only talk to her . . .'

'Of course I will!' Aurian cried impulsively. 'Listen – I'll come to supper after all. I'm sure I can set her mind at rest. In the meantime I'll take these and make a start.' Gathering her armload of heavy old volumes from the table she dashed out, forgetting, as usual, to say goodbye. Finbarr sighed. Well, he had tried. Perhaps Meiriel could talk some sense into her.

The heat struck Aurian like a blow as she emerged from the library into the dusty, sunlit courtyard. The weather was rarely this good so far north, but the hot spell had been going on for over a month now, and showed no signs of abating. At first the farmers outside the city had been pleased, but now all the hay was in and the parched corn was drooping in the fields. The river had dried to a stinking, muddy trickle, and for the first time in living memory, water was rationed in Nexis. The

Mortals had started looking to the Magefolk to solve the problems, and rumours of unrest were growing daily as the drought continued.

Aurian gave the matter little thought. She was absorbed in her work, and blithely confident that Miathan could solve any problem. She had no idea of the hardships that Mortals were suffering, as the academy was supplied by its own deep underground springs and the Magefolk had no lack of water. Since she rarely left the hilltop complex, she was unaware that her people were now discouraged from going into the city alone. Speeding across the courtyard, Aurian decided to spend the rest of the afternoon studying in Miathan's garden – a privilege that was uniquely hers, so close had she come to the Archmage. But when she reached the little door she heard Eliseth's voice coming from the other side of the wall.

'Miathan, I've done what I can. I can't make it rain just like that – the nearest clouds are hundreds of miles away! I've set things in motion, but it will take them days to get here, and I'm exhausting myself in the process. Those clods in the city should be grateful! Frankly, had you not insisted, I wouldn't even bother. Who cares about their stupid drought? The Magefolk are all right.'

'Eliseth, I explained why.' Miathan sounded weary and exasperated. 'You know how volatile the situation is down there. Water is already rationed, and Meiriel says that if the river gets any lower there's a serious risk of disease. There have been some isolated outbreaks already, and they're blaming the Magefolk. If we have an epidemic, the city will go up like tinder, and I'm not ready to deal with an angry mob. Rioch came to see me last night, and this time he's determined to retire. He says he's too old to cope with the unrest. And Vannor! I suspect that secretly he's one of the main fomenters of the trouble. He used to be bad enough, but since his wife died last year he crosses me on the council at every opportunity. Because Meiriel failed to save her, he blames the Magefolk.' Miathan sighed. 'It would help if we could find a successor for Rioch, but there is no sympathy for our people at the garrison just now. Eliseth, if you can't manage some rain soon, I daren't contemplate the consequences.'

'I'm doing my best!' Eliseth snapped. 'If you didn't plague me with your problems, I would have more time . . .'

Aurian walked away, frowning. Poor Miathan! Perhaps if she made some progress with her studies in Weather-magic she would be able to help him. Suddenly decisive, she shifted the heavy stack of books to her other arm and headed for her rooms. It was stifling in the tower, and for once Aurian found herself wishing she lived nearer the ground floor as she dragged herself up the endless spiral of steps. By the time she reached her door she felt weak and dizzy. A servant passed her on his way down from Miathan's chambers, and, with Finbarr's warning in mind, Aurian detained him. She hadn't eaten all day, but as she was on the point of asking him for some food she hesitated. It was too hot to eat. I can get something later, she thought. 'Bring me a cool drink,' she told the man, and went into her rooms, dropping the books on the table with a grateful sigh.

The study was like an oven. The green and gold curtains hung limp at the open window, and dust motes hovered in the thick bar of sunlight that pooled on the moss-green carpet. Aurian reached for the pitcher of water on her table, but discarded its stale and lukewarm contents with a grimace, deciding to wait for the servant's return. If Miathan would give me my own servant, she thought, I wouldn't suffer such neglect! She pulled up a chair and sat down at the table, deciding that she might as well get started.

Whoever had written the ancient volume had atrocious handwriting. Aurian rubbed her eyes, which ached from trying to decipher the illegible scrawl. The lines seemed to undulate across the page as the brassy sunlight poured through the window, striking the parchment with a dazzling glare and scorching the back of her head. Aurian wondered irritably when the servant would bring her drink, then turned her attention back to her work. Thank goodness Finbarr had taught her that spell to clarify these archaic scribbles! Frowning with concentration, she focused on the page, reaching deep within herself to access her powers.

At first Aurian was unaware that anything was amiss. Then she noticed that, instead of becoming clearer, the words

78

seemed to be getting smaller. With a shock, she realized that the periphery of her vision had clouded so that the writing seemed far away, at the end of a long, dark tunnel. When she tried to wrench her eyes away, her body would not obey her. Everything was speeding away from her, and she was falling – falling into the dark . . .

'I'm sorry, Archmage. I can't do any more. I warned her this would happen if she pushed herself too hard.' The healer sounded upset, and Miathan stifled his anger. This is my fault, he thought, for letting Aurian overextend herself.

'Are you sure?' he asked. 'It's been three days, Meiriel!'

Meiriel sat down wearily on Aurian's bed. 'Physically, there's nothing wrong with her. As far as I can tell, there's no loss of her powers. But something within her has withdrawn to stop her abusing them. I think she is aware of what is happening around her, but she's trapped within herself, and we can't get through to her.'

'How long will it last?'

Meiriel shrugged. 'Who knows? To be honest, Archmage, if you can't reach her, the situation looks bad.'

'What about her mother?'

Meiriel shook her head. 'I doubt she'd be much help. Apart from you, the only person close to Aurian was that Mortal.'

'Forral! Of course!' Miathan drove his fist into his palm. His quick brain had the glimmerings of a tremendous idea. 'Forral could be the solution to all our problems. Can you have Finbarr scry for him at once? I'll arrange for a messenger. The sooner we can send for him, the better.'

The light from the glowing crystal on the table before the archivist threw sharp shadows on the wall behind him. The Archmage hovered at his shoulder, seething with impatience. 'Will you get out of the way, Miathan?' Finbarr's voice was uncharacteristically sharp. 'Your emotional aura is enough to block reception for miles around!'

'Just get on with it!'

Finbarr unfolded from his chair and turned to glare into the Archmage's eyes. He pointed a long, bony finger at the door.

'Out!' Miathan blinked in astonishment. He had forgotten the fondness that had always existed between Aurian and the archivist. Swallowing an angry reply, he headed for the door, and began to pace up and down the corridor outside. After several minutes, Finbarr's head appeared round the door. 'All the way out!' he said. 'When I find your swordsman, I'll send for you.'

Forral sighed wearily, and pushed the stack of documents away from him. There was no more space on the overcrowded desk, and a pile of papers at the back slid over the edge and rearranged themselves across the floor. Forral swore. What had possessed him to take command of this dead-and-alive hole at the back end of nowhere? The southern coast was quiet these days, and the troops at the hill forts had nothing to do but ride out to quell the occasional uprising of the Hill Tribes: the rough, fiercely independent folk who mined minerals and metals from these bleak southern slopes. And since the Tribes, savage though they were, were utterly disorganized and constantly feuding with one another, that left Forral with little to do but cope with a flood of trifling administration that was slowly driving him crazy.

The swordsman bitterly regretted, now, that he had ever come to this place. It had seemed a haven at first, for without Aurian his life had held little purpose. For about a year after leaving the Valley, he had wandered aimlessly, picking up work here and there as he could, mostly guarding caravans or warehouses for merchants. Dull work it had been, and sometimes degrading, but he had cared little, save that he had a dry place to sleep and food in his belly – and sometimes a few spare coins over, to spend on drink and women. The latter, in the end, had finished it for him. Sick of loneliness, and squalor, and morning-after awakenings with a throbbing head and a strange face next to him on the pillow, he had taken the post at the fort to provide himself with some purpose in life. It had seemed like a good idea at the time, he thought ruefully.

Forral picked up the flask of wine, then set it down with a grimace. Boredom and inaction were driving him to drink, and that wouldn't solve anything. He frowned at the walls of thick grey stone that had become his prison. It was definitely time for a change. Absently, he picked up the flask again, poured a cup of wine and began to review his options. Mercenary work, with its danger and hardships, no longer attracted him as it had done when he was younger. There was no doubt about it – life at the fort had made him soft.

A knock on the door interrupted his gloomy thoughts, and a young soldier entered somewhat timidly. Forral was aware that his troops were giving him a wide berth nowadays. Afraid of the old man's uncertain temper, he acknowledged ruefully to himself. 'Yes, what is it?' he snapped.

The soldier saluted. 'Sir, a courier has arrived for you. He bears an urgent message from the Archmage himself.' The young man's tones were hushed with awe, and Forral felt much the same. What could Miathan want with him? Aware of the young trooper's eyes on him, he schooled his features into a semblance of unconcern.

'You'd better send him in, then.'

The dust-caked messenger was stumbling with weariness. Forral suggested that he go to the mess hall to refresh himself, but the man hesitated. 'The Archmage said to be sure you read it at once, sir. He said it's very urgent.'

'All right. Sit down then, man, before you fall over.' Forral poured him a glass of wine, then sat down and broke the seal on the crumpled scroll.

'Great Chathak!' Forral's eyes widened in disbelief. He was actually being offered command of the garrison, with its position on the ruling council of Nexis! But the import of the news was lost in the remainder of the message. Aurian needed him! 'Take a day's rest before you start back,' he told the courier. 'I have to leave at once.' Overturning the chair in his haste, he shot out of the door, bellowing for his second in command.

Aurian was lost. She was trapped within a maze whose dark walls enclosed her endlessly, keeping her mind circling in an agony of hopeless frustration. She heard voices sometimes; those of Meiriel and Finbarr, and even Miathan, but she was helpless to respond. She lost track of time and reality, slipping away into bizarre and frightening dreams, or sometimes returning to her childhood. The voices faded in and out of her consciousness, sounding hushed and worried. Aurian clung to them desperately, fearful for her sanity.

Then, out of the darkness, a new voice called to her – and an old one. A dear, familiar voice that she had despaired of ever hearing again. It shook with emotion. 'Aurian? Aurian, love, it's me.' It was a dream – it had to be – but her mind yearned desperately towards it. The voice grew stern. 'They tell me you've been neglecting your sword practice. How do you expect to become the world's best swordswoman if you lie around in bed all day?'

Ah, that was it. She had been wounded. All that stuff about the Academy and the Archmage must have been fever dreams. Gods, they had seemed real. But now Forral was calling to her, and she must be getting better. Aurian opened her eyes, and blinked in confusion. It was Forral all right, but he seemed older now. His body was heavier, and his hair and beard were grizzled.

'Forral?' She struggled to sit up.

'Ah, love!' Forral's voice was choked with emotion as he enfolded her in an enormous hug, crushing her tightly to his breast. Aurian felt her heart thudding strangely. Never before had she been so aware of his touch. Over his shoulder she glimpsed the white walls of the infirmary, and the familiar figures of Meiriel and the Archmage, and her mind reeled, trying to slot it all into place. She pulled away, touching the swordsman's face with tentative fingers.

'Forral? You've come back? You've really come back?' He nodded, unable to speak. Aurian's eyes brimmed over, and she threw her arms around him in a fierce hug of her own.

'I do like to see a happy ending.' Miathan's dry voice interrupted their reunion, and Aurian wondered why he was frowning.

Forral turned to the Archmage with a scowl. 'If it is a happy ending, it's no thanks to you,' he said flatly. 'How could you let this happen to her?'

Miathan's face darkened. Aurian winced, knowing all too well the Archmage's temper, but Forral glared back at him, unimpressed. 'Now that I'm back I'll make bloody sure it doesn't happen again!'

'That depends on you,' Miathan said coolly. 'When I put my proposition to you, you seemed far from enthusiastic. How can you help Aurian if you are elsewhere?'

'What is this?' Aurian interrupted.

Forral sighed. 'The Archmage has offered me the post of commander of the garrison,' he said.

'That means you'll be staying in Nexis!' Aurian could hardly contain her delight. 'Oh, Forral, that's wonderful! I've missed you so much!'

Forral looked at her helplessly, and shook his head. 'All right, Miathan, I give in. I accept. But it'll be on my terms. And before I start, I'm taking Aurian out of here for a holiday – a long holiday – at your expense.'

Aurian and Forral left the Academy unaware that they were being watched from a window high in the Mages' Tower.

'Curse her!' Bragar snarled. 'Why could the arrogant bitch not have died? Why did Miathan bring that wretched swordsman here? The fewer pieces there are in this game, the better; especially where Aurian is concerned.'

Eliseth laughed; a soft, smug, silvery laugh. 'I wouldn't be too concerned, Bragar.' She laid a cool hand on his arm. 'I have a feeling that before too long Miathan's little pet will remove herself from the game.'

'What do you mean?' Bragar was frowning.

Eliseth laughed again. 'You men. So obtuse! Did you not notice the way she was looking at that oaf of a Mortal?'

'What?'

'Spare me the indignation, Bragar! You've had Mortals many a time, and so have I. But we had the sense to hide the evidence.' Eliseth purred. 'Aurian won't, I'll wager. And our dear Archmage will never brook a rival. He has plans in that direction himself.' She shrugged. 'All we need do is wait. Eventually the pieces will fall right into our hands. And speaking of pieces, I think we ought to recruit a pawn of our own.'

'What do you mean? What are you plotting now, Eliseth? Meiriel and Finbarr would never . . .'

'Not them, moron!' Eliseth's voice dripped scorn. 'I was talking about Davorshan.'

Bragar burst out laughing. 'My dear Eliseth, how do you propose to get him away from that twin of his? And even if you did, what earthly use would he be? Those two haven't the power between them to light a candle.'

'Between them, no. But if there were only one? I believe that's the problem, Bragar. They have sufficient power for one Mage, but their minds are so closely linked that neither can use it. But I want that power to come to us, and Davorshan is the likelier candidate of the two. As for parting him from D'arvan . . .' A smug little smile tugged at the corners of Eliseth's mouth. 'I believe he has reached the stage where – certain inducements – might work.'

Bragar reached out to embrace her. 'By the gods, but you're devious!' he said approvingly.

'True.' Deftly, Eliseth avoided his grasp. You fool, she thought scornfully. Little do you know how devious I can be.

Forral took Aurian to stay at the Fleet Deer, one of the finest inns in Nexis. From the start, the swordsman forbade her to use the slightest hint of magic – not even to light a candle – but now that she was reunited with her beloved Forral Aurian never missed it. On the first night, over the best supper the inn could provide, she and Forral brought themselves up to the present, and the swordsman spoke of his reluctance to accept the garrison post. 'It's a tremendous honour,' he said, 'but I don't fancy it much. I accepted because I couldn't turn down the chance for us to be together again. Oh, gods, lass, but I've missed you!'

Aurian reached across the table and took his hand. 'And I missed you,' she said softly. 'If you only knew the tears I've shed . . .' Her eyes flashed. 'How could you just go away like that?'

Forral looked abashed. 'I'm sorry, love, truly I am. I honestly thought it was the best thing. I felt so bad about what happened, I just couldn't think straight. Then the healer and your mother said . . .'

'Mother? I might have guessed!' Aurian contained her anger

with an effort. 'I'm sorry. I won't spoil tonight. The main thing is that you're back. But why don't you want to take command of the garrison?'

Forral smiled. 'How you've grown up! All these years I've thought of you as a child, and now I find a woman. It'll take some getting used to.' The look he gave her was lingering, and Aurian found herself blushing as the intimacy of his gaze kindled a new and disturbing warmth within her.

'The garrison?' she prompted, to cover her sudden, unaccountable shyness. To her relief Forral shook himself, as though waking from a dream, and took up her cue.

'It's not the responsibility that worries me.' He grimaced. 'It's the bloody paperwork! I hate administration.'

Aurian laughed. 'Is that all? Then don't do it!'

'Aurian, I don't think you realize . . .'

'Of course I do. But as garrison commander, you'll have so much influence. Hire someone else to do the paperwork, then you'll have more time to do what you want – and to spend with me!'

Forral's face was a study in amazement and relief. 'Aurian, you're a genius!'

They talked all night, revelling in each other's company, and for the first time in her life, Aurian got drunk. Forral introduced her to peach brandy, and she took to it all too well. The way she felt next morning came as a shock. She awoke with a churning stomach and pounding head, and a quick, wincing glance between the curtains showed that the sun had already reached the zenith.

When Aurian came down to the private dining-room reserved for guests at the inn, she discovered that Forral had beaten her to it – but only just. One look at his pale face and bleary eyes showed that at least they were suffering together. At the sight of him, Aurian found herself hesitating. She'd had such dreams last night! Dreams where Forral had kissed her, held her . . . You fool, she told herself firmly. Why, he practically brought you up! It must have been the wine. But he looked up and smiled, and she found that she was shaking as she sat down. It was the wine, she repeated determinedly. Only the wine . . .

'Great Chathak, love, you're white as a sheet!' Forral sounded concerned. 'Poor lass – it's the first time you've drunk too much, isn't it? And it's my fault.' As he took her hand, a jolt of tingling fire sped through Aurian's body. Gods, she thought, what's happening to me? Forral pushed a steaming cup towards her, and she buried her face in it to hide her confusion. It was taillin, a tea made from the leaves of a bush that grew in the south-east that was the staple stimulant of the city-dwellers. Aurian took a sip, grimacing at the acid taste. How she missed her mother's teas, made from a variety of berries, flowers or herbs, each with a specific benefit to confer. None the less, at that moment, Aurian was grateful for taillin.

Just then one of the inn's serving men approached, all apologetic deference. They had already discovered Forral's identity, and as for having a Mage as a guest . . .

'I'm sorry, sir and Lady,' he said. 'This is the best we could do for breakfast, it being so late, and times being so bad . . .' He plunked down two plates of what Aurian could only describe as curdled eggs, and beat a hasty retreat. She stared in disbelief at the slimy yellow spoonful on her plate, swallowing the bile that rose in her throat. Times being so bad? What did he mean? Surely things weren't that bad in the city, despite the drought? Supper last night had been all right. Although, she acknowledged wryly, she'd been so immersed in Forral that she wouldn't have noticed if . . .

'Sir! Commander Forral!' It was the landlord of the inn, and by the look of him, the man was in a rare panic. Aurian blinked in surprise at his red-faced, dishevelled appearance. Could this be the same urbane, self-possessed man who had welcomed them last night? He tugged at Forral's arm, completely abandoning the servile courtesy with which the Fleet Deer treated its guests. 'Sir, come quick!' he panted. 'There's a riot in the market!'

'What?' Forral flung back his chair and leapt to his feet. 'Stay there,' he told Aurian, and was gone.

For a moment, the Mage's childhood habit of obedience to the swordsman held firm. Then her brows knotted, and her jaw began to clench. Stay here, indeed, as though she were still a child? Sit and drink taillin while he went into danger? 'Some chance!' Aurian muttered. Rising swiftly, she hurried after Forral.

6
Stormbringer

The mess hall of the Nexis garrison tended to be busy during the hour of the midday meal. The noise was usually close to deafening as the cheerful clatter of knife on plate and the din of competing talk and ribald jests echoed round the bare walls of whitewashed stone. Today, nothing could be heard but a desultory murmur of conversation and the buzz of the fat black flies that clustered round the discarded food on the tables. Because of the drought, the imminent change of commander, and the looming threat of civil unrest, morale at the garrison was at its lowest ebb.

Maya looked at the rows of empty tables and benches and frowned. She was not surprised that no one was eating. Rations were short because of the drought, and food went rancid quickly in this heat. Vegetables and fruit were in short supply, going mostly to the well off, who could afford the inflated cost; to inns like the Fleet Deer, that catered to the rich; or – the small, dark-haired warrior scowled – to the blasted Magefolk! Maya clenched her fists beneath the table. What had happened to justice? Everywhere else in Nexis, including the garrison, folk were mainly living on the stringy, fly-blown carcases of the beasts that were dying like flies in the scorched countryside.

'What a bloody awful life!' Maya muttered, hardly sure whether she was speaking to herself or to Hargorn. The ageing warrior, well aware of what lay behind her gloom, gave her hand a sympathetic squeeze.

'Don't take it to heart, lovey. It's no reflection on your abilities, or the fact that you're a woman, that the Archmage won't have you on the Council of Three. In fact, to the troopers, it's a compliment. At least it proves that you aren't in the old bastard's pocket. And second in command to so great a swordsman isn't such a bad promotion, is it?'

Maya grimaced. 'It is if you'd planned to be commander! Besides, Forral may be a great swordsman, but we all know he got the post because he's so matey with the Magefolk!' She banged her fist on the table. 'Miathan might as well take command himself and be done with it. If it wasn't for Vannor, the poor bloody Mortals who live in this city would have no representation at all!'

'Woman or no, you'd never have got the post with those views,' Hargorn told her bitterly. 'They were what ruined my career at the garrison. Mark my words, lassie – stay out of city politics!' He adjusted the band that held back his long, grey-shot mane of hair, and stood up. 'I'd better go. If Parric doesn't get back soon I'll be needed.'

'He's not back from seeing Vannor?' Maya wished that she had drawn that duty. She both liked and respected the tough, stocky little head of the Merchants' Guild, with his wry sense of humour and uncompromising attitude to life in general and the Magefolk in particular.

Hargorn shook his head. 'Why Rioch sent Parric up there with word about his successor, I don't know. As if it makes any difference to Vannor who the Archmage has picked.'

'Here comes Parric now,' Maya interrupted.

It was a long-standing garrison joke that the wiry little cavalry master could never enter a room quietly. This time, he was in a paroxysm of coughing from the white dust that blew endlessly around the dried-out parade ground. He was also in a tremendous hurry. Crossing to their table, he wiped the dust from his tanned face and balding head and downed the flat, lukewarm remains of Maya's tankard of ale in a single gulp. 'There's trouble,' he said, 'and I can't find Rioch anywhere.'

It had been a long walk from the mill to Nexis. It seemed like an even longer climb from the river path up to Greenmarket Square, where the farmers from outside the city came to sell their produce. Sara tucked stray wisps of sweat-damp hair back into her kerchief as she trudged up the steep cobbled lane, and shifted the clumsy basket to her other arm. She stamped her foot in annoyance as the loose weave snagged the thin fabric of her gown. Why had her mother made her trail all this way on a fool's errand? As if there'd be any produce to buy! Is it my fault we're short of food? she thought irritably. Did I make the wretched drought? To add to her list of complaints, her usually indulgent father had given her a thorough scolding for not getting up early enough to reach the market as soon as it opened. Sara scowled. There'd been no living with the man since the shrunken river had left the mill-wheel high and dry. And since Anvar no longer came in his cart for flour, she'd had to walk all this way. Not, she mused, that Anvar was any fun nowadays. He was always working, as if that would get him anywhere! The trouble was, he had no ambition!

Nearly there. Sara sighed gratefully as she started to drag herself up the steep flight of steps that led to the entrance of the square. Hot, footsore and hungry, she was far too busy nursing her grievances to notice the rising hubbub of angry voices. Entering the square, she walked straight into a riot.

Vannor galloped through the city streets at breakneck speed, having flogged his poor horse all the way from his home on the south bank of the river. He'd received word from the frantic market stallholders who, on seeing the ugly mood of the crowd, had sent for the head of the Merchants' Guild. 'Stupid idiots!' Vannor muttered in exasperation. Why hadn't they sent to the garrison, which was closer? It was sheer luck that Parric had been with him when the flustered messenger arrived.

Not daring to waste time in taking a longer way round, the merchant urged his reluctant horse straight up the stone steps that were the quickest route into the market. By the time Parric had managed to alert the troopers, the situation could be well out of hand. Reaching the square, Vannor discovered that it already was. A huge bonfire of torn-down stalls burned in the centre of the market place. The square was filled with a seething mass of people. Some bore cudgels, while others, to Vannor's alarm, were armed with torches, axes and knives. 'Down with the merchants!' they chanted. 'Down with the Magefolk!'

Vannor cursed. He agreed, in his heart of hearts, with the latter sentiment, but as head of the Merchants' Guild he could hardly condone the former. The merchants were huddled behind a barricade of upended carts, the target of missiles and abuse. It was easy to see what had sparked the riot. Behind the traders was a wagon laden with produce: boxes of summer fruits; root and leaf vegetables, shrivelled but sound; assorted cheeses; and two crates of live poultry. The cart was stamped with the mark of the Magefolk, and had clearly been destined for the Academy. The merchants, even in the face of the mob, were too terrified of Miathan's wrath to renege on their bargain with the Archmage, and were still trying to defend the wagon with its precious cargo.

Struggling with his shying horse, Vannor paused at the edge of the square. What can I do, he thought, against this? Where are the troopers? The trouble was that, having fought his way out of a childhood of squalid poverty to his present high station, he sympathized with the desperate, hungry folk in the square. Yet he was head of the Merchants' Guild now, and his people were in danger. He had a responsibility to them. He must get through to the traders, and force them to abandon that wagon. Not daring to think of the consequences, he began to urge his shrinking mount through the impacted crowd.

It was hard going. The horse was understandably reluctant; terrified of the mob. That makes two of us, Vannor thought grimly, as he fought off clutching hands and fended off the missiles as best he could. Faces, pale and pinched with hunger, turned towards him. Somewhere in the crowd, a cry went up. With a hollow sickness in the pit of his stomach, Vannor realized his mistake too late. To these people, his horse meant food. A stone hit his face, and he tasted blood. They surged behind him, blocking his retreat, but too scared, yet, to approach the flashing heels of his mount. Though he tried to thrust a way forward, he could make no headway. He shouted to attract the traders' attention, but they would never hear him over the din.

Suddenly Vannor's horse gave a shrill scream and reared, lashing out with its hooves. The crowd shrank away from it in panic. As he wrestled with its reins, another shriek drew the merchant's eyes downward. A young girl had fallen beneath the flailing hooves of his mount. Wrenching the beast aside with a yank that nearly pulled his arms from their sockets, Vannor reached down, grabbed her wrist, and pulled her out of danger.

She scrambled up into his saddle, weeping, bruised and terrified – surely nothing to do with this wild mob. 'It's all right,' Vannor assured her, as she clung to him, sobbing hysterically. 'You're all right now!' It was an outright lie. His horse lurched, buffeted by the crowd, and the girl gave another terrified scream. Oh gods, the merchant thought, how am I ever going to get us out of this?

Forral took in the situation in a single glance. Coming from the Fleet Deer, he had reached the square from the opposite side to Vannor, emerging from a narrow alley behind the traders' barricade. 'Chathak's balls!' he swore. What a start to his garrison command! And where were the troopers? They should be here. The swordsman knew that nothing could be done to calm this mob. The merchants would have to retreat, and fast, A gang of men, their faces distorted with hysterical rage, were lighting torches at the bonfire. Ducking to avoid the barrage of refuse and uprooted cobbles hurled by the crowd, Forral dodged into the cramped space behind the wagons. The terrified merchants were doing their best to hold off the mob by thrusting their swords through the spaces between the carts. Forral grabbed the nearest trader by the shoulder and spun him round. 'Get out of here, man, before they think of the alley and block your retreat. The food will delay them.'

The merchant's face, already pale, twisted into a mask of terror. 'We can't leave the cart! The Archmage will . . .'

'Bugger the Archmage!' Forral roared. 'You'll be killed!'

It was too late. With a crackle and a roar, the tinder-dry barricade of carts burst into flame. As the traders fell back, screaming, the mob prepared to charge.

Aurian had followed Forral until he entered the square. She paused then, wondering what to do next. If she tried to join him, she knew he would send her back – and have a thing or two to say to her when the fuss had died down. But he was in danger – she should be with him! She felt sick with terror at the thought of losing him again. Yet Aurian knew from past experience that Forral would be furious if she risked her own life. Too bad. She started towards the end of the alley, but just as she reached it she noticed that the side door of one of the houses that lined the square was standing slightly ajar. Aurian stopped. She rarely came down into Nexis, but if she remembered rightly these houses had balconies that looked over the square. Without hesitation she slipped inside. Luckily, the house was empty. Perhaps the occupants had gone to join the riot, Aurian thought.

The once grand houses that lined the market were shabby and crumbling now, for the district was no longer fashionable. Aurian hunted through spacious, well proportioned rooms until she found one with tall windows leading to the balcony. Opening the shutters, she stepped out, and recoiled from the chaos below. Across the square, a man on horseback was struggling against the crowd, who threatened to drag him down. A fair-haired girl perched before him on the saddle, and the little fool was clinging to him hysterically, hampering his sword-arm as he tried to strike at his attackers.

Aurian snorted, and turned away to look down to her left, hoping for a glimpse of Forral. She spotted him below her, arguing with one of the merchants. Then her blood froze as she saw a thin, deadly ribbon of flame winding through the crowd as the torch-bearers advanced. Gods! If the barricade burned, Forral would have no defence! Aurian's mind raced with the impetus of fear. There was one chance to stop this madness – and only she could do it. Rain, she thought. I must bring rain! Yet her guts knotted in terror as she remembered what had happened when she had last tried to use her magic. She recalled the hopeless circling in the dark maze – her terror – her helplessness. She'd never used her magic since then – would she still be able to function? Would she suffer the same fate again? She'd had no real experience with Weather-magic, which was a difficult and exhausting business. But she had to save Forral . . .

Her fingers clenching tight around the bevelled metal railing of the balcony, Aurian pushed her awareness out beyond her body, as she had been taught. Scanning the sky, she swore under her breath. Blue. Bright, unblemished blue, paling to white-heat near the horizon. Where were the clouds that Eliseth was supposed to be moving? Aurian recalled what she had learned of weather patterns from Finbarr's archaic books. They should be coming from the west. Able now to focus all her power in a single direction, Aurian pushed her mind out further and further. Ah! There – far out over the western ocean . . .

An explosion of flames and a wild cheer from the crowd wrenched Aurian back to herself with a jerk. She clung to the railing for a moment, dizzy and disorientated from the abrupt return to her body. Then she saw. The wagons were burning! *'Forral!'* Aurian was unaware that she had called his name aloud. The clouds were too far away – how could she move such a mass of air and water in time?

In that frantic split second, Aurian felt the heat of the flames as they consumed the carts – felt the anger of the mob, like another wall of fire, beating up at her with pulsing hatred. Suddenly the face of her father, Geraint – long-forgotten from her babyhood – seemed to hang before her. She could hear his voice: *'Energy takes many forms, and the wise Mage can utilize them all. Strong emotions – anger, fear, love – all of these can be used to fuel the powers of magic . . .'*

Aurian never stopped to question. There was no time. She reached out to the mad, frenzied energy of the mob, to the raw heat-energy of the fire – and pulled . . .

It was strange to her, this taking-in of power. It was, strictly speaking, against the Mages' Code – yet there was so much energy surging around the square that she could easily take what she needed, and do no harm.

The tricky part was to pull energy into herself and push her consciousness outward at the same time. She had to forget her body completely; her consciousness almost . . . She had to become a pipe, a conduit, a vessel, and simply let the energy flow through . . .

Her seeking mind encountered the clouds once more. Would it be easier to push, or pull? But the clouds were moving in this direction anyway. Pull, then. But how? What was there to grasp in a cloud? Ah! Of course! Aurian stationed her will between the clouds and the front of cold pressure that preceded them, and pushed with all her strength towards Nexis, driving the air away to create a vacuum. Air was lighter

94

to move than water. Gleefully, it seemed, the clouds rushed in to fill the space.

It was almost too easy, with all this energy at her disposal. Later, Aurian was to realize that what had taken ages in her out-of-body time was scant seconds in reality. When a thick layer of cloud had capped the city like a black and sinister lid, she returned to her body, gathered her power, and struck.

A bolt of lightning arced down, splintering into forks as it came. In the distance, a rumble of thunder rolled down the valley. *Rain!* Aurian thought, reaching up to the low-trailing streamers of cloud. It felt as though she was clawing at the blue-black canopy; using her fingers to drag the precious moisture down from the skies . . .

She was jerked abruptly back to herself as the downpour hit. It came all at once, in a solid, heavy sheet. Instantly, Aurian's hair was flattened over her face. It was hard to breathe, as though she were underwater. The rain was cold. It extinguished the fire in an instant.

Reluctantly, Aurian pulled herself away from the glory of the elements. Only then did she hear the cheering of the crowd. The riot had ceased in an instant, as though the rain had washed the fear and fury away. People were capering in the square, swinging each other about in wild, giddy dances, men and women alike. The man on the horse was picking his careful way through the celebrating crowd, heading towards the merchants' position.

'*What have you done?*'

Aurian whirled, shocked, to find herself face to face with Forral. He'd used the crumbling brickwork of the building to pull himself up to her balcony.

'How did you do it? It was you, wasn't it? How dare you put yourself in such danger? Don't you remember why I was called back here in the first place?' Forral's smoke-blackened face was grim and his voice was harsh with anger as his big hands gripped her shoulders. Aurian shrunk away, remembering the day when he had caught her playing with fireballs. Then her Magefolk pride asserted itself, and she pulled herself erect. How dared he treat her as if she were a still a child!

It was the last thing Forral had expected. Aurian wrenched

herself violently out of his grasp, and for the first time he realized that she was as tall as he, if not slightly taller. Her chin tilted proudly, and her eyes blazed with cold fire in a face that was white with anger. In her wrath she was a true Mage, and truly intimidating. The storm above him seemed to swell in sympathy with her rage. A bolt of lightning splintered the roof of a nearby building. 'How dare you!' Aurian spat. 'How *dare* you abandon me all this time, and return for less than a day, before trying to kill yourself! And what gives you the right to try to keep me from helping you?'

Forral backed away hastily, and knew it for a retreat. By no means a stupid man, he suddenly realized that his relationship with Aurian was going to need a lot of rethinking. But gods, she was magnificent in her rage – standing proud and tall and beautiful, like a spirit of the storm, with fire-ice flashing from her eyes. In that moment, Forral was lost. 'I . . .' he stammered. Whatever he had meant to say was drowned in a thunder of hooves as a company of warriors rode into the square. The troopers had arrived at last. Forral turned back to Aurian. She was still facing him, proud and uncompromising, with a challenging question in her eyes. The swordsman grinned, and clapped her hard on the shoulder – the typical comradely gesture between warriors. He chuckled as he saw her eyes widen with surprise. 'Well done, lass!' he told her. 'Well done indeed! You've saved the day!'

An hour later, a solemn conference of leaders gathered in the private dining-room of the Fleet Deer. The room was warm with lamplight, for the heavy black clouds of Aurian's storm still hung overhead, turning the summer afternoon into twilight. Rain drummed on the streaming pavements outside, and ran in rivulets down the diamond-leaded casements.

The fawning landlord, obviously flattered by having so many influential people beneath his roof, served them with brimming tankards of dark ale, and platters of fruit, cold meats, and cheese. Aurian looked sourly at the food. Granted, there wasn't a lot here, but to the hungry folk who had started the riot it would have been a feast. For the first time, she wondered why the Magefolk rations had been singled out in the market.

As everyone settled round the table, Aurian looked at the assembled faces, searching her memory to put a name to each of the folk who had so recently been introduced to her. Seated on Forral's right was a tough-looking, stocky man with close-cropped hair and beard: Vannor, head of the Merchants' Guild. To Aurian's left sat a small, slender woman in leather fighting garb. Her tanned limbs were corded with muscle, and her dark braids, still jewelled with raindrops, were wrapped round her head warrior-fashion. This was Lieutenant Maya, second in command of the garrison. She was frowning and ill at ease, biting her lip and twisting her hands in her lap. Beyond her was Parric, the cavalry master: a short, brown, wiry figure (were all these garrison warriors small? Aurian wondered) with thinning brown hair and laugh-lines on his face. But he was not laughing now.

Aurian felt uneasy herself, among these grim-faced strangers. Never before had she been surrounded by so many Mortals. To ease her anxiety she picked up the huge pewter tankard from the table before her. She had never drunk ale before – the Magefolk, who drank wine, scorned it as common stuff and only fit for Mortals. It took both hands to lift the tankard, and she grimaced as she took a sip of the foaming brew. Gods! How could the others sit there and quaff this bitter stuff? She took another hasty sip to stop herself choking, reluctant to lose face before the Mortals. But Vannor had noticed. He grinned at her sympathetically, and gave her a sly wink, miming that she should keep on drinking. Shyly, Aurian smiled back, and tried again. Ah, this time it didn't taste quite so bad. Maybe it was something you had to get used to.

Vannor cleared his throat and stood up, resting his hands on the table. 'Well,' he said bluntly, 'we didn't come here to sit all afternoon drinking ale. We'd best get started – and I can't think of a better way to start than by thanking the Lady Aurian for bringing the rain, and for releasing that Magefolk food to those in need of it. Lady, as head of the Merchants' Guild, I'm most grateful, as are the folk of Nexis.' Turning to her, he bowed.

Aurian felt her face grow hot with embarrassment at such a public compliment. Moreover, he'd used her honorific title, and it was the first time she had been formally addressed that way. 'I . . . ' Lost for words, she spread her hands helplessly. 'What else could I have done?'

'Well said, Lady!' Vannor's voice rang out in approval.

Aurian thought it might be a good time to broach the question that had been bothering her. 'Sir,' she began.

'Vannor, please, Lady.' He smiled at her. 'I've got no use for these fancy titles. Just call me Vannor.'

Aurian returned his smile. 'Then call me Aurian – just Aurian.' She wondered why he looked surprised at her words, and why Forral was beaming with approval. 'Anyway,' she went on, 'I wondered . . . Well, this place has food – ' she pointed at the plates on the table, 'and it can't be the only one, I'm sure. Why wasn't this shared among the people? And why was the wagon of the Magefolk singled out by the mob?'

Vannor seemed taken aback, and seemed unable to meet her eyes. Forral, a half-smile on his face, was watching the exchange with keen interest. At last the merchant found his voice. 'Lady – Aurian – in a way, you're right. There's injustice in Nexis. The rich look after themselves, and the poor – well, they manage as best they can. Those who can't must sell themselves as bondservants for a term of years, or, in the case of heavy debt, for life. It's nothing but legal slavery!' He scowled. 'I do what I can on the council – I was poor myself once – but the trouble is, as head of the Merchants' Guild I represent a lot of rich people. If they don't like what I do, I'll be voted out, and they'd replace me with someone who didn't give a hang about the poor. So I walk a fine line.' He sighed. 'Aurian, I have to tell you that I get no help on the council from the Archmage, or from his puppet, Rioch.' He directed a piercing glance at Forral, and Aurian saw the big man suddenly stop smiling. Vannor turned his gaze back to Aurian. 'Can you deny that Miathan despises all Mortals, rich or poor?'

Now it was Aurian's turn to blush. He was right – Miathan had said so often enough, and it made her uncomfortable. The Archmage had always represented Mortals as being conniving, idle, shiftless, and downright dangerous, and Vannor the worst of the lot. The acts of today's mob had supported his words, and yet – she looked at Vannor and, through his blunt, rough-and-ready manner, saw a kind, caring, honest man. She looked away from him, more confused than she'd ever been in her life. Suddenly she remembered the unpleasant incident last year, when Meiriel had refused to help Vannor's wife through a difficult childbirth. It was unnecessary, the healer had insisted, but the woman had died. Aurian's face grew hot with shame. No wonder Vannor had little use for her people! Suddenly she began to understand why the Magefolk had been the target of the mob's resentment. She only hoped her action in bringing the rain and releasing food to the Mortals had done something to redress the balance.

'Look here, Vannor.' Forral rose, scowling, his gruff voice betraying his irritation. 'Aurian is a very young, and very minor, member of the Magefolk. You can't go blaming her for the Archmage's . . .'

'I don't, I don't!' Vannor held up his hands in a conciliating gesture. 'My apologies, Aurian, if I suggested that! What you did today is more than good enough for me!'

'And another thing,' Forral cut in. 'If you think that I'm Miathan's puppet, just because Rioch was . . .'

'Well, he chose you, didn't he?' Maya flared, her voice harsh with bitterness. 'What are we supposed to think?' Forral looked at her coldly. 'Ah yes, Lieutenant Maya. I'd meant to get round to you, before we were sidetracked! Rioch is retired, and as I hadn't taken charge yet, you were in command of the garrison today! Why were there no duty patrols on the streets? Can you explain why you didn't arrive until the emergency was over? As second in command you haven't impressed me so far!'

Aurian, seated next to Maya, was aware of the woman's distress at the charge. The warrior's face burned, and her hands were shaking. She squirmed beneath Forral's accusing gaze. Her mouth opened, but she couldn't speak. Aurian felt sorry for her. She knew how intimidating Forral could be when he was angry. In an instinctive, impulsive gesture – for she was not generally given to such intimacy with strangers – she clasped Maya's hand beneath the table, offering support and comfort. The pressure was returned, and Maya flashed her a grateful smile, seeming to find her voice at last. 'Sir, I . . .'

'Now just a minute – sir!' Parric leapt angrily to Maya's defence. 'It wasn't Maya's fault! You say that Rioch had retired, but it's not true – not where we were concerned! He was still hanging around, giving the occasional order when he felt like it. True, he expected Maya to handle all the dull, nitpicking jobs he couldn't be bothered with, but he didn't back her authority, and he wouldn't let her act on her own. The poor lass was in an awful position! And today those dumb bastards didn't even think to send for us. By the time I'd managed to get word to the garrison, Rioch had disappeared, bag and baggage, and nobody knew where you were, and there's poor Maya trying to organize the troops, but everybody's running around like chickens saying "Where's Rioch?" and "Who's giving orders?" Well, it was a miracle that she got them out at all – especially when you consider that she was in line for this command, and should have had it, and how much she wanted it, but got turned down out of hand . . .'

'Parric!' Maya looked stricken.

Parric shrugged. 'Well, it's true, and he should know it! Maya's a bloody good soldier, sir – the best! She deserves better than this.'

Forral's expression was rueful. 'So that's how it is.' He sighed. 'I wish I'd known before I accepted this post. My apologies, Lieutenant, I was unjust.' He took a deep breath, and looked around at them all. 'Grievances have been aired today among the five of us that need to be dealt with. It's no good squabbling amongst ourselves while the city falls apart around us. We must support each other, for *we* – he hit the table with his fist, then gave a wry smile – 'for lack of anyone better, are the ones who must set Nexis to rights! And since we must trust each other, let me make it clear once and for all that I don't plan to be a puppet for Miathan, or anyone else!'

Suddenly they were on their feet, cheering. The tensions in the room had vanished like smoke. Aurian looked proudly at Forral. This is his doing, she thought, much impressed. Look how he's brought us together!

'Now.' Forral brought the meeting to order. 'Maya, you left Hargorn and his troops in charge of the market, and handing out the Magefolk food. You reckon he's a good, experienced man, so there should be no problems there.'

'If there are, he'll soon let you know!' Maya smiled.

'Good. I like dependable people around me. Now Parric – you organize a troop of mounted foragers, and get into the countryside at first light. Don't starve the farmers by any means, but I doubt you'll have to.' He grinned. 'The drought hasn't been going on *that* long! I suspect they're keeping the best stuff for themselves – and to push up the cost. By majority vote of the council' – he caught the merchant's eye, and Vannor chuckled – 'rationing is in force during the emergency, and their produce is requisitioned – and don't put up with any nonsense! Mind you, don't get carried away and start taking seed crops or breeding stock – we have to think about the future. Take some extra troopers to cart the stuff back as soon as possible –'

'And send it to me.' Vannor's face was alight with mischief. 'I'll set up fair distribution through those merchants of mine – and don't worry, I'll make the misers behave! No profit-squeezing at the expense of the poor. It'll be a new experience for them, doing good deeds.' He slapped his knee and chortled. 'Gods, this'll upset them.' He winked at Forral. 'I'll say it's your fault, of course.'

'Of course,' Forral replied solemnly, with a wink of his own. 'Right, Parric – it'll take you a while to sort things out, so you'd better get started!'

'At once, sir!' the cavalry master replied with brisk good humour, and emptying his tankard in one gargantuan, well practised swallow he went off, grinning from ear to ear.

'Maya.' Forral turned to the warrior. 'I want you to take charge of the day to day running of the garrison.' He smiled at the warrior's dumbfounded expression. 'As Aurian will tell you, I'm no administrator – my skills lie in practical warfare and teaching – so we might as well play to our strengths. And don't worry about me supporting your authority, because I'll back you every inch of the way – in fact, I'll draft a set of orders before you leave, so there are no more doubts about who's in charge.'

'Thank you, sir.' Maya's voice was level, but her face was alight with joy. 'I'll do a good job, I promise.'

'Call me Forral,' the swordsman smiled. 'I've no doubt that you'll do a good job – as I said, I want dependable folk around me!' He paused. 'There's one more thing – I'm supposed to have a month's leave with Aurian before I take command, and I'd still like to do that if I can. Of course, I hadn't foreseen the present crisis, but you and Vannor, with Parric's help, should be able to handle things. If there's any trouble, of course, I'll be completely at your disposal – but saving that, you'll be acting commander of the garrison in my absence, and –'

'Who has dared to steal Magefolk provisions, already bought and paid for, to feed the unruly rabble of this city?' The Archmage's entrance was unexpected, and his rage was awesome. He stood tall before them with blazing eyes, his expression thundrous. Aurian knew a sudden stab of fear for Forral and Vannor. She had never seen Miathan so angry.

The merchant and the swordsman exchanged a glance. 'I did!' Both of them spoke together, and as Miathan's face darkened further Aurian knew she must act quickly in support of her friends. Though her knees were trembling at the thought of Miathan's stupendous wrath falling upon her, she stood up and faced the Archmage squarely.

'That's not true,' she said, in a small but steady voice. 'Neither of them had the authority to release that food, so I did it, for the honour of the Magefolk. You see, the –'

'You – did – *what?*' Miathan spoke through gritted teeth. Aurian quailed, suddenly robbed of words by the soft menace in his voice.

'Let her finish, Archmage.' Forral's voice was quiet, but his face was set like stone. As the swordsman spoke, Aurian felt the bracing grip of Maya's hand, and knew that the warrior was on her side, returning help for help. The unexpected support gave her the courage to continue.

'Miathan, it's not your fault. You can't have known how bad things were in Nexis. If you had, you'd have done something about it. If you'd seen those poor, starving folk, I know you would have released the food yourself! I, of all people, know how kind you are! Please don't be angry – I knew it was what you'd have wanted!'

As Vannor was later to comment rather irreverently, her words took the wind right out of Miathan's sails. The Archmage was, for once in his life, completely lost for words.

'Archmage, the city appreciates the generosity of the Magefolk.' Vannor spoke softly and persuasively. 'This Lady has earned you a lot of gratitude today – for her kind heart, and for bringing the rain.'

Miathan gasped. 'You did that?'

Nervously, Aurian nodded. 'I – I hope I did it right,' she faltered.

'Right? My dear girl, Eliseth has been trying for days to accomplish what you have done. Most impressive! Most impressive indeed! But as for the rest, you must learn not to act without thinking. Our people needed that food . . .'

As Miathan's brows began to knot once more more into a frown, Vannor spoke up again. 'Don't worry on that score, Archmage. Commander Forral has organized foraging parties, and food will start coming into the city tomorrow. You've my word that your food will be replaced as a matter of priority. Don't be angry with the Lady Aurian – she acted from the best of motives.'

'I'll support that,' Forral added. 'She prevented great loss of life today.'

Miathan, seeing that he was outnumbered, shrugged, and managed a grimace that might have passed for a smile. 'Very well,' he said stiffly. 'It seems I must concede – this time.' Turning on his heel, he left. Aurian, guilty about her part in his rout and anxious to know if he had really forgiven her, almost ran after him, there and then. Almost.

'Phew,' Vannor said. 'That was nasty! Aurian, you're a hero! You've saved our bacon again.'

Glowing at the compliment, Aurian took a long swig of ale to dispel her shakiness. Forral was here, after all, and she *was* supposed to be on holiday . . .

'By the gods, lass, that was the bravest thing you've done all day!' the swordsman told her, his face glowing with approval. Maya caught her eye and smiled. Aurian knew, in that moment, that the seeds of friendship had been sown between herself and this small, dark-haired warrior, and the thought pleased her inordinately. She'd never really had a woman friend before. Smiling shyly back at Maya in acknowledgement of the wordless understanding between them, Aurian decided that nothing, not even the Archmage, was going to part her from these new and special friends.

It was long past nightfall when Vannor rode back towards his home. Though Aurian's rain was still coming down in sheets and he was soaked, it seemed, to the very bone, the merchant was smiling to himself as he crossed the white bridge near the academy and headed up the tree-lined, lamplit lane towards his mansion on the southern riverbank. For the first time in over a year, since the death of his beloved wife, Vannor felt at peace with himself. He was delighted, of course, that he'd achieved such a good understanding with the new garrison commander; and having one of the Magefolk on his side, for once, boded well for the future – and what a brave, delightful lass she was, at that. But the true cause of the merchant's quiet joy was Sara, the girl he had rescued from the riot.

During his meeting with the other leaders, Vannor had left the girl in the care of the innkeeper's wife. When he saw her again, she had been fed, and had her bruises tended. The innkeeper's lady had loaned her a gown to replace her ruined clothing, and her hair had been newly washed and combed. The merchant had been amazed by the transformation. He had stood, agape like the rawest apprentice-lad, in appreciation of her fragile, ethereal beauty. Gods, but she had reminded him of his own dear, lost, lovely wife!

Now, Vannor was returning from taking her home to her worried family. His heart beat faster at the memory of her slender form perched before him on his saddle, his arms clasped tightly around her waist. It would be a while before he could see her again, to be sure. With so much to settle in Nexis after the drought he'd have his work cut out for him in the coming days, but afterwards . . . His children needed a mother again, Vannor assured himself, shrugging aside the uncomfortable thought that Sara could not be much older than his eldest daughter. Where love was concerned, age was never a problem. Her family had clearly been impressed by their daughter's new friend, and Sara herself had hardly been discouraging . . .

As he rode up the curving, gravelled drive of his mansion,

Vannor's face split into a grin of pure joy. He knew where she lived now, and by all the gods, once this crisis was over, he meant to see her again.

7

Death By Fire

With the coming of the rain, the threat of unrest in the city soon died away. Regular supplies of food, small at first but gradually increasing, began to trickle into Nexis as Parric's bands of foragers warmed to their work, and the reluctant merchants (browbeaten into cooperation by Vannor) began to oversee the fair distribution of rations. At last the people of Nexis could eat again – though it was sheer, contrary human nature, perhaps, that led them to give the credit for the happy change in their circumstances to the young, fire-haired Mage who had brought the rain.

Word of Aurian's actions had spread through Nexis like wildfire, and wherever she and Forral went the young Mage was embarrassed to find she had gained many new admirers. Though the Magefolk, with their dramatic, finely sculpted appearance, could not be anonymous in a Mortal crowd, Aurian was stunned that time and again people would recognize her: picking her out to thank her; or, in the case of the crafters, pressing their finest wares on her as gifts. The last straw, however, was a woman who emerged from the crowd in a tightly packed market and handed her a grimy, bawling, and very wet baby that apparently she was supposed to kiss. Gods, it had been hard to extricate herself from that with good grace. Later, when Aurian complained about it to Forral over a much-needed flagon of ale, the swordsman shrugged. 'Don't worry, love,' he said. 'It's only a nine days' wonder. The excitement will soon die down. In the meantime, be glad that they're grateful, for once, to the Magefolk. You've done your people a lot of good, and I hope Miathan appreciates it.'

In fact, Forral thought, Aurian had done the most good through her influence with Miathan, for her exchange with the Archmage seemed to have affected him for the better. To the surprise of the swordsman and the merchant, Miathan had backed them on the council when the first of the farmers arrived in the city complaining about a visit from Parric's warriors. Miathan had sanctioned the foraging, and it had been the farmers' fear of the Archmage that had allowed it to succeed. After that, word sped through the countryside as fast as it had flashed across the city, and the troops experienced little resistance. Also, Miathan was happy for the Magefolk to take the credit given to Aurian for ending the drought, and Forral had been relieved that relations between the Mage and her mentor seemed to be back on a friendly footing.

After a while, Aurian found that Forral had been right. The people of Nexis had their own lives to lead, and before very long she had cased to be the victim of their embarrassing attentions. Spared of their unwelcome curiosity and her new notoriety, and with the garrison prospering in Maya's familiar, capable hands, she and Forral were soon free to resume their interrupted holiday.

After a while, their days settled into a pattern. Sometimes they would simply walk around the city and see the sights, and Aurian discovered a new fascination in hunting around the merchants' booths, with their silks and velvets, their jewels and perfume and combs. Now that she was in Forral's company, she suddenly found herself taking an unprecedented interest in her appearance. Though she considered the elaborate gowns that were currently in fashion among the city's women too fantastic and impractical for words, the landlord of the Fleet Deer was more than ready to direct her to the best dress-makers, and his wife, who considered herself an expert in taste and style, was happy to advise her, and help her in the choice of fabrics. The grey Mage's robes that Aurian usually wore were soon consigned to the back of the closet in favour of bright, well cut new garments, and she was staggered by her own transformation. Forral was very tolerant. 'You spend what you like,' he grinned. 'The Archmage is paying for it, after all.'

Though Aurian possessed more than her share of Magefolk pride, she had never been particularly vain about her looks. The swordsman's reaction to her new finery was both gratifying and disturbing. Time after time, she was aware that

107

he was looking at her, but when she caught his eye he would quickly turn away. To make matters worse, Aurian found herself playing this watching game; discovering a strange new fascination in the white flash of Forral's smile through his grizzled beard, or the play of muscles in his brawny, sword-scarred limbs as he moved, despite his bulk, with the silent grace of the born swordsman. She would see his powerful, blunt-fingered, capable hands and marvel that so much strength could be combined with such gentleness. She'd imagine them touching her, caressing her, holding her . . . and would check herself sharply, perplexed and dismayed by her wildfire imaginings.

Gone was the close, carefree comradeship they had shared in Aurian's childhood. Since Forral's return, a new restraint had grown between them, a tension, half guilt, half excitement, that underscored their friendship. Yet for all that, they were inseparable; each trying their hardest to pretend that nothing had changed, though Aurian's heart would lift in the most unsettling manner whenever he entered the room, and her senses were swamped by a giddy, breathless feeling of happiness when he was close to her. But she had always been glad to see him . . . hadn't she? 'It's all right,' Aurian would tell herself as she lay awake in the night in her small, white-walled room at the inn. 'It's only that we've been apart for so long. We need to get used to each other again, that's all.' And as time went on, she almost started to believe it. With use and familiarity, the tensions between them seemed to be easing – a little.

On some evenings, they would meet Vannor, or Maya and Parric, if he was in the city, and spend happy hours talking and carousing in one of the city's many inns. Aurian found herself warming more and more to Maya's company, and the two women soon found themselves well on the way to becoming the closest of friends.

On days when the weather was fine, the Mage and Forral, and sometimes Maya, if she could spare the time, would borrow horses from the garrison and take a picnic into the hilly countryside around Nexis, or hire a boat to sail the dozen or so miles downriver to the sea. Aurian had never seen the sea before, but she loved it. They would swim in the invigorating, strangely buoyant waters, and spend hours basking on the sands. Her body lost the pallor it had gained from years of indoor study, and her muscle tone began to return. Hoping it might help to get their friendship back on its old, familiar footing, Aurian, with Maya's enthusiastic support, nagged Forral into agreeing to resume her sword training. He was reluctant at first, because of her accident, but she knew that he was secretly pleased. She still had her sword, which Miathan had returned to her, and the thought that she'd soon be using it again helped to cheer her up when at last the vacation was over.

Finally the day arrived when Forral was due to take up his new duties as commander of the garrison, and the young Mage had to return to the Academy. Seeking an excuse to linger a little longer in one another's company, they decided to delay Aurian's return with a last shopping expedition in the Grand Arcade, an interconnecting series of pillared stone halls housing hundreds of little shops and stalls that catered to the well heeled section of the Nexis community. It was said that virtually anything could be bought there, if one had enough money. Most of the endless variety of goods on display were far beyond the means of Aurian and Forral, but they enjoyed wandering up and down the brightly lit aisles, planning what they would buy if they ever became rich.

At last, footsore and hungry, they stopped at a baker's shop, lured by a glorious aroma of warm, fresh bread. While Forral was buying pasties from the woman behind the counter, a young man emerged from the back of the shop carrying a tray of loaves. Aurian saw him stop and stare at the swordsman, his blue eyes suddenly widening. As they walked away from the shop, Aurian noticed that Forral was frowning. 'Never mind,' she said. 'The holiday may be over, but we can still see a lot of each other.'

Forral shook his head. 'It isn't that,' he replied. 'It was that lad in the baker's shop – I'm sure I know him from somewhere, but I can't think where.'

Anvar was disappointed. He'd hoped for some acknowledgement from the swordsman, but Forral had obviously failed to remember him. But a man who kept company with one of those arrogant Magefolk – even if it *was* the one who was said to have brought the rain (which he privately doubted) – would scarcely have time for a common baker's son. He shrugged, and set down the heavy tray. 'That's the lot,' he told his mother. 'I'll mind the shop now, if you want to rest.'

Ria smiled. 'Thank you, dear, but I'm fine. Why don't you go now? I know you're meeting Sara this evening.'

'Are you sure?' Since Torl had bought the shop, Ria's life had become much easier, but Anvar still liked to spare his mother whenever he could.

Ria hugged him. 'Of course. It's almost closing time anyway, and it's a lovely evening. You two youngsters enjoy yourselves – oh, and give my love to Sara.'

'Thanks, mother.' Anvar hugged her back, and, taking off his white apron, he dashed out of the shop.

As he made his way out of the arcade and down to the river, Anvar couldn't help reflecting on the changes that had taken place in his life since he had last seen Forral. When grandpa died, Torl had found a chest in the old man's room filled with clever, wonderfully detailed carvings of birds, animals and people. As was often the case, the death of the artist pushed the prices up, and grandpa's consummate works of art quickly became fashionable among the rich folk of the city. With such patronage, Torl soon had enough money to put the next phase of his business plan into action. His idea was simple but cunning. He bought the shop in the arcade, and though the only premises he could afford were too small for a bakery, he installed a single oven in the back. Stocks of almost-baked loaves were brought down from the old bakery by horse and cart to be finished in the little shop, and soon the mouth-watering smell of fresh bread was wafting through the arcade, bringing in the customers in droves.

Despite the temporary hardships caused by the drought, the business had taken off like wildfire, keeping the whole family busy. Ria and Anvar worked in the shop while Bern and Torl laboured in the bakery. Bern loved the trade, and was set fair to becoming as good a baker as his father. Anvar knew that his brother wished him out of the way so that one day he could

110

inherit the business, and to be honest it only seemed fair. Anvar wanted to be a minstrel, and had no interest in becoming a baker. But while his father lived, he had little say in the matter.

Apart from his music, Sara was the main consolation of Anvar's life. On these long summer evenings they would meet down by the river and stroll along the tree-shaded banks that smelled of damp earth and wild garlic. Sometimes they would take a bottle of wine and some of Torl's bread and stay out all night to make love under the stars.

The thought of his love made Anvar's feet fly faster along the dusty towpath. How he longed to see her! During the drought, he had missed his visits to the mill. His father had kept both himself and Bern busy, riding into the countryside or scrounging round the markets of Nexis to find enough food to support the family through the crisis. In fact, Anvar had been out of the city on just such an errand when the riot had occurred, and he had missed the so-called miracle of the bringing of the rain. Sara had been there, though – his heart chilled at the thought of her exposed to the dangers of the riot – although he could never persuade her to speak of it.

Afterwards, when they had started to meet again, Sara had seemed different somehow. More moody and discontented, less happy to see him than of old, and inclined to fall into long and secretive silences. It worried Anvar a little, but he told himself that her strangeness was probably due to trouble at home. He knew her family had suffered during the drought, and wished he could have done more to help them.

When he reached their meeting place by the old stone bridge beyond the outskirts of the city, Sara was waiting for him, her small body lithe and slender in a thin summer dress and her long golden hair unbound like a blaze of sunbeams. Anvar ran towards her, his heart pounding, but the expression on her face stopped him dead.

'What's wrong, love?' Anvar put his arms around her, trying to stifle his hurt at the stiffening of her body and the way her eyes avoided his.

'I'm pregnant. I'm *pregnant*, Anvar!'

'But that's wonderful!' Her words had shocked him, true, but nevertheless Anvar felt a fierce, overriding surge of pride.

111

Sara turned on him, her eyes wild. 'Wonderful?' she cried. 'What's wonderful about it, you idiot? What will father say? This is all your fault!' Tears poured down her cheeks. 'What am I going to do?'

Anvar led her down the grassy bank to the riverside and sat her down gently, putting an arm around her. 'Don't worry, Sara,' he said. 'I'll talk to your father. It'll be all right, I promise. Oh, there'll be shouting from our families, and a few things said about being more careful, and what will people say, but it'll blow over. They know how things stand between us, and they've always approved. We'll just have to bring our plans forward, that's all.'

'But I didn't want to get married yet! I'd hoped that . . . I mean I – I haven't lived!'

Sara's words cut him to the quick. Anvar stared at her, suddenly feeling icy cold. 'But I thought you wanted to marry me,' he said. He took a deep breath. 'Sara, have you changed your mind?' He saw the quick flare of panic in her eyes.

'No!' she said hastily. 'No – look, Anvar, I'm sorry. I didn't mean it like that. I'm just upset, that's all. And frightened.' She stared up at him with huge violet eyes. 'Anvar, please. I – I need you.'

Sara's lovemaking that night had a frenzied, almost desperate quality. Again and again she wanted him, as though to blot out her worries with the physical act. Anvar had no objections. He thought he understood, and besides, the fact that the one he loved was now bearing his child made her doubly precious to him.

He awoke late next morning, cold and stiff and damp from the dew, and in the harsh light of day he began to worry, after all, about what their families would say. 'Look,' he said to Sara, 'why don't you come with me now and we'll talk to my mother. She's the best person to break the news to.'

Sara bit her lip. 'Do I have to? Can't you tell her?'

'No.' Anvar took her firmly by the hand. 'We'll have to face this sooner or later. Come on – I'm late already, and mother will have to open up on her own. She never could manage to light that blasted oven.' He set off quickly along the path, with Sara trailing reluctantly behind him.

112

When they arrived at the arcade, a crowd of impatient customers had gathered outside the shop, and Anvar and Sara had to shoulder their way through. As they entered, Anvar saw Ria kneeling amid a haphazard pile of kindling and tinder; struggling, as usual, to light the oven.

What happened next would be etched on Anvar's memory for ever, returning over and over to haunt his worst nightmares. As they entered, he saw his mother take the oil lamp from the shelf and pour its contents over the logs. 'No!' he screamed, but it was too late. Ria struck a spark and the oven exploded in a sheet of flame, trapping her behind a wall of fire with her hair and clothes alight.

To the end of his days, Anvar had no idea how it happened. Afterwards all he could remember was shouting '*Stop!*' in a superhuman voice. A huge surge of force came out of nowhere, flattening him against the wall, and the flames went out. Immediately. Totally. Anvar crumpled to the floor, weak and dizzy. He tore his eyes from the blackened, smoking thing that was his mother to see Sara staring at him, her eyes filled with horror, her mouth open in a soundless scream.

Someone fetched the baker. Anvar vaguely remembered his father's hands around his throat, and Torl's voice screaming, 'You did this! You killed her!'

Still in shock and sick with guilt, Anvar made no move to defend himself. It took four men to drag the baker off him. Even when he was calmer, and had heard exactly what had happened, he eyed his son with cold hatred. People in the arcade rallied round. Someone offered to take the weeping Sara back to her family, and the cheesemaker from the next stall took Anvar and his father home. Ria's body followed, wrapped in blankets, on another cart. A kindly neighbour put Anvar to bed, and gave him a draught to make him sleep.

He was awakened by voices. 'I've housed your bastard long enough,' Torl was saying, his voice thick with venom. 'It was my one chance to get a woman like Ria to accept me. She'd never say who the father was – I thought it must be some merchant who was too grand to marry her after her family lost their money. But after the way Anvar put that fire out – and a

113

dozen witnesses will back my word – it's clear that his father was one of your people, sir.'

'Indeed?' The other voice was gruff and harsh. 'This is a grave accusation, baker. You know that matings between Mortal and Magefolk are not acceptable to either community.'

'I know, sir. But I think that was why Ria was abandoned when she became pregnant. And what Anvar did today proves it – so he's your responsibility now. I don't care what you do with him just so long as you get him out of here. I never want to set eyes on him again!'

There was a long pause, then the other spoke again. 'Very well – on condition that you deny the whole story. If there was a lapse by one of the Magefolk, I don't want it to become common gossip. Will you sign an indenture bonding him to my service for the rest of his life?'

'I'll sign anything if it'll get rid of him.'

'Then I'll take him with me now.' A rough hand shook Anvar's shoulder, and he found himself staring up into the craggy, eagle face of the Archmage. 'Get up, boy,' he snapped. 'Come with me!'

'Get a move on, fool!' In temper, Miathan jerked the rope that bound the wrists of his new bondservant and kicked his horse forward, increasing the pace. The young man fell with a cry, skinning hands and knees already scraped raw from previous falls during his stumbling journey through the city streets. The Archmage had ridden on for several yards before he realized that this time the boy had failed to get up, and was being dragged behind like a sack of bones.

Miathan reined in with a curse. It only needed one interfering guard to come along, and he'd be the centre of far more attention than he wished. He dismounted, thanking providence that the hour was late and most folk were off the streets. Anvar lay in the gutter – where he belonged, the Archmage thought spitefully – sobbing quietly. 'Get up, you!' Miathan unleashed his rage with a vicious kick, but his victim simply whimpered, and lay there unmoving. 'Oh, gods – this is all I need!' Miathan muttered savagely. With angry, magically impelled strength, he lifted Anvar and threw him roughly across his saddle. He tried not to look at the boy's face, with its resemblance to Ria. She's dead now, he reminded himself. Dead at last.

As he led the horse down the steeply sloping lane towards the bridge, Miathan found himself wondering how she had managed to hide herself and her son for all these years. Had she guessed that he would never have allowed her to bear this half-breed abomination of an offspring? Gods, what a fool he had been, to allow himself to be lured by a Mortal in the first place!

It was part of Miathan's Magefolk arrogance that he had nothing but contempt for the Mortals with whom he shared his world and his city, thinking of them as little more than animals. It was particularly unfortunate for Anvar that his discovery had come at this time, when the Archmage was still smarting from Aurian's defection and her unfortunate, unanticipated friendship with the despised and lowly race. Because he was anxious to retain her respect and goodwill, in order to foster his future plans for her, he had been forced into the invidious and humiliating position of making concessions to Forral and Vannor that he would never otherwise have countenanced.

Already, the Archmage was beginning to regret bringing the swordsman back into Aurian's life – the very same who had corrupted his one-time friend Geraint with those ridiculous ideas of rights for Mortals. But at least Aurian was younger, more easily influenced, Miathan mused. And she must be influenced! This very day, his plans had taken a new and unexpected turn, when the young Mage had returned to the Academy. A mere month's absence had turned the child into a woman. Miathan had been stunned by the difference that was not merely due to her new clothing. He saw her sudden awakening; the new innocent air of maturity; the awareness of her female self that cloaked her in an aura of unconscious sensuality, stirring feelings within him that he believed he'd put away long ago in favour of cold ambition.

How it had galled the Archmage, that some clod of a Mortal – and one that he himself had summoned, at that – had been the one to bring this transformation about. Now, suddenly, he found that he wanted Aurian for himself – and by all the gods, she belonged to him, not to that unworthy, low-born animal of a swordsman. Still, he had both the will and the opportunity to win her back, and in the meantime he had another Mortal – one to whom he also owed a debt of revenge, for daring to exist in defiance of his wishes – upon whom to vent his wrath.

It was night outside the Mages' Tower. Anvar stood blinking in the warm lamplight of the Archmage's opulent quarters, still half drugged and hardly aware of what was happening to him. His body was scored and bruised from being brutally hauled through the streets, and his legs ached from climbing the endless spiral of steps that led to his room. His arms and wrists were in a fire of agony from the merciless pulling of Miathan's rope, and he was confused and terrified. What was he doing here? Why had the Archmage taken him away from his home? Were the Magefolk intending to punish him for his part in his mother's death? Anvar choked back a sob. Why, *why*, had he not been on time this morning? It was all his fault. But why had his father sent him away with Miathan? Did Torl really hate him that much?

Miathan propelled him roughly to a seat and stood glaring down at him with the cold of a thousand winters in his eyes. Anvar began to tremble.

'So,' the Archmage said harshly. 'After all these years you've turned up to plague me. I had planned to have you destroyed before you were born, had your wretched mother not run away. Still, you may have your uses.'

He placed a hand on either side of Anvar's head. Anvar gasped with pain. It felt as though his brains were being wrenched inside out. Doubling over, he vomited on to the floor. 'Imbecile!' The blow from the Archmage's fist rocked his head back on his shoulders. Anvar tried to cringe away, but Miathan caught hold of his hair and hung a sparkling, flattish crystal on a silver chain round his neck. 'I will not tolerate a mongrel joining the ranks of the Magefolk,' he said. 'You may have power – but I'll soon take care of that!' He lifted his staff, crying out some words in a strange and convoluted tongue.

The crystal round Anvar's neck blazed with a sudden, unearthly light. Anvar screamed in agony and collapsed on the

116

floor, clutching at his head and feeling as though the very life was being sucked out of his body. He was dimly aware that Miathan was removing the crystal, and when the pain subsided and his vision cleared he saw the Archmage hanging it around his own neck with a smug smile. 'So much for your powers,' he said. 'Now they belong to me. Just one more refinement, I think, before we send you where you belong, you half-breed bastard!' Once more he put his hands on Anvar's head, and held the boy's terrified gaze with burning eyes. Anvar felt as though a band of icy steel was being clamped tightly about his brow.

'Can you feel it?' the Archmage asked. 'It will be with you for the rest of your life, Anvar. Normally you won't even notice its presence – but if you try to tell anyone what you did today, or about your Magefolk heritage – if you even try to *think* about it – that band will tighten, causing you unspeakable agony. If you persist, it will kill you, make no mistake.'

There was a knock at the door. 'Enter,' Miathan called. A huge man with greasy black hair and a brutish face entered the chamber. He bowed deferentially to the Archmage, flicking a puzzled glance at Anvar, who still huddled, groaning, on the floor. 'You sent for me, sir?'

'Indeed I did, Janok,' Miathan beamed. 'I was told of your complaint that you're short of help in the kitchens – for your Archmage is aware of even such trifling matters – and I have a new bondservant for you. He comes from a baker's family, so he may be of some use to you. His father gave him over to me after he killed his mother.'

Janok frowned. 'Sir, you want me to take a murderer into my kitchen?'

'Don't worry,' Miathan said blithely. 'He's a cowardly little brute at best. Treat him as he deserves, and you should have no trouble. If he proves too much for you to cope with, you may, of course, refer the matter to me.' His eyes were steely with an unspoken threat.

'Very well, sir,' Janok mumbled, defeated but obviously unhappy. 'Come here, you.' He went to Anvar and, taking a handful of his shirt, lifted him bodily off the floor. As he was

117

dragged out, the last thing Anvar saw was a smirk of cruel satisfaction on Miathan's face. The Archmage was gloating.

8
Bondage

As usual, Anvar never saw the sly foot that tripped him. He was carrying the heavy bin full of offal and vegetable peelings towards the kitchen's outer door when there was a sharp pain in his ankle. Then he was down; sprawling on the flagstones that he had scrubbed only this morning, in a welter of blood and stinking garbage.

The head cook's furious bellow silenced the titters of the other kitchen workers. 'Stupid clumsy oaf!' Janok's heavy boot caught Anvar hard in the stomach, in the ribs, and in the face. Seizing a broom that had been propped against the wall, he began to beat him, cursing him all the while. Anvar howled as the heavy shank struck down repeatedly on his back and shoulders. He tried to crawl away to escape the blows, but his hands slipped on the slimy offal and he went face down into the bloody mess, cracking his chin hard on the stone floor. Dimly, he heard someone laugh. It saved him. Raging, Janok turned on the watching servants. 'What are you standing there for? Get back to work, before I beat the lot of you. It lacks but two hours to the solstice feast!' He threw the broom across Anvar's body and gave him one last kick for good measure. 'Get this mess cleaned up, you!'

Anvar struggled to rise, afraid of the consequences if he did not. He felt sick and breathless; his body clenched in a knot of pain. Gently he probed the side of his face, where Janok's boot had struck. Nothing seemed broken, but his jaw hurt, and he would have another bruise to go with the marks that Janok's fists had left yesterday, and the days before. Using the broom for support, Anvar hauled himself shakily upright. No one offered to help him. Stiffly, painfully, he began to sweep up the mess. Now he would have the floor to scrub again.

The four months that Anvar had spent in the kitchens of the

Academy had been a living nightmare. There were only eight Magefolk, but they were very awkward in their eating habits; wanting different and elaborate meals at separate times and places, and refusing to eat together in the Great Hall adjoining the kitchen. This made a great deal of work, and Janok gave Anvar the worst tasks. The head cook was an evil-tempered bully who brutalized all the kitchen menials, but he had selected Anvar for special attention.

Each day Anvar scrubbed the greasy stone floors, peeled root vegetables, and washed an endless succession of dishes until his hands were cracked and raw. Janok made him scrape and polish the blackened copper pots until they gleamed. He cleaned the silver, took out the rubbish, and fetched and cut wood for the ovens and ranges until his back ached. All he was given to eat were kitchen scraps. If Anvar dropped or broke anything, he was beaten. If he managed to drag his way to the end of the day without getting into trouble, Janok found an excuse to hit him anyway.

Things might have been easier if Anvar had made any friends among the other servants, but they were a miserable, surly lot, and letting someone else bear the brunt of the head cook's temper suited them very well. Janok had made a point of telling them that Anvar had murdered his mother, and, kitchen gossip being what it was, the tale grew with every telling. No one spoke to him, except to curse him or give him orders, and they went out of their way to get him into trouble with cruel practical jokes. When his back was turned, they poured boiling water into the pots he was washing, so that he scalded his hands. When he cleaned the silver, tarnished items would vanish, to reappear when Janok entered the room. If he was carrying hot food or trays of dishes, he was tripped or pushed so that his burden went flying. They blamed him for their own mistakes, too. If anything went wrong in the kitchen, it was Anvar's fault.

The boy was in constant torment over what the Archmage had done to him. How had he come to be here? Whenever he tried to remember what had happened in Miathan's quarters, his thoughts were erased by the agony that knifed through his skull. After a while, it became easier to believe that he was

120

being punished for Ria's death. Anvar was consumed with grief for his mother, and he truly believed he was to blame. If he had been on time, she would still be alive. He might as well have murdered her. So great was his despair that only the thought of Sara kept him from taking his own life. What had become of her? He had let her down when she needed him. Anvar fretted himself sick over her fate, and that of her unborn child. But he was helpless – imprisoned here with the conspicuous Magefolk bondmark tattoed on the back of his left hand in indelible dye. In the early days, before his spirit was utterly broken, Anvar had considered trying to escape in one of the carts that brought fresh produce from the markets to the Academy each day, but it was hopeless. Janok had him watched constantly, and even if he had managed to get away the penalties for runaway bond-servants were severe.

Now the winter solstice was upon them, but the holiday brought no joy to Anvar. Once they had finished preparing the Mages' solstice feast, the kitchen menials were free to celebrate the festival. Casks of ale were broached, and a lively party was soon under way. There was eating, drinking – lots of drinking – and a great deal of horseplay. Drunken couples cavorted on tables where food would be prepared tomorrow, and Janok had the youngest laundrymaid face down over the bags of flour that were stacked in a corner, his flushed, sweating face contorted in a slack leer as he lifted her skirts. Judging from her muffled shrieks, she was not enjoying the experience, but Janok was king of his little domain, and gave her no choice.

Anvar, watching from his damp and squalid sleeping-place beneath the stone sinks, felt sick with disgust. They had excluded him from their festivities, and for once he was glad. It was now, when everyone was celebrating, that he missed his home and family most keenly. Anvar crouched in his dank, cramped refuge, nursing his bruises and his grief. Had he not been late that morning, Ria would be alive now. He and Sara would be married, and looking forward to the birth of their child in the spring. Anvar wondered where she was tonight, and how she was spending her solstice. Overcome with despair, he wept.

He was exhausted. His body was weak and aching from grinding toil and Janok's brutal beatings, and activity in the kitchen that day had been frantic. Despite the din, he eventually dozed. When he awakened everything was quiet. The fire had burned low and the servants were snoring where they lay, sleeping off the ale. Anvar sat up, his pain and weariness forgotten. This was his chance to escape! At last he could see Sara, and set his mind at rest. Perhaps they could run away together!

D'arvan thought the Great Hall looked magnificent in its festive finery. He loved this vast, imposing chamber. For some reason, it had always been the place where he felt most at home. Its double row of supporting pillars, cunningly carved from dark stone in the shape of trees whose branches interlaced to support the ceiling, had been decorated with bright-berried evergreens, and Magelight blazed golden in crystal globes on the walls. The dancing flames of scarlet candles were reflected in the polished wood of the tables, and a huge log fire roared in the massive fireplace.

It was late, and most of the Magefolk had already retired. Elewin, the academy's chief steward, was up in the gallery serving mulled wine to the tired musicians, to fortify them for their journey home through the snow, and servants were clearing away the remains of the solstice feast. Though traditionally, only the fruits of the wildwood were eaten at solstice, Janok had outdone himself this year. D'arvan had been staggered by the variety of foodstuffs served. Haunches of venison and a roast boar stuffed with herbs and wild apples; roast pheasant and swan decorared with their own plumage, and pigeon and rabbit pies. Succulent trout from forest streams had been broiled with flaked nuts, and there were wild roots and winter greens, dried mushrooms in a sauce of wild garlic, and a mound of truffles. During the growth season, Janok's most trusted workers had scoured the woods near the city seeking ingredients for this feast, and had preserved fruits and berries in syrups and fortified wines for cakes, tarts, and sweetmeats crystallized with honey. D'arvan sat back, and loosened his belt. What a feast it had been!

Aurian's yawn pulled him back from his thoughts. 'Well, that's it for me,' she said. 'I'm worn out. Forral almost battered me to death in sword practice this morning, and I have to be up early tomorrow for more of the same, Solstice Day or no. Goodnight, D'arvan.'

'Goodnight, Aurian, and – ' D'arvan cursed the wretched shyness that kept him tongue-tied. 'And thank you for keeping me company tonight,' he finished softly.

Aurian smiled. 'Thank *you*, D'arvan. I don't know what I'd have done without you. Gods, but these Magefolk feasts are dull!' The wealth of feeling in her words was a comfort to him. She had stayed with him for most of the evening, telling him about her current healing studies with Meiriel, and her new Mortal friends at the garrison, but all the time he had thought she was doing it from pity, since Davorshan had so hurtfully ignored his presence. His twin had spent the whole night dancing with Eliseth, dining with Eliseth, laughing and flirting with her. He had eyes for no one else. Now the pair were seated near the fire, lingering over their goblets of wine, deep in conversation.

Aurian, as if she knew what was troubling him, frowned at Eliseth and her rapt companion. 'D'arvan,' she said, 'It's none of my business, but maybe you spend too much time with your brother. If you want, you would be welcome to visit the garrison with me sometimes. They're good people, you'd like them, and I think you need a change of company.'

D'arvan stared at her, startled and lost for an answer. Go among a lot of strangers? Alone? The notion terrified him. He had never done anything without his brother! Yet he appreciated the kindness of her offer. It seemed she had noticed that, during these last months, Davorshan had been spending more and more time with Eliseth and her friends.

D'arvan twisted his hands together beneath the table, fighting despair. Davorshan had said that the Weather-Mage was teaching him to bring forth some of his dormant powers. If it was true – and his brother never lied to him – then he, D'arvan, was now the only powerless Mage in the academy. He shivered. How long would Miathan let him stay, if he had no powers? Where would he go if the Archmage cast him out?

123

'Are you all right?' Aurian sounded concerned.

D'arvan longed to confide in her and ask for her help – oh, gods, he needed a friend right now! But his crippling shyness kept him silent, and he didn't want her to blame his brother. For some reason, she had never like Davorshan. 'I must be tired,' he prevaricated. 'Perhaps I'll go to bed.'

Aurian raised a sceptical eyebrow, then shrugged slightly. 'Good idea – that's where I'm going. Anyway, think about what I said. The offer is always open. And if you ever need someone to talk to – well, I'm available.'

After she had gone, D'arvan sat alone, waiting for his brother. Eventually, growing weary, he went to bid his twin goodnight. Davorshan sat beside Eliseth, his arm around her shoulders, their heads very close as they talked in soft voices. The Magewoman was stunning in a gown of shimmering ice-blue. Her long hair was intricately braided and coiled with a thin interlacing silver chain. At D'arvan's hesitant approach, Davorshan looked up sharply. Attuned as always to his twin's thoughts, D'arvan sensed annoyance, a flicker of guilt – and something else. Something wrong. Before he could identify it, Davorshan's shields slammed down, shutting him out for the first time in their lives. D'arvan reeled as though he had been struck. He had never felt so alone – as if a part of himself had been brutally torn away. The isolation – the loss – the uncertainty – he was too overwhelmed by pain and confusion to speak.

'How dare you spy on me!' Davorshan shouted, his face flushing crimson. 'I'm sick of you following me around with that pathetic expression on your face! Get away from me, do you hear? Leave me alone!'

D'arvan was stunned by the bitter hostility of his brother's tone. As he fled, gulping back sobs, he was pursued by the sound of Eliseth's silvery laughter.

Anvar tiptoed across the floor of the cavernous kitchen, carefully avoiding the sleeping bodies. The door opened silently to a swirl of fine, wind-driven snow. He grabbed an empty flour sack to cover his head and shoulders and slipped outside, closing the door quietly behind him. The night was bitterly cold. The darkened courtyard was empty, and no lights burned in the Mages' Tower. The two guards at the upper gate were huddled over a brazier in the gatehouse with a shared bottle, playing dice and keeping out of the icy wind that pierced Anvar's filthy, ragged clothing as he lurked in the shadows. Every minute or so, one of the guards would look up from the game, keeping an eye on the gate. Anvar cursed. He had to escape – he *had* to! But how? The bitter wind was rapidly sucking the heat from his body, and every minute he lingered here increased his chance of being discovered.

Voices! Anvar jumped. His heart hammering wildly, he peered round the corner of the building, to see the door of the Great Hall open, spilling golden light on to the snow. A group of figures came out, all cloaked and hooded, and bearing a variety of oddly shaped burdens, well wrapped against the cold. Of course! Anvar remembered hearing that there would be musicians at the Mages' feast. Now they were going home. Going out!

Not daring to consider the risks, Anvar hid in the shadows of the narrow alley between the infirmary and the kitchens until they had all passed him, heading for the gates. He darted across the intervening space, keeping low, and tagged on to the end of the group, hoping his sack would pass for a hood in the dim light. The tired musicians, muffled in their cloaks and only concerned with getting home out of the cold, never noticed the addition to their number. Nor did the tipsy guards. 'Joyous solstice,' they called as the musicians went through. As the gate clanged shut behind him, Anvar sagged with relief.

There was a new watchman in the gatehouse at the bottom of the hill, younger than the one Anvar remembered from years ago. He was mulling ale at his small fireplace as the musicians approached, and was more concerned with his steaming jug than anything else. He opened the spiked iron gates with scarcely a glance, and waved them impatiently through. Free! Anvar's heart soared. The musicians passed over the causeway and into the tree-lined avenue leading to the bridge that crossed back into the city. Anvar detached himself from the group and hid until they were well away before crossing the slender stone span himself. Once across the river, he circled

125

through the back streets to give the wharves a wide berth, keeping a watchful eye out for patrols from the garrison. Avoiding groups of drunken revellers, he angled back towards the towpath and made his way upriver.

The journey seemed longer than he remembered. The snow fell more thickly now, and was heaping in drifts across the path. Visibility was poor, and Anvar was forced to stay near the thickets on the bank with their clutching, thorny limbs or run the risk of blundering into the river. The exertion of his escape had intensified the pain of his battered body, and he shook with cold and fatigue as the wind blew into his face, blinding him with its burden of snow. Stubbornly he staggered on, drawn by the thought of seeing Sara again.

The shadowy figure of a woman, cloaked and hooded against the snow, stood by the mill looking down at the speeding, glimmering waters of the millrace. Anvar's heart beat fast. 'Sara?' he whispered. The woman spun round with a sharp exclamation. It was Verla, Sara's mother. 'Anvar!'

'Please,' Anvar begged her, ignoring the hostility in her voice, 'I've got to see Sara. Is she all right?'

'How can you ask? How *dare* you come here, after all the anguish you've caused us?'

'What do you mean?' He grasped her shoulders. 'What has happened? Tell me!'

'All right!' Verla spat. She shook herself free from his grip. 'After what happened,' she said grimly, 'Jard refused to let Sara bear your child. He took her to a back-street midwife in the city.'

'No!' Anvar cried out in horror.

'Oh, yes. The woman got rid of the babe, but things went amiss, and now Sara will never bear children.'

Anvar sank to his knees on the snowy path, his head in his hands. 'Oh, gods,' he whispered. Sara! His child!

'After that,' Verla continued remorselessly, 'Jard sold her in marriage to Vannor.'

'What?' Anvar gasped. No one crossed the most powerful merchant in the city – especially if they had heard the dark rumours about his violent past on the wharves, before he became rich and respectable. 'The same,' Verla said bitterly.

'He didn't mind that she was barren. He has children from his first wife. He wanted Sara in his bed, and he was prepared to pay. I don't know whether she's happy – we never see her. I hope you're pleased with what you've done. Now get away from here. I never want to set eyes on you again!'

Anvar was opening his mouth to protest when a heavy blow cracked across the back of his head. Stunned and half blind with pain, he collapsed on to the snow. The last thing he heard was Jard's voice. 'Well done, Verla! Tie him up, while I go for the guards.' The miller seized his hand, examining the brand by the light of the torch he carried. 'There's sure to be a reward for a runaway bondservant.'

It was Midwinter's Night, the longest of the year, and D'arvan, lying awake, had counted many dark hours before Davorshan returned with the dawn to the rooms that he shared with his brother. D'arvan had been left in no doubt as to the way in which his twin had passed the night. With his concentration distracted by passion, Davorshan's shielding was fitful; his link with his brother too strong and reflexive to be broken on a whim. D'arvan had been tortured by such thoughts – such feelings – such glimpses of Eliseth, lying naked on a white fur coverlet – the chiming silver of her laugh – the burning of her touch, imprinted on his skin as it was on his brother's – the slippery touch of cool satin sheets – his own lone and shameful spending, that had echoed the climax of Davorshan's frantic lust and in its passing left him drained and guilty, and sick at heart.

Even after the storm of Davorshan's passion had finally and mercifully spent itself, D'arvan had passed a wretched night. His thoughts, still scattered by the shock of the brutal, abrupt isolation from his twin's mind and the maelstrom of lust that had followed, had been wavering back and forth between grief and anger and guilt – blaming his brother, blaming Eliseth, and blaming himself. *Davorshan is all I have* – the thought wove through and through the others in an endless litany of despair. *It's always been that way, but now he has someone else . . . What will I do without him?*

Throughout their lives, the twins had been forced to depend

127

on one another. D'arvan could barely remember his father and mother – Bavordran and Adrina had elected to pass from their lives when he had been very small, but the fact that they had chosen to bear two infants, and then abandoned them so precipitately, made no sense to the young Mage. The older Magefolk would never speak of it, but his parents had not been happy together, D'arvan was sure – as sure as he was that his mother, at least, had not wanted to leave him. He had a vague, confused memory of a savage quarrel, and Adrina's face all streaked with tears as she rocked him to sleep. He had never seen her again. With their parents gone, the twins had been raised, in a careless fashion, by Meiriel and Finbarr and the Academy's servants, and had very naturally compensated for the lack of parental love by their devotion to one another – a bond that had been suddenly, and savagely, severed by Eliseth.

Before Davorshan entered their rooms, D'arvan had sensed his return. He always knew when his brother was close. And though he dreaded seeing his twin, he was glad of any respite from his anguished thoughts – until the brother of his soul crept in, grinning smugly, and reeking of wine and Eliseth's heavy perfume. He tiptoed past D'arvan's bed without sparing him a single glance.

'It's all right – I'm awake. You needn't bother to creep!' The venom in his own voice surprised D'arvan, but the anger had won out, after all. Davorshan lacked even the grace to look guilty. Not for a moment did his complacent expression alter. Shrugging, he sat down on the bottom of D'arvan's bed, all openness and charm; his hostile shielding seemingly banished.

'You have good reason to be angry with me,' he said. 'Listen, D'ar – I'm sorry about what happened earlier, at the feast. It was just that I wanted to be alone with Eliseth – you'll see how it is, when you find someone of your own. I never meant to shut you out so suddenly, but there are some things that you just cannot share – not even with your own dear brother.'

Even a few short hours ago, D'arvan would have believed him. Would have trusted him, and rejoiced that their differences had been explained, and dismissed. Davorshan's mind was open to him once more, in all its old comforting familiarity. Except. . . Acting on pure instinct, D'arvan swept

128

up all the bitterness and treachery and pain that had formed the dregs of this wretched night, and fashioned them into a lancelike probe of will that stabbed searchingly into his brother's mind. Davorshan had no warning – no time in which to react. 'Curse you!' he shrieked, recoiling and slamming up a block with which to foil the piercing attack. But it was too late. D'arvan's probe had already encountered the hard, dark, pulsing core of secrets that his brother had so cunningly concealed behind his open guise.

Shaking, D'arvan snatched back his probe as though he had been burned. Gods – why did I do it? he thought despairingly. Why couldn't I leave well alone? This second betrayal hurts even worse than the first!

'Why did you do that?' Davorshan's sorrowful whisper echoed his thoughts. 'I want this – I want *her*, and nothing – not even you – will keep me from her! But truly, brother, I had no wish to hurt you.'

It might have been the truth – Davorshan certainly seemed sincere – but D'arvan had had enough of lies and treachery. He could not risk a third betrayal. 'Leave me alone – just leave me alone!' For the first time in his life, he closed his mind to his brother, and turned his face away, staring steadfastly at the wall through tear-blurred eyes until he heard Davorshan seek his bed. It was the hardest, most painful thing he had ever done. To distract his mind from the crushing weight of loneliness, he fuelled his faltering courage with his anger against his brother, and forced himself to think of Aurian and her offer. Perhaps she was right – if he could no longer count on his brother, perhaps he ought to meet other people. After the solstice, he would ask her to take him to the garrison. Until then, he would simply mourn.

9

A Warrior's Heart

The muscles in Aurian's back and shoulders screamed in protest. The sword felt unbelievably heavy in her tired hands. She stepped back to give herself a little extra time to react, her blade lifted defensively as she watched Forral through narrowed eyes, trying to anticipate his next move. It was a quick sideways strike – low, almost taking her legs out from under her. Aurian jumped back, parrying clumsily, feeling the shock of the clashing blades run numbingly through her hands. She caught the quick white flash of Forral's grin through his curling brown beard.

Lifting her blade again, Aurian cursed the swordsman's tirelessness; cursed his insistence that they practise even on Solstice Morn; cursed her stupidity in drinking too much the previous night, and not going to bed sooner. Drat that D'arvan! Sweat ran down stinging into her eyes and dripped on the sands of the garrison's great, barnlike practice arena. Trembling with weariness, she forced her sword up to parry Forral's lightning thrusts. Why on earth had she nagged him to resume her sword training? She would never have believed that she could be so out of condition, so out of practice; and four months of sweaty, back-breaking torture on these sands seemed to have brought little improvement. Would she ever get her old skills back?

Forral drove in suddenly, his heavy sword a flickering swirl of light as he employed the famous circling twist of the blade – his own trademark, which neither Aurian nor anyone else could seem to master. She gasped with pain as her wrists snapped round, and her sword flew spinning from her hands to land some distance away. Forral shook his head. 'You're dead!' he said. Before Aurian had time to react, he spun her round by the shoulder and whacked her hard across the backside with the flat of his blade. It was a trick she was all too familiar with – one that he used on all his pupils as an incentive not to repeat their errors. 'Ow!' Aurian wailed indignantly, rubbing at the sting. Tears of exhaustion and frustration sprang into her eyes.

Forral's arms went comfortingly around her, one big hand kneading the tight, aching muscles across the shoulders and in the back of her neck. 'Never mind, love,' he said softly. 'I know it's hard, but you simply can't afford to make mistakes that will kill you. It's coming back to you, though – I can see the improvement. You're making up a lot of lost time, that's all. Just stick at it, and we'll soon have you back in fighting shape.'

Aurian leaned into his chest, smelling clean sweat and the tough, scarred leather of his fighting vest. His words of encouragement warmed her, and she was grateful for the support of his brawny arms round her weary body. 'All right, Forral,' she murmured trustingly. Lightly, he kissed the top of her head, and at his touch Aurian's heart gave a dizzy lurch. A tingling heat swept through her body. Again. It happened now whenever he was close to her. Oh, Forral! She'd loved him since she was a child, but after his return the change in the quality of that love had left her baffled and thwarted. She had finally admitted to herself that she wanted more, now, than the affectionate comradeship they had always shared. Aurian tightened her arms around his neck and looked up searchingly into his face, unable to hide her longing. As always, his eyes met hers for an agonizing instant, then flicked away.

'Come on,' he said gruffly, stepping back from her. 'Vannor's coming this morning, remember? We'd better get cleaned up for that snooty wife of his.' Without looking at her, he walked away. Her throat tight with misery, Aurian retrieved her fallen sword and followed him out of the arena.

Vannor and his lady had arrived early, and were waiting in Forral's rooms. Aurian felt a stab of annoyance as the elegant young woman wrinkled her nose fastidiously at the sight of her in her battle-scarred leather vest and breeches. Aurian had taken an intense dislike to Vannor's new wife. The slender, blonde young woman looked around Forral's wood-panelled, workmanlike quarters with an air of distaste, as though disgusted to find herself in such a lowly place. Sourly, Aurian wondered how, since the girl was so much shorter than herself and Forral, she could still manage to look down her nose at the two of them. With her own feelings still stinging from Forral's latest rebuff, she found the besotted look in Vannor's eyes as he gazed at his wife very hard to take.

Aurian was fond of the blunt, straightforward merchant. Short and stocky, his beard and hair cropped very short, Vannor resembled exactly what he was – a former dockside tough come good. His rough voice was still edged with the gritty accent of the wharves, and he took no pains to alter it. But his hard exterior disguised a warm, generous heart. He plainly doted on Sara. She was magnificently clad in rich, fur-trimmed velvet, her hair done up in an elaborate knot, her fingers, wrists and ears dripping with the jewels he had bought her. She looked flawlessly beautiful – except for her haughty expression, and the hard, calculating look that came into her eyes whenever she looked at her husband.

Vannor, as head of the Merchants' Guild, had planned this solstice visit to the garrison as a courtesy to the new commander. The Archmage, the third member of the ruling council, was expected later. It was not a lively gathering. Though Vannor and Forral were good company as a rule, the normally bluff and hearty merchant seemed constrained by his wife's presence, and Forral was unusually quiet, frowning more than he smiled. Aurian, nursing her heartache, was wondering if she should excuse herself and go back to the Academy, when there came a knock at the door. Forral went to answer it, and Aurian, relieved at the interruption, followed him into the outer chamber.

It was Parric, the cavalry master. The leathery, balding little man was duty officer for the day, and his manner was apologetic. 'Sorry to disturb you, Forral, but a miller along the river has caught a runaway bondservant. We've just brought him in.'

Forral sighed. Aurian knew that he loathed the practice of bonding, but unfortunately he had been unable to influence the council against it. The Archmage supported it, and Vannor was forced to bow to the wishes of the merchants he represented, who increased their profits through not having to pay their bonded labour.

'For goodness sake, Parric!' Forral said testily. 'Why bother me with this now? Just lock him up, and we'll deal with him tomorrow, after the holiday.'

Parric looked uncomfortable. 'Sir – I think you should see him. The poor sod's in an awful state – beaten black and blue. Honestly, I don't blame him for trying to run away. I wouldn't treat a dog the way he's been treated.'

Forral frowned. 'Sorry, Parric – that's different, of course. We had better look into it. I won't have people getting away with that kind of abuse. Who is he bonded to?'

Parric hesitated. 'Well, it's a bit awkward, you see . . .'

'Come on, man, you've seen his mark! Stop maithering and tell me.'

The cavalry master glanced uneasily at Aurian. 'He's bonded to the Academy.'

'What!' Aurian was stunned. 'But he can't be.'

'He is. And it's a bloody disgrace, let me tell you.' Parric's look was plainly accusing.

'Steady on, Parric,' Forral intervened, putting his arm around the indignant Mage. 'Just bring him in, and we'll get this straightened out.'

'He's outside.' Parric beckoned through the open doorway, and two guards entered, supporting a limp, ragged form between them. The lad stank. His clothing was tattered and filthy, and soaked through. He was shivering violently, and his skin had a bluish tinge. His face was swollen and covered in bruises. Aurian was horrified. Who at the Academy had treated the poor wretch so badly? Suddenly his eyes opened – the most brilliant, piercing blue that Aurian had ever seen. They looked straight past her, and stretched wide in joyful astonishment. 'Sara!' he gasped.

Aurian whirled to see Vannor's wife standing in the inner doorway, her face deathly white. Drawing herself upright, Sara looked down on the runaway servant with icy contempt. 'Who is this person?' she demanded coldly. 'I never saw him before in my life!'

'But he knows your name,' Forral pointed out with a frown.

Sara shrugged. 'I'm married to the most important merchant in the city. Lots of people know my name. Vannor, take me home. This revolting creature is making me ill!'

Vannor shrugged helplessly. 'All right,' he said. 'Forral, you'll excuse us?' Taking his wife's arm, he led her out.

As they passed the prisoner, he struggled free from the guards and fell at Sara's feet, clutching at the hem of her gown. 'Sara, please . . .' he begged. With an exclamation of disgust, the woman twitched her skirts from his grasp and swept out of the door. Aurian closed her eyes against the naked hurt and betrayal on his face. Sara was lying, she was sure. The lad buried his face in his hands and began to sob. Aurian, galvanized by the tortured, hopeless weeping, dropped to her knees at his side, her heart aching for him. 'Poor thing,' she said softly. 'Don't worry, we'll take care of you. And whoever did this to you . . .' her voice grew fierce. 'I'll make sure it never happens again!'

Anvar looked up at the tall, red-haired woman. He could tell from her appearance that she was a Mage, and recognized her as Forral's companion when the swordsman had come to the shop, that day so long ago. Her eyes were flinty with anger. In his horror at Sara's betrayal, he had failed to hear her comforting words, and thought her rage was directed at him. He made a strangled sound of fear deep in his throat, then broke out into a sudden fit of sneezing. The Mage frowned, and fished in her pocket for a handkerchief, which she handed to him. No ladylike scrap of lace, this, but a large square of white linen that, judging from the oily smears, looked as though it had last been used for cleaning a sword. As he blew, she placed a cool hand on his brow. 'Forral, he's ill!' she said sharply. 'Help me get him inside. Parric, fetch some broth from the mess hall. He looks half starved. Hurry!'

Anvar saw the two men look at each other and shrug, then he was hoisted up by Forral himself, and half carried into a snug inner room where a bright fire burned.

'Put him on the couch.'

Anvar wondered who she was, to be giving orders to the garrison commander. Imprisoned as he had been in the

134

Academy kitchens, he had never come into contact with any of the Magefolk.

'But Aurian, he's filthy,' Forral protested.

So this was the Lady Aurian, said to be the Archmage's favourite! Anvar felt sick with fear. When he had been brought before Commander Forral, he had hoped to be able to plead his case. But now he was back in the hands of the Magefolk, and who knew what punishment the Archmage would have in store for him?

The Mage spread a blanket on the couch and helped him sit, putting an arm around his shoulders – right on the bruises where Janok had beaten him with the broom. The pain made him cry out. In one swift movement, she ripped away the remnants of his tattered shirt. Anvar heard her make an inarticulate retching sound, then she swore viciously. 'Who did that?' she growled, turning him to face her. Anvar could feel her anger beating against him like a physical presence. She seemed to grow in stature, and her green eyes glowed with an icy grey light. With a sudden thrill of fear, he realized that she was not the Archmage's protégée for nothing. He began to tremble.

'Steady, love. He's terrified. Don't worry, lad, she's not angry with you.'

Forral's gentle voice gave Anvar courage. 'It was Janok,' he whispered.

'The *bastard*!' Aurian exploded, leaping up and striking her fist on the high marble mantelpiece with such magically impelled force that the thick stone corner broke off in a flash of light. Anvar was awestruck, but Forral simply sighed.

'Aurian,' he said, in tones of mild reproof. Guiltily the Mage retrieved the broken piece from the hearth and set it back into place.

'Sorry, Forral.' As she passed her hand across it, the stone fused together without a trace of a join. She shook her head. 'I can't believe this could happen in the Academy,' she said. 'Wait until Miathan gets here! In the meantime – ' she returned to Anvar as she spoke – 'I'll see what I can do to help this poor soul.'

'Aurian, no!' Forral's voice was urgent.

'Why ever not?' Aurian sounded astonished. 'I've learned enough from Meiriel to be able to heal . . .'

'It's not that,' Forral said. 'He's a runaway, and . . .'

'It makes no difference!' Aurian insisted angrily.

'Look, love, I know it's hard, but Miathan has the right to punish him. If he sees what's been done to him, it should go easier on the poor lad. Besides, the Archmage should know what's going on in his halls.' Forral's voice was stern. 'This has got to be stopped.'

Sara stormed into her bedroom, venting her temper on the door with a vicious slam that in a lesser home would have shaken the building to its very rafters. Not here, though. Vannor's mansion had been constructed by master craftsmen out of the best materials that gold could buy. Despite the entire weight of her body behind the shove, the heavy slab of oak swung ponderously shut on its oiled and balanced hinges, and slipped smoothly into its frame with a barely audible click. Robbed of its expression, the pressure of Sara's rage could only increase. Screeching obscenities like a dockside fishwife, she picked up the nearest object to hand – a white porcelain vase filled with hyacinths and winter roses – and flung it at the offending door.

She gasped, her rage stifled for an instant by horror at the damage she had caused – the shattered vase, a gouge in the door's silken panelling, the crushed and twisted flowers and the water stains that dimmed the jewelled colours of the room's rich carpet. Then her shoulders straightened in defiance. So the carpet was ruined – so what? This place was hers now, as well as Vannor's. And she would treat it as she pleased. It would serve him right if she tore his precious house apart with her bare hands!

As her anger flared up anew, Sara paced the room, heedless of the splintered porcelain and broken blooms that she was treading into the carpet's deep pile. How dared Vannor take her to task for her rudeness in so brusquely leaving that uncouth oaf of a soldier and that hoydenish scarecrow Mage! How dared he give her such a dressing-down – and in front of his wretched, smirking children!

But at the thought of her husband, Sara's recalcitrance faltered a little. This had been their first real quarrel. In all the months of their marriage, Vannor had never before raised his voice to her. She'd been a fool today, she suddenly realized – careless, overconfident; too certain that she had him in her power. She would have to make it up with him, and as soon as possible. He was her security – her wonderful, newfound wealth and luxury – her protection against her father, and what he'd done to her; against squalor and poverty and endless brutal toil; against the scandal of having been pregnant by some stinking wreck of a bondservant who was no better than an animal . . .

As the vision of Anvar rose up in her mind's eye, Sara began to tremble. Her shock at seeing him so unexpectedly after all this time, her horror when he had called her by name, had completely scattered her wits. All she could think of was flight – of putting as great a distance as possible between herself and the bruised and filthy bundle of rags who had called her with Anvar's voice, and beseeched her with those blazing blue eyes.

With hands that shook violently, Sara unlocked the delicate lacquered cabinet that stood by her bed and pulled out a crystal decanter that shot splintered rainbow sparks into the room's wintry light. It was her solace and her secret. Her maid had been well bribed to keep it filled, and keep her mouth shut. On the nights – most nights – that Vannor visited her bed, she would lock the door when he had finished and gone, and sit through the long wakeful hours, drinking wine and piling the white counterpane with all her jewels, in little heaps that sparkled warmly in the candlelight.

Oh, gods. She splashed wine into a goblet, drank it off, and poured again. I'd give anything, she thought, if this morning had never happened. At last she knew what had become of Anvar. Torl had simply claimed that he'd gone and most people believed that he had run off in the aftermath of Ria's accident, and left Nexis for good. Her parents, of course, had assumed that he was fleeing his responsibilities to his sweetheart and her unborn child. Sara, too, had preferred to think of his departure in that light; that way, she could accept Vannor's suit without any bothersome feelings of guilt . . .

'At the wine again, stepmother?'

Sara spun round with a curse. Zanna! Vannor's younger daughter stood in the doorway, glowering, as usual, through her unkempt fringe of thick brown hair that had defied the efforts of a battalion of maids to keep it tidy. Sara bit her lip in vexation. How had the brat crept in so quietly?

'What do you mean, again?' she said, trying to brazen it out. The girl detested her, as she very well knew, and the feeling was mutual. The last thing Sara needed today was the little wretch stirring up more trouble for her with Vannor.

Antor, the merchant's young son whose birth had cleared the way for Sara to marry Vannor, was no trouble. He was too small to really know who she was or care, and Sara simply left him to his nursemaids. Corielle, the older daughter, had been easily managed. She was of an age with Sara, and the two girls shared a similar golden beauty. She was also of an age to be extremely interested in men – and not just the scions of the rich merchant houses that her doting father had marked out as suitable suitors. A few instances of careless chaperoning – of turning a blind eye to the odd love-note and secret tryst – and Sara had won her over. Not so with Zanna, however. Taking after her father in looks, the child was as plain as a pikestaff, but she was too clever by half, and far too knowing for fourteen. It simply wasn't natural!

'Next time, you should tell Gelda to hide the bottle better when she brings it upstairs.' Though Zanna spoke respectfully to her stepmother when Vannor was in earshot, her tone, in private, was pert and mocking. Sara's hands clenched tight around the fragile crystal of the goblet. Gods, how she'd like to strangle the little bitch! When she spoke, her voice was low, and shaking with fury.

'Listen, brat – you mention a single word of this to your father, and I'll make you sorry you were ever born! Do you hear me?'

Zanna's eyes, beneath the flopping curtain of hair that irritated Sara so, narrowed in calculation. Vannor's blood ran true in her veins, all right! The minx was a merchant through and through. 'I might not,' she said carelessly. 'I'm sure that someone as clever as you can think of some way to make it worth my while!'

It was all too much. 'Get out!' Sara shrieked. 'Get out now – and send Gelda up here to clear up this mess!'

Zanna looked down at the shards of porcelain that littered the floor, and her expression changed from smugness to a stony hatred that was shocking in one so young. 'That was mother's favourite vase,' she said in a small, tight voice. 'Gods, I hate you.' It was the first time she had actually said the words out loud. Then she was gone, leaving a shaken Sara to pour herself another drink and wonder how, after her own failure to slam the door, the child could have managed it so effectively.

Anvar fought to stay conscious, out of fear of what the Archmage might do to him if he were asleep and helpless. The Lady tried to feed him broth, propping him with one arm while she held the cup of warm liquid to his lips with the other. He couldn't swallow it. His head throbbed from Jard's treacherous blow, and his body ached all over. It hurt to breathe. His stomach was knotted in trepidation. When he heard Miathan's voice, talking to Forral in the outer room, he began to struggle violently, sending the cup flying and drenching both himself and the Mage.

Then the Archmage was in the room, towering over him, his eyes burning with rage. 'You!' he snarled, reaching out to haul Anvar to his feet. Anvar cringed back, whimpering.

'Miathan, no!' Aurian sounded shocked.

'Aurian, don't interfere,' Miathan said sharply. 'The wretch has broken his bond, and must be punished.'

'Punished?' Aurian's voice rose in disbelief. 'He's been punished enough! Have you seen what Janok did to him?'

'She's right, Miathan,' Forral said. 'This goes beyond the bounds of all reason.'

'You mind your own business!' Miathan snapped.

'It is my business.' Forral scowled. 'It's my duty to enforce the law in Nexis, and Magefolk or not, I won't turn a blind eye to such brutality. Even a bondservant has some rights. How would you look if word of this got out?'

Anvar felt a surge of hope. They were defending him. They

were both defending him, even the Mage! Miathan seemed taken aback, but he recovered quickly. 'My dear Forral, you misunderstand me,' he said. 'Of course there must be no repetition of this unfortunate incident, and I assure you that I will look into the matter – in detail.' He frowned at Anvar as he spoke. 'You should know, however, that this Mortal is a troublemaker, and very dangerous.'

'He doesn't look dangerous to me,' Forral said bluntly. 'The poor beggar's scared out of his wits. Surely you could pardon him this time, Archmage. He's suffered enough.'

'Please, Miathan – for me?' Aurian added her own plea, looking trustingly at the Archmage. Had it not been for the desperate extremity in which he found himself, Anvar could have laughed at the trapped expression on Miathan's face.

'Oh, very well,' the Archmage muttered at last. 'I shall speak to Janok on my return.'

At the sound of the head cook's name, Anvar moaned. Not the kitchens again! He couldn't! Desperate, he caught hold of the Magewoman's hand as she stood by his side, and levered his weak body down on to his knees. 'Don't let them send me back there,' he begged. 'He'll kill me. Please . . .'

'Anvar!' Miathan's voice was like a whiplash. 'How dare you! Leave the Lady Aurian alone!' He bore down on Anvar, who cowered away, burying his face in his hands.

'No!' he shrieked. 'Please! Don't hurt me again!' He screamed again as Miathan's spell took hold; its icy band of agony clamping tightly around his brow. Helpless, he fell twitching to the floor.

'Dear gods!' Aurian exclaimed, kneeling beside him. Suddenly the pain was gone. Anvar, able to breathe again, looked up and saw a clear message in Miathan's glinting eyes. *If you tell, you'll die!* And he knew that Miathan had removed the pain before Aurian could investigate.

'It's all right,' he muttered helplessly. 'I'm all right.'

Aurian frowned. 'What the blazes was that? I don't understand. . .' She looked at the Archmage. 'What did he mean, Miathan? You haven't hurt him, have you?'

The Archmage laughed harshly. 'Don't be ridiculous! The lad is clearly insane.'

140

'I don't think so.' Slowly, Aurian shook her head. 'No, he's just terrified, I'm sure. It's very strange, though. Where did he come from?'

'Really, Aurian, is all this fuss necessary?' Miathan said testily. 'Let me send him back to the Academy, and then perhaps we can enjoy the rest of the day.'

'Miathan, you can't send him back to the kitchens,' Aurian pleaded. 'Not after what he's been through. Wait – I know!' Her face suddenly lit up. 'You've been promising me my own servant for ages. Let me have him!'

'What!' Miathan thundered. 'Certainly not! It's absolutely out of the question!'

Aurian's eyes widened with surprise at his refusal. She got to her feet, confronting the Archmage, her jaw jutting stubbornly. 'I don't see why not. It seems a perfect solution to me. Please, Miathan.'

'Aurian, no. I shall find you another servant, but Anvar is most unsuitable. What he needs is discipline.'

'Discipline my eye!' Aurian snapped. 'He's had too much discipline, if you ask me. What he needs is kindness.'

'I will be the judge of that!' The very air seemed to crackle and spark as the two Mages stood, eye to eye, glaring furiously at one another, while Anvar held his breath.

'Aurian,' Forral intervened urgently, 'perhaps the Archmage is right. If he's truly dangerous . . .'

'Don't you start!' Aurian snapped at the startled swordsman. 'I'm sick of the pair of you. I'm no longer a child, to be constantly deferring to your so-called wisdom.' Her voice curdled with scorn. 'I'm right in this case, I know it. I want to help this poor lad – to restore the honour of the Magefolk. It's our fault that he ended up this way. But instead of letting me trust my judgement, all I get from you two is specious quibbles. It's pathetic.'

Miathan looked thundrous. 'Aurian!' he roared. 'How dare you speak to me in that fashion! Get back to the Academy at once!'

'I will not!' Aurian shouted. 'You may rule the Academy, but you don't rule the world, and you don't rule me! My father and my mother left, and so can I!'

Miathan went white at her words, and Anvar was puzzled by the sudden flicker of panic in his eyes. Abruptly, he seemed to shrink. 'Very well, my dear,' he said. 'Since it obviously means so much to you, Anvar is yours.'

Aurian seemed staggered by his sudden capitulation. As the tension drained from the room, she blushed, shamefaced. 'Miathan, thank you,' she said softly. 'You're so good to me. I shouldn't have lost my temper, and I'm truly sorry.'

'So am I,' Miathan said feelingly. He held out his arms, and Aurian ran to hug him.

'I'll make him behave,' she promised. 'I swear I will.'

Miathan looked at her gravely. 'Indeed you must. You are now responsible for this Mortal, and I hold you answerable for his conduct. If he misbehaves, he goes straight back to the kitchens.' He glowered at Anvar. 'Anvar, I trust you will not abuse the Lady Aurian's kindness.'

Anvar, meeting that steely gaze, shivered. Miathan smiled coldly. 'Now, before I permit you to enter this Lady's service, you must swear, before these witnesses, that you will not try to escape again.'

Anvar froze. Trapped! The Mage was smiling at him encouragingly. Unwittingly, she had trapped him with her kindness. He had no choice, and he knew it. With a sinking heart, he gave his word.

The Archmage was seething as he returned to the Academy through the snowy streets. How dared Aurian defy him! And over his own, accursed half-breed bastard! Miathan ground his teeth. He wanted to kill Anvar, to bury once and for all the mistake of his younger days – but he could not. If Anvar should die, then the power that he had stolen from the wretch would be lost for good. Miathan had to keep him alive. He needed that power.

Aurian's words still stung. So I don't rule the world, he thought. Well, one day I will – and then Aurian will pay for her defiance! And it was fitting, that Anvar should provide the means. Miathan smiled. With the additional powers he had stolen, nothing could stop him. It was simply a case of biding his time and waiting for the right moment to strike.

142

Miathan was obsessed with power. His ambition was to restore the great old days when Magefolk had used their power to rule the Mortal race. To achieve this, he had wormed his way into the position of Archmage with merciless cunning and stealth. He and Geraint had been friends until Aurian's father, with his subversive liking for Mortals, had been nominated as the next Archmage. It had been simple to engineer the 'accident' that had removed his rival, but Miathan had not reckoned with the guilt that had pursued him at the murder of another Mage. In atonement, he had originally planned to make Aurian his successor, but now he had evolved a new plan for Geraint's daughter. He wanted her as his consort, at his side – and in his bed! A surge of desire consumed the Archmage at the thought. Her threat to leave still turned him cold.

Miathan knew he had erred in bringing Forral to Nexis. He had thought that, by using Aurian as a lever, he would retain control of the garrison's voice on the ruling council, but his plan had backfired. Because of her allegiance to her Mortal friend and teacher, his pupil was becoming increasingly intractable, and her loyalty, which he had fostered with such painstaking care over the years, was weakening. Unfortunately, there was no way at present to solve the problem. If he was implicated in Forral's removal, Aurian would never forgive him.

Miathan resigned himself to patience. Sooner or later he would find an opportunity to deal with the swordsman. In the meantime, he must at all costs keep Aurian's love and trust. With Forral out of the way he would soon break her to his bidding, and use her powers to further his ends. Miathan smiled to himself. How difficult could it be, to rid himself of one man? Forral was only Mortal, after all.

Aurian was weary but satisfied. This had been her first essay in the skills that Meiriel was teaching her, but everything had gone well. Those long hours studying the intricate workings of the human body and learning to channel her power to repair damage and speed natural healing had not been in vain. Though she still had much to learn, her first independent efforts had been a success. As though dusting off her hands, Aurian banished the last flickering blue traces of Magelight that marked her healing spells.

Her new servant rested comfortably between clean sheets in a room that had been provided by a rather tight-lipped Forral. Now that he was clean, she could see the bruises fading rapidly against his pale, fair skin. Soon they would be gone, and the Mage blessed her powers that could work such miracles. His eyes flickered open, and Aurian caught her breath at their vivid blue intensity.

'How do you feel?' she asked.

'It doesn't hurt,' he said wonderingly. 'It really doesn't hurt! Gods, I'd forgotten . . .'

Aurian swallowed sudden emotion. How the poor wretch had suffered! 'It won't hurt any more,' she assured him. 'I've taken care of it.'

'Magefolk don't heal Mortals!' His voice rose in disbelief. 'Lady Meiriel wouldn't heal my grandpa, and he died!'

Knowing Meiriel, Aurian was uncomfortably aware that he could be telling the truth. 'Well, Lady Aurian heals Mortals,' she said briskly, 'and you certainly needed it!'

'Lady – what's going to happen to me?'

Aurian gave him a reassuring smile, trying to soothe away the fear that showed on his face. 'Don't you remember? From now on you'll be my servant, and I'll make sure you're never hurt like that again. You're safe now.'

'Oh.' He sounded far from convinced.

Well, what did you expect from a bondservant? Aurian thought to herself. Gratitude? She smiled at her own folly. If I were him, she decided, I probably wouldn't trust me either.

This time he managed to swallow the broth she gave him, and soon afterwards he fell asleep. Aurian also needed to eat, to replace the energy expended in her healing, and after the appalling business of getting her patient clean she badly needed a bath herself. But she lingered for a while, watching him as he slept and trying to shake off the nagging feeling that she had seen him before. Anvar, had the Archmage called him? His body was long in the bed and broad-shouldered, but dreadfully thin. Well, that could be remedied. He looked younger than she had first thought; probably not much older than herself. His face, even in repose, seemed melancholy; with fine lines between his brows, and at the corners of his generous mouth. His jaw was firm, though his nose was rather big, and his fine bronze hair curled into the nape of his neck. And those eyes! Aurian had never seen such eyes on a Mortal.

Forral entered the room, and found Aurian regarding her patient with an oddly tender expression. He was rocked back on his heels by a violent surge of jealousy. What was it about this bloody man anyway, that she had defended him so fiercely against the Archmage – and himself?

Aurian looked up quickly, her expression suddenly clouded. 'I didn't hear you come in.'

'I noticed.' He couldn't keep the gruffness from his voice.

Aurian winced. 'Forral, I'm sorry I lost my temper with you. I'm really grateful for your help . . .'

'You've a warrior's heart, to defend what you believe in so fiercely – and to take on the Archmage, too! I'll always help you, you know that, but . . . Aurian, are you sure this is a good idea?'

'Forral, not again! Don't you understand that I'm no longer a child?' Her meaning was all too clear. She sounded so sad, so wistful, that he had to fight the urge to tell her that he loved her; that he wanted her as she so plainly wanted him. Forral pulled himself together. It was impossible. There were reasons for the proscription against love between Magefolk and Mortals – reasons that she had not considered. He had to protect her. He steeled himself against the longing in her eyes, forcing himself to be genial.

'I'm sorry, love,' he said. 'I've looked after you since you were a little scrap of a thing, remember? Us old folk tend to forget how fast our charges grow up.'

She looked away, and Forral knew she was trying to hide her hurt from him. It lanced his heart. He left the room hastily, closing the door behind him. Leaning against the polished panels, he swore softly and continuously for several minutes. How much longer could this go on? He should never have come back! Seeing how things were turning out, he should have left at once. He should leave now, but . . . He couldn't. He couldn't leave her again. With a sigh, Forral turned away from

145

Aurian's door and went off to find himself a very large drink. These days, it was the only thing that helped.

10
A Shadow Of Evil

When Anvar returned to the Academy as the Lady Aurian's servant, he found that his life had changed completely. He no longer had to suffer the bullying of the kitchen workers, for the personal servants of the Magefolk lived apart from the menials, and under very different conditions. The chief steward Elewin, a tall, gaunt, silver-haired old man with a gentle expression, ruled the household servants with a rod of iron, but he was scrupulously fair, and tolerated no gossip among his charges. As long as Anvar worked hard and kept out of trouble, Elewin made sure he was left alone.

He had a bunk in the servants' dormitory next to the Mages' Tower, and regular, hearty meals were served in the adjacent refectory. (It gave Anvar a smug feeling to think that Janok and his surly workers were now cooking for him.) Personal servants were issued with clean, neat working clothes every day, and because they came into contact with the Magefolk they had to be decent and well mannered.

Anvar was torn between gratitude and resentment for the Mage who had rescued him. She had saved him from the Archmage's wrath, and thanks to her his life had improved considerably; but by asking him to swear Miathan's oath, she had trapped him here. On the other hand, he had no other life, since Sara had rejected him so cruelly. Yet how could he blame her? His fathering of a child on her had led to her being sold in marriage to that brute of a merchant. Even if she had dared to help him with Vannor present, why should she? She had every reason to hate him. Anvar was heartbroken and bereft. Now he had nothing—not even hope. All he had was work. So he worked as hard as he could, wishing that his Lady would give him more to do, so he would have less time to think. Elewin was pleased with him, and Anvar welcomed the steward's kindly praise after Janok's abuse.

The other Magefolk took little notice of the servants. On the rare occasions when he came into contact with them, Anvar found Meiriel brisk and efficient, Finbarr kindly but vague, and Eliseth cold and scathing. D'arvan rarely spoke. Davorshan and Bragar were the two to avoid. Davorshan was simply a bully, but there was a streak of cruelty in Bragar. He regularly abused servants, who were all afraid of him. Even Elewin gave the Fire-Mage a wide berth.

Anvar had expected that the Lady Aurian, having settled his fate with typical Magefolk arrogance, would have little time for a mere servant, but he was wrong. She always had a smile and a kind word for him, and invariably thanked him for his efforts. Her consideration earned her little respect from the other servants, and this so puzzled him that he plucked up courage to ask Elewin about it. 'It's simple enough,' the steward said. 'The household staff, I'm afraid, are somewhat lacking in imagination, and the Lady Aurian differs from other Mages because of her association with Mortals. It violates what the servants see as the natural order at the Academy, and it makes them nervous.' His grey eyes twinkled. 'Personally, I find it refreshing, but don't you go repeating that, young Anvar. And never confuse her kindness with softness. If you take liberties, you'll soon find that she has the usual Magefolk temper.'

Anvar took the advice to heart. He was still wary of his Lady, who was one of the hated Magefolk, and not to be trusted. He lived in constant dread of what would happen when the tale that he had murdered his mother spread from the kitchen to the servants' quarters, and thence, gossip being what it was, to his new mistress. He wondered why the Archmage had not told her himself, especially during their confrontation at the garrison. But one morning, within a month of his joining the household staff, he found the other servants whispering in corners and avoiding him, and he knew that the secret was out. Even the kindly Elewin was looking at him with a frown. Anvar was glad to collect the Lady's breakfast – the warm, soft, fresh-baked rolls that were all she ate at this early hour, and a huge pot of taillin – and hurry away to the sanctuary of her room.

The Mage rose early for her sword practice at the garrison,

and on these iron-hard winter mornings her room was dark and chill. Anvar laid the table and lit the lamps, and was cleaning the fireplace when Aurian, never at her best at this hour, entered looking cross and bleary-eyed. Anvar busied himself at the hearth, trying to make himself inconspicuous and praying that the rumours had not reached her. He heard her footsteps crossing the floor behind him, the scrape of her chair on the carpet, and the bubbling, liquid sound of taillin pouring into a cup. After a moment, she cleared her throat. 'Anvar – I want to talk to you.'

Anvar's heart lurched as his terror of the Magefolk blazed up within him, renewed. He dropped the bucket with an ear-splitting clang, and to his horror the ash flew up in a cloud to cover every surface. The Mage leapt up from her ruined breakfast with a blistering oath, her hair and face turned powdery grey. Anvar threw himself at her feet, quaking. 'Lady, please,' he begged, 'it was an accident.'

'Of course it was.' Aurian knelt at his side. 'Don't cringe like that, Anvar – I'm sorry I frightened you. I was half asleep, and that noise startled me out of my wits.'

She was apologizing – to him? Anvar looked up at the Mage in astonishment, and her lips began to twitch. 'Gods,' she chuckled, 'you look like the offspring of a ghost and a scarecrow!' She ran her hands through her abundant red hair, and was immediately enveloped in a choking grey cloud.

'Lady, I'm so terribly sorry,' Anvar said in dismay, as she coughed and spluttered.

'Not to worry. We'll soon fix it.' She gave a flip of her fingers, and instantly every speck of ash was back in the bucket. Throwing logs into the fireplace, she ignited them with a careless gesture. 'We Magefolk are so used to people running around after us, we forget we can do things for ourselves.' Then her manner sobered. 'Come and sit with me, Anvar. There's something I need to ask you.'

The Lady led him to the table, and gave him taillin in her own cup. His hands were shaking as he took it. Aurian sat down opposite, holding his eyes with her steady green gaze. 'Elewin tells me you murdered your mother,' she said bluntly. 'Is it true?'

149

Anvar bit his lip, not knowing how to reply. He was terrified of invoking Miathan's spell if he tried to tell the truth. Besides, she would never believe him.

'Well?' The Mage broke the lengthening silence. 'Why won't you speak? Are you afraid?' She reached across the table to take his hand. 'Look,' she said gently, 'I can't believe this, and neither can Elewin. When he heard from Janok, who was apparently told by Miathan, that you're a murderer, he was so concerned that he came straight to me with the tale. It seems wrong to me, too, Anvar. If you were accused of murder, your case should have come before Forral, but it never did. I want to hear your side. If you were wrongly bonded, I'll do my best to set things straight.'

Anvar stared at her, unable to believe that she was on his side. 'It's no good,' he said at last. 'My father was within his rights to bond me. I wasn't old enough – by a month – to be considered a man under the law.'

'And the rest?' Aurian said softly.

Anvar struggled to hold back his tears. 'How could I have killed her?' he cried. 'I loved her!'

With infinite patience, Aurian coaxed the story of his mother's death from him, though he couldn't tell her how he had put out the fire. 'It was an accident,' he finished, 'but it happened because of me. My father blamed me, and signed my life away for revenge.'

Aurian shuddered. 'Your father is a bastard,' she said.

'No.' Anvar shook his head, his face burning with shame. 'I'm the bastard. That was why he did it.' It was the closest he could come to telling her the whole truth.

'Anvar!' Aurian's grip on his hand tightened, and her expression grew fierce. 'Listen. Even if I can't do anything about the bonding, I won't have you unjustly accused of murder! I'll talk to Forral this morning. At least we can clear your name.'

From that day, Anvar's relationship with the Mage began to change. Aurian had Forral investigate his story, and after questioning the shopkeepers of the arcade the commander ruled that Ria's death had been an accident. Aurian announced

150

the fact within the Academy, and at last Anvar was freed from the sideways looks and accusing whispers. Only when it had gone did he appreciate the extent of the strain he had suffered with the false accusation hanging over him; and Mage or no, Anvar was truly grateful to his Lady.

Aurian's kindness to him became more marked, as if she was trying to make amends for the misery he had suffered. Often, as he worked in her rooms, she would make him sit and have a glass of wine or some taillin with her, and Anvar became aware of a new peril. As they talked, Aurian would drop in a question about his past or his family, and he'd be lost for an answer. She was so easy to talk to that he found himself in constant danger or bringing the Archmage's terrible spell into effect. Sometimes he longed to try to confide in her, and ask her help, but though she had done so much for him she was still a Mage, and Miathan's favourite, and somehow he could never quite bring himself to trust her.

None the less, as time went by, Anvar became increasingly concerned about his Lady. She worked too hard, as though she, like himself, was trying to drive away her troubles with activity. She would come from her sword training, or her healing work with Meiriel, looking utterly exhausted; and Anvar, no stranger to sorrow, often wondered at the sadness that shadowed her face. She began to spend less and less time at the garrison, eventually only going there for her morning practice. Anvar noticed this, and wondered if Aurian's unhappiness was somehow connected with Forral.

He knew for certain, however, that Miathan was worrying her with his attentions. As the year went on, the Archmage began to visit Aurian at odd hours – late at night, or in the morning when she was bathing after her session at the garrison. He plied her with gifts, and was always finding excuses to touch her. Anvar saw the gleam of possessive lust in the Archmage's eyes, and he feared for her.

Since his terror of Miathan was undiminished, Anvar was unnerved by his frequent visits. When the Archmage was present, Aurian began to find excuses for her servant to be in her rooms, inventing any number of trifling tasks to keep him there. Anvar could hardly blame her – in fact, he was relieved that she had some instinct of self-protection, though he could see that she was confounded by Miathan's behaviour. Unbelievable as it seemed to him, she looked on Miathan almost as a father, and simply could not believe that he would betray her trust in him.

Aurian may have been reluctant to face the truth, but Anvar had no doubts. As he worked, he could feel Miathan's eyes boring into his back, and if he turned around he was confronted by a savage glare filled with loathing and hostility – and an unmistakable threat. The thought of crossing the Archmage made him quake with terror. Miathan was not one to be thwarted for long, and Anvar's only protection was Aurian, for the Archmage was not ready to upset her by depriving her of her servant. But it was only a matter of time. Anvar knew that Miathan's patience was limited, and sooner or later matters would come to a head.

When he heard that Aurian usually visited her mother during the summer, Anvar was tormented by fear. While he knew it would benefit his Lady to get away from both Forral and Miathan for a time, he was terrified that she would leave him behind, defenceless and in the Archmage's power. He was sure that if she did, he would not be there when she returned. He doubted that he'd even be alive.

The day before Aurian was due to leave, Anvar was sitting on her bedrom floor with an oily rag in one hand and one of her riding boots in the other. He gave a final polish to the soft brown leather, then set the boot down beside its companion and turned with a sigh to the neatly folded clothing on the bed. He was supposed to be packing Aurian's saddlebags, but was finding it impossible to concentrate on his task. The Mage had still not told him whether he could go with her – she'd said that for some reason Miathan had refused to allow it, but she still hoped to persuade him. Anvar knew what that meant. He was not surprised, therefore, when he heard Aurian enter her rooms like a hurricane. The door slammed shut with a resounding crash, followed by a string of lurid curses. Anvar shuddered. Obviously, Miathan had said no again.

Aurian stormed into her bedroom, still swearing, and pulled up short at the sight of him. 'Anvar! I didn't think you'd still be here!'

'I'm sorry, Lady – it's taking longer than I thought.'

'Never mind – there's no rush.' Aurian returned to the other chamber and came back with two goblets of wine. Handing one to him, she sat down on the bed. 'I'm sorry, Anvar. The Archmage just won't budge. I don't know what's come over him lately – he never used to be like this.'

Though he tried to hide his fear, the glass began to shake in Anvar's hands, and Aurian gave him a knowing, sympathetic look. 'Don't look so worried,' she said hastily. 'I know you're afraid of Miathan, but you won't see much of him while I'm away. Finbarr and I were talking last night, and he suggested that you could help him in the archives. He's sorting documents just now, and it's too much for one person to manage. Would you mind?'

Would he *mind*? Anvar felt giddy with relief. Ever since she had discovered that he could read, Aurian had given him the task of organizing her own researches, so by now he knew Finbarr very well. Although he was a Mage, Anvar could not help liking the clever archivist, and as Finbarr's servant he knew he'd be safe. Down in the catacombs, he would be well out of Miathan's way, though he wondered whether Finbarr would have much use for him. Knowing his Lady, Aurian had probably talked the archivist into the idea.

When Anvar went to take up his new duties, Finbarr's dirty, dishevelled appearance disabused him of the notion. The archivist greeted him with relief. 'My, but you're a sight for sore eyes, Anvar! Aurian offered to help me with this appalling task, but I insisted that she went away as usual. I've been worried about her lately – she will insist on working too hard. Besides, all I need is a quick brain and an extra pair of hands – though you're not so good to look at, if you'll forgive my saying so. Come this way – I'm working right down on the lower levels.' He held out his dusty hands with a grimace. 'There's stuff down there that hasn't been disturbed in centuries.'

The days of Aurian's absence passed quickly for Anvar. He had to work harder for Finbarr than he had done for his Lady, but he found endless fascination in sorting the ancient documents. The archivist was delighted to have his assistance, and more than happy to encourage his interest.

Finbarr was attempting to use the much-neglected sorting of the lower levels to further his research into his own pet subject – the ancient history of the Magefolk. 'If you look into the annals, my boy,' he told Anvar, 'you will find that every archivist has had his particular obsession. It's an odd position, this – the holder's magical talents are of small importance, except that they can be used to further the work in hand. My own powers, for instance, mainly encompass Air and Fire, but my predecessor was a Water-mage, and the work she did in drying out these very lower levels, so that we can work in them, was invaluable. No, what counts is a love of order, and an insatiable thirst for knowledge – that's what makes an archivist!'

While they worked, Anvar would listen happily, as Finbarr expounded his theories on the disastrous wars of the ancient Magefolk. 'So much was lost,' the archivist would mourn, 'in the destruction of Old Nexis. There are vague, unsubstantiated hints, you know, in some of the chronicles, that we were not the only race of Magefolk at that time. Of course, we know that the Dragonfolk existed, though our knowledge of them is scant, but certain sources – alas, discredited as the blackest of heretics by many previous archivists – hint that the Cataclysm was actually set in motion by a Mage who could fly, if you can believe it! Still others suggest that there were Mages who could live beneath the sea, and that all these races had a part in the forming of the four legendary Weapons of the Elements . . .' He sighed. 'If only I could find something that might decrease our ignorance of those times . . . If those four Implements of Power really did exist, then surely they must still be at large in the world – and should they fall into the wrong hands, then history could easily repeat itself . . .'

Though Anvar, unlike Finbarr, refused to lose sleep over the possibility of another Cataclysm, he hoped that the archivist would find what he sought. There was a time, he knew, when Finbarr's pursuit of knowledge for knowledge's sake would have angered him, given the poverty and suffering that existed among so many Mortals. But the archivist meant well, and in all honesty he found Finbarr's enthusiasm very contagious.

154

On a bright, crisp day that presaged the turning of the season to autumn, Finbarr decided it was time to tackle the lowest level of all. 'I must make the most of you before Aurian gets back,' he smiled. 'She is due any day now. I wonder what she'd say if I decided to steal you for good?'

For a moment Anvar was tempted by the idea. He had enjoyed assisting the archivist, but, more to the point, he had seen nothing of the Archmage while Aurian was away. He'd be safer as Finbarr's servant, and he would also escape the torment of Miathan's visits to his Lady. None the less, he felt a strange pang of reluctance at the thought of leaving Aurian. Lately, he had found himself looking every day for her return, and finally been forced to the astonishing conclusion that he missed her.

Anvar followed Finbarr down through the maze of passages and stairways that had been hewn out of the living rock of the promontory. They passed beyond the upper levels where the archivist had set lights of glowing crystal, until their only illumination was the glowing ball of Magelight that Finbarr sent before them. Their shadows, cast by the iridescent, silvery globe, bobbed and danced like puppets on the rough stone walls.

'I thought we would make a start in here.' Finbarr ducked through a doorless archway, and Anvar followed him into a small stone chamber whose walls were filled with crumbling wooden shelving. The place was shrouded in dust and cobwebs, and many of the shelves had collapsed beneath the weight of documents. Scrolls and papers littered the floor in haphazard piles. The archivist sighed. 'By Ionor the Wise,' he muttered, 'my predecessors neglected these lower levels disgracefully. It's a lifetime's work to put it right, Anvar my friend – and that being the case, we'd better get started.' He felt in the pockets of his robes, and grimaced in irritation. 'Drat! I forgot to bring any crystals with me to light our labours.'

'I'll go,' Anvar offered. 'I know where you keep them, sir.'

'Never mind. If you trek all the way up to the library and back again, we'll lose half the day. Besides, it's a tricky route for the uninitiated.' Finbarr's eyes twinkled. 'Aurian would never forgive me if I lost you in the bowels of the earth. We'll manage.' He tossed the ball of Magelight towards the ceiling, but it went too high, splattering against the buttressed stone in an explosion of sparks and plunging them into utter blackness.

'Festering bat-turds! I'm always doing that.' Finbarr's voice echoed, sharp with annoyance, out of the darkness.

Anvar caught his breath. His night-vision had always been excellent, but he had never experienced such absolute darkness. It pressed on him as though the entire weight of the hill was resting on his shoulders. In panic, he turned to flee. His foot caught in a pile of scrolls and he overbalanced, falling hard against the wall. The shelves above him collapsed in an avalanche of papers and splintered wood, and then an entire section of the wall gave way beneath his weight, in a cloud of dust and a rumble of stone.

Finbarr struck a new light. 'By the gods, Anvar! See what you've found!' His young-old face was alight with excitement. Anvar scrambled out of the wreckage, brushing off the rubble and dust. Beyond the wall was a chamber – no, a cave! A tunnel led from it at the far side, promising further secrets beyond. Finbarr's eyes glowed with rapture as he looked at the treasures within. Ancient volumes, their gilded bindings winking in the Magelight, were piled in chests and scattered across the floor, as though they had been abandoned in a hurry. Tapestries lay stacked in a corner, and a pile of artefacts – personal belongings by their look – were tumbled against the opposite wall. As Anvar looked, a beautiful golden chalice toppled from the pile and rolled across the floor towards him. He stepped forward to catch it, but Finbarr thrust him back. 'Wait! There's magic here! This place is protected!' Seizing his arm, the archivist hauled Anvar out of the chamber. 'If I'm not mistaken,' he said, 'you have just made the most valuable discovery of our age! We must fetch the Archmage at once!'

Before she entered the Mages' Tower, Aurian took a good long look around the familiar courtyard of the Academy and decided that she was glad to be back. Although she'd enjoyed her visit with Eilin, she had missed Forral dreadfully, and had also been worried about Anvar, and how he had managed in her absence. Once again, she wondered why he was so afraid of Miathan, and why the Archmage seemed to have taken such a marked dislike to him. If Miathan had truly believed that Anvar was a murderer, it would explain the mystery – but if that was so, then why had his attitude not altered when her servant's name had been cleared?

As she lugged her heavy saddlebags up the stairs of the Mages' Tower, Aurian found herself wishing that Anvar had been there to help. Somehow, she'd been disappointed not to find him standing in the courtyard waiting for her. 'Aurian, you are an idiot!' she told herself, as she panted her way up the steps. 'How could he possibly know you were coming? Besides, he has better things to do.'

All thoughts of Anvar vanished as she let herself into her rooms. Miathan was already there, waiting for her. 'My dearest Aurian!' The Archmage stepped forward, hands outstretched in welcome. 'I saw you ride into the courtyard from my window. How glad I am that you're safely home!' Aurian stepped back hastily from his effusive greeting, dropping her saddlebags. As Miathan's arms went round her, she felt herself stiffen with panic. How had he managed to get into her rooms? She'd thought that she and Anvar had the only keys. Had something happened to her servant? She flinched away from the fey brightness of Miathan's eyes; the excitement betrayed by his jerky movements. It had been easy, while she was away, to convince herself that his odd behaviour had all been her imagination, but suddenly she knew better. And now, at last, he had her alone.

As he left the library, Anvar saw Aurian's horse standing patiently outside the door of the Mages' Tower, and all thoughts of his amazing discovery in the catacombs fled. 'My Lady!' he cried joyfully. 'She's back!' He raced across the courtyard and up the tower stairs, followed by a smiling Finbarr.

'No! Get away from me, Miathan!' Aurian's cry rang out just as Anvar and Finbarr reached her quarters. Anvar gasped with horror. The Archmage! He tugged frantically at the handle of the door, but it was locked. Without thinking, he threw himself at the door, hammering loudly on the wooden panels, and heard the Archmage curse. After a moment, the door was flung open. The hem of Miathan's robe was tattered and smouldering, and his hands were blistered and black with soot. His face was livid with rage. 'How dare you interrupt me,' he snarled, raising his hand to strike, but Finbarr stepped forward quickly between the Archmage and his prey, and Anvar blessed the archivist's presence of mind as Miathan drew back quickly with a stifled oath.

'I interrupted you, Miathan,' Finbarr said calmly, for all the world as though nothing was amiss. 'You must excuse the servant's excitement – we've made an incredible discovery in the archives that you must see at once.' Without waiting for a reply, he pushed past the dumbfounded Archmage and entered the room. Anvar followed him quickly, and stopped dead at the sight of his mistress.

Aurian was backed into a corner, her clothes torn and her eyes blazing with anger. Her hair, untangled from its intricate braiding, swept almost to the floor in a tide of crimson. Her hand was drawn back like a claw, clutching a searing fireball, and a smoking scar on the carpet proved that it was not the first. As she saw Finbarr and her servant, the Mage slowly extinguished the flame between her fingers and leaned back against the wall, white and shaking.

Anvar went rigid with fury, but Finbarr laid a restraining hand on his arm. 'Is anything wrong, Aurian?'

He gave the Archmage a hard look. Miathan shrugged. 'A simple experiment with Fire-magic that got out of hand,' he replied calmly. 'I was trying to help her when you arrived.'

'Shall I send for Meiriel?' Finbarr addressed the Archmage, but his eyes went to Aurian as he spoke.

'That won't be necessary,' Miathan snapped. Then he turned to the door, all smiles again. 'Well, shall we go and look at your amazing discovery? I'm sure the Lady will join us, too.' It was little short of a command, and Anvar knew that the Archmage was reluctant to leave her.

'She'll follow when she's recovered,' Finbarr said blithely. 'I know how draining these – experiments – can be. Come, Archmage – this won't wait.' He shepherded Miathan out of the room. Once the Archmage had gone, he turned back to

158

Anvar with a frown. 'Take care of your mistress,' he whispered. 'I'll deal with Miathan.' Then he was gone.

Aurian crossed the room and sat down on the couch, shuddering, her face hidden in her hands. 'He was waiting for me,' she whispered. 'When I got back, he was here. He – he just seemed to go mad, Anvar! He said he'd been patient long enough, and he didn't want to wait any longer. Oh, gods!' Her gasp was half a sob. 'How could he! He was always like a father to me!'

Not knowing what else to do, Anvar poured her a glass of wine. She took it gratefully, and he knelt at her feet. He could hardly bear to look into her horrified, pain-shadowed eyes. 'Lady – he didn't . . .'

Aurian grimaced, and shook her head. 'No,' she said shakily. 'He had a damned good try, though! It's a good thing I know how to fight!'

Anvar saw the gleam of tears in her eyes, and a startling surge of protectiveness swept over him. Greatly daring, he took her hands. 'Don't worry, Lady. Finbarr saw what had happened. He said he'd speak to the Archmage. Besides,' he added fiercely, 'Miathan won't get another chance – I'll see to that! I'll stay with you, no matter what he says. I'll never leave you alone with him, I promise.'

'Thank you for that, Anvar. I know it's hard for you because your're afraid of him – and after today, I can begin to see why!' Aurian shuddered.

'It'll be all right, Lady. Surely he couldn't do anything in front of a witness.' Anvar wished he could make himself sound more confident.

Aurian sighed. 'I only hope you're right. Otherwise I don't know what I'm going to do.'

11

Trial By Combat

It's truly autumn now, Aurian thought, as she rode through the deserted streets towards the garrison. The weather was fine and clear as dawn stroked the city's roofs with golden fingers; but the light was paler now, the air clear and crisp. For the first time in months Aurian wore her cloak, and was grateful for it. Miathan had given her a new one, a luxurious mantle of thick soft wool dyed her favourite emerald green, but it hung neglected behind her door while Aurian wore Forral's sturdy old soldier's cloak made from the tough oily wool of mountain sheep. She knew it was foolish, but wearing his cast-off cloak seemed to bring him closer to her. The swordsman was still keeping a discreet, unbridgeable distance between them, and she was close to despair. She had loved him for so long! Ever since her childhood. She hadn't known, then, that it was forbidden for a Mage to love a Mortal, and now it was too late. How could she ever love anyone else?

Which brought her back to her other, far more pressing problem. Miathan. Since the Archmage had first adopted her as his pupil, he had treated her like a favourite daughter, and she'd loved and respected him as such. But yesterday's happenings had changed everything. Aurian shuddered, unable to shake off a crawling feeling of uncleanliness. Though she had never taken a lover, she'd been well educated by her earthy friends at the garrison, and the idea of sharing Miathan's bed filled her with revulsion. His cruelty to Anvar had first given her cause to doubt him – and had he deliberately lied about the servant being a murderer? Aurian knew that she would never be able to trust the Archmage again, and her relationship with him was now tinged with an undercurrent of fear. Last night, in the excitement caused by Anvar's discovery, she had managed to avoid being alone with Miathan, but how long could she keep avoiding him? He was the most powerful person in the city, and what he wanted he could take.

Apart from Finbarr, Aurian dared confide in none of the Magefolk. If this had been Miathan's intention all along, any or all of them might be in the plot. To be chosen by the Archmage was deemed the greatest of honours. Eliseth would give her right arm for it, Aurian thought wryly. She thought of discussing it with Maya, but then Forral would be sure to find out, and she wanted to avoid that, knowing full well how he would react. He was no match for the Archmage.

It's no use, Aurian thought despairingly. I should leave Nexis and go back to the Valley. But though it was the only sensible option, she could not stop the tears coming at the thought. How can I leave? What will happen to Anvar without me? But he belongs to the Academy – I wouldn't be allowed to take him! And how can I leave Finbarr, and Maya and Parric and Vannor? And, oh – Forral! How could I bear to lose him again? Weary as she was after yesterday's shock and a sleepless night, her thoughts circled in hopeless misery, without ever coming near to a solution.

Absorbed in her troubles, the Mage rode through the great stone gateway of the garrison, scarcely aware that she had arrived. Too late, she heard the thunder of hooves bearing down on her. Her training saved her – that, and blind instinct. She felt the wind from the sword-stroke whistle over her head as she dived beneath the belly of her horse; one foot still in the stirrup, one hand clutching the reins and the pommel of the saddle. Drawing her dagger with her free hand, she sliced the girth of her assailant's mount as it passed, then hauled herself upright and wheeled her horse around in time to see the other's saddle rock and tip, dumping the rider into the dust of the parade ground. Aurian grinned. Parric, with whom she had lately been training, sat on the hard-packed earth, swearing horribly.

'Got you!' Aurian crowed, her troubles, for the moment, vanished. 'You owe me a beer, Parric.'

The little cavalry master gave her a sour look, and spat out a mouthful of dust. 'Pah! Beer, indeed! You were so bloody slow, I could have had your head off if I'd wanted!'

161

'Rubbish!' Aurian retorted. 'What are you doing down there, then? Go on, admit it, I won.'

'Didn't!'

'Did!' She looked around for support, and saw Maya over on the archery range at the far side of the parade ground, watching D'arvan shooting at targets with Fional, the garrison's crack archer. 'Maya, did you see it?' she called. 'I did win, didn't I?'

Forral's second in command – a slender, dark-haired young woman whose luminous, delicate beauty belied whiplash reflexes and one of the most aggressive, effective fighting styles that Aurian had ever seen – stood little over five feet tall, but she had no trouble keeping order – even the biggest trooper feared her acid tongue. Yet she was quiet and shy among strangers, preferring the company of a few intimate friends. Since their first meeting in the Fleet Deer, she and Aurian had become very close. What was more, Maya seemed to be acquiring a taste for Magefolk. Since D'arvan had started coming with Aurian to the garrison, he and Forral's second in command could usually be found together.

Aurian was delighted that the shy young Mage had found a friend outside the Academy. He had grieved so hard, at first, over Davorshan's defection to Eliseth. D'arvan's early visits to the garrison had been strained and awkward, and for a while she had despaired, but his shyness had eventually been vanquished by the discovery of an incredible talent for archery, of all things. Then Maya had won his trust at last, and taken a weight of worry from the Mage's shoulders. The twins, at this point, seemed to have called a truce – though they had moved to separate rooms, they had apparently learned to live with the differences that had alienated them from one another. And Aurian, to her surprise, had been well repaid for her kindness to D'arvan, for she had gained another friend within the Academy where she had least expected to find one.

Aurian was brought back from her thoughts by Parric's voice. 'Well, you heard her – did she win?'

Fional simply shrugged, and D'arvan, intent on his shooting, gave the two assailants an absent-minded wave. Maya, however, sauntered across to them, grinning. 'Parric's right. You were slow,' she said to Aurian.

'See?' the cavalry master jeered. Aurian's face fell.

'But,' Maya went on, 'you were effective. Cutting that girth was the neatest trick I've seen in ages! Face it, Parric, you've taught her too well. I give the result to Aurian.'

'Ha!' Aurian pointed at the little man. 'Told you!'

'Bloody women!' Parric muttered disgustedly as he picked himself up, beating the dust out of his clothing. 'Always stick together!'

Aurian dismounted with a smile. An outsider, she thought, would have been horrified by the incident, but within the garrison such surprise attacks were commonplace. The troopers were a close-knit family. They policed the city and its surrounds, dealt with any trouble, and fought any battles or wars that the council needed fighting; and they were well aware of the dangers of their profession. Hence the potentially lethal tricks they played on one another. They pushed themselves and their comrades to the limits out of friendship – to sharpen their wits and skills, and increase their chances of survival. It was very effective. Now, thanks to Forral and her comrades-in-arms, she was a better fighter than she had ever been, and the friendships she had made were worth more than gold.

Aurian suddenly became aware that Maya was speaking to her. 'What did you say?'

'I said, how was your visit to your mother?'

'Oh, I don't know – about the same as usual.' Gods, had she only returned yesterday? It seemed unbelievable to Aurian.

'Honestly, you're miles away this morning,' Maya said. Linking arms, the two women strolled towards the barn-like building that housed the garrison practice floor.

'I've been up all night, as D'arvan might have told you, had you been able to get his attention away from his archery,' Aurian told her. 'There's great excitement at the Academy. Finbarr found some caves beneath the archives, filled with old documents that might hold the lost history of the Magefolk, before the Cataclysm.'

Maya shuddered at the mention of the long-ago magical wars that had almost destroyed the world, and made a sign against evil. 'Gods,' she said, 'I thought everything had been destroyed.'

'We all did, but apparently someone had the sense to hide this stuff away out of danger. Although the Academy of that time was levelled along with the rest of the city, these artefacts survived the centuries,' Aurian said. 'It took us half the night to unravel the spells protecting them, just so that we could touch them, and then they started to disintegrate. We spent the rest of the night working preservative magic so that we wouldn't lose the lot.'

'If you ask me, you should have left them well alone,' Maya said darkly. 'Mark my words, Aurian, no good will come of digging up ancient evils.'

At her friend's words, Aurian felt her skin prickle. The day seemed to darken with the presentiment of some impending catastrophe. She shivered.

'What's wrong?' Maya asked sharply.

'Nothing. I'm tired, that's all.' She tried to convince herself that it was true.

'Are you sure you should fight this morning?' Maya sounded anxious. 'Tired people make mistakes, you know.'

Aurian stopped in her tracks. 'Great Chathak! I'd forgotten all about that!'

'Wonderful,' Maya said drily. 'This year Forral chooses you, out of everyone in the garrison, to partner him in the demonstration duel for the new recruits, and you forget. It's only an honour given to the best warrior in the place. No wonder such a little thing slipped your mind!'

'Oh, shut up, Maya!' Aurian snapped.

'Staying up all night hasn't made any difference to your legendary grouchiness first thing in the morning!' Maya teased, then her face grew serious. 'I'm sorry, Aurian. I can see that something's bothering you. Look, do you want to talk about it? We have time. Forral overslept again.' She made a wry face.

Aurian sighed, as her friend's sympathy tempted her to spill out all her worries. With an effort she pulled herself together. 'Thanks, Maya, but it's something I'll have to sort out for myself,' she said. 'If we have time, though, I could kill for some taillin.'

As they sat in the deserted mess hall cradling their steaming cups, Maya returned to the attack. 'It's not this business with Forral, is it?' she persisted.

'What?' For an instant Aurian thought her friend had discovered her feelings for the swordsman, but Maya's next words disabused her. 'He's managed to hide it from most of the garrison, but no one can drink like that without it coming to light sooner or later.'

Aurian's heart sank. 'How long has this been going on?'

Maya shrugged. 'Weeks – months, really. But lately it's been getting worse, and as Forral's friend, as well as his deputy, I'm worried. He's losing his edge, Aurian. I can see it already, and you know what it's like around here. Sooner or later somebody will pull a stunt on him like Parric did to you this morning, and he's going to get hurt.' Maya stopped short at the horrified expression on Aurian's face. 'Damn my big mouth! You didn't know, did you?'

'It's all right,' Aurian said weakly. 'I wish you'd told me sooner. Maybe I can talk to him about it.'

'Thanks, Aurian. I'm sorry to burden you with this, but he might listen to you. He . . .' Maya suddenly shut her mouth, her eyes narrowing. She stood up abruptly. 'Come on,' she said. 'It's time we were going.'

The banks of wooden benches around the practice floor were packed to capacity. The new recruits sat on one side, and the remaining seats were packed with every off-duty member of the garrison who could squeeze in. The annual no-holds-barred exhibition fight, to show the newcomers what would eventually be expected of them, was always spectacular, and no one wanted to miss seeing the world's greatest swordsman in action – especially this year. Forral always chose the best warrior as his opponent, and in nominating Aurian he had risked the charge of favouritism. The troopers, however, knew better, and the wagering (strictly illegal) on the fight was heavier than usual.

The atmosphere was tense with excitement as Aurian entered the arena. She'd done the exercises and meditations to prepare her body and mind for the coming fight, but still she found herself glancing worriedly at Forral as he entered. Apart from a slight puffiness about the eyes, he seemed well enough, and Aurian forced herself to put it out of her mind until later. The two contestants, clad alike in sleeveless leather fighting vests, leather breeches and soft boots, bowed to each other formally, and the fight began.

Aurian circled warily, knowing better than to commit herself too hastily with a warrior of Forral's calibre. Suddenly he lunged, finding an opening she could have sworn was never there. She leapt back, feeling his sword's very tip graze the tough leather of her vest just over her ribs. Good thing she was fast on her feet. She feigned a stumble, then drove in to one side. A trickle of blood appeared on Forral's left arm, and the audience's startled gasp echoed Aurian's own. First blood to her, and so soon! He should never have fallen for an old trick like that. She had to do something. She drove in again, straight this time. Forral blocked her blow with his upraised sword, and they strained against each other, nose to nose, blades locked. Aurian heard the spectators gasp again. They thought she had made an error in closing with the burlier, stronger man, but her move had been deliberate. 'Slowing up, old man?' she taunted softly. 'Today's the day I beat you, Forral.'

She saw shock and anger flick across his face, but there was no time for more. In a whirling flurry of steel he disengaged, almost wrenching Aurian's blade from her hand. Then the fight was on in earnest. To Aurian, time seemed to slow as she and Forral wove their intricate dance of death across the sands. All other concerns were forgotten as the world narrowed to herself, her opponent, and the gleaming steel they wielded.

Coronach screamed its deathsong as it clove the air, and Aurian exulted with the blade – and *became* the blade with its clean, sharp flicker followed by the jarring impact that ran up her arms as the two swords clashed again and again. She registered the warm trickle of blood from a dozen minor wounds, then forgot them. Forral was also bleeding in several places. He was red-faced and panting now, his movements less fluent than her own. With a sudden shock, Aurian realized that she could beat him. The split-second's distraction almost cost her the fight. She saw Forral's downswing just in time, tucked in her head and rolled, coming up again, sword still in hand, to press the attack. Step by step, she began to force him backwards.

The awareness that he was losing began to dawn on Forral's face, and with it the atmosphere of the fight was changed. He was proud of her – Aurian knew it as though she had picked the thought from his mind. As they fought, the air was charged with a tension between them; a bond so close that they were almost fighting as one, and Aurian knew that they were no longer fighting against each other – they were fighting *with* one another, though each was striving their utmost to win. Despite her wounds and the tiredness that was creeping over her, the feeling was like heady wine. A slow smile spread across Forral's face, and she found herself grinning back in answer. Never had they been so utterly together.

The fight went down in garrison legend. Those fortunate enough to witness it said afterwards that the moves were so fast that they could hardly be seen. No one knew how long it took – Aurian lost all track of time in the exhilaration of the contest. Then, abruptly, it was over. Forral was sprawled on the sand at her feet, the tip of her sword at his throat.

The audience was stunned into silence as Aurian lifted her blade to salute him, sagging with exhaustion as the tension of the fight drained from her limbs. Leaning on her sword, she put out a hand to help Forral to his feet. As he rose, their eyes met, and in that one glance, all the words, all the feelings that they had hidden in their hearts for so long, passed between them. There was no more hiding now. Supporting each other, they left the arena. The crowd, as if released from a spell, leapt to its feet and burst into tumultuous cheers. Aurian exchanged a startled look with Forral. They had forgotten all about them.

Without a word, they limped back to Forral's quarters. Before the door had time to close, they were in each other's arms. They made love right there on the floor – blood, sweat, sand and all. The touch of Forral's hands sent delightful shivers over Aurian's skin as he discarded her bloodstained clothing, and his own. She remembered crying out once, as he first penetrated her, and later she found bruises on his shoulders where her fingers had clenched in that instant of pain. Forral cried out as his body tensed and shuddered; he had longed for this moment for so many years that he could delay no longer. Then he relaxed against her, kissing her eyes,

167

her neck, her mouth. Aurian moaned, still tense, wanting . . . She felt his hand caress her breasts, her thighs, then between her thighs, and as he brought her to her own release he entered her once more, and this time, when the moment came, they were together; their passion firm and lasting and strong with friendship and respect and the deep, deep joy of an old love turned new.

They lay in each other's arms, letting the world drift slowly back to them. Aurian was filled with awe. She had passed through the most important event in a woman's life – and Forral loved her. Not as the young girl he had known, but as a woman. She felt transformed; and so, somehow, was he. Aurian felt unaccountably shy in the presence of this muscular, hairy man – her lover. Then he turned to her, his face alight with tenderness, and he was Forral again, whom she had always loved and trusted.

'Ah, love,' he murmured, 'if you only knew . . .'

Aurian reached out to touch his face. 'I've known ever since I was a little girl. I told you then, remember?'

'Aye, so you did. I thought it was just a childish fancy, though. I didn't take into account how stubborn you can be. And what a fighter! Gods, but I was proud of you today.'

'You taught me, Forral – and now you've taught me something else.' Aurian's eyes danced. 'Who do you think won this time, then?'

'Wretch!' Forral laughed. 'Who do *you* think won?'

'I think,' Aurian said happily, 'it was a draw.' And she kissed him.

They bathed, and doctored each other's wounds from the duel. Aurian wanted no magical healing today. She had magic of another kind, and every one of these scars was precious to her. None of the cuts was serious, but now that Aurian was noticing them, they stung. She was beginning to stiffen up after being sweated up in a battle then making love on a draughty floor. But it made no difference. She and Forral were stupefied with wonder. They could hardly stop touching each other, and gazing into one another's eyes. To Aurian it was like coming home – and so perfectly right that she had never known before what rightness was.

Their ministrations might have developed into something more, but they were interrupted by a discreet knock on the door. Forral swore, and went to answer it. No one was there, but a large tray, laden with food and drink, had been left on the floor. As Forral put it on the table, Aurian spotted a slip of folded paper propped against a flask of wine. Forral opened it, and burst out laughing. 'I might have known!' He handed the note to Aurian, who recognized Maya's neat, compressed hand. 'About bloody time!' it said.

After they had eaten, they decided to see if their love felt as good between clean sheets. It was even better. Dusk found them sitting up in bed, sipping peach brandy as the sound of Maya's voice drilling the hapless new recruits in the parade ground drifted through the open window. Aurian sipped the mellow spirit. The warm glow as it trickled down her throat matched the glow she felt inside. But it reminded her of more serious matters, and she turned to Forral. It was best to get things right out in the open. 'Why have you started drinking so much?' she asked him.

Forral almost dropped the glass. His face flushed guiltily. 'Who told you?'

'Maya. She's worried, Forral, and so am I.'

'Gods, does that wretched woman know everything? Between the two of you, a man doesn't stand a chance.'

'That's because we care about you,' Aurian said softly.

Forral put his arm round her. 'I know, love, and I'm sorry. A man gets defensive when he knows he's been acting like a fool. It was just – well, it was you.'

'Me?'

He nodded. 'I don't know when I stopped thinking of you as a child, but when I did – well, I've had women before . . .'

'Oh?' Aurian's voice had a dangerous edge. His previous lovers were the last thing she wanted to discuss.

'But not for a long time,' Forral said hastily, ruffling her hair. 'Anyway, I knew you felt the same. I tried to avoid this happening, to protect you, but I knew I was hurting you, and it hurt me too – and so I started drinking.'

'Well, why didn't you say something?' Aurian demanded. 'Think of the time we've wasted!'

Forral sighed. 'Look, let's talk about this another time. We've been so happy today, I don't want to spoil it.'

'No,' Aurian said fiercely, 'I want to know. You said yourself that I'm not a child any more. Is it something to do with this stupid Mage-Mortal proscription? Because I've already thought about that, and I don't care. If need be, we can go away together. Miathan doesn't own the world.'

'No, it's not Miathan, though we'll have trouble enough when he finds out about this. But there's something that you haven't considered.' Forral's face was very grave. 'Aurian, you're Mageborn. Unless something kills you, you can live as long as you want. It's different for me – I'm a Mortal. I'm not a young man – I'm over forty now – and even if I survive the dangers of a warrior's life, how many years do you think I'll have left? I tried to stop this from happening because I love you, and all too soon I'll be dead, and I can't bear to think of you left alone to grieve.'

Aurian felt a dizzy lurch in the pit of her stomach. She had never considered Forral's mortality. As she stared at him in horror, the room seemed to vanish around her, and she felt the same premonitory shiver of dread that she had experienced that morning. It seemed as though his features had been overlaid with a vision of that same dear face, but pale and still, the eyes closed in the sleep of death. 'No!' Her own tearing cry brought her back to reality. The vision vanished as she buried herself in Forral's arms, sobbing.

He held her tightly, and it seemed as though his warrior's strength was flowing into her. She stiffened her spine and wiped her eyes, and her chin went up in the old stubborn gesture. 'If grief is the price of our love,' she said, 'then I'll pay it. Not willingly, maybe, but in full. I love you, Forral. I've waited years for this, and I'm not losing you now. Even Magefolk don't live for ever. We may be parted for a while, but some day I'll find you again, I promise, in the worlds beyond. I already have Miathan to fight over this – I'll take on death too, if need be.'

There were tears in Forral's eyes, but he smiled. 'My warrior,' he said gruffly. 'I'm glad you're on my side.'

'Always. And I'll be there for a long time yet!'

Forral hugged her. 'The gods help anyone who tries to come between us. One thing though, love. When I'm dead . . .'

'Don't say that!' Aurian cried.

'Just this once,' Forral said firmly, 'and I want you to remember what I'm going to tell you now. You don't know grief yet, but I do, and I want to warn you. When I die, at first you may want to follow me. Don't. You've been blessed with the gift of years, Aurian, and many other gifts besides. It would be a grave sin to throw those gifts away. I can't go on with our love if it will rob you of your future. No, love – when I'm gone, I want you to find someone else, if you can, and be happy.'

'How can I?' Aurian protested bitterly. 'How could you ask such a thing of me?'

'Because I love you, and I don't want you to go through the years alone. That would be foolish and unfair. I've seen people waste their lives moping around the graves of their loved ones. I'll be with you, wherever you are, in your heart. If I ever catch you at my graveside, I'll – I'll make it rain on you, see if I don't!'

Despite her anguish, Aurian had to smile at that, and as the moment lightened they turned to talk of happier things. But Aurian kept his words in her heart. She felt older now, and sadder, but stronger and more determined than ever. Now that she understood its transience, her love for Forral was bittersweet, but infinitely precious.

Miathan had missed Aurian the previous day. As soon as she entered the room, hand in hand with Forral, he knew where she had been, and why. Forral did not bow. 'Archmage,' he said calmly, 'Aurian and I have become lovers.'

At the words of this upstart Mortal, Miathan felt his guts twist with icy rage. Aurian met him eye to eye, her face pale but her expression unrepentant. He turned his fury on Forral. 'Seducer!' he hissed, his voice shaking with anger. 'Lawbreaker! Transgressor!'

'What?' Aurian was aflame with indignation. 'You dare accuse Forral . . .' She bit off her words with a sideways look at the warrior, and Miathan saw her fighting to conquer her anger. Ah, he thought. So she has not told him.

'What you have done is forbidden,' he snapped.

171

'Nonsense!' Aurian retorted. 'The Mage-Mortal proscription isn't a law, and it's not in the Mages' Code. It's a recommendation made for practical reasons. If Forral and I can live with the problems, what affair is it of yours?'

Miathan was beside himself with rage. 'It will be the scandal of the whole city! How dare you embarrass the Magefolk, and me, in this way?'

'Not so, Miathan,' Forral intervened. 'The people view Aurian differently from the other Magefolk, after that business of the drought. They see her with me, or going to and from the garrison, and frankly they find her much more acceptable than the rest of you. My people already think of her as one of themselves, and the troopers will soon deal with any loose talk. Vannor is fond of her too, so there'll be no trouble from the merchants . . .'

'Well, there will be trouble from the Magefolk!' Miathan stormed. 'I'll break you for this, Forral. I'll have you thrown off the council! Banished from the city . . .'

Forral smiled coldly. 'I don't think so, Archmage. You see, it's no longer up to you to arrange the military presence on the council. You might be interested to know that I've already appointed my successor, in case anything should go amiss. You know Maya, my second in command? For some reason, she has no time for this idea of the Magefolk running Nexis. You'll really have fun wrangling with her on the council. Vannor is looking forward to it already.'

'But – but you can't do that!' Miathan spluttered.

Forral grinned. 'Oh yes I can. Vannor seconded the nomination, and we had it set down in the official records.'

The Archmage was aghast. He took a step towards Forral, intending to blast him into oblivion. But Aurian stepped quickly in front of the swordsman, raising her hand in a sweeping gesture. Miathan saw the air blur and shimmer as her magical shield snapped into place. There was a look of pure hatred on her face that he had never seen before. 'Just try it, Miathan,' she growled. 'I'm not your pupil for nothing. Let's see how much you've taught me!'

She meant it. Miathan was on the verge of losing her completely, and his carefully tended plans would be lost with her. His age-old cunning reasserted itself. He was an expert in deceit, and he was ruthless. He knew now that he had erred badly in letting his lust get the better of him when Aurian had returned from the Valley. Somehow, in her absence, he had persuaded himself that once he possessed her body, he would win her heart. Witless fool! This was no simple Mortal girl, to be overawed by his position and his powers. And now, thanks to his clumsy haste, he had driven her right into the arms – and the bed – of the swordsman. A just punishment indeed for his own stupidity.

Miathan knew he must win back Aurian's trust – and in order to do so, he'd have to swallow his pride. Trembling with strain, he forced down his anger and schooled his features into a semblance of regret. 'Aurian, please forgive me. I'm truly sorry – for everything. I have behaved very badly to you, and I wish to make amends. Forral, my deepest apologies. I should have anticipated this long ago, knowing how Aurian feels about you.' He sighed. 'I cannot say that I approve – but I love Aurian, and I value your support. If this is what you want, I must accept it. Be happy, then, for as long as you can.'

Aurian hesitated, suspicion written clearly on her face.

'My dear, I beg you.' Miathan forced tears into his eyes. 'Don't punish me for my hastiness. I would rather lose anything in the world than your good opinion. I swear by my very magic that I accept and respect your decision.'

'Thank you, Archmage.' Though her reply was spoken calmly, the Archmage saw Aurian relax a little, and heard relief in her voice as she lowered her shields at last. But where she would once have come running to hug him, she remained where she was, with one hand on Forral's arm. Miathan gritted his teeth against the surge of possessive desire that welled up in him. By the gods, when he finally took her, this humiliation would be repaid a thousandfold . . .

Once Aurian and Forral were safely away, the Archmage took out his fury in a blast of force that shook the tower to its foundations. He strode across the smoking carpet, kicking the splintered furniture aside, and pressed a section of the blackened wall. A panel flew open with a click, revealing a hollow space. Miathan reached inside and took out a golden goblet. He sat by the window on the one undamaged chair, staring blindly out and caressing the rich, intricately chased metal. The cup was wide and shallow, with a slim golden stem and a broad, heavy base. It hummed with power – a power so ancient and so great that it brought the very air alive. Miathan smiled. Not all was lost – he had found this precious thing in the cave that Finbarr had discovered, and had stolen it secretly away before the others saw it. He knew what it was, and it changed everything.

In the dark years following the Cataclysm, most of the history and lore of the ancient Magefolk had been lost. All that remained of the shining Elder Age were vague, colourful legends, so corrupted by time that it was impossible to sift the truth from minstrels' lays and old wives' tales. One legend, however, Miathan now knew to be true. It spoke of the four great magical Weapons of the Elements: the Harp of Winds, the Staff of Earth, the Sword of Fire – and the Cauldron of Rebirth. Although it now took the form of this golden chalice, Miathan was sure that he held a fragment, possibly refashioned to disguise it, of the Cauldron. He was also certain that it held the Cauldron's power, and that, given time, he could learn to master it.

Miathan's eyes burned. Let them wait, those who dared defy him! Aurian, Forral, Vannor – and Anvar, that accursed abomination who had thwarted him when he'd been so close to his goal. Let them enjoy their petty victory for a while. Let Finbarr labour like a blind mole in his archives, unwittingly providing his Archmage with the very information that he needed to bend the world to his will. Let Aurian copulate like an animal with that thrice-damned rutting swordsman, blithely unaware of the fate in store for her . . .

Fear pierced Miathan's heart like a sword of ice. How history repeated itself! He thought of Ria – so sweet, so compliant beneath him – and remembered his disgust when she had told him he was to be the father of a half-breed monster. What if it should happen again – to Aurian? The thought of her bearing Forral's brat turned him sick to the very core. But wait – what if the child, if child there were, should really be a monster? That would suit his ends, for such a creature could hardly possess magical powers, and it would also punish Aurian and Forral for their perfidy.

Miathan drew his power around him, and as he did so he felt the chalice quiver in his hands. Choosing his words carefully, he summoned a deadly bane against any such babe, that it should take the form, not of the human that had fathered it, but of the first beast that Aurian set eyes on after she had given birth. As he spoke the curse, the grail flared with a brief, cold light and there was a noise like a thunderclap far across the city. Triumph swelled within the Archmage's heart. So the thing could be used! It would take much study to learn how to wield it effectively, but in the end this weapon would give him mastery over the world – and over Aurian. After that, he would have all the long ages to make her pay for what she had done.

12
The Nightrunner

It was the day before Solstice Eve, but Vannor's daughter Zanna was finding that seasonal goodwill was in short supply. She and Dulsina, the housekeeper, had been forced to make a special trip to the food markets of the Grand Arcade for Vannor's cook, who had been in a rare old taking. It was Sara's fault, of course. The meals for the festival required considerable planning in advance, and Hebba, who had cooked for the family for years, had her solstice routine organized with immaculate timing, right down to the last delicious morsel. Her reaction, therefore, when Sara had decided, the day before the solstice celebrations were due to begin, that it was time to make some changes, had been a mix of horror, outrage and utter panic. Vannor was out, and his eldest daughter Corielle had recently wed the son of a wealthy sea-captain, and moved to the port of Easthaven with her new husband. It had been left to Zanna, as usual, to deal with the trouble as best she could.

As Hebba would not trust the kitchen maids with the errand ('What? Send them girls down there to dawdle and dally all day?') Dulsina and Zanna had been sent off with a long list of delicacies by the frantic cook, who was turning the kitchen upside down in her frenzy. Zanna was glad to escape – the two kitchen-maids had already been in tears. She couldn't blame poor Hebba, but Zanna resented the fact that the rest of the household, and herself in particular, had to bear the brunt of the cook's temper, while Sara, as usual, had escaped the consequences of her thoughtlessness. While Hebba might call Sara 'a little guttersnipe' behind her back, she was not prepared to cross the mistress of the house.

Because it was almost solstice, the Grand Arcade was crowded to overflowing. At first, Zanna had enjoyed the bustle. The long, colonnaded aisles were brightly lit by endless lines of

176

glowing lamps, and the air was fragrant with the mingling aromas of spices, cheeses, smoked meats and seasonal fruits. The stallholders were shouting to draw attention to the best of their wares, and people called out cheerful greetings to friends that they met in the crowd.

As time wore on, however, and the stocks of delicacies were depleted, folk became tired, cross and despondent. The crowd seemed to be increasing all the time, and the building, for all its vast size, became unbearably stuffy and hot. Zanna, over-burdened with purchases, felt sweaty and bedraggled. Her ribs were bruised where she had been elbowed by the thrusting crowds. Her feet had been trodden on repeatedly, and were sore from trudging the hard stone floors of the arcade. Her head ached, she was desperately thirsty, and the tottering pile of packages in her aching arms was hampering her progress through the crush of people. Really, she decided, this is impossible! We've done enough, and if Sara wants anything more she can bloody well come and get it herself. She turned to say as much to Dulsina – and discovered, to her horror, that the housekeeper was nowhere in sight. I must have lost her in the crowd, she thought. Dear Gods, how will I ever find her again in this?

Zanna tried to stop, and was cursed by impatient folk who jostled her roughly aside. Because of her short stature, she couldn't see a thing, and she was carried along helplessly; forced to move with the flow in order to stay on her feet. Zanna bit her lip, determined not to panic. I have to get out of here, she thought – but how?

'Ho, Zanna? Are you all alone?' A steadying hand grasped Zanna's shoulder. A slight but respectful space opened around her in the crowd, and to her relief she found that she could breathe again. She looked up, with gratitude, into the kindly face of the Lady Aurian, who was accompanied by Lieutenant Maya from the garrison. 'Gods, what a dreadful crush,' the Mage said cheerfully. 'I'm not surprised you were struggling! Maya and I slipped down here to buy a gift for Forral, and we've been just about trampled to death!' Her arching brows twitched together in a slight frown. 'Could Vannor not spare a servant to send with you?'

Zanna, who had met both the Lady Aurian and Maya on several occasions when she had wheedled her father into taking her with him to the garrison, admired both women tremendously – but the Mage, in particular, was everything that Zanna wished to be. Feeling rather overawed at finding herself in such exalted company, she explained about losing Dulsina, and found herself telling her sympathetic rescuers the whole story of her disastrous day. At the mention of Sara's name, she saw the two women exchange a grimace. Aurian opened her mouth as if to comment, but, on catching Maya's eye, closed it grimly again, with a slight shake of her head.

'Right,' Maya said briskly. 'Let's get you and your parcels back to your carriage. If Dulsina has any sense, that's where she'll be. I expect she's in a rare panic by now!'

The Mage and Maya divided Zanna's purchases between them, and escorted her out of the arcade. The crowd seemed to melt away before the two grim-faced women in their fighting clothes, and Zanna was tremendously impressed. As Maya had predicted, they met the housekeeper in the great arched entranceway. Dulsina, frantic with worry, had been just about to go back inside to search for her missing charge. Zanna was heartily embarrassed by her fussing, and everlastingly grateful to Aurian for cutting her short. 'Oh, you had nothing to worry about,' she said airily. 'Zanna's a sensible girl. She was already making her way out when we ran into her, but you know what a time it takes to get through those crowds!'

The Mage herself helped Zanna into the carriage, and settled her packages around her. Vannor's daughter looked back wistfully as the carriage drove off, calling out her thanks again to the two women, who were already turning away to walk along the street. The sound of their conversation floated back to her on the still evening air.

'Gods, Maya,' she heard the Mage say. 'That wife of Vannor's is such a bitch.'

'You're telling me. If it were up to me, I'd drop her in the river – in a sack! Do you fancy a beer now?'

Zanna smiled to herself. Somehow, it helped a lot to know that she was not alone in her opinion of her stepmother.

The errand had taken longer than Zanna had expected, and

dusk was falling as they clattered across the Academy bridge and turned to climb the wooded hill that led to home. It looked as though it might snow again. The hazy sky above Nexis was suffused with an unearthly copper glow, etched by lines of smoke that rose straight as penstrokes in the still air. Zanna snuggled into the thick fur of the carriage rug, fidgeting with the discomfort of frozen fingers and aching feet. She sighed wistfully at the thought of the cookfires glowing in the city's different homes; the scents of citrus and spices and roasting meats, and the bright, excited faces of children. She knew that she would be going home to a very different scene. Hebba never worked well when she was flustered, and after today's upheavals this year's solstice celebrations at Vannor's house were likely to be a disaster.

The lamplighters were at work, and as the carriage laboured up the steep, snowy hill a string of golden globes burst into life one by one, to mark the road ahead. The coachman swore as the horses slipped on the slushy road, and Dulsina, who had been tight-lipped all day, poked him crossly, her brows drawn down in a disapproving frown.

The snow had been raked from the curving sweep that led to the mansion, and the coachman, relieved at getting up the slippery hill without injuring Vannor's precious black horses, finished the journey in style, rattling up to the door in a spatter of gravel. Zanna had meant to accompany him to the back door, to help unload the precious packages, but Dulsina was having none of it. 'No you don't, my girl,' she said. 'Get inside and I'll fetch you a nice hot drink. Put your feet up for a while. It's bad enough you had to traipse round the market like a serving-wench. Your poor mother, bless her, would turn in her grave.'

Zanna let her rattle on as they went inside, knowing that the housekeeper's indignation was really for them both. Dulsina bore her years well; her skin was clear and unlined, and her dark hair without a trace of grey. She had been very close to Zanna's mother, and it was that friendship, so kitchen gossip said, that had kept her feelings hidden from Vannor after his wife's death. The other servants, however, had looked upon her eventual marriage to the merchant as a certainty – until Sara had come along.

As Dulsina bustled off down the kitchen stairs, Zanna paused in the spacious hall to unwrap the cloaks and shawls in which the zealous housekeeper had swathed her. She sighed. Dulsina meant well, but she was tired of being coddled like a child. Inevitably, her thoughts turned to the Lady Aurian. Mage and warrior, she could ride and fight like a man, and you wouldn't find anyone wrapping her in half a shipment of wool. I wish I could be like her, Zanna thought. She was unwrapping her scarf from around her ears when she heard a resounding screech of rage. Gods! Not another disaster. Zanna ran. She was halfway upstairs when she heard the howls of her little brother.

The noise came from Sara's room, and in other circumstances Zanna might have laughed. Antor, now a mobile and mischievous three-year-old, had escaped his nursemaid, and found his way to Sara's open door. Unfortunately, she had been out at the time, but the collection of jars on the mirrored night-table had proved an irresistible temptation to the child.

The reek of spilled perfume hit Zanna as she entered. She took in the whole scene at a glance – the powder spilled across the carpet; the upended jars and bottles, their lotions pooling on the table; a frieze of greasy, coloured handprints that tracked across the wall, the furnishings and even the counterpane. And Sara, her face contorted and flushed with rage, was hitting Antor over and over again.

Zanna did not stop to think. Her resentment of Sara and her fierce protectiveness towards Antor fused in a flash of rage. 'Leave him alone, you bitch!' She flew across the room and dragged the child away. She had never meant things to get out of hand – this was her stepmother, after all – but when Sara slapped her Zanna lost all sense of restraint. She got in one good hard blow before Sara started hitting back, and then they were on the floor; biting, scratching, pulling each other's hair and screaming like wildcats, with Antor, in the background, adding his shrill wails to the commotion.

Neither of them heard Vannor enter. The first they knew of his presence was when he waded into the fray and flung his daughter and wife apart. One look at his face, and the fire of Zanna's rage turned to ashen horror. Antor's howls were the only sound that broke the silence, until a chuckle came from the direction of the door. 'On my oath, Vannor, you've a pair of hellions here! I had no idea your home life was so interesting!'

To Zanna's horror, a stranger stood in the doorway, witness to the disgraceful brawl. Despite her acute embarrassment, she felt her heart turn over at the sight of the handsome young man. Vannor scowled, looking angrier than ever, then turned to the visitor and forced a smile. 'Why don't you go downstairs, Yanis, while I sort this out,' he said. 'You know where the drink's kept.'

The interruption had given Sara time to gather her wits. As soon as the stranger had gone, she seized her husband's arm. 'Vannor, she attacked me! And look what that wretched brat has done! I insist that you punish them, or . . .'

'Or what? You'll go back to the poverty I took you from?' Vannor's face was bleak as stone. Sara turned white at his words, and shut her mouth abruptly. Zanna sighed with relief. Her dad was so entranced by his new wife that she had feared he would take Sara's part, but her relief was short-lived. When Vannor turned to look at her, Zanna realized with a sinking heart that Sara was not the only one in trouble. 'Get to your room,' Vannor growled. 'I'll deal with you later!'

Zanna had been prepared for her father's anger, but his disappointment was more than she could bear. 'I thought I could depend on you to be sensible,' Vannor stormed at her. 'I know you miss your mother – don't you think I miss her too? I know you don't want Sara in her place. But I won't have my home turned into a battlefield, Zanna! Sara is your stepmother, and you'll treat her with respect!'

Zanna, choking with tears, was unable to speak. Vannor, who had been about to leave, turned quickly and came back to her, putting his arms around her as she sobbed. 'Look, lass, don't cry. I'm not such a fool as to put all the blame on you for what happened. I've spoken to Sara.' He looked so grim that Zanna wondered what had been said. 'She'll not mistreat Antor again, I promise. But she isn't used to children, and . . .'

'Curse it, dad, why must you make excuses for her? Can't you see she's – ' The mad, untimely words spilled out of Zanna before she could stop them, and were silenced abruptly by Vannor's slap.

'You watch your mouth, girl, or by the gods I'll – ' His face twisted with rage and anguish, Vannor stamped out, slamming the door behind him.

He went downstairs, completely at his wits' end; ashamed of what he had just done; sickened by his earlier scene with Sara. He adored both his wife and his daughter, but why couldn't they try to get along? He rubbed his aching head. Gods, what a night! When he'd left that morning, everything had been running smoothly as usual. He had come back a few short hours later to find the house in an uproar.

In the brief time since his return, Vannor had calmed his bawling son and turned him over to a bristling Dulsina (who, judging by the look on her face, meant to have words with him before the night was out). He had dismissed the nursemaid, who'd been outside, flirting with the gardener, while Antor was getting into mischief. Having sent the girl packing, in tears, he had found himself confronted by a furious cook, with baggage, who announced that if her solstice feast was no longer good enough for him, he had better make his own in future. Hebba had marched out, leaving him gaping. As if these disasters were not enough, he had followed them up with a blistering row with Sara, who was no longer speaking to him, and had hurt his favourite daughter. What a bloody awful solstice this is going to be! Vannor thought bitterly.

It was only then, as he was heading for the welcome sanctuary of his library, that he remembered the visitor. Vannor groaned. If that idiot was desperate enough to come to the house, it had to mean trouble.

Yanis, who was sitting by the roaring log fire, leapt to his feet when Vannor entered the library, his handsome face taut and anxious. 'Vannor, I'm sorry to come here like this. I know what you said about secrecy, but . . .' He looked away, biting his lip. 'Oh, gods,' he muttered. 'It wasn't my fault, I swear! How was I to know they would . . .'

'Whoa, whoa!' Vannor held up a hand to stop the young man in mid-protest. 'If this is more bad news, Yanis, for the gods' sake let me get myself a drink first!'

Vannor had not been Zanna's only visitor that night. Her

stepmother had come close on his heels. Sara's visit had been brief, and she had said very little, but her words had turned Zanna cold with fear. 'Well, brat – since you are so protective of children, perhaps you ought to have some of your own,' she had said with vicious sweetness. 'Now that you've turned fifteen, I must take my duties as a stepmother more seriously, and start casting around for a suitable husband for you!' And with a whirl of skirts, she had gone.

Long after Zanna had wept herself out, she lay awake in the darkness, dreading the future. She knew that Sara would never rest now until her troublesome stepdaughter was out of the way for good. Vannor's daughter was a practical girl, and she faced facts squarely. Marriage was the obvious solution to Sara's problems, and Zanna felt a chill go through her. Oh, gods, she thought. She'll dress me up like a stupid doll, make Vannor give me an enormous dowry, and hand me over to the first witless, overbred merchant's son who wants the money! The thought filled her with such panic that she wanted to run – but where could she go? Suddenly, for no apparent reason, the face of her father's mysterious visitor came into her mind: his shaggy dark hair falling across those dark grey eyes, that had crinkled at the corners when he smiled at the scene in Sara's bedroom.

The door of her room opened quietly, and Zanna started, blushing as though her thoughts must be transparent. To her surprise, her visitor was Dulsina. 'Shhh,' the housekeeper whispered. 'Light the candle and get dressed. You're going away for a while.'

'What?' Zanna froze. Horror congealed like a choking lump in her throat. 'Dad?' she could hardly form the whispered words. 'Is he sending me *away*?'

'No, you goose – as if he ever would! Listen, Zanna. Your stepmother is as furious as a wasp in a bottle tonight. Now that you've made trouble between her and Vannor, she'll –'

'I know what she plans to do,' Zanna said wretchedly, 'and it's worse than you could possibly imagine. She wants to marry me off, Dulsina!'

'I heard,' Dulsina said grimly. 'It's a housekeeper's privilege to eavesdrop! Not that Vannor is such a heartless dolt as to force you to wed against your will . . . But you know how desperate he is for his daughters to make good matches – there would be pressure on you to consent. Anyway, you're young yet to be thinking of husbands, no matter what the custom is among these witless merchants! I thought to send you to my sister Remana, until the fuss dies down. Antor can go too – doing without the pair of you for a while might bring that old fool Vannor to his senses.'

Zanna wondered if she was dreaming. Though it might be wise to get away until Sara had calmed down, it was not like level-headed Dulsina to come up with such a wild idea. And never before had she heard the housekeeper criticize dad. In a daze, she dressed herself warmly and began to pack some clothes under Dulsina's direction, while the housekeeper explained: 'You've a good head on your shoulders, Zanna – I know you can be trusted with the secret. My sister Remana is – was, I should say – wed to Leynard, leader of the Night-runners.'

Zanna gaped at her, a nightgown, half folded, forgotten in her hands. The Nightrunners? The elusive smugglers who traded with the prohibited Southern Kingdoms for silks, gems and spices and had driven generations of garrison commanders to despair? Prim Dulsina had a sister wed to a *smuggler*?

'You may as well know,' Dulsina was saying. 'Your dad made his fortune through trading in partnership with the Night-runners. His visitor tonight is my nephew Yanis – he became leader last year when Leynard was lost at sea. When he goes back, he'll be taking you with him.' She paused, her eyes twinkling. 'Mark you, he's afraid of Vannor, so the less he knows of the truth, the better. I'll give you a note for my sister – Remana will take care of you.'

'But what about dad?' Zanna protested. 'He'll be so angry! And what if Sara arranges a husband for me in any case? Anyway, if I know dad, he'll come and fetch me straight back again. Besides, I'll miss him so. How can I leave him – and at solstice, too?'

'Child, you worry too much.' Dulsina hugged her. 'Vannor won't blame you – it's me he'll be angry with. And Sara will be much too busy to make mischief.' She grinned. 'With you away,

Vannor will see who was really running the household – and I won't be taking up where you left off! Let Sara occupy herself with all those tiresome details that you and I have been taking off her shoulders. If she wants to play the great lady, it's time she learned that there's far more to it than sitting around counting her jewels!'

'But what if dad comes after me?' Zanna persisted. 'Impossible,' Dulsina said briskly. 'The smugglers' hideout is a deadly secret – so much so that Leynard wouldn't even tell his partner. Vannor won't know where you are, and I won't tell him – not unless there is a real emergency. Just trust me, my dear, and all will be well.'

Zanna hesitated. Then she thought of what her future would be like, married to a dull merchant's son who did not love her. She had no illusions about her looks – she was short and sturdy, like her dad, with a plain, no-nonsense face: a far cry from the willowy, delicate creatures which the well-heeled merchant classes liked to decorate their opulent homes. She was clever and quick-minded, and it was her greatest frustration that her dad would never let her work with him in trade. 'Whoever heard of a lady merchant,' he would chide her gently. 'Why, it's just not done.'

There are lady Magefolk, though, Zanna thought resentfully – and lady warriors. Why not a lady merchant, I'd like to know? Inevitably, her mind went back to that afternoon, and her meeting with Aurian and Maya. Well, you wanted to be like them, she told herself – maybe this is your chance! Lifting her chin, she turned to Dulsina. 'You're right,' she said. 'I'm ready to go!'

Yanis left the mansion in a hurry, by the back door, his ears still ringing with Vannor's epithets. Dear gods, but when his father's old partner flew into a rage, it was enough to scare the wits out of a man! 'It wasn't my fault,' he muttered helplessly. After the unpleasant evening he had just spent with Vannor, the excuse was starting to sound rather thin, even to himself.

'Where am I going wrong?' he sighed as he made his way back to the river, slinking through the merchant's terraced garden with his sea-boots crunching softly on the snowy ground. It had all seemed simple when he had accompanied his father to the south. Leynard had taught him how to find his way to the remote, secluded bay that was the clandestine rendezvous with the southerners. Yanis knew the series of lamp-flashes that were the secret signal to grant him safe passage in southern waters. Unfortunately, the one vital piece of information that his father had not passed on was how not to get swindled by those slimy southern bast –

'Hist! Yanis!'

The smuggler whirled abruptly, his hand on his sword. He was astonished to see his Aunt Dulsina beckoning to him from the bushes at the bottom of the garden, near the small, ornate boathouse where Vannor kept his pleasure-craft. In the dim snowlight, it looked as though she was carrying a large bundle, so thickly swathed in shawls that it looked almost circular. Grabbing his arm with her free hand, she pulled him into the shelter of the shrubbery.

'Listen,' she told him without preamble. 'Vannor wants you to take his children to stay with Remana for a while.'

Yanis blinked. 'He does? He never mentioned it. And why are you all hiding in the bushes, Aunt Dulsina?'

His aunt sighed. 'Because you shouldn't be here, remember? Vannor thought that if you left the house with the youngsters, it would attract too much attention, so I brought them down here to meet you. Off you go now – take good care of the children, and remember to give my love to your mother. And, Yanis, be careful. Don't get caught.'

Before Yanis could say a word, she had dumped Vannor's son into his unready arms and bustled away, with a quick parting hug for the cloaked and muffled figure that must be the merchant's daughter. Yanis, speechless, thrust his squirming burden at the girl, and bent to pull on the rope that tethered his small boat beneath the concealing sweep of willows at the water's edge. Somehow, he managed to get them, with their several bundles, off the frost-slick jetty and into the little craft. The girl was sniffling into a lacy slip of a handkerchief, and the smuggler's heart sank. 'Are you all right?' he asked nervously.

'Yes.' The voice was little more than a whisper. Then, to his relief, she sat up straight, settled the infant on her lap, and put the handkerchief away. 'Yes,' she repeated firmly. 'I'm fine. I don't like leaving dad, but I always wanted adventure. I'm sick of sitting at home sewing, and all that tedious female stuff.'

Yanis grinned. She was going to be all right, after all. 'You sound like my mam,' he told her. 'She wanted adventure, too, and ended up marrying a smuggler.'

A chuckle emerged from the shadows of the girl's hood. 'At least I'm going to the right place, then!'

She was a droll little thing, and no mistake. Snorting with laughter, Yanis picked up his oars and set off to row swiftly downriver through the frost-glittering night, to his fast little ship that was moored in a quiet cove around the headland from the port of Norberth.

Yanis, thankful that it was solstice, and the hours of darkness were so long, ordered the ghost-grey sails to be unfurled. Steering his sleek little ship out of the twisting inlet that had shielded it from prying eyes, he headed, with a tremendous sense of relief, out to sea. His passengers were safely asleep below, tired out from their journey. Two children would only be in the way as he dodged along the treacherous coastline in the darkness, avoiding the safer sea lanes that were crowded with fishing fleets from the villages and the clumsy, wallowing vessels of the legitimate merchant traders.

Besides, it was best to keep the youngsters out of sight of the crew, who were in a state of near-rebellion after the disastrous voyage to the south. They had made it clear to Yanis that they were far from happy with the responsibility of these unexpected passengers. Vannor might have made the Nightrunners rich through his trading connections, but they were still in awe of his reputation as a dangerous man to cross.

'What if there's a storm?' Gevan, the mate, had asked. 'What happens if the young'uns fall overboard and drown? What will Vannor say if we're caught with his brats on board by one of Forral's patrols? That big bastard from the garrison is getting too clever by half.'

'What if – what if!' Yanis had mocked. 'Why, Vannor himself sent his youngsters with us.'

'And what about that girl?' Gevan had continued, undeterred. 'I always said a ship's no place for a woman.'

'You'd better not let my mam hear you saying that,' Yanis grinned. 'She'll stretch your guts for rigging.'

'I don't count your mam as a woman. She's a sailor born and bred, that one, which that little lass below is not.' The mate stumped off, still muttering darkly.

In truth, Yanis had his own misgivings, but they differed from those of his crew, who had only seen Zanna's small figure muffled up in cloaks. They thought she was still a child – but he had seen her up at the house, brawling with Vannor's wife, and she was older than she looked.

During the long and tiresome trip downriver, Yanis had been putting two and two together, and he was far from happy with the result. Why had Vannor suddenly decided to send his children to the smugglers? Why had he not mentioned it earlier? Why had Aunt Dulsina appeared with them so unexpectedly, and hurried them off so quickly? There could only be one answer. 'That cunning bastard,' Yanis muttered. 'He's sending his daughter to spy on me.'

It was all too clear. Vannor, angry because Yanis had been cheated by the Southerners, had sent his wretched girl to mingle with the smugglers and probe their secrets. And then – Yanis swore. The leadership! Vannor meant to depose him, and take over the smuggling operation himself.

'Oh – we're sailing!'

The voice, so close at hand, made Yanis jump. That wretched girl had crept up so quietly while he stood at the wheel that he was taken completely by surprise. Startled and unthinking, he gave voice to his suspicions. 'Spying already, eh? Well, I know what you're up to, girl, and it won't work, see?'

Yanis had been so kind to Antor and herself on their way downriver that Zanna was shocked by his sudden hostility. Biting her lip, she fought back tears. The rest of the crew had looked so unfriendly when she ventured up on deck that she had been counting on the support of their leader. What had she done to earn his anger? Remembering the grave, dignified manner with which Dulsina deflated Vannor's fierce rages, Zanna drew herself up to her full, albeit scant, height. 'If you 'know what I'm up to,' she said coldly, 'I hope you'll tell me, for I'm sure I have no idea.'

'You have no idea, indeed,' Yanis mocked. 'You and Vannor didn't think I had the wits to work it out, did you? Poor daft Yanis – he'll never guess he's being spied on. He's so thickheaded that he gets cheated by southerners!'

Most of this outburst was a mystery to Zanna, but she heard the bitterness in his voice, and caught the name of Vannor. 'Dad? But he doesn't even know I'm here.'

Horrified, she caught herself up with a hand to her mouth, but it was too late. Yanis looked at her with narrowed eyes. 'What?' he yelped. 'He doesn't know you're here?'

Gods, but he looked so fierce! Zanna backed away from him, the words tumbling out of her as she tried to explain. 'Well, he must know now, of course, because Dulsina will have told him, but he didn't know when we came away.' Her words trailed off. Yanis looked at her, stony-faced, not helping at all.

'I had to get away from Sara,' she protested. 'She meant to marry me off to some moon-faced merchant's son.'

'Vannor didn't send you?' Yanis was gaping at her. Zanna sighed. No wonder he was cheated by the southerners, she thought.

'No,' she repeated. 'Dulsina said you wouldn't take us if you knew, so – ' She shrugged. 'I'm afraid she didn't exactly tell you the truth.'

'Gods' teeth! I have to get you back, before he finds out.' Yanis spun the wheel, and the ship lurched and shuddered, heeling over as the wind spilled from its sails. Curses and shouts of protest could be heard all over the deck as the crew were tumbled about.

'No,' Zanna cried. 'You can't!' Without thinking, she tried to wrench the wheel from his grasp, to return the ship to its original course. For a grim moment they grappled while the vessel wallowed and tipped.

'You idiot!' Yanis bellowed. 'You'll have us over!' Giving in to her, he let the ship swing round, heaving a sigh of relief as the tilting vessel straightened, the wind swelling its shadowy grey sails once more. 'Get below!' he snapped at Zanna. 'I ought to throw you overboard!'

189

'Not until you've heard what I have to say.' Zanna stood her ground. 'You can't take us back.' Didn't this fool realize that she was trying to keep him out of trouble? Yanis was not to blame for the disappearance of Vannor's children – but her dad wouldn't see things in that light. Desperately she tried to think of a way to change the young smuggler's mind. 'Do you want your crew to see how you were taken in? You'll be a laughing-stock!'

'What in the name of all the gods are you playing at, Yanis? Are you trying to send us to the bottom?' Gevan thrust forward, his weatherbeaten face pale with anger.

'It was my fault,' Zanna said quickly, trying to look meek. 'I – I thought I could steer it, but . . .'

'You let this child take the wheel?' Gevan turned on Yanis. 'Have you lost your mind?' The crew, limping and rubbing their bruises, were gathering round, awaiting the outcome of the confrontation with avid curiosity.

'You can't blame Yanis. I told him I knew how to do it,' Zanna insisted.

'What?' Yanis looked baffled. 'But . . .'

Zanna kicked him sharply in the ankle. 'I'm truly sorry, sir – I only wanted to try.' She turned her most winning smile on the mate, and jumped as Yanis whispered in her ear: 'Take the wheel a minute – just keep her exactly as she is.' Before she knew it, Zanna, rigid with anxiety, was hanging on to the wheel with trembling hands.

'Thara's titties!' Gevan spat disgustedly. 'I don't know which of you is the bigger fool . . .' His words ended in a choking gurgle as Yanis lifted him off the deck with a twisted handful of shirt and pinned him, struggling, across the ship's rail with a knee in his groin and his head hanging down towards the waves that surged and foamed along the vessel's side.

'Now,' said Yanis, 'you'll apologize to the lady for your foul language, and then you'll apologize to me!' He loosened his grip slightly on the pop-eyed mate's collar, still holding him in his perilous position while Gevan gasped out his apologies. Yanis lowered the terrified man to the deck and stepped back to look at his dumbstruck crew. 'I know you don't think much of me, compared with my dad. Oh, yes – I've heard you muttering and whispering in corners. But there can only be one captain of this ship, and one leader of the smugglers, see? If anyone else wants to take over, you can speak up now or not at all. But you'll have to fight me for it first – and you'll take the leadership over my dead body!' For a long, grim moment he held their eyes, until one by one the crew turned and slunk away.

Zanna felt like cheering. She gazed at Yanis with shining eyes, but he was looking past her at . . . 'Look out!' Pushing her roughly to one side, he seized the wheel and wrenched it hard over. The ship swung and heeled, its timbers creaking in protest, and Zanna, as she tumbled into the scuppers, caught a glimpse of a dark, jagged shape against the starry sky, and the thundering crash of waves on rock.

As the vessel straightened, Yanis turned to her with a grin, and extended a hand to help her to her feet. 'Got to keep your eyes skinned, sailing this close to the coast at night,' he said cheerfully. Zanna, her heart still hammering, looked at him open-mouthed. 'Apart from that, though,' he added condescendingly, 'you did very well for the first time. We'll make a sailor of you yet.'

'I wouldn't count on it,' Zanna said weakly. 'Gods, Yanis – I never saw that rock. It was so dark. How did you know?'

Yanis winked at her, and his teeth flashed white as he laughed. 'See – not as daft as you thought, am I? Even though I did get cheated by the southerners!'

'I never said you were daft,' Zanna protested.

'No, but your dad did, and a lot more besides.' Though he spoke lightly, she could hear an undercurrent of bitterness in his voice. 'What happened?' she asked him softly.

Yanis sighed. 'It's been going on for an awful long time, this trade with the southerners – in the family, you might say. When Vannor came in with dad, and found us new markets, we really started to prosper. We trade with the Corsairs, who are supposed to defend their coast, but who are really the worst bunch of knaves and scoundrels you'll ever see. They'll do anything to line their pockets.'

'What do you trade?' Zanna was fascinated.

Yanis shrugged. 'Various things. Theirs is a hot, desert country and not much grows there. We trade wood and wool

191

and grain, mostly – common enough stuff here, but worth a fortune to the southerners. In exchange, we get spices, silks and gems – or we're supposed to,' he added glumly. 'This time, when we got back and opened the caskets, they had the good stuff on top, and the rest was worthless sand!'

'But didn't you think to check?' Zanna asked in amazement.

'Check?' Yanis glared at her fiercely. 'It's not a bloody game, you know. It's deadly serious, and deadly dangerous. We have no time to check! We slip in, exchange the goods as fast as possible; then we run for home as fast as we can!'

'Hmm . . .' Zanna frowned thoughtfully. 'Then the whole operation depends on good faith.' A surge of excitement ran through her. This was a real challenge. 'Leave it to me,' she told Yanis. 'I'll think of a way to beat those crooked southerners, I promise!'

The young smuggler's mouth twitched for an instant, but he failed to hide his smile. 'Of course you will,' he said kindly, as though addressing a very small child. Drat him, Zanna seethed. He doesn't believe I can do it.

Still, Yanis had only just decided not to take her back to Vannor – she wouldn't risk a quarrel now. She turned away from him. 'I ought to get back to Antor,' she said mildly. It was an excuse to go below and do some hard thinking. I'll show him, she thought. Just wait. He may not know it, but he needs my brain. I can make a place for myself among these smugglers, I know I can. I'll make them respect me if it's the last thing I do.

13

A Solstice Gift

Aurian leaned back in her chair and took another pull at her flagon of ale. 'I'm still astonished that Miathan has been so understanding about you and me being lovers, especially after – ' She stopped abruptly, biting her lip. She had still not dared to tell Forral about Miathan's attack on her. 'If he was only pretending to approve, I think the façade would have slipped by now, but after almost four months . . .' She shrugged. 'Admittedly I haven't seen much of him lately – he's busy with some pet project of his own – but when I do, he's as kindly as ever. And the way he turns a blind eye to you sleeping at the Academy with me, and defends us from the other Magefolk . . .' She broke off with a sigh.

'This unpleasantness with Meiriel is still bothering you, isn't it?' Forral prompted.

'I can't help it, Forral. I don't mind about the others – Eliseth and Bragar were always rotten to the core, not to mention Davorshan, but Meiriel . . . I would never have believed she could be so prejudiced! She even refused to teach me any more until Miathan intervened. It's awful to lose a friend like this, but not even Finbarr can talk her round.'

'Never mind, love.' Forral covered her hand with his own. 'If she wants to be like that, there's nothing we can do about it. If she had been any sort of friend in the first place, she would be glad for you.'

'That's what Anvar said.' Aurian managed a smile. 'He's come a long way from that terrified creature we rescued last solstice. You must admit, I was right about him.'

'You were indeed, and I'm glad. He turned out to be a good lad, Aurian, despite what Miathan said about him.'

'I wonder about that.' Aurian frowned. 'He does a marvellous job of looking after me, but he rarely smiles, and he's still

193

terrified of the Archmage, but he won't tell me why. What's more, he won't talk about his past, his family – anything. I'd like to help him – he always looks so unhappy – but how can I if he won't trust me?' She glowered into her beer. 'Gods, how I hate mysteries.'

It was Solstice Eve, and the two of them had started the seasonal celebrations early with a visit to the Invisible Unicorn. Conveniently close to the garrison, the tavern was the favourite haunt of the off-duty troopers. The long, low taproom was shabby but homely with its ceiling of sturdy, lamp-hung beams and huge arched fireplace of red brick that always housed a welcoming blaze. The once white walls were mellowed by a patina of smoke, and the floor was covered with a thick layer of sawdust to soak up spilled ale and the blood from the occasional rowdy brawls that were (usually) overlooked by the tolerant landlord. The company was good, and the beer was excellent. It was one of Aurian's favourite places, but tonight she had too much on her mind to be able to relax and enjoy herself.

Forral reached over and topped up their mugs from the big pewter jug on the table. 'You can't really blame the lad, you know. It must be terrible to be a bondservant, even with the kindest of mistresses. He's lost his family and future – and supposing he had a girl, before? What happened to her? Gods, this bonding is barbaric!'

It was a sore point with Forral; one over which he had clashed repeatedly but unsuccessfully with the other council members, especially the Archmage, during the past year. 'But if Anvar won't confide in you, what can you do?' he added. 'After rescuing him the way you did, I find it odd that he won't trust you, at least.' The swordsman frowned. 'You're right, though – it's strange how Miathan hates him. The other servants are beneath his notice.' Seeing Aurian's gloomy face, he sought to lighten her mood. 'Don't worry about it now, love. It's Solstice Eve, and we should be enjoying ourselves. I'll tell you what – why don't I take Anvar out with me tonight while you're at the Mages' feast? I wish you didn't have to go to the damned thing, but we'll have our own celebration later. And it might cheer that poor lad of yours up to get out with me and the troops.'

Aurian brightened. 'That's a kind thought, Forral. I'll tell Elewin when I go back to the Academy. There are always enough servants in attendance at the feast, so Anvar won't be missed. I wish I could come with you, but I daren't risk upsetting Miathan – not when we're on such shaky ground with the Magefolk. Anyway, Finbarr and I have a plan to cheer up D'arvan tonight – he could use the company. He's had a rough time of it this year, what with his brother joining Eliseth's clique, and still no sign of his powers surfacing, *and* Miathan is looking on him with greater disapproval every day. I suspect that Eliseth is trying to persuade the Archmage to get rid of him so that she can have Davorshan to herself. It's a blessing that D'arvan has made some friends at the garrison – Maya, especially – but at the Academy he's becoming increasingly isolated. I do feel sorry for him.'

'More good deeds, eh?' Forral chuckled, but she saw the gleam of pride in his eyes, and knew that he approved.

'Well, it is the season of goodwill and all that.' Aurian made a face. 'I think I had better start fortifying myself. Is there any of that beer left?'

Anvar sat alone on his bunk in the servants' dormitory, playing a mournful air on the little wooden flute that his grandfather had carved for him so long ago. It was the only one of his instruments that he'd been able to bring with him to the Academy, and oh, how he missed them! Elewin, at the Lady Aurian's request, had excused him from serving at the feast, and while he appreciated her kindness in giving him the holiday, what was the point? He had nowhere to go. As usual, at this time of year, his thoughts were with the loved ones he had lost – Grandpa and his mother – and Sara, who was equally lost to him now. Trying unsuccessfully to put them out of his mind, Anvar played on, merging his loneliness with the achingly sad notes of Grandpa's flute.

Suddenly the door was flung open, and Commander Forral stood there. 'There you are!' he said. 'I've been looking all over for you. What are you doing here all alone, lad? Aurian has to attend the feast tonight, so we thought you might fancy keeping me company while I have a few beers with the lads and lasses

195

from the garrison.' He tugged the astonished Anvar to his feet, barely giving him time to snatch his cloak from its peg on the wall. Its threadbare appearance stopped Forral in his tracks. 'What's this?' he said, frowning. 'You can't go out in that dishrag, lad. It's snowing! Here – ' He unclasped his own thick, weatherproof soldier's cloak and draped it round Anvar's shoulders, kicking the offending old garment under the bunk. 'That's better. It suits you, too, us being about the same height and all. I know – you keep it. A solstice gift, for looking after Aurian so well. I've a spare in her room, so we'll just go and get it, and then we can be off.'

Anvar was overwhelmed. This was his second solstice at the Academy, and in all that time no one had ever given him a gift. Swallowing hard, he tried to stammer his thanks, and Forral clapped him on the shoulder in a comradely fashion. 'Not at all, lad. You deserve it. Now let's get off to the tavern. There's good ale just begging to be appreciated, and it's our duty to do our share!'

Anvar had a wonderful time at the Invisible Unicorn. The troops from the garrison were full of solstice cheer, and the talk and laughter and ale, bought by the generous Forral as a solstice treat for his troops, flowed in equal quantities. Then someone discovered that Anvar could sing, and a battered old guitar was borrowed from its usual strictly decorative place on the wall, despite feeble protests from the long-suffering landlord. The pleasure of playing a real instrument soon overcame Anvar's diffidence about performing, and the troops joined in with great enthusiasm. Soon the walls were ringing to the sound of rowdy, bawdy barrack-room ballads whose general subject matter and volume soon sent the tavern's more sober-sided customers scurrying for home. (The landlord, noticing the rate at which his ale kegs were emptying, had long since ceased to object.)

All too soon, the evening had flown and Anvar's new friends were saying farewell. Reluctantly he hung the borrowed guitar back on the wall. It took several attempts, because he couldn't see which of the two nails was the real one and couldn't hit it anyway. Then he and Forral made their unsteady way back to the Academy through the crisp new snow, leaning against each other at an acute angle with their arms draped round one another's shoulders. They each carried a large bottle of wine in their free hands and sang as they went on their way, trading rude folk ballads for scurrilous soldiers' songs, and threatening to awaken the entire city with their noise. Anvar didn't care. Tonight, for once, he was truly enjoying himself.

Meiriel was not enjoying the Mages' feast. She swirled the meagre ration of wine around in the bottom of her cup and took a chaste sip, glowering across at the merry group who occupied the opposite table.

'Finbarr seems happy tonight.' Eliseth slid into the empty chair beside the healer. Meiriel frowned. She could have done without the Weather-Mage and her sly insinuations. She shrugged, forcing the appearance of nonchalance. 'It's a rare occasion where Finbarr can be dragged out of his archives to a celebration. He isn't used to all this wine.' Despite her efforts to hide it, her anger broke through. 'It's all very well for Aurian – she's accustomed to carousing all hours with those low-born Mortal scum from the garrison . . .'

'Don't we all know it!' Eliseth said sympathetically. 'Believe me, Meiriel, we can see the shape of things to come. Why, that wretched swordsman of hers already spends half his time here, profaning our halls with his presence. Before long, she'll be inviting the rest of her Mortal friends, and our peace and seclusion will be gone, for ever. Why does Miathan not put a stop to it?'

'You know why,' Meiriel said sourly. 'Aurian has the Archmage wrapped around her little finger.'

'And not only the Archmage, it seems.' Eliseth indicated the next table, where Finbarr and D'arvan were laughing and drinking with Aurian. The gibe hit home. Meiriel, her emotions already inflamed by the wine, felt her face flush hot with rage. 'You mind your own business, you bitch!'

Eliseth's sympathetic expression did not alter. 'I simply wished to warn you,' she said smoothly, 'but if you've noticed . . .' She left the thought hanging; the more powerful for being unstated. 'Has it occurred to you,' she went on, 'that if Aurian should abandon her Mortal lover for ambition's sake – for she

197

could never be the next Archmage with such a scandalous encumbrance – she would need to seek a mate among the Magefolk?'

Meiriel stared at her. 'Just what are you trying to say?'

Eliseth shrugged. 'Only that the possibilities are limited. She hates Davorshan and Bragar, D'arvan is next to useless, and it's rumoured that she has already rejected Miathan, fool that she is.'

'Finbarr would never leave me!' It hardly sounded convincing, even to herself. Meiriel had been harbouring jealous thoughts of late, since Finbarr had taken Aurian's side over the disgraceful business with the Mortal.

'Well, that's all right, then. You have nothing to worry about,' Eliseth said heartily. 'I was about to offer a small suggestion that might be of interest, but . . .'

'What?' It came out more sharply than Meiriel had intended, and she cursed the slip as she saw the Weather-Mage smile.

Eliseth leaned close. 'You know Miathan's abhorrence for half-breeds. If Aurian were to bear the swordsman's brat, then the Archmage would surely exile her for good.' She drew back, looking closely into Meiriel's face.

'But Aurian would never let that happen – and her control of such matters is too good. I taught her myself.'

'But you are the healer, Meiriel. You must have the power to undo what you've taught – that is, if you want to. Just think – one small counterspell would rid us of Aurian and her unsavoury influence for good. Really, it would be a favour to everyone concerned. Aurian's feelings are pulling her more and more towards the Mortals, unthinkable though it is. With the decision made for her, she'd be happier elsewhere, and she and Forral could be together in peace.' Eliseth shrugged. 'And what better opportunity could you have than tonight? Aurian has already drunk a good deal – she is enjoying herself too much to notice your interference. She'll think she has made the slip herself when she finds out. She would never suspect you.'

As she rejoined Davorshan and Bragar, Eliseth was smiling. 'Well?' Bragar asked her. 'How did it go?' The man would never learn subtlety.

'It could scarcely be better.' The Weather-Mage seated

herself, smoothing her skirts with fastidious care, and poured herself a goblet of wine. 'As I thought, it was no trouble at all to make Meiriel's ridiculous jealousy work in our favour. Oh, she protested of course, and said she could never contemplate such a thing, but the seed has been sown. She'll do it, never fear.'

She turned to Davorshan with a dazzling smile, smugly noting the anger on Bragar's face. While the fools were at each other's throats vying for her favours, she could easily control them both. 'Well, Davorshan,' she purred, 'now that Aurian is taken care of, we can turn to the business of removing your unfortunate brother. Why don't you fetch some more wine? Suddenly I feel like celebrating!'

When they got back to the Academy, having been sternly 'shushed' by the guards at the gate, Anvar and Forral came to an unsteady halt outside Aurian's rooms. 'Come in, lad,' Forral said gaily if somewhat indistinctly. 'Come and have a drink with Aurian. You haven't had a drink with Aurian yet, and she'll get mad if you don't. And we don't want to make her mad,' he added in an exaggerated whisper, making such a face that Anvar had to prop himself weakly against the wall, he was laughing so much. Forral opened the door and the two of them practically fell into the room.

Aurian had been doing a fair amount of celebrating herself, judging by her flushed face and the brilliance of her sparkling green eyes. She'd discarded the sombre Mage's robes or practical warrior's garb that she usually wore in favour of her holiday finery – a tawny gold gown of velvet with a deep neckline and long flowing sleeves. Her wealth of fiery hair was caught back in a loose web of gold, and she glowed like a living flame in the soft candlelight. Anvar felt his heart give a couple of unsteady thumps. He had never realized that she was so beautiful.

Forral swooped down on her and, totally unembarrassed by Anvar's presence, covered her face with kisses. She laughed and, flinging her arms around him, kissed him back. 'You look as though you've been having a good time,' she said with a smile.

'Me an' Anvar have been down to the Unicorn with the lads and lasses,' Forral informed her, 'but we missed you.'

·'And I missed you two – er – too,' Aurian laughed. 'I've been pining for my solstice kiss all night.' She made a doleful face, and Forral kissed her again. Then she discovered the bottle of wine that he held. 'You love! Is that for me?'

'We couldn't celebrate without you,' Forral declared grandly. 'I'll open it.' Divesting Anvar of cloak and bottle, he poured wine for the three of them and they stood in front of the fire and lifted their glasses to each other. 'Joyous solstice, love,' Aurian said to Forral. 'Joyous solstice, Anvar.'

And to Anvar, for the first time in two years, it truly was.

They sat together round the table and, to Anvar's embarrassment, Forral told Aurian about his impromptu concert. 'Truly, love, it was amazing,' he said. 'Anvar here played that guitar like – like you handle a sword – all rhythm and fire and flow. I wish you could have heard him.'

'So do I,' Aurian said. 'It sounds wonderful. Wherever did you learn to play like that, Anvar?'

Because Anvar felt so happy, and because the wine had loosened his tongue, he found himself telling them about Ria teaching him music, and how his grandpa had made instruments for him that he had lost when he came to the Academy. Tears filled his eyes as he spoke of the two people he had loved so much, who were both dead now. Gently, Aurian reached across and brushed a tear from his face. 'Don't be sad, Anvar. They're still with you, in the gift of music that you love so much. They'll always be there – in your hands, and in your heart.' She exchanged a look with Forral – a look filled with such depths of love and sorrow that Anvar, suddenly understanding, became uncertain whether his tears were for himself, or for these two who had been so kind to him, and whose love was doomed some day to end in tragedy.

Their glasses were empty, and Aurian got up a little unsteadily to fetch some wine that she said was perfect for a special occasion. 'Miathan gave me this for solstice,' she said, uncorking the dusty bottle. 'It's one of his special vintages. He would have fifty fits if he found out who'd been drinking it!' The two men chuckled, and thanks to the Archmage's gift, the party soon cheered up again.

The three of them sang together, unaccompanied and softly,

because the hour was late. A fleeting thought of having to get up to serve the breakfast crossed Anvar's mind, but he ignored it. How could tomorrow ever come? This night was held for ever in a timeless web of delight. Aurian's contralto voice thrilled him. He'd never known that she could sing. By the time they reached the bottom of the bottle they were back to bawdy ballads and silly children's songs, and all three were laughingly helplessly.

'Oh dear,' Aurian gasped, wiping her streaming eyes. 'I haven't had such a good time in ages!' She tilted the bottle to refill their glasses, but only a few drops trickled out. 'Bat-turds!' She muttered Finbarr's favourite curse. 'That's the last!'

'I should go anyway,' Anvar said, struggling to his feet. 'I have to get up in the morning to bring you lazy lot your breakfast!' He had spoken thoughtlessly, confident for once that his words would not cause offence, but Aurian's face fell. 'Oh Anvar, I'm sorry. I wasn't thinking . . .'

Forral frowned. 'Look, lad,' he said, 'you know it's not Aurian's fault. She can't release you from your bond and my hands are tied. I'd have this bondservant business stopped tomorrow if I could, but I'm outnumbered on the council. Don't think I haven't tried. And why blame poor Aurian? She didn't make you a bondservant – she only tried to help you. Does she treat you like a slave? She's been worrying herself silly over you these last months, did you know that? She'd like nothing better than to free you if she could, and this is no way to treat her in return.'

That was too much. 'I know that!' Anvar cried angrily. 'But how would you feel if you were in my place? You don't know what it's like to have nothing – no freedom, no future, no hope! To be respectful all the time, to watch each word lest you're punished for speaking out of turn; to be always at someone's beck and call. You and the Lady Aurian have a place in the world. You have respect; you have each other to love. Can I ever hope for that? I'm a bondservant – I'm not free to love. Can you imagine how lonely that can be? For the rest of my life I'll have nothing to look forward to – nothing and no one of my own!'

'Oh, Anvar.' Aurian's eyes brimmed with sympathy. Going

to him, she took his hands. 'I wish there was something I could do,' she said softly. Anvar, already ashamed of his outburst, felt guiltier than ever.

'Lady, I'm sorry,' he said. 'I didn't mean to sound as if I was complaining about you. You've been so kind to me . . .' He struggled to find the words. 'I wouldn't have missed tonight for all the world.'

'Nor would I,' Aurian reassured him, and he knew his apology had been accepted. She dug into a drawer and produced a small packet of herbs which she tucked into his pocket. 'Make that into a tea in the morning,' she said. 'It's one of Meiriel's cure-alls – wonderful for aching heads. I'm sure I'll be in no state tomorrow to attempt any healing. Sleep as late as you want, Anvar, and when you get round to it, bring enough breakfast for three.'

Anvar assumed that Miathan must be breakfasting with Aurian and Forral, and suddenly the evening was ruined. With a sigh, he turned to go. But Forral detained him, putting an arm around his shoulders. 'We understand, lad,' he said softly. 'Both of us do. I don't know if we can influence the Archmage, but maybe next year we can try to get you down to the garrison. I know you said that Aurian has been teaching you a bit of swordplay. If you look as if you can learn, and it suits you, maybe Miathan would let you join my troop. You're too good a man to waste your life drudging for bloody Mages – begging your pardon, love,' he added quickly, glancing at Aurian and covering his mouth in embarrassment. 'I didn't mean you, of course.'

To Anvar's surprise, Aurian, far from being angry, was delighted. 'Forral, what a splendid idea!' She hugged the swordsman fiercely. Anvar felt as though a heavy weight had been lifted from his heart. In an excess of gratitude he hugged Forral too, joining in the general embrace, his face cracking in a grin so wide it almost hurt. Then Aurian was hugging him, and Forral suddenly said: 'Here, you haven't given Anvar a solstice kiss yet. Fancy forgetting that!'

'Goodness,' Aurian said, 'you're absolutely right.' She put her arms around Anvar's neck and he felt her lips brush his cheek, light as a butterfly's wing.

'That's pathetic, lass!' Forral roared. 'Can't you do better than that? Go on, it's solstice! Kiss him properly!' And she did. Not a kiss of passion, such as Forral had received, but a gentle, generous kiss none the less, and to Anvar strangely precious. Once again, he felt his heart pound unsteadily, the touch of her soft lips on his making him tremble.

'That's more like it!' Forral said, and suddenly Anvar remembered his presence. 'You've brought back his smile, love,' the swordsman said to Aurian.

'Well, I should hope so!' the Mage replied. For an instant she looked deep into Anvar's eyes. 'You should smile more often – it suits you. Well, if things work out, maybe you'll have more reason to smile in the future.'

'I'll drink to that,' Forral said. 'Oh, curse it – we can't!' So they said their goodnights instead. That night Anvar's bed seemed less hard and cold than it usually did, and his dreams were sweet.

Anvar paid for the previous night's celebrations on Solstice Morn. His head was pounding fit to fall off, and he wished it would – anything to be rid of the pain. But Aurian's remedy worked wonders, and soon he felt able to get her breakfast tray ready, though the smell of the food gave him some queasy moments. As he carried the tray up the tower steps to Aurian's door, Anvar heard the sound of hurrying footsteps behind him and turned to see the Mage herself, cloaked and booted for a trip outdoors. She was out of breath and carried a large, flattish wooden box in her arms. He wondered where she had been so early, especially if she felt as delicate as he did. As she approached, Anvar saw that she looked rather tired and drawn, but the cold had brought a glow to her cheeks and a little of last night's sparkle back into her eyes. Snowflakes were melting into brilliant diamond drops in her wind-tangled hair and the spicy, musky perfume that she favoured was overlaid with the fresh, invigorating scent of the snowy open air.

Thinking of her kiss the previous night, Anvar felt himself blush. Would she regret what had happened under the influence of the wine? Would she turn away in embarrassment or scorn? But the smile she gave him was frank and friendly –

and sympathetic. 'You too?' she said with a wry smile, putting a hand to her forehead. Anvar nodded. 'Never mind. It was worth it. I enjoyed every minute of last night.'

Anvar was startled. Did she know what he'd been thinking? Did her words carry some hidden meaning? Frowning, he followed the Mage into her rooms.

'Gods, what a mess!' Aurian grimaced at the litter of bottles and goblets, and went to open the curtains. Anvar put down the tray and began to tidy the debris while she lit the fire – a task that never took her long. The sound of their bustle must have awakened Forral, for Anvar heard a groan from the bed in the adjacent room. Aurian ran to the swordsman, her face full of sympathy, and Anvar cursed his own stupidity. Hidden meanings indeed! What a fool he was. Thoroughly ashamed of himself, he turned to go.

Aurian's face appeared round the bedroom door. 'Don't go yet,' she said. Anvar waited reluctantly as she mixed some of Meiriel's medicine and took it in to Forral. The loving closeness of the pair highlighted the emptiness of his own life, and he felt left out and, in truth, a little jealous. Besides, he didn't want to risk meeting Miathan.

'When are you expecting the Archmage, Lady?' he asked, as Aurian came back into the room.

'Miathan? Is he coming? Has there been a message?' Aurian frowned.

Anvar gestured at the table set for three. 'No, but I thought . . .'

The Mage's face broke into a grin. 'Gracious, no,' she said. 'Miathan won't eat with me while Forral is here. I thought you might like to join us this morning, since it's Solstice Day. Go on, sit down. Forral's just coming.'

When the swordsman appeared, his haggard face turned quite green at the sight of the food. 'Do I have to eat that stuff?' he asked plaintively.

'Go on, try it,' Aurian urged. 'It's just what you need.'

'Bossy!' Forral grumbled, but sure enough, the food and Aurian's medicine soon began to work, and by the time the last plate was cleared everyone was feeling much better.

Aurian turned to Anvar. 'Forral and I exchanged gifts last

night,' she said, 'and it occurred to me that I hadn't given you anything so . . .' She leaned across and lifted the box that had been propped in the corner. 'This is for you.'

Anvar held the box on his lap, not knowing what to say. It was almost too much. Forral, last night, had given him the cloak – and now this. Slowly he opened the lid. There, cradled by a thick padding of cloth, lay a beautiful guitar, its gleaming wood rich with intricate inlay – work of real quality. He stared at Aurian, not daring to believe. 'Is it all right?' she asked. 'I should have let you choose for yourself, but I wanted to surprise you. I'm sure he would change it if you don't like it, even though he wasn't too pleased at being dragged out of bed this morning.'

Anvar lifted the instrument carefully out of the box and struck a chord. It needed tuning after its journey in the cold, but the tone was mellow and sweet. 'Oh, Lady, thank you,' he whispered. His throat felt tight, and his eyes filled with tears. No matter how much he feared and hated most of the Magefolk, he knew now that Aurian was a very special exception. If he had to be a bondservant, he could not have hoped for a kinder mistress.

In the snowy weeks that followed solstice, Anvar's life was brightened by the Lady Aurian's gift. The Mage suggested that he keep it in her rooms, rather than leaving the precious instrument unattended in the servants' quarters, and since she was away from the chambers so much he could practise there to his heart's content. At their suggestion, he began to accompany Aurian and Forral down to the Invisible Unicorn in the evenings to play for the troopers, and his talent was so well appreciated that he suddenly found himself gaining many new friends.

One night, Anvar was at the Unicorn with his Lady and her warrior friends, Maya and Parric. Forral was absent; occupied at the garrison with work for the next day's council meeting. Since he and Aurian had become lovers, the swordsman had been clashing more and more with Miathan, and Anvar knew that Aurian was becoming increasingly concerned. She was quiet and abstracted that night, her brow clouded with a frown that not even Parric's most outrageous sallies had been able to lift. The arrival of Vannor, however, brought a new animation to the Mage's face. 'Well?' she demanded, as the merchant settled down with his ale. 'Did you find Dulsina? Did you ask her to come back?'

Vannor gave her a mock-fierce scowl. 'Did I have much choice, after that tongue-lashing I got from you and Maya? Yes, I found her – she was staying with a cousin who has a lodging-house near the garrison. Yes, she consented to come back – after she'd made me grovel.'

'Serves you right for dismissing her in the first place,' Maya snorted. 'We have no sympathy, do we, Aurian?'

'Not a bit!' the Mage chuckled. 'You must admit, Vannor, it wasn't a very clever move, considering that Dulsina is the only one who knows where your children are. You said she had sent them to stay with her sister, didn't you?'

'That's right,' the merchant said, with a heartiness that Anvar, looking on, found oddly false. 'But there's no mystery. She lives up the coast somewhere near Wyvernesse. Dulsina didn't want to tell me at first – I think she expected me to go charging up there causing trouble.' He sighed. 'I miss them, you know – especially Zanna – but Dulsina's sister will take excellent care of them. It'll do them good to get out of the city for a while, and I must admit that it's restful not to have Sara and Zanna squabbling all the time. On reflection, Dulsina was right to do what she did – I should have known that she was acting in the best interests of everyone.'

'I'll wager that Sara's glad to have Dulsina back!' Aurian's eyes glinted wickedly, and Anvar pricked up his ears.

'I'll say!' Vannor snorted. 'In truth, we're all glad to have her back – the household was falling apart around our ears without her. Even Sara said . . .'

At this point, Anvar went to fetch a new jug of ale. Listening to Vannor talking of Sara as his wife was too painful. He was returning to the others at their favourite table by the fireside, when a pale, faltering figure appeared in the tavern doorway. Anvar caught his breath in astonishment. D'arvan! What was he doing here?

'Aurian – thank the gods you're here!' The Young Mage

staggered to the table, flinging himself on Aurian, who had leapt to her feet. 'Miathan threw me out! And Davorshan – he . . .'

'D'arvan!' Aurian had automatically put her arms around the distraught Mage's shoulders. Anvar saw her recoil as though she had been stung, and her hands, when she took them away, were covered with blood. The Mage recovered herself quickly. 'Hurry,' she hissed at Anvar. 'Help me get him out of here before anyone notices!'

'Do you want me to help?' Vannor asked, but Aurian shook her head. 'No, Vannor – just avert suspicion, if you would. I don't want the word to get out that a Mage was attacked.'

'We'll follow in a moment,' Maya whispered, looking alarmed. Anvar helped the Mage catch D'arvan as he collapsed, and she made her hasty goodnights to Parric and Maya. They headed for the door, supporting his limp body between them. 'Honestly,' Maya was saying to Vannor in a loud voice as they left, for the benefit of anyone who might be curious. 'She's told him time and again about drinking so much!'

Aurian was relieved when they finally reached the door to Forral's quarters. D'arvan's breathing was becoming more and more laboured, although, since he had managed to get from the Academy to the Unicorn, she didn't think the wound was too serious. She had acted decisively in the tavern, getting him away before the other customers had time to become interested, but now the shock was taking its toll, and she was weary from half-dragging D'arvan through streets filled with slippery slush, taking a circuitous route through the back lanes to avoid the stares of passers-by.

'Aurian! What the blazes has happened?' A tired-looking Forral opened the door, his mouth slack with astonishment. Without answering, Aurian helped Anvar to lay D'arvan on the couch. Forral put his arms around her, and she relaxed for a moment, leaning against his shoulder. 'Are you all right, love?' he asked her, and she pulled herself upright and kissed him, glad that he was there.

'I am, but D'arvan isn't,' she said. 'He's been hurt. Forral, will you light another lamp and get us all some wine while I see to him? Anvar will tell you what happened.'

Sitting on the edge of the couch, Aurian pulled away the torn remains of D'arvan's robes to expose his back, feeling a mixture of relief and consternation. The wound was a long slice, bloody but shallow, obviously done with a knife. It wasn't serious, thank the gods – but who in the world had tried to stab the Mage? Aurian was well aware that most of the Magefolk were unpopular with the city's inhabitants, but this was unthinkable!

By now, Aurian was well advanced in the skills of healing. As she concentrated her powers, the wound was suffused with a faint, violet-blue glow, and she had the satisfaction of seeing the sundered tissues start to knit before her eyes as the bleeding stopped and the gash began to close. As D'arvan's pain ceased, she felt his body relax beneath her hands, and his eyes flickered open. She helped him to a sitting position, supporting the healing wound with cushions, and Forral handed him a cup of wine.

Just then Maya entered with the cavalry master. 'Don't worry,' Parric assured Aurian. 'Whoever attacked him didn't follow you here.'

'Is he all right?' Maya asked anxiously. 'Has he told you how it happened?'

'Not yet.' The Mage frowned. 'I'm just about to ask him.'

D'arvan's fine-boned face was even paler than usual, but he was conscious, and seemed fairly alert. 'You'll want to sleep,' Aurian told him, 'but drink your wine before you rest.' She sat down beside him, gratefully taking a goblet of wine from Forral. 'You're safe now,' she said. 'We're in the garrison. Can you tell me what happened?'

D'arvan shuddered. 'Miathan,' he whispered. 'He sent for me. He said that I was never going to be any use, and told me to get out of the Academy.' His hands trembled so that wine slopped out of the cup. 'He had the guards throw me out of the top gate. I – I didn't know what to do, so I was coming to find you. Then, as I was crossing the causeway, Davorshan leapt out from behind the wall and tried to stab me.'

Aurian caught her breath. Davorshan? A Mage attacking another Mage? And his own brother? One thing was certain, she thought grimly. Eliseth was behind this somehow.

'I knew he was there,' D'arvan went on. 'We're so closely linked, it saved me. I saw my murder in his mind, and I dodged, but the knife caught me, then we struggled and I managed to get away. The guards at the lower gate heard the disturbance, and he had to stop to talk to them. We've always been so close, Aurian – how could he do this?' He dropped the cup, burying his face in his hands.

Aurian put her arms around him. 'You say you knew his mind,' she prompted gently, when he became calmer. 'Do you know why he did it?'

D'arvan nodded. 'He – he's been working with Eliseth, and making some progress with Water-magic,' he said. 'He had decided that we must have only enough power for one Mage between us, and, since Miathan had banished me, he could kill me, so that all the power would be his.'

'But that's ridiculous!'

'I don't think so,' D'arvan said. 'I've suspected as much myself. It's the only explanation. We've been tangling up the power between us, but since Davorshan discovered where his skills lay, he's been able to access some of it. Maybe I could, if I had any talents, but I've tried everything . . .'

'Wait a minute!' Aurian sat up abruptly. 'No you haven't! Gods take me for a fool, why didn't we think of it sooner? You haven't tried Earth-magic, for the simple reason that there's no one at the Academy who teaches it. D'arvan, we'll send you to my mother. No one will know where you are, so you'll be safe. Eilin can shield you, and she'll teach you. And it would be a great help for her. She won't admit it, but she desperately needs some company.'

'But I'm not sure . . .' D'arvan began doubtfully.

'Oh, nonsense. You have to try, don't you see? At least you'll know for certain. And you can't let that brother of yours get away with this without a fight!'

'Well . . . I've always liked plants and things . . .'

'Of course you have.' Aurian noticed that D'arvan's eyelids were drooping. 'Look, get some rest now. I'll fetch a blanket and you can sleep on the couch. You'll be safe here, and in a day or so we'll see about smuggling you out of the city. At all costs, the other Magefolk mustn't find out where you are.'

'I'll send Maya with him,' Forral suggested. 'She'll see that he gets there safely.'

'Of course I'll go,' Maya said. Stooping, she embraced the young Mage. 'Don't you worry,' she told him. 'We'll take care of you.'

When Maya and Parric had gone to their beds, Aurian and Forral stood with their arms around each other, looking down at the sleeping Mage. 'Poor fellow,' Forral said softly. 'Thank goodness he had you to turn to – but you always were one for taking on other people's troubles. My dearest love, what an Archmage you'd make!'

Now that D'arvan was asleep, Aurian could no longer contain her rage at the way he had been treated. 'I don't want to be their bloody Archmage! I don't like what's happening up there. Nothing's as it should be any more, and as for Miathan – well, after the way he treated Anvar, and – and now this . . .' Still she couldn't bring herself to tell Forral about the Archmage's attack on her. But her decision had crystallized. 'Forral, I've had enough! I'm sick of the Academy – and the Magefolk, most of them. We have so many powers, but we never think of using them to help people. Think of the good we could have done, if we had not been so arrogant and self-absorbed. I want to leave – to find my own way in the world. And I want to be with you – all the time, not just for these snatched moments!'

Forral looked at her gravely. 'Maybe you're right,' he said softly. 'I've felt that way about the Magefolk for so long – gods, if it hadn't been for you, I'd have left years ago. Of course we can go, love. But we'll have to make our plans carefully, and we must flee fast and far to escape Miathan. He won't let you go easily.'

'We must take Anvar with us, too,' Aurian said urgently. She looked around at her servant, who had fallen asleep in a chair. 'At least we can give him back his freedom.' Gently, so as not to wake him, she covered him with another blanket from Forral's bedchamber.

'We could all do with some sleep,' Forral suggested. 'Once D'arvan and Maya are safely on their way, we'll be able to make some plans of our own.' He yawned. 'Come on, love. Come to bed. We're too tired to think straight – and I want my wits about me tomorrow. I have another wrangle to face in council with that bloody Archmage – can you believe he wants to raise the sewer tax again? He won't be satisfied until he's bled this city dry. If this is to be my last fight with him, I mean to make it a good one – especially after what I've seen tonight!'

Aurian climbed gratefully into bed with her lover, ruefully noting the scarcity of covers. 'You'd better not steal the bedclothes tonight,' she told Forral. 'I'll have trouble keeping warm as it is.' She snuggled close to him. 'It reminds me of when I was little, when I gave you all my blankets so that you wouldn't have to leave the Valley.' She flung her arms around him. 'Oh, gods, Forral, I love you! I couldn't bear to think of losing you.'

Forral held her close, stroking her hair. 'You'll never lose me,' he reassured her. 'Never, while I live.'

As he spoke, Aurian again felt that premonitory prickle of dread, like ice sheeting over her bare skin. She shuddered, and tightened her grasp on Forral until he grunted a sleepy protest. It can't be true, she assured herself desperately. I'm tired and worried, that's all – I'm imagining things. She closed her eyes firmly, and did her best to thrust her fears from her mind. But weary as she was, Aurian got no sleep that night.

14

The Death-Wraiths

The meetings of the Council of Three were held in the Guildhall, a magnificent circular building near the Grand Arcade. The decisions that ruled the city were made round a small gilded table in the very centre of the vast round chamber, and anyone wishing to observe the proceedings could watch from the gallery of the hall, though usually only a few stalwarts were present. Narvish, the city recorder, sat with the Three to record what took place.

When Forral arrived at the Guildhall, every seat was taken. Interest in this meeting was unusually high because the matter under discussion would affect every man, woman and child in the city. The Archmage wanted to raise the sewer tax. This nominal sum was paid to the Magefolk by every citizen in Nexis, in return for the upkeep of the sewer system that made life so pleasant and healthy for them. Magic kept the water circulating, pumping the city's waste away downriver, and no one objected to giving the Magefolk a small amount for the convenience, but Miathan's new demands were extortionate, especially for those with large families. There was a great deal of anger among the city's people at the prospect, and feelings against the Archmage and the council were running high.

Vannor had already arrived, and was seated alone at the table, looking uncomfortable. When Forral took the garrison commander's chair, the head of the Merchants' Guild leaned towards him, his low voice masked by the general hubbub in the room. As usual, he came straight to the point. 'Forral, no offence, but I know that Miathan has you in an invidious position on this council because of Aurian. I've never said anything about it before, because you've done your best in a tough spot – but have you thought this sewer business through? The tax will cripple the poor people of the city, and it'll be your job to enforce it. What will happen to those who can't pay? What if they all refuse to pay it – and the way feelings are running at the minute they well might. If this law goes through, we'll be up to our necks in shit, in more ways than one!'

In spite of himself, Forral grinned. 'You have a wonderful way with words, Vannor.'

'So they tell me.' The blunt-faced merchant returned his smile, and Forral regretted that his relationship with Aurian had always prevented him from outfacing the Archmage in a public display of opposition. Vannor deserved better. It would be a real pleasure to help him out this time.

Miathan swept into the room, making his grand entrance as usual, flanked by that obsequious little toad Narvish. Forral's mouth tightened at the sight of the city recorder – a stringy, gap-toothed old fossil who was the bane of the swordsman's life. Rumour had it that Narvish took bribes from Miathan, and to Forral's certain knowledge the records of recent meetings had been slanted in favour of the Archmage. Nothing major, of course. Nothing that could be proved. But an altered emphasis, perhaps, or an odd word or two displaced, that threw the account of a straightforward discussion into confusion and doubt. Well, there would be no chance of that today, Forral thought grimly. This would be a public debate, settled by a simple majority vote, and now that Aurian had decided to leave the Magefolk the swordsman no longer had to dance to the Archmage's tune. Miathan was going to be in for a big surprise, Forral thought. He was looking forward to it immensely.

The debate took up the whole of its allotted three hours, and Forral could feel the surprise emanating from the audience. Such a thing had never been known during the Archmage's tenure. Miathan had always made sure that he had at least one supporter on the council, and had always had his way, sweeping any opposition easily aside. But not this time. After a while, Vannor no longer bothered to hide his smile, as the two Mortal men systematically destroyed every one of the Archmage's suave arguments between them. Forral contented himself with smiling inwardly as he watched Miathan's expression grow blacker and blacker.

At last the voting bell was rung, putting an end to any further debate. Narvish, who had been looking increasingly alarmed as the discussion continued, rose to his feet and addressed the meeting. 'The Archmage Miathan has put forward a motion to this council to increase the sewer tax by ten silver pieces,' he intoned. 'Those in favour of accepting the motion into the city's statutes, please rise.'

There was utter silence as the Archmage rose to his feet – alone. Forral saw Miathan turn to him, expecting him to have risen also. With a show of nonchalance, he leaned back in his chair, and put his booted feet up on the gilded council table. A gasp echoed through the room. The Archmage's expression changed from complacency to baffled rage. Narvish, completely at a loss, looked wildly around, as if searching for a means of escape. 'Er . . . Is that everyone?' he squeaked.

'Get on with it, man,' Vannor growled, but his eyes were twinkling. The merchant appeared to be enjoying himself hugely. The greasy little recorder sidled away from the fuming Archmage. 'Er . . . All those against?'

Slowly, Forral removed his feet from the table and stood up with Vannor, as the chamber erupted into tumultuous applause. The Archmage, his face absolutely livid, opened his mouth to speak, but Forral held his glare with a look of stony defiance. Miathan turned on his heel and stormed out of the hall, for once in his life utterly defeated.

The Archmage paced the floor of his chamber, barely able to contain his rage. This time, Forral had gone too far. How dared he stand with that upstart Vannor, flaunting the supremacy of those Mortal scum over one of the Mageborn! Miathan knew that the rule of the city was slipping out of his grasp, along with all his greater plans. Enough was enough. Aurian or no Aurian, Forral had just signed his own death warrant.

Miathan frowned, remembering something else. Something that he had not previously connected with Forral's defiance. Since he had exiled D'arvan last night, the Mage had simply vanished. Where could he be? Miathan's spies had failed to locate him in the city, and the Archmage wondered if he had made the right decision in acceding to the pleas of Eliseth and Bragar to get rid of D'arvan, who, they insisted, was impeding his brother's progress. Better to have one working Mage loyal to us, they had said, than two who are useless. But Miathan wondered now. Someone of Mage blood was still a potential source of power, and it disturbed him to have D'arvan away from his influence. What if he was hatching some plot with Forral and – Miathan winced at the thought – Aurian? And what did Eliseth and Bragar mean by 'loyal to us'? Was Davorshan loyal to the Archmage, or simply to them? Miathan wrestled with the possibilities, falling into the classic trap of those who spend their lives plotting and scheming against others. He was convinced that the others, in their turn, were plotting to overthrow him.

Eliseth and Bragar appeared to be loyal, but he did not completely trust them. Certainly not enough to tell them about this. Miathan stroked the burnished golden rim of the chalice that stood on the table before him. This would serve him well, if they should move against him. Finbarr's research had provided him with the answers he needed. Here indeed lay the power of the Cauldron, and, like all the tools of Gramarye, the High Magic, it could be used as boon or bane. Miathan smiled. The Mages' Code was for simpletons. Here, under his hand, lay a weapon so formidable . . .

His deliberations were interrupted by a soft knock at the door. Miathan cursed, and quickly pulled an embroidered cloth over the chalice to hide it. 'Enter,' he called. It was Meiriel. She bowed low. 'Your pardon, Lord Archmage,' she said, 'I must speak with you urgently.'

'This is very formal, is it not, Meiriel?' Miathan forced joviality into his voice. There was no evidence that the healer was against him, and he might need all the support he could get. 'Come, sit. Let me pour you some wine.'

Meiriel seemed very disturbed. Her jaw worked; her eyes darted everywhere as she sat and accepted the cup from him. Before he had time to sit again she had blurted her news. 'Aurian is with child, Archmage!'

Miathan froze, half seated as he was. The room seemed darker, and suddenly chill. 'Are you sure?' he whispered.

'I'm certain,' Meiriel said. 'The aura of a Mage changes once a child is conceived. A healer can see it, though

Magewomen themselves are later than Mortals in making the discovery, since we are trained to suppress the cycles that would otherwise warn us. It can be little more than two months yet and I don't think Aurian knows – she can hardly have expected it. But soon – very soon – she will know.'

Miathan fell heavily into the chair. 'Oh, gods,' he whispered. 'Gods – not this!'

The healer, braced as she was for a furious outburst, looked at him in confusion, then took a sudden, gulping breath.

'How could you let this happen!' she spat. 'With a Mortal!'

'Be silent!' Miathan snapped, not listening. He was remembering a day long ago when a blue-eyed Mortal girl had wept before him, as she told him similar news – and, more urgently, a day not so very long ago, when he had conceived a terrible curse . . . His Aurian, gravid with that cursed Mortal's monstrous spawn – a monster that he himself had helped to create, just as much as they . . .

'Archmage?' The healer was tugging urgently at his sleeve.

'Curse you, Meiriel, get out – no, wait!' He crushed her hands in an iron grip. 'You are a healer – could you get rid of this child? Without Aurian knowing?'

'What?' Meiriel stared at him. 'What are you saying?'

'Listen.' Miathan leaned close. 'You said that Aurian is unaware of her pregnancy. We must end it, Meiriel, and as a healer it would be a simple matter for you. But if Aurian finds out, she would never allow it, and she has power enough to prevent you. So we must act quickly. I'll summon her now, and put spells of deep sleep on her while you dispose of the child. When she wakes, she will be none the wiser. We can say she was taken ill – that she overtaxed herself again, and' – the Archmage shrugged – 'the matter will end there.' His eyes met those of the healer. 'After that, I shall deal with that thrice-cursed swordsman once and for all. This must not be allowed to happen again!'

The healer gaped at him. But . . .' she floundered, 'you weren't supposed to – I mean, I . . .'

'Meiriel!' the Archmage barked. 'Can you do it or not?'

With an effort, the healer got hold of herself. 'I suppose so,' she whispered unhappily.

'Excellent.' The Archmage smiled. 'My dear Meiriel, I am well pleased with you. This will not go unrewarded. Are you sure that no one suspects? Finbarr? Anyone?'

'As if I would tell Finbarr!' Meiriel's lip curled. 'He'd be no friend to us in this. He's besotted with the wretched woman!' Her eyes flashed angrily.

Miathan's eyes narrowed. So she was jealous of Aurian? He filed the information away in his mind for future use.

'Very well,' he said. 'I'll send for her now.'

'Blasted, bloody thing!' Aurian tugged fiercely at the brush that was inextricably tangled with a snarl of her hair. Then in temper she threw the whole thing away from her – brush, hair and all – with the inevitable result. 'Ouch!' She banged her fist hard on the table, making the poised mirror tremble.

'Lady, let me.' Anvar hurried to her side, hastily retrieving the brush that swung in mid-air, dangling from the tangled lock of hair. He freed it carefully, then, while she rubbed at her head, he brought her a glass of wine, taking the brush with him to forestall a further outburst. For some reason, his mistress seemed to be growing awfully moody of late.

Aurian took a huge gulp of the wine and smiled at him. 'Thank you, Anvar. I don't know what I'd do without you.' She rubbed irritably at her forehead. 'Stupid of me, to carry on like that. I don't know what's the matter with me these days. You had better give me the brush back, or I'll never be in time to meet Forral.'

'Shall I do it, Lady?' Anvar offered. 'I used to brush my mother's hair . . .' He flinched from the memory. Why did it still hurt so, to think of her? 'Anyway,' he went on hastily, 'she always said I was gentle.'

'Perhaps you should,' Aurian agreed. She looked surprised at the mention of his past, but Anvar knew that she had given up trying to question him about it.

Anvar took up the brush and began to work on her hair, carefully unknotting the snags with his fingers before carrying on. He enjoyed the feel of the long, thick strands that slipped like heavy silk through his hands. Soon he was brushing in long, smooth strokes, and he saw the rigid set of Aurian's

217

shoulders beginning to relax. 'That's lovely,' she sighed. 'Bless you, Anvar. I can't think how it got so tangled – it usually doesn't when it's braided. It must have been Parric's cavalry practice. I've been on the horse, off the horse, underneath it even, all day – and that's not counting the times when I fell, or was knocked off!'

'Is fighting on horseback very different, Lady?' Anvar asked. Lately, she had been teaching him the rudiments of swordsmanship, and he was determined to excel.

Aurian nodded. 'Completely different,' she said. 'For one thing, you aren't on your own feet – you're on a great heavy thing that's far less manoeuvrable, so you count on force rather than agility. There are different fighting styles, depending on whether your opponents are mounted or on foot – if they're on foot, they'll be trying to get in underneath and disable the horse, which in itself is a very formidable weapon – warhorses are trained to fight as well as their warriors – ' She broke off with a rueful smile. 'Sorry, Anvar. I didn't mean to start a lecture. Parric has me eating, sleeping and breathing horsemanship at the minute.'

Anvar smiled back at her reflection in the mirror, enjoying the ease that existed between them nowadays. 'Shall I braid it again?' he asked.

'You can do that too?' Aurian sounded surprised. 'Gods, Anvar, is there no end to your talents?' She chuckled. 'I suppose you realize that you've just talked yourself into another job? All that braiding makes my arms ache!'

'I'd be happy to do it, Lady,' Anvar said, and was surprised to realize that it was true.

'Thank you, Anvar. I appreciate that. But not tonight. We're dining with Vannor, and I think I'll look like a lady, rather than a warrior.' She slipped a fillet of twisted gold over her burnished hair to hold the fiery mass in place, and stood, smoothing the skirts of her emerald-green gown. 'Well,' she said, 'I must be off. See you later, Anvar – oh, drat! Who can that be?'

Anvar went to answer the door. It was a servant, summoning the Lady Aurian to the presence of the Archmage. Aurian scowled when he gave her the message. 'Bat-turds! I'm going to be late! Did he say what Miathan wanted?'

'I'm sorry, Lady.' Anvar shook his head. The Mage gave a longsuffering sigh, but he had glimpsed the flicker of fear behind her casual pose. 'Lady, if you want to get away, I'll go and tell the Archmage that I made a mistake, and that you've already gone,' he offered.

'Thanks, but I'd better go myself. Miathan is the sort to blame the messenger for the tidings! I'll come back for my cloak before I go – I hope this won't take too long.'

When Aurian had gone, Anvar busied himself about her rooms, tidying away the clothing she'd discarded on her return from the garrison. He picked up her leather fighting clothes and her sword belt and boots, rolling them into a bundle with the cloak that had once belonged to Forral. He left them by the door, near the sword that stood propped against the wall. He'd clean them later, he thought. They stank of horses. He emptied her bath, built up the fire, and placed a new flask of wine on the table, ready for her return. His tasks completed, Anvar was about to reach for his guitar to while away a solitary hour or two when he saw her staff, which had rolled beneath the bed, forgotten.

A staff was a vital tool for a Mage, serving to focus and concentrate their power. Each of the Magefolk, on reaching a certain degree of aptitude, would make a staff from one of the traditional magical trees – from a branch or a root, as they preferred – and fuse it with their power and personality. Aurian had delayed long over making her staff, knowing she was clumsy at carving and afraid that the result would be a disaster. Seeking a way to repay her generous solstice gift, Anvar had gone to the woods south of the river and found a twisted root of beech, Aurian's favourite tree. He had carved it carefully, using the skills his grandpa had taught him and following the natural twists of the wood to form the two Serpents of the High Magic – the Serpent of Might and the Serpent of Wisdom – that coiled, intertwining, up the length of the staff from bottom to top. It was the most beautiful thing he had ever made, with a force and life of its own, even before it was imbued with magic. Aurian had been overjoyed with it, and her delight had been reward indeed for Anvar.

Anvar bent to pick up the staff – and dropped it as though it had burned him. When his fingers had touched the wood, he'd felt a jolt of fear, a flash of panic as though Aurian had cried out to him in helpless desperation. Cautiously, he reached for it again, but this time there was nothing. Turning the staff in his hands, Anvar frowned. What had happened to Aurian? She had been gone for ages. Was something wrong? Had she managed to reach out to him via this implement that he had made, and she had infused with her power? A knot of pain formed between Anvar's eyes at the thought, but he refused to be put off, remembering the flash of fear on her face when she was summoned by Miathan. Terrified though he was of the Archmage, Anvar knew he would have to find out if she was all right.

With dragging feet, he climbed to the topmost floor, trying without success to convince himself that he'd imagined the whole thing. Miathan's door was slightly ajar. Anvar was lifting his hand to knock when he heard voices within. The Archmage – and Meiriel? Where was Aurian? He froze, one hand lifted, chilled by what he heard.

'It isn't working, Miathan.' Meiriel's voice was strained. 'Even under your spells, she instinctively fights to protect the child.'

'Plague on it! Is there nothing you can do?'

'Well . . . There's a drug that I could try. It would work on her mind, to make her malleable to our commands. We might be able to make her expel the brat herself.'

'Do you have it with you?'

'Of course!' Meiriel snapped. 'We must hurry, though. It will take the drug about an hour to take effect, and if we should be discovered in the meantime . . .'

'Don't worry. Eliseth and her companion will no doubt be occupied in plotting their usual mischief, and you know that Finbarr never leaves his archives. Get on with it, Meiriel. Forral's child must not survive this night.'

Anvar gasped, steadying himself against the cold stone wall of the tower, his mind spinning with confusion. Aurian's babe, destroyed as Sara's had been, and for similar reasons . . . His child – Forral's child . . . Forral! Turning, Anvar ran soft-footed until he was well around the first curve, then descending the spiral stairs at a breakneck pace. Without thinking, he thrust the staff into his belt as he reached the bottom, then pelted across the torchlit courtyard to the stables next to the guardhouse. 'A horse, quick!' he yelled to the startled guards. 'I'm on an urgent errand for the Lady Aurian!' They knew by now that he was the Lady's trusted servant, and did not hinder him. He snatched a bridle and forced it on to the nearest animal, then without waiting for a saddle he vaulted astride, ducking beneath the stable doorway. He spurred out of the gate just as the guards raised the signal lantern that would alert the gatekeeper to open the lower gates.

Anvar reached the garrison, pursued by several mounted troopers who had taken exception to his hurtling through the city streets, heedlessly scattering the passers-by who got in his way. Two guards stood forth to bar his way, and Anvar wrenched at the horse's mouth, throwing himself off the startled beast before it had time to skid to a halt. He thrust the reins at the astonished soldiers. 'Commander Forral!' he gasped. 'Quick – where is he?' Luckily one of the guards was Parric.

'In his quarters, but . . .' He was talking to empty air. Anvar had gone, shouldering past him and running across the parade ground to the officers' quarters. The troopers, arriving close on his heels, looked at Parric, who simply shrugged.

Anvar hammered frantically on Forral's door, almost hitting the commander in the face as he opened it.

'Anvar, what in the world . . .'

He almost fell into the room, barely noticing Vannor seated by the fire. Clutching at Forral's tunic, he gasped out his story. The result was unexpected. Anvar, knowing Forral as a cool, capable, professional soldier, had failed to realize that the swordsman might have a blind spot where Aurian was concerned. Forral's face went absolutely white; all reason fled from his eyes. '*Miathan*,' he howled in an inhuman voice, and, snatching up his sword, he fled from the room. Vannor and Anvar stared at each other, horrified; then, as one, they rushed out after the berserk swordsman.

By the time they had found horses and made their way through the crowded streets of the city, Forral was well ahead of them. The gatehouse on the causeway showed the horrific evidence of his passing: the gatekeeper lying huddled and twisted in a pool of blood. In the courtyard above was a worse scene of carnage, with dead guards and servants littering the bloodstained paving stones. Forral's warhorse stood by the tower door, its sides heaving, its ears laid back and nostrils flaring at the scent of blood. Anvar and Vannor hurled themselves from their mounts and dashed up the steps of the tower, only to stop dead on Miathan's threshold, frozen by the horror within.

Aurian was lost in a dark dream, fighting with all her strength against something dark and nebulous, twisted and unspeakably evil – something that strove to possess her very soul. She fought, desperate, weaponless, knowing that she was gradually beginning to weaken, feeling her will slowly slipping away in the face of the dark terror, the voice that strove to master her. Then another voice reached her, crying Miathan's name. Forral! She clung to his voice – a lifeline pulling her up – up and out . . .

Aurian opened her eyes; saw the lamplight of Miathan's opulent quarters; saw Meiriel cowering in a corner – and saw Forral, splattered with blood and clutching a gory, dripping sword, advancing on the Archmage. Miathan retreated behind the table, snatching at a cloth that covered something . . . A chalice of graven, burnished gold. In a chilling voice, the Archmage began to intone the words of a spell, in a language ancient and steeped in evil. Aurian felt an agonizing buzzing within her skull as the build-up of dark, obscene magic permeated the chamber. 'Miathan, no!' she shrieked, struggling to throw off the effects of the drug, and rise from the couch where she lay. Forral continued his slow, inexorable advance, murder in his eyes. Desperate, Aurian sent out a frantic mental call for help to Finbarr, the only Mage she could still trust.

The air thickened and grew dark. In the gloom, the outside of the cup began to glow with a pale, sickly luminescence like rotting fungus, its inside enclosing a black, bottomless pit from which issued a hideous stench. The air was chill with a cold from beyond the grave, and reeked of rot and putrefaction.

Something stirred in the depths of the chalice. A shadow, like a drift of black, oily smoke, poured over the rim. A single red eye burned steadily within the moiling, churning vapours as the spectre expanded and coalesced. Forral shrank away as its deadly light fell upon him. A freezing wave of malevolence filled the room, striking the swordsman to his knees as the creature drifted slowly in his direction. He screamed once, horribly, his face contorted.

'Miathan, no!' The Archmage turned at the sound of Aurian's shriek, to see her struggling to rise from the couch, her eyes fixed in horror on the abomination that he had summoned. Then she turned to him, and the agony on her face struck straight to his heart. 'Take it back!' she cried. 'Please, Miathan, spare him! I'll do anything – I swear it! I beg you, take it back!'

For a moment, the Archmage hesitated, and his creature paused, hovering. He already owed Aurian a blood-debt for the murder of her father, and in his own, grasping way, he truly loved her. Anything, she had said – and he had her oath on it. Having won her gratitude for sparing Forral, surely he would win back her heart?

He turned, fully intending to call the creature back, until he saw the swordsman trapped in his corner. All at once, the memory of his humiliation at Forral's hands that morning returned in force. This filthy upstart Mortal was Aurian's lover! He had laid hands on her body, had filled her with his seed, and now she carried his monstrous brat. Enough! The Archmage's mind was utterly consumed by the searing flames of jealousy, and his one chance to redeem himself from evil was utterly lost.

Aurian saw Miathan turn to the abomination, and saw his face contort into a hideous mask of hatred. 'Take him!' he shrieked. Forral huddled flat against the wall, staring wild-eyed at the thing that stalked him. Utterly fearless in the face of any human foe, this was beyond him. Aurian gasped, her body breaking out in an icy sweat. Never had she seen anything like this! It took all her courage not to break and run; to flee in mindless panic from this manifestation of evil that was advancing on her love with deadly intent.

It was like a wisp of dark cloud – a smoky wraith that writhed and undulated with a sickening pulsation, twisting and recombining in a series of leering, malevolent demon faces that flickered and shimmered in a way that tortured and wrenched both the eye and the gut. It was impossible to look at it; impossible to look away. Aurian felt her head beginning to throb. The thing was surrounded by a swirling vortex of cold evil that sucked at her, leeching the warmth and strength from her body, and she suddenly knew she had little time in which to act.

With the strength of desperation, she wrenched herself to her feet and leapt across the room, hurling herself in front of the swordsman and snapping her magical shield into place to protect them both. The thing kept advancing, slow and inexorable. Aurian bit back a scream as it hit her shield – and passed straight through as though nothing was there! Forcing down her panic, she backed towards Forral, snatching the sword from his nerveless fingers.

The blade thrummed, flaring into fiery light as Aurian infused it with the force of her Fire-magic. She went for the abomination with a great, two-handed swipe, cleaving it straight through the middle. Her blade met no resistance, as though it had passed through smoke. The spectre gave a deep, chilling chuckle, and the two halves rejoined, flowing effortlessly back together. Shock exploded through her as her blade went dark and dead. She staggered back weakly, dropping the sword, her hands and arms numb with a pervasive chill that was quickly spreading. The abomination advanced, seeming to grow in size, blotting out the room with its massive, shadowy form. Passing over her as she lay helpless, it swooped upon the swordsman, engulfing him in its reeking darkness. Forral gave one last, strangled cry – her name – as the dark mass flowed over him. Then there was silence. Slowly, the abomination lifted.

Forral lay, white and still, as Aurian had seen him so long ago, in a dread vision. 'Forral!' she shrieked, a cry wrenched with anguish from the depths of her soul, as, heedless of her own danger, she flung herself upon him. But it was too late. Forral's body beneath her was lifeless, an icy husk, his breathing stilled, his great, generous, loving heart stopped for ever.

Anvar reached the doorway in time to see Forral fall. He saw Aurian, oblivious in her grief, hurl herself across his body, weeping as she tried to revive him, seeking desperately with her healer's senses for one last spark of life to which she could cling. With a jarring whine, the dark, roiling monstrosity swooped down towards her, its black maw gaping. 'No!' Miathan screamed. 'Not her, you fool!' The thing ignored him. Strengthened by the life-force of its victim, it was now beyond his control. With an inarticulate cry, Anvar leapt forward, only to be shouldered aside by the tall lanky form of Finbarr, bearing his staff. He lifted it, facing the monster, and cried out some words in a strong, ringing voice.

The abomination gave a startled flicker, suddenly finding itself enclosed by a misty blue aura. Then it stopped, frozen, hanging helplessly in mid-air scant inches away from Aurian's face, taken completely out of time by Finbarr's preserving spell. Miathan recoiled with a vile curse, and lifting his hands uttered a spell of his own. More dark shapes, more and more, began to pour over the rim of the chalice. Finbarr countered them with his own spell, freezing each wraith as it emerged, his damp face contorted with strain. 'Nihilim!' he shouted. 'The Death-Wraiths of the Cauldron! Anvar – get her out of here!'

Meiriel, in her corner, was shrieking.

Anvar needed no second telling. He dashed across to Aurian, ducking around the frozen form of the hideous monstrosity that loomed over her. She clutched frantically at Forral as Anvar tugged her arm. 'Aurian, come on,' he yelled. 'Please – there's nothing you can do for him!' His own face was flooded with tears. Aurian looked up at him, and her eyes suddenly cleared, as though she recognized him for the first time. She dragged a sleeve across her tear-stained face and nodded, then turned back to Forral, touching his face in farewell with a gentle hand. 'Safe journey, love,' she whispered, 'until we meet again.' Then, with a sob, she tore herself away, leaning heavily on Anvar's arm as they staggered towards the door.

225

Finbarr was still fighting the Archmage's endless succession of Wraiths. He was staggering with weakness now. Vannor stood at the door, paralysed with horror, his face deathly white. Anvar thrust Aurian into his arms. 'Help her,' he yelled. 'Hurry!' He ran ahead of them down the stairs and ducked into Aurian's room, snatching up her bundle of discarded warrior's clothing and her sword. There was no time for more. He caught up with Vannor and Aurian at the bottom of the stairs and helped the distraught Mage mount one of the horses. Vannor mounted the other, and Anvar passed his bundle to the merchant before leaping up behind Aurian and snatching up the reins.

'My place!' Vannor shouted, and spurred towards the gates, trampling the fallen bodies of the guards in his haste.

As they passed the gates, they heard a terrible shriek from the tower – Meiriel's voice. Aurian stiffened in Anvar's arms and gasped, flinching as though she had been struck. 'Finbarr. He'd dead,' she said in a small, bleak voice, as though this last grief was the utter end and nothing could ever touch her again. As Anvar looked back at the tower, he saw the sinister black shapes of the Wraiths already beginning to pour out of the upper windows, heading for the city.

They thundered across the causeway, away from the horror behind them, and, turning right, took the lamplit road that climbed away amidst the trees, never once pausing in their wild flight until they reached the sturdy carved doors of Vannor's mansion. Pushing past the bewildered servant who opened the door, the merchant led them across the tiled hallway and into his study. Dropping Aurian's bundle on the floor, he gestured for Anvar to help the Mage to the couch, and poured strong spirits for each of them before dropping shakily into his own chair. 'Gods,' he said. 'What are we going to do?' Pulling a handkerchief from his pocket, he mopped his brow. 'It's obvious,' he went on, with the calm of deep shock, 'that Miathan is insane. He's broken the Mages' Code and unleashed a horror such as this city has never seen. He always wanted power – he'll take it now, make no mistake. And he'll be after us – Aurian in particular. You'll have to get her away from here, lad. The only question is, where? Could you go north, Lady, to your mother?'

Aurian sat stiffly beside Anvar on the couch, staring at nothing, her eyes wide and blank, her face grey. Her knuckles were clenched white about her untouched cup. 'Lady?' Anvar prompted gently. Putting an arm around her shoulders, he guided the hands that held the cup to her lips, encouraging her to drink. As she swallowed the fiery liquor a tremor passed through her, and the terrible tension of her body eased a little. 'Forral,' she whispered longingly. Her eyes began to focus, and Anvar could hardly bear to meet that lost, pain-filled gaze. Then she looked away, and with a shaking hand held her cup out to Vannor to be refilled, and downed the liquor in one swift gulp.

'Anvar, what happened?' she asked. 'What did the Archmage do to me? Why were you and – and Forral there?' Briefly, his voice trembling with emotion, Anvar told her, and saw her eyes grow wide with shock. 'Child?' she gasped. 'What child? I'm not . . . I can't be!' For a moment her expression clouded, and Anvar guessed that she was probing within, with her healer's extra sense. 'Dear Gods,' she murmured. 'Solstice! It must have been at solstice. We were drunk that night . . . so happy. But I couldn't have been so careless – it's impossible.' Suddenly her eyes flared with a terrible anger. 'Meiriel!' she snarled. 'Meiriel betrayed me! It's the only possibility. By all the gods, she'll pay for this before I'm done.'

Leaping to her feet, she whirled towards Vannor, suddenly grimly decisive. 'You go north, Vannor, if you will,' she said. 'My mother must be warned that the Archmage has turned traitor and renegade. We'll need her powers before this is done. Gather together any who'll support us as you go. I'm going south, to the hill forts, to raise an army. I swear to you that I'll never rest until Miathan has paid in full for his deeds tonight!'

'What!' Vannor sprang upright in turn, white and shaken. 'Aurian, will you break the Mages' Code for revenge? Don't you remember the bitter lessons of the Cataclysm? You can't unleash that horror again!'

The Mage met his gaze without flinching. 'I have no choice,' she said. 'Miathan has already broken the Code. Finbarr said those – things – were Nihilim, the Death-Wraiths, and that can only mean that he possesses the Cauldron of ancient legend, and has turned its power to evil. If we don't stop him, he'll eventually hold the very world in his hand.'

Vannor sat down abruptly. 'How could you hope to defeat him, when he holds such a powerful weapon?'

'I don't know,' Aurian admitted. 'But I have to try, or die in the attempt.'

There was no swaying her, and time was too short, danger too near, for argument. Anvar, afraid to his very soul, knew that he would have to accompany her. Who knew what the Mage might do in her grief? And she hardly seemed to be considering her unborn child. Someone had to take care of her, and it was the very least he could do, in atonement.

Having had some little time to reflect on what had passed, Anvar was consumed with guilt over his part in Forral's death. Had he paused to consider the consequences before rushing to seek the swordsman, Forral would still be alive, and so would Finbarr. And Miathan would not have unleashed the terror of the Wraiths. True, the babe would have perished, but hard though the choice was Anvar knew that Aurian would always have chosen her love. Just now, she had submerged her grief in the need to act, but eventually it would occur to her, as it had to him, who was truly responsible. He shuddered at what she might to do him then. But it would only be what he deserved. Anvar closed his eyes in grief. Was he doomed always to be the bane of those dearest to him? First his mother, then Sara – and now Forral and Aurian. He truly wished that he had died instead of the swordsman, and he was certain that Aurian would feel the same way.

Aurian and Vannor made their plans swiftly. Vannor would take his personal guards and try to locate Parric in the city, and gather support there to resist the Archmage. Anvar shuddered, marvelling at the merchant's courage. He was shamefully glad that he would not have to venture into those Wraith-infested streets. He and Aurian were to take Vannor's little boat, a light pleasure craft, and escape downriver to the port. The Mage had decided that the quickest way to reach the southern forts would be by sea, and Vannor provided her with gold to pay for their passage on a ship. Then the merchant made a request of

Aurian that snapped Anvar out of his introspection with a jolt. 'When you go, will you take Sara with you? She'd be safer in one of the southern forts than with me.'

Aurian frowned. 'Vannor, I can't,' she said bluntly. 'Though Forral – ' her voice trembled at the mention of his name, 'though he taught me a lot about adventuring, this will be the first such journey that I've made, and having Sara with me would endanger both us and herself. Truly, she'd be safer with you.'

'Aurian, please,' Vannor begged. 'I know she's not made for hardship, but she'll be in worse danger if she stays here.'

Aurian sighed. 'Very well, Vannor. I owe you that much, and more besides – but bear in mind that we won't be able to cosset her.'

Vannor's face brightened. 'Thank you, Lady,' he said. 'I'll have her brought here at once.'

Sara, on hearing what had passed, had hysterics. She rounded on Vannor like a fury, accusing him of all kinds of stupidity for becoming involved in the first place, for incurring the Archmage's wrath and ruining their lives. The merchant looked thoroughly ashamed of her behaviour, and Aurian's lip curled in disgust. Anvar stayed silent in the background, his heart pounding as he drank in her beauty once more. Though she was ignoring his presence, he had seen her face turn white at the sight of him, and was tortured anew by the memory of her repudiation the last time they had met. Yet had it stemmed from hatred of him – or fear of Vannor discovering the shameful secret of her past? It was plain from the scene before him that all the love in the marriage was on Vannor's side. When Sara addressed her husband, Anvar saw nothing but coldness and scorn. Her mother had said that Sara's father had sold her in marriage to Vannor. Had she been forced against her will? Was she a prisoner in these rich surroundings? It would explain her behaviour towards the merchant, whom Anvar knew to be a kind and decent man at heart. And if she hated Vannor, how would the girl react when she discovered that she would be travelling with her former lover, who had fathered a child on her and left her to face the consequences?

Vannor's explanation never got as far as including Anvar.

229

When the merchant managed to get a word in edgewise to tell Sara their plans, she refused point blank to go. 'Why should I?' she snapped, stamping her foot. 'I'm not wandering the world like a vagabond, with her.' She glared at Aurian. 'None of this is my fault – the Archmage can't blame me. I didn't choose to marry a fool – or an outlaw!'

Anvar saw the hurt on Vannor's face, saw Aurian curse and step forward, her hand upraised. He leapt forward, certain that the Mage was about to strike her, but Aurian simply laid her hand on Sara's head and said: 'Sleep!' Sara crumpled to the ground. 'Don't worry,' Aurian said, catching Vannor's worried glance as he knelt by his wife. 'It'll keep her out of mischief for a while. Send for someone to carry her down to the boat, Vannor. We've delayed too long already.'

'Is she all right?' the merchant asked.

'Of course she is. Better than she deserves to be,' Aurian replied irritably. 'She's only asleep. But I warn you, Vannor – the next time she starts carrying on like that, I really will hit her – with the greatest pleasure!'

The wind was rising, driving ragged tatters of cloud across the face of a sickly half-moon whose fitful, flickering light afforded glimpses of dark, bare branches tossing against the sky. Patches of unmelted snow still lingered on the wooden river banks by Vannor's little boathouse and the river ran swiftly, sending choppy waves lapping hungrily against the edge of the low wooden jetty. One of Vannor's guards held a shielded lantern aloft, and another pulled the small boat out of its shelter and held it steady while the merchant gently laid the sleeping, warmly wrapped form of his wife inside, pillowing her head on the pathetic bundles that contained their belongings.

Anvar shivered. He was wearing a cloak borrowed from Vannor, but between the chill of the night and the shock that had finally caught up with him, he was seized with an uncontrollable trembling. Aurian stood beside him, huddled miserably in Forral's old cloak, her face pale and set like stone. Only her indomitable will, he knew, was keeping her from collapse, and he feared for her.

Vannor looked long at Sara and kissed her in farewell, then turned to Aurian, catching her up in a rough hug. 'The gods go with you, Lady,' he said in a choked voice, tears running freely down his cheeks.

'And with you, dear Vannor.' Aurian's voice caught on a sob. She swallowed hard. 'Take care of yourself,' she said softly and, wiping her eyes, she drew her hood over her head and climbed down into the boat, careful of the sword that she now bore at her side. She thrust her staff, which she had reclaimed from Anvar, into her belt, and took told of the pole, ready to push off. Vannor came to Anvar and seized his hand in a warm grasp. 'Take care of them, lad,' he said. 'Take care of them both.'

Anvar nodded, speechless. He climbed aboard the frail little craft and took up the oars. Aurian pushed with the pole and the boat swung out into the current of the dark river. As they gathered speed, Vannor's form quickly dwindled, and passed out of sight.

15
Flight and Pursuit

Keeping close into the shadows of the bank, Aurian poled the boat swiftly downstream as Anvar laboured at the oars. Running with the current, they fled the horror behind them, skimming first past trees, then the finely tended gardens of merchants' mansions, then past more trees. Aurian gripped the pole tightly and put her back into the work, steeling herself against the heavy, burning pain of her grief; blind to the dark, choppy waters that swirled around them. Forral's face was all that she could see. Forral – left behind, but gone much further than that – gone for ever. She'd never see his beloved features again, alight with life and love. Never feel his arms around her, never . . . 'Stop that, you fool,' she muttered to herself through clenched teeth. 'Not now. Not yet.'

Anvar looked up, concern on his face. 'Lady, are you all right?'

'Shut up,' Aurian said tightly. 'Shut up and row.'

It was some twelve miles to the port of Norberth at the river's mouth, and they concentrated on covering the distance as quickly as possible; passing mills and villages, meadows and woods; aided by the swift current that was swollen by winter's melting snow. Aurian's muscles ached, her hands were blistered, and sweat stung her eyes. Once, Sara moaned and began to stir as Aurian's spell weakened. The Mage cursed. That should never have happened! What was wrong with her magic? Laying her pole down in the bottom of the boat, she squatted beside the girl. 'Sleep,' she commanded in a ringing voice, laying her hand on Sara's forehead. Sara relaxed once more, her eyes closed, her breathing slow and even, and Aurian sighed with relief. When she took her hand away, the girl's forehead was dark with blood. Anvar gasped.

'Don't worry, it's only mine,' Aurian said, looking ruefully at her raw and bleeding palms. She picked up the pole again, and went grimly back to work.

Time passed. Aurian could feel nothing, now, through the haze of pain and exhaustion that enveloped her. Surely they must be nearing their destination? This black, bitter night seemed to have gone on for ever. Suddenly, her long pole found no bottom, and she flailed wildly, unbalanced by the force of her thrust. As she fell, one hand hit hard wood and she clutched it with all her strength, losing her pole as she struck the icy water. It was deep here – too deep – and the force of the current plucked and buffeted at her numbing body as she clung, one-handed, to the stern of the boat. Already she could feel her grasp beginning to weaken, her fingers starting to slip on the wet wood . . .

In that moment, a curious peace came over Aurian – a strange, relaxed clarity of thought. All she had to do was let go, and she would be safe; out of reach of Miathan, who had betrayed her so bitterly, away from all this grief and strife. And Forral, dearest Forral, would be waiting . . .

'Hold on, Lady, I'm coming!' Anvar's voice was like a slap in the face. Strong fingers grasped her wrist, then her arm. Strong hands were hauling her back aboard the rocking boat. Aurian tried to protest, but she was too weak to fight. She slithered down in a shivering, sodden heap on the bottom boards.

'Lady, the weir!' Anvar's voice was shrill with panic above the river's roar. Aurian wiped water from her eyes. White foam streaked past on the dark water as the frail craft began to rock wildly, picking up speed. Anvar was struggling with the oars, blinded by flying spray, and even as she looked the left one slipped from his grasp, whirled greedily away by the rushing waters. Immediately the boat swung round, spinning violently and listing dangerously to one side, out of control. Aurian smiled. Forral, she thought, yearning. Only a moment more . . . Then, out of nowhere, she seemed to hear the swordsman's voice. *You'll want to follow me. Don't.* She looked at Anvar. He had just saved her life. No matter how deep her own despair, what right had she to take him with her?

Cursing bitterly, Aurian grabbed her staff. 'Get out of the way,' she yelled. She barged past Anvar into the bows, over the top of Sara, struggling to keep a grip on both her staff and the lurching boat. A glimmer of white stretched across the river ahead of her, desperately close. The roar grew to a booming thunder. Aurian placed her staff crosswise in her lap, across the bows of the boat, gripping it tightly in both hands, her knuckles clenched white around the polished wood as she concentrated with all her might. The calm sound of her chanting cut across the thunder of the weir. The staff began to glow, shimmering with a blue-white light that spread, like tiny fingers of lightning, to encompass the entire boat as it reached the edge of the weir and began to tip . . .

Aurian heard Anvar's grasp of fear – and then, as she made one last, wrenching effort, the boat straightened itself, floating serenely above the churning maelstrom, supported upon a surface of pure light. Gently they were borne forward, over the danger, then just as gently the little craft came to rest in a stretch of quiet water in the shallows beyond the force of the weir.

Aurian blinked, and collapsed panting across her staff, letting the darkness swallow her as the light of her magic was extinguished. She had bitten her lip, and her mouth was filled with the metallic taste of her own blood. Dimly, she felt Anvar pull her into his arms. Gently he pulled her soaked, tangled hair back from her face, and wiped the trickle of blood from her chin. 'Aurian? Lady?' His voice was anxious. With an effort she opened her eyes. 'Are you all right?' Anvar said.

'Tired.' That one word cost her an enormous effort. 'Get us there, Anvar.' Her voice seemed to be coming from far away. Had he heard her? But Anvar nodded. He settled her as best he could in the cramped space of the bows, pillowing her head on his wet cloak, and turned to pick up the single remaining oar. Gratefully, Aurian closed her eyes.

When she opened them again, buildings lined the river banks. They passed dwellings, warehouses and mills and then, rounding a curve, they swept beneath the great bridge that marked the boundary of the port of Norberth. A mighty arch of white stone, it sprang across the river that by now had grown broad and sluggish. Rippled reflections from the lights of the town covered the underside of the arch with an ever-changing network of dappled silver, and the river chuckled hollowly beneath the echoing stonework. Once the bridge was behind them, they passed quickly through the town itself and swept out into the pool of the port. The masts and rigging of sailing vessels webbed the sky, and Aurian wondered which of these ships would be the one to take her south. Anvar paddled a zigzag course towards a rotting and abandoned wharf on the south side of the harbour, and grabbed at the slimy pilings to pull the boat underneath the little pier, where its shadows would hide them.

Aurian dragged herself wearily upright and rummaged in one of the bundles that lay in the bottom of the boat, finding a little silver flask and a hastily wrapped package of meat, bread and cheese that was beginning to disintegrate from the soaking it had taken at the weir. She took a deep swig of Vannor's fierce liquor, feeling its heat course through her stiff, chilled body. She handed the flask to Anvar, who took it gratefully. In her Mage's night vision he looked grey and haggard, his eyes dark-circled with weariness, his blond hair dark and straggling from the river's spray. Aurian divided the sodden food between them and they ate in silence, both of them too tired to speak. The Mage felt better for eating, feeling the food restoring, temporarily she knew, a measure of the energy she had lost in using her power to save them from the weir.

The weir. Ah, she'd come so close then – so close to escaping all this. Suddenly Aurian was overwhelmed by her grief, by all her burdens; by the peril and the near-impossibility of the task she had set herself. She turned to Anvar, consumed with rage at his interference, and hit him as hard as she could, across the face. 'That's for saving my life!' she snapped. She saw surprise and hurt on his face, then his mouth tightened grimly as his hand lashed out to hit her back.

'And that's for saving mine!' he retorted. The sound of the slap echoed sharply across the water, and Aurian rocked backwards, one hand pressed to her stinging cheek, her eyes wide with shock.

Anvar looked away, shamefaced. 'Lady, I'm sorry,' he mumbled. Slowly, Aurian shook her head. How could she fault his response, that mirrored her own despair so exactly? For the first time she realized that she was not alone, that he shared her predicament, and her suffering. She held out her hand to him – a gesture between equals, between friends.

'I'm sorry too, Anvar,' she said softly. 'I had no right – it's just that I don't know how I'll ever find the strength to go on with this.' Her voice faltered, as the rigid control she had maintained all through the night began to crumble. Anvar took her proffered hand.

'Then we'll do it together,' he said, and gathered her into his arms as she began to sob, giving in at last to all her grief as she accepted the burden of continuing to live.

After a time she pulled away, wiping her face on her sleeve. 'That's a terrible habit,' Anvar said, with a crooked grin, and she managed a shaky smile in return.

'Someone forgot to pack the handkerchiefs,' she said.

'Disgraceful,' Anvar said. 'I'd beat your servant, if I were you.'

'Oh, he has his good points. At least he remembered to bring my proper clothes.' Aurian rummaged in the bottom of the boat, hauling her bundle out from beneath Sara's head. 'I'd better get moving and find us a ship. It'll be getting light all too soon, and I want us safely out of sight before too many people are up and moving about. Thank goodness the nights are so long just now.' As she spoke, she pulled her fighting clothes out of the pack, and began to strip off the soaked, tattered remnants of her green gown. Anvar averted his eyes politely, but Aurian was forced to enlist his aid in donning her warrior's gear, since the leather was damp from their encounter with the weir and her fingers were stiff with cold.

'Right,' she said briskly, when she was ready. 'I'll try to be as quick as I can.'

'Lady, surely you don't mean to go alone?'

'Can't be helped.' Aurian looked down at Sara's unconscious form with a frown. 'You'll have to stay here and keep an eye on her.' She grimaced. 'Gods, but she's going to be a nuisance.'

'Lady, I . . .' Anvar found himself flushing guiltily. How could he even begin to explain about Sara – about the love they had once shared?

Aurian looked at him quizzically. 'You do know her, don't you?' she said. 'That day, when they brought you to the garrison – when we first met – she was lying, wasn't she, when she said she'd never seen you before?'

Miserably, Anvar nodded, wondering how she would react when he told her that he and Vannor's wife had once been lovers. Luckily, Aurian spared him. 'More complications, eh?' she said ruefully. 'Well, you can tell me about it later, Anvar. I really must get going.' Fastening her damp cloak around her shoulders, she climbed carefully up the tangle of half-collapsed timbers that supported the old pier and vanished among the shadows of the wharf.

Anvar settled back into the bottom of the boat and lapsed into his own worried thoughts. Aurian's sudden briskness had not fooled him in the least. He knew how deeply she was grieving for Forral, and was concerned about the effect that it would have on her judgement. This whole plan of hers, to raise an army to defeat the Archmage, was pure insanity. But he had no better plan to offer – only to flee, as far as fast as possible. Well, they were doing that now, and perhaps in time she would come to her senses.

Anvar wondered where Vannor was. Had the merchant managed to escape? Suddenly, it occurred to him that if Vannor was killed, then Sara would be free . . . Guiltily, he stifled the thought. Vannor was a good man, Anvar knew. He wondered how the merchant would react to the knowledge that he had given his beloved wife into the hands of her one-time lover. Sara, he was sure, didn't care two pins for her doting husband, and Anvar wondered what she would do now that she was free from him. He looked down at her as she slept, her golden hair tumbled around her shoulders. She looked so fragile – so beautiful. With a pang, Anvar remembered the old days, when they were young and in love, happy with each other and confident in their future. Was there no hope that they could be that way again? Had he not a right to some happiness?

The light of a damp, grey day was growing by the time Aurian made her way back along the wharf, keeping close to the cover of the derelict warehouses. It had taken for ever to find a vessel whose captain would convey them, and his price had been extortionate – far more than the gold Vannor had given her. She'd given him all she had, and done some fast talking to convince him that the remainder would be waiting at the journey's end. As she returned to Anvar, the Mage worried about the company they would be keeping on board the rat-infested, leaky old ship. She had never in her life seen such a villainous-looking crew, but she knew she had no choice but to risk it. If Miathan was not already searching for them, he soon would be. By the time she reached the boat, Aurian felt faint with weariness, her mind fuzzy and slow. Anvar scrambled up, offering his hand to help her descend the slick, rotting timbers, and she was grateful for his steadying grasp. 'Come on,' she said, when they had reached the safety of the boat. 'I've bought us passage to Easthaven. We can travel overland from there.'

'What about Sara?'

'We don't have time to argue the issue. I'll take care of it.' Aurian snapped her fingers near the sleeping girl's face. 'Come,' she commanded. Sara's eyes flicked open, her expression utterly blank. She rose stiffly to her feet, and Anvar grabbed quickly at a piling to steady the rocking boat.

'We can't take her aboard like that!' he protested.

'We have to. Pull her hood down over her face and take her arm. You'll have to guide her.' Aurian's expression brooked no argument.

They had a dreadful struggle to get the girl up on to the pier, but after that she walked along quite naturally, steered by Anvar's guiding hand while Aurian carried the packs. The one or two early passers-by they met paid them little heed, and Anvar began to breathe more easily. But when Anvar saw the ship that was to take them he stopped dead, his face a picture of dismay. 'Oh, Lady, no,' he said. 'You can't possibly be serious.'

'Anvar, what do you want from me?' Aurian snapped, close to tears. 'Look at the state of us! We hardly look respectable, do we? Did you think any decent captain was going to take us? I did my best – and it's better than waiting here for Miathan to find us!'

To that, she knew, Anvar could have no answer. Shaking

238

his head, he led Sara up the narrow, slippery gangplank that led to the deck of the dilapidated little sailing ship.

Captain Jurdag had side whiskers and greasy ginger hair tied in a pigtail. Gold rings glinted in his ears, and his narrow face and feral expression reminded Aurian of a stoat. He bowed to her with leering mock courtesy, and the rest of the lounging crew – a shabby, scarred, pockmarked bunch – snickered. Aurian gave them a level, steely glare, and there was a sudden tense silence. 'Show us to our cabin, captain, and prepare to make sail,' she said coolly.

'Very well, *Lady*.' The captain turned the word into an insult, and Aurian, seeing Anvar's face flush with anger, gripped his arm tightly and shook her head.

They were shown into a tiny, filthy cabin in the stern of the ship, which the captain had obviously vacated for their use. Aurian picked up a pile of stinking unwashed clothes from the floor and handed them to him. 'Yours, I imagine,' she said. 'That will be all for now.' He left, scowling, and Aurian barred the door behind him with a sigh of relief. 'Dear gods!' she said. 'I'm sorry about this, Anvar.'

Anvar was struggling with the catch of a tiny salt-encrusted pane set in the stern wall. It was the only means of ventilation in the room. 'How long does it take to get to Easthaven?' he asked faintly.

'With good winds, about four days,' Aurian said gloomily. 'If we don't get our throats cut in the meantime.'

The Mage led Sara to the only bunk, and laid her down. 'Rest,' she said softly, and Sara's eyes closed again. 'There,' Aurian said wearily. 'She'll sleep naturally now, and wake when she's ready. Pray gods it won't be too soon.' Drawing Coronach, she sat down on the floor, resting her back against the bunk, and fell instantly asleep, her sword in her hand.

Aurian was rudely awakened by the sound of Sara's wails. 'I won't stay here, I won't! It's filthy and it stinks and it's infested with bugs! I want to go home! This is your fault, Anvar. If you hadn't . . .'

The Mage leapt to her feet, confronting the raging girl who was sitting on the bunk, her skirts drawn tightly around her ankles. 'Shut up!' she ordered sharply. Sara stopped short in

239

the midst of her tirade, glaring up at her. Aurian registered the rocking motion of the ship beneath her feet and, ignoring Sara, leaned past her to look out of the tiny stern port. 'There's the land, back here,' she said calmly, pointing out of the window. 'I suggest you start swimming now, before it gets any further away. I don't think you'll fit through the window, but I'm sure we can arrange to have you thrown over the side.'

Sara's face twisted with rage. 'I hate you!' she snapped.

'Hate away,' said Aurian evenly. 'It doesn't bother me. But just bear in mind that you don't have a home any more. This stinking, louse-ridden hole is all you have, and this is where you'll stay until we reach Easthaven.'

Sara's mouth fell open. 'You mean I'm a prisoner?' she shrieked. 'You can't do this! How dare you! When Vannor hears of this . . .'

'Vannor sent you with me for your own protection. Your safety is my responsibility, and I'm telling you that you won't leave this cabin for any reason. If anyone comes to the door, get into the bunk and cover yourself with the blanket – especially your face. Whatever happens you must not show yourself to any of the ship's crew. I've told the captain you're sick with the pox – that should keep them . . .'

'What?' Sara yelled, outraged.

'Lady,' Anvar protested, 'it isn't fair to . . .'

'Have you two ever seen a young woman raped by a gang of pirates?' Aurian's matter-of-fact tone brought the others up short. There was sudden fear in Sara's eyes. 'I haven't,' Aurian went on, 'and I don't want to see it now. This ship is crewed by the most villainous, vicious-looking gang of cutthroats I've ever set eyes on, and if they get one look at you, I won't be able to stop them, and neither will Anvar. I know it's hard on you, Sara. Anvar is right, it isn't fair, and I'm sorry. But do it my way, please – for all our sakes.'

Sara stared at her for a moment, then fell face down on the bunk and burst into tears. Anvar rushed to comfort her. Aurian glanced at him in surprise, then turned with a shrug and left the cabin.

The Mage sat with one leg tucked beneath her on the narrow bench that curved around the bows of the ship. So far, the crew seemed to be giving her a wide berth, although she often felt their eyes on her as she watched the hazy sun making its slow descent towards the dim horizon to her right. She was thinking back to the previous night, trying her best to sort the hard facts from the haze of anger, grief and fear that overlaid her memory of all that had happened. The child – that was one matter. Wonderingly, Aurian turned her thoughts inwards, to touch that dim spark of life – so tiny, yet, that she hadn't even known it existed. Try as she might, she was unable to stifle the resentment that flared within her. If it had not been for this child, Forral would still be alive . . . Yet now it was all that was left of him. It should be precious to her. And it had hardly asked to be brought into being. That was her fault, her own carelessness in letting Meiriel betray her. All the poor thing had was enemies – the Archmage would take its life as he had taken its father's . . .

How could she ever hope to defeat Miathan? Aurian shuddered. It had been all very well, in the heat of the moment, to swear that oath, and she meant to bring it home to him in any way she could – but how? The Archmage was mad, and renegade, and he possessed a weapon far beyond her capabilities. How powerful was the Cauldron? What was the point of raising an army against such power? Thousands of people would be killed to no purpose. But what had happened to the other lost artefacts of the High Magic? Ah. If she could only trace even one of them . . . But where could she start to look? They had been lost for centuries. Aurian's thoughts circled in hopeless frustration. This is too much for me, she thought. If only Forral were here . . .

As she thought of her love, his image suddenly came into her mind – not dead, as she had last seen him, but alive, and sitting, of all incongruous places, in the taproom of the Invisible Unicorn. He was leaning across the beer-stained table towards her, explaining something, and Aurian realized that she was remembering a conversation that they had had some time ago. 'If a problem seems too big,' he was saying, 'you'll never get anywhere by battering yourself against it. Break it up into steps, and deal with the first thing first. Then, more often than not, you'll find that the other steps will fall into place.'

It was good advice, and timely. Aurian smiled, remembering. 'Thank you, love,' she whispered, and the image seemed to smile in return as it faded from her mind. Aurian blinked at the ocean before her, and shook her head. Had it been a memory? A vision? Imagination? She had no idea, but it had left her feeling more at peace, and obscurely comforted. And her path was suddenly clear before her. Do the first thing first. Well, the first thing was to get this journey safely over – to escape from the pirates and the Archmage and get to the hill forts, where she could find some help and some measure of safety. And after that? Well, she would see.

Aurian whirled at the sound of soft footsteps behind her. Her sword was halfway out of its scabbard before she realized that it was Anvar, who stepped back, startled. She shrugged apologetically, and moved to make room for him on the bench. 'How is Sara?' she asked.

Anvar made a wry face. 'Still upset,' he said. 'Cursing Vannor, and you, and me, and just about everybody she can think of.'

Aurian sighed. 'As long as she curses inside the cabin, I'm not going to waste time worrying about it. We'll never get the wretched girl to realize that she's not the only person in the world with troubles.'

Anvar looked concerned at the reminder. 'How are you, Lady? I didn't like to leave you alone for so long, only she . . .'

'I'll survive. I suppose I'll have to, really.' Aurian tempered her grim words with a smile for him. 'And I didn't mind being alone, Anvar. The crew aren't bothing me – they seem to have some respect for this' – she patted the hilt of her sword – 'and I needed to do some thinking.'

'Lady, what are we going to do?'

'I don't know.' Aurian could see no point in lying to him. 'I wouldn't worry about it too much at the moment, Anvar. We have to get off this ship alive first. Let's just concentrate on that for now. I wonder what passes for food around here?'

What passed for food turned out to be a greasy, nauseating grey slop that went by the name of 'stew'. Sara, in particular, was far from impressed, and said so in no uncertain terms. 'I can't eat this!' she protested. 'It's disgusting! I'll be sick!'

'If you're going to be sick, be sure and do it out of the window,' Aurian said brutally, forcing another spoonful of the vile stuff down and trying not to think of dead rats. Sara retired to her bunk in offended silence, and soon the sound of sobbing could be heard coming from beneath the blanket.

'Lady,' Anvar whispered awkwardly, 'couldn't you be – well, more gentle with her? It's hard for her – she's not used to this . . .'

Aurian swore. 'Anvar, may I remind you that we aren't on a picnic? We're fleeing for our lives, and we have no time to cosset Sara. It's the same for all of us, you know. She'll just have to get used to it – and bloody quick!' Hurling her empty plate across the floor, she stormed out of the cabin, slamming the door behind her.

Anvar winced, wondering whether to follow her or not. After a moment's hesitation he went to comfort Sara. 'Sara, don't cry. She doesn't mean it. She's going through a great deal of suffering just now, what with Forral . . .'

'Shut up about her!' Sara sat up abruptly, hurling the blanket aside, her eyes wild in her flushed face. 'In fact, don't talk to me at all! You kidnapped me, you and her – just when I thought I'd never have to set eyes on you again.'

'Let's not start that again,' Anvar said wearily. 'Vannor begged us to take you. I don't think you understand the danger we were in. We had no other choice.'

'Vannor!' Sara spat. 'That beast! That imbecile! I despise him!'

'Sara, Vannor loves you.'

'What would you know about it? You told me that *you* loved me, once. And how did you prove your love? You got me pregnant, then abandoned me to be sold to that uncouth brute. So don't sit there and talk to me about love, Anvar.'

'That wasn't my fault!' Anvar thrust his left hand, the one that bore the hateful mark of the bondservant, in front of her face. 'Do you think I – '

'Anvar!' The cabin door banged open. Aurian stood there, her hair wild and tangled from the wind, her face white and strained. 'Anvar – the Archmage! He's searching for us! I think he knows where we've gone!'

'What?' Anvar leapt to his feet. 'How?'

The Mage closed the cabin door, and leaned back against it. 'He's scrying, probably with a crystal – that's the most powerful way. I had no idea that he could even do it. It was always Finbarr's special talent.' Her mouth twisted with pain at the memory of her dead friend, slain by the Archmage. 'He must have picked up our trail on the river, from the residue of the magic that I had to use to get us over the weir, and guessed the way we would take. He's searching the ocean now – I was up on deck and I felt his mind sweeping across.'

'Gods! Did he find us?'

Aurian shook her head. 'I managed to shield us in time. His power felt tentative; not too strong. I think this is new to him. But it won't take him long to learn, not with the power of the Cauldron to draw on. And he won't give up until he finds us.'

'What will he do?' Anvar felt sick with dread. 'Will he send those – things after us?' Seeing the stricken expression on Aurian's face, he cursed himself for reminding her of the monster that had killed Forral. But when she spoke, her voice was steady. 'No. I doubt it. He seemed to have very little control over the Nihilim, once he had unleashed them.' She shuddered. 'When I think of those abominations loose in Nexis . . . But I don't think they'll bother us. The gods only know what he will send after us, Anvar. He could strike at us in any number of ways. The only thing we can do is to stay hidden. I'll have to shield us all – the whole ship – constantly from now on.'

'But Lady, you can't!' Anvar was appalled, remembering how the effort of her magic had exhausted her on the river. 'We have at least three more days to go, and you're worn out already!'

'I know. But it can't be helped. We have to try, for our very lives, and I'll need your help.'

'Me?'

Aurian nodded. 'I'll have to stay awake. If I sleep, my shields will crumble, and leave us open to discovery. You've got to keep me awake, Anvar, and I'm afraid that means staying awake yourself. Talk to me, sing to me – if all else fails, hit me – but don't let me fall asleep, whatever you do, or we're lost. Promise me, Anvar.'

'I promise, Lady,' Anvar assured her. But I don't know how, he thought, dreading the long, gruelling vigil that lay before them.

16

A Rendezvous with Wolves

The day was darkening into evening as Eliseth swept un-
announced into the Archmage's tower room. Miathan was bent
with slit-eyed concentration over a crystal that lay on a black
cloth on the table. He looked up, dark eyes flashing, as the
Magewoman entered. 'For pity's sake, Eliseth, can you not
leave me in peace? Don't you know how difficult this is? If it
were not for Finbarr's notes . . .'

'Were it not for Finbarr, your blasted abominations would
have slaughtered us all by now!' Eliseth snapped. 'By the gods,
Miathan, why did you not tell us about this?' She gestured at
the Cauldron, which stood on the table. It was no longer a thing
of beauty; its finely wrought gold now black and tarnished.
'You of all people should know the dangers of tampering with
High Magic,' Eliseth went on. 'Bragar and I could have helped
you to research its powers and their mastery; but no – you had
to do it by yourself. And see what has happened! One Mage is
dead, one's missing, and one is a raving wreck. The gods only
know how many Mortals your creatures killed in the city last
night. The whole place is in an uproar.'

'*Enough!*' Miathan roared. He paced the room, breathing
deeply, striving not to lose control as he had done last night,
with such disastrous results. 'What is the situation in the city
now?'

'That's why I came – to report on your dirty work.' Eliseth sat
down, rubbing her eyes wearily. 'Bragar and I have been
combing the city, trying to seek out and immobilize your
creatures. The gods know whether we got them all – I doubt it,
myself. We've been spreading the tale that no one knows where
they came from, but the heroic Magefolk are risking life and
limb to defend the citizens of Nexis.' Her voice dripped scorn.
'They seem to be swallowing it – at least for the moment – so

this would be a good time to consolidate your hold on the city, while people are still terrified.'

'What of the garrison?' Miathan asked sharply. Eliseth shrugged. 'The troops are reeling from the tragic death of their beloved leader – I had his body dumped where you told me, and it didn't take them long to find it. They have their hands full keeping order just now, what with panic and looting and such, and there seems to be a distinct shortage of leaders. Maya, Forral's second in command, is away on some mysterious errand or other, no one knows where, and the cavalry master, Parric, seems to have disappeared. Deserted, probably, if he had any sense. There has been no sign of his body so far, at any rate.'

'Excellent.' Miathan rubbed his hands together. 'We may salvage this yet. Well done, Eliseth.'

'If we do, just remember who helped get you out of this mess,' Eliseth replied shortly. 'What shall we do with all your frozen Wraiths, Miathan? You have no idea how to get the wretched things back into the Cauldron, and we can hardly leave them all over the city.'

'Use an apport spell – it worked on the ones that were here.' Miathan gestured round the room, now empty of Wraiths. 'I have them stored down in Finbarr's archives for the present – what place more fitting?'

Eliseth frowned. 'Frankly, I dislike the idea of sitting on top of those things. We all know how to undo the preserving spell and bring them back into time again. You'd better be careful, Miathan.'

'I'm always careful.' Miathan's voice held a thinly veiled threat. 'I intend to have that section of the catacombs sealed, and only you, Bragar and I will know the whereabouts of the creatures. And I'm sure I can trust you – can't I?'

'Of course you can.' Eliseth swallowed uneasily. 'How is Meiriel, by the way?'

'Still out of her mind.' Miathan sighed. 'Finbarr's death affected her badly. I've wasted half the day persuading her that Aurian was responsible, and not myself. She's in such a vulnerable state right now that I succeeded in the end. Which, if Aurian can be located, may prove useful to us.'

247

'Is there any sign of Aurian?'

'No – but I shall find her, never fear. She escaped by river, that I do know. I found traces of her magic by the weir. I could not locate her in Norberth, so I've extended the search to the ocean. It would seem that Vannor has gone with her, unless you found any trace of him in the city.'

Eliseth shook her head. 'Miathan,' she ventured, 'should you not be concentrating on Nexis just now? This is a critical time for us, with Vannor gone and Forral dead.'

'No!' Miathan's eyes blazed with a mad light. 'I must find her, Eliseth. You know that she will not let Forral's death go unavenged. Besides, there is still the matter of that acccursed child! It must not be allowed to survive.'

'I'm sure you'll find her in that case. In the meantime, I can take care of things for you here. I must have help, though. Elewin says that most of the servants and guards are either dead or fled.'

'See to it, then.' Miathan, already turning back to his crystal, waved an absent gesture of dismissal.

'One more thing.' Eliseth hesitated. 'Must you send Davorshan away just now? The Magefolk are spread very thin and I could really use his help.'

The Archmage glanced up at her. 'Yes, as a matter of fact I must. He has to go to the Valley, Eliseth, for Eilin is the only remaining threat to us here. I intend to be rid of the Lady of the Lake – for good.'

Maya was limping as she climbed the wooded slope that bordered the rim of the moonlit Valley. She tugged at the reins of D'arvan's horse, which she was leading. It had been unbelievably bad luck, her own horse going lame that morning, after they had made such good time on their journey north. It was one more thing to cope with on top of the trouble she'd been having with D'arvan. Stopping for breath, she glanced worriedly back at the Mage, who sat limply on the horse, his delicately moulded face expressionless, his eyes blank.

Maya muttered a barrack-room curse. She wished he would snap out of it. He had almost scared her to death three nights ago, taking that strange, sudden fit. One minute they had been sitting quietly by their small campfire; the next, he had gone absolutely rigid, his face contorted, his eyes rolling back in his head until only the gelid whites were showing. He had screamed out something about Finbarr being dead, and monsters, and Miathan, before collapsing. Since then, he had been as impassive as stone. He could ride if she put him on the horse, eat if she put food into his mouth, and sleep, or so it seemed, if she closed his eyes and laid him down; but for all the response she'd been able to get from him, Maya might as well be lugging a corpse around. The thought sent a shiver through the warrior. She was truly fond of the young Mage, and had been trying hard not to dwell on the possibility that his condition might be permanent. Maya bit her lip. I hope I find Aurian's mother soon, she thought. Surely she will be able to help D'arvan?

Catching her breath, Maya trudged doggedly on towards the head of the slope. Whatever the trouble was, she hoped that the Lady Eilin would be able to sort it out, and let her get back to the city. She had a feeling that something was badly wrong, and her instincts, developed over a dozen years of soldiering, rarely let her down. She knew from Aurian that if a Mage died, all other Magefolk felt that death. Had D'arvan been reacting to Finbarr's passing? And what about the Archmage, and the monsters? If there was trouble in Nexis then Maya knew that her place was with her troops, and she was seething with frustration. Close as she and D'arvan had grown over the last months, she was ashamed to find herself wishing that she had never volunteered for the task of nursemaid.

Suddenly the Valley stretched below her, vast in the moonlight. Maya gasped. It was immense! What sort of destructive force could have caused this huge crater to be formed? She led the horse along the edge, seeking a safe way to descend the steep black walls. Then, to her horror, a blood-chilling sound shrilled through the forest behind her. The eerie song of many wolves, hunting. The horse threw up its head and reared, spilling D'arvan to the ground. Maya swore and hung on grimly to the reins, fighting the terrified beast. 'No you don't,' she muttered. 'I'm not losing you, too!' Somehow she got the reins wrapped round a sturdy tree limb, and tied them firmly. The horse plunged and screamed at the end of its tether as she ran back to where D'arvan lay. There was no sign of any injury – he seemed as unaffected by the fall as by anything else. She hauled his limp form over to the tree, propped him against the trunk, and straightened, panting. The howls grew nearer; turned shrill with excitement. They were on her trail! Greak Chathak, they were all around her!

Maya considered letting the horse go, hoping it would lure them away from her, but decided to save that as a last resort. She still had to get D'arvan across the Valley, and she would never manage it on her own. Stooping, she scrabbled together a small pile of twigs and dead leaves for tinder and struck a spark, feeding her fire with the larger dead boughs that lay beneath the tree. Wolves feared fire. Drawing her sword, she thrust it point down in the earth in front of her, ready to her hand. Then, unslinging her bow from her shoulder, Maya nocked an arrow and stood at bay beside D'arvan, her back against the tree.

Like a shadowy tide, the wolves surged through the trees, yelping triumphantly. Then they saw the fire. The grey wave broke; hesitated. One wolf stepped out into the firelight, a huge, silver beast whose eyes flared green-gold in the glow of the flames. Maya pulled back the bowstring to its full tension, aimed, and – 'Wait!'

'What the . . . !' Maya jumped, and the arrow went wide. Bloody D'arvan! Why had he chosen that split second to wake up? Feverishly she groped in her quiver for another shaft.

'Maya, wait!' D'arvan's voice was urgent now. 'It's all right. I can talk to him. He won't hurt us.'

Maya set the arrow to her string, then hesitated, staring at the wolf in utter disbelief. It sat on its haunches, its mouth gaping in a wide grin, its tongue lolling from the side of its mouth, for all the world like that friendly hound that cadged scraps at the door of the garrison kitchen. The rest of the pack sat in similar postures, or lay, relaxed, on the ground. Maya did not move. 'D'arvan,' she said quietly, through gritted teeth, 'would you mind telling me what the blazes is going on?'

The young Mage struggled to sit up. 'They guard the

Valley,' he said. 'Eilin set them to watch after – after what happened the other night.'

'What did happen the other night, D'arvan?'

D'arvan grimaced with pain. 'Finbarr . . .' He shook his head, his eyes veiled and haunted. He was spared having to answer by the sound of hooves that first sounded ringingly on rock, then softer on the loam of the forest floor. Maya tightened her bowstring, and the wolves leapt to their feet.

A white horse sprang forth between the trees, bearing the cloaked figure of a wild-haired woman. The staff in her hand blazed with unearthly green light. The tip of Maya's arrow burst into incandescent flame, and the warrior dropped it hastily, cursing.

'Who are you?' The woman's voice was tense.

Maya took a deep breath, and forced herself to stay very still. 'Maya, Lieutenant from the Nexis garrison, and friend to the Lady Aurian. I bear a message from her to her mother, the Lady Eilin.' Slowly, she reached inside her tunic for the tightly rolled scroll and bowed as she held it out to the Lady. One of the wolves padded forward and took the scroll in its mouth. It walked softly across to Eilin, and delivered its burden into her hand. By the light of her staff, Eilin examined it, and nodded. 'That is her seal,' she said softly. Breaking the seal, she unrolled the sheet, quickly scanning its contents.

'Are you D'arvan?' The Lady turned to the young Mage, who scrambled to his feet and bowed. 'Yes, Lady Eilin.'

'Stay there!' Eilin's voice cracked across the clearing, and the big wolf gave a low, warning growl. 'How do I know that I can trust you?' the Lady said. 'After what happened the other night?'

'Will somebody please tell me what happened the other night?' Maya interrupted.

Eilin glanced at her sharply. 'You mean you don't know?'

'My fault, Lady,' D'arvan said. 'Finbarr's death shocked me so badly . . .' He shrugged. 'I knew nothing after that, until I awakened and saw the wolves.'

'As well for you that you woke up then,' Eilin said drily. 'Aurian says in her message that your powers never surfaced. How is it, then, that you can speak with my wolves?'

'I don't know,' D'arvan confessed. 'I never tried to communicate with animals before. I didn't know I could.'

'Well, there may be hope for you yet,' Eilin said. 'That is, if you are telling me the truth. Will you be tested?'

D'arvan nodded, and stepped forward, his expression strained. The Lady held out her glowing staff, and he reached out his hand to grasp the iron-shod heel. The green glow flared into a dazzling aureole that consumed the body of the young Mage, and D'arvan gasped, falling to his knees. Through the scintillating glare, Maya saw sweat break out on his forehead, and stepped forward, an involuntary cry escaping her lips; but the big wolf barred her way, and others advanced to circle her. Then it was over. The Magelight died away, leaving only the flickering flames of Maya's little fire, as D'arvan relinquished his hold on the staff with a sigh of relief, his shoulders slumping.

Eilin smiled. 'Bravely done, young Mage,' she said. 'The Test of Truth is not a pleasant experience, or an easy one.' She turned to Maya. 'My apologies, Lieutenant Maya, for suspecting you both. But grave times are upon us – the gravest the world has faced since the Cataclysm.'

'Lady, what has happened? Maya begged. 'If there's trouble in Nexis, I should go back at once.'

Eilin shook her head. 'No, child. It would be a grave mistake to rush back to Nexis, unrested and uninformed as you are. In fact, it would probably be pointless for you to return at all. Be patient a little longer. Come home with me, and I will tell you what I know, ill news though it is, then we can decide what to do for the best.'

'Very well, Lady.' Maya curbed her impatience, forced to accept the sense of this. The Lady Eilin took D'arvan up on her own horse, and Maya carefully buried the remains of her fire and, mounting the other skittish beast, followed in their wake. The wolves remained behind, on guard.

The warm red glow of the stove in Eilin's kitchen dispelled the chill of the wintry night outside. The Lady soon had them seated in comfort, eating bread and cheese and cradling cups of fragrant, steaming tea. As the Mage sat down with her own cup,

Maya leaned forward, desperate for news. Eilin opened her mouth as if to begin, then paused, with a little shrug of helplessness. 'I'm sorry,' she said. 'I haven't spoken to anyone for so long; one gets out of the habit.' She sighed. 'Still, it must be done.' She closed her eyes, remembering. Maya wanted to shriek with frustration, but held her tongue, schooling herself to patience.

'I generally go to bed with the sun,' Eilin said at last. 'Three nights ago, I awakened suddenly – I thought I heard Aurian calling me. Calling for help. She sounded so desperate – I knew it was not a dream. I could hear nothing more, but I was afraid to my very soul. I got out of bed and sought my crystal. It's been years since I last attempted scrying – what need had I to look out at the world outside? As long as I had the occasional visit from Aurian I knew she was all right. But that night I looked, and I saw . . .' Her voice cracked, her hands whitening in their tight grasp round the cup.

'What did you see?' Maya pressed. 'Lady, please – '

Eilin drew a long, shuddering breath. 'Abominations,' she said. 'Creatures of horror beyond all imagining. The Archmage has tampered with an ancient artefact from the past. Out of legend, out of history, he has unleashed the Death-Wraiths of the Cauldron.'

Maya knew little of such matters, but beside her she saw the shock on D'arvan's face, and the look of dread that he and Eilin exchanged.

'There was more,' the Lady went on, her eyes shadowed with grief. 'Maya, I'm sorry to have to tell you this. The Archmage set one of those hideous creatures on Forral. I saw him fall, and saw him die.'

'No,' Maya whispered. The world stood still around her. 'Oh, Lady, no.' As a warrior, she had thought herself inured to the loss of comrades in battle, but now she felt her throat tighten with unshed tears. Not Forral! She had never known a better man. Not only was he her commander, but he had also become her close friend over the last few months, as had Aurian. Poor Aurian! Maya caught her breath. 'What of Aurian?' she gasped.

'Alive. Finbarr came in time to save her. Somehow he found

253

a way to disable those monstrosities, and two men – Mortal men – got her away.' Eilin's voice was strained. 'I have no idea what happened to her afterwards. They fled, I suppose. She lives, I'm certain, but I cannot find her. I lost my link when poor Finbarr died. The Wraiths were too many for him. He fell in the end, and D'arvan must have felt his death as all we Magefolk did.'

'Yes,' D'arvan whispered. 'I felt his passing. Dear gods, Lady, what are we to do? How could Miathan be capable of such an act?'

'Miathan was always capable of far more than most people gave him credit for.' Eilin's eyes hardened. 'I had no proof that he had a hand in Geraint's death, but I had my suspicions. That was one of the reasons why I fled to this place when Aurian was a baby. But as the years passed, I persuaded myself that it was a foolish fancy, born of grief, and that was why I permitted my daughter to go to the Academy when she was older. Folly! I should have trusted my instincts. But I wish I knew why the Archmage has so suddenly turned to this new evil. D'arvan, you were at the Academy. Can you shed any light on this matter?'

'Not really, Lady, though Miathan has been acting oddly of late. What he did to me – he and my brother . . .' D'arvan told her his story, and Eilin frowned.

'Ridiculous!' she said. 'Of course you have power, he should know that.' Then she paused. 'Ah, but does he?' she murmured. 'D'arvan, did your mother ever tell you about your father?'

The young Mage blinked, puzzled. 'Tell me what, Lady? They both passed when I was very young – about the time that Miathan became Archmage – but I can remember my father quite well. Bavordran was a Water-Mage; clever, yes, but not special in any way. What should she have to tell me about him?'

Eilin seemed lost in thought for a moment, then she straightened, her expression suddenly decisive. 'Perhaps I am the only one who does know,' she muttered to herself. 'Perhaps Adrina chose to confide only in me.' She looked straight at D'arvan. 'Prepare yourself for a shock, young Mage,' she said. 'Davorshan is not your twin, and only half your brother.

Bavordran was his father, but yours . . . well, that is quite a different matter.'

The cup fell from D'arvan's hands and splintered on the floor without his even noticing. 'What do you mean?' he gasped. 'It can't be true! How can it?'

'Oh, we Magewomen can manage these things if we must,' Eilin said. 'Having conceived you, Adrina was quick to see that Bavordran had a son of his own, to allay his suspicions. You were brought into being within mere days of one another, and it was fairly simple for her to arrange for you to be born at the same time – as well as her Earth-magic, she had a singular healing gift.' She shrugged. 'It was a bold move on her part. From the very start people wondered why the two of you looked so different.'

'But . . .' D'arvan floundered, as though the words were choking him. 'Then – who is my father?'

Eilin smiled. 'Hellorin, the Forest Lord.'

'Lady, that is not amusing!' Maya had never heard D'arvan sound so angry. 'How dare you mock me with such a jest! The Lord of the Phaerie, indeed! What nonsense! They have no existence outside legends and children's stories!'

Eilin gave him a stern look. 'Lad, do you think I'd jest over such a thing? You are completely mistaken, as are most folk. The Phaerie do indeed exist, and have existed far longer than either Mortals or Magefolk. They have their own powers, different from ours, and if they use them to remain apart from us I cannot blame them. Your mother never told me how she met and fell in love with Hellorin, though it was no secret in the Academy that she and Bavordran bore little love for one another. She only agreed to become his soulmate at the insistence of Zandar, her father, the Archmage before Miathan. He was concerned that the Magefolk were dying out, and Bavordran was the only available mate.' Eilin sighed. 'Well, she joined with him in the end, out of love and respect for her father, but she gained no happiness from it. Bavordran was the dullest, most self-centred Mage I've ever met, and he made her life a misery in a thousand ways. As Adrina's friend, I'm glad she found love, however briefly, with her Phaerie Lord. And you

255

were the result, D'arvan. Your brother was her child of duty, but you were the child of her heart.'

D'arvan shuddered. 'But Lady,' he cried despairingly, 'what does that make me?'

'Unique!' Eilin replied briskly. 'In my opinion, D'arvan, you are by no means inferior to the rest of the Magefolk. Aurian believes you may have a talent for Earth-magic, and your being able to speak with my wolves would seem to confirm that. We'll soon see how far you can develop in that direction. As for any abilities you may have inherited from your father's side – well, I scarcely know where to begin. The powers of the Phaerie are far beyond the experience of any Mage. Let us concentrate first on what I can teach you, then I suggest you go and ask Hellorin.'

'What?' D'arvan gasped.

'I don't see why not,' Eilin replied. 'I know that the Phaerie are close to us in this valley. They approve of my work here – bringing back the trees and such. If his own son were to call him, then surely their Lord would answer. But . . .' She held up a warning hand. 'I beg you not to rush into such a meeting, D'arvan. The Phaerie have a reputation for being tricky folk, and I don't want to risk losing you to them just now. Miathan must be opposed, and with Aurian missing and Finbarr dead that only leaves you and me. I wouldn't trust the rest of them as far as I could spit.'

'But Lady, what can we possibly do against the Archmage?' D'arvan said.

'Just now, I have no idea. I think we may have to wait and see what happens. Anyway, I'm tired, you're tired, and you have had far too many shocks in one night to be able to think straight. And poor Maya looks as though she could fall asleep at any second.' Eilin gave the warrior a kindly smile. 'I suggest we all go to bed for what's left of the night, and make our plans in the morning.'

No one argued. Too many shocks indeed, Maya thought, as Eilin showed her to the little room off the kitchen that had once been occupied by Forral. D'arvan had been given Aurian's old room. The painful reminders of her two lost friends made Maya realize that there was one piece of news she had not imparted to the Lady. 'Lady Eilin,' she said abruptly, unable to think of a gentle way to break the news. 'Did you know that Aurian and Forral were lovers?'

'Lovers?' For a terrifying moment Eilin's eyes blazed into her own, then the Magewoman dropped her face into her hands. 'Dear gods,' she whispered. 'Why did I never foresee it? There was always such a depth of love between them – but how could they have been so foolish?' She turned to Maya, her eyes dim with pain. 'Well, they cannot be blamed for the Archmage turning to evil, but now we know what made him act when he did. Miathan, being so obsessed with the purity of our race, would take such a joining ill indeed.' She shook her head. 'My poor child,' she murmured. 'My poor, poor children.' As Eilin mounted the tower stairs, Maya heard the soft sound of her weeping.

In the dead of night – the dark, oppressive time when it seemed that dawn would never come – Maya left her room to sit by the embers of the kitchen stove. Weary though she was, she had finally given up trying to sleep. Her thoughts were filled with sorrow for Forral, who seemed so close to her in the room that had once been his; with fear for Aurian, now a fugitive. Gods, how she must be grieving! Maya also worried about her city, in the grip of an evil madman, and her troops, who would be bearing the brunt of the disaster. Between grief and worry, she was finding it impossible to think clearly. The more she tried, the worse it became. What's wrong with me? she thought despairingly. I'm a bloody soldier. I'm trained to deal with emergencies! There must be something I can do! But whatever it was, it eluded her. Never before had she felt so alone – or so utterly, wretchedly helpless.

The sound of a door opening made her reach for her sword – but the intruder was only D'arvan, coming out of his room. He looked haggard and haunted. 'You too?' Maya said ruefully, suddenly glad of the company.

D'arvan glared at her. 'How could I possibly sleep, after what I've been told tonight?' he snapped.

'How indeed? I can't sleep after what *I've* been told, and you've had it far worse than me.' The self-pity in the Mage's voice had served as a salutary reminder to Maya of just how close she had come to sinking into that same trap herself. 'Want some tea?' she offered.

'No! I want this not to be! I want to wake up and find myself in my bed in the Academy, with everything safe and normal – and none of this ever to have happened!' He sank to the floor beside Maya's chair and leaned his head against the arm. Though he was trying to conceal it from her, she could feel him shaking with sobs. Maya stroked his fine, pale hair. 'Me too, pet,' she murmured sadly, 'me too.'

D'arvan looked up at her quickly, dragging a hand across his eyes. 'Gods, how you must despise me!' he choked.

Maya was taken aback. 'Whatever for?' she said.

'Because I'm good for nothing. I'm a useless coward – I can only weep like a maid and make a nuisance of myself. But you're a warrior – you're brave – I know how brave you are. You would never shame yourself by giving way like this.'

Maya chuckled. 'Little do you know. Less than an hour ago I was lying next door bawling my heart out!'

D'arvan's eyes went wide. 'Truly?'

'Of course, daftie. We've had terrible news – treachery heaped on tragedy – and you've had some shocks to cope with on top of that. This is the best time for us to give way to our feelings – here, where we're safe for the moment. It's never wrong to need – or take – comfort, D'arvan. That's something we both need right now.' As she spoke, Maya slipped to the floor beside the young Mage and put her arms around him. He turned his face away.

'How can you bear to touch me?' he muttered. 'You don't know what I am.'

'Balls! I know exactly what you are – I've known for months. You're shy and good-hearted, you like music and flowers, and you have the most amazing aptitude for archery I've ever seen. I couldn't believe it when you tried my bow that first day at the garrison, then told me you'd never handled one before. So that's one thing you're good at, for a start. You can talk to wolves, and the Lady Eilin thinks you'll be fine at Earth-magic – and who knows what talents you might have inherited from your father? I know what you are, D'arvan. You're very special indeed.'

It started with her simply comforting him. As she spoke, Maya felt D'arvan relax, and gradually his arms crept around her. Rather to her surprise, that comforted her, and she found her mind turning to just how attractive she had been beginning to find him lately. Stop! her commonsense warned her. This is folly. You know what happened to Aurian and Forral. But Maya didn't care. She had no delusions about their plight, and suddenly it seemed to her that this might be the last chance, for both of them. 'Do you know,' she murmured to D'arvan, 'you have the most beautiful face I've ever seen?' And she kissed him.

The Mage froze, his lips unresponsive against her own, then suddenly he tore himself away. 'No!' he gasped. 'I can't!'

Feeling unutterably foolish, Maya tried to make light of the situation, wondering how she could manage a dignified escape. 'That bad, eh?' she said with a shrug.

D'arvan's face went crimson. 'Maya, no! I mean – don't think . . . It wasn't you . . .'

'Well, that's a comfort, anyway.' Her attempts to rescue him from his floundering seemed to be making matters worse. He turned his face away, refusing to meet her eyes.

'I'm sorry,' he muttered. 'I can't. I mean, I've never . . . Oh, curse it, I don't even know where to start!'

Maya smiled. 'If you want,' she said softly, 'I would consider it both an honour and a pleasure to teach you.'

He was clumsy at first – clumsy and awkward and painfully shy. But Maya was patient. Gently, unhurriedly, she encouraged and instructed him, and the look of wonder on D'arvan's face first at his own pleasure and later when she taught him to pleasure her, was more than reward enough. Seeing his glowing expression as the dawn light crept through the window of his room, Maya was flooded with a feeling of tenderness so intense that it took her breath away. Selective though she'd been about her lovers in the past, never had any of them evoked such a feeling within her. She reached out to touch his face. 'There,' she told him. 'Now we've found something else you're good at.'

D'arvan blushed, but his eyes gleamed with delight. 'Oh,

Maya. I never dreamed . . . Maya – you won't go back to the city, will you? I won't be parted from you now.'

Maya's brows knotted in a frown as she realized how badly she had complicated matters. 'D'arvan,' she said gently, 'the time will come when we'll have to fight. You know that, don't you?'

To Maya's surprise, the Mage met her eyes with a clear, steady gaze. 'I know – and I'm ready for it,' he said. 'It's difficult to explain, but after my – after Davorshan betrayed me, it was as though I had no reason for existing. I felt empty, like a shadow. But now it's different.' He smiled. 'For the first time in my life I feel like my own, whole self, and now I have something to fight for. All I ask is that, whatever form the battle takes, we face it together. And if you really feel that you must return to Nexis, my magic can wait. I can still shoot a bow, you know. I've had the best possible teacher – in all things.'

Maya was stunned by his words. At last she found her voice. 'I can think of a hundred reasons why I should go back,' she said. 'But somehow . . . Well, maybe it would be best if I stayed for a while. The Lady Eilin seems to think that my returning to Nexis would serve no purpose, though I do feel guilty about leaving my post. But I don't want to leave you either, dear heart. Perhaps, together, we could work out some way of combining our talents against the Archmage – depending, of course, on whether Eilin will approve this arrangement. She'll probably be horrified, and throw me out of the Valley at once.'

'In that case,' D'arvan said firmly, with a new, joyous ring to his voice, 'she can throw us both out together.'

They were asleep when Eilin found them in the morning, curled together on the rumpled bed like two cats. D'arvan's skin was very white where his arms encircled Maya's brown, wiry body, and he was smiling as he slept. The warrior's long dark hair, loosed from its braid, fell across them both like a cloak. The Lady stared at them in silence for a long moment, her brows creased in a frown. 'Not again,' she sighed, then shrugged helplessly and cast her eyes heavenwards. 'Oh, gods,' she murmured. 'Why do you keep doing this? Now I have three of them to worry about.'

17
Shipwreck

The lantern rocked on its ceiling hook with the motion of the ship, its dim circle of light swinging back and forth across the wooden floor and walls with hypnotic regularity. Aurian sat bolt upright, cross-legged, in the centre of the tiny cabin, holding her shield in place to conceal the vessel from the force of Miathan's seeking will. Occasionally she felt the pressure of his mind brush across her shield, and held her breath until he had passed on, away over the dark waves. Yet time and again, despite the peril, despite the fact that she had chosen her position so that she could not fall asleep without falling over and wakening herself, Aurian felt her leaden eyelids beginning to close.

This was the second night of her vigil. She had passed the first night successfully by drawing deep on the hidden wellsprings of her magical power to keep herself awake and her shield firm; and she and Anvar had spent most of the intervening day on deck in the bracing sea air, until the looks and mutterings of the increasingly restive pirate crew had driven them back to the cabin. Sara was still scorning to speak to them, and had remained huddled in sour misery on her bunk, so at least there had been peace from that quarter. By unspoken consent, they had avoided speaking of Anvar's connection with Vannor's wife, though Aurian still wondered. Now she had insisted that Anvar sleep for a time, while she could still be confident of staying awake, and he dozed beside her, stirring restlessly as though he also felt the power of Miathan's seeking mind that passed and repassed across them. Aurian was reluctant to awaken him, but eventually, when her leaden eyelids refused to stay open any longer, she knew that she must. 'Anvar,' she whispered, prodding him awake. 'Anvar, I need your help.'

'All right.' He sounded bleary and dazed, and Aurian wondered if she looked as bad as he did: dishevelled and dirty, his face drawn and grey with weariness. He passed the water flask to her before drinking himself. 'Is he still out there?' he whispered.

Aurian nodded. 'It's best we don't speak of him when he's seeking for us,' she warned. 'When I talk, it weakens my concentration on shielding, so we should choose subjects as far as possible from the things we're trying to escape.'

Anvar groaned. 'It's impossible not to think of him,' he said. 'What can we talk about, then, Lady?'

Aurian shrugged. 'The weather?' she suggested ruefully. 'That should occupy us for all of two minutes.'

'Let's pretend we're going far away – to another place entirely,' Anvar suggested. 'That might confuse him, if anything should leak through your shields. You know, Lady, I can't help but feel that I would like to go away – far, far away from all this trouble. Do you know anything about the southern lands beyond the sea?'

Aurian did, having picked up the information from Forral, who in his younger days had been a secret gatherer of intelligence in the south. (It was just such a mission, in fact, which had kept him away from home for so long at the time of Geraint's death.) The garrison tried to stay informed, because the belligerent southern races were always a potential threat. Glad of the distraction, the Mage was only too willing to tell Anvar what she knew.

The bleak hills of the south coast ended at the ocean that divided the northern landmass from the vast Southern Kingdoms beyond. There was little congress or communication between the two continents, though spies, if they returned at all, had testified to the belligerence and superior numbers of the warlike inhabitants of the larger continent. Luckily, the southerners feared the powers of the Magefolk, and so far that had been enough to keep them at bay.

It was known that there were at least three kingdoms in the south, though beyond that, where the deserts gave way to impenetrable jungle, all was mystery. A range of high mountains near the northern coast were said to be inhabited by the legendary Winged Folk, who guarded their peaktop eyries with savage determination. Between the mountains and the sea, where the peaks dropped down to green, pine-clad valleys, was the kingdom of the Xandim. Trapped between mountains and ocean, their space was limited, and it was said that they coveted the northern lands with their rich pastures for the fabulous horses that they bred. South of the mountains was a desert, beyond which lay the country of the Khazalim: a fierce warrior race ruled by a savage tyrant king. With such neighbours across the sea, it was not surprising that the ruling council of Nexis kept the bleak hills of their southern coastline well defended.

'I wonder if the southerners really are as dangerous as all that?' Anvar mused.

'It's said that they bear no love for my sort,' Aurian said, 'so it would be as well if I didn't try to find out. But I know what you mean. I would like to visit new lands – to try to leave the past behind. But for me that's impossible, though you might do it some day.'

'Me?' Anvar's eyes went involuntarily to the bondmark on his hand. 'But I'm only a servant. I couldn't expect – '

'Nonsense!' Aurian retorted. 'Because you're a servant? Why should you be inferior, because of the work you do? Why, you're a far better man than some of the Magefolk. If I were Archmage, I would . . . Oh!' Aurian felt sick with dismay as she realized what she had done. 'Oh, Anvar, I had the chance, didn't I? I could have changed things for the better . . .'

'You never thought of that?' Anvar asked in surprise.

'It never crossed my mind. I didn't care about that kind of power. Like a fool, I never considered the good I could have done. I threw it all away, when I took Forral as my lover. Gods, it was me who brought this disaster down on us. Forral even warned me . . .' Aurian buried her face in her shaking hands.

Anvar, alarmed by her bitter self-recrimination and afraid that in her distracted mood she would drop her shield and bring discovery on them, reached out and pulled her hands away from her face. 'Lady,' he said firmly, 'don't blame yourself. The Archmage is evil – the Mortals in Nexis have always hated and feared him. He would have grasped power in the end, whatever you had done, and the results would likely have been the same. You would have fought him – you and Commander Forral, and Vannor and Finbarr. People would have died in any case. Thank the gods that you're alive to fight him now. Don't give in like this, Lady – we need you. We all need you.'

For a moment hope dawned on Aurian's face, then she sighed. 'Kind words, Anvar, but if Forral and I hadn't . . .'

Anvar gripped her shoulders. 'Don't say that, Lady. Don't ever say that! What happened between you and the commander was inevitable. Any fool could see how much you loved each other, and if the Archmage had cared about you, he would have rejoiced for you. Can you tell me honestly that you, or Forral for that matter, would have had it any other way?'

'No,' Aurian confessed after a long moment. 'You're right, Anvar. At least we had what we had, but . . .'

'Then stop feeling sorry for yourself and get that bloody shield back up!' Anvar snapped. The Mage recoiled as though he had struck her, anger flaring in her eyes. Then suddenly she began to laugh – a low chuckle that accompanied the relaxing of the tension in her face and shoulders.

'Ah, Anvar, you're good for me,' she said. 'If anyone can get me through this, you can. I'm glad you're here.'

Somehow they made it through the night, each keeping the other awake when they began to falter. Using Aurian's dagger to scratch on the floorboards, they played all the childhood games of words and wits that they could remember. When it became too much of an effort to concentrate, they told jokes instead, and sung their way (softly, so as not to awaken Sara) through all the old songs and ballads they knew. But they were always aware of Miathan's restless will, ceaselessly combing the oceans in search of them.

By the time the dawn light was creeping through the tiny stern port, Aurian's eyes felt gritty, and her voice was scratchy and hoarse. She stopped singing, and Anvar followed her example. He rubbed his eyes and stretched, yawning hugely. 'Thank the gods it's getting light,' he said. 'I know we still have a long time to go, but it feels as though we've passed another hurdle, at least. You know, in spite of everything, I enjoyed last night.' He seemed shy and hesitant, unsure of his right to say such a thing.

Aurian smiled. 'So did I. You make a good companion, Anvar.'

'You too, Lady,' Anvar said. 'I wish I had seen that sooner, instead of being so preoccupied with resenting my position as a servant . . .'

'You two are up early!'

Aurian spun round, startled, to see Sara scowling from the bunk. 'We've been up all night,' she snapped, nettled by Sara's tone. 'Since you're awake, let Anvar have the bunk,' she added. 'He needs to sleep. I'll walk around on deck for a while – it might wake me up a bit.'

'That's not fair!' Anvar protested. 'I slept last night . . .'

'Anvar, we have at least two nights to go,' Aurian said gently, warmed by his concern. 'I can't count on you to keep me awake if you're dropping from exhaustion. If you get some rest now, we might manage.' She fished in the pack that Vannor had given them, and brought out a small packet. 'Before you do, could you get the dreadful cook to make me some taillin? It might help keep me going.' Then in the act of handing it over, she stopped. 'Would you look at me?' she said ruefully. 'After all I said about being companions, I've still got you running around after me. I'll go myself, Anvar. You get some sleep.'

'No.' Anvar took the packet from her hand. 'I'll get it. If you're staying awake, it's the least I can do.'

Sara looked sourly after him as he went out. 'Ever the devoted servant,' she sneered. 'That's all he's good for.'

'What do you mean by that?' Aurian was furious.

Sara shrugged. 'Ask Anvar,' was all that she would say.

Aurian rubbed a hand over her face. I can't cope with this just now, she thought. 'Sara, don't make trouble,' she warned. 'If you can't treat Anvar decently, just leave him alone.' With that, she left the cabin, unable to spend another minute in Sara's company.

The Mage sat in the bows, drinking taillin and watching the rose-gold glow of sunrise flood the ocean. It was some time since she had felt Miathan's presence, and she wondered if he was asleep, or perhaps occupied in ordering a city that must

266

have gone mad with panic when his creatures had attacked. She wondered what was happening in Nexis, then thrust the thought firmly from her mind. She couldn't be certain that the Archmage had given up, and she dared not relax her vigilance. In order to keep awake, she got to her feet and began to walk back and forth across the narrow, pitching deck, ignoring the curious stares of the few crew members who were up and about at this early hour.

After a time, the wind freshened enough to make pacing impossible on the lurching deck, and Aurian went below to the cramped, greasy galley to coax another unpalatable meal from the ship's cook. The smell that assailed her as she climbed down through the narrow hatchway was disgustingly familiar. Not stew again! Aurian felt her stomach heave. Gritting her teeth against the surge of nausea, she shot back up the ladder and rushed to be sick over the side, too wretched to care about the sniggers from the ill assorted crew. When it was over, she sat limply on her bench in the bows, drinking cold taillin straight from the jug and blotting her damp brow on her sleeve. Gods, she thought, that wasn't seasickness! For the first time, the problems of being pregnant while on the run truly came home to her. She touched her belly, where the tiny scrap of life lay, snug, and uncaring, and sighed.

'Lady, wake up!'

Aurian jumped at the sound of Anvar's voice, catching up her fallen shield in panic. Horrified, she cursed her own carelessness and weakness. If Miathan had found them . . . She shuddered. 'What a fool I am!' she said. 'I'm sorry, Anvar. How long have I slept?'

Anvar squinted at the sun. 'Most of the morning, it looks like. Don't worry, Lady, it was for the best. The Archmage hasn't found us, and you needed the rest. In your condition . . .' He stopped, blushing.

'I know,' Aurian said ruefully. 'First the little pest made me throw up, then it made me sleep. At this rate, it's going to be more of a nuisance than Sara.'

'Lady, you don't mean that,' Anvar chided.

Aurian sighed. 'I suppose not,' she admitted. 'Even though it is true.'

She shared the last of the taillin with Anvar, and they breakfasted on iron-hard slabs of biscuit that he'd coaxed from the cook. The Mage felt better for the sleep. Her nausea had gone, and she was cheered by the sparkling day. The green waves danced in the stiff following wind that bowed the canvas of the old patched sails. The pale sun beamed, playing tag with mountainous bluffs of cloud that raced like driven sheep across the sky. The brisk wind was refreshing, blowing away the last cobwebs of sleep. When they had finished the daunting task of chewing their way through the meal, Anvar pulled a little wooden flute from his pocket. 'Would you like me to play for you?' he asked.

'That would be lovely.'

So Anvar played – funny, lively little tunes of his own devising, to go with the brisk, bright day. His music soon attracted the crew, who began to find excuses to lurk within earshot of the merry pipe. Aurian was amazed to see their faces break into smiles as they clapped their hands and stamped in time to the music. Soon they were teaching Anvar shanties and hornpipes, and dancing with wild abandon to the tunes. When the captain came to berate his men for leaving their posts, he too was caught up in the festive spirit. Casting an eye over the perfect weather, he ordered that a cask of rough spirits be broached.

It was due to the drink that things got out of hand. Since Aurian and Anvar needed to stay alert, they did not join in the drinking. Anvar had left his seat in the bows to be nearer the dancers, and Aurian was watching them, keeping her concentration firmly on her shield. Suddenly an arm went round her shoulders, and there was a blast of foul breath in her face. A tin cup brimming with liquor was thrust in front of her. 'Have a drink, darlin',' a slurred voice said. Aurian turned to look into the leering, unshaven face of a filthy pirate.

'No, thank you,' she said, trying to keep matters in hand.

'I said, have a drink!' Grabbing her hair, he forced the cup to her mouth with his other hand, spilling the sticky stuff down her chin and the front of her shirt. Because of the concentration involved in keeping up her shield, Aurian was slow to react. Before she could move, Anvar was there. He jerked the man to his feet and punched him squarely in the face, sending him crashing on to the deck. There was a chill glint in his eye, a set to his jaw that Aurian had never seen before.

'Keep your hands off her,' he growled.

The cutthroat scrambled up, a wicked-looking curved dagger in his hand. Aurian's heart sank. She got quietly to her feet, her hand on her sword hilt.

'Why should you have two, an' us have none?' the pirate snarled. 'Well, I'll have 'em both – once I've gutted you!' Anvar stepped back, drawing his own weapon: a pathetically in-adequate belt knife that Vannor had given him. The pirates crowded round like wolves closing in on their prey.

The tension was broken by a slithering hiss as Aurian drew her sword. She stepped up beside Anvar, her voice calm and level. 'You'd better stop them, captain, if you want to continue this voyage with a crew.'

'Bollocks, lads – 'tis only a maid,' the brigand with the dagger roared, and charged. Aurian's blade flicked through the air so quickly that it hardly seemed to move, and the curved dagger flew over the side and into the ocean as its owner collapsed, howling, on the deck, clutching his knife hand.

The Mage pointed the tip of her sword at the hapless pirate. 'The next time you try that,' she said into the dumbfounded silence, 'it won't be your hand. It'll be those bollocks you were mentioning. Yours or anyone else's who dares to interfere with me.' She locked eyes with the captain, who hesitated, glaring. 'Do you want to live to spend the gold I gave you?' Aurian asked.

Cursing, he spat on the deck. 'Get below, boys, and leave the passengers alone. Their gold'll buy you plenty of whores in port.' Muttering darkly, the crew dispersed, Aurian's bleeding attacker being dragged away by his comrades.

To Anvar's amazement, Aurian turned to the captain with a smile. 'Thank you, Captain Jurdag,' she said. 'I'm most grateful to you. You've spared us a lot of unpleasantness.' Anvar gaped at her, staggered by her dissembling, and even more astonished to see it working.

'No trouble, Lady,' the captain said, though he looked rather tight-lipped. 'If you and the gentleman have any problems with the crew, I'll be glad to deal with them. I'm sure you needn't carry such ironmongery about.' His voice held an unmistakable threat.

'I wouldn't be without it,' Aurian assured him, a similar edge to her own voice. 'It's much too useful.'

The captain stared at her, then at Anvar. 'Gods' blood!' he said. 'You're a brave man to take her on!'

Anvar started. So the captain thought they were a couple? Well, it wouldn't do any harm. Bluffing for all he was worth, he put a nonchalant arm around Aurian's shoulders. 'Oh, I think I can handle her,' he said coolly. Giving them a dark look, the captain went below.

'Why, you – ' Aurian turned on Anvar, all indignation, but there was laughter dancing in her eyes. 'So you can handle me, eh?'

'Lady, I wouldn't dare try,' Anvar confessed ruefully. 'I certainly gave a poor account of myself today. I never thought about that animal having a knife. When I saw him maul you, I just wanted to smash his teeth down his throat. And don't say you could have done that yourself – I know. I wanted the pleasure of doing it, that's all.'

Aurian smiled. 'I don't mind, Anvar. It was a true act of chivalry, and I'm grateful. But if you're going to make a habit of it, beware of hidden weapons. I don't want to lose you too.' Her smile gone, her eyes suddenly shadowed with sadness, she turned abruptly and walked away to the opposite rail of the ship. Anvar cursed under his breath, wishing that everything didn't remind her of Forral; wishing he could do something to ease her sorrow.

Aurian stood with her hands locked round the rail, gazing across the endless ocean. Were there other lands across that vast expanse? Why had no one gone to look, and if they had, what had become of them? She found herself wishing that she could go – that she and Forral could have gone together. She remembered the time they had talked about his death. *I'll always be with you*, he had said. Aurian felt a prickling in the nape of the neck. Could it be true? She had never managed to master his odd, circling flick of the blade – and yet today, when

270

she had needed to disarm the pirate, it had come to her as naturally as breathing. Could it be true, that he was still with her? But if it were, surely she should be able to feel something – feel his presence? She shook her head, confused; unwilling to let her heart fool her into accepting a lie, just because she needed it so badly. And yet . . .

Anvar came to stand beside her, not speaking, the breeze ruffling the tawny curls at the nape of his neck. 'Is Miathan still up to his tricks?' he asked at last, and Aurian knew that he was as anxious as she to break the mood that had fallen between them.

'I haven't felt him for several hours now, luckily for us,' she said. 'I suppose he has to rest some time – it's hard work, scrying. I daren't relax my guard again, though.'

Anvar was about to reply, but Aurian grasped his arm, forestalling him, turning towards a new, strange sound that caught her attention. It came from out at sea – wild, high swirls of song that sent thrills through her body, rooting her to the spot in rapt attention. 'Listen,' she breathed, clutching at his arm. 'Oh, listen! Can't you hear it?'

Anvar peered out to sea, trying to find the source of the haunting sounds. 'What is it?' he asked her. 'Why – they're singing!'

They waited, listening intently as the sounds gradually drew nearer. Then, far out across the waves, a series of immense dark shapes erupted from the water; leaping high, twisting in the air and falling back into the sea amid fountaining walls of white foam. Feathery white plumes shot skyward, twice as high as a man, filling the sunlit air with rainbows. 'Whales!' Aurian exclaimed. 'Forral told me about them. Oh, Anvar, how beautiful!'

She gripped the rail tightly in her excitement. As the creatures drew nearer, she saw that they were indeed immense, the largest of them longer than the ship. They numbered about half a dozen, including, to her delight, two babies. The Mage gazed at them, lost in wonder, admiring the huge, streamlined bodies that moved with delicate grace through the water; the perfect arching curves of the tail flukes which beat the surface with exuberant power as they dived. She noticed the tender

271

care that the giant family showed for the two babies, warding and watching them always.

She was so enthralled that she forgot the shield. And as it fell away, unnoticed, the first thoughts touched her mind. Thoughts as great and deep as the ocean itself. Thoughts of surprise and curiosity, full of deepest love, boundless joy, and endless sorrow. She, Aurian, was the first of her people in aeons to communicate with the People of the Sea. People who made no wars, who did no violence; who spent their days playing and singing songs, making love and caring for their children, thinking their deep, wise, gentle, thoughts. And their wisdom! The Mortals and Magefolk who squabbled and scurried across the face of the earth gave themselves neither time nor peace to develop their minds, to become one with the oneness of all things. But the race of Leviathan carried in their mighty brains the wisdom of the universe – these beings that mankind called animals. And with that wisdom came love.

Aurian never saw the lookout awaken from his rum-fogged sleep, never heard his cry of: 'Whales! Whales ho!' She only came back to herself when the crew came tumbling out on to the deck, falling over each other in their haste to lower the long, sharp-nosed wooden boat that hung from the side of the ship. Her joy turned to horror as she saw them reaching for the wicked harpoons with their steel barbs.

'No!' she cried, reaching for her sword, desperate to stop them. Then Anvar was in her way, blocking her path, grabbing her by the shoulders. 'Lady, don't!' he said. 'It means gold to them – lots of gold. They wouldn't hesitate to kill you over this!'

Aurian struggled with him, reluctant, despite her desperation, to hurt him. 'Get out of my way,' she cried, 'I've got to stop them.'

'You'll have to kill me first.' Anvar's voice was quiet, but his eyes met hers without flinching. 'I'm not letting you destroy us all over this, Aurian.'

It was too late. The boat had been lowered. The men were climbing in. Eight strong rowers, four on each side, and a man in the bows, clutching a harpoon. Aurian glared at Anvar. 'Damn you!' she spat. 'Run!' she screamed at the whales, projecting the thought with all the force of her mind. 'Run, oh,

272

run!' The whales, discovering the danger, turned and fled, diving for safety beneath the surface. But the boat was swift, the oarsmen propelling it through the water with mighty strokes. And the whales had to surface to breathe. Aurian was holding her own breath. The captain and the three remaining crew members worked frantically, trimming the sails to follow the flight of the stricken creatures as closely as they could.

For a moment Aurian thought the whales would escape. Then she saw the smallest baby, left behind, exhausted. It swam feebly on the surface, uttering plaintive cries for help as the boat closed rapidly. The man in the bows raised his arm, clutching the harpoon, another ready in his left hand. Why? Then Aurian saw what he had already seen, the whale-child's mother, racing frantically back to her stricken baby, as he had known she would. The harpoonist pulled his arm back for the cast . . .

Aurian cried out, raising her hand in a sharp gesture, and the boat disintegrated, every plank flying apart from its neighbour, pitching the floundering men into the sea.

'Bring her round!' Jurdag bellowed. 'Get some ropes!'

In the confusion, the mother whale, joined now by her mate, managed to round up her lost child. Helping the baby along, one on either side, they followed the rest of their family to the safety of the open sea, their cries of gratitude ringing in Aurian's mind as she relaxed, weak with relief, against the rail – and felt the triumphant grasp of Miathan's mind as he located her through the use of her magic.

'Get out!' she screamed silently, striking back with all the force she could muster. She felt his pain and shock, felt his clutch slip away, and slammed her shield back into place. But she knew, with a sinking heart, that it was too late. She had betrayed them. He knew where they were, and he would be back.

Then Anvar was upon her, his face rigid with fury. 'You did that! Don't you know that sailors can't swim? You've probably drowned them all. And what if they realize they've got a bloody Mage on board? How could you be so stupid – and so callous?'

It was more than Aurian could take. 'How dare you question my deeds?' she snarled.

273

Anvar's lip curled. 'Ah,' he said bitterly. 'Now it comes out. How dare I, a mere servant, criticize one of the great and lordly Magefolk! All that talk about being companions. Pah!' He spat contemptuously on to the deck. 'When it comes down to it, *Lady*, you're no less arrogant and despicable than the rest of them.' Shouldering her roughly aside, he stormed back into the cabin, slamming the door behind him.

Sara was startled by the violence of his entrance. 'That Mage,' she heard him mutter. 'That bloody bitch!' She stifled a smile of triumph. So he had quarrelled with Aurian. In the long hours spent in this dingy hole, she had done some hard thinking. She knew that she was very much alone; cut off, possibly for ever, from the luxuries of her former life. It was unlikely that she'd see that ass Vannor again, so she was going to need someone to take care of her, and at the minute Anvar was her only option. At least she had always been able to twist him round her little finger. The problem had lain in getting him away from that red-haired harpy. But now here he was, upset and off-balance. Easy. 'Why, Anvar,' she said, 'whatever has happened?'

He told her, at great length, pacing back and forth in the cramped confines of the cabin. Sara could make little sense of it all, but that didn't matter. 'I can't believe it,' he kept saying, shaking his head in baffled dismay. 'I just can't believe it of her.'

'Who knows what the Magefolk are capable of?' Sara said insinuatingly. 'They've never had our interests at heart. What does it matter, anyway? You're free of them now, don't you see? Free of her. What can she do about it? When we dock at Easthaven, we can do what we like; go where we want. We could be together . . .'

'Sara?' Anvar turned to her, stunned. Did she mean it? Could it possibly be true, that she still loved him after all? The few feet of space between them was a gulf of years, of hurt, of heartache, but Sara seemed to fly over the intervening gap, and at long last her small, slight form was in his arms once more. As he turned her face to him, the lamplight glowed on her fine-spun hair and her eyes glistened with tears.

'Thank goodness,' she whispered. 'Thank goodness I've found you at last.'

Anvar could hardly believe it. Were all his dreams finally coming true?

'I was so afraid,' Sara went on. 'But you've been so brave. You've been wonderful.' Breathlessly she hurried on without giving him a chance of speak. 'Oh, Anvar, I've missed you so much!'

At last Anvar found his voice. 'But I thought you hated me, Sara. After what you said . . .'

She sighed. 'Anvar, I was deeply hurt. I – I hardly knew what I was doing. Forgive me, please. You're the only man I've ever loved . . .' Her tears overflowed, spilling down her flawless face.

Anvar crushed her to his breast, wanting never to let her go, his heart soaring. 'Sara, my love, don't cry. That's all over now. We'll do whatever you say; anything you want. We'll go away, and be together . . .'

Sara smiled. Then, putting her arms around his neck, she kissed him, long and deep, with all the lost passion of their youth. For a moment Anvar was completely taken aback, but her kiss awakened all the frustrated longing he had kept buried in his heart. His arms tightened around her as he returned her kisses with increasing urgency and fervour. His heart began to pound, and he found himself going rigid with excitement as he fumbled at the fastenings of her bodice to touch her breasts, her . . .

'What is this?' Aurian stood in the doorway, her voice stern, her expression thundrous. 'Is this how you repay Vannor for his love?'

Sara gave a little cry of fear, her hands fumbling at the open neck of her dress.

Anvar put himself between the two women. 'You mind your own business,' he told the Mage flatly. 'Sara and I were lovers once, and parted through no fault of our own – I was sold into slavery to you, and she was sold into slavery of another kind. We've suffered enough, and now we're going to take what's due to us. Don't you try to interfere.'

'Not interfere!' Aurian cried. 'By the gods, Anvar, how could you sink so low? Another man's wife – a good man, who trusted you!'

'Don't you lecture me!' Anvar yelled, beside himself with rage at the insidious guilt her words had raised. 'You – you murderess!'

Aurian stared at him, her mouth open, her face white and blank with shock. Then she whirled, and was gone. Sara smiled a smug little smile.

Everything was quiet on deck. Not a soul was about, except the captain at the helm and the solitary lookout perched high on the mainmast. The rest of the crew were below, greatly subdued by the loss of two of their comrades in the accident that afternoon. One of the dead had been the harpoonist, and Aurian could not bring herself to be sorry for his loss. She went quickly to her accustomed place in the bows, her mind reeling from the shock of what she had just witnessed, and the venom of Anvar's attack.

'Murderess!' The accusation rang in her ears. How could he possibly understand? He thought of the Leviathan as animals. He'd be quick enough to act to save a human child. And Anvar had not been trained as a warrior, as she had. People needed warriors to do their killing, so that they could keep their own consciences clear, and lay the blame at someone else's door.

Forral had understood. He had told her once: 'It's a dirty job, when you come down to it. They use you to wade through the blood and muck and corpses, while your friends get slaughtered around you. They use you to deal with the people who stand in their way so that they don't risk their flabby bodies and snow-white consciences; and then, if you have the gall to survive – to be there afterwards as a living reminder – they turn on you and cry "atrocity"!'

'Then why do we do it?' she asked him.

He had smiled. 'Think of the people at the garrison,' he had said. 'There's nothing like the comradeship that warriors share. And do you remember the fight we had, the day we first made love? If you remember how that felt, then you know.' And she had known.

Gods, how she missed Forral! How she wanted him. She had nothing now; her heart was filled with a bleak, aching void.

How could she live with this pain for the rest of her life? She saw the keg of spirits that had been left behind, forgotten, on deck. An empty tin cup was rolling round in the scuppers by her feet. A voice at the back of her mind warned of danger, of the need to be alert, but she ignored it. What does it matter? She thought dully. I've made a total mess of everything anyway. Picking up the cup, she went to fill it. It was poor comfort, but it might help to dull the pain for a while.

They had made love. When the Mage had left, Sara had seized Anvar with savage ferocity, pulling him down with her on the bunk and tearing at his clothes. It had been so long . . . How could he resist? Like animals, they had taken each other in the sordid cabin, mindless in their lust. Now it was over, Anvar felt drained and guilty, and somehow used. The old, sweet innocence of their love had vanished. Then he chided himself for his folly. He and Sara loved each other, and now, at last, she was his again. What did anything matter in comparison to that? He rolled over to take her in his arms. Perhaps this time it would be better . . .

'Not now.' Sara's words were like a slap in the face.

'Why not?' Anvar exclaimed in injured tones, and reached for her again.

Sara slapped his hands away, then favoured him with a smile. 'There'll be time for that later,' she said, 'when we're off this rotten ship. But now you must go and make sure that the Mage is staying awake.'

'What? She won't want to see me now, after what I said to her.' Anvar felt a pang of guilt.

'Who cares what she wants.' Sara's voice was hard. 'The important thing is that we survive this journey. Don't you see, the Archmage isn't after *us*. Once we dock, we can be free of her, and him, for ever.'

Not to see Aurian again? Somehow, Anvar could not imagine it. But Sara was right, he supposed. After tonight, the Mage would never want to see him again anyway. Everything had changed so suddenly . . . But Sara was right. The main consideration was that the Archmage should not find them yet. Sighing, he rummaged on the floor for his clothes, and dressed hastily. Sara gave him a farewell peck on the cheek, sending him on his way.

Anvar crossed the deck, feeling a dreadful reluctance to face the Mage. But all such thoughts fled from his mind when he saw her asleep in the bows with her head on the ship's rail and a half-empty cup of liquor by her side. Traces of tears glistened on her face. A chill ran down Anvar's spine, a sudden feeling that danger lurked very close. He leaned over to awaken her, shaking her shoulder.

It happened with unbelievable speed. Aurian was on her feet, her hands fastened in a crushing grip around his throat – and the eyes that blazed into his were not her own! Anvar fought for breath, clawing in panic at the choking fingers. Aurian's mouth opened, her face contorting into a horrible parody of itself, and his blood froze as Miathan's voice issued from her snarling lips. '*Anvar! I should have known. I should have ended your miserable life long ago. And how fitting it is that I use her hands to slay you!*'

The grip around Anvar's throat tightened. At the last instant, while he still could, he screamed, 'Aurian, no!' He couldn't take another breath. His lungs burned; his vision was darkening. Then suddenly the hands released him, and he was pushed violently away to fall on the deck, wheezing as he tried to suck air down his bruised throat. From a distance he heard a voice. Oh, mercy, it was Aurian, calling his name. As his vision cleared, he saw her face above him in the dim light. Her own face, frowning. She looked very shaken. 'Are you all right?' she said.

He nodded, and let her help him up on to the bench. His throat felt crushed. He reached for the cup of rum, and took a painful swallow. 'Are you?' he whispered hoarsely.

'I am now.' She sounded very grim.

'Lady, what happened?' he asked her. 'Can you remember?'

Aurian looked away from him, speaking in terse, emotionless tones. 'I fell asleep. And suddenly I wasn't in my body any more. I was somewhere else, all grey and misty, not in this world at all.'

'Is that possible?' Anvar gasped.

'Of course it's possible!' the Mage snapped. For all her

278

efforts at control, she was shaking. 'Miathan – he had taken me there. He was holding me somehow, and I couldn't move; couldn't get back. I tried to fight, but I couldn't do anything. Then I heard your voice, and it seemed to break his concentration. I fought him then, all right!' She shook her head. 'But I shouldn't have won – not on ground of his choosing. It seemed as though he wasn't using all his power . . .'

'Probably because he was occupying your body at the same time,' Anvar suggested.

'So that's why I was trying to kill you!' Aurian cried. 'Oh, gods – the thought of him inside my mind – using my body – ' She turned away, retching violently. Anvar offered her the cup of spirits, but she waved it away.

'How did you get back?' he asked her, in the hope that it might distract her from the horror.

'I don't know – there was a kind of jolt, and I found myself with my hands around your throat.'

'Where is he now?' Anvar felt a sudden stab of alarm.

Aurian frowned. 'I don't know, and I don't like it. He – '

A huge wave crashed up over the bows, drenching them both in shockingly cold water. Gasping, Aurian pulled her streaming hair out of her eyes and looked up, aghast. Black, boiling clouds streamed across the sky, blotting out the stars with unbelievable speed. A mighty gust of wind tore at the sails and the masts creaked dangerously as the ship heeled over at an alarming angle. The lookout fell with a shriek from the tilted mast and vanished among the churning waves. Another wave swept over the deck as the bows dipped into a deep trough. Aurian and Anvar found themselves in a tangled heap in the scuppers, knocked there by the wall of water. The crew came racing up from below. 'What the blazes is going on?' Jurdag yelled. 'No storm comes up that fast!'

The strength of the gale was increasing, and with it the height of the waves that tore at the little ship. Once again she heeled dangerously, and Aurian clutched at Anvar as a torrent of water crashed over the side. 'Cut it loose!' Jurdag was screaming, and the Mage looked up at the panic in his voice. The soaking mainsail had jammed in place, and the wind was

279

pushing it inexorably over, threatening to capsize the ship. Two men scrambled up the rigging to do his bidding, but the next mountainous wave washed them away. The mast dipped alarmingly once more, the heavy sail almost going under.

Aurian knew she must act swiftly. Rising to her feet she made a scrambling dash for the foremast, clinging to it for dear life as the deck pitched and lurched beneath her. Biting her lip, she tried to focus on the straining sail, but it was impossible to concentrate on her magic and keep her hold on the mast. She looked round for Anvar. 'Anchor me,' she yelled above the shrieking storm. 'Hold me!' In a moment he was at her side, putting one arm around the mast and bracing himself against the tilting deck while holding her firmly round the waist with the other arm.

'Now!' Aurian lifted her hands, and with a sound like a thunderclap the sail split up the middle, ripping apart from top to bottom. Immediately the ship began to straighten as the canvas wound itself round the mast in a tangle of ropes. The captain stood gaping for a moment, then began to order the remaining crew to cut away the wreckage and reef the foresail. Even with a single slip of canvas on the foremast, the ship ran hideously fast before the storm.

Anvar put his mouth close to Aurian's ear. 'It's bad,' he shouted. 'We'd better get Sara.' Holding firmly to each other and whatever else happened to come to hand, they staggered and crawled across the wave-swept deck, in constant danger of being swept away by the solid sheets of water that threatened to swamp the ship. It seemed a lifetime before they reached the sanctuary of the cabin.

The door was blocked by a tangle of flotsam, washed across the deck by the invading sea. Aurian cursed and raised her hands again. 'Protect your eyes!' she yelled at Anvar. Shards and splinters flew as she blasted the mass away. Anvar wrenched the door open and they rushed inside, a swirl of icy water at their heels.

Sara screamed and scrambled on to the bunk as the flood rushed across the cabin floor. Anvar, fighting the force of the water, struggled to close the door without success until Aurian also put her shoulder to it. Between them they forced it shut, preventing any more of the ocean from entering. Aurian, gasping for breath, looked ruefully down at the dirty sludge that lapped around her boots. 'Well,' she said, 'at least the floor's had its first good wash in ages.' She ducked across the room for her staff, and thrust it securely into her belt. 'Let's go,' she said tersely. 'We can't be caught in here if the ship goes down.'

'Lady, surely this must blow itself out?' There was a tacit plea in Anvar's voice.

Aurian shook her head. 'No, Anvar. This storm is Eliseth's doing, and it won't end until she runs out of strength, which won't be for some time – or until the ship is sunk. Miathan wants us dead.'

Sara gave a frightened little cry, and burst into tears. Anvar looked at the Mage, grey-faced. 'Lady, I can't swim,' he said.

Aurian stared at him, bracing herself against the heaving floor. 'What do you mean, you can't swim?' she said.

'I can't. Sara can – she had to, living beside the river – but my father always kept me too busy to learn.'

Aurian smacked an exasperated palm against her forehead. 'As if we hadn't problems enough!' she said. 'Stay by me. I'll try to help you, but to be honest, Anvar, you'll only be out of this mess a little quicker than the rest of us. Nobody could survive a sea like this.' She felt bitter, and wretched, and utterly defeated.

A volley of thunder overhead made them jump, and a vivid flare of lightning brightened the window. There was a rending crack overhead, followed by a crash that shook the entire ship. The lamp went out, plunging them into darkness. Aurian was thrown abruptly foward, falling with Anvar and Sara in a tangle of bruised limbs. She scrambled to her feet, clinging to the bunk to keep her footing, and formed a ball of Magelight. The floor was canted at a steep angle towards the bows. Aurian swore. Anvar was still hampered by Sara, and the Mage pulled her away to let him rise. 'Hurry,' she yelled. 'We've got to get out!'

When they reached the deck, utter chaos met their eyes. The mainmast had been struck by lightning. Catching fire, it had snapped halfway down, falling into the rigging of the foremast, which had collapsed in turn, pulling with it a splintered area of the deck, and smashing the bows on the starboard side. It protruded across the water, unbalancing the ship and causing her to to swing broadside to the battering waves that were already beginning to break her up. The sea was flooding in across the shattered bows. The captain was still clinging desperately to the wheel – a futile gesture, since the rudder was out of the water.

The ship was going under. As they stood, paralysed by the sight before them, she began to turn over. The deck was slanting too steeply – they were falling! Aurian felt Anvar grab her shoulder then lose his grip as she plummeted into the icy sea; felt the current trying to draw her down with the foundered ship. The water closed over her head in a froth of bubbles, and she struck out desperately, trying to get clear of the danger. But the pull was too strong. She held her breath as she was sucked beneath the waves, and then Miathan was back. She felt the grasp of his will, like icy claws sinking deep into her mind.

It was too much. When she was so close to drowning, when she needed all her resources to survive, he was there again. Aurian felt rage building within her like a crimson tide. She remembered Finbarr's brave stand; remembered Forral, brutally slain by the Archmage's vile creatures. Miathan had deprived him of a decent warrior's death. Unthinking in her blind fury, she opened her mouth to curse him aloud. Salt water seared her throat; flooded burning into her lungs. Well, she'd do her best to take him with her. With a wrench she broke from his grasp, ripping her consciousness free of her body and arrowing her will back to Nexis. He was there, hunched like a spider over his crystal. Aurian entered the crystal and, gathering all the force of her Fire-magic, she launched a bolt of energy straight at his eyes. Miathan shrieked – a horrible, tearing sound – and clasped his hands over his face. Smoke leaked between his fingers as he reeled away, blinded.

Not enough. Damn this weakness! As her dying body pulled her back, Aurian tasted bitter failure. He still lived, she knew. There was only one comfort to cling to with the last shreds of consciousness as she was sucked back into the agony of her body. She had blinded him – destroyed his eyes irrevocably. That's for Forral, you bastard, she thought. Then the darkness took her.

18
Leviathan

She was swimming. What the blazes was going on? This couldn't be death – not another dark, freezing ocean. Some inner sense of time told Aurian that only a few seconds had passed since she'd lost consciousness – in fact, it was little longer than that since she had fallen into the sea. Then, to her utter astonishment, she realized that she was breathing easily. Breathing underwater! Aurian laughed out loud, the sound muffled and distorted as her lungs forced water through her mouth. So the legends were true, that you couldn't drown a Mage. Her body must have made the change instinctively, adapting her lungs to deal with the new medium. I'll wager Miathan doesn't know about this, she thought triumphantly. He'll think I'm dead, and I've given him too much to worry about for him to suspect otherwise. Gods, I hope he's in agony.

Then she remembered Anvar and Sara. Their lungs would not adapt. They would be drowning. Heading back to the mass of floating wreckage from the stricken ship, she dived, trying to ignore the insidious thought that it would probably be useless. But she had promised Vannor that she would take care of Sara, and it was herself who had brought Anvar to this fate. She had to try. But it was impossible to see anything beneath the dark waves. Even her Mage's night vision could not penetrate the murk. She wished she could be like the whales, with their ability to sense shapes in the blackest depths . . . Of course! Beneath the water, she sang; a song she had only learned today but seemed to have known all her life. She called the Leviathans in her mind, begging for their aid. And, to her relief, they answered.

They were with her in an amazingly short time, combing the wreckage-strewn waters to find what she sought. One of them was soon beside her, his immense bulk dwarfing her as she swam. She recognized his thought-patterns as those of the father of the whale-child she had saved. His deep, kindly voice echoed in her mind. 'I have the man. My mate seeks the other. Can you climb on to my back, little one? The man needs help.'

Aurian thanked him and headed for the surface, where the whale rested with his broad back just out of the water. She scrambled up with some difficulty, hoping that she wouldn't hurt him, and had time for an instant's surprise at the warmth of his sleek skin beneath her hands before she found herself gasping and choking, unable to breathe. She was drowning – drowning in air!

This time Aurian did not lose consciousness, though the panic-filled moments while her lungs adjusted seemed to last a lifetime. She tried to stay aware of what was happening, knowing that some day the knowledge might stand her in good stead. *'Have you considered the implications of this thing?'* The words she had once said to Finbarr came back with startling clarity as she choked and wheezed.

The Mage looked around dazedly. She felt cold and exhausted, but was relieved to be breathing normally once more. She lay on the whale's broad, barnacle-encrusted back, rocking gently with a sea that was already growing calm. And there was Anvar, lying limp and motionless not far away. Balancing carefully, she crawled over to his side. He felt cold – very cold – and he was not breathing. A chill passed through Aurian. Was she too late?

She tried to reach out with her healer's senses – and found, to her horror, that she could not. Cold and exhaustion had taken their toll, and she had thrown every shred of her power into her attack on Miathan. The effort of contacting the Leviathan had completed the drain. Aurian cursed, hammering a fist into her thigh in frustration. Now, at the time of her greatest need, her body had betrayed her! Until food and rest had restored her, she would be unable to summon the intense energies needed for healing.

Fighting panic, Aurian racked her brains. Surely there was an alternative? Remembering Meiriel's instructions for such an emergency, she turned Anvar over and pressed hard and repeatedly on his back. Water trickled from his mouth, but still

285

he did not breathe. Aurian pushed harder, the exertion warming her despite the icy wind. 'Breathe, blast you!' She was tiring quickly; cold sweat trickled down her face.

At last, as the Mage was on the verge of despair, Anvar's chest heaved once, then again. He coughed and retched, spitting out seawater and taking great, gasping breaths, his eyes staring wide at the calming sea and the vast, curving back of the whale. He struggled in Aurian's arms and tried to speak, but could only splutter and choke.

'Steady, Anvar. You'll be better soon.' With sympathy, Aurian remembered her own terrifying moments on the whale's back, before her lungs had adapted back to breathing air. 'Rest for a minute, and get your breath back while I tell you what happened. Anvar, the whales aren't just beasts, they're intelligent. I can talk to them, in my mind, and this one saved your life – '

Anvar interrupted her. 'Sara?' he asked in a faint, hoarse voice.

Aurian shook her head. 'I don't know, Anvar. Wait, and I'll – '

'Why didn't they save her?' Harsh and accusing, his voice cut across her own. 'Did you ask them to try?'

Aurian recoiled in indignant rage. Why, the miserable, ungrateful . . . He had no thought of how close she had come to losing her own life, or thanks for saving his. For an instant her mind went back to that dreadful night on the river, when she had lashed out at him in her grief over Forral. Maybe Anvar was doing the same thing – but no. He had called her a murderess, and the memory still burned. Goaded beyond bearing by this new proof of his lack of trust in her, she could only react with anger. That does it, she thought. When we get to land, I'm finished with him!

'Anger, little one?' The whale's warm tones echoed chidingly through her mind.

'The other member of our party has been lost, mighty one,' Aurian explained. 'The man blames me.'

'He blames you?' Wry humour bubbled beneath the thoughts of the giant. 'He must think a great deal of you, to believe you capable of shouldering such awesome responsibilities!'

286

Aurian, once she was was over her surprise at the notion, was quick to deny it. 'I fear not, mighty one. Where I am concerned, his mind seems filled with doubt.'

The Leviathan laughed. 'Little one, when we doubt our own selves greatly, we often find it more comfortable to transfer that doubt to another. The man will learn, in time. As for his lost friend, you may tell him to put aside his fears. My sister has her safe, and she will reach land before we will. For this, he has you to thank.'

As Aurian had expected, Anvar's face lit up at the tidings. But when he reached out in an excess of joy to hug her, she moved angrily away from him. 'Stay away from me!' she snapped. 'You've already made it clear what you really think of me. Once we reach land, you and that selfish little featherhead are on your own – and I wish you joy of her, Anvar, for one day she'll betray you as she's already betrayed poor Vannor!'

Anvar's face darkened. 'How dare you talk about Sara like that?' he said. 'You've been unfair to her from the start. You have no idea what she's suffered . . .'

'No, and I couldn't care less. I can see what she's become and that's enough for me. She'll use you, you fool, and drop you as soon as it's expedient, but at least I won't be around to see it this time. I'm finished with both of you, and I hope I never see you again.'

Furious as she was, the expression on Anvar's face gave Aurian pause. She had never seen him look so angry. 'That suits me!' he retorted hotly. 'I notice that you had no objections to using me over the last year or so. Well, let me tell you this, Lady – I'm done with slaving for the bloody Magefolk! After today, Sara and I will make our own way in the world – without your interference!'

At this point the whale intervened, saying that the anger emanating from their minds was causing him great distress. Aurian, instantly contrite, apologized to the massive creature. She moved as far away from Anvar as the Leviathan's broad back would permit, and, for the first time in days, settled herself for a good sleep. Surprisingly, it was long in coming. She had lost Forral's thick cloak in the shipwreck, and her wet clothes clung to her like a sheath of ice. The Mage admitted a passing wish that she could curl up with Anvar, so that at least they could share what paltry heat remained to them. A surreptitious glance showed him huddled tight in his own lonely place, visibly shivering, but refusing to make a move towards her. Well, I'm not going to ask him, Aurian thought. If he wants to get warm he'll have to come over here. So she stayed where she was, with nothing to sustain her but empty, stubborn Magefolk pride, until finally her exhaustion claimed her.

Dawn found them approaching land. The sky had cleared to the palest blue. The sea was flat calm, and the air surprisingly warm. Aurian awakened, bleary-eyed and unrested, to see a beach of fine silvery sand broken by clumps of jagged rock. A lush, dense strip of unfamiliar forest lay behind it, and beyond that towered cliffs of convoluted grey stone that soared to a staggering height. The silky, perfumed air was alive with the shrill calls of unknown creatures beneath the forest canopy. Shock ran through Aurian. This was no northern shore. The violent storm had blown them right to the fabled southern lands!

The whale halted an arrow's flight from the shore, where the water was still deep enough to float his massive bulk. Aurian turned to Anvar. 'This is where you get off,' she said tersely. 'He says that his sister left Sara here, so she should be about somewhere.'

Anvar looked astonished. 'You really can talk to that thing, can't you?' he said.

'Thing? He's a friend, Anvar, and I find his conversation infinitely preferable to yours, so go away.' Aurian set her jaw, averting her eyes from Anvar's injured expression. It's a bit late now to be looking hurt, she thought grimly.

Anvar looked down into the water, which was crystal clear in this sheltered bay. Following his gaze, Aurian saw a myriad of bright fish darting through the lapis-blue depths.

'Aurian, it's too deep here! I can't . . .'

The Mage could see the panic in Anvar's eyes, and belatedly remembered his inability to swim. She remembered her terror the previous night, when the choking water had surged into her tortured lungs, and shuddered. Anvar was shaking, and she fought in vain against a surge of pity for him. 'All right,' she sighed. 'I'll help you. I'll go first . . .'

Suiting word to deed, she slid off the whale's sloping back and into the water. After the bitingly cold seas of the northern climes, its warmth came as a pleasant shock. After a brief consultation with the whale, she turned to Anvar. 'Now, I want you to slide down here. His fluke's just . . .'

'His what?'

'His fin, then, if you like. It's just under the water, so you can stand on it, and you won't go under.'

Anvar hesitated, biting his lip.

'Go on – he says it doesn't bother him,' Aurian urged.

'Maybe, but it bothers me,' Anvar muttered through clenched teeth.

'Look, it's perfectly safe. I won't let your head go under, I promise. Trust me for once.' She couldn't keep the edge out of her voice.

Finally she managed to coax him on to the fluke that the patient whale was holding steady. The water came up to his chin. Thank goodness he's tall, Aurian thought as she swam to his side. 'Don't grab me!' she warned, realizing what he was about to do. She righted herself and stood beside him on the fluke, and discovered his problem. It was difficult to stand upright in the buoyant, salty water. The body wanted to tilt itself and float.

Aurian placed her hand on the back of Anvar's head.

'What are you doing?' he gasped.

'I'm holding your head out of the water. All you have to do is take a deep breath and lean back – just relax and your feet will come up naturally. You'll float, I promise, and you won't go under. I'll have you safe.'

After a time, Anvar thought he had plucked up enough courage to do as she said. Aurian was swamped by a flurry of foam as he immediately panicked, floundering and thrashing and clutching at her. At the expense of a ducking, she managed to keep him from swallowing too much water and got him right side up, back on the fluke. Pushing the heavy, clinging curtain of hair out of her face, she found an indignant Anvar glaring at her with red, salt-stung eyes. 'You said I'd float!'

289

'I said relax, you fool, and *then* you'd float!'

'I can't relax! I'm terrified!

It took a while, but finally they managed to get the floating part of the operation sorted out. Anvar lay back, his face breaking into an astonished smile.

'Anvar, don't forget to breathe!'

More floundering. But eventually they managed it, and after that towing him to shore was a comparatively simple matter. Within minutes they found themselves standing knee-deep in a gay lacework of surf that tumbled and danced up the beach.

'Well,' Aurian said. 'If you ever get into deep water again, at least you'll be able to float.' On an impulse, she reached down and pulled a long, lethal dagger from her boot, handing it to him without looking him in the eye. 'Take this,' she told him. 'At least you won't be unarmed.'

It struck them both at the same time that this was the moment of their parting. There was a sudden, tense silence as they stood and looked at one another. Suddenly, Aurian was tempted to reconsider. How could she leave Anvar? She found herself unable to turn away from him, and he too seemed unhappy and undecided, biting his lip while he fidgeted with her dagger. Oh, damn this, Aurian thought. We're behaving like children! An apology was out of the question – after all, he was in the wrong – but she was about to open her mouth to tell him that they ought to stay together when Sara erupted from the forest and dashed down the beach towards them, calling Anvar's name.

'I was so afraid! Those beastly sea monsters – I though I'd be eaten for sure!' She gave a sudden shriek. 'Oh! Look out – there's one right behind you! Quick, get out of the water!'

'Sara – thank the gods you're safe!' Forgetting the Mage, Anvar left the water in a flurry of foam, and ran to her. Aurian cursed, and turned away in disgust. Breasting the warm waves, she swam out to the Leviathan and climbed on to his back, her heart weighing her down more than her wet clothes.

When she looked back, Sara was in Anvar's arms. Her shrill voice carried clearly across the water. 'Well, who cares if she goes! We don't want her with us anyway!' The Mage gritted her teeth and braced herself against the warm body of the whale.

'Let's go,' she said. She never heard Anvar's frantic voice, calling her back.

Anvar was furious. 'Be quiet! She'll hear you!' He could not believe that Aurian was actually leaving. He felt somehow lost; anchorless. He called to her, begging her to wait, but the whale was sounding; exhaling deeply in a roaring geyser of water and air. She could not have heard him. Sara's arms twined persuasively round his neck as she kissed him, turning his face from the ocean, effectively stopping him from calling again.

'Never mind her,' she murmured. 'Think of your freedom, Anvar. Think of us.'

The Leviathan could move very fast when he wanted to. Anvar broke away from the kiss, but Aurian was already out of earshot. 'What in the name of the gods do you think you're doing?' he snapped at Sara. 'It's not a question of freedom, you idiot. Not just now. We should be sticking together.' In his heart he knew, with a sickening sense of shame, that it was he himself who had driven the Mage away.

'How dare you speak to me like that!' Sara flared. 'How is it supposed to be my fault? It wasn't me who called her a murderer. I thought you wanted us to be together, just the two of us.' Her face crumpled, and tears spilled from her guileless violet eyes. 'I thought you loved me, but it was her you wanted all along.' Picking up her tattered skirts, she ran away from him, along the beach.

Gods, what else could go wrong? With a groan, Anvar hastened to follow her. The early sun blazed down from a vibrant, cloudless sky. Its silky heat was already enough to dry the clothes on Anvar's body, but the chill of last night's stormy waters seemed to have settled immovably into his bones. The drying salt and sand made his skin feel stiff and gritty, his eyes smarted, and he ached all over. Panting in the heat, he caught up with Sara, and put an arm around her. 'I'm sorry,' he told her. 'Truly I am, and I do want to be with you.'

After a while, Sara allowed herself to be mollified, but there was a certain hard look in her eye that made Anvar feel as though he would be treading on thin ice for a while. Bloody women! he thought sourly. He looked out to sea, but Aurian had vanished. They were alone. 'Come on,' he said resignedly. 'Let's go and find some water.'

Luckily, fresh water was plentiful in the forest. It drained from the cliffs behind, forming streams that passed through the lush fringe of forest on their way down to the sea. Anvar and Sara only had to walk a little way along the beach before they stumbled on the first of these streams where it entered the ocean. They followed it up into the shadowed forest, where the air was cool and moist, the broad-leaved trees and tangle of thick vegetation overhead cutting off most of the sunlight.

The air was filled with a zithering chorus of insect noises, interspersed with strident shrieks and calls from the canopy overhead. Sara shrank fearfully against Anvar, unnerved by the strange sounds. 'It's all right,' he reassured her. 'They're only animals and birds.' But he used Aurian's dagger to cut them two stout staves from a nearby tree, thinking as he did so how annoyed the Mage would be at this abuse of her good blade.

The waters of the brook gathered in a hollow to produce a small, deepish pool. Around its sides the vegetation had been nibbled back, leaving a strip of earth and leaf-litter. The mud at the brink was cross-stitched with the tracks of animals who had come down to drink. Anvar stopped to examine them. Small rodent prints, the slots of tiny deer, sinister s-tracks of snakes – and what were these? They looked like prints of hands – tiny human hands! Anvar felt a prickle in the back of his neck. Suddenly the forest seemed full of unseen eyes. He hastily scuffed the tracks away with with his boot before Sara could see them.

Parched by the heat and the seawater he had swallowed, he flung himself down to drink, splashing cool, fresh water on his salt-tightened face. Once his first, urgent thirst had been quenched he looked around, fearful of losing his way in the forest, until he remembered, sheepishly, that he only had to follow the stream. If Aurian should change her mind . . . But she would not, not after the way he had treated her. He regretted his harsh words of the previous night. If only he had kept his temper, instead of flying to the attack because she had made him feel guilty. Surely she would have understood . . .

Gods, but he was hungry! Desperate to ease the gnawing

emptiness inside him, Anvar pondered the possibilities of finding food in this alien place. Sara must have been thinking the same thing. 'Anvar, I need something to eat.' It was little short of a command, and Anvar felt a stab of irritation. Aurian had never spoken to him like that, and he had been her servant.

Striving to keep his voice calm, he said: 'So do I. Let me think a minute.'

'But I'm hungry. I want something to eat now!'

Luckily, Anvar's long-departed grandpa came to the rescue. He had filled the boy's childhood with tales of his own youth in the country. By the time he was nine, Anvar had been fully conversant with the skills of trout-tickling – in theory, at any rate. 'Come on,' he said to Sara. 'We'll catch some fish for dinner.'

In practice, it proved to be a lot more difficult than it had sounded. Out in the open sea, the fish seemed to have developed some magic of their own. Again and again, as Anvar's careful hand almost closed on their sleek, shining bodies, they suddenly vanished, leaving the exasperated hunter with a handful of empty ocean. Anvar stood waist-deep in the sea, growing more irritated by the second. Why wouldn't the wretched things stay still? His eyes ached from peering into the dazzling waters, and the sun beat fiercely on his unprotected head and back. He seemed to have been doing this for hours. Try as he would, he could not shake off the notion that the fish were mocking his bumbling efforts. As he lifted his hands out of the water, he saw that the skin on his fingers was white and wrinkled.

'Anvar? Anvar!' Sara's voice rang out from the shore. What did she want? He was vaguely aware that she'd been calling for some time. He turned, and there she stood, laughing, holding up a bag made from a white square of linen torn from one of her petticoats. It was bulging and squirming in her grasp. 'Look! I've caught some!'

For a split second he could cheerfully have strangled her. Then the import of her words sunk in, and Anvar was both astonished and relieved. Moving as quickly as he could against the clinging pressure of the water, he waded back to her through the shallows. 'How in the world did you manage that?' he said, trying not to sound as indignant as he felt.

Sara dumped her writhing bundle down on the white sands and put her arms around his sunburnt neck, making him wince. 'Easy,' she smirked. 'Aren't you proud of me?'

'Of course!' he snapped, glaring at her, and Sara relented. 'Did you not notice?' she said. 'The tide's turned.' She gestured to a reef, now exposed, that pointed out like a finger into the ocean. 'There are lots of fish over there, trapped in the rock pools.'

'The tide?' Anvar felt stupid. He knew of tides, but having been born an almost penniless city dweller, and become a slave, he had never understood their import.

The realization hit Sara at once. 'Oh,' she said. 'You've never been to the sea before, have you?'

'How could I?' Anvar snapped. 'The Magefolk don't give their servants outings to the coast, you know. How do you know so much about it, anyway?'

Sara looked away for a moment. 'Vannor used to take me every summer.' Seeing the look on Anvar's face, she hastily changed the subject. She couldn't afford to alienate him. 'Anyway,' she added brightly, 'I'm useless. I may have caught them – I couldn't help but do that – but I can't kill them. And as for dealing with the horrid bits, well, it always makes me sick.'

She had obviously said the right thing, because Anvar smiled. 'I'll do that. I learned how to do it in the kitchens at the Academy.'

Sara shuddered. She wished he wouldn't keep reminding her that he had been a bondsman. Living with Vannor, she had grown used to having servants around; had ceased to think of them as human beings. They were just, well, there – polite, anonymous, and at her beck and call. It made her feel unclean, somehow, to be making love to one of them. Still, for expediency's sake, she could put up with it. Turning to Anvar, she gave him her brightest smile, which had always worked with Vannor. 'It's a good thing there's somebody practical around,' she said. 'I'm afraid I'm just hopeless. Do you know how to get this fire started?'

Before his ill-fated fishing attempt, Anvar had left his tinder and flint with his discarded shirt (he was regretting the latter, now, as the sunburn began to bite) on a sun-baked rock to dry

294

out. There was plenty of wood between the forest's edge and the high tide mark, and Anvar soon had a fire going. He used Aurian's dagger to gut the fish, feeling guilty again, for he knew she had given him the weapon for more important purposes than this. He baked the fish on flat rocks at the fire's edge, and they feasted in the shade by the stream, where the lush foliage protected them from the midday sun.

Anvar awakened in the cool, fragrant dusk. The last blush of sunset glowed behind the tall cliffs, and bats swooped over the beach, hunting insects lured by the glow of the fire. Now the sun had gone, hordes of tiny scuttling crabs were making off with the remains of the fish. Anvar shuddered, and scrambled hastily to his feet, wincing at the fiery stiffness of his sunburnt back, and trying to clear the fuzz of sleep from his brain. All that staying awake with Aurian had finally caught up with him, he supposed. He must have fallen asleep before he had even finished eating.

Then he realized, with a start, that Sara was missing. Anxiously, Anvar scanned the beach. Surely she wouldn't be so stupid as to wander off alone? Taking a branch from their firewood pile, he kindled one end at the embers, and examined the spot where she had been sitting. There was no sign of a struggle, so no beast from the forest had seized her. He saw her footprints, leading to the stream, then away into the trees. With a curse, Anvar plunged into the shadows, following the course of the water.

The forest at night was far more eerie than the glowing emerald jungle of the daytime. Roots writhed up to trip him; vines (snakes?) brushed his face, almost startling him into dropping the torch. Branches grasped at his clothing. Faces leapt out from trees, seeming to grimace in the flickering light. The mould underfoot was slick with the evening's dew, and sickly glowing growths sprung from rotting logs, reminding him horribly of the chalice from which Miathan had released his Wraiths. Anvar's heart hammered; his breath came short and gasping. What was that ahead? A strange, flickering ghost-light. Anvar slowed his pace, creeping carefully up to the clearing that cradled the little pool, and stopped enchanted.

A nymph was bathing in the still, dark water. She was pale-skinned and golden-haired: surrounded and waited upon by a court of fallen stars that danced above the water, crowning her with silver. Anvar held his breath. An errant star danced close to him, and he saw that it was a flying insect whose body glowed with cool, white fire. Then the nymph turned to face him, standing naked in the enchanted pool, her golden hair streaming across her shoulders. Sara.

Anvar was enraptured, helpless in the face of such otherworldly beauty. He had meant to chide her for venturing alone into the forest at night; to rebuke her for her lack of common sense. Instead he found himself moving inexorably towards her, a sleepwalker drawn by the lure of an elusive dream. Throwing down his guttering torch and casting aside his clothes, he joined Sara in the pool.

She stiffened, a protest half-articulated on her lips. Then, with a shrug, she lifted her face to his kisses; her arms to return his embrace. They made love on the brink of the pool. Anvar was afire, carried away on the wings of love, of passion, of the beauty of Sara and the lambent night which combined to form a single transcendent whole. It was only in the instant of climax that he felt an uneasy lack of certainty that Sara was with him. Oh, her body, yes. Supremely responsive, making all the right moves, the appropriate sounds. But in that explosive instant her eyes flew open, and looking into them he realized that Sara herself was far away.

Anvar let his body relax, his heart thudding rapidly against her breast. Sara smiled, and ran her fingers idly through his hair. You imagined it, he thought. Trick of the light with those damned fireflies. But his joy had fled, and his heart's ease was replaced by a desperate awareness of how much he needed her. From his childhood she had been his – and now, at last, he had her to himself. The idea of losing her was unthinkable. But for the first time, he felt an insidious touch of doubt, like an icy finger. Had Aurian been right? Had Sara been using Vannor for her own ends? And now, was she using him?

'I'm cold,' Sara complained. 'Cold and muddy.' She grimaced, and tried to wriggle out from beneath him. 'Now I'll have to bathe again!'

With a sigh, Anvar let her go, joining her in the pool to bathe.

The unexpected chill of the water, now that he was in a state to notice such things, sent the last remnants of the night's magic fleeing as quickly as it had come.

Without speaking they walked back to the beach, where Anvar rekindled a huge blaze.

'I'm hungry again,' Sara said. But the last of the fish had been carried away by the crabs, and Anvar knew they had no chance of finding food in the dark.

'Try to sleep,' he said. 'We'll find something in the morning.'

'And then what?' she demanded. 'We can't stay in this dreadful wilderness for ever, you know.'

To Anvar this place was a paradise, if he didn't count the sunburn, but he supposed she was right. 'I don't know,' he said. 'If we climb the cliffs tomorrow . . .'

'What? Climb up there? You must be joking!'

Anvar sighed. 'Well, we can make our way along the shore, then, camping as we go. The cliffs can't go on for ever.'

'And which direction do we take?' Sara countered. 'You don't even know what lands we're in!'

'Neither do you,' Anvar retorted, nettled, 'and you've travelled further than I have, or so you say. Why don't you make a suggestion?'

'You're absolutely useless, Anvar! You don't know anything! I wish I'd never – ' Sara bit the words off abruptly.

'You wish you'd never what?' Anvar felt an ominous chill at her words. But Sara turned away from him, refusing to say more, and he was reluctant to press her. Within a matter of minutes she was asleep, or at least pretending to be.

Anvar stared miserably at the night sky. The stars seemed closer here; mellow lamps set in a velvet canopy. It was a far cry from the glittering star-crazed sky of his northern home, and suddenly he felt lost and, despite Sara's sleeping form huddled next to him, very much alone. He wondered where Aurian was, and was bitterly sorry for his hurtful words. She'd have known what to do. Forral had taught her well. Even when she found herself at a loss, her courage made up for the lack of knowledge. In truth, he admitted ruefully, it was the near-arrogance of her self-belief that sometimes annoyed him so much. That and the fact that she was a Mage; one of the race that had robbed him of his place in the world. He toyed with the dagger she had given him, its clean, sharp, businesslike lines reminding him of its previous owner. Where was she now, he wondered. How would she manage, pregnant, alone and grieving, with Miathan in close pursuit? He began to worry about her, feeling that he had failed in his responsibility. But the days of terror and flight had taken a greater toll than Anvar realized. Long before he could awaken Sara to take a watch, he fell asleep in the midst of his reverie.

Had they known to which lands they had come, and what race inhabited them, Anvar and Sara would never have built a great fire, like a beacon on the beach. Had they been aware of the danger, they would have hidden in the forest and been more careful about setting watches. As it was, they slept innocently on, their fire visible for miles from the open sea. When the long black galley glided up to the beach they were unaware of it, and even the light crunch of boots on the sand and the hiss of drawn steel failed to wake them.

Anvar was awakened by the clutch of hands on his body, and the sound of Sara's scream ripping through the night. He struggled violently, gaining his feet for a moment and groping for Aurian's dagger. But the blade had fallen from his hand while he slept, and was lost in the sand. He had time for a glimpse of flickering torches, swarthy faces, and white, grinning teeth before a heavy blow on the back of his head knocked him unconscious.

19

The Cataclysm

The Leviathan's name was Ithalasa. Sensing Aurian's need for rest, he told her that he would take her to a sheltered sea-lagoon further south, where his people often found sanctuary. As they went on their way, the Mage saw the cliffs behind the shoreline to her right gradually coming closer to the sea until they formed the coastline itself, and her view of the Southern Kingdoms consisted of a high wall of sharp-edged grey crags with the odd touch of dark green where tough, scrubby bushes had found a foothold within the many crevices. Sometimes the cliffs would curve inward, forming deep, sheltered bays, but Ithalasa kept going, passing them one after another. An indecipherable murmuring on the very edge of Aurian's thoughts told her that he was communicating with other whales as he travelled.

Her head ached from the dazzle of the sun on the sparkling blue waters. She was ravenously hungry, and very miserable. Try as she would, she could not get Anvar out of her mind. Whenever she closed her eyes to try to sleep, she saw his face with the unhappy expression it had worn when they stood together on the beach. Then, just as she was on the point of asking Ithalasa to turn back, she'd remember what had happened between the two of them and Sara the previous night, and her anger would come boiling up all over again. And if she was not thinking of Anvar, she was thinking of Forral, which was even worse. At last, because she had no idea what to do next, and was desperate to distract herself from her loneliness and the guilt of having abandoned the others, she decided to confide in Ithalasa, and ask his advice. To her relief, he proved amenable to the suggestion, confessing that he had been curious as to the source of her distress, and the reason for one of the Magefolk's travelling so far south.

Ithalasa's response to Aurian's tale was startling. She was drenched all over again as his massive tail lashed the water in agitation. 'The Cauldron is found? It has passed into evil hands? Oh, rue this bitter day!' His distress washed over the Mage, almost swamping her consciousness with its intensity.

'You know of the Cauldron?' she asked, balancing with difficulty on his slippery, pitching back. Stupid question, she chided herself. Obviously he does.

'I know,' Ithalasa replied gravely. 'My people carry in their minds all the lost secrets of the Cataclysm. It is our burden and our sorrow. That part of the past is best buried and lost.'

He knew. Dear gods, he knew! The Leviathan had the answers that Aurian sought. But she could sense, without any need for further words, his reluctance to speak of the matter. Still, she had to try. 'My sorrow to distress you, great one, but will you tell me? If I hope to fight this evil, my ignorance puts a deadly weapon into the hands of my foes. And fight I must, or die in the attempt. I have sworn to bring the Archmage's evil to an end.'

'Child, how can I?' Ithalasa's thoughts were tinged with deep regret. 'I understand your need to oppose this evil, but all the races of the Magefolk swore never to revive this perilous knowledge, lest the Cataclysm come again. I cannot tell you. Would you have the world's destruction on your conscience, and mine?'

Aurian sighed. 'Mighty one, wise one, I may be young and untutored by your terms, but I understand the fearsome responsibility that rests with me. I know what devastation a war between the Magefolk could unleash. But if I should gain the three lost weapons, surely Miathan could be subdued without too much damage being done? I tell you frankly that I am trained in the arts of war. But I was taught by one who had no love for violence or destruction. He was the best and gentlest of men, and the greatest of the many great gifts he gave me was respect for my fellow beings, no matter what their race, and a hatred of senseless death and bloodshed.'

The Leviathan paused a long while in thought, but his mind was veiled from the Mage. At last he sighed; a mighty sigh that threw a sparkling, iridescent fountain from his blowhole.

'Little one – let us suppose you found the weapons. Let us suppose you used them to defeat the Archmage, and in doing so gained the fourth also. What would you do then?'

'I would give the weapons to you,' Aurian told him without hesitation. 'Your people would be far better guardians than mine of such perilous things. I would leave it to you to judge whether they should be kept, concealed, or destroyed. I seek no power – only the fulfilment of my task.'

'Are you certain of this?' Ithalasa's thoughts were tinged with surprise.

'I swear it. Great one, you may read me if you wish, so that you can be sure I speak the truth.'

'You would submit to that?' The Leviathan sounded astonished. Reading was hardly ever done. Far deeper and more intense than the Test of Truth, it was said to reveal the depths of a person's very soul – and in the hands of a skilled practitioner it was open to dangerous meddling and abuse. In even suggesting such a thing, Aurian had declared her absolute trust in Ithalasa.

'I would – and I will,' she said firmly.

'Very well, little one. I accept – and I am honoured.'

Steeling herself, Aurian opened her mind to Ithalasa's probing thoughts. It was worse than her worst imaginings – a wrenching intrusion far deeper, far more intimate, than any physical rape could ever be. The Leviathan sifted through her mind, turning over the very silt and dregs of her soul, all that was unworthy or petty, all the faults of pride and temper and stubbornness that were so much a part of Aurian's makeup. All the things that she had denied, or kept safely hidden from herself, were churned up like clouding mud disturbed from the bottom of a clear stream. When it was over, she found herself huddled in a tight ball on the behemoth's knobbly back, sickened and shaking.

'Little one, be easy.' The Leviathan's words spread like a soothing balm through Aurian's ravaged and abraded consciousness. 'Even the gods themselves, they say, never attained perfection. It is not pleasant to confront one's faults, but therein lies the path to true wisdom – and that is why so few ever attain it. There is great good in you – great honesty and honour and courage, coupled with a loving heart – that far outweighs the bad. Keep a balance between both aspects of yourself, daughter, and all will be well.'

Daughter – he had called her daughter! Aurian's wretchedness was lightened by a fierce surge of love and pride. She tried to gain control of herself, at least enough to ask for his answer, but he spared her the effort.

'For my part, you have my trust,' he told her, 'and I owe you a great debt for saving my child. But I may not make this decision alone. See, we are near the lagoon – there, beyond that tall point that juts into the ocean. It is safe there, and you must eat and rest. While you sleep, I will consult with my people, and plead your case, for this decision must be made by all our race, not one alone.'

Aurian's heart sank. After all she'd gone through . . . But she knew that Ithalasa had done all he could, and it would be wrong to press him further. With a tremendous effort, she summoned the grace to thank him as she ought. There was a smile behind the Leviathan's reply, and she knew that he approved of her efforts. 'See?' he told her. 'Already your wisdom grows.'

The lagoon was almost a complete circle, hemmed in by reefs on the ocean side and tall cliffs on its landward edge. It was as safe as it could possibly be – nothing might come to this place except by sea or by air. Aurian swam to the strip of stony beach that curved round the farthest edge, and Ithalasa herded fish into the shallows for her to catch. She was grateful for his help, knowing that she would never have managed otherwise. As she was starting her fire the Leviathan took his leave, promising to return as soon as possible.

The Mage was bone-weary. She ate her fish half asleep, and after drinking from a spring that trickled down the cliff she lay down to rest, trusting to the powerful sun to dry her clothes on her body. This time, she fell asleep at once, and while she slept, she dreamed. A wondrous dream of the past, set in the dawning ages of her own world.

The Magefolk were numerous and powerful, and ruled the world. They controlled the weather and the elements, the seas and the crops in the fields, the birds and beasts and Mortal men without magic who, little more than animals themselves, were their servants and slaves. All across the lands and seas dwelt the four great races of the Magefolk – one race to control each of the four elemental magics.

The Human Magefolk, or Wizards, as they then called themselves, ruled the element of Earth. They had speech with all creatures of the earth, and the trees and all things that grew. The most skilled among them could even communicate with the very rocks of the mountains. Their task was to keep all things fruitful; all that lived or grew upon the earth in balance, so that each might prosper and thrive, and fill its rightful place in the interlinking web of life.

Their brethren the Winged Magefolk, or Skyfolk as they chose to be known, controlled the element of Air. They dwelt in lofty eyrie-cities in the tallest mountains, and were responsible for the birds and all other creatures that flew. Their powers harnessed the mighty winds that bore the rainclouds to make the world fruitful.

In the essential business of weather, they worked with the masters of the element of Water – the Magefolk of the Race of Leviathan, in whose charge were the waters of the world and the creatures that dwelt therein. They controlled the seas, rivers and lakes and, using the Cold Magic in the days before it was turned to evil, the great icecaps in the far north and south of the world. Theirs was the gift of rain, which was borne where it was needed by the winds of the Skyfolk. The Leviathans, because of their aquatic home, were not human in shape. Since the water bore their weight, some developed to immense size. They were streamlined and sleek, with great curved flukes to steer and flat horizontal tails to propel them at great speed. But they were warm-blooded and air-breathing, and bore their young alive. It was said that they were the oldest race of Magefolk, from which the others had sprung. They certainly possessed the deepest wisdom of all, and the most profound joy in life.

The element of Fire was the province of the Dragonfolk, who dwelt in the broad desert lands. In appearance, they were most dramatic of all. Long-necked, long-tailed, sinuous creatures, they were winged, and their scales glowed with a

303

metallic sheen. Their bulbous, glowing, gemlike eyes allowed them to see all around without turning their heads. They were born pure silver, and chose their preferred colour in infancy, retaining that hue ever after. Though some chose blues, greens and blacks, most preferred the colours of their element of Fire – shades of red or gold.

The Dragonfolk could produce two kinds of fire. They could turn the energy stored within them into a long jet of flame to be exhaled. Their other fire was more lethal, focusing energy through the crystalline structure of their eyes to form a slender, concentrated beam with appalling destructive capacity. Their teeth and claws were deadly too, but these were for defence only, for the Dragonfolk ate no flesh. Instead they spread out their massive translucent wings, ribbed like those of a bat, to absorb pure energy directly from the sun itself, as a plant does with its leaves. The wings were ill adapted for flight, but an adult dragon could glide for short distances. The young, being lighter and smaller, could fly further.

Within the province of the Dragonfolk's Fire-magic lay the art of storing power within gems and crystals that had been formed by heat and pressure within the earth, and the skill of working and smelting metals. All forms of fiery energy lay within their art, and they were capable of producing the most deadly and terrifying weapons. But being a peaceful folk, they kept these a closely guarded secret.

Because of the very nature of the universe, the four elemental magics had four negative magics to balance them, and it was the responsibility of the Magefolk to keep these under control, and, if possible, turned upon themselves to positive ends. None of these powers was the specific domain of any one race of Magefolk, but each was the responsibility of all, since all of the negative magics were wild, unpredictable, and potentially very destructive.

The first and most primeval of the negative powers was the Old Magic. This called upon ancient, elemental forces as old as time, which had stalked the chaos of the newborn universe before the Guardians brought the Magefolk into the balance to provide order. The Old Magic was the power of these ancient spirits – the rock spirits or Moldan, who once walked in giant, form; the tree spirits or Veridai; and the Naiads, the spirits of the waters. These ancient spirits had long been brought under control by the Fathers of the Magefolk, and were now trapped and powerless, unless deliberately called into the world.

More lately born were other races who called upon the Old Magic: the Merfolk and the Phaerie and Dwelven races, who lived in peace with the ancient spirits in the deep waters, in the heart of primeval forests, and beneath the hollow hills. These could, as they wished, dwell either in the mundane world or in the Elsewhere inhabited by the elemental spirits. It was rumoured that they were the offspring of matings between early Magefolk and the ancient spirits, but whether or no, the Magefolk had seen fit to imprison them in the mysterious Elsewhere of the Old Magic, to protect the peoples who later came to inhabit the world, for they were said to be tricky, false and dangerous.

To call on any of these elemental beings was a perilous business. Released back into the world from their long imprisonment they wielded great power, but were likely to turn it upon summoner as well as foe. But some of them, to the consternation of the Magefolk, did still wander free, occasionally appearing to turn the tide of history in some new direction. And rightly so, for without chance as well as balance the universe would grind to a halt.

The second of the negative magics was of a much more sinister nature, its origins shrouded in mystery. It was necromancy, the Death Magic, by which a sorcerer could sap the very life-force of another being. Like the Death-Wraiths, who used this magic to feed themselves, an evil Mage could use another's life-energy to fuel his power, making it temporarily stronger. The vampirelike annihilation of life was so grossly against the very grain of the universe that few of the Magefolk even knew of its existence, and those who did guarded the secret to their utmost capacity.

Then there was the Cold Magic. This was the magic of entropy, which drew its power from the chill, lifeless black depths of the universe. In the hands of a powerful Mage, the Cold Magic could sap the very heat of the sun itself, plunging the world into the darkness of eternal winter.

The Wild Magic was the fourth of the negative magics. This governed the primeval forces of nature – tempests, hurricanes and whirlwinds; floods and tidal waves; earthquakes, volcanoes and lightning. It was said that by employing the Wild Magic, a Mage could make the very soul of the world rise up as a living force; but to make it biddable – ah, that was another matter.

In her dream, Aurian saw these matters acted out in a panoply of history that spanned generations. At last she saw how, in defence against the negative magics, the four races of Magefolk had created the Weapons of the Elements. She saw how the Race of Leviathan crafted the Cauldron of Life, that was to be a defence against the very necromancy for which Miathan had used it. She saw the Skyfolk's Harp of Winds, that was made to master the Wild Magic, but which in evil hands could be used to summon it, for the Magefolk, in their pride, had forgotten a fundamental fact – that a weapon has two edges. She saw the Wizards, her ancestors, create the Staff of Earth to control the Old Magic, and saw with horror how it turned on them to release an elemental free upon the world – a Moldan, that had cracked open the sea-filled rift between the northern and southern lands. It was only then that the Magefolk realized their error.

The powerful Dragonfolk, masters of weaponry, turned aside then from their task to create a ward against the Cold Magic. Instead they created a master weapon – the Sword of Flame, whose powers were manifold, and transcended those of the other three weapons. This ultimate weapon was judged to be too dangerous to fall into the wrong hands. A Dragon seer foretold a time when the Sword would be needed to save the world from evil, but that was unimaginably far into the future. Under his guidance, the Sword was crafted for One alone to wield. The blade had a mysterious intelligence of its own, and was made to know the hand for which it had been created, but to reduce the risk it was sealed in a great, imperishable crystal. To gain the Sword, the One had to discover a way to release the blade. When all was done, the Dragonfolk hid the Sword beyond all seeking, and the few who knew where it had been bestowed took their own lives. Thus did the Sword of Flame pass out of all knowledge.

Aurian blinked, and saw dawnlight gliding the silver of the lagoon. Every detail of the dream was etched clearly in her mind. She shivered in the slight dawn chill and stretched limbs that were stiff and bruised by the rocks upon which she had lain. Turning her powers within, she examined the tiny spark of life that was her child and Forral's. Ah, Forral. Would she awaken every day for the rest of her life to be crushed yet again by the bleak knowledge that he was gone? But the child – their child – seemed well. It slept, safe and snug within her, and Aurian prayed that it would remain so. Then she saw the dark bulk of Ithalasa surface above the brightening waters of the lagoon, and all other thoughts fled from her mind.

'Is it well, father?' she asked him, trying to keep the urgency from her mental voice. 'What did your people say?'

He chuckled – she heard it quite clearly within her mind. 'Foolish child – think! You know their answer already.'

'I do?' Aurian, never at her best on first awakening, was baffled.

Ithalasa chuckled again. 'Of course you do. Half of what you sought, you have already been told!'

'My dream! Of course!' Aurian, filled with excitement, ran down the beach and dived into the cool water to swim close to the Leviathan's massive head, wishing that he wasn't too big to hug. His bright, deep eye twinkled at her. 'We thought it the best and quickest way,' he said.

'Oh, thank you, great one,' Aurian gasped. 'Thank you with all my heart!'

Ithalasa sighed. 'It was not an easy decision, but we pray that it was the right one. I beg you, daughter – if you succeed in your task, do not forget the vows you made me. We have no wish to create a tyrant from our deeds this day.'

Aurian was sobered. Now that she had seen for herself the scale of the powers that she would be presuming to deal with, she understood all too well what a great trust the Leviathans had placed upon her. Treading water, she reached out to touch Ithalasa's knobbly head. 'I understand, father. I won't fail you, I swear it.'

Once again, Ithalasa helped her catch fish for her breakfast.

Aurian had slept for half a day and a whole night and was ravenous, her body responding to the needs of the child within her. As she ate, she spoke further with the Leviathan. 'Father, I'm confused,' she said. 'I never knew there were four races of Magefolk. At the academy, we were taught that we were the only ones. We call ourselves the Magefolk, rather than Wizards, as you say we used to. What happened to the other races? Why don't we know about you? What happened to the weapons?'

'Ah. That, as they say, is another story, within which the answers to all your questions are inextricably linked. It is the tragic history of the Cataclysm, and it is that, to my sorrow, which I must tell you next.'

But Aurian's conscience was troubling her. Since she had seen her faults through Ithalasa's reading, her anger with Anvar had cooled and congealed into a choking mass of guilt. She knew how her arrogance had stung him, and she had no idea of the truth behind the affair with Sara, over which they had quarrelled so bitterly. They had both been at fault, but how often had Forral told her never to desert her comrades, no matter what? Aurian was ashamed, and, that apart, there was a prompting voice within her, some instinct that insisted she return at once. There was nothing for it. No matter how it galled her, she would have to go back for them. The idiots would never manage on their own, and she had promised Vannor that she would look after his wretched, faithless wife.

'Wise one; before you tell me this tale, I must find my companions. I should never have left them, and I fear they may be in trouble.'

Ithalasa sighed. 'Ah, little one, did I not say that you were learning wisdom? But now, I fear, you must learn something else – how to choose between a lesser good and a greater one. I dare not delay in telling you the remainder of the tale. Though my voice was enough to sway my people, they had many doubts. They may change their minds at any time, and if even one of them should do so I would be unable to tell you more. That is why we must act with all speed. The tale of the Cataclysm is long, and there would be little point in travelling by night. Besides, you are still weary, and the child within you requires

308

that you rest after such intense mental communication. If you wish to hear the history, we may not seek your friends until tomorrow.'

Aurian bit her lip, trapped between conscience and necessity. She had to know the rest. The future of the world might depend on it. Anvar and Sara would be all right, surely? Ithalasa had landed them in a safe place. But that inner voice would not be silenced, and told her that she was wrong. Aurian shook her head, wrestling with herself. Finally, she made her decision. I must do this – it's too important to lose. When I've found out what I need to know, I'll go back for Anvar and Sara.

Ithalasa waited, as near inshore as he could come, staying silent and detached until Aurian had resolved her dilemma and turned to him. 'Very well,' she said, 'I will stay and hear what you have to tell me.'

'You are right, I think. This will give you the knowledge that your people lost long ago. Use it wisely, child.' And with that, Ithalasa's thoughts overwhelmed her mind, filling it with words and visions that unreeled before her, showing her the terrors and tragedies of a time long gone.

In the days of the golden past, all was peace and harmony. The four races of the Magefolk laboured together in their great task, to keep the world peaceful and prosperous and fair. But chance ever lurked, wolflike, outside the gates of balance, waiting to swing Fate to a new course. Evil stars heralded the births of Incondor and Chiannala.

Incondor was one of the Skyfolk, handsome, muscular and lithe. His great feathered wings had the iridescent darkness of a raven's plumes. Though young, he was mighty in sorcery and showed promise of becoming even greater, until, overcome by his arrogance, he fell. For a wager – a stupid, drunken wager with his wild friends – he stole the Harp of Winds to summon the forbidden Wild Magic, creating a whirlwind to bear him to the heavens, higher than any of his folk had ever ventured before. But the whirlwind, fuelled by the errant power of the Wild Magic, proved too mighty for him to control. Its forces tore and smashed his wings beyond repair before flinging him to earth in a tangle of crushed and broken limbs. It went on to wreak great havoc, killing many, before it could be brought under control by the wise ones of the Skyfolk.

As for Incondor, it was deemed that he had been punished enough. The sky would now be denied to him for ever, and without the freedom of the air the lives of the Winged Magefolk became bleak and without meaning. Earthbound, crippled and disgraced, he was exiled from the lands of his people and sent to Nexis, the greatest city of the Wizards. It was hoped that there, along with the healing for which the wizards were famed, he might also find wisdom at last. The former was accomplished, as far as it could be, although his body would be for ever twisted and his wings were beyond saving. Before the latter could take place, however, he met Chiannala, and chance brought balance down.

Chiannala was the offspring of a Wizard and his Mortal servant. Such pairings were possible, given the physical similarities between the races, but they rarely occurred because the brevity of Mortal lifespans could cause the Mage partner much grief. It must also be said that, pride being an integral part of the Magefolk nature, the Wizards looked down on the Mortals as lowly, primitive creatures, powerless in a world where magic was all. However, not all wizards thought in this way, and unions did occasionally take place. The offspring of these could favour either parent, turning out to be Mortal or Mage, as chance allowed.

Chiannala favoured her father, and at an early age rejected her Mortal mother completely, throwing herself obsessively into the study of magic and the development of her powers in an attempt to eradicate the lowly Mortal stain on her ancestry. However, though she excelled in her studies to such an extent that she became the obvious candidate to be the next Chief Wizard, she was rejected by the council because she was a half-breed. Bitter and thwarted, she came to meet Incondor in Nexis and found him of a like mind, and the seeds of disaster were sown. For revenge on the Magefolk who had rejected them both, they plotted to seize power and rule the world.

Turning the powers of healing to destructive ends, Chiannala engineered a plague that swept through the Wizards like a scythe, killing many and throwing their entire society into turmoil while they desperately sought a cure. In the confusion, the Staff of Earth was discovered to be missing, and none knew where it had been bestowed. Incondor, meanwhile, unleashed Wild Magic upon the mountain eyries of the Skyfolk, battering them with hurricanes and blizzards which left them besieged and helpless, unable to free themselves from his spells.

While the Mages of the two races were occupied in dealing with these menaces, the evil pair smote the Dragonfolk with the Cold Magic, almost annihilating their race, for they needed the sun's energy to survive. At last, the few survivors, worn beyond endurance by weakness, grief and suffering, gave up the deadly secrets of Fire-magic, including the making of explosive weapons and the knowledge of storing power in crystals.

The world was in turmoil, all balance irrevocably upset. In the oceans, the gentle Leviathans turned, too late, from their meditations to find themselves beset by Fire-magic. Explosions ripped through the depths, slaying without mercy. The survivors were beset by armies of Merfolk, called up with the Old Magic by Chiannala. Peaceful to the core of their beings, the Race of Leviathan could not retaliate. Instead they retreated, dwindling in number all the time. And somehow, during the retreat, the Cauldron of Life, which had been their creation and chiefest charge, was stolen by the Merfolk, and found its way into the hands of Incondor and Chiannala.

Turning the Cauldron to negative ends, they summoned the Death-Wraiths – spirit-vampires that sucked the life-force from living souls. This power of necromancy they turned upon the besieged Winged Magefolk. The desperate Skyfolk gathered all their remaining numbers down to the smallest child and joined minds in one last, desperate throw – a single, co-ordinated blast of power aimed at the evil pair. But Incondor and Chiannala had prepared for this. Using the Dragonfolk's fire-magic they had constructed a great crystal to absorb the magic of the Skyfolk and trap it, rendering their race powerless for ever.

The Magefolk were in desperate straits, their numbers diminished to a handful, their weapons lost or in the hands of the enemy. But the last hope of the universe is that evil will always turn upon itself. With their goal in reach, Incondor and

Chiannala came to vie between themselves for leadership. Using the Cauldron, Chiannala sapped the life-energy of vast armies of Mortal slaves to fuel her power. Using the great crystal that stored the stolen magic of the skyfolk, Incondor increased his own power, and by now all the powers were their province. The world was blasted with fire and ice, flood and tempest, earthquake and lightning as the two strove. Mighty armies of elementals were unleashed to turn upon each other to their mutual destruction and that of any living thing that chanced to be near. And finally, inevitably, Chiannala and Incondor destroyed one another, and the universe breathed once more. The few survivors crept out into the ruins of a changed and blasted world.

The Leviathans, in desperation, had saved themselves by breeding a small, fierce race of warriors – the Orca – to end the threat of the Merfolk and restore peace to the seas. But fearsome though they were, the gentle Leviathan hearts of the Orca abhorred the killing, and the blood upon their consciences was an intolerable burden. So, when their task was complete, their race was granted the mercy of eternal sleep and hidden away in a deep undersea cavern, ready to be called to life again should the need ever arise. This accomplished, the Race of Leviathan resolved never again to have dealings with the aggressive, destructive land peoples. They shut themselves away from all contact with the outside world and returned to their meditations and play. And the peoples of the ruined world soon came to forget that they were anything other than simple beasts.

In atonement for giving away the secrets of the Fire-magic which had wrought such havoc, the few remaining Dragonfolk also cut themselves off, retreating to the deserts and vowing to abandon magic for ever. They wished to avoid contact with other peoples, but were frequently disturbed by warriors with more courage than sense. At this time, many of the Dragons broke their vows and used the power of the Fire-magic to take themselves to other worlds. Sometimes a curious Dragon, hungry for outside contact, would kidnap a Mortal pure in spirit and gentle in nature for a companion.

The remaining Skyfolk, bereft of their powers, turned the

Harp of Winds over to a Guardian who dwelt beyond the world – the Cailleach, or Lady of the Mists, who lived outside time on the shores of the Timeless Lake. Diminished and without their magic, their martial skills grew perforce. They kept to their own territory but defended it ceaselessly and ferociously against outsiders, for they were shamed by their fall. The world soon learned to leave them well alone.

And the Wizards? Well, theirs was a different story. When the plague struck, the Chief Wizard prepared for the worst. He called upon his son, Avithan, who was renowned for his wisdom, to choose six of his folk with special skills – three men and three women, to carry on the race if all should be lost. Avithan chose Iriana, whose speciality was the beasts of the earth; Thara, who cared for growing things; and Melisanda, whose healing skills made her reluctant to leave her people in this time of crisis. With them went three men – Chathak, who loved the Dragons and had knowledge of their magic; Yinze, a friend to the Skyfolk; and Ionor the Wise, ambassador to the Leviathan race. Avithan went to the Cailleach and beseeched her to take the Six out of time for a hundred years, and she agreed on condition that he himself would leave time for ever to be her soulmate, for the Timeless Lake was a lonely place and Avithan was fair to look upon, and a good and wise soul besides. He agreed, and passed out of the world, to re-emerge in legend as Avithan, Father of the Gods.

For, when a century had passed and the Six returned, they found that the world had changed beyond recognition. The other races of Magefolk had gone into their self-imposed exiles, and the race of Wizards had been wiped out by the plague and the Cataclysm that followed it. The lesser race of Mortals, breeding like rats in the ruins of the scarred planet, were kings of the world, such as it was.

The Six put aside their horror and grief, and bravely set about their task of healing. Iriana and Thara worked to restore the beasts, and make the world green and fertile once more. Melisanda healed the disease-ridden Mortals and animals. The men travelled widely, garnering the surviving knowledge of the disciplines of Fire, Air and Water; for all powers must now rest in the hands of the Wizards, who took the sole title of

Magefolk. Between them, the Six set about restoring their race – a pleasant task, but one to be undertaken with care and planning. As a ward against future misuse of their powers, they formulated the Mages' Code, and passed it on to their descendants as an incontrovertible law which each of the Magefolk must swear, on their very souls, to uphold. And, accepting the inevitable – that the age of freedom had finally arrived for the despised Mortals – they set about teaching them all they could, that their race might grow in wisdom and responsibility.

For a thousand years they laboured, and then, too weary to do more, they chose to pass from their lives together and fell into legend as gods and goddesses – Iriana of the Beasts, Thara of the Fields, and Melisanda of the Healing Hands; Chathak, God of Fire; Yinze of the Sky; and Ionor the Wise, who became to the southern races the Reaper of Souls, because he possessed a part of the Leviathans' lore, and they had created the Cauldron, which was said to control the rebirth of souls. Avithan became known as the Father of the Gods, and the Cailleach as the Mother.

But what had become of the four great Artefacts of Power? The Sword was hidden, awaiting the One for whom it had been forged, and the Harp had been sent beyond time. The Staff of Earth was lost, and it was believed that the Cauldron had perished in the Cataclysm. People little thought that a fragment had somehow survived, once again to cast chance into the teeth of balance in ages to come.

Aurian surfaced from Ithalasa's tale, dazed by what she had seen and heard. The history of her people had been spread out before her like an open book. But for all that, her goals seemed less attainable than ever. Miathan held one weapon, and two of the others were seemingly unreachable. Even the Staff of Earth had been lost for ages uncounted. Only the presence of the Leviathan stopped the Mage from a furious outburst of swearing. Instead, she contented herself with a disconsolate sigh. 'Well, father, you needn't have worried about what I'd do with the weapons. I can't see any hope at all of gaining them. I'll just have to go against the Archmage without them – but the gods alone know how.'

'Do not despair, little one,' Ithalasa comforted her. 'You now know more than your enemy about the nature of our world, and the powers and peoples within it. Maybe you will find unexpected allies. And now that you know the fate of the weapons, it may be that they will come to you in the end.'

Some chance, Aurian thought sourly, but was careful to hide it from Ithalasa. He had done his best, and she was grateful. His next words made her more grateful still. 'I can do one thing more to aid you, daughter, though neither I nor my people can fight for you. Such a thing is beyond our natures. But I will give you a spell – the ancient spell to summon the Orca from their rest. Though I beg you, out of pity for their suffering, do not use it unless you are in the direst need. But I know you would not.' His thoughts washed over her, full of love and approval, and mingled with them the spell came into her mind – the long-unused call to wake the warriors of the race of Leviathan from sleep.

'Ithalasa, how can I ever thank you?' Aurian said. Truly, she was overwhelmed with gratitude for all he had done.

'Prevent another Cataclysm, daughter. Restore peace to the world, if you can.'

Night was falling, and Aurian was hungry once more, and very tired. The Leviathan insisted that she eat and sleep before returning to her companions. The following morning they set out northward once more, the Mage riding on her friend's broad back and trying to curb her anxiety and impatience. But when they reached the forest-fringed beach where they had left Anvar and Sara, there was no one there.

20
The Slavemaster

From the familiar way in which the floor rocked and heaved beneath him, Anvar realized that he was on board a ship once more. He was tightly bound with coarse rope, and his aching head was throbbing in time to a hollow, muffled booming that assailed his hearing with ceaseless monotony. He lay still for a moment, not daring to open his eyes, his cheek resting on damp, splintery boards. It was suffocatingly hot. He could smell tar and reeking bodies, vomit and excrement. As well as the booming thuds that echoed painfully through his skull, he could hear the clink of chains and the occasional crack of a whip, punctuated by screams of pain.

He opened his eyes. He lay in a long, narrow, torchlit space that took up, he guessed, most of the below-decks area of the ship. Chained slaves, in rows of four, sat at benches on either side of a narrow aisle, each row of men wielding a heavy oar between them. The hulking figure of an overseer prowled up and down, flourishing a vicious whip, while at the far end a bald giant with skin like dark-tanned leather pounded on a heavy drum, setting the pace for the rowers. Anvar had been thrown into the cramped space in the narrow bows, where there was no room for oarsmen. A quick glance round showed no sign of Sara, and his stomach tightened with fear.

Someone was coming down the ladder that was attached to the wooden bulkhead behind the behemoth with the drum. From the sudden smartening of the overseer's attitude, the quickening of the drumbeat and the richness of the man's loose robes, Anvar decided that this must be the captain. He was a tall, emaciated-looking man with a hook nose and a thin, straggling beard. His head was shaved completely bald, except for a braided pigtail at the back, and his skin glowed like polished wood in the dim red torchlight. His voice was deep and guttural as he addressed the drummer. 'Pick up the beat, you! Get these sluggards moving, or you'll find yourself joining them!'

Anvar was stunned. The man was speaking a language that was completely strange to him, yet he could understand every word! The ability to understand and speak any language was a talent common to all the Mageborn . . . Anvar felt a warning pain lance through his skull, and had to clench his teeth to keep from groaning out loud. To turn his mind from such dangerous thoughts, he concentrated on the captain's words.

'And swill this pigsty out! How can you endure the stench? I will not have us coming into port smelling like a cattle-boat. We are Royal Corsairs, and we have a reputation to uphold.'

A groan of protest came from the overseer. 'It's bad enough having to live with these animals. Why should I have to clean up after them?'

The crack of the captain's fist hitting his underling's jaw echoed in the confined space. He staggered and fell, dropping his whip and hitting his head on the edge of one of the benches. A murmur of appreciation ran through the shackled slaves.

'Because, you stupid son of a donkey, if you leave them to wallow in their own filth they will sicken and die,' the captain said testily. 'They wear out too quickly as it is, and if I have to squander our profits replacing any more galley slaves I intend to take it out of your bonus.'

'But that isn't fair,' the overseer whined.

'Think of it as a favour. If the crew lose out through your carelessness, they'll slit your throat for you.' The captain grinned evilly. 'Get busy, Harag. And you, Abuz, pick up that cursed beat. I want to be in time to catch the Khisu's procurer tonight. He should be very interested in buying the pale-haired wench for His Majesty's collection, and the man will fetch a good price in the market. With the Khisu building his summer palace, the price of slaves is as high as the stars. The slave master will find a place even for an illegal northerner, and his gold will line our pockets. So think of that while you work. It might help to speed things along.' He left, whistling.

Having been doused with several pailfuls of seawater during Harag's rough swilling out of the slave area, Anvar could no longer pretend to be unconscious. As he choked and spluttered, Harag seized a handful of his hair and pulled his head backwards, giving a low whistle of astonishment. 'Souls, Abuz, you want to see this one! It's true – northerners do have eyes the colour of the sky!' With a shudder he dropped Anvar's head. 'Ugh! Unnatural, I call it. I'm glad the captain is selling him – with eyes like that he's bound to be unlucky.'

Abuz nodded, never losing the rapid beat of his drum. 'I know what you mean. I saw one when I was young – a captive spy about to be executed. When his head was struck off, those pale eyes stared right through me. Gave me nightmares for ages. Northerners are bad luck, I think. Good thing we're nearly home.'

'Should we feed him?' Harag wondered. 'The captain will have our hides if he arrives in poor condition.'

'Nah. He'll only be sick, and you've just cleaned up. They can feed him in the slave pens – at their expense.'

Anvar closed his eyes in utter wretchedness. A slave! Oh, gods, no! And what of poor Sara? Cursing inwardly, he struggled against his bonds until a vicious kick in the stomach from Harag stopped him. Anvar doubled up, vomiting bile on to the boards. Harag howled in fury. 'Filthy swine! I've just cleaned that!' He raised his whip and Anvar cringed, awaiting the blow.

'Stop that, Harag!' Abuz bellowed. 'I don't intend to lose my bonus through your temper!'

Harag turned, his whip still raised, his face livid with rage. 'You mind your own business, you lumbering ox!'

Abuz laid the massive sticks down on top of the drum and rose to his feet. He was so huge that he had to bend beneath the low ceiling. The slaves stopped rowing immediately, relief on their pain-racked, sweat-drenched faces. 'Do I have to come down there and deal with you, Harag?' Abuz said. 'Because you're beginning to make me angry, and you know what happens when I get angry!'

Harag's swarthy face paled. Slowly, he lowered the whip.

'What in the name of the Reaper is going on down there?' the captain's angry voice bellowed through the open hatchway above. 'Why have we stopped?'

318

Abuz flinched. 'Sorry, captain. Just having a little problem with the new slave.' Without waiting for a reply, he sat down hastily and picked up his drumsticks, resuming a rapid beat. Harag, taking his temper out on the gasping, glassy-eyed slaves, strode up and down, lashing them into greater efforts. Anvar curled around his bruised stomach and abandoned himself to utter misery.

A cascade of cold water awakened him abruptly, washing away the pool of vomit in which he had been lying. He heard the captain's voice rising in anger. 'I thought I told you to clean this place up!' There was the sick thud of a fist striking flesh. 'But I did,' Harag whined. 'The mangy dog threw up again.' 'Never mind. Just get on with it.'

A stinking sack was thrust over Anvar's head, and he was lifted by rough hands. As they bundled him through the hatch, he heard the hubbub of what must presumably be the docks. The sun's heat hit him like a hammer-blow as he was carried down a sloping, bouncing gangplank and thrown forward roughly, so that all the breath was knocked out of him. Suddenly he was in motion – from the jolting, it seemed that he was in a cart – and the multitude of sounds around him seemed to indicate a town or city of some sort. He thought he understood why they had put the sack over his head – even if he should escape, he would have no idea of where he was, or where to run. Not being familiar with the customs of this land, he failed to realize that it was also to hide the fact that the captain was bringing an illegal foreigner into the slave-markets instead of turning him over to the city's authorities as the law demanded.

The cart bounced along, jarring Anvar's aching head, the motion making him feel as though he would be sick again at any minute. His body was baking in the heat of the sun, and he was near suffocating inside the smelly sack. But at last the sun's heat vanished abruptly, and the faint light that filtered through the weave of the sack dimmed. The cartwheels echoed hollowly on smooth stone, then stopped.

'Greetings, captain.' The light voice dripped false honey. 'You had a profitable voyage, I trust? Are we buying today, or selling?'

319

'Selling, Zahn. Just the one this time.'

'Only one? Tut tut, captain. You are usually one of my more dependable suppliers.'

'Be reasonable, Zahn,' the captain said irritably. 'What could we possibly gain from two months' duty patrol up the coast? We are the Khisu's Corsairs, you know. Sometimes we must do our duty, and forget profit for a while.'

'Your loyalty does you credit, captain,' Zahn replied smoothly. 'Shall we inspect the merchandise, then?'

The bonds were cut from Anvar's feet, and he gasped with pain as blood ran back into the numbed tissues. He was pulled from the cart and hauled upright by strong hands, and the sack was wrenched from his head. A short, wizened man with a face like a steel trap stared at him open-mouthed.

'Reaper of Souls!' he gasped. 'A northerner! How dare you bring an illegal slave into my premises!'

'Spare me your righteous protests, Zahn,' the captain said impatiently. 'I know how desperate you are for slaves – any slaves – just now.'

His words seemed to deflate the slave master. 'Where did you find him?' Zahn asked with a frown.

'Washed up along the coast. Shipwrecked, by the look of it, in that freak storm. We saw some corpses and floating wreckage. They must have been blown far off course. Normally, they have more sense than to venture into our waters.' He grinned wolfishly. 'Anyway, enough of this. Do you want him, or shall I turn him over to the Arbiters like a good little Corsair?'

The slave master pursed his lips and began to walk around Anvar, looking him carefully up and down with an occasional pinch and prod. 'Strip him,' he ordered, and one of his handlers drew a knife and began to slit away the ragged remains of Anvar's clothes. Anvar struggled wildly until, feeling the bite of cold steel against his naked flesh, he froze, swallowing hard as he realized where his guard had positioned the knife.

'What are you doing?' the captain protested.

Zahn grinned evilly. 'Don't worry, I can sell him just as well as a eunuch, but there will probably be no need. He may not speak our tongue, but I think he understands.'

Sweat broke out on Anvar's brow. Though he was sickened by the touch of Zahn's over-familiar hands on his body, there was nothing he could do. His arms were still bound, and there was a burly handler on each side of him, one holding the knife in its perilous position. Anvar clenched his fists and shuddered. To take his mind off the examination, he concentrated instead on his surroundings.

He was in a large, circular chamber built of stone, with a domed ceiling. In the centre was a raised, roped-off platform, to one side of which stood a row of large iron cages, empty at present. The walls of the chamber were pierced at regular intervals by a series of shadowed archways. Only one of them was filled with the glare of bright sunlight, leading to the outside world.

'Well . . .' Anvar heard Zahn say, and snapped his attention back to the slave merchant, who was eyeing him thoughtfully. 'He's in fair condition, considering,' he told the captain, 'and he seems strong enough, with that height, and those lovely broad shoulders.' Zahn was eyeing Anvar in a frankly speculative fashion that made him shudder. 'Unfortunately,' the slaver continued, 'I cannot sell him to a private client – those eyes would put people off. Besides, there would be too many questions asked. But as you know, the Khisu is desperate for more labourers. The Reaper only knows how they go through so many slaves out there. Sheer mismanagement, if you ask me. Still, this summer palace is the best thing for trade in years, and His Majesty pays well. I think we can come to an arrangement. Of course, he will not last long in this climate, but that is not our problem. Come, my friend. Let us discuss the price over a glass of wine.' He snapped his fingers at the two husky men holding Anvar. 'Take him,' he said.

To Anvar's utter relief, the knife was removed. He was dragged through one of the shadowy archways and forced down a long, echoing corridor lit by lamps that hung from chains set in the ceiling. Bars of sunlight filtered through a latticed wooden door at the far end. His captors unlocked it and Anvar was thrust out into a dusty yard edged with open-fronted workshops. A potter sat in one, turning a rough clay bowl on his wheel. In the next, a draggled woman stirred a cauldron of vile-smelling swill over an open fire, pausing only to flick away myriads of great black flies which swarmed around her greasy face. Outside another booth, a man was plaiting long, thin strips of hide into a whip. Anvar turned his eyes away, not liking what that portended.

On one side of the courtyard was a smithy. A skinny, sweating little boy worked the bellows, keeping the forge at white heat while two dark-skinned men in leather aprons hammered out chains and manacles. There was no mistaking the smith himself. A squat black man, his skin tanned like wrinkled leather from the heat of the forge, he was twice as broad across the shoulders as Anvar, his muscles standing out like rough-hewn rocks. The two guards approached him with respect. The smith's eyes widened at the sight of Anvar. 'Reaper take us!' he growled disgustedly. 'Zahn is getting desperate!' He advanced on Anvar, holding a hinged metal collar that looked like a child's bracelet in his great hands. One of his assistants followed, bearing a glowing, white-hot iron.

Anvar struggled desperately, flinching away as the broad collar was placed around his neck and the ends were closed together, but the guards held him firmly. The smith was well accustomed to this delicate task, and caused him little pain, though Anvar whimpered in fear as he felt the collar grow hot when the edges were welded together with the searing iron. But the little boy, who had left his bellows, was standing ready to douse him with cold water from a jar, and the heat vanished at once. The child gave him a cheeky grin as he returned to his former task, and Anvar felt like a craven fool. The coarse rope binding his hands was cut away, and his hands were drawn round to the front and fitted with manacles joined by a few metal links. One of the guards produced another chain which he attached to a ring on the collar. Nodding brusque thanks to the taciturn smith, he gave a sharp tug, preparing to lead Anvar away.

Like a dog! Anvar, furious, humiliated and still shaking from the jolt of fear that had gone through him when the collar was sealed, gripped the chain in his manacled hands and pulled back as strongly as he could. Instantly the other guard took a short, thick whip from his belt, and the heavy lash fell once, twice, three times across Anvar's back and shoulders. He staggered, crying out with pain, and the guard pulled sharply on the chain. The hard edge of the iron collar cut into his neck and the lash fell once more, branding a line of fire across Anvar's back as he staggered after the guard. The other handler followed, his whip flashing down whenever Anvar stumbled or slackened his pace.

They took Anvar back inside the building and down a steep flight of steps into the cellars beneath. He was thrust into a bare and gloomy cell that housed several other slaves, all men. Their collars were attached at waist height to rings on the wall by a hand-span of chain, so that they were forced to remain sitting up at all times. Ventilated only by an iron grille set high on the wall, the place stank of human excrement. Gutters led down to a dip in the centre of the floor, in which was set a noisome open drain. Anvar was later to learn that the cell was swilled out, slaves and all, twice a day, and that was the limit of the sanitation.

The guards chained him by his collar to a vacant ring in the wall and left him, bolting the door behind them. None of the other slaves reacted in any way to his presence. They were sorry specimens mostly; filthy, half starved, and covered in sores and scars. Some wept and some dozed, while others stared blankly at nothing with hollow, vacant eyes.

Anvar tried to reach behind him to grasp the links which fastened him to the wall. He managed to get a grip at last, though the iron collar almost throttled him. He tore at the chain until his fingers bled, but it was firmly attached to the collar at one end and to the ring that was bolted into the wall at the other. At last he abandoned the unequal struggle and, hiding his face in his bleeding hands, he gave himself over to despair. There was no escape. What would become of him? What was happening to Sara? And most of all, where was that faithless Mage? In his self-pity, he imagined Aurian continuing her journey, free and uncaring about the two she had so callously abandoned to their fate.

Despite his anger with her, the thought of Aurian steadied him. At least she faced things with courage and determination. What would she say if she could see him giving way like this?

Nothing, Anvar suddenly realized. She would simply free him from these chains and spirit them both out of here – and it wouldn't be the first time she had saved him. Anvar thought of Aurian's past kindnesses; remembered the closeness they had briefly shared on board the ship. He recalled that in bringing him on this journey she had saved him from the Death-Wraiths, and remembered why she had left him in the first place. It was his own fault. He had driven her away, and wherever she was she would be facing difficulties of her own. At least he could take courage from her example. Anvar vowed then that whatever happened, he would endure, as he knew that she would endure. 'I will survive this,' he promised himself fiercely. 'And one day I'll see Sara and Aurian again.'

Sara cringed back as far as her bound limbs would let her, shrinking into the corner of the narrow bunk as the cabin door opened. The captain entered with a bundle in his arms, followed by two brawny sailors carrying a large tub of water between them. Another followed with a plate of bread and fruit and a tarnished cup, which he set down on the table. The captain waited until his men had left, and then, with a sweeping gesture, he drew a jewelled dagger from the sleeve of his loose-fitting robe. Sara uttered a little shriek, but he merely leaned forward and cut the ropes that bound her feet and hands. Standing over her, he made motions for her to undress. Sara clutched the neck of her tattered gown and shook her head wildly. 'No!' she gasped. 'Please, no.' The captain laughed, and pointed at the tub of water, the bundle that he had dumped on the bed, and the food on the table. Then, with an ironic bow, he turned and left the cabin, locking the door behind him.

After a moment Sara slipped from the bunk and ran to try the door, knowing the futility of the act even as she did so. It was locked, of course. She was not sure whether to be glad or sorry. In a way it was a comfort to have this solid piece of wood between herself and the men who had laid hands on her on the beach. She shuddered at the memory. After Aurian's warning about the sailors on the first ship, she'd been half crazed with terror, but when the captain set eyes on her he had shouted some orders in his harsh foreign tongue and they had brought her down here. Apart from sleeping for a while – she had no idea how long – she had lain here, trembling, ever since, the sound of every footstep filling her with dread.

Now it seemed that the captain wanted her for himself. Well, Sara decided, it was better than being raped by his unsavoury-looking crew. He'd been courteous, at least. Fear was such a familiar companion by now that practicality asserted itself. The fruit on the table, though strange to her, looked ripe and luscious, and it smiled so good . . . Oh well, she thought. Might as well be ravished on a full stomach. The cup held a light, spicy wine that Sara found delicious, although in her de-hydrated state she would have preferred water. The contents of the tub looked clean enough, but she had no intention of risking it.

After her meal, Sara felt much better, and turned to examine the bundle on the bed. It contained cloths for washing and drying herself, a bar of coarse soap, a comb carved from some white, bonelike substance, and a richly embroidered hooded robe that tied at the waist with a silken sash. As she shook out the folds of the robe, something fell out and rolled across the cabin floor. It turned out to be a little glass vial of perfume. Sara sniffed the fragrance appreciatively. Despite the dangers that lurked all too close, things seemed to be improving.

Although the water in the tub was shallow and only lukewarm, the bath was a glorious luxury. She washed her hair, too, drying it afterwards as best she could with the damp cloths and combing out the tangles and snarls until it fell in its usual glimmering cascade of lustrous gold. The robe felt wonderfully soft and cool against her bare skin, and the perfume was rich and sweet. It felt so good to be clean again. She only wished she had a mirror.

The sound of the door opening made her jump. She backed hastily away, belatedly wondering if it had been a mistake to make herself presentable once more. The captain stood in the doorway, smiling approvingly. Then he gestured towards the door. 'Where are you taking me?' Sara asked suspiciously, forgetting that he could not understand her.

The captain shrugged. Abandoning all pretence of patience,

he swept down on her in three rapid strides and grabbed her wrists, tying them in front of her with the trailing ends of her sash. Ignoring her shrieks and struggles, he called on a brawny sailor to hold her still while he fitted a veil of some unfamiliar diaphanous material over her head and pulled the deep hood of the robe down to cover her face. The sailor threw her over his shoulder with careless strength, and she was carried away.

Like Anvar, Sara was placed in an uncomfortable, jouncing cart, travelling blind. After a while, she knew from the tilt of the vehicle that they were climbing a steep hill. Then the road flattened, and the cart drew to a halt. Sara heard voices, followed by the grinding creak of huge gates opening. Then they were in motion once more.

They stopped, and Sara heard the cheerful patter of a fountain. The captain helped her down, and she found herself standing on glassy stone that felt delightfully cool to her bare feet. He pulled the hood from her head. She saw his outline through the translucent veil, and that of another man to whom he was speaking with rapid eloquence. Then he lifted the veil and the other man gasped. Sara, blinking, echoed his gasp at the sight of him. He was short and chubby, his face elaborately painted with cosmetics, his eyes outlined with kohl. He wore many glittering necklaces over brightly coloured robes, and gold earrings pierced his ears. His shaven head was painted with intricate swirling designs in gold. The overall effect was dazzling.

At least, Sara thought smugly, her appearance seemed to dazzle him too. He was almost jumping up and down with excitement. There was a rapid volley of talk between the two men, then the fat man gave the captain several bags that clinked, and seemed to be heavy. Sara felt a sudden stab of panic. He was selling her? As he turned to leave she tried to grab his sleeve, forgetting that her hands were bound. She didn't think much of him, but he was the only familiar thing in this strange place. He shrugged her off, and leaping aboard his cart manoeuvred the donkey carefully round in the narrow space of the white-walled courtyard. The high, sturdy gates were closed and locked behind him by two slender young men with shaven heads and curiously effeminate, painted faces.

Sara felt a wild urge to run, but there was nowhere to run to. The walls that surrounded her were very high. Her eyes filled with tears that spilled unchecked down her cheeks, since her hands were still bound to her waist by her sash.

The fat man clucked in concern, and patted her arm. 'Weep not,' he said, in a high, reedy voice.

Sara stared at him in astonished relief. 'You speak my language?'

He nodded vigorously. 'Little,' he beamed. 'Khisu, speak good. He teach. You like Khisu. Weep not, Lady. Spoil.' With a gentle hand, he stroked the tears from her cheeks. 'Be proud. You for Khisu – your word, king.'

'King?' Sara gasped.

The fat man nodded again. 'Khisu many beautiful lady. Want always beautiful lady. Want you, for sure.' He gave her a dazzling smile, showing a gold tooth at the front. 'Come,' he said. 'Bathe. Dress. See other lady. Many lady. See Khisu this night. Weep not. He like.'

The ladies' quarters were a labyrinth of many interconnecting rooms, their walls and floors richly decorated with pastel tiles and intricate mosaics. There were rooms with silk-covered couches, and tables, chairs and chests that were inlaid with gold; rooms with wide low beds curtained in drifting white muslin; rooms with fountains, pools and huge circular marble baths. There were shady courtyards and gardens full of exotic flowers and vivid butterflies. The air was laden with mingled perfumes and the sweet piercing song of bright-hued birds in cages of gold.

The women drifted in and out, some like silent ghosts in their diaphanous robes, others who gathered in chattering flocks around the edges of pools or splashed and soaked together in the communal baths with a complete disregard for their nudity, several who gossiped together on the soft cushions of couches. There were more of them than Sara could count, and each was more beautiful than the last.

Sara's companion detached half a dozen dusky beauties from one group, jabbering to them in their own language, with an occasional gesture towards herself. Their amazement at her golden hair seemed no less than his had been, and they crowded round her, exclaiming loudly and fingering her heavy tresses. The little man silenced them sharply and issued what seemed to be a stream of instructions. Then he turned to Sara with a smile. 'Zalid I,' he said, pointing at himself. 'You want, you send. You?'

'Sara,' she told him, realizing that he wanted her name.

'Sara. Good. Like desert wind. Go with lady now. Bathe, dress, eat. Later, see Khisu.' Unbinding her hands, he delivered her into the care of the girls.

Sara was ushered into a luxurious suite of rooms. She ate first, the chattering girls serving her with spiced meats, fruit, and strange, flat, leathery bread. She drank wine from a jewelled goblet, and looked around the sumptuous chambers, wondering if she had strayed into a dream. Then she bathed again, in a deep pool of steaming water scented with flowers and herbs. After her bath, two of the girls massaged her body with fragrant oils.

Sara relaxed beneath their hands, enjoying the pampering. As Vannor's wife she had been used to such attentions, and over the last few days she had missed them dreadfully. After the terrors and hardships of her flight from Nexis, the harem was a haven, not a prison. She was not concerned about meeting the – what did they call him? – the Khisu. She knew she was beautiful. She had used her looks to twist Anvar and that lout Vannor around her little finger, and had no doubt that she could do the same with the king. She felt a flutter of excitement. A real, live king. It was the chance of a lifetime! Sara stretched like a cat, thinking how far she had come in the last few years. This was a far cry from marrying the baker's son!

Anvar indeed. Sara scowled, irritated by the slight pang of guilt that marred her self-congratulation. She had not seen him since their capture. She shrugged. He'd been alive then, so they must have plans for him, and he was already a servant, so things couldn't get much worse. Besides, it served him right for dragging her off on this insane journey! She meant to survive; to take care of herself. With that, she put Anvar out of her mind.

They brought great heaps of clothes for her to choose from – embroidered robes of translucent silk in myriad colours; veils with less substance than a summer morning's mist. They brought gilded sandals, perfumes, cosmetics and more jewels than Sara had seen in her life. She took her time choosing, combining the materials for maximum effect. She was in her element now. This was what she was best at.

At last she was ready. She gazed at herself in a full-length mirror of polished silver, and the vision that stared back at her took her breath away. Gods, she thought, I'm stunning! I've never looked so beautiful. Although her heart was beating rather fast, Sara waited with calm confidence to be summoned into the presence of the king. The dazzling creature in the mirror smiled at her enigmatically. This was going to be child's play.

21
The Bracelets of Zathbar

Inch by inch, Aurian searched the deserted beach, and found the remains of a fire and signs of a violent scuffle. Her heart turned over. What had happened here? A few clear tracks – the prints of strange, pointed boots – still remained. A dull gleam in the sand caught her eye. Digging down, the Mage unearthed her own dagger. With a sinking heart, she tried to reconstruct what had happened, toying absently with the knife as she thought. No strange prints leading to or from the forest. The invaders had come by sea, then. Sure enough, there was a deep rut at the water's edge, where the prow of a boat had been pulled up on to the sand. No bodies. No blood. Had Anvar and Sara been captured alive? If so, where were they now? Aurian, full of self-recrimination, cursed her tardiness. Why had she not returned sooner? Why had she ever left them?

'Such thoughts are foolish, daughter, and ultimately destructive,' Ithalasa chided her gently. 'You did what you had to. If you wish to find your companions, perhaps I can set you on the proper track.' He told her that the ships in these waters came and went down a great river that emerged further down the coast. His cousins, the river dolphins, had reported a city, many days' journey upriver. If her companions were anywhere, they would be there. 'Though you were right to describe them as foolhardy,' he added dryly. 'Only an imbecile would light such a beacon in an alien land, to summon who-knows-what! But now you must decide your own course. If you wish to travel north in search of the weapons, I can take you a goodly distance, though we do not venture into northern waters as a rule. But if you seek your companions, your way lies south, and I will bear you to the mouth of the river Khazala – the Lifeblood.'

Aurian was in a dilemma. She ought to head north with all

speed, for time was against her. As her pregnancy progressed, her powers would gradually wane, vanishing at about six months to leave her bereft of magic until the child was born. Aurian had no wish to linger in the Southern Kingdoms, with their hostility towards Magefolk; nor to have her babe born here. Ithalasa could take her to her own lands in easy stages, with little risk of trouble on the way. But the Mage blamed herself for the plight of Anvar and Sara. She should never have left them. Though it meant a greater risk and a grave setback to her plans, her conscience would not let her rest if she abandoned them now. Eventually, heavy of heart and filled with doubts, she asked her friend to take her to the river's mouth.

'Take comfort, little one,' he told her, as they resumed their journey. 'Who can fathom the workings of fate? It may be that you have tasks to perform in these lands, and you may even find part of what you seek. Such an act of friendship and honour will surely turn to good.'

Aurian thought of her love for Forral, which had begun in friendship and honour and ended in tragedy, and forebore to reply. But parting with Ithalasa was hard. When she left him, with many tears, at the broad delta that formed the river's mouth, Aurian felt as though she was leaving part of her soul behind. She thought of Forral and Finbarr; of Vannor, Maya, D'arvan, and even her mother – and of Meiriel and the Archmage, who had betrayed her so bitterly. Was her life always destined to be filled with grievous partings? 'Stop that, idiot!' Aurian chided herself as she sloshed through the sticky red mud of the delta. 'Self-pity won't help.' She wiped her tears on her ragged sleeve, smiling a little as she recalled how Anvar had once scolded her for that habit. In this case, perhaps she was heading for a reunion, not a parting. Aurian prayed it would be so.

The Mage had not reckoned on the journey upriver taking so long. The valley was broad and flat-bottomed, hemmed in on either side by towering cliffs of reddish stone. She wondered what lay beyond them, but a mortal dread of heights meant that climbing was to be avoided wherever possible. Besides, she had neither time nor the energy for side-trips. The journey was tough enough as it was.

Aurian could see why the river was named Lifeblood. Its broad, sluggish waters were tinted with the same rusty red as the cliffs that towered on either side. The thin strip of land between the cliff and the river was a flat expanse of stinking russet mud and stagnant, reed-choked pools, and because of the treacherous, swampy ground Aurian was forced to travel by day. She felt horribly exposed on the naked mudflats. The sun hammered down on her like a great weight, burning her pale skin, and the air seemed too thick to breathe. She was unable to shed her clothes because of the whining, biting insects that swarmed around her, settling to feed on any exposed flesh. Her hands and face were soon swollen with itchy red blotches, and the effort of will it took not to scratch them was tremendous. Aurian knew that she could use her power to create a shield between herself and the little horrors, but she was reluctant to expend her waning energy in the use of magic, and was wary of using it in a land where it was forbidden.

By the second day, Aurian was already exhausted, and suffering badly from the heat. Though she had braided her long, thick hair out of the way, its sweat-soaked weight pulled painfully at her scalp and made her dizzy head ache. By noon, she could stand it no longer. She stopped to rest, but found no ease beneath the broiling sun. There was no shade anywhere, and she was unable to immerse herself in the river to cool down. While hunting the small, eel-like fish that were the only food supply to hand, she had encountered great lizards, bigger than herself and armed with long toothy jaws. Apart from that, the river was full of leeches. Of the two, Aurian thought she would almost prefer to deal with the lizards, but was anxious to avoid both.

Her head throbbed. The back of her neck, where the braid hung down, was unbearably hot. It was no good. Her hair would have to go. Such a decision no longer involved the heart-searching it would have once, since her recent choices had encompassed much graver issues. Using a stagnant, reed-fringed pool as a mirror, she took out the dagger she had given Anvar and hacked off the braid. Oh, the blessed relief!

Aurian felt literally light-headed. The discarded braid lay pathetically on the ground like a dead snake, caked with dried mud and sweat, and snarled with bits of weed and other nameless things. Aurian stared at it in dismay. Gods, she thought, what am I coming to? She had always taken such care of her hair, as Forral had taught her when she was a little girl. It seemed as though she had cut away part of her life with him. *I don't want a stupid prince. I'm going to marry you.* The memory of those childish words twisted in her guts like a jagged knife.

On an impulse, Aurian picked up the braid and washed it in the little pool. It immediately unravelled from the cut end, and the mass of hair floated in the water like a cloud at sunset. Leaving the other end tied, she fished it out and whirled it around her head to dry it as best she could. Then, coiling it tightly round her hand, she stowed it in one of the deep pockets of her leather tunic, where its clammy dampness soon seeped through to her skin.

'Idiot!' Aurian told herself. 'Sentimental fool! You cut the wretched thing off so that you wouldn't have to carry it around.' But all the same, she felt better about the whole business, until the pool settled and she saw her reflection. What a mess! Although she had never been vain about her appearance, Aurian was appalled. Painstakingly, she used her dagger to trim away the bits that straggled round her face, until it didn't look so bad. And it was certainly more comfortable and practical in this climate, she comforted herself, as she got to her feet and trudged on.

That day she also solved the problem of the insects, quite by accident. Catching sight of a ship in the distance coming downriver, Aurian had no recourse other than to fling herself face down into the mud and roll, camouflaging herself, and then lying perfectly still on the ground until the galley was out of sight. It was then that she realized that the stinking mud that coated her skin was a perfect shield, not only against sunburn, but against the bloodsucking gnats that had plagued her so. Thanking providence, she went on her way much relieved, stopping now and again to renew her protection as the mud dried and flaked in the strong sun. My own mother wouldn't know me now, she thought, and wondered what was happening to Eilin, so far away in her northern home. Would the Archmage take out his spite on her? Aurian shuddered, wishing that she had some way of warning her mother. However, there was nothing she could do but grit her teeth, and go on with the task in hand.

By the fourth day, the land was gradually becoming less boggy. Aurian began to come across little strips of cultivated land with the odd tethered goat, and crude huts of woven rushes: the hovels of peasants and fishermen. This meant that she was forced to switch to travelling by night, hiding in the leech-haunted reed-beds by day for lack of anywhere better. The constant danger of discovery placed a terrible strain on her nerves. She had hoped to be able to steal food from the peasants to supplement her inadequate diet of fish, but these people were so desperately poor and wretched that she could rarely bring herself to do it.

On the sixth night, Aurian came to land that was totally cultivated. Every precious bit of soil between the river and the cliffs had been used. The dwellings that she came across had a more solid appearance, constructed as they were from withy and daub, and thatched with the ubiquitous rushes. Stunted trees had begun to appear, and in addition to the welcome cover they provided in this more populated area, Aurian was delighted to discover that they bore a harvest of nuts, though in her own lands these would be well out of season. Aurian thanked the gods for such a boon.

Two nights later, as she rounded a bend where the long river valley kinked back upon itself, Aurian came upon the city. The sight of it took her completely by surprise, making her forget the weariness of eight days' hard travel. She had never seen anything like it. Bone-white in the moonlight, the buildings clustered thickly on the flat ground on either side of the river, then rose almost vertically on perilously constructed terraces hollowed back into the cliffs that loomed above the valley on either side. Narrow, sinister-looking warships crowded the riverside wharves, together with smaller craft and low, flat barges whose workmanlike appearance was much more comforting.

The city was much bigger than the Mage had expected, and

its architecture seemed strange to her. The roofs were flat, or domed, or twisted into slender, fluted spires. Doors and windows tended to be arched, rather than the square utilitarian shapes with which she was familiar. Impossible bridges, looking insubstantial as threads from the ground, were suspended across the chasm hundreds of feet, even a thousand, above. The very thought of them made Aurian feel sick and dizzy with her irrational terror of heights. She was puzzled by the lack of protective walls, not realizing that beyond the cliffs the city was guarded by something more powerful, more terrifying, than any defence that man could devise.

Aurian pushed her draggled hair out of her eyes and tried to get her tired brain to work. It would be easy enough to get into the city, but once inside – what then? How could she find Anvar and Sara in a place that size? Were they there at all? Were they even still alive? Why had she left them in the first place? The questions circled in her mind, but she found no answers.

Belatedly remembering her exposed position, Aurian turned right, towards the cliffs, and took shelter in a grove of low, twisted trees. She recognized them from others she had encountered on her way upriver, and as she had expected they held a bountiful crop of ripe nuts. With the child in her belly sapping her energy, Aurian was starving. Hurriedly, before she lost the last of the moonlight behind the dizzying cliffs, she gathered a large pile of nuts, then sat down in comfortable concealment among the roots of an old tree to eat, cracking open the hard shells with the hilt of her dagger.

She felt better for the food. Turning to the problem in hand, she began to employ Forral's method of breaking it into manageable stages. So what were the first steps here? Stop worrying, to begin with. If Anvar and Sara were there, she would find them. If not, she'd deal with that when the time came. First things first. In order to enter the city without arousing suspicion, she must steal some clothes to replace her ragged fighting gear. She had to pass as one of the natives, so she would need to see what they looked like and come up with an appropriate disguise. Since she was Mageborn, the language would be no problem. Having accomplished her disguise, she would need whatever passed for money in these parts. Aurian realized with grim amusement that she was about to add thievery to her growing collection of skills, both magical and martial. Stretching her aching limbs, she allowed herself to relax. Now that she had a plan of sorts, she could rest for a while, hidden in the sheltering trees.

Exhausted, she fell dead asleep among the roots of the tree. She was still asleep at dawn, when the bird-hunters came with their dogs and nets. The dogs were on her in flash, their yelps awakening her just in time to draw her sword and defend herself against their masters. The hunters were no warriors. Aurian killed one, and put another two out of action before their comrades managed to bring her down in their nets. By that time the commotion had attracted other peasants from the fields around, and Aurian found herself lying, helplessly tangled in the nets, in the midst of an astonished, vociferous crowd.

'See that pale skin!'

'Look at that hair – the colour of blood!'

'A warrior?'

'A demon?'

'A *woman*?'

'She killed poor Harz!'

'Fetch the Elder!'

Elder be damned, Aurian thought, and moved her hand a little to summon Fire-magic to burn away the nets. The movement was injudicious. The peasants saw, and a heavy blow from a stave sent her down into unconciousness.

Aurian awoke with a blinding headache, to find herself lying on the marble floor of a long, white hall. She was trussed in the nets, which had been bound tightly with rope. Her staff was still in her belt, but her sword was gone. The Mage cursed softly. It looked as though she had been brought to the city, and a brief period of observation told her that she was in some kind of hall of justice. The judges, she discovered, were respectfully addressed as Arbiters. There were three of them, dressed alike in long white robes and flowing white headdresses, sitting behind a table on a raised platform at the far end of the chamber. Their faces were masked in white, rendering them anonymous and expressionless. To Aurian it was an unnerving sight. In her country, white was the colour of death.

From tales that Forral had told her, Aurian thought that the brown, dark-haired, fine-boned people must be the Khazalim. In that case, the use of her magic would mean instant death; she had already seen the bowmen who stood guard on the balcony that circled the upper gallery of the hall. She decided to leave magic as a last resort – to wait, and see if she could bluff it out. While her captors awaited their turn, Aurian heard the Arbiters deal with other cases. The punishments were unremittingly harsh. The loss of a man's hand for theft; castration and stoning, respectively, for an adulterous couple. Gods, what would it be for murder? Fear clenched a fist of ice in Aurian's stomach, and she tensed herself, ready to sell her life dearly. Not here though, not with those bowmen. If they wanted to execute her, surely they would take her outside . . .

It was Aurian's turn. Her captors dragged her before the impassive Arbiters and placed her upon her knees, still bound, while the village Elder, his face haggard through hardship and pitted with the scars of disease, told his story. When he had finished his tale the Arbiters turned to the Mage, and she felt their cold eyes pierce her, taking in her alien appearance. Then the man in the centre of the trio spoke. 'Have you aught to say for yourself?'

Aurian's brain had been working with the lightning-speed of desperation to concoct a plausible story that might save her life. Since they seemed so keen on fidelity, she had decided on rape. Haltingly, she explained that she had been travelling with her husband and his sister (in case Anvar and Sara were somewhere in the city) when they had been blown south by the storm and shipwrecked. She had lost the others and made her way upriver in search of them. Eventually, she had fallen asleep beneath the tree and had awakened to find herself molested by a gang of ragged men (that part was true, at any rate). Half asleep and believing that she was about to be ravished, she had defended herself as best she could, prepared to die rather than yield herself to any man but her husband.

The Arbiters conferred in low voices, then the spokesman in

337

the centre turned back to Aurian. 'This tale does not explain your prowess at fighting.'

Aurian fought to stay calm, wishing that she could see his face. 'In my country, many women train as warriors.'

'I see.' Resting his arms on the table, he leaned forward, and she saw his eyes narrow behind the mask. 'And how do you explain your knowledge of our language? Only the demon sorcerers of the north have such facility with our tongue. Can you deny that you are one of those sorcerers?'

A low babble of astonishment came from the onlookers. The people closest to her backed hastily away, their eyes wide with fear. Aurian gulped. She had betrayed herself. She took a deep breath, thinking quickly, hazarding her life on a gamble. 'I was. But I fled their corruption to be with my husband.' What would he make of that?

'And is your husband also a sorcerer?'

'No. He is a Mortal, and our joining was forbidden. That is why I fled, renouncing the evils of sorcery for ever. I never intended to trespass in your lands, and bear no ill-will towards your people. I deeply regret what I have done, but truly it was an accident. All I want is to find my husband and leave this place. I am alone and bereft and afraid. For compassion's sake, will you not let me go?'

The Arbiter drew himself upright. 'Compassion? There is no compassion for wrongdoers in this city. You have taken a life. Forbidden! You are a foreigner trespassing in our lands. Forbidden! You are a sorceress. Forbidden! What right have you to compassion?'

Aurian dropped her eyes. 'None; yet I ask it anyway. It may be – it is – all I have left.'

Again, the Arbiters conferred. The man in the centre, who obviously wielded the greatest authority, seemed to be arguing with the other two. At last he turned to her. 'I believe that you are telling the truth, at any rate, for had you not renounced your sorcery you could have used your evil powers on those who captured you, or to escape from us. You have not done so, which implies that you mean no harm. And truly, I pity you, for you are alone and bereft indeed. Your husband has not reached

338

this city. If he had, he would have been brought to us, in accordance with our law.'

His words hit Aurian like physical blow. She had no need to feign grief or dismay. Anvar and Sara must be dead. She was to blame, and all this had been for nothing. When the Arbiter spoke again, his voice was less harsh. 'By law you should die for your crimes, but surely the Reaper of Souls would look upon us harshly for condemning a woman in your straits. Yet we cannot let you go. So we will give you a choice. As an alternative to execution, you may risk the arena, where criminals like yourself fight to the death for the entertainment of the Khisu and the people. You are said to show skill as a warrior. Perhaps, if you fight well, you will win your freedom – or, if you wish to seek your husband further, you will have the choice of following him to the Granaries of the Reaper. Do you accept this judgement?' It was not a question, and Aurian knew it. But at least it left her with one slim avenue of escape.

'I accept – and I am grateful for your mercy,' she said.

'One thing more . . .' The Arbiter beckoned to an official of the court and spoke to him in a low voice. The man left the room, and presently returned bearing a grey metal box, intricately chased with strange, arcane symbols that made Aurian shudder. The Arbiter blew away the coating of dust and raised the lid, withdrawing something that she could not see. He ordered her guards to unbind her, approached her cautiously, and with a surprisingly gentle touch fastened something around each of her wrists. As the second catch snapped shut, Aurian lurched and fell, her scream of agony echoing in her ears. It felt as though she was being wrenched inside out. A creeping weakness overwhelmed her, as though her very soul was being leeched away. She felt strong arms beneath her as the Arbiter lifted her to a bench by the wall and held a cup of wine to her lips. Aurian sipped it gratefully. Her muscles would not support her, and her head was swimming. But far worse than that, somewhere within her, unplaceable, there lurked an absence – a cold grey void that seemed ever to slip away from her seeking mind.

'What have you done to me?' she whispered.

The Arbiter sounded shaken. 'I have placed upon you the

bracelets of Zathbar Wizard-Bane – artefacts won from a Dragon's hoard, long ago. The secrets of their making are lost in the mists of time. I had no idea that they would affect you so severely, but they are necessary, if you are to live within our lands. They are set with spellstones that negate your sorcerous power, drawing it into themselves, and they will act as a safeguard for my people against any attempt on your part to employ your evil powers upon us.'

Aurian felt a flash of rage. These people who protested so strongly against the use of sorcery had actually employed negative magic to bind her power. Oh, gods, Aurian thought despairingly. How am I ever going to get out of this?

The warriors' quarters at the arena were pleasant – for a prison. Aurian's cell had barred windows and a sturdy door, but the smooth white walls and brown tiled floor were spotless, and there was a table, a chair, a chest and a narrow bed. Pegs were attached to the walls to hang clothing, and a gay woven rug on the floor provided a splash of bright colour. Aurian remembered little of her journey to this place. Someone had helped her here and removed the bonds that had been placed upon her, and she had fallen asleep on the bed, utterly spent.

When she awakened it was dusk. An oil lamp burned in a niche high in the wall, enclosed behind an iron grating, presumably in case she decided to set herself on fire, she thought wryly. The pain and weakness had passed, leaving only the hideous grey void – the absence of her magic. Aurian fought the panic that threatened to choke her. Don't be a fool, she told herself, or you'll never get out of this. But oh, that drear, chill emptiness . . . Get used to it, she told herself implacably. Fast.

She sat up, scanning the room, and saw a generous meal on the table. Ah, that looked good! She seemed to have been hungry for ever. Though it had cooled, it was good. There was some kind of spiced, savoury porridge made from cooked pulses, a haunch of roast meat that turned out to be goat, and strange, flat bread. There was a bowl of fruit, and white cheese so strong that it made her eyes water; and wine, a rich, dark red, fruity and strong. Aurian gorged herself, making up for her days of fasting. Then she returned to the bed with a brimming cup of wine and the bottle, propped her back against the wall and put her feet up, squinting at the dancing flame of the lamp that doubled and blurred in her vision. Gods, that wine was strong! Or was it simply affecting her because she was so spent?

The Mage felt curiously numb and detached. The theft of her powers, her current predicament and the loss of Anvar and Sara – she couldn't face any of them yet. She knew she ought to be making some kind of plan, but she simply could not bring herself to care. Since her flight from the Academy she had been constantly driven, constantly on a knife edge. Now she was imprisoned and forced to be still, and her mind and spirit were making the most of the opportunity to rest and renew themselves. The wine helped, too. She found herself drifting into a doze . . .

There was the sudden snick of a key turning in the lock. Aurian shot bold upright, blinking in the dazzling sunlight that poured through the barred window of her cell. She reached for her sword, but it was gone, of course. A tall, brown-skinned man of middle years entered, bearing a tray. The Mage made no move, but watched him as he went to the table and set his burden down. His head was completely bald, and he wore a red patch over his left eye. A pale, jagged scar ran down his face from beneath the patch. Beneath his loose red robes, his body was broad in the shoulder and rangy, reminding her, with a pang, of Anvar.

He turned to her, bowing deeply. 'A propitious day to you, warrior.' His voice was deep and smooth. Aurian, reacting instinctively to his courtesy, inclined her head in reply.

'A propitious day to you, sir – and yours will be more propitious than mine, I fear,' she added dryly.

The man smiled. 'That remains to be seen. Eliizar am I, sword master of the arena.' He bowed again. Aurian got to her feet, rubbing her painfully stiff neck, and responded in kind.

'Aurian am I – and a fool, it seems, for going to sleep sitting up.' As she spoke, she wondered why the bracelets had not impaired her ability to understand the local language. Could there be a loophole in the spell?

Eliizar smiled. 'You were weary indeed – and hungry, too, it

341

seems.' He cocked an eyebrow at the scant debris from her previous night's supper. 'I thought it best to let you sleep. We have masseurs here who can remedy your stiffness, but first let us break our fast together. I am curious as to your history, and I feel sure you have many questions that you would wish to ask me.'

Breakfast consisted of eggs, hard-boiled and shelled; the ubiquitous flat bread; cheese, honey and fruit – and a covered pot from which issued the most tantalizing aroma.

'What's this?' she asked Eliizar. His eyebrows went up in surprise.

'You do not know liafa? Why, you have never lived! This is the warrior's boon – it gives strength, alertness, sustenance.' He poured a cup of steaming black liquid and handed it to Aurian, who grimaced. It looked like mud. Inhaling the heady aroma, she took a sip, and choked. The taste was strong, and very bitter.

'It – it doesn't taste the way it smells,' she said sheepishly.

Eliizar smiled, and ladled a spoonful of honey into her cup, stirring vigorously. 'Try again,' he prompted. Aurian picked up the cup as though it were a viper, but, not wanting to lose face, she drank again. This time her face lit up with delight. With the honey smoothing out the bitterness, the drink was delicious – and stimulating, too. Aurian, who had such difficulty waking up in the morning, approved. She began to tackle her breakfast with a will.

'How came you here, Aurian?' Eliizar asked, drawing her attention from the food. 'How comes a lady to be a warrior? Swordswomen are unknown in this land.'

Aurian repeated the story she had told to the Arbiters. When she mentioned her two missing companions, Eliizar's good eye narrowed thoughtfully. 'Ah,' he said. 'Then there may be some truth in the rumours after all.'

Aurian pounced on the words. 'What rumours?'

The sword master hesitated. 'It may be nothing,' he said at last. 'You know how a rumour can grow from nothing . . .'

Aurian clamped her hand round his wrist. '*Tell me!*'

Eliizar looked away. 'Very well,' he said reluctantly. 'There was talk in the market some days ago that a Corsair ship had found outlanders further up the coast, and that one was a woman of surpassing fairness. But no outlander has been seen in the city to my knowledge, save yourself.'

'If they had been captured, what would have happened to them? Please tell me.'

'They would have been brought before the Arbiters, as you were. That is our law,' the sword master said brusquely.

'But if they were not?' Aurian persisted.

'Well, there have long been rumours of an illegal trade in slaves, but in that case the woman would have been sold to a house of pleasure. You can be sure that she has not. Word of such a wonder would have reached every man in the city by now, without a doubt. Leave it, Aurian. Whatever has happened to them, it cannot affect you.' Eliizar swallowed hard, looking unhappy. 'Warrior, you must concentrate on your own survival in this place, for as long as you can. The minute you entered the precincts of the arena you came under sentence of death, be it soon or late.'

Aurian, dismayed, let go of his arm. 'But the Arbiter said I would have a chance to win my freedom.'

The sword master shook his head. 'It was cruel and wrong on his part to tangle such a hope before you,' he said flatly.

'Then he lied? There is no way . . . ?'

'Impossible!' Eliizar rose abruptly. 'Here, you are naught but sword-fodder for the Khisu's entertainment. He is a cruel man, as I know to my cost. First I must place your level of skill against the other warriors. I have your sword, to return to you. You will train with them under supervision. We only fight to the death in the arena. Be warned. When you do fight there, if you overcome your first opponent you will then fight two together, then three. If, by some miracle, you survive all that, we pit you against the Black Demon.'

Aurian's scalp prickled. 'And if I defeat this Demon?'

'Then you win your freedom. But it is impossible. No one has ever defeated the Demon. No one can.'

Aurian stood, straightening her shoulders. 'I will defeat him,' she growled. 'When do we start?'

Eliizar shook his head sadly, and left without another word. Aurian heard the key turn in the lock. She shrugged and returned to her breakfast, refusing to countenance the insidious fear she felt for herself, and for her child. She would need to keep her strength up. After she had eaten she rested for a while, then began to put herself into the deep meditation of Forral's long-neglected swordsman's exercises. Whatever was to come, she would be ready. She had to be.

22
The Invisible Unicorn

'Again!' Maya shouted. D'arvan gathered his exhausted limbs and rushed towards her across the forest clearing, swinging his wooden sword wildly. The warrior sidestepped neatly, stuck out a foot and tripped him. The Mage went down like a felled tree, sprawling face down in the mud and last year's leaves. 'I think that's enough for today,' Maya said tactfully, the corners of her mouth twitching with suppressed mirth as she went over to help him up.

'You – you vixen!' D'arvan spluttered, wiping the mud from his eyes.

'I'm sorry, pet, but it is a standard move.' Maya offered him her hand. 'If you like, I'll teach it to you tomorrow.'

'Why bother?' D'arvan scrambled up and retrieved his cloak which hung from a nearby bough, wiping his glum face on the end of it before slinging it around his shoulders. 'We've been at this for about two weeks now, and I still hardly know one end of a sword from the other.'

'It'll come, don't worry. Two weeks is no time at all in sword training – especially when starting from scratch at your age.'

Her words did nothing to soothe his irritation. 'So it's my age, now, is it? It seems I can't win. When she teaches me magic, Eilin treats me like a child, and now you tell me I'm in my dotage!'

'When you act like this, I can't help thinking that Eilin has the right of it!' Maya snapped.

Seeing the scowl on her face, D'arvan made an effort to shake off his gloom, afraid of jeopardizing the love that was blossoming between them. He managed a lopsided smile. 'I'm sorry, Maya – I know I'm out of temper this morning.' He put his arm round her shoulders as they began to walk back towards the tower. He shivered, and it was not just the cooling of his body in the chill grey winter's day. 'I didn't sleep well last night. Every time I closed my eyes I had nightmares.'

'Why didn't you wake me?' The warrior tightened her arm round his waist, her voice full of sympathy. 'What were you dreaming about that was so dreadful?'

'It was my brother – well, half-brother. I kept dreaming that he was creeping up on me with a knife – trying to kill me, as once he tried before.' D'arvan swallowed hard, still in thrall to the dregs of his dreams, feeling a tension between his shoulder blades and dry tightness in his throat – the lurking, all-pervasive terror of the stalking assassin, of the hidden knife in the dark.

'Well, I'm not surprised, considering – ' Maya stopped in mid-stride and turned to him, her eyes very wide. 'D'arvan, you don't think it could be true, do you? I mean, the two of you were so closely linked. You don't think he has found out where you are, and he's coming to . . .'

D'arvan gasped as he acknowledged the truth to which his own fear had blinded him. Her instincts were always much surer than his own. 'Dear Gods – Eilin!' he shouted. 'He'll come to the tower. Quick!' Snatching Maya's own sharp blade from her scabbard, he plunged away through the trees, leaving the warrior, with her shorter stride, straining to catch up.

'D'arvan, you fool, wait!' she called after him. 'You can't . . .' But he had already left her far behind.

D'arvan had almost reached the border of trees that hemmed the grassy sward beside the lake when Eilin's mental shriek for help rocked him back on his heels. Panting, he redoubled his pace, forcing his way through branches that sliced, whiplike, across his chest and face; over roots that seemed to rise and reach out for him, twining about his ankles and knees. He was too preoccupied with thoughts of his brother to wonder why the forest seemed to be so much denser, his way through it far longer, than it had been before. Davorshan! How had he managed to pass the wolves that guarded the valley? What sorcery had he used to creep up on them like this? D'arvan gasped out a curse. If only he had paid more attention to his dreams!

When he reached the lakeside he stopped dead, confused

and dismayed. The border of trees now ended right by the shore, digging in with writhing roots to churn and obliterate the smooth, grassy slope that had been there before. It was not the only change. The island tower had been transfigured beyond all recognition. Huge vines snaked up round the once smooth walls, scratching the stonework and tapping at the hardened crystal of the windowed rooms. Thickets of thorny bramble and sloe choked the wooden bridge and the ground before the tower door.

Round the mainland end of the bridge, the apple trees from Eilin's orchard had gathered in a tight knot. D'arvan watched in amazement as unseasonal fruit swelled on each bough with uncanny speed, but the reason failed to occur to him until a branch whipped back with snakelike speed and hurled an apple like a stone from a slingshot. He dodged, but the hard fruit drove with bruising force into his shoulder, missing his face by inches. A fusillade of apples followed it, forcing him to duck behind a tree for his own protection; but the roots began to tug themselves out of the ground in a shower of soil as his shield moved to give the orchard trees a clear shot at their target. The entire Valley was in turmoil, every growing thing hastening to protect Eilin, mistress of earth-magic. And, mistaking D'arvan for another intruder, they were blocking him from going to her aid. Taking a firm grip with both hands on Maya's sword, he began to hack at the surrounding branches, frantic and unthinking in his haste.

A sinister rustle passed through the ranks of the assembled trees. A crimson mist began to loop and roil among the reaching branches – the rage of the forest. A sound like the whistling howl of a gale filled the Mage's ears as the boughs began to toss and sway, their twigs like bony fingers grasping at his hair and tearing at his eyes and clothing. His knuckles dripped blood as branches clutched and smote at his hands, trying to knock the sword away. Far away, it seemed, beneath the snarling, raging din of the forest's fury, he heard Maya crying for help. Torn, D'arvan tried to turn back to her, but his way was blocked by a thicket of holly trees that bristled with glossy, dagger-pointed leaves. Taking advantage of his hesitation, the forest flung roots like earth-encrusted tentacles around his ankles. One sharp jerk and he was down, and the roots began to tug him away, further back into the deep heart of the forest. Briars looped round his hands, digging clusters of sharp thorns into the tender skin of his wrists and the backs of his fingers, which still clutched the hilt of the sword. Dust-devils swirled across the ground, flinging dead leaves, earth and pebbles stingingly into his eyes.

'Help me!' Once again Eilin's cry seared D'arvan's mind, weak now and despairing.

'I can't!' he gasped out loud, tears of pain and frustration running down his face. Already the knees and elbows of his clothing had been torn to ribbons on the rough ground, and the skin beneath was scraped raw. His hands were numbing, their circulation cut off by the ever tightening loops of vine. Soon he would lose his grip on the sword, and then he would be helpless to go to his teacher's aid . . .

Of course! Fool! What had he been thinking of? He was an Earth-Mage too! No wonder the forest had taken him for an enemy, hacking at it like some stupid, untutored Mortal! Straining to focus his whirling thoughts, to remember what the Lady Eilin had taught him over the past weeks, D'arvan gathered his power and reached out with his mind, trying to contact the heart – the very soul – of the forest.

It beat back at him furiously, its intelligence obscured behind a mist of seething red rage. But D'arvan persisted. *'I'm a friend! A friend! I'll help you to help the Lady! See, I'm an Earth-Mage, her own pupil. See?'* Beseechingly, he held his powers out, as Eilin had shown him, open to the scrutiny of the forest. He summoned the moist, heady scents of spring's burgeoning and the ancient musk of the mother-soil that cradled the seed; the dapple of sunlight in the beech tree's shade and the diamond-dance of the lively stream; the silver of moonlight and the silk of morning mist; the stark white shroud of winter's mourning and the poignant exuberance of autumn's fire.

And something changed. Like the snick of a key unlocking a door, like the falling away of chains, like the relaxing of winter's claws upon the land with the coming of spring, the forest accepted him. The howling died away to a muted murmur, and D'arvan felt relief like the lifting of a massive weight as the ire of the trees ceased to hammer at him. The roots and vines loosed their grip and fell away, and a clear avenue opened before him, across the churned ground and over the bridge, leading right to the door of the tower. Scrambling to his feet, D'arvan ran, a single errant branch poking him hard in the back to hasten him on his way.

The vines across the door fell back with a slithering rattle as D'arvan approached, sword in hand. As he jumped past them into the kitchen, he wondered if they would come after him, but some force seemed to be preventing them from entering the building. When he reached the bottom of the spiral staircase, the young Mage discovered the reason. He staggered back, gagging on the reek of evil magic. Choking, with streaming eyes, he pulled himself upright using the smoothly curving stair-rail and began to haul himself, step by step, up the metal stairs.

The upper rooms that led off the staircase were utterly devastated. D'arvan flinched at the chaos of room after room. The windows were cracked, the wooden benches overturned and splintered; the tender young seedlings torn and trampled underfoot. Now that he had opened his mind to the use of his powers, the Mage could feel their distress acutely; their tiny, soundless cries of pain piercing his mind and wringing at his heart. But each room was empty of people, and, reach though he might, he could no longer touch Eilin's mind. Chamber after deserted chamber he passed during his ascent, and found the same appalling destruction. Then, rounding the final curve of the staircase, he stopped. At the top of the stairs was a figure bearing in its left hand a sword that was dripping with blood. Davorshan. At the sight of D'arvan, his face contorted into an evil, leering grin. 'Hail and well met, brother', he said. 'It took longer than I had thought to find you – but the days of wandering lost on those blasted moors will be well repaid by your death.' Raising the blade he stepped forward, murder in his eyes.

Davorshan had the advantage of the height – Maya had taught D'arvan that much. Grasping his blade in a hand that was suddenly wet and slick with sweat, the Earth-Mage began to back slowly down the stairs, feeling his way with careful feet since he knew better than to take his eyes from his brother, even for an instant. Davorshan's hatred scorched into his brain, like the rage of the forest but deeper, closer, far more intimate. They had been linked for so many years – how well his brother knew him. Inexorably, Davorshan's malice ate into his mind, working on his fears and self-doubts, chipping away at his confidence and courage. 'Half-breed!' his brother spat. 'Spineless, gutless, powerless mongrel! Did you really think it would work, D'arvan – running away to hide behind the Lady's skirts? And what have we here?'

His merciless, rummaging will unearthed a memory – to D'arvan the most precious of all. 'So!' Davorshan's cruel laughter mocked him. 'What have you been up to, brother mine? Rutting with a little Mortal bitch, since you can't manage anything better. Is she any good, D'arvan? Perhaps I'll try her, after I've killed you. Or maybe I'll do it first, so you can watch. Where is she, eh? Where have you hidden your Mortal slut?'

Red rage flooded D'arvan's mind. His hand, holding the sword, began to shake. Yet Maya's training held firm. She had taught him better than to be gulled by a transparent gibe. Instead he began to gather his powers as he continued to back away, wondering which aspect of his Earth-magic he could use against his brother. The plants upstairs were too small, but . . . Could he bring the vines that enveloped the tower to his aid? If they could break through a window . . .

'Oh, no, you don't!' Davorshan's voice was a snarl. 'I won't waste my time on a contest of magic, D'arvan – not on *her* ground.'

'Really?' D'arvan lifted his hand, ready to strike.

'I warn you! Do you want to be responsible for Eilin's death?'

D'arvan stopped in mid-gesture, his eyes flicking involuntarily past his brother to the top of the stairs.

'Well done,' Davorshan sneered. 'It has finally occurred to you. Had she been dead, you would have known it.'

'Where is she?' D'arvan cried. 'What have you done to her?'

Davorshan shrugged, and held up his dripping sword. 'Don't depend on her coming to your aid, though you gave me no time to finish the job. But if you want to bring magic into this, remember where my talents lie. I can raise the waters of the lake to swamp this tower. And when the tower collapses, where will Eilin be, eh?'

'Bastard!' D'arvan grated through clenched teeth.

'No, brother. You're the bastard. Eliseth told me that much. You've leeched my power all our lives – the power that should have rightfully been mine – and when I kill you it will all be mine. *You should never have been born!*'

So that was how Eliseth had subverted him. D'arvan felt his brother's resentment; his burning greed and the unreasoning rage that consumed him. When it reached a climax, Davorshan would attack. D'arvan felt carefully with his foot for the next step down, and found it to be the broader landing of one of the tower rooms. The glimmerings of a plan came into his mind. He stretched his lips wide in a mocking grin. 'Oh no, my brother, you're wrong. Eilin told me the whole story. I'm the child of our mother's love. She hated Bavordran, and she only had you to allay his suspicions. I may be the bastard, but you're the one who should never have been born!'

'*Liar!*' Davorshan charged heedlessly down, his face twisted, his bloody sword flailing. D'arvan wrenched himself to one side, into the open doorway of the room, and stuck out his foot as he had seen Maya do only that morning. He felt the hot wrench of tortured muscles as his brother's momentum twisted his leg to one side, unbalancing him; but as he fell, he heard thudding and clanging as Davorshan tumbled headlong down the metal staircase. It had worked!

D'arvan used an upturned bench to help himself to his feet, sweat springing out on his brow as fire and ice lanced agonizingly up the injured leg, which would not bear his weight. He staggered, falling again.

Spitting out one of Maya's favourite oaths, he pulled himself to the stairs and began to slide down, step by step, on his rump, as he and Davorshan had done so often as children. The memory hurt like a knife twisting in a wound, but childhood was over now, and the soul-companion of those days had turned into a murdering monster. He had to get to the bottom to finish Davorshan, if yet he lived, for otherwise his brother would surely finish him.

By the time he reached the bottom, his face was soaked with

sweat and tears. Davorshan lay face down on the broad kitchen flags at the foot of the steps, unmoving. D'arvan prayed he might already be dead. The hilt of the sword was ice in his trembling hand as he perched on the lowest step, directly above his brother. 'Oh, gods,' he prayed, 'please don't force me to do this!' But Davorshan moaned just then, and stirred, rolling on to his back. Though his eyes were glazed, the hatred, unconquerable, still twisted his mind. Still and always. D'arvan faced it at last, and accepted. Lifting the sword high in both hands, he drove the point down through his brother's heart – and felt pain unspeakable ram through his own breast as their minds linked for the last time. Screaming, he convulsed, his arms clutched round his chest as he doubled over.

'*Brother* . . .' Davorshan's broken whisper fled through D'arvan's mind, as his brother's soul fled his body. D'arvan felt the pain in his chest give way to the searing wrench that marked the passing of a Mage. One who had died by his hand.

'D'arvan!' Maya's gruff voice was a ray of light that pierced the dark well of the Earth-Mage's grief. Numbly, he lifted his head to look at her. Dropping down beside him on the step she put her arms around him. The tears that he himself had been unable to shed flooded her face, and he knew she understood. Yet her voice, when she spoke again, was surprisingly matter-of-fact. 'You killed him.'

It needed no answer.

'The way things stand, he won't be the last,' Maya went on. 'It's never an easy thing, for most of us. It never should be. All we can do is try to distance ourselves a little and get on with our lives as best we can. But I promise you that never again will it be as bad as this first time. The worst is over now, love.'

D'arvan clung to her, oddly comforted by her blunt words. How like his Maya, to dispense compassion and common sense in the same breath. How lucky he was to have her, in all this ruin and death . . . 'Eilin!' His voice cracked. 'Maya, she's upstairs. Hurt – badly, I think.'

'Seven bloody demons!' Maya leapt to her feet. 'Where?'

'At the top.' He tried to get up, and sank back down again with a yelp of pain.

She whirled back sharply. 'You're wounded?'

'Wrenched my leg, doing that tripping move of yours. You go on – I'll follow as best I can.'

Maya bit her lip, nodded, and fled upstairs.

D'arvan made slow and painful progress, hauling himself along by his good leg and the stair-rail. He was only halfway up when he heard the ring of booted feet on the metal treads and Maya reappeared round the curve, abruptly stopping her headlong descent when she saw him. 'She's dying.'

Maya was right. D'arvan knew it as soon as he saw the Lady, who lay in the wreckage of her chamber like a crumpled bundle of rags. He had not known that one body could hold so much blood. It was everywhere; splattered and smeared across the bed and walls, pooled on the floor, soaking her robes which were rent and sliced in a dozen places. Her skin already held the pale translucence of imminent death. Maya propped him against the wall with his weight balanced on his good leg, and ran back to Eilin. The old D'arvan would have retched and turned his eyes away from the horror. The new D'arvan felt his guts twist, but with outrage. In one grim instant, his grief and guilt at killing Davorshan vanished.

'I will not let this happen.' His voice sounded alien and distant, even to himself.

'D'arvan, there's nothing we can do for her.' Maya was on her knees beside Eilin, her voice choked with grief. 'Even a healer couldn't . . .'

'My father can.'

'What?'

D'arvan felt very calm. It was a dangerous thing to try, a desperate thing, but it was their only chance. 'Maya, get out of here. You mustn't be caught up in this.'

'Damned if I will.' She scrambled to her feet, her hands and knees stained with blood. 'You haven't time to fight me over it.' She picked up the Lady's staff from the floor and handed it to him. 'Here. You'll need this for support – in more ways than one.'

'Stubborn bitch!' He kissed her mouth, overwhelmed by love for her, and felt the tension of her lips melt as she returned his embrace.

353

'Pig-headed bastard!' she retorted. 'Be careful, D'arvan.' She stepped back, unsheathed her sword, and flung it out of the door. 'You can't have iron near the Phaerie, the legends say,' she explained.

'Really.' D'arvan was annoyed with himself for not knowing. 'Do they say anything else useful?'

'Umm . . . yes. You have to call him by three true names. Hurry, D'arvan.'

Leaning on the staff to support his injured leg, D'arvan gathered his powers and hurled his mind and spirit forth, trying somehow to reach the mysterious other place where the Phaerie were said to dwell. Once more he invoked the essence of the forest – its scents and colours; all its moods through the changing days. The sounds of drowsy bees and bright birds; the rustle of leaves and ripple of stream; the scuttling dash of rabbit and squirrel; the soft, careful footfall of deer and stealthy glide of fox and weasel. Taking a deep breath, he called, using both voice and mind. 'Hellorin! Forest Lord! Father! In the name of Adrina, my mother, I summon you!'

Nothing seemed to be happening. Yet so clear, so real was his vision of the forest that he could almost see it taking shape around him. The ruined chamber faded from his sight, and as if through a shifting mist he saw trees take shape – the stately silver columns of beeches; a study oak gnarled like the thews of a giant; supple willow and martial holly bristling with spears. Gay hawthorn like a flower-decked maiden and slender rowan, ethereal as a dream. Through the trees starlit water glinted – with a start he recognized the lake and its island, though the tower had vanished. He could smell the heady summer scent of the grass that covered the solid earth beneath his feet. But it was winter outside. How could this be? D'arvan's eyes widened. Maya was standing to one side of the forest clearing, her mouth agape, her hand reaching automatically for her missing sword. And at her feet lay the still form of Eilin.

'*Who summons the Forest Lord?*' The voice was deep and sad as the autumn wildwood; as light and merry as a summer breeze amid the treetops. Before the mighty oak a figure stood, obscuring the great tree with his immensity. He was cloaked in shimmering, ever-changing grey and green, and so vast was he that the silver glinting in his long dark hair was the light of stars. His brow was circled with a diadem of golden oak leaves, and above them towered the shadowy branches of the proud stag's crown. Once more he spoke, his voice like winter's bite; like the gladsome warmth of a new spring day. 'Who dares summon the Lord of the Phaerie?' D'arvan, awestruck, almost dropped to his shaking knees. He took a firm grip on Eilin's staff and reminded himself that this being was his father. He bowed deeply, at a loss for words. This was far beyond his wildest imaginings. What could he possibly say to one such as Hellorin?

'My Lord, allow me to present the Earth-Mage D'arvan – your son.' Maya's gruff voice cut through the silence.

'What?' the Forest Lord thundered, transfixing her with his glare. Lightning flashed in his eyes, beneath darkly frowning brows. As he raised his hand, the very trees seemed to quail. D'arvan suddenly found that he could move. Leaning on the staff, he limped across to Maya, placing himself protectively in front of her.

'It's true!' he cried. 'I called you by your true name of Father, and you answered. My mother was Adrina of the Magefolk, and in her name I summoned you, for we have dire need of your help. The Lady Eilin, my mother's friend and guardian of this Valley, is dying.' It all came out in a rush. Before D'arvan's astonished eyes, the awesome figure vanished.

D'arvan looked wildly around. Then, from behind the oak, stepped his father, shrunk now to normal, mortal size, but not a whit diminished in might and majesty. Great muscles etched and shadowed his bare chest beneath the cloak. Strong legs, clad in dark leggings and tall boots, were planted wide apart on the forest floor. A ghostly image of the antlered crown still rose above his oak-circled brow. His stern, kingly features and hard mouth were gentled now, and the expression in his dark eyes was indecipherable. 'My son?' The deep voice was soft, and lilted with a thousand questions.

The Forest Lord strode forward, and strong hands clasped D'arvan's shoulders. Dark, fathomless eyes searched his face, and D'arvan found his own eyes brimming with tears. 'My son,' Hellorin murmured, the beginnings of a wondering smile lifting the corners of his sculpted mouth. 'My own son, and I never knew I had you.'

'Father . . .' D'arvan whispered. Dropping the staff, he flung his arms around Hellorin's broad shoulders, and there, in the starlit forest clearing, father and son embraced at last.

'D'arvan? Lord Hellorin?' Maya's hesitant voice broke into their silent communion. The tears in her eyes were evidence that she was far from unmoved by their reunion but, ever practical, she gestured towards Eilin's stricken body. 'My apologies, Lords, but the Lady's condition is desperate. We may already be too late.'

The Forest Lord lifted an eyebrow. 'Who is this temeritous person?' he asked his son.

'This is Lieutenant Maya, a peerless warrior, a brave and true companion, and' – D'arvan's voice rang out with proud defiance – 'my own Lady.'

The Forest Lord burst out laughing. Maya was scowling, and D'arvan gestured urgently for her to be silent, fearing the furious outburst that he knew was coming. 'I fail to see what is so amusing,' he said icily.

Hellorin took a deep, gasping breath, wiping his eyes. 'Ah, my son,' he chuckled. 'How good it is to see you already carrying on the ancient traditions of our people.'

'What?' D'arvan was stunned.

'Do you pay no attention to the legends?' his father asked, his eyes dancing with mirth. 'All those stories about the Phaerie luring Mortals away to be their brides? And bridegrooms, for that matter, for the ladies of my people would make my life a misery indeed if I were to deny them their chance at the occasional lusty Mortal stud!'

He turned to Maya with a deep bow. 'Lady Maya, I am honoured to meet my son's chosen, and I apologize for my unseemly mirth. In my opinion, he has chosen very well indeed.' His gaze travelled over her like a caress; so blatantly, potently lecherous that D'arvan found himself grinding his teeth. Maya crimsoned, uncertain whether to be indignant or flattered. Then, drawing herself up to her full height, she looked Hellorin coldly in the eye.

'My thanks for your courtesy, Lord, but this is hardly the

356

time. Might we, perhaps, consider the urgent business at hand?'

D'arvan groaned and covered his eyes with one hand, and Hellorin whooped with mirth. 'An excellent choice indeed! D'arvan, you have a she-wolf on your hands.' His voice became sober. 'Fear not, little warrior. The Lady Eilin will come to no further harm. The Phaerie honour her for her work in this vale, and I would not allow her to die. In summoning me, you brought yourselves into my kingdom, where time holds no sway. Her life is suspended here – suspended and preserved. But I must know who is responsible for this atrocity, and why. You are right – this is no light matter, and my instincts tell me it is part of a greater pattern of mischief. So let us make ourselves comfortable, children. Tell me what has come to pass in the world outside.'

He waved his hand, and the clearing in which they stood wavered and blurred. The surrounding trees became the pillars of a great hall, their branches linking overhead to form a roof. At one side, where the crimson-berried hollies had stood in splendour, a fire blazed in a huge fireplace. The floor was covered by a deep green carpet. D'arvan gasped. 'Why, it's like the Great Hall at the academy!'

'And from whom do you think the Magefolk stole the design?' Hellorin's voice held a grim edge that vanished with his next words. 'Come, sit.'

D'arvan retrieved Eilin's staff, and Maya helped him limp to the deep, comfortable chairs beside the roaring fire. A huge grey hound was sprawled before the flames, taking up all the space in front of the broad hearth. Though Hellorin had made no visible summons, the doors at the far end of the hall opened, and a tall, copper-haired Phaerie lady entered, gowned in green and as slender as the willow she resembled. Her eyebrows went up at the sight of the bloodstained strangers. 'Melianne, will you bring refreshments, please?' Hellorin asked her. 'And convey the Lady Eilin to our healers.'

Her brown eyes widened at the sight of the Earth-Mage. 'Lady Eilin! My Lord, what evil is this?'

'That is what I intend to find out.' He waved her away. 'Summon the Phaerie, my dear. I believe that this event may mark the end of our long waiting.'

The Phaerie woman's eyes burned. 'At once, my Lord!' In a soundless explosion of golden light, she vanished. Hellorin chuckled at Maya's dumbfounded expression.

'We generally use the doors,' he said dryly. 'Melianne is rather excitable, however.'

D'arvan was utterly exhausted; drained in body and spirit by the events of the day. At first he thought the ripple in the air before the hearth was a trick played by the firelight on his tired eyes. Then he heard Melianne's sharp voice coming, it seemed, out of thin air. 'Barodh, you oaf, get out of the way.' The hound leapt up and slunk guiltily to its master's side. Where it had been lying, the shimmering air began to glow, forming a globe of golden light which cleared to reveal a low round table. On its snowy cloth reposed a flask of clear yellow wine and three crystal goblets. Bread and fruit took up the remaining space, and the fragrance of the food made D'arvan's mouth water. But his attention was diverted by Maya's anguished cry. 'Eilin!' He swung round in his chair to see the body of the Earth-Mage surrounded by the same golden light. Even as he looked, she was gone.

'Do not worry, Maya.' Hellorin's voice was soothing. 'My healers far outstrip those of the Magefolk in skill. Eat, children, and rest yourselves – and tell me your tale.' He poured wine for them, and handed them the sparkling goblets. Maya, about to take a sip, suddenly hesitated, and the Forest Lord smiled. 'Legends again, Maya? Well, you need not worry about that one. Tasting our food and drink will not put you any further into my power than the two of you have already put youselves by summoning me.'

D'arvan met Maya's eyes and shrugged. This was his father, after all, and he had helped them so far. He took a sip of the wine and saw Maya do likewise, though she still looked suspicious. Somehow, the thought that she would follow him even into this warmed him as much as the drink, which was potent enough. D'arvan felt it course through his body as though his veins were running with liquid fire. His weariness fled, and the room seemed to come into sharp and vivid focus around him. The tight, hot ache of his injured leg vanished as though it had never been.

Hellorin pressed food on them, and as they ate D'arvan told of Miathan's perfidy, the breaking of the Mages' Code, and the fall of the Magefolk into evil. Hellorin said nothing until D'arvan reached the end of his story, speaking of Davorshan's attack on Eilin and his brother's death, followed by the desperate summoning of the Phaerie Lord. As he faltered into silence, his father leapt from his chair, one fist pumping skywards in a gesture of victory. 'At last!' he exulted. '*At last!*' Outside the hall, a chorus of glorious Phaerie voices cried out in wild celebration. Maya leapt to her feet with an exclamation of dismay.

'Father!' D'arvan's shocked voice cut through the Forest Lord's rejoicing. Breathing hard, Hellorin resumed his chair. 'Oh, my son,' he gasped, 'if you only knew how we have waited down the endless years for this news! For goodness sake sit down, girl.' He waved an irritable hand at Maya who was still on her feet, her eyes casting round the hall for a weapon of some kind.

'My Lord, how can you rejoice at such a grim tale?' D'arvan asked in cold reproof. 'Have you forgotten my mother? I'm Mage as well as Phaerie, and you mock both my grief and that of all folk who suffer because of this evil.'

Hellorin looked at his son expressionlessly, but his words were soft. 'My deepest apologies to you both. Please, Lady, sit down and let me explain, then perhaps you will understand my unseemly joy.'

Maya gave him a savage look. 'I hope so,' she growled.

'You have been taught that the universe is shaped by chance and balance,' Hellorin began, pouring himself a cup of wine. 'You may not know that the Magefolk were brought into this world to maintain and guard the balance, as others were on other worlds, lest chance gain a stranglehold, and the universe be destroyed by chaos, chance's bastard child.'

The warrior's fingers drummed irritably on the arm of her chair.

'Patience, Maya. To shorten a lengthy tale; we Phaerie have always been, well, rather unpredictable, and we wield great powers of the Old Magic. The ancient Magefolk feared us, believing us agents of chance, which was, in a way, quite true.

359

They contrived to shut us out of the world – to imprison us in this Elsewhere, which we cannot leave unless summoned, and from which we may not influence the events of the world. We are also unable to bear children among ourselves in this place – hence our need for the occasional Mortal or Mage to increase our race.'

D'arvan froze. 'You mean you used my mother . . .'

'No – never!' Hellorin reached out to grasp his arm. 'Do you think we Phaerie are monsters? No child is born to us save through deepest love. It tore my heart when Adrina returned to Nexis to fulfil that ridiculous promise to her father. I wept, and raged, and cursed. I was desperate to go to her – to find her, and bring her home. But I could not go unless I was summoned, and no one summoned me – until it was too late.' His voice was choked with grief.

'Oh, father,' D'arvan whispered, too moved to say more.

Hellorin took a long swallow of his wine. 'Now it may be clear to you why we are unfriends with the Magefolk. They have robbed us of our freedom over many a long age, and they were wrong to do so. You see, chance is as essential to the world as balance. Without us, the Magefolk began to stagnate, becoming more introspective, more proud and self-willed. In their pride, they created the four great Artefacts of Power, of which the Cauldron is but one. When the Cataclysm came, we almost escaped them, but failed. Then, in our bitterest moment, came our greatest hope. The Sword of Flame, the greatest of the four weapons, was given into our keeping by its makers, who desired that it should be taken out of the world until it was claimed by the One for whom it had been forged. When the time was right, they told us, we must return it to the world, setting traps and guards about it to ensure that it would only fall into the proper hands.

' "But how shall we know whose hand was meant to hold this thing?" we asked.

' "That will be your test," they told us.

' "How shall we know when the Sword is needed?" we begged.

' "You will know," they said. "A time will come when the Magefolk will dwindle and fail, and fall upon one another like wolves. Brother will slay brother, and ambition betray trust, and the world will fall into great evil. That will be the time."

' "But how shall we return the Sword to the world?" we asked. "How can we guard it, where we are powerless?"

' "That," they said, "is your problem." So I asked them: "What is to be our reward for undertaking this great task?" '

Hellorin paused, his eyes gleaming. 'They promised us our freedom, using the Sword to circumvent the ancients' spells and bring us back into the world. We swore fealty to it, and to the One who will wield it. When he claims it, we will follow him back into the world, to fight at his side against the evil. Having overcome it, we will be free, as once we were. Free, my children!'

'When brother slays brother,' D'arvan whispered. 'So the time is at hand. But how will you return the Sword, father? How will you guard it?'

The Forest Lord would not meet his eyes, but simply sat, staring into the fire, his face shadowed by sorrow. The silence stretched between them.

'I take it, my Lord, that you intend to use us, somehow,' Maya said bluntly.

Hellorin looked up at last, nodding. 'D'arvan, I'm sorry,' he said. 'There are age-old laws governing dealings with the Phaerie. Laws I made myself, long ago, for the sake of my people. When you summoned me, you put yourself under those laws, and I cannot alter them, even for my son. You asked a boon of me – the saving of Lady Eilin's life – even as the Lady herself once begged me to find her child, and I have helped you both. Now you are beholden to me, and I can demand a service from you. Do you understand?'

'You want us to guard the Sword.' D'arvan's disappointment in his father warred with his understanding of the Forest Lord's predicament. A ruler should obey his own laws, and Hellorin had the responsibility for his people on his shoulders. 'I'll try,' he said at last. 'But father, I ask only this – I beg you, leave Maya out of it.'

'No, D'arvan. We're in this together.'

'D'arvan, I cannot.' The voices were simultaneous in their protest.

The Mage looked from his father to his lover with mounting annoyance. 'Will you two stop that.'

Maya and Hellorin looked at one another and burst out laughing. 'Ah, what a woman!' Hellorin said. 'How I wish I could keep you both here with me. But we are in the grip of events much larger than any of us.' He held out his arms and gathered both of them in a close embrace. 'I promise you will not be parted, though you must be sundered as lovers until our tasks are complete. That being so, the large events must wait a while. You need time together – as far as time applies here – and a room is ready for you. Go, children, and rest – or not, as the case may be!' His eyes twinkled wickedly. 'I will call you when it's time to go.'

They met again in the great hall, after the passage of a night by worldly standards, though far too short a time by those of D'arvan and Maya. Hellorin embraced them once more. 'Are you ready, children?'

They nodded. They were, as far as they might be. During their time alone they had shared fears and secrets, exchanged their own private vows, and loved one another endlessly, trying to store up memories for the time they must spend apart. 'Will Eilin be all right?' Maya asked, and D'arvan marvelled once more at her courage as she stood, straight and composed, before his father.

Hellorin nodded. 'Our healers say she will recover, and she will stay with us in safety and honour until this business is done.'

'Thank you,' Maya said simply. 'Have you any idea how long that will be?' There was a catch in her voice, and D'arvan suddenly realized that she was as afraid as he.

Hellorin shook his head. 'Until the One claims the Sword, that is all we know. Let us hope, for all our sakes, that he hurries!'

Maya's eyes twinkled. 'What makes you so sure that it's a man, my Lord?' She stepped back to let D'arvan say his own farewells.

Hellorin embraced him roughly. 'How it grieves me to lose the son I have only just found.'

'It grieves me to lose you,' D'arvan whispered. 'I hope, when this is all over, we'll be able to make up for it.'

362

Hellorin nodded gravely. 'And now, my son, you must take us into your world,' he said.

D'arvan stared at him. 'Me? But how?'

'Do as you did yesterday. Summon the forest. The real forest. Use the Lady Eilin's staff which you bear – it has more power than you imagine.'

It was easier than D'arvan had expected. Eilin's staff seemed to want to go home. Within a few breaths, they stood on the banks of the lake at sunrise. The grass was scarred where tree roots had gouged it, and though the vines had retreated from the tower the stonework was scored and the windows broken, leaving the building open to the elements. 'It would break Eilin's heart to see this,' D'arvan murmured.

'She will not.' As Hellorin spoke, the tower blurred and vanished. In its place stood an immense red crystal. As it caught the sun's first rays, it glowed with pulsing brilliance and hummed with power, dazzling the eye. Within its glittering facets, the outline of the Sword could be glimpsed, shimmering with its own ghostly light.

'That will never do.' Hellorin waved his hand, and the massive gem clouded and turned grey, taking on the appearance of a huge, rough boulder. Vegetation swarmed up to cover its sides, and moss and lichen appeared on its grainy surface.

Maya gasped. 'How did you do that?' she demanded. 'I thought you had no power in this world.'

'I do it through D'arvan,' the Forest Lord explained. 'He brought me here, and he is part Phaerie, like me, and part Mage; and the Magefolk made these rules. But we must hurry. I can only bend their magic so far.' Already strain was showing on Hellorin's face. 'Now, my dearest daughter . . .'

'Wait!' Maya ran to D'arvan and threw her arms around him. 'I love you,' she whispered.

'I love you, too.' He kissed her one last time, and stepped back reluctantly as the Forest Lord raised his hand.

Maya vanished. In her place appeared the most beautiful creature that had been seen since the dawning of the world. A unicorn, insubstantial, made up it seemed from all kinds of light: starlight's glimmer, gossamer moonlight, silken dawn

363

mistlight, and incandescent sunbursts where her hooves touched the ground. On her forehead was a long, slender, wickedly pointed silver horn.

'See?' Hellorin said softly. 'Our warrior still bears her sword – for it will be her task to protect the Sword of Flame. Only you can see her – to all others she will be invisible. To be worthy of the Sword, the wielder must be wise as well as courageous. In order to approach it, the One must discover a way to see the unseen, for in no other way can our invisible guardian be passed.'

'Passed?' D'arvan shouted. 'Killed, you mean?'

'No, I do not mean killed. It is part of the spell that while Maya is visible to any person save yourself her guardianship will be suspended. There will be no need for killing. Besides,' Hellorin added, 'would a being who was worthy of the Sword of Flame wantonly slay such a beautiful creature? I think not.'

D'arvan shook his head. 'And what do you have in store for me?' he asked tightly.

'You? You are Earth-Mage and son of the Forest Lord. You bear the Lady's staff, and the forest will do your bidding. You must bring back the wildwood to this valley; fill it with an impenetrable barrier of trees. The wild things will dwell here, and be sustained, and the wolves will be your friends and share your task. You will guard the Sword from all enemies, and the forest will shelter the enemies of evil whom you will also guard and sustain – yet they will never see you, or know of your presence. You and Maya will share your guardianship until the One comes for the Sword, when you will be freed and reunited, as we all will be at that time.' As he spoke, Hellorin's outline began to shift and shimmer. 'I can stay no longer. Farewell, my son – and forgive me.' He vanished.

D'arvan looked at the unicorn. The fierce, beautiful creature snorted and pawed the ground, flinging up clods of turf in sunburst explosions. Then she trotted to the Mage and rested her head on his shoulder, and her huge dark eyes were fathomless pools of sorrow. D'arvan flung his arms round her strong, arching neck beneath the sweeping mane, his throat tight with tears. 'Oh, my love,' he murmured, 'how I'll miss you.'

The invisible unicorn snorted and tossed her head.

'You're right,' D'arvan said. 'I had better get started.'

Turning, he lifted the Lady's staff and began to summon the forest.

23

Demon

The area buzzed with the noise of the excited crowd. The sweeping tiers of marble benches were tightly packed with sweating bodies, all crushed together. Excitement was at fever pitch, the crowd's attention alternating between the sanded circular fighting area on the floor of the massive stone bowl and the flower-decked royal balcony where sat the frowning Khisal, heir apparent to the throne, and the smiling Khisu Xiang and his new queen the Khisihn, whose wedding was being celebrated today. The crowd gawked at the balcony with great curiosity. It was indeed a day of wonder – that the Khisu, content for so long with his harem of beauties, should have finally elevated another lady to be his consort in place of the old queen, dead these many years. Rumour said that she had been slain by the Khisu's own hand.

Wrinkled, sharp-eyed crones nodded sagely to one another. 'The young prince'll have to watch his step now,' they were saying. 'He never had his father's favour. If the new queen drops a son, Khisal Harihn will find himself in a sack at the bottom of the river, like his mother.'

They watched the early bouts with scant attention and less patience, waiting for the real entertainment to start. There was a new warrior to fight today. A foreigner – and, Reaper preserve us, a woman! A sorceress, and as fierce as the Black Demon itself. Rumour had it that she had laid an entire village to waste, downriver. Because of this tale, the arena had filled early that day. Outside the gate, hundreds of disappointed people were still being turned away.

In the warriors' yard beneath the stone tiers of the arena it was shady and cool. Aurian, alone in a corner, was going through Forral's exercises, trying to prepare her body and mind for the coming ordeal. It was difficult to suppress the fear

366

she felt for her child, knowing that this day's exertions and peril might spell the end for the hapless mite. If only she had her magic, she might have been able to protect it, but as it was . . . 'Oh, Chathak,' she prayed, 'protect this child: the child of warriors.'

Aurian was vaguely aware of the eyes of the other combatants fixed curiously upon her. They were strangers to one another, kept apart lest unfortunate friendships develop between them. They met only in closely monitored training sessions, and even then were not allowed to speak to each other. She had trained with several of them over the last weeks, astonishing even Eliizar with her prowess. Apart from training, her days had been spent pleasantly enough in eating, resting, and bathing in the arena's large pool. She was as ready as she could be. She forced all thoughts of her erstwhile companions, and even her child, from her mind, in order to gain the inner calm and poise that she would need to save her life and regain her freedom; for, despite Eliizar's warning, she was determined to try.

Despite his initial reluctance, Eliizar had become a friend, as had his plump, motherly wife Nereni, who took care of Aurian, the only female warrior. Through their talks, Aurian had discovered that Eliizar had been an officer in the Royal Guard. He had lost his eye during an assassination attempt on the Khisu, when he had singlehandedly killed all four attackers. Since cripples were not tolerated in Khazalim society, Eliizar's only options had been slavery or death for himself and his beloved wife. Fortunately, in a rare gesture of gratitude, Xiang had intervened, and Eliizar had been rewarded with the post of sword master at the arena. 'And a cruel, backhanded reward it was,' he had confided to Aurian. 'I am forced to send strong, healthy young warriors to their deaths to pleasure a blood-thirsty mob. How can a man live with such a thing and still sleep at nights? Yet I have no choice but to remain. To leave this post would mean death or slavery, and for poor Nereni also. Truly, I hate the Khisu for what he has done to me.'

'Are you ready?' Eliizar's voice brought Aurian back to the present. The large wooden doors that led to the killing grounds had been opened. A warrior was limping in, aided by two attendants and bleeding from several wounds. Two armoured arena guards carried his opponent, a mauled and bloody corpse. Aurian recognized the twisted features of a brave, laughing young man against whom she had sparred only two days before.

Eliizar wiped his face with a shaking hand. 'May the Reaper forgive me,' he murmured, and Aurian's heart went out to him. Impulsively, she laid a hand on his arm.

'Eliizar, you must get out of here. When I win my freedom, you and Nereni should come with me to the north. I will have need of a true friend and a good warrior, one eye or no.'

Eliizar looked at her in amazement, then turned away as the great gong sounded, summoning the Mage to combat. 'Forgive me, Aurian,' he whispered.

'Nothing to forgive,' said Aurian lightly. 'If this is my only road to freedom, I would choose it in any case. See you later, Eliizar – and think on what I said. I meant it.' She dropped a daring kiss on the top of his bald head, then, striving for calm, she stepped into the tunnel, whispering a warriors' prayer that Forral had taught her long ago. She was ready. She had to be.

Aurian trod out of the shadowy tunnel into the white-hot glare of the arena. A mighty roar went up from three thousand throats, echoing and re-echoing within the confines of the bowl until she was rocked, buffeted, borne aloft by the sound. She lifted her sword – her own Coronach, which had been returned to her – to salute the crowd. Sunlight ran like liquid fire down the keen edges of the blade. Aurian raised her face defiantly, shaking back her hair, which was too short now to braid. The stench of sweat, dust and blood was in her nostrils – the scent of battle.

Then Aurian saw her opponent, and was brought up short. She had been expecting one of the hulking warriors she'd sparred with when Eliizar was placing her level of skill. Instead she faced a stranger – a wiry little man whose muscles stood out like knotted rope on his arms and legs. The top of his head barely reached her tightly laced breasts. What is this? the Mage thought scornfully. Do they mock me? Even as she was thinking it, he darted in, his blade a silvery blur. Cold fire coursed down her left arm, followed by a drench of hot blood as he danced back out of striking distance. Aurian, for a split second, gaped at the gash, just below her shoulder, where the point of his sword had sliced down. Forral's voice rang in her mind. *Never underestimate an opponent, however he may look.*

Icy common sense doused Aurian's battle-heated blood. She circled the little man with newfound respect, trying to gauge his next move; probing for a weakness in his stance. Then the wretch was in again, like quicksilver. Aurian dodged, swinging her own blade by instinct, feeling the draught of his sword's tip against her thigh. There was a ripping noise, and the hem of the ridiculous fighting kilt that the gladiators wore was flapping in tatters against her bare skin. Again she felt the warm, telltale trickle of blood as she backed away. Not serious this time. A mere graze, it stung, no more. But her own swing had caught him. She was too tall – her instinctive decapitating stroke had just caught the top of his head. A strip of flesh hung over his left eye, and blood streamed from the scalp wound down his face. He was circling now as she was, awaiting an opening. As he caught her eye he grinned – a brave smile; saluting her. Aurian smiled back, returning his salute with a barely perceptible tilt of her blade. He had courage, and he knew that she had. Aurian found herself wishing that she could fight at his side, rather than against him.

She lunged – he feinted. Stalemate. Circle once more. The crowd were restless; they wanted action. A scatter of boos and catcalls could be heard. The little man lashed out and Aurian rolled beneath his blade, swearing as hot agony shot down her wounded arm. She landed on her feet, facing her opponent. Her blade had caught his ankle as she rolled. Pure accident, or Forral's unstinting training taking over? He was limping badly, his foot half-severed and losing a lot of blood. The crowd roared, hungry for the kill. To Aurian they were the enemy, not the courageous warrior. Stop that! she warned herself. This isn't the garrison. Sentimentality here will mean your death.

Aurian braced herself, taking the weight and grip of the sword with her right hand and balancing it as best she could with the next to useless left that was locked in a death grip around the hilt. The little man was reeling, his face glazed with sweat and blood. Without warning Aurian moved swiftly to her right so that his vision was blocked by the hanging flap of scalp over his left eye. He turned, but too late. Aurian felt a screaming agony in her left arm as her sword bit through bone, and then his head was rolling, bouncing across the sand as his body swayed and toppled in a welter of blood that fountained from the severed neck. The death-howl from the crowd almost knocked her flat beside him. Rocked back on her heels by the din, Aurian stood over her dead opponent, lifting her streaming blade and kissing it, a warrior's salute to the fallen.

It was lucky that the crowd's roar warned her. Blinded by tears, Aurian had not seen her next opponents leave the tunnel's mouth. Now they were nearly upon her. Dashing her bloody hand across her eyes, she turned to face the new challenge. What was this? Two men, one armed with a long spear, the other with only a net. Aurian blinked in confusion. This was completely outside her experience. They fanned apart, right and left, until she could not watch both. Then, too late, she understood. The warrior with the net was a blind – a distraction. She had to watch the one with the lethal spear that was levelled at her chest. If she took her eye off him, he could hurl his spear, or rush her. But while she watched the spearman, the other could creep up behind her with the disabling net.

Rage swept through Aurian like a forest fire. Unfair! But this time she caught herself, forcing herself to stay calm and think. Never mind fair – she had to win her way out of this. All the time she was thinking, Aurian had been backing away, trying to keep both men in her field of vision. Soon they would have her trapped against the stone wall that ran round the edge of the arena. She caught the glance of understanding that flashed between her two foes. So they wanted her there! Aurian didn't understand why, but if that was their idea she was having none of it.

She feinted right, then made a sudden dive to her left, towards the net-bearer. From the corner of her eye, she caught a flash of movement as the spearman made his cast. Aurian felt the heavy point go through her calf, grazing the bone and tearing the muscle. She almost fainted with pain and shock, but the desperate leap had taken her far enough. Her wrists were jarred as the keen edge of her sword hit the netman's knees. He crumpled to the ground in a pool of his own blood, crippled and screaming.

The spearman, weaponless now, ran to grab the net while Aurian was disabled. Once enmeshed in its fold, she would be finished. There was no help for it – she needed the spear, with its longer reach, to defend herself. Aurian dropped her sword and seized the wooden shaft, wrenching the barbed metal blade out through her leg, feeling flesh and muscle tear as she did so. Dizzying, nauseating agony engulfed her and her vision blurred. There was no time to get to her feet. Almost blindly, she flipped the spear around, plunging the butt end into the fallen net. With a sharp sideways tug, she twitched the tangled meshes right out from under the spearman's reaching hands.

It was the last thing he had expected. To gain the net now, he would have to come closer than was wise without a weapon. In the split-second of hesitation while he weighed the odds, Aurian acted. Sliding the smooth spear-butt out from under the net, she reversed it – and threw.

The spearman had fathomed her plan. He was already running, and Aurian, still on the ground, was not in a position of strength. But the range was short, and it was enough. He stumbled; fell forward; the bloody point of the spear embedded in his back. Could she have killed him? Surely not, Aurian thought dimly. But, dead or not, he did not rise. On the other hand, if she failed to get to her feet, it would not count as a win for her, either. She remembered the exhausted young warrior who had left the arena before she entered it, doomed to a repeat performance as soon as his wounds had healed.

The howling of the crowd receded as a welcoming veil of darkness swirled around her head. It would be easy to let go, to slip into unconsciousness . . . Maybe she would live to fight another day . . .

What, and go through all this again? 'No!' Aurian told herself firmly. 'Get on your feet, warrior!' Groping for her sword, she set its point in the bloodstained dirt and dragged herself blindly upright, leaning on the strong blade. The pain brought tears to her eyes. Her injured leg would not support her, her back ached where she had wrenched it in her fall, and her left arm was next to useless. She was weak from exertion and loss of blood. Oh, gods, she thought. How can I face another opponent like this? Fleetingly she longed for her lost powers. If it weren't for these accursed bracelets, she thought bitterly, I could save myself yet. But wait! The bracelets stopped her from putting forth her powers, but would they stop her from taking power in? She remembered the riot in Nexis, and how she had used the anger of the mob to bring the rain . . .

Aurian concentrated with all her might, turning her will inward to pull, as she normally turned it outward to manipulate . . . And it was coming! She drew in energy from the heat of the sun; from the very life-force and blood-lust of the mob that surrounded her. To them it seemed like a sudden chill in the air, a brief shadow passing across the face of the sun, though no clouds marred the sky . . .

Aurian's ragged breathing steadied; her vision cleared. She could not heal her wounds or even still the pain, but the weakness of blood-loss had left her and her body felt the renewed strength of her borrowed energy. For the first time, she wondered why there was such a delay, though it had given her the respite she so badly needed. The cries of the crowd returned to her consciousness, crashing against her like a tidal wave. What were they chanting? 'Demon! Demon!' There seemed to be some confusion. No more opponents had appeared. Aurian leaned on her sword, husbanding her strength. She saw Eliizar, standing on the sands before the flower-decked royal balcony. He seemed to be caught up in some kind of debate with the king.

A solution was reached, apparently. The sword master approached her, shaking his head. 'Unheard of,' he said. 'The crowd want you to miss out the last ordeal of combat with human warriors. They demand that you face the Black Demon, and His Majesty has concurred. The new Khisihn, for some reason, disagreed, but the Khisu has prevailed.'

Aurian pulled herself upright, and looked Eliizar in the eye. What a farce! she thought with some irritation. My fate hanging on a royal quarrel. 'All right,' she said resignedly. 'Bring on your Demon.'

A tear ran down from Eliizar's one good eye as he embraced

Aurian briefly. 'Farewell, bravest of warriors,' he said. 'I am sorry it had to end thus. May the Reaper be merciful to you.' And he was gone.

Thanks for cheering me up, Eliizar, Aurian thought ruefully. The westering sun beat down on the back of her neck as she waited. Flies buzzed, hovering around the blood that trickled stickily from her wounds. The crowd was hushed now; expectant. Aurian took one unsteady hand from her sword hilt to wipe the sweat and dirt from her face. She was desperately thirsty, but told herself sternly that that was the least of her worries. What was this Demon that they all seemed so afraid of? What form would it take?

A rumble of wooden wheels echoed in the tunnel mouth. A great iron cage, pulled by a dozen strong slaves, was wheeled into the arena. As the procession halted, one slave darted up and pulled out the thick iron pin that held the door shut, then scurried away with his fellows as fast as he could into the safety of the tunnel mouth. The wooden gates boomed shut behind them, sealing off the only exit. Aurian waited. The thick bars of the cage were set close together, preventing her from seeing what was inside. A dark, shadowy shape stirred restlessly within.

There was a sudden, rumbling roar that made the earth tremble beneath Aurian's feet. A blood-freezing sound, full of fury and menace. The crowd shrank back, buffeted by the noise. Then slowly the cage door swung open, its metal hinges screeching, and a huge black shape with eyes of flame flowed lithely down on to the sand. A great red mouth opened in a snarl of defiant challenge, exposing curved ivory fangs longer than Aurian's hand. The Mage gasped, and her grip tightened on the hilt of her sword.

The Demon was a great cat, larger than Aurian could have imagined in her worst nightmares. Twice the length of a man from nose to tail, it stood as high as her waist. Its yellow eyes blazed like fire as they fixed on their prey. Slowly, deliberately, it began to stalk her, its claws like great steel scimitars gleaming against the bloody sand.

Aurian planted her feet firmly and lifted her sword, fear sending her heart banging wildly against her ribs. How could anyone hope to fight such a creature? How could she fight it, hampered as she was by injury and exhaustion? Then her eyes met those of her foe and, with a sudden shock, her mind touched the mind of the massive cat. It was intelligent. Or rather she. A queen – the matriarch of her people – captured, humiliated, and bent on vengeance.

The Mage gathered her scattered wits and reached out with her mind. 'Wait,' she said.

'Why?' The reply was loaded with derision, but Aurian sensed the astonishment concealed beneath. The cat was coming closer; nearly within pouncing distance. Aurian was almost glad that her injured leg prevented her from running. She tried again.

'I'm not your enemy. I am a captive too.' Steady, Aurian. Don't plead.

'All men are my enemies.'

'I am not.' The Mage kept her mental voice firm. 'The people here are my enemies too. Why kill each other, when we have the same foes?'

The cat paused with one huge paw uplifted, seeming to consider. Then it fell into a menacing crouch. 'You lie!' it snarled. 'Die!' And sprung.

But Aurian, a lover of cats, had seen the telltale wriggle of the haunches before it launched itself, and was already diving forward beneath the pounce. She felt claws rake her side like white-hot irons, and heard a yowl of furious pain as her sword point grazed the cat's ribs. She tried to get to her feet to turn and meet her enemy, but the injured leg collapsed beneath her, and then the cat was on her, flattening her face down in the dirt and knocking the sword out of her grasp – out of reach. For the space of a few heartbeats, neither moved. The crowd held its breath. Again, the Mage sought the mind of her foe. 'You're making a big mistake.' If her plight had not been so desperate, she would have laughed at her own temerity.

The cat's cruel amusement flicked across her mind like a whiplash. 'Surely,' it mocked.

Slowly, very slowly, Aurian eased herself up a little, not even daring to spit the sand from her mouth. Like a searing brand, the great claws raked lightly across her back, shredding her leather vest and scoring the tender skin beneath. Aurian cried out in pain, unable to stop herself, but she had achieved her goal. Her right hand was now beneath her, groping for her dagger, which she had stolen back from Eliizar and concealed inside her vest. The cat had unwittingly helped her by all but annihilating the garment, and the long, flat blade slid easily into her hand.

Suddenly a mighty swat from a huge paw knocked her rolling, over and over; the cat was playing with her as a domestic pet plays with a mouse. This time Aurian landed on her back, a sharp catch of pain hampering her breathing. Her ribs? Or the child? Unable to place the location of the pain, Aurian felt a jolt of fear. The great cat leapt on top of her, tensing its claws to disembowel her; and froze, the tip of the Mage's dagger pricking its throat.

Aurian stared into the fierce golden eyes only inches from her face. 'Stalemate, I think,' she said. There was no reply, but she caught the faintest flicker of doubt behind those blazing eyes. The crowd, to a man, was on its feet. Aurian forced herself stay calm; to take the gamble. 'They say that if I slay you, I will win my freedom,' she told the cat. 'Have they offered you the same? Of course, if I make a move, you may kill me – or you may not be quick enough.'

The cat growled menacingly. Aurian's thought cut through the sound. 'You have nothing to gain from my death but a quick meal – and I assure you, you'll find me very tough.' This time the cat seemed to respond to her humour, relaxing a fraction. Aurian pressed her point home. 'But what if we refuse to kill each other? Do you think we could fight our way to freedom? If not, we could certainly take a lot of them with us into death. What have we got to lose? Do you want to stay here, caged and captive for always?'

'Men are not to be trusted.' The cat's tone was flat.

'Very well.' Aurian had been hoping it wouldn't come to this. She looked once more, frankly, into the cat's eyes. 'You must decide that for yourself. But you are the most beautiful, the most brave, the most magnificent creature I have ever seen. I would be your friend, but if that is not possible I will not be responsible for your death.' Moving with careful deliberation, she removed her dagger from the cat's throat and flicked it away from her, sending it bouncing and skidding across the sand.

The crowd gasped. For a moment, everything was still; then the cat opened its huge jaws, its long, lethal fangs gleaming white in the sun. The Mage flinched and closed her eyes against the sight of her approaching death, but at the last second the great head swung to one side, and a rasping tongue like a steel file licked the oozing blood from the wound on her arm. Aurian opened her eyes in astonishment, and the cat's golden gaze met her own.

'My name is Shia,' she said. 'Drink my blood, and be friend.' She backed away slightly, removing her weight from Aurian's body. Murmurs of confusion welled from the crowd. Aurian sat up weakly, unstrung with relief. Placing her mouth to the cat's ribs she licked salty blood, mixed with sand.

'My name is Aurian,' she said, 'and I am honoured.' Then, greatly daring, she reached out her bloodstained fingers and caressed Shia's broad, sleek head. And a sound that had never been heard before echoed across the stunned arena – the slow, bass rumble of the big cat's purr.

The crowd, cheated of a death, erupted into wildness. Boos and jeers resounded, and missiles rained down into the arena – fruit, sweetmeats, drinking goblets, even shoes. The tunnel doors swung open, admitting two dozen armed and armoured guards. They approached reluctantly, fanning out to form a loose circle around Aurian and Shia as the Mage struggled to her knees. Shia trotted obligingly over and retrieved Aurian's sword from where it lay, dragging it back with the hilt held carefully in her mouth. Propping herself with Coronach, Aurian tried out her injured leg. She could balance herself without support while standing still – but moving? Not a chance. But they didn't know that. Sword in hand, she stood back to back with Shia as the ring of guards tightened around them. 'Right,' she called out grimly. 'Which of you sons of pigs wants to be first?' Shia snarled a menacing echo to her words. Their assailants looked at each other doubtfully. Apparently no one wanted to be first.

Eliizar emerged from the tunnel at a run and crossed the

sands to the royal balcony. The Khisu got to his feet, and all sound ceased. 'Your Majesty,' the sword master cried in a quaking voice. 'The decision of life or death for this warrior rests with you. Death is the usual penalty for one who fails to slay his foe, but this woman – this warrior – has honoured us with the bravest performance in the history of the arena. None will forget this day. Will you, on the joyous occasion of your wedding, grant her clemency?'

Bless you, Eliizar, Aurian thought.

On the balcony, the king considered, wavering. It would be a munificent gesture, and worthy of a Khisu, but the Arbiters had told him about this dangerous foreigner, and he wasn't sure that he wanted her at large in his land.

Aurian watched the Khisu, holding her breath. This was her first good look at him. He looked younger than he must be, but his expression was wolfish and feral. Beneath level brows his dark eyes glinted with pitiless cruelty. Black hair, falling past his shoulders, showed no sign of grey, and he sported a drooping moustache. He had a lean, lithe, hard-muscled killing machine of a body and looked as though he used it frequently – and well. Gods, Aurian thought. I wouldn't like to fight him. I might like to bed him, though. The thought, so inappropriate to her desperate situation, shocked her. But it was undeniable. His aura was irresistibly sexual, and equally dangerous. He was like a magnificent wild beast.

Then suddenly the queen – the new Khisihn – stepped forward from the shadows of the balcony and murmured into the Khisu's ear. Her face was veiled, but the bright flash of golden hair was unmistakable. Sara! Aurian sagged against Shia's flank, dizzy with shock. How in the name of all the gods had the wretched woman managed this?

Sara had been equally stunned by the sight of Aurian in the arena. What evil luck! If that damned Mage should tell the Khisu that she was already married, all the hard work she had done to win him would have been for nothing. She stepped up to him and whispered in his ear, glad that he was proficient in her language, though she was making progress at learning his own. 'Kill this woman, Lord,' she said. 'Make me a gift of her death.'

Xiang stared at her in amazement. Was this the gentle creature that had so charmed him?

'Please, my love.' Sara smiled beguilingly, and the Khisu, as always, found her impossible to resist. His thumb began to turn down in the traditional signal of death.

'Stop!' Prince Harihn strode forward from the rear of the balcony. 'It is the Khisu's custom to bestow gifts on his wedding day,' he said. 'Somehow, I seem to have been overlooked so far.' He smiled at his father without warmth. 'Give her to me, father. Grant me the gift of this woman's life.' His voice, deliberately loud, rang across the arena, and the Khisu found himself the focus of hundreds of curious eyes. He glared at his son.

'In the Reaper's name, why?'

Harihn shrugged. 'You've been telling me for long enough that I need a woman of my own. This foreign warrior presents a challenge that I can't resist.'

Sara, who had managed to follow most of the exchange, felt the moment slipping away from her. 'Lord,' she protested. 'I beg you, give me this woman's death.'

'There, my son.' The Khisu shrugged. 'See what a coil you have me in? I must disappoint my heir – or my new bride.' He bestowed a dazzling smile on Sara before turning back to the prince. 'Surely this woman cannot be so important? She is hardly a beauty, and any man would think twice before bedding such a she-devil. Come.' There was a hard edge in his voice. 'Choose another gift, Harihn. If it is a woman you want, I will give you the choice of any in my seraglio. Every one is in the fullness of beauty, and skilled in the arts of love.'

Harihn's jaw clenched. 'No,' he said flatly. 'I want that one.' Father and son glared at each other, all pretence of friendliness abandoned. The Khisu thought rapidly. What was Harihn up to? Was he simply trying to embarrass his royal father in public, or make trouble between him and his new bride? Or did he have some other motive in taking this sorceress into his household?

Xiang made his decision. Most likely the witch would stick a dagger into her benefactor at the first opportunity, which would solve his problem. If not . . . well, there were other, less public ways of dealing with the matter. 'Very well, my son,' he said loudly, for the benefit of the rapt crowd. 'I cannot refuse you. I give this brave warrior into your care.' He raised his thumb in the gesture of life, and the crowd applauded. Sara gasped.

'My father, I thank you,' Harihn said, and, vaulting dramatically over the balcony, he crossed the sands towards Aurian.

The Mage consulted briefly with Shia. 'It seems our lives have been saved – for now. Shall we go with this man?'

'I trust him not.'

'Nor do I. But I think we should risk it. It's better than being hacked to pieces by these idiots.'

'Agreed.'

As the Khisal approached, Aurian bowed low, wincing with pain and gritting her teeth to keep her temper at the speculative way his eyes lingered on her breasts, exposed by the ruination of her leather vest. 'I thank Your Highness,' she said.

He smiled. 'Bravely fought, warrior. The honour is mine. Will you come with me?' He extended a hand to help Aurian, and the great cat growled warningly.

'I'm afraid you've also inherited my friend,' Aurian said.

The Prince glanced doubtfully at Shia. 'Willingly,' he lied, 'save that my father did not include her in our bargain.'

Aurian was heartily sick of this charade, and she knew that she had reached the end of her strength. 'Where I go, Shia goes,' she said flatly. 'Would you like to try to stop her? Or perhaps you're more afraid of your father.' Harihn scowled, and glanced up at the crowd. Aurian knew that he feared the cat, but was afraid of looking a fool if Shia should ruin his triumphant exit. 'She will not hurt a friend of mine, and your people would be impressed by a prince who could tame such a creature,' she suggested.

Harihn brightened at her words. 'Very well. Will it let me help you?'

'She will.'

The prince scooped Aurian theatrically into his arms and left the arena with the great cat pacing watchfully at his heels. The crowd cheered delightedly. They seemed to have forgotten that only a few minutes before they had been howling for Aurian's blood. The last thing Aurian saw as they entered the tunnel was the Khisu and Sara glaring savagely, naked fury on their faces. Aurian felt an uneasy chill creep up her spine. What did this prince intend for her, anyway? 'Keep hold of my mind,' she warned Shia. 'I daren't pass out yet.'

24
The Search for Anvar

Anvar had been spared the humiliation of the slave market. After several days spent languishing in the squalor and despair of the noisome cellar, he and some fifty other slaves had been chained together in groups of ten and marched, by night, down through the narrow, twisting alleys of the city to the wharves. As dawn was breaking, they were herded into open barges and rowed some miles upriver in the broiling heat to the site of the Khisu's summer palace.

The area was a hive of activity. The huge new edifice was being built on a series of terraces that had been hewn by hand, at the cost of many lives, back into the face of the towering red cliffs. The air was thick with dust and rang with shouted commands. The beat of hammers and chisels, the crack of whips and the groans of the tortured slaves echoed in a ceaseless cacophony between the canyon's walls, which trapped all sound and heat in a simmering cauldron of suffering.

Already the massive blocks of white stone that had been ferried down from the upland quarries were being set into place. Teams of exhausted slaves were hauling on the ropes of the great hoists that lifted the blocks, while others swarmed over the stepped banks of wooden scaffolding that lined the half built walls, or mixed vast quantities of mortar that stood in constant danger of drying out in the baking sun. Whole camps of masons and master carvers and carpenters laboured at their crafts, and architects strode around the site carrying rolls of parchment and an air of self-importance. A huge outdoor kitchen had been built on the flat ground near the river to feed the labouring hordes, and sweating cooks worked ceaselessly, seemingly oblivious of the stench and dust, amid a cloud of swarming flies.

Anvar's group was offloaded at one of the flimsy wooden piers that projected out into the sluggish water, and the site slave master came to look them over, his expression sour. 'Is this all?' he demanded of the barge-train captain. 'I need three times as many. The palace will never be finished at this rate. Slaves last no time at all in these conditions.'

The captain spat on the dusty ground. 'Don't take it out on me,' he grumbled. 'I only bring them, however many. Maybe if you treated them better they'd last longer.' He glanced disparagingly round the dusty, noisome worksite.

'Don't tell me how to do my job, you dockside layabout. If the Khisu's accursed palace isn't finished on time heads will roll, and I'm not taking the blame. How I'm expected to work with the rubbish you people have been sending up here ... Look at that one!' The slave master's finger shot out in the direction of Anvar, whose light skin and hair made him conspicuous. 'What in the name of the Reaper is that supposed to be?'

The captain shrugged. 'How should I know? I only bring them, remember? Zahn doesn't tell me where he gets his slaves, and I don't ask questions – it's not healthy. As long as he keeps sending them, you'd be wise just to use them, and keep your mouth shut. Who cares what colour one bloody slave is anyway? Zahn? Not if there's profit in it. The Khisu? All Xiang cares about is getting his god-blasted palace finished. Just do what you usually do – work the bastard till he drops and bury him out of sight somewhere, or throw him in the river for the lizards. If anybody asks, I never saw him. I'm off now. This place stinks!'

'Some help you are,' the slave master grumbled. 'Tell Zahn I need more – and the quality had better improve, or someone just might whisper in the Khisu's ear that someone has been importing illegal northerners.'

The captain spat once more. 'I don't tell Zahn anything – and I would watch my mouth if I were you. Knowing him, you're likely to wind up buried under your own foundations.' He turned on his heel and left.

The slaves were put to work at once. One by one, each man was unshackled and questioned as to whether he had any

382

particular skills, such as masonry or carpentry. If he had, he was lucky, for he was sent to assist the artisans and spared much gruelling labour in the brutally hot climate. As the overseer worked his way towards him, Anvar found himself in a dilemma. Should he pretend to be ignorant of their language, in the hope that it might give him a chance to escape, or should he claim the knowledge of carpentry his grandpa had taught him, and so survive longer in this terrible place? He was spared the decision. As the overseer approached him, the slave master intervened. 'Not that one,' he snapped. 'I don't want him around too long. Put him on the pulley gangs.'

The pulleys were the worst work on the site, as Anvar soon discovered. Twenty slaves at a time hauled on thick ropes which raised the massive stone blocks up the half finished walls. The more blocks that were raised, the higher the walls became, and the greater the effort required from the struggling, exhausted slaves. The death toll was appalling. Once a block had begun its ascent there could be no stopping, for if momentum was lost the stone would fall, and might crack as it hit the ground, incurring a huge waste of time and labour to hew and transport another from the quarries. And the Khisu wanted his palace finished. So if a slave was unlucky enough to lose his footing or collapse from exhaustion in the line, he would be trampled by those behind him, who would in their turn struggle desperately to keep their own bare feet from slipping on the slimy, bloody pulp that had once been a man.

It was a nightmare unending. From dawn to dusk, the work rarely halted. Food was scarce and unsatisfying – a thin mush of cooked grain doled out morning and evening. Water was insufficient for the slaves' needs in the burning sun, and many collapsed from heatstroke. Brutal overseers with whips stalked the lines, never permitting the pace to slacken. Clouds of biting insects assailed the labourers, and snakes and scorpions came scuttling from beneath the shelter of the blocks as they began to lift, scattering at random towards the bare feet and legs of the helpless slaves. It took many agonizing hours for a man to die from their venom.

By the end of the first day, Anvar's fair skin was burned and blistered by the fierce sun. His hands and shoulders were bloody and raw from the friction of the coarse ropes; his bare feet scored and lacerated from the uneven, gritty ground. His back was striped with whip-cuts, his head throbbed from the relentless heat, and his tongue was swollen in his parched mouth. His pain-filled world had shrunk to a single thought: keep moving. Endure.

In the blessed cool of evening, another gang replaced the exhausted survivors at the pulleys, and the work went on by torchlight. Anvar and the other slaves who made up the day-teams were herded into a high-walled stockade. No attempt had been made to provide sanitation, and the place stank like a cesspit and swarmed with flies. A handful of gruel was doled out to each man as he passed through the gate, and a long stone trough within the compound was filled with muddy river water. Anvar fought for a drink at the trough, where men crowded and jostled like beasts for the unsavoury water. Then he staggered away from the mob and lay in the filth where he fell; too exhausted to think, or even register the pain in his abused body. It seemed that he only slept for an instant before he was awakened with a kick to begin another day of toil and torture.

There was no doubt that if Anvar had been a true Mortal he would never have survived this terrible place for two days together. But somehow, while he slept, his Mage-blood worked automatically to heal and restore him enough to face another day of dreadful suffering. Still, it could only do so much. Anvar had not been trained in the healing arts, and Miathan had stolen the active element of his powers. Food and rest were needed to restore the energy used in the healing process, and these were in desperately short supply. So, day by wretched day, his condition began to deteriorate; the healing becoming less and less effective and only serving to prolong his misery. Yet the overseers were amazed by his endurance, and wagers began to be made concerning how long this strange, pale-skinned northerner would last. Anvar was oblivious of it all. His exhausted, pain-racked mind and body only worked at survival level, and the luxury of thought was a long-forgotten dream. All that remained was a faint spark of consciousness; a stubborn, relentless manifestation of the will to live.

Aurian opened her eyes. Moonlight shone in dazzling star-and-diamond shapes through the lattices of delicately carved shutters, forming lacework shadows on the pale, thin sheet that covered her bed. She was confused – her coming here was all a daze, and she was still half asleep. But something had awakened her. Something wrong. What? The back of her neck prickled with some vague, formless fear that brought back the irrational childhood urge to hide her head beneath the covers, hoping that the unknown terror would be unable to find her there. Aurian tried to pull herself together, reminding herself sternly that she was a warrior. She lay very still, concentrating with all her senses to locate the source of the wrongness.

Ah. She had it now. The silence. Each night since she'd come to these lands, the darkness had been filled with the rhythmic, creaking chirrups of nocturnal insects that formed a shrill night-time chorus. Now everything was still. Aurian could hear herself breathing in ragged, shallow gasps; could hear the thunder of her own heart. Despite the warmth of the room, icy sweat slid down her spine. What else? She was missing something. Shia! Aurian could hear only the sound of her own breathing. No one else was in the room. Shia was gone!

Aurian looked wildly around her, but the room was growing darker. Something was sapping the moonlight from her window; consuming it, drowning it in an overwhelming wave of utter blackness. Something stirred in the corner – she could feel it as it moved, creeping – no – gliding silently towards her. It passed in front of the window, and her blood congealed to ice at the sight of the shape that haunted her most nightmarish memories. Nihilim! Miathan had sent the Death-Wraiths!

Aurian tried to move, to reach for her sword – no, that was no good. The Wraith advanced, uttering the weird, cruel bass chuckle that she remembered so well. The wave of leaching coldness and terror that spun out before it washed over her. The spell! Finbarr's spell! What was it? Her mind was in a whirl of panic – she couldn't think. She couldn't move. Her tongue was frozen in her mouth, her limbs were frozen to the bed. It swooped down on her, its great maw drooling long ropes of slimy, clinging darkness to engulf her, as it had engulfed Forral. . . 'Forral! *Forral!*'

'For pity's sake, Lady, wake up!'

Aurian blinked, and her vision cleared. She was sitting up in bed, in a room aglow with lamplight. Before her, instead of that hideous shape of evil, was Harihn, shaking her shoulders, his tanned face grey with shock. Her left arm was bound up in a sling, and her throat was raw with screaming. Shia was by the bed, her snarling face a demon-mask of fear and fury, her slitted yellow eyes glaring at something that wasn't there. It wasn't there! As Aurian's nightmare faded, the great cat suddenly relaxed, shaking her head in bewilderment, her ears still flattened, the tip of her black tail twitching back and forth. And as the bitter tide of reaction to her dream flowed over her, Aurian began to shake uncontrollably, weakened by her wounds and undone by the vivid memory of Forral's hideous death as the barely healing scars in her emotions were ripped asunder by what she had just experienced. Unable to help herself, she collapsed in a storm of hysterical weeping.

She heard Harihn curse; heard him call a servant to fetch the surgeon. Then he was back at her side, patting her shoulder awkwardly as she wept. 'Hush, Lady, hush,' he soothed her helplessly. 'It was only a dream – a bad dream from the fever. I am here – your Demon is here. Nothing can hurt you, I promise.'

Then the surgeon came. Aurian vaguely remembered the round-shouldered, wrinkled old man who had stitched the torn muscles of her calf, quaking all the while under the baleful glare of Shia, who had barely been able to restrain herself from attacking this puny creature who was causing her friend such pain. Now he was all bustling efficiency despite the comical long white nightgown he wore. The sight of him was so ludicrous that Aurian wanted to laugh, but she couldn't stop crying, and somehow the laughter and sobs mingled so that she couldn't get her breath. She fought free of Harihn and clutched her bandaged aching ribs, wheezing helplessly as tears poured down her face.

Aurian heard the surgeon tsking, then a cup was forced between her lips and she choked on a coldly burning brew, coughing and spluttering and causing further pain to knife between her ribs. 'Deep breaths, Lady, if you please,' the surgeon chanted patiently, speaking to her as though she was a small child. Then she heard Shia's voice in her mind, sensible and comforting.

'Enough, my friend,' the cat said, 'or you will harm yourself.'

With a superhuman effort, Aurian got control of herself, enough to swallow the rest of the draught. The tight knot within her unravelled, and she could relax, though she was still shaking as she leaned back against the pillows and wiped her eyes.

Harihn looked relieved. 'By the Reaper, Lady, but you frightened us all!' he said.

'Nonsense!' the surgeon said briskly. 'It was only the fever. You have been very ill, Lady, for several days.' He leaned over to place a hand on her forehead. 'It has broken now, so you should have no more bad dreams. And you will be pleased to know that your child is safe.'

The child! She had forgotten all about it. And days, he had said. There was something she should be doing – something urgent – but the memory of Forral haunted her, and she felt weak and confused by the aftermath of her dream. Oh, gods, that hideous creature! Aurian shuddered. 'Wine?' she gasped, trying to force the memory away.

The surgeon smiled. 'I know my patients are mending when they ask for wine. Is there any here, Your Highness?'

'Should she have it?' the prince asked anxiously. 'I mean, what about the drug – and she has not eaten anything . . .'

'That can soon be remedied.' The surgeon went to the door and gave orders to a hovering servant.

While she waited, Aurian tried to piece together what had happened. 'How badly was I hurt?' she asked the surgeon.

His wizened face creased in a frown. 'Lady, you gave me some work! But your arm is healing, and your ribs were simply cracked, not broken. They will soon improve with care. As to your leg, the muscles were badly torn. I fear there will be some scarring.'

'Never mind that. Will it be all right?'

The surgeon hesitated. 'It should,' he said at last. 'That is, if you give it a chance to heal, Lady. You must stay off that leg for ten days at least, and more if possible.'

'What!' Aurian shot bolt upright, wincing at the pain from her cracked ribs. 'I don't have that kind of time.'

'Lady, you must.'

'But there's something I have to do – it's important!' Desperately she tried to remember what it was.

The surgeon frowned at her as though she were a petulant child. 'Suit yourself,' he replied frostily. 'But if those muscles have no chance to heal properly you will be crippled for life, or at best that leg will always be weak. You must stay in bed until I tell you otherwise. If not, you have only yourself to blame for the consequences.'

Aurian swore viciously and thumped the pillow with her fist, frustrated by the limitations of Mortal medicine. If only she had her powers, she could heal her injuries in no time!

Just then the servant returned with a cup of warm broth. 'Drink this, Lady,' the surgeon told Aurian, 'then you may have your wine.' Despite her frustration, Aurian realized that her stomach was churning, not just from emotion, but from hunger. She drank the broth down eagerly, and the surgeon handed her a goblet of sweetish red wine. 'Have no fear, Highness,' he told the prince. 'Together with the drug it will make her sleep again, which is what she needs. Perhaps then we can all return to our rest.' His voice held an acid undertone. Aurian's hand tightened round the stem of the goblet in panic. She couldn't sleep! What if it returned in her dreams? But it was too late. Already she had drunk most of the wine, and she could feel a drowsy euphoria stealing over her. It felt good, after what she had just undergone. She heard herself giggling as she held out the cup for a refill. The surgeon tsked disapprovingly, then shrugged. 'It may be for the best,' he sighed, and poured more wine. 'Whatever she dreamed about, it gave her a severe shock. You ought to have some too, Highness. You look exhausted. Why not have a servant watch this ungrateful woman? You have more important things to concern you, and you must sleep.'

Harihn dismissed the surgeon with brusque thanks. The wretch was so officious! But since he was so skilled in his art, he invariably managed to get away with it. The Khisal rubbed wearily at his gritty eyes, and turned back to the mysterious lady he had rescued so impulsively from the arena. She was already sleeping peacefully, the terror that had haunted her face smoothed away in repose. What had she dreamed, to cause such anguish? Had it been her husband's name she had cried out? His inquiries to the Arbiters had revealed that she had probably been widowed, and the surgeon had told him that she was with child. That had come as a shock. Given her condition, her performance in the arena had been near miraculous. Silently saluting her courage, he bent over and tucked the thin sheet more closely around her shoulders.

The Demon lifted her head and snarled, baring long white fangs. 'Hush, you,' Harihn soothed, keeping a wary eye on her. 'You should know by now that I will not harm your friend.'

The cat dropped her head back to her outstretched paws, contenting herself with a black look for the prince. She had remained on guard throughout Aurian's illness, treating all who tended her friend with similar suspicion. Most of the servants were afraid even to enter the room.

Deciding to take the surgeon's advice after all, Harihn poured himself some wine. Opening the carved shutters that stretched from the floor to the ceiling, he took his cup out into the balmy, moonlit peace of the garden. Ah, how he loved this place! The small walled area with its grassy lawn and flowering plants and trees was a haven of green in this arid city. His mother had created it when she came here, a captive bride, to this small but exquisite palace on the south side of the river – the opposite side from the arena and the Khisu's sumptuous dwelling. Her refusal to live in the same house with her lord and his harem had been but one of the reasons for her murder. Xiang, used to the subservient women of his land, had not been able to deal with her pride, and her contemptuous hatred, never concealed, of the man who had taken her by force from the Xandim, her own people.

Harihn crossed the lawn to sit on the low marble coping that circled the pool where carp swam in gilded splendour. The scent of huge white blossoms from the tree that overhung the moon-silvered water was intoxicating, but his thoughts were elsewhere. After all these years, he still missed his mother. He remembered her vividly – her long brown hair, her flashing eyes, the indomitable spirit that his father's brutality had never quenched. Harihn dwelt here for the same reasons she had – to maintain his independence and to keep as far from Xiang as possible. But it hurt. This place was haunted by his mother's memory, and perhaps that was his own fault, for he had never allowed it to be changed. There had been some raised eyebrows, to say the least, among his servants when he had placed the flame-haired foreigner in his mother's old suite of rooms. Somehow, though, it had seemed the right thing to do. Her spirit, her courage and pride and refusal to surrender in the arena had called back such powerful memories of his mother that he had been compelled to intervene, to help this woman, though he had been too young to save the other.

Since then, of course, he'd had time to consider his rash act, and had wondered, more than once, what had possessed him. All he'd got out of the lady so far was her name – Aurian. Where had she come from? What was her history? How had she – a mere woman – learned to fight so well? The fact that she was one of the witch-breed of northern sorcerers made him very nervous, despite the bracelets she wore which, he had been absolutely assured, would negate her magic. Not for the first time, Harihn wondered if he had bitten off more than he could swallow. He had never thought, for instance, that it would mean giving house-room to the fearsome Demon. And the Khisu, of course, was furious with him, but that was nothing new.

Thinking of Xiang, Harihn had to admit that there were advantages to his deed. It had been most enjoyable to see that look of thwarted rage on his father's face, and that of his bride. Now why did she want the warrior dead? Harihn was convinced that the women must have been travelling on the same ship. Two foreigners appearing in the city at the same time? It was more than coincidence. He smiled to himself. If his mystery lady could provide him with information to the new Khisihn's disadvantage, it might give him a new, and very necessary, lever to use against the Khisu. Harihn's mouth twisted in a bitter grimace. The hatred his father bore for him was no secret. In that respect, this Aurian could prove useful indeed. She could fight like a demon – that much he had seen for himself – and she had her own Demon to help her. Between them they made a formidable team. The Khisal smiled to himself. Perhaps, in saving her, he had made the right decision after all.

When Aurian awakened, it was broad daylight. The prince had gone, and a stranger was drowsing in a chair by her bed. Aurian gasped. The man was huge. But Shia was asleep on the bottom of the bed, curled up with her tail wrapped over her eyes, and the Mage took it as a sign that her new warder could be trusted. She wondered if he would bring her some food. Her mind felt clear now, but her insides were cramped with hunger. She reached out to touch his arm, and the big man snapped to attention at once, his face a picture of guilt. Aurian saw the fear in his eyes, and instinctively sought to soothe him. 'Don't worry,' she said. 'There's no harm in your being asleep. Everyone else was.' She smiled at the oblivious Shia. 'Only – I'm terribly hungry. Do you think you could arrange for some food? And some liafa?' While at the arena, she had become addicted to the stuff. The giant leapt to his feet, nodding fit to loosen his bald head, his broad brown face breaking into a shy smile. Aurian's eyes widened. He must have been almost seven feet tall, his shoulders so broad that she wondered how he could fit them through the door. He bowed, and left the room with a speed which belied his enormous bulk.

He returned very shortly, bearing a tray almost as wide as his shoulders. From the contents, Aurian decided that, whatever time of day it was, it was not breakfast time. But she didn't care – her mouth was watering. There was a thick soup, a roast fowl, and the meal was rounded off with fruit, cheese, honey, and the usual flat bread. A flask of wine and a brimming jug of liafa competed for the small amount of remaining space. 'Why, this is a feast!' Aurian exclaimed. 'Thank you – thank you very much!'

Shia stirred, smelling the food, her golden eyes lighting up as they fixed on the tray. Aurian sighed. It wasn't that she begrudged sharing with her friend, but . . . But her friendly giant had even thought of that. Tucked beneath his arm, where he had been carrying it to leave his hands free for the tray, was a bulky, cloth-wrapped object. He unwrapped it with a flourish, presenting it to the cat without a sign of fear. It was a haunch of raw meat. Shia, to Aurian's utter astonishment, purred loudly and rubbed the side of her face against the man's hand.

'Thank you,' Aurian told him with a smile. 'That was very considerate. Shia! Not on the bed, please!'

'Why not? I'm hungry too.' Shia gave her a black look, and dragged her meat out into the garden.

Aurian could wait no longer to attack the food. 'What's your name?' she asked the huge man indistinctly, her mouth full. He simply looked at her, shaking his head and waving his hands in front of his face.

'His name is Bohan. He cannot answer you, for he cannot speak.' As Harihn entered, Bohan prostrated himself, touching his forehead to the floor. The prince gestured negligently, and the huge man left the room. 'I set him to serve and to guard you. He is a eunuch, as is proper.'

'Poor man!' Aurian gasped. 'How cruel!'

Harihn looked surprised. 'Cruel? How so? All ladies of rank are served by eunuchs. How else would the sanctity of their persons be guarded?'

Aurian shuddered, thinking of Anvar. Anvar! Great Chathak, how could she have forgotten him?

The prince shrugged. 'It is of no consequence. I trust he is satisfactory?' He settled himself comfortably on the bottom of her bed and casually helped himself to a leg of her fowl. Aurian took another huge mouthful, reluctant to lose any more of the bird.

'How are you feeling?' Harihn asked, and Aurian choked trying to answer. She took a gulp of wine and a deep breath.

'Hungry,' she replied pointedly, then regretted her churlishness. After all, she was very much indebted to him, and dependent, at the moment, on his continuing goodwill.

The prince smiled tolerantly. He was handsome, Aurian thought, with his black curling hair, thick level brows and dark, lustrous eyes. His face was gentler, less angular and wolfish, than that of his father, but the same pride was in his bearing, and his body was lithe and strong. She was, however, beginning to find his condescending manner very irritating, and had to force herself to keep a rein on her temper. 'My apologies, Your

Highness,' she said. 'I'm afraid I'm never at my best when I first wake up.'

'You may call me Harihn,' he told her, with the air of one conferring a singular honour, 'and I have no objection to you eating while we talk.'

Thanks a lot, the Mage thought sourly. 'Thank you very much,' she said out loud. 'You may call me Aurian.'

Harihn raised an eyebrow. 'Of course.'

With an effort, Aurian restrained herself from flinging her breakfast in the complacent idiot's face. It was good, and she needed it. Instead she gave him a very direct look. 'Harihn, why did you rescue me?'

The prince smiled. 'Lady, you have naught to fear from me. You are more valuable to me alive than dead. You see, I need you – and your Demon, if she will help. I saw you fight in the arena, and I need your skill to protect me. My life is in danger from my royal father – not to mention his new wife. If she should give him another heir . . .' He made a slicing motion across his throat.

After a moment, Aurian discovered that her mouth was open, and hastily shoveled some food into it, to give herself time to think. She had almost started to tell him why she couldn't possibly stay, but she realized that the self-absorbed young prince would hardly take her problems into consideration. Besides, she could not leave until she had found Anvar; and, even more important, discovered a way to remove these bracelets which crippled her powers.

The prince was frowning, obviously wondering why she was not overcome with delight at the prospect of being his bodyguard. 'Excuse me, Your Highness,' Aurian said hastily, managing to dredge up a smile from somewhere. 'I'm almost speechless at the honour you do me. But . . . the surgeon must have told you of my condition. How can I defend you adequately when I've grown great with child?'

Harihn shrugged. 'I appreciate your frankness in discussing this delicate matter with me, of course.' The distasteful curl of his lip gave the lie to his words. 'However, it may not be a problem. You have your Demon to assist you, and besides, your condition may lull any would-be assassin into a false sense of security. After all, who would suspect a pregnant concubine of possessing warrior's skills?'

Aurian choked again. Whan she had regained her breath, she pushed the tray away, her appetite abruptly gone. 'Did you say concubine?'

Harihn's eyes widened. 'Surely you did not expect me to marry you? My people would never countenence a foreign sorceress as their Khisihn!'

'Of course I didn't! I thought you wanted me for a bodyguard, not – ' Aurian spluttered angrily, all restraint scattered to the winds. 'You must be out of your mind!'

Harihn assumed such an air of benign patience that Aurian wanted to throttle him. 'The surgeon warned me you might react in this way,' he said. 'Being pregnant, you are not in control of yourself at present, and I have your history from the Arbiters. I appreciate that, as one newly widowed, your sensibilities may be raw, but it is not permitted for a woman to be without a man to govern and guard her. How could it be otherwise? You need a man's protection, a home and a future for your child. If you leave here, you will be at the mercy of the law, and the best you can hope for is slavery – or a return to the arena. Could your child survive another such bout? Could you? I think not. I have no idea how things are managed in your own land, but here, as a widow, your husband's brother, or some relative, or even his closest friend, would take you into his family as his concubine, or even as a wife, if he wished. You are a stranger here, and have no one to render you this service. Surely you cannot be insensible of the honour I do you?'

Great gods! He was actually preening! Aurian cursed her imagination, which had come up with the idiotic story of a missing husband. She cursed the ridiculous laws of this land that passed women around like possessions, and cursed this arrogant young booby who thought he was doing her such a favour. What gall! Then she pulled herself together, and started thinking with frantic haste. Maybe the tale about Anvar being her husband would stand her in good stead, if he could be found . . . She took a deep breath and crossed her fingers beneath the sheet. 'But, Your Highness,' she blurted, 'what about my husband?'

Harihn frowned. 'Aurian, your husband is dead.'

'But what if he isn't? We don't know for certain.' At her words, the image of Forral's face rose before her with such painful clarity that she gulped back a sob. Oh, Forral, forgive me, she thought. 'What happens if he comes here only to discover that I've become another man's concubine?' She was unable to suppress the quiver in her voice. 'Please, Your Highness, surely you could put a search in motion? I beg you . . . As a woman alone in a strange land, I throw myself upon your mercy.' Well, grovelling had worked with the Arbiters. If only the prince would take the same bait . . . But as Aurian forced tears into her eyes, she saw Harihn's expression harden.

'Lady,' he said flatly, 'to find the one you seek would be impossible.'

I've outfoxed myself. He has no intention of finding Anvar, Aurian thought, because he wants me himself. She had no other recourse but to persist. 'What, with light skin and light hair, and blue eyes? I'd have thought he would stand out in this city. If he was brought here with Sara, surely someone must remember having seen him?'

'Exactly! And in all this time, there has been no word of such a man . . . What did you say? He was with Sara? The Khisihn? Why?' Harihn leaned forward, his eyes suddenly intent. What had got into the man, Aurian wondered. Could she use this sudden interest to her advantage?

'Did Sara not mention him?'

'She most certainly did not! Should she have? Were they together? Why did she not speak of him? Is this something I could use to discredit my father?' Harihn's questions tumbled over each other in his eagerness.

So that was it! Aurian fought to suppress her relief. If she handled this right . . . She assumed what she hoped was a shocked expression. 'I'm not surprised she didn't mention Anvar to the Khisihn. She's his concubine. That's why she wants me dead, Harihn – in case I betray her secret. Of course, if poor Anvar is dead, it won't make any difference, but if he's still alive, it would put your father in a very embarrassing position . . .'

The prince let out a whoop of triumphant laughter. 'Ah!' he

said. 'You are repaying my investment already. I wondered, when I rescued you, if you two knew one another. Two outlanders arriving so close together was too much of a coincidence. I wonder what my father will say when he hears that his precious new Khisihn is another man's concubine.'

Aurian sighed. What an innocent! 'Sara will say that I'm lying, or that you are lying, and the Khisu will believe her, of course, and then we'll both be in trouble,' she said flatly, and Harihn's face fell. 'What you need is proof. If you could only find Anvar . . .'

The prince's face lit up. 'By the Reaper, Lady, but you are clever! I never would have thought of that. What a pity that you are a foreign sorceress. You would make a far better Khisihn than that she-jackal of my father's! You are worth your weight in the treasures of the desert.' It seemed an odd sort of compliment, but Aurian let it pass. Harihn leapt to his feet. 'I will send a man down to the docks at once – the trail should start there, if anywhere.'

'Harihn, I don't know how to thank you,' Aurian told him, in an excess of relief. 'As soon as I'm on my feet, I'll repay your kindness, I promise. With your permission, I'll start training your personal guard in northern fighting skills. Then, if your father should make a move against you, you'll have as much protection as possible.' And when I go away, she thought, at least you'll still be defended.

'Lady, you have my heartfelt thanks.' Harihn faced her, his front of arrogance replaced by gratitude. Aurian realized that he was very much afraid of his father – and very much alone. And now she intended to betray him; to win his trust and use what aid he could offer her, and then, as soon as it was expedient, to leave him. In that moment she hated herself. How far would the ripples of Miathan's evil spread? Were they beginning to engulf her, too? Aurian forced a smile, but she was shuddering inwardly, despising herself for what she was doing.

'Your Highness,' she said, 'it will be my privilege to help you.' And may the gods help me, she thought.

25

The Prisoners

The Nightrunners had made their home in a safe and secret honeycomb of caves, reached from the ocean via a tunnel where waves beat into a shadowed opening in the cliff. This access, with waters deep enough to float a ship, opened into a vast cavern, hollowed out aeons ago by the sea's ceaseless pounding in the constricted space beneath the cliffs. A gently sloping beach of shingle narrowed as it curved round, to be lost in the deep waters that lapped the sheer, sea-smoothed walls at the rear and opposite sides of the cave. Anchored in the pool were four small ships, their lines lean and swift, the figureheads at their prows carved and painted with skill and love in the shapes of legendary beasts. A cluster of smaller boats were moored by the beach, which sloped up to a broad shelf of flat rock, the wall behind it pierced with dark entrances to the maze of corridors and chambers where the smugglers dwelt.

The cavern was lit by lamps and torches fixed in brackets to the rock itself, or mounted on tall wooden poles planted firmly in the shingle. Their flickering light was picked up by glittering fragments of mica and fine veins of ore in the walls, and thrown back in splintered rainbow gleams that echoed the sparkle of tears in Zanna's eyes.

She didn't want to leave. In three short months, this place had become her home. They let me have a life here, Zanna justified herself against the guilt that dogged her love of this place. Though Dulsina's sister Remana had been kind and welcoming, she had not tried to coddle Zanna as though she might break apart. In the secret world of the Nightrunners, everyone made themselves useful.

Zanna paused in the entrance to the massive cavern, assailed by memories of the day she had first arrived in this place. She had been weary and chilled to the bone, and not a little afraid.

Despite Dulsina's assurances, the reluctance of the smuggler crew to accept her had left her uncertain of her welcome in their hideaways. But from the moment Vannor's daughter had stepped unsteadily down the springy gangplank with a fretful Antor in her arms, Remana had been a fount of comfort and reassurance.

The tall, grey-haired woman, older and stouter than her sister, but with the same upright carriage, brisk manner and shrewd, twinkling grey eyes, had taken Antor in one arm and put the other around the tired girl's shoulders, cutting short Zanna's attempt at an explanation with a flood of brisk and friendly chatter. 'Never mind that, child – you look quite worn out. I don't suppose these useless men even thought to feed you, did they? No? I thought not. Men! The only way to drive any sense into them is to hit them over the head with an oar. What? Dulsina gave you a letter for me? Wonders will never cease! I know it's not easy to get messages to this place, but my sister is the worst correspondent . . . Here you are, my dear – the kitchen – we'll get you fed and warm in no time . . .'

As she had been speaking, Remana had been leading the bemused Zanna through what had seemed, at the time, to be a maze of interconnecting caves and tunnels. At last they reached a low arched entrance at the end of a corridor, and passed into the warm, fragrant cavern that was the communal kitchen. In the Nightrunner community, even kitchen duty had its place. It was left to those unable to perform the more arduous tasks of survival: the old and the very young. In this way, everyone, even the children, contributed to the welfare of the close-knit group. A sense of belonging was fostered at a very early age. It was a good system, in Zanna's opinion – better than that of the city, where the poor were bonded like slaves, and little children and folk too old to do manual work begged in the stinking streets, or were forced to turn to crime in order to survive.

The kitchen was loud with chatter and brightly lit with many lamps, its smoke-stained walls glowing a soft red with the warm light of the cookfires. Even at this early hour, the place was filled with a businesslike bustle. A budding young girl, one of the goatherds who tended the small flock that grazed on the cliffs above, was pouring warm, fresh milk into cans which stood in an icy pool at the back of the cavern, where the sea penetrated through some subterranean chink in the rocks. A boy sat at the edge of one hearth, stirring a cauldron of porridge. By its side steamed a kettle of fragrant tea, made from dried flowers and sea-grass that grew at the top of the cliff. An old man with gnarled hands was gutting fish in a corner, and the fruits of his labours were baking on griddles at a nearby fire, supervised by his wife. One old woman was beating gulls' eggs in a basin, watched hungrily by the small boy and girl who had climbed the sheer cliffs to collect them. The mouth-watering aroma of new bread filled the air.

Antor caused a sensation. Within seconds, the little boy had been taken over by a vociferous group of delighted old fisherwives, and was being bathed and fed, pampered and cosseted and exclaimed over. Remana, having made sure that they were not neglecting the business of breakfast in their zeal, turned her attention to Zanna, seating her by the fire with a large bowl of porridge, a cup of the steaming tea, and a hunk of warm new bread and pungent goatsmilk cheese. Pouring some tea for herself, she sat down on the other side of the hearth to read Dulsina's letter while Zanna ate.

'Well! My poor dear girl, you have had a time of it, haven't you?' Zanna blushed beneath her scrutiny as Remana looked up from the letter with lifted brows. 'Don't worry, child – we'll take good care of you both, and you can stay as long as you like. Be sure that you are welcome here, my dear – very welcome indeed.'

And so began one of the happiest times in Zanna's life. She was given a chamber close to Remana – a tiny curtained cubicle that had, like many of the living areas, been chipped pain-stakingly out of the rock during the many years that the Nightrunners had dwelt in this labyrinth of caves. The delightfully eccentric furnishings were made of driftwood, and brightly coloured rag rugs covered the floor. Thick woven hangings helped take the chill from the walls, for only the kitchen and the main living and work rooms had fireplaces, vented via natural faults in the cliff.

'But aren't you worried about the smoke being seen?' Zanna had asked Remana.

'Not a bit, my dear. For one thing, by the time it filters up through all that rock, there's very little smoke left; for another' – Remana's eyes grew large and round as she lowered her voice – 'no one ever comes to this desolate part of the coast. You see, the area is haunted.'

'Haunted?' Zanna gasped.

Remana burst out laughing. 'Zanna, if you could see your face! It's naught to worry about. There is a massive standing stone nearby, out on the far headland of the bay – a great, towering black thing that looks very sinister, especially in the moonlight. Leynard's grandfather, the first of the Nightrunner leaders, discovered that the local fishermen and herders were very superstitious about it, so he arranged some "hauntings" –you know, mysterious lights around the stone at night, ghostly voices on the wind, the sound of invisible horsemen passing by – all the usual old rubbish. Now, no one will come within miles of it. Mind you . . .' For an instant, her brow creased in a frown. 'I must admit that the animals are afraid of it, but truly, there's nothing to worry about. In fact we bless the stone, because it keeps us safe. I'm only warning you in case you go riding up there. The vicinity of the stone is best avoided, if you don't want a spill . . .'

'I can learn to ride?' Zanna, the stone forgotten, could barely contain her delight.

'You mean that father of yours never taught you?' Remana looked shocked. 'I've heard Dulsina say that Vannor was over-protective of his daughters, but by the gods, that's going too far. Of course you can learn to ride – it's something every girl should know. Later in the year, when the weather improves, I'll teach you to sail, too. . .'

And so it proved. Remana, as good as her word, lost no time in recruiting a young smuggler named Tarnal as Zanna's instructor, and she soon became an insatiable horsewoman, going out with the tow-headed lad every day the uncertain midwinter weather permitted. The Nightrunners kept a troop of swift, sturdy, sure-footed ponies that usually ran wild on the grassy headlands, but came happily down a narrow, sloping tunnel whose entrance was concealed in a clump of gorse at the top of the cliff to be stabled safely below in the caves when the eastern coast was lashed by storms.

Zanna adored her rides with Tarnal. From the clifftop above the smugglers' cave, the view was glorious. Below and to the right was a pale sweep of crescent beach, embraced by cliffs and cradling the shining sea. Some half-league away on the opposite horn of the crescent was a green knoll crowned by the stark and sinister standing stone, and behind were the vast, curving, green-grey swells of the empty moorland. Astride her beloved pony, a shaggy, gaily marked piebald she had named Piper, Zanna would ride for miles across the moors with the smuggler boy, their hair, dark brown and palest gold, streaming behind them in the winter wind. They would return at dusk, tired but exhilarated, their hands and faces tingling painfully from the cold, to hot soup in the kitchen and an affectionate scolding from Remana for staying out so long. Though she missed her father, Zanna felt as though she were truly coming home.

She had wondered, at first, why she could see no evidence of actual smuggling, but a chuckling Remana had soon put her right. 'Oh, not in winter, dear child. This is our quiet season, you might say. The seas are far too rough to risk our ships at this time of year, and to be honest there's little to trade.'

She had explained to Zanna that the chief activity of the smugglers was to ply between the coastal villages, transporting locally grown foodstuffs and crafted wares between the communities on a barter system, thus cutting out the ruinous tariffs charged by the Merchants' Guild, and allowing the poor peasants to enjoy a few of the luxuries that would otherwise be denied them. 'Of course your dad, as head of the Guild, is officially against such criminal behaviour,' Remana had remarked. 'Fortunately, he holds the private belief that the merchants make profit enough, and the peasants should enjoy the fruits of their labours. Besides' – she winked at Zanna – 'there's also the little matter of our southern partnership! At least there was.' Her face had clouded over, and she had said no more, but Zanna knew that she was thinking about Yanis. She vowed to herself that before it was time for him to set out again she would come up with some kind of plan for him to defeat the southerners.

As the winter days sped by, Zanna learned many things from

her smuggler friends. The old men had taken her to their hearts, and showed her how to fish with a line in the tidal pools outside the cavern. At low tide, they fought for the privilege of teaching her to set crab-pots along the rocky reefs near the mouth of the cave, which protected the hideout from the close approach of other ships. In the spring, Remana had promised her, when it was calm enough to teach her to sail, she herself would show Zanna the secret of navigating the one safe route through the treacherous maze of submerged reefs.

In winter, much of the work for the younger, fitter men involved repair and maintenance of the ships and their gear. While snowstorms raged outside, the women showed Zanna how to mend nets and ropes and sails, and how to make the rugs that protected their feet from the cold stone floors by hooking shreds of rag through coarse sacking. They also taught her the secrets of their beautiful and intricate weaving, which they used to make the warm wall hangings that brightened up the gloomy darkness of the caves.

These were companionable times, filled with chatter and laughter, gossip and teasing among the younger women. There was a great deal of talk about the handsome, wind-bronzed young men, and who was in love with whom, and who would marry. At these times, Zanna was content to listen and keep her own counsel. Though Tarnal had become her devoted shadow, she had already decided that she would marry none but Yanis, for she had loved him from the first day she had set eyes on him. Fortunately, or perhaps unfortunately, the leader of the Night-runners had no idea, as yet, of the fate she had mapped out for him – and now he might never know, for Zanna had to leave.

Zanna paused in the shadowed entrance to the great harbour cavern, paralysed by the rush of happy memories that had assailed her with such pain. Angrily she shook her head, and brushed her tears away. This was doing no good. For three short months she had been happy, until word had come of the recent catastrophe in Nexis. Word of monsters, hideous beyond imagining, which had caused many deaths. Word of the Archmage seizing power, and holding the city in a grip of terror. And no word of Vannor, who had been missing without trace since that horrific night when so many had died.

When Remana had told her the news, Zanna's guilt at leaving Vannor had returned to overwhelm her. She had known at once what she must do. She must return to Nexis to find her dad, or at least find out what had happened to him. Of course, if the Nightrunners discovered her intentions, they would never let her go – that was why she was sneaking around now, late at night, preparing to make her escape.

It was fortunate that there had been several days of stormy weather, and thus the horses were stabled below in the caves. The bizzard raging outside would make the journey both difficult and dangerous, but Zanna was sure she only needed to get as far as some kind of shelter that night – then, having lost the pursuers that Remana would no doubt send after her, she would be able to continue in daylight. Surely it wouldn't be too difficult to find her way over the moors to Nexis? She hoped not.

Zanna peeped around the side of the archway to look for the watchman who guarded the ships at night. He came into view, his footsteps crunching on the shingle beach, and she heaved a sigh of relief. So far, her plan was working out. She had forced herself to wait, with scant patience, until the night when Tarnal vould be on duty. Taking a deep breath, Zanna stepped out to meet him.

'You're up late!' Tarnal sounded surprised but, as she had expected, his brown eyes brightened at the sight of her. Oh dear, Zanna thought – I hope I don't get him into too much trouble. She arranged a smile on her face.

'I couldn't sleep,' she told him ruefully. 'Even though we're underground here, the storm still seems to bother me.'

'Ah, that happens to a lot of us,' Tarnal assured her. 'It means you're weather-wise, as we call it. You have the makings of a good Nightrunner, Zanna.' He grinned at her shyly, and she understood all too well what was on his mind. He'd been mooning after her for ages, but of all the times to start getting romantic . . .

'Anyway,' Zanna said briskly, 'since I couldn't sleep, I thought I'd come down to the stable to see if Piper is all right.'

Tarnal's face lit up. 'Good idea,' he said. 'You never know with horses in this wild weather. Tell you what – I'll come along in case you need any help.'

Oh no you don't, Zanna thought grimly. If you get me alone in that nice, warm, bracken-filled cavern . . . 'That's very kind of you, Tarnal,' she said swiftly, 'but if Yanis found out that you'd left your post, you'd be in a lot of trouble.' She gave him a conspiratorial wink. 'Stay here, Tarnal – I'll be back shortly.' With that, she beat a hasty retreat, praying that he wouldn't take it into his head to follow her.

The stable cavern was warm with the press of animal bodies. As she entered, replacing the heavy hurdle that barred the exit behind her, Zanna could hear the soft huffing sound of horses breathing in the shadows, followed by a rustle of straw and a scrape of hoof on stone as the sleepy creatures became aware of her presence. Great, lustrous eyes swung in her direction, gleaming like jewels as they reflected the light of the lamp she carried. Stretching up on tiptoe, Zanna reached up and placed the lamp very carefully in a deep niche carved high in the rocky wall on her right hand side. There were very strict rules about keeping any kind of flame away from the tinder-dry bracken that covered the cavern floor. One spark, and the cave would become an inferno within seconds.

Shuffling thrugh the deep-drifted bedding, Zanna moved along the wall until she came to the row of pegs, hammered into a natural transverse crack in the stone, that held saddles and bridles. Rummaging under a pile of bracken, she unearthed her warm cloak and the bundle of food and belongings she'd hidden there earlier in the evening. Rather than lugging the whole lot, along with the ungainly, flapping saddle, through the mass of restless animals, she decided to catch Piper first and bring him here. Unhooking his bridle from its peg, she took an apple from the pocket of her skirt and wriggled her way carefully between the milling horses, calling softly for the piebald pony.

Piper came to her calling – she had been teaching him to do this by bringing a him a treat every time she wanted to ride him. Zanna smiled as he snuffled greedily into her palm and scrunched the fruit in a single bite. While he was looking for more, she slipped the bridle into place and fastened the buckle quickly. Then, despite her hurry, she threw her arms around Piper's arching neck, burying her face in his streaming black and white mane to stifle her sobbing. Oh, gods, she did love him so! And Remana, and Yanis and Antor and Tarnal, and all the others . . .

The pony snorted, and turned his head to nibble at her pocket, his ears cocked forward hopefully. She had no more apples, however – all he found was her handkerchief, which he tugged out anyway. Zanna's sobbing turned to shaky laughter. 'Why thank you, you clever creature!' she told him. Having retrieved her chewed and rather soggy possession, she led the pony to the place near the wall where she had left her belongings.

Tethering Piper to a handy peg, Zanna turned to lift the saddle down – always a stretch for one of her short stature. Placing it carefully on the pony's back, she stooped under his belly to find the dangling girth – and jerked upright with a yelp as a hand grasped her shoulder. Zanna spun round, her heart hammering with shock, to find herself in the arms of Yanis.

'I've been waiting for you to make a run for it ever since we told you about your dad,' the smuggler said, but there was sympathy, not anger, in his face.

'Yanis, please don't stop me,' Zanna begged. 'I must go – I can't bear it! I have to know, don't you see . . .' Her eyes overflowed with tears.

'I know, girl. In your place I'd feel the same,' Yanis told her gently, 'but rushing off all alone in a storm is no answer. Why, there's hard men, experienced men, been lost out on those moors in the blizzards, and all we've found come spring was their bones picked clean by wolves – if we found anything at all, that is.'

Zanna stared at him in dismay. For a moment she had hoped to persuade him . . . But though it was obviously not to be, her agile brain was already at work on a new plan. Yanis would be watching the horses like a hawk at first, but if she could allay his suspicions long enough . . .

'All right.' She sighed, and wiped her eyes. 'I'm sorry, Yanis – I didn't know the moors were so dangerous, but now you've explained it to me . . .' She caught her breath, suddenly very conscious of his arms around her; aware that this was the first time he had touched her since the day of her arrival. She didn't want him to let her go, but if her new scheme was to work it was imperative that she fool him into thinking she was resigned to her fate. Sighing, she pushed him away, and turned to leave.

'Wait!' Yanis caught hold of her arm. 'I know what you're thinking. You only need wait a while and then you can try again – only it won't work, see?'

Zanna gasped, furious that he had outguessed her. 'And just how did you manage to work that out?' she said acidly.

The young smuggler's face darkened. 'I know what you think of me,' he said stiffly, 'but that's the first time you've come near calling me daft to my face. Well, let me tell you something – there's stupid and stupid, and it didn't take much for me to realize what you were up to. All I did was put myself into your shoes for a minute. I would never have given up so easily, and I knew for sure that you wouldn't, loving your dad like you do. You were the stupid one, to underestimate me.' His grip around Zanna's arm tightened as he continued: 'The Nightrunners can't let you go running off to get killed, you little idiot! *I* won't let you! I'm a patient man, believe me, and it's winter, so I've nothing better to do. Get used to having me around, girl, because I plan to be your shadow from now on.'

Zanna stared at him open-mouthed, for a moment too outraged to speak. She stared into that rugged, handsome face, those dark grey eyes that were sparking with anger, the mouth that was hard now, and unyielding. Not long ago, Vannor's daughter would have been overjoyed at the thought of having Yanis constantly at her side. Now, the idea filled her with rage and frustration. 'Damn you!' she yelled, and kicked him as hard as she could in the shin. 'I might just as well be your prisoner!'

With a stifled curse, Yanis let go of her arm, and Zanna fled from the cavern with tears of anger streaming down her face.

'I might just as well be your prisoner!' The Earth-Mage Eilin glared at the Forest Lord. 'You deliberately took my staff and gave it to D'arvan, so that I could not return to my Valley. You could hardly wait to seize the chance to tamper with the fate of the world outside once more!'

Hellorin looked at her steadily, but made no reply to her charge. The suspicion dawned on Eilin that he was simply waiting for her anger to run its course – after all, what need had he to waste his breath in fruitless debate? No matter how much she might storm and argue and protest, she was utterly in his power.

The Mage found that she was shaking with rage. 'Meddler!' she spat. 'It was ever so with the Phaerie! It's of no consequence to you that the Archmage rides roughshod over all the world! Just so long as you can exercise your influence on events, what do you care? Don't you realize that I am the only Mage left in the north to oppose Miathan? You've let those two children loose in *my* Vale with *my* staff to face the Archmage alone. In the name of all the gods, my Lord – they need me!'

'No, Eilin – they do not need you.' Hellorin spoke softly, but the underlying power of his voice sent a shiver across the smooth, silver-grey bark that coated the walls of the chamber. The Mage fought to hold on to her anger: the legendary temper of the Magefolk was the only thing that had saved her from being overawed by this stupendous immortal. She folded her arms and her lips thinned into an obdurate line.

'Why not?' she demanded. 'Give me one good reason why not!'

'Because I am Lord here, and I say that they do not!' When Hellorin frowned, it was as though a cloud had passed over the sun – though there was no sun in this changeless, timeless Elsewhere. As his dark brows drew together, Eilin shivered at the sound of a distant growl of thunder. 'Have a care, Magewoman – I do not *meddle*, as you call it, through idleness or spite – though the debt your people owe to mine is a sore temptation.' Hellorin's voice was a blade of ice, and Eilin took an involuntary step backwards, rubbing at the gooseflesh that pricked her skin.

'So that's what this is about!' she hissed. 'Revenge, pure and simple. Oh, you may protest your innocence, Lord, but if I had not been a Mage – '

'Had you not been a Mage, you would never have survived the murder attempt by one of your own people,' Hellorin told her flatly, his eyes glinting with irritation. 'Had you not been a Mage, you would never have come here to plague me!'

'If I plague you, let me go!' Eilin countered swiftly.

'By all the gods, Eilin, is there no telling you? *I – can – not!*'
Hellorin threw out his arms in a gesture of defeat, and stamped
across the mossy green carpet to the deep window embrasure,
where a flagon of wine and two goblets stood on the sill.
Throwing himself into the window-seat, he poured wine for
them, and held out a cup to her. 'Here – sit down, you wretched
woman, and stop bristling. Let us end this wrangle, once and
for all.'

'But . . .'

'Eilin, please?'

The Earth-Mage was disarmed by the change in Hellorin's
voice. Biting her lip, she crossed the room to him, and perched
tentatively on the edge of the window-seat.

'You look just like a little brown bird, poised and ready to fly
away at the slightest hint of danger.' Hellorin's chiselled mouth
softened in a smile, and Eilin, much to her dismay, found the
last shreds of her righteous anger melting like sunrise mist.

'Little brown bird my eye!' she retorted tartly, but despite
her best efforts she found that her lips were twitching as she
took the goblet from his hand.

Hellorin's eyes never left her own. 'Rest you, my Lady,' he
said softly. 'Your healing is but lately accomplished, and you
need time to regain your strength. It does you no good to agitate
yourself in this way.'

'Is that why you won't let me go yet?' Eilin seized eagerly on
his words. 'Do you mean that when . . .'

'No.' The word held a terrifying finality. Hellorin sighed.
'Lady, I have put off this explanation lest you be distressed
beyond the limits of your strength – and because I feared that
you would not believe me.' He took her hand in a firm, warm
grip, and his fathomless eyes bored into her own. 'Eilin, you
must try to understand. What I am about to tell you is the
absolute truth – I swear it on the head of my son. When you
were brought to us, your injuries were fatal, even to one of the
Mageborn. My healers brought you back from the brink of
death – in this place, where the Phaerie are empowered and
time holds no sway, it was possible for them to do this. But
thanks to your Magefolk ancestors, their power – *our* power –
no longer extends into the mundane world. In short, you have

been healed in this world, but not in your own. If you try to return . . .'

'No!' Eilin choked on the cry. Her blood was ice in her veins. 'It can't be true – it *can't*!' But the lines of sorrow on the Forest Lord's face, the overflowing sympathy in his eyes, convinced her beyond any words that he spoke the absolute truth. Eilin, after the tragedies of her life, had believed herself more than a match for any disaster that fate flung into her path, but this last cruel jest on the part of destiny felled her with a single, lethal stroke.

The impenetrable citadel of fierce Magefolk pride with which Eilin had surrounded herself after the death of Geraint began to crumble and totter at last, and the Mage felt as though she was falling into pieces along with it. 'I cannot leave?' she whispered. 'I can't go home – ever?'

The pain in Hellorin's eyes said everything. 'I fear not, Lady,' he told her sorrowfully. 'At least, not unless – '

But Eilin never heard those vital, final words. They were drowned in a sound of endlessly breaking glass, as her adamantine fortress exploded into shards that were falling, falling like her tears . . .

Hellorin could only hold her helplessly while she trembled and wept. She had been dreadfully weakened, of course, by her injuries – far more, in fact, than she realized – but he was shocked by such profound distress. To see Eilin brought so low was more than he could bear: she who was so fierce and proud. How he admired her for that. No one had stood up to him so well in aeons, save little Maya, of course. We have been out of the world too long indeed, he mused. They seem to have produced a wild and wonderful breed of woman in our absence. But even the strongest of women occasionally needed help.

The Lord of the Phaerie gathered his powers, and '*Enough!*' he roared. The air was ripped apart by a tremendous thunderclap, and lightning arced across the chamber in a searing flare. Eilin jerked to her feet, cramming her knuckles into her gaping mouth, her tangled hair a bristling aureole from the residue of power in the room, her eyes enormous in a chalk-white face. Hellorin smiled at her. 'Much better!' he said briskly. 'And now that I have your attention, Lady . . .'

Seizing the hand of the startled Mage, the Forest Lord pulled her after him out of the room and rushed her, clattering, down the wooden spiral of stairs that twisted down inside the walls of the slender tower. Ignoring the incredulous stares of his subjects, he towed her through the seemingly endless series of halls and chambers that made up his citadel, until at last they crossed the great hall where Maya and D'arvan had rested and burst through the great, arching outer doorway and into the open. Without pausing, he hurried her down the steps of the outer terraces, and across the meadow towards the misty outline of the woods beyond.

'Hellorin, wait! I can't . . .' Eilin's breathless wail halted the Lord of the Phaerie. He turned to see that she was in real distress; her legs were shaky, and her chest was heaving with the unaccustomed exertion, which had come too soon after recovering from her dreadful wounds. But at least she was speaking again, and that irate glint in her eye promised well for the resurgence of her fiery spirit.

'Well run, my Lady,' he told her, thinking it was just as well she had no breath for the blistering retort that was written all too clearly across her face. Putting his arm around her, he turned her back to face the way she had come, and was gratified by her gasp of pure delight. 'Forgive me for rushing you out in such a rude and rough fashion, Lady,' he said gently, 'but I wanted very much to show you this.' There, before them, climbing up and up from the gentle swell of the grassy meadow, was the pride of Hellorin's heart – the citadel and home of his people.

The Phaerie, consummate masters of illusion that they were, had excelled themselves; combining nature with magic to create a true entity that actually lived and breathed around them, unlike the oppressive heaps of soulless, murdered, hacked-out stone that formed the dwellings of Mage and Mortal. Glowing like a jewel in the strange, golden half-light that was an unchanging feature of this timeless Otherworld, the citadel took the outward form of a massive, craggy hill. Its walls and balconies were cliffs and ledges, its windows were concealed by glamourie from outward view, and its many delicate wooden towers, such as the one in which Eilin had been staying, were groves of soaring, living beech. Level areas boasted glades and gardens with translucent, bright-hued flowers that sparkled like spun glass in the eerie amber light. Streams and fountains decked the hillside in diamond-glitter, cascading down the sheer rock faces like drifting silver veils.

Hellorin let out his breath in a contented sigh. Down through the ages, this sight had never failed to move him with a pleasure so intense it was almost pain. He smiled at Eilin, who stood beside him as though she had been turned to stone. Her face was rapt and glowing. 'Beautiful, is it not, beyond all words?' he murmured. 'Though your exile must be bitter, can such a place as this not ease your sorrow, Lady?'

Eilin sighed. 'A little, perhaps – in the course of time.'

'Ah, time – but time, at last, may mend all things.' Seeing the Mage's quizzical frown, Hellorin was swift to enlighten her. 'Your exile need not last for ever, Lady – only for as long as we ourselves are imprisoned here.'

'What?' Eilin gasped. 'I don't understand.'

'It is all to do with our magic, and its limitations,' the Forest Lord explained. 'The power of our healers cannot yet extend into your world, but when we Phaerie are released from our own exile our healing powers will also be freed from their restrictions. You can return in safety then, and be well and whole again as you were before.'

Eilin was still frowning. 'But I thought the ancient Magefolk had imprisoned you here for all eternity.'

'Ah, of course! Now I perceive your confusion. I explained the prophecy to Maya and D'arvan, but I had forgotten that you would not know. But you are weary, and the midst of a meadow is no place for lengthy tales. Come back with me now, my Lady, and be refreshed and rest in comfort. Then I will tell you all that you wish to know.'

'So your – our – freedom depends on the One who comes to claim the Sword of Flame?' Eilin felt crushed all over again with disappointment. Almost, she wished that Hellorin had spared her these ridiculous notions. A Phaerie prophecy was too fragile a thread on which to hang her hopes.

'You must have faith, Lady.' Hellorin took her hand.

411

'Believe me, had you known the Dragonfolk as I did, their words would not have failed to comfort you. Events are in motion – we have only to wait.'

'Yes, but for how long?' A tear trembled on Eilin's lashes. 'Events are in motion as we speak, out there in the world. My child is lost and in danger, Nexis has fallen, the Magefolk have been corrupted – and Maya and D'arvan are out in the forest doing the gods know what with this magic sword of yours . . .' Her words were lost in a sob. 'They need me, Hellorin! While I am forced to kick my heels in this – this Nowhere, and don't even know what is happening . . .' To her dismay, she was weeping again.

'Hush, Lady, hush,' Hellorin comforted her. 'There, at least, I can ease your mind. Come, Eilin – I have one more wonder to show you.'

Taking the Mage's hand, he led her away from the fire towards the far end of the hall. There, to Eilin's puzzlement, a short flight of stone steps ended in nothing. They simply went halfway up the wall, and stopped. Above them, the wall was hidden by a rich hanging of green-gold brocade. Hellorin mounted the steps, taking her with him, and pulled the curtain aside.

Eilin gasped. There, set high in the wall, was a glorious window of glittering, many-hued crystal shaped like a sunburst. Around the edges, the richly coloured panes sent pinpoints of jewelled light cascading into the chamber. In the centre was a single, circular crystal, set at eye-level from the vantage-point of the stairway.

'Here.' Hellorin guided her forward with an arm around her shoulders. 'Look through my window.'

'Oh!' The Mage blinked, rubbed her eyes, and peered closer. 'By all the gods – it's Nexis!' She swung around to face him, suddenly suspicious. 'Is this more of your Phaerie trickery?'

'Upon my oath it is not!' The Forest Lord's eyes glinted with annoyance. 'Gods, but if you are not the most contrary, stiff-necked creature ever to come within these walls . . .' Suddenly he began to laugh softly, shaking his head. 'Nay, but I have not enjoyed such a battle of wits and wills since I lost my poor

Adrina. Trust me, Lady Eilin – you I would not deceive. This is my window upon the world – left me by your wretched ancestors, no doubt to tantalize me with all that the Phaerie were missing. It was through this casement that I first saw Adrina, collecting her healing herbs in the forest.' He sighed. 'I had the casement covered on the day I lost her, and have never looked through it again until now. But if it will ease you, Lady, we will come here whenever you wish and keep vigil together, until our exile is ended at last.'

The Earth-Mage looked up at the Lord of the Phaerie, suddenly and utterly moved by his kindness. How could her ancestors have been so cruel as to shut this magnificent, kindly, great-hearted being away from the world? Her fingers tightened on his hand, and, for the first time in their acquaintance, she smiled at him. 'Thank you, my Lord,' she said simply. 'I would like that very much.'

26

A Bargain with Death

Anvar's endurance had finally reached an end. After many days – he had lost count of how many – in the slave camp, he was laid low by a fever carried by the whining, biting insects. One morning he found himself unable to rise, his body racked by shivers and delirium. The overseer rolled him over with a sandalled foot. 'This one is finished.' The words echoed weirdly in Anvar's receding consciousness. 'Get the others to work, and we'll see to him later. What a pity – already he has won me a month's wages. Had he lasted a little longer it would have been more.'

These were the last words that Anvar heard as he was drawn down, down into a spiralling blackness. In that moment, all pain and sorrow and weariness lifted from his heart, and gladly he let go, to commence the final journey.

For several days after her talk with Harihn, Aurian did little but eat and sleep, and argue with the surgeon about when she could get out of bed. The search for Anvar had made no progress, and she was anxious to get matters moving at her speed. But the surgeon remained obdurate, and to her dismay she was prevented from trying out her injured leg by Shia, who had come down unexpectedly but firmly on the side of the wrinkled little man. Since the great cat never left her side, Aurian found herself helplessly confined to bed, waited on hand and foot by the gigantic Bohan. Out of gratitude for his devotion, and the well-meaning concern of both Shia and her host, Aurian tried to curb her irritation, but her frustration was mounting with each passing day.

Harihn spent a good deal of time with the Mage, and in the source of their conversations told her about the city-state of Taibeth to which she had come. It was the capital city and northernmost outpost of the Khazalim, most of whom lived a nomadic life in the arid wilderness to the south of the great river valley, or dwelt in scattered settlements to the west, further up the river. 'It is a difficult land,' he told her, 'and the Khazalim are a difficult people – fierce, warlike, and merciless to their enemies. My father is a good example of our race.' With that, he went on to speak of his unhappy childhood. The prince's mother had been a princess of the Xandim, who lived far across the desert and were renowned for their legendary horses. She had been captured on a raid and wedded to Xiang, but her spirit had proved too proud and independent to suit the Khisu. When Harihn was still a boy, Xiang had finally had his mother drowned in the river by assassins, claiming her death as an accident. Her son had spent his childhood roaming the royal palace, lonely and unloved, a constant victim of his father's brutality. But the Khisu had never taken another queen, and as sole royal heir Harihn's life had been preserved – until now.

The prince, to Aurian's dismay, refused to let go of the idea of somehow using Anvar to discredit the new queen. 'Truly,' he said, 'your husband may yet prove to be a weapon for me against my royal father.'

'Now wait a minute,' Aurian broke in. 'I'm not having Anvar put in danger because of this feud of yours.'

'Danger? Feud? Aurian, you do not understand.' Harihn leaned forward, his eyes intense. 'Your husband is in the gravest of danger, if yet he lives. If the Khisu discovers the connection between this man and his new Khisihn, then Anvar's life will not be worth a grain of sand. And what of the Khisihn herself? I saw her ruthlessness when she pleaded for your death. She would never leave your man alive to give away her secret. Nay, I must intensify the search at once. I would rather have this pawn in my hands as soon as possible, not only for your peace of mind and for my benefit, but for his own safety.'

None the less, it was another four days before the search yielded any results. Aurian, driven mad with impatience, had finally won the right to be allowed out of bed. Her persistence had worn down Harihn, the surgeon, and Shia, to the point where it had been decided that Bohan should carry her outside, and settle her on a comfortable chair in the walled garden, with her injured leg propped up on a footstool. She was sternly forbidden to get to her feet, however, and the eunuch remained in constant attendance on her to see to her every need. Well, it's progress at least, Aurian though glumly. At first she had badgered the prince to remove those accursed bracelets and let her heal herself, but he had told her that the secret of their unlocking had long been lost by the Khazalim. Besides, according to an ancient law, the freeing of a sorcerer within the bounds of the kingdom would result in all parties concerned being flayed alive. Though the Mage had grudgingly dropped the matter, it only served to increase her despair.

Aurian sat by the ornamental pool in the shade of a flowering tree, inwardly fuming. Shia, having lost patience with her irascible friend, had taken herself off to sleep in the shade. The Mage was moodily shredding the waxy, perfumed, trumpetlike blossoms between her fingers and throwing the fragments into the pool, where they were instantly seized by the greedy golden carp and as instantly spat out again. But the fish kept trying, all the same. Stupid things, Aurian thought grouchily. You'd think they'd learn. Just then Bohan, who had been sitting on the grass nearby, leapt to his feet at the sound of approaching footsteps, and hastily prostrated himself before his prince, who came hurrying along the terrace, his face alight. 'News, Aurian,' he cried. 'I have news at last!'

Aurian tried to rise, but he pushed her gently down again into the chair. Pain lanced through her strapped ribs, but she ignored it. 'Tell me!' she cried. Harihn dropped to the grass beside her, panting in the enervating heat, and poured two goblets of wine from the jug on the low table beside her.

'We located the captain of the Corsair ship last night,' he said. 'Naturally he was reluctant to admit to illegal trade in foreigners, but a brief sojourn in my dungeon soon changed that.' His eyes sparkled with a savage glee that Aurian found distasteful. Like father, like son, she thought. I ought to be more careful.

'It seems,' Harihn continued, 'that he sold your Anvar to a notorious slave trader named Zahn. My men paid him a visit this morning. At first he denied all knowledge of the matter, but when offered a simple choice – a large bribe on the one hand, or a visit to his friend the captain in my dungeon on the other – he became most helpful. It is just as well.' He frowned. 'Had I been forced to arrest Zahn, it would have attracted the Khisu's attention – Zahn is the main source of slaves to build his summer palace. If my father had found out about your husband, things might have gone very badly for us all.'

'Never mind that,' Aurian prompted impatiently, not interested in any of this – a mistake, as she was later to discover. 'Where is Anvar? What did you find out?'

'Try not to hope too much, Aurian.' Harihn's face grew sombre. 'Zahn sold him to the work gangs building my father's summer palace upriver. The Khisu wants it finished, and cares not how many lives he wastes to gain his ends. I visited the place once. The brutality with which the slaves were treated made me sick.' He took hold of the Mage's hand. 'Aurian, your Anvar went there several weeks ago, and slaves die in that place like flies. And you northerners have not the constitution for this climate. It is almost certain that he is dead, Lady.'

'No!'

Seeing her stricken face, he went on quickly. 'But I have readied a boat, and I will go myself, at once, to see.'

Instantly the old glint was back in Aurian's eyes. 'Good,' she said. 'I thought I would have to talk you into it for a minute. How soon can we start?'

Harihn stared at her, taking in the strapping on her ribs which was visible through the gauzy white robe she wore; the leg tightly swathed in bandages; the left arm still in a sling to immobilize it as much as possible. Fading bruises lingered on her arms and her pallid face. 'Aurian, you cannot go,' he told her firmly.

Aurian's jaw tightened. 'Would you care to wager on that, my prince?'

At any other time, the journey upriver would have been very pleasant. Aurian and Harihn reclined on cushions beneath a shady canopy, the ever attentive Bohan fanning away the swarms of insects that hovered over the sluggish waters. Though Harihn had forsaken his extravagant royal barge for a plainer craft in order to attract as little attention as possible, there was an unmistakable air of luxury about the voyage. Fruit and wine had been provided, but the Mage was far too anxious to eat. She sat bolt upright, gazing upriver, willing the bargemen to row faster. Never in her life had she bitten her nails, but she was doing it now. Harihn watched her, a frown on his face. 'Aurian,' he said at last. 'Must you fret so?'

'What do you think?' Aurian snapped. 'How can I not fret when Anvar is suffering so badly? I blame myself for this.' Her voice was bitter.

'Aurian, what could you have done?' The prince sat up and laid a soothing hand on her arm. 'You take too much upon yourself. What's done is done – remember how near you came to losing your own life. You might have turned your back on Anvar, as the Khisihn has done, but you did not. What more can you do? Whether we come in time or no, we will not come any quicker for your worrying.'

'I know,' Aurian said miserably. 'I just can't help it.'

As the barge approached the jetty at the site of the summer palace, Aurian could see for herself how badly the slaves were abused, and how much they suffered. Her throat constricted with fear. Surely Anvar could never have survived this? Why had she ever left him? Her knuckles tightened, the nails of her clenched fingers digging into the soft wood of the barge's rail.

When they were safely moored, Bohan carried the Mage ashore and set her down on the dusty ground while Harihn sent for the slave master. They waited, Aurian in a fever of impatience. Shia, to her disgust, had been made to stay behind, but Harihn had brought his surgeon with them. The little man was frowning, his lips pursed in disapproval at what he saw. When Aurian caught his eye, he responded with a slight shake of his head. 'Oh, please,' she began to pray, even though she knew now that the gods she had grown up with had only been Magefolk like herself. 'Please . . .'

The slave master duly arrived. Recognizing his prince with a start, he dropped to the ground, quaking all over. Harihn hastily summoned him to rise and drew him to one side, out of earshot. Their discussion seemed interminable to Aurian. Though she was unable to hear, she could see the slave master spreading his hands in denial and shaking his head vehemently.

At last Harihn tired of the argument, and snapped his fingers. Immediately two grim-faced palace guards, armed with great curved scimitars, climbed out of the barge and positioned themselves on either side of the slave master with drawn blades. The slave master sank to his knees, pleading. Pointing! Aurian turned her eyes in the same direction. The slave compound.

Harihn returned to her, his expression grim. 'Anvar is here,' he said. 'Bohan will take you to him at once, for the news is grave. The slave master says he is dying.'

The stench in the compound was overwhelming. Bohan set Aurian down beside the solitary occupant huddled on the far side, in the scant shade afforded by the wooden palisade. Aurian gasped. Anvar was scarcely recognizable, his reddened skin peeling and blistered, his lips cracked, his body covered in bruises and sores beneath the sweat and grime. He barely breathed. Aurian took her arm out of its sling and pulled his head on to her lap, wiping the dust from his face with the trailing sleeve of her robe. Her vision blurred with tears. 'Quick!' she snapped at Bohan. 'Fetch some water!' The eunuch hurried off, and Aurian beckoned the surgeon over. His face was grave as he made his examination.

'This man is dying,' he said flatly.

'Surely you can do something?' Aurian pleaded, and for the first time in her experience the surgeon's professional mask slipped. He laid a sympathetic hand on her shoulder.

'Lady, I can do nothing – only end his suffering and speed him on his way. It would be by far the kindest thing.'

'Damned if you will!' Her eyes blazed with such fury that the surgeon threw himself flat on the ground in terror. 'Get out of here!' Aurian spat. 'Go!'

As the little man scrambled away, she reached forward and took Anvar's scarred hands in her own. As her tears fell on his face, Aurian's heart was wrenched by a stab of excruciating memory. She had been through this experience before, when Forral died. Her indrawn breath was a sharp hiss. 'Curse you, Anvar, don't die on me too. I can't face this again. I won't let you die!'

She gripped Anvar's hands in an iron grasp, as though she

419

could drag him back to life by main force. Desperately she fought to access her power – to reach him, to heal him – but her will slipped away like water trickling through her fingers, drawn into the dead grey vortex that was the power of the bracelets. Aurian gritted her teeth against despair. But the harder she tried, the more she felt herself weakening as her power poured into the bracelets. Her vision darkened, her awareness of this foul place and the sun's merciless heat slipped away until her consciousness hung, it seemed, by a single thread of will. But that thread was made of adamant. She struggled on, down a tunnel of endless blackness, refusing to give in.

A gentle touch on Aurian's shoulder snapped her back. She found herself slumped, faint and dizzy, over Anvar's motionless form, her mind reeling from the shock of the sudden transition. She could no longer feel him breathing. No! It couldn't be over! Bohan swam into focus, kneeling beside her on the filthy ground, a jug of water beside him. With a gentle finger he touched the tears on Aurian's face, his own eyes brimming with sympathy. And something clicked in the Mage's mind. She remembered the arena – remembered drawing strength from the crowd around her. 'Bohan,' she whispered, 'will you help me?'

The giant hesitated for a moment, fear in his eyes. Then he nodded.

'Put your hands on mine,' Aurian told him. He did as he was ordered, his great hands engulfing both those of the Mage and Anvar. Aurian took a deep breath. 'Good. Now stay absolutely still and relax. Lend me your strength, Bohan, to save Anvar's life.'

Aurian concentrated as she had never done before, straining to breach the barrier that was the power of the bracelets. Then it came. Like a floodgate opening, Bohan's strength flowed into her, supplementing her own. Through a reddish haze, she saw the rust-coloured stones of the bracelets pulse and glow like tiny embers as they sated themselves on her magic. A scorching heat ate at her wrists, but she paid no heed. With a sudden shock, she realized that the bracelets stored power – not just her own, but the powers of all the Mages who had borne them

420

before her. If she could access that power, even for an instant, she could break down the very walls of death itself. But how to release it – what was the key? Come on, Aurian urged herself. Think! Anvar's life depends on it. She found her thoughts turning to him, then; reaching for the essence of the man. Anvar. Those piercing blue eyes that held his smile; his rare smile itself – the way it transformed his face. The memory of that smile went like an arrow to her heart, and her heart turned over in her breast . . .

And Aurian's vision was suddenly blocked by a vast, darkly shrouded form that loomed over her, towering into the sky. 'Aaaah,' it said, its voice a deep, dry, rustling whisper like leaves turning in a midnight graveyard – like worms that seemed to eat into her very soul. 'So – once more you think to cheat me?'

Aurian swallowed hard, gathering her courage to answer back, to defy death itself. And from somewhere the courage came. 'If that's what it takes,' she replied. 'You have had enough from me and mine. Seek your prey elsewhere!'

Death laughed like a blade drawn up Aurian's spine. 'A fool you are, to believe that matters are so simple. Yet in your ignorance you have found the only coin which will permit you to bargain with me. Many before you have tried to make such a bargain, but I warn you that my price is high – and both of you will pay it ere we meet again!' The spectre loomed forward threateningly, and Aurian bit her lip, steeling herself not to shrink away from his overwhelming presence.

'You have courage, Lady.' This time the voice held an undertone of respect. 'And for all my evil reputation, never believe that death is merciless. Far from it. If your coin – the coin that you and this man both possess – is good, and not counterfeit, you may yet have the best of the bargain. Remember that, when you come to pay my price!'

The figure disappeared in a blinding flash of red light. The power within the bracelets, suddenly released, coursed through Aurian – through Bohan, throwing him backwards – then through Anvar. Aurian felt her soul rushing outwards to meet the soul of her companion – to enfold it safely, and bring him home again.

The Mage blinked, baffled for a moment to find herself back

in the squalor of the slave compound. Then she saw that her wrists were bare. The bracelets had crumbled away to fine, powdery ash that was already dissipating as she watched.

Anvar stirred beneath her hands, his brilliant blue eyes opening to meet her own. All traces of his hurts had vanished. Later, Aurian would realize that in that flash her own hurts had also been healed, but now she was simply consumed with relief, and gratitude, and wonder for the miracle that her own indomitable will had wrought.

'Aurian?' Anvar's voice was barely a whisper in his parched throat.

'I'm here.' The Mage could scarcely find her own voice. Bohan was at her elbow, proffering a cup of water, but Aurian's hands were shaking too much to take it, and she was afraid to lose her tight grasp on Anvar, lest by doing so she let him slip away from her again. Instead she propped him, while the eunuch held the cup to his lips.

'Witch! You've betrayed us all!' The sun was blotted out as Harihn's shadow fell across the little group on the ground. His eyes, stretched wide with horror, were fastened on Aurian's wrists, where the bracelets of Zathbar had been.

'Harihn . . .' Aurian began urgently, but the prince's jewelled sword had already flashed free of its scabbard. She tried to get to her feet, but was hampered by Anvar, who had seen the danger and was also struggling weakly to rise as the blade arced down.

Bohan moved with an agility that belied his immense size, flinging himself between the Mage and Harihn's blade. He had drawn his own short sword, and metal clashed with metal, showering Aurian and Anvar with sparks as he turned the blow aside. Harihn's wrist twisted down and outwards from the backshock of the blow, and Bohan's left hand shot out to grasp it, tightening his grip until, with a cry of pain, the prince dropped his weapon. Aurian saw his chest swell with a deep breath as he prepared to call his guards.

'Stop!' Her voice, though not loud, was like a whiplash. From her kneeling position, she addressed the prince, speaking low and rapidly. 'If you kill me, Xiang will want the bracelets back. What will you say to him? You can't produce them – they're gone. He has waited for a chance like this. He'll say you removed them. He has a new Khisihn now, remember – a chance to have other heirs. He'd enjoy having you flayed alive. Think about it.' Harihn paled as her words spelled out his dilemma so succinctly. Aurian pushed her advantage. 'We're ready to leave, aren't we?'

He nodded.

'Good. Then let's get out of here before anyone notices what has happened. We can work something out when we get back to the palace.'

'The surgeon saw.' The words grated from between Harihn's teeth. 'He came gibbering to me with some tale of sorcery. Others must have heard.'

Aurian frowned. 'Right. Get something to wrap Anvar in, so no one will see that he's been healed. Bohan will carry him to the barge, and you can take me. I'll cover my wrists with my sleeves so no one will see that the bracelets are gone, and when we get to the barge you will curse the surgeon for lying – be really angry with him.'

'I think I can manage that,' Harihn muttered grimly.

'Just make sure nobody believes what really happened and get us out of here as quickly as possible. You can offer the surgeon a bribe or something later. All right?'

Harihn scowled. 'Very well – for the present. But this matter is not ended between us, Lady.'

'Fair enough,' Aurian said evenly. 'Just get on with it.'

Bohan fetched a blanket from the artisans' camp and carried Anvar down to the barge while the prince followed with Aurian. He carried her stiffly, his face averted, his jaw clenched with anger. When he had stowed her safely on board, Aurian watched with horror as he carried out his charade with the hapless surgeon, who backed away in terror, right down to the very end of the jetty, as his prince bore down on him in wrath. His screams rang out as Harihn seized a whip from a nearby overseer and lashed him across the face and shoulders, punctuating the blows with shouts loud enough for the entire camp to hear. 'Liar! Fool! How dare you come to your prince with such a tale!' The surgeon fell on his face, wailing. The prince threw away the whip and advanced on the poor man, and

Aurian gasped with horror as he lifted the surgeon bodily and hurled him into the river. Hordes of the great toothed lizards appeared as if by magic, converging on their helpless, thrashing victim. The surgeon's last despairing wail was cut short in a flurrying maelstrom of tails and teeth as he was pulled beneath the surface and ripped to pieces. Then there was only silence, and a spreading red stain on the waters.

Harihn, stony-faced, leapt into the barge and signalled the oarsmen to pull away. There was not a sound from the shocked onlookers as his voice echoed across the water. 'So perish all who lie to their prince. Remember that.'

Aurian, utterly sickened, turned away from the carnage and made Anvar comfortable on the cushions, pulling the blanket away from his face.

'Are you all right?' he whispered. Aurian nodded, bemused by the irony that he should be asking her. She patted his arm gently.

'You rest – I'll be back in a minute.' She turned to Bohan. 'Take care of him, please.' The eunuch nodded, and she took his hand. 'Bohan, I can't thank you enough for your help today. I'm for ever in your debt.'

The big man smiled, shaking his head.

'Yes,' the Mage corrected him firmly. 'Somehow I'll find a way to repay you, my friend.'

Steeling herself, Aurian made her way to the bows where the prince sat, staring sightlessly at the muddy river. 'I hope you're proud of yourself,' she hissed. 'How can you justify such a monstrous act?'

Harihn spun to face her, wretchedness and disgust on his face. His eyes glinted with unshed tears. 'The man was a surgeon!' he flung at her. 'He thought he had seen a miracle! How could he resist telling others, and proving our undoing in the process? The slave was dying – dead, in fact. Your actions were against all nature.' His voice curdled with bitterness. 'Did you not think there would be a price to pay? A fair bargain, was it not? A life for a life – my servant in exchange for your man. You robbed the surgeon of his life, Aurian, by your deed. I was merely the agent. Only hope it ends here – for the Reaper may exact a higher price for the soul that you snatched from his grasp!'

'Superstitious nonsense!' Aurian snapped, unnerved by his words. She seemed to remember something – something about a price, and true coin – but it eluded her. Death had already wiped his words from her mind. 'I simply acted in all good faith to save a life,' she protested.

'And how many lives may be lost in the future because they will be denied the surgeon's skill?' Harihn's voice was rising to an hysterical pitch. 'How will his family take comfort from your *good faith*? And when my father has me flayed alive for loosing a foreign witch on his people, what will you – '

'*Enough!*' Aurian leapt to her feet, rocking the barge. Her voice was shaking. 'Very well. The fault is mine. I take responsibility. But your law put those accursed bracelets on me in the first place, and the same law brands me a criminal for using my powers to save a life, and condemns you by default because I did it whilst in your custody. Were I faced with the decision again I would do the same thing – not only for Anvar, but for you, or for anyone else I cared about!'

She sat down beside him once more, her voice softened. 'I'm sorry, Harihn, for bringing such trouble upon you. This is a shabby way to repay all you've done for me, and I'll try to think of a way to protect you from the consequences. But can't you see I had no choice?'

Harihn tore his eyes away from hers. 'Lady, I fear you,' he said frankly. 'You talk of repeating the same act, had you the need – but I tell you plainly, were you before me in the arena once more, I would not lift a hand to save you, knowing the consequences as I do now.'

Aurian tried desperately to think of a way to mend matters. 'You speak of consequences, but the thread has not unravelled yet, and the tale of our lives is unfinished. I hope that in the end you won't have cause to regret saving my life, Harihn. It may be that I can help you, now that my powers are unfettered.'

Harihn flinched. 'No!' he cried. 'Do not tempt me with your evil. I would never gain power by such ends.'

'Now you see what an awesome responsibility the Magefolk carry,' Aurian said. 'Such power is a constant temptation – and a constant burden. Think of the slaughter, if I backed you in a revolution. Think of the deaths on my conscience then. But o

425

use my power to save a life – I cannot believe that to be an ill deed.'

Harihn sighed. 'I think I understand – a little. Lady, leave me for a while; go tend to your husband. I have much to think upon – and much to regret.'

They had almost talked the journey out. Aurian was surprised to see the city around them once more, and the ornate contours of the Prince's boathouse in the distance. But she could not begrudge the time she had taken to reach some form of understanding with Harihn. His fear of sorcery was the fear of all his people, and in a way they were right, she thought, remembering with a shudder the Nihilim that Miathan had unleashed, and the terrifying ferocity of Eliseth's storm. Those two had sold their souls for power, and the thought sickened her. Would she finally come to that? Never, Aurian vowed to herself. Not wanting to think about it, she went to the stern to check on Anvar.

He was sleeping, but his eyes opened at her approach, as though in some way he sensed her proximity. Perhaps he did. When she had pulled Anvar back from death, their very souls had touched. Who else could say they had shared such closeness? Yet Aurian found herself reluctant to approach him. She was stricken with guilt that she had abandoned him to such suffering. How could she face him now? He must hate her, surely? But as she hesitated, he reached for her hand, holding on to it with surprising strength, as though she was still his only anchor on life. 'I thought you wouldn't come,' he whispered. 'I almost let go. I'm sorry, Aurian. I should have known better.'

Aurian stared at him, tears in her eyes. *He* was sorry? 'Oh, Anvar,' she murmured. 'How can you ever forgive me?'

'You came,' he said. 'You're always there when it matters. Why did it take me so long to realize that?'

Aurian was completely taken aback. 'You almost died because of my temper this time,' she insisted. 'I should never have left you like that. You can hit me when you're feeling better – I deserve it.'

'No.' The stubborn set of Anvar's jaw was an echo of her own.

'Then I'll do it myself!' She made a parody of punching

426

herself in the jaw and falling over, and he laughed. Oh, thank the gods that he was all right; that she had arrived in time. In an excess of relief she hugged him, and felt his arms tighten round her shoulders.

'Have you found Sara?' His words were like a drench of icy water. Aurian pulled away from him, frowning. Always Sara! And how in the world was she going to tell him that Sara had betrayed him – had abandoned him for a king and not lifted one finger to find him, let alone help him. It would break him. She looked away from the hope in his eyes.

'Sara is fine,' she evaded. 'She came out of this better than any of us.'

To her intense relief, at that moment the barge bumped up against the edge of Harihn's jetty. 'Here we are!' she said briskly. 'Let's get you inside, and have you cleaned up and fed. 'Bohan – that's the enormous fellow – will take care of you. Don't worry, you can trust him. When you've rested, I'll tell you everything that's been happening.' Quickly she beckoned to Bohan to take Anvar up to her rooms, and got out of the way before he had time to ask her any more awkward questions.

Anvar lay in bed, watching the light breeze stir the filmy gauze canopy that protected him against insects. Silken sheets felt cool and luxurious against his newly bathed skin. This time, for some reason, the healing had not had its usual enervating effect, and he felt alert and tingling with life – and fabulously hungry. Not surprising, he mused, feeling his protruding ribs with bony fingers. His body tensed as he recalled the horrors of the slave camp, and his hands flew automatically to the unyielding iron collar, the mark of slavery that had still to be removed from his neck. No! he told himself firmly. He mustn't think of that. It was all over now. Aurian had come for him, as he had prayed she would. She had saved him again.

Anvar was reminded of his first meeting with the Mage, when he had run away from the academy's kitchens. He had awakened between clean sheets in a room in the garrison, with all his hurts healed, to see her smiling at him. He had not trusted her then – but this time I'll do better, he promised himself. He would repay her by taking care of her, at least until her child was born. The gods knew she needed him, though he would have a hard time convincing her. She was so bloody stubborn and independent! He would just have to make her understand – and Sara, he thought guiltily. How could he reconcile the two? Sara would never tolerate having the Mage with them.

'That's her problem!' Anvar, speaking aloud, startled himself with his own vehemence – and his own conclusions. But the truth had begun to dawn on him during his imprisonment in the cells below the slave-market. Sara, the love of his childhood, tugged at his heart. How could she not? But she was no longer an innocent girl. She had hardened. There was a calculation, now, in her manner – something tainted, that he dared not trust. It had taken their time alone, when they were shipwrecked, to show it to him. Aurian's absence then had left a void within him, as though a part of himself had gone. Gods, how he had missed her! How his heart had lifted, to see her again! The thought of the Mage had given him courage – had given him hope through all the terror and torment. He had known that she would come. It was Aurian that he trusted. Not Sara. Aurian.

But you love Sara, part of Anvar's mind protested, and he knew it was true. But did he love what she was now – or what she once had been? And did he love Aurian? She was a friend, a true companion, but ... Could I love a Mage? he asked himself. Gods, I don't know. I just don't know. But I know who I'd rather have beside me in a tight spot!

Anvar heard the door opening, and the rattle of a tray being set down. Someone moved on the other side of the gauze that shrouded his bed. It must be the taciturn Bohan, bringing some food. But to his surprise it was Aurian who thrust aside the curtains. Anvar smiled, delighted to see her again, even after only an hour's absence.

'How are you feeling?' she asked. He thought she looked worried. Was she still feeling guilty about his suffering in the slave camp?

'I'm fine,' he hastened to reassure her. 'In fact, I don't need to be in bed at all – except that your friend Bohan put me here and made me stay.'

Aurian made a droll face. 'He did that to me, too,' she told him sympathetically. 'Sometimes he's a little overzealous! Here, I've brought you something to eat.' She put the tray down on the bed, forestalling him as he made a grab for the food. 'I know you're ravenous, but take it slowly,' she warned him. 'We don't want you making yourself sick.'

Anvar nodded, knowing that she was right. 'Where are we?' he asked her between bites. 'What is this place?'

Aurian grinned. 'Ostentatious, isn't it? It belongs to the Khisal – the prince. He rescued me from the arena, and . . .'

'He rescued you from what?'

Aurian paused to pour herself some wine. 'I suppose I had better start from the beginning,' she said. While he ate, she told him of her dealings with the Leviathan, her discovery that he had been captured, and her terrible trek upriver in search of him.

'I'm sorry about your hair,' Anvar interrupted. 'It was so beautiful.'

Aurian shrugged. 'It just wasn't practical in this heat,' she said, but the compliment made her smile, none the less. 'Besides,' she went on quietly, 'I missed having you around to brush it for me.'

Anvar reached out and took her hand. 'In that case, you'd better start growing it again,' he said firmly.

Aurian was staring at him as though she could hardly believe her ears, and he was shocked to see tears in her eyes. 'I didn't think you'd want . . .' she whispered.

It tore Anvar's heart to see her so vulnerable. She was always so brave, so self-sufficient, that he tended to forget she needed comfort and support just like anyone else. He gripped her hand more tightly. 'Aurian, what happened was just as much my fault as yours,' he told her firmly. 'I behaved abominably to you on the ship, and afterwards. Let's put it behind us. We need each other. I'll make Sara understand somehow.'

She flinched and looked away at the mention of Sara's name. 'I'd better tell you the rest,' she said grimly. Anvar felt alarm tighten his throat. But she'd said that Sara was safe. Seeing the bleak look in the Mage's eyes, he decided it would be wiser to let her tell the story in her own way. Aurian spoke of her capture on the outskirts of the city, and how they had used the bracelets to take her powers, and condemned her to fight in the arena. She had reached the climax of her fight with Shia when she was interrupted by a fearsome clamour. They heard shouts from outside, and the sound of weapons clashing.

Aurian spun round. 'What the . . . Xiang!' She was up off the bed and running for her sword, which stood propped in the corner, but even as she moved the door burst open and several men at arms rushed in, bearing loaded crossbows. Anvar's warning cry froze in his throat. Aurian whirled and fell, clutching at her shoulder, above her right breast. Blood spurted between her fingers. The bolt, which had torn through her flesh and right out the other side at this short range, clattered off the wall behind her and fell to the floor, leaving a blood smear. Instantly, the Mage was surrounded by a circle of soldiers, their crossbows cocked and aimed at her. Anvar, who had leapt from his bed regardless of the danger, only had time for a brief glimpse of her motionless form before he was seized and dragged from the room.

27

Revelations – and Betrayal

Anvar's captors bound his hands tightly behind him, with cords that cut painfully into his wrists. The soldiers were far from gentle, leaving him with a new set of bruises to replace the ones that the Mage had healed, but Anvar had more to concern him than his growing discomfort. What had they done with Aurian? How badly was she hurt? Were these the prince's guards? Had he repented of his hospitality? Why had he tried to attack them back at the slave camp? The Mage had had no time to explain. Anvar wished she had been able to finish her tale. As it was, he had no idea what was happening. But he had time enough to worry about it. They left him in Aurian's chambers, guarded by two grim-faced, taciturn soldiers, and there he remained for over an hour, with only his fears for company.

Xiang swept regally into Harihn's audience chamber, arm-in-arm with his Khisihn, and surrounded by an entourage of guards. Seating himself in the prince's gilded chair, he motioned for someone to fetch a seat for Sara as the captain of his guard approached with a deep bow, and began to make his report. 'The palace has been secured, Your Majesty. The Khisal is in our custody, and his sorceress has been disabled by our bowmen. We have her below in the dungeons, unconscious, but under heavy guard.'

'Well done,' Xiang smiled his approval. 'You have captured the Demon?'

The captain nodded. 'Indeed, sire. It cost us several men to overcome it, but we have it unharmed as you ordered. It, too, is imprisoned below, awaiting transport to the arena.'

'Excellent! And the slave?'

'My men are bringing him now, Your Majesty.'

'Very well. You may bring in the Khisal also.'

431

The Khisu settled back in his son's chair, smiling triumphantly. As soon as the message from his slave master had reached him, he had put his plans into action. Harihn had overplayed his hand this time. What a fool the boy was, to free the sorceress from the bracelets, and allow her to practise her evil arts before witnesses. And all to save the slave who, according to the Khisihn Sara, had kidnapped her from her native land. It had been part of some plot to overthrow him, Xiang had no doubt. Harihn was in league with the two foreigners, but he had underestimated his father, and now he would pay. For releasing the sorceress, he had put himself under automatic sentence of death. Xiang wondered whether to keep his son alive for a while, to suffer the terror of the threat hanging over him. The sorceress, of course, would be executed as soon as possible. Unfettered, she was too much of a threat to be left alive.

There was a stir at the doors of the chamber, and the guards dragged Harihn into the room and cast him, white-faced and trembling, at the Khisu's feet. Xiang smiled with cruel enjoyment, savouring the terror in his son's eyes.

At last the soldiers came for him. Dragging Anvar through a long series of corridors, they thrust him between a pair of huge doors inlaid with bronze. The vast, high-ceilinged room beyond seemed filled with soldiers. The young man that Aurian had identified as Harihn was cowering before a man enthroned on the low platform. If Harihn was the prince, this could only be the king.

Then all thoughts fled from Anvar's mind at the sight of the golden-haired figure seated to one side of the throne, regal and resplendent in jewels and fine silken robes. 'Sara!' he shouted joyfully. He struggled to reach her, but the guards held him fast. The cold aloofness of Sara's demeanour did not waver as Anvar was hurled to the floor by the prince's side. With his hands bound behind him, he was unable to save himself, and his forehead cracked against the marble floor. As he staggered to his knees, blinking to clear the exploding lights that obscured his vision, the king began to speak, addressing Harihn.

'Well met, my son,' Xiang sneered. His eyes gleamed with triumph. 'I am informed that you have laid yourself open to a charge of treason, by releasing a known sorceress from the bonds that constrained her power, against the laws of this land. What answer do you make to this charge?'

Anvar managed a sidelong glance at the prince and saw the young man's face contort with shock and panic. 'No!' he howled. 'It isn't true! I did not release her. She escaped from the bonds herself.'

'You lie.' The Khisu's voice cut through his son's terrified protestations, and Anvar saw sweat break out on Harihn's forehead. 'Furthermore,' Xiang went on, 'you have stolen one of my slaves – a rare specimen from the northlands. My Khisihn has told me that this creature was responsible for kidnapping her from her home, in league with your sorceress. I can only assume that you are consorting with the Khisihn's enemies for one reason: to bring about her overthrow and mine.' He turned to Sara. 'Is this the slave, my queen?'

The words hit Anvar like a death-bow. 'Queen!' he shouted, too horrified to consider the consequences. One of the guards hit him hard across the mouth. 'Silence!' he roared. Anvar went sprawling, tasting blood in his bruised mouth. Sara's gaze flicked contemptuously over her former lover.

'That's the one,' she said coolly.

'Very well,' Xiang replied. 'What shall we do with him, beloved? The choice of his punishment shall be yours.'

Sara shrugged. 'Kill him,' she said offhandedly. Anvar went cold all over at her words. He could not, would not, believe that she had so callously ordered his death.

'Wait!' Harihn cried. 'The slave is mine.'

'What did you say?' Xiang's voice was grating and cold as a knife against stone.

'Your informant lied, Your Majesty,' Harihn said. 'I own the slave.' Tearing an arm free from the grip of the guards, he produced a crumpled parchment – the deed of ownership for a slave. 'I bought him from your slave master with good gold, not three hours ago – and with good reason.'

'You have already been condemned as a traitor,' the Khisu snapped. 'Your ownership counts for nothing.'

433

'Father, hear me out,' Harihn shouted, his voice cracking with strain. 'I did this for your benefit. This slave is the living proof that your Khisihn has betrayed you, and must die! She is his concubine.'

Anvar gasped.

'No!' Sara shrieked. 'He's lying.'

'Silence!' the Khisu roared. His face was livid. 'Now,' he growled at his son, 'I will have the truth of this, before I end your miserable life. Where did you get such a preposterous tale?'

Harihn trembled as he faced his father. 'From Aurian – the sorceress. Did you not think it strange that the Khisihn wanted her death so badly when she fought in the arena? It was because she knew the truth – as well she ought. This man is her husband.'

Anvar, already reeling from the revelations of the day, was stunned. Aurian had told Harihn he was her husband? Why had she lied to the prince?

The sound of the Khisihn's mocking laughter echoed shrilly through the room. 'She said he was her husband?'

'You deny it?' Harihn suddenly seemed less sure of himself.

'Of course,' Sara replied calmly. 'She lied to spare herself a traitor's death. This man is not her husband, he is her bondsman; her accomplice in my kidnapping. Do you think I, the Khisihn, would lower myself to lie with a mere servant?' The scorn in her voice went like a knife through Anvar's heart, and he missed the look of shock and outrage on Harihn's face. He steeled himself against the pain, telling himself that she didn't mean it – that she was at the Khisu's mercy, and only trying to save herself.

The Khisu turned his glowering gaze on Anvar, and spoke to him in the northern tongue. 'Well, slave? What say you? On the one hand, my son says that the Khisihn is your concubine. She, however, accuses you of being her kidnapper. Weigh well your reply, for lives depend on it – including your own miserable existence!'

Anvar hesitated, so confused by this tangle of betrayal and lies that he didn't know what to say. If he supported Sara's story, it would mean his own death, not to mention Aurian and

434

the prince. On the other hand, Sara's life was at stake . . . He wavered, trapped in the dilemma, only knowing half the facts and unable to make a choice.

'See?' Sara shrilled triumphantly. 'He can't say I'm lying. He's only keeping silent to protect his mistress. My Lord, believe me. I would never betray you. But your son would – indeed, he already has, by conspiring with the sorceress against both of us.'

A look of relief crossed the Khisu's face, and he smiled at his queen. 'You are wise as you are beautiful, beloved. How could I doubt you?' He gestured to his guards. 'Kill these traitors. Then I will deal with their sorceress.'

Darkness. A cold, damp floor beneath her. Agony in her right shoulder, spreading fire down her arm and side. Nausea clutching at her throat. Aurian caught her breath against a moan. There must be guards about. Better if they believed she was still unconscious. No one could see her in this black hole – not without Mages' sight. She had recognized the livery of Xiang's soldiers, and could hazard a fair guess at what must have happened. She lay very still, face down on the hard stone floor where she had been carelessly tumbled. With her extra healer's sense, she checked first on the child within her. To her relief, all seemed well. The mite must be hardy indeed to survive all that had recently befallen its mother.

Mother. It was the first time she had used the word, even in her thoughts. Despite her pain and discomfort, despite her peril, Aurian's lips curved in a smile. She had accepted the child at last, and her love and pride for this tough little survivor heartened her considerably. It was taking after its indomitable father, she decided, and the thought of Forral strengthened her resolve. She turned her attention to the wound on her shoulder, and began to control the searing pain. Without that to impede her concentration, Aurian set about repairing the damage. She would be needing to use that arm; her sword arm, she thought grimly.

It was more difficult than she had expected. Aurian had never tried to heal herself, but she knew from her lessons with Meiriel that there was considerable risk involved. Healing took

435

a great deal of energy, partly from the healer, but partly from the patient. That was why magical healing was so debilitating to both parties. In healing herself she had only her own strength to draw on, and she knew that, unless she was very careful, she stood in grave danger of burning herself out completely and killing herself. There were precedents. But oh, it was difficult to school herself to patience, to proceed with care, stopping frequently to rest. Aurian was keenly aware that time was very much against her. What was happening up above? How long had she been unconscious? Not long, she comforted herself. The blood from her wound had still been fresh and flowing. But Harihn had said that his father sought his death, and if Sara was involved, Anvar's chances of survival were slim. Forcing herself not to think about it, Aurian returned to her work. It was her only chance of helping them. Step by step, working as fast as she dared, she set the damage to rights, painstakingly reconstructing the torn flesh and muscles, knowing that a mistake made in haste could cripple her arm for good.

Done at last! Aurian moved the wounded arm and shoulder experimentally, wishing she had time to rest the repaired tissue. Never mind. It would do. Not quite as good as new yet, but it would serve her purpose, and improve with time. But there was no doubt that the work had taken its toll. She felt limp with exhaustion, only wanting to lie where she was on this filthy, freezing floor and sleep until her body had recovered itself. Well, no chance of that. Mindful of the risks of overtaxing herself and being unable to return to her body, Aurian extended her consciousness carefully outwards, seeking the sparks of human awareness that would mean guards.

She had gone no distance at all when she encountered a set of thoughts that made her heart leap with joy. Shia! The great cat was imprisoned in the next cell.

Shia's thoughts were scorching with fury. 'There were too many of them! They used nets!' Aurian could feel her friend's pain as she struggled against the entangling bonds.

'Patience,' Aurian soothed her. 'I'll get you free – only stay still, and don't attract attention.'

436

'Very well,' Shia grumbled reluctantly. 'But when you do, those men are my meat!'

Aurian had no quarrel with that.

Now – how to get out of the cell? The Mage regretted that her powers had been weakened by the healing. Impelled by her growing sense of urgency, she'd have liked nothing better than to demolish the heavy door in a single blast. However . . . Again she sought for the guards. Ah. Over a dozen of them, but in true mercenary style they were all congregated in the guardroom on the upper level, away from the damp, noisome chill of the dungeons. There was only one on this floor, stationed at the bend in the passage by the foot of the stairs, ready to give the alarm if anything stirred. Even better, she could sense the angry, frightened presence of other captives – a good number – occupying other cells further down the passage. She fervently hoped they were Harihn's guards, imprisoned down here out of the way.

Aurian crept to the door of her cell. Instead of blasting it, which was not only physically impossible for her at this time, but would also bring all Xiang's guards down on her, not to mention the low ceiling, she turned her remaining power to manipulating the lock, feeling for the worn, stiff tumblers with her healer's senses much as she would probe a wound for damage. Ah. Pressure here – and there – the Mage gathered her will and pushed.

The rusty lock grated open. Aurian froze, her body tensed for combat. Had the guard heard? Apparently not. Disgust at his inattention briefly warred with her relief. Opening the door only enough to squeeze herself through, lest the rusty old hinges betray her with their squeak, Aurian sidled along the low, arched passage on silent feet, suppressing a wish for her warrior's clothing. Not only would this thin robe be awkward in a fight, but it was useless against the piercing cold of the dungeons, which was already stiffening her muscles and eating its way into her very bones.

Aurian could see the profile of the guard silhouetted against the yellow torchlight at the bottom of the stairwell. The fool's eyes were turned away from her to look longingly up the steps towards the warm guardroom, instead of down the corridor he

437

was meant to be guarding. Aurian's arm went around his throat in the quick, lethal throttling hold that Maya had taught her so long ago. But she had never killed with her bare hands before, and was unable to suppress her shudders as he slid soundlessly to the floor, his windpipe crushed and eyes staring-wide with shock. Clenching her teeth, the Mage quickly rifled the still twitching corpse for sword, knife and keys, trying to avoid the accusing stare of those dreadful eyes. Then she ran, as quickly as she could, back down the corridor to Shia's cell, feeling keen relief at leaving her grisly handiwork behind.

As Aurian sliced through her restraining bonds, the great cat exploded into motion like an uncoiling spring, and fell heavily on her side, her numb limbs refusing to support her. Aurian knelt to rub the cold legs and paws. Though curses seemed not to be a part of the cat's mental vocabulary, Shia's tirade of low, spitting snarls sounded so much like a stream of human invective that the Mage had to smile. 'Listen,' she told her friend, 'once you're on your feet, go to the bottom of the stairs and guard this corridor. Wait for me there, while I free the other prisoners.'

'Those men!' Shia's eyes blazed with a savage light.

'Not those men,' Aurian said firmly. 'Once I've freed the good men, we'll deal with the bad ones, I promise.'

'What good men?' Shia sulked.

'Trust me.' With a hug, Aurian sent her out, taking the opposite direction herself, towards the other cells.

A low, nervous murmur of voices betrayed the presence of the men occupying the cell. 'Who's within?' Aurian called softly, and the sound ceased abruptly.

'Yazour, captain of the Khisal's guard. Who are you?' The voice was young, but firm and strong, despite the fact that its owner was imprisoned to await the dubious mercy of his cruel king.

'The Lady Aurian, the Khisal's sorceress,' Aurian whispered back. At her words, a frightened muttering broke out among the men in the cell, and she heard Yazour hushing them hastily.

'Lady, can you release us? His Highness has dire need of our help.'

Wasting no time, Aurian opened the door, struggling a little with the heavy lock. She belatedly remembered that the men would be unable to see in the dark passage, and spotting a burnt-out stump of torch affixed to a bracket on the wall lighted it with a careless wave of her hand.

'How did you . . . Lady, that is forbidden,' a stern voice chided her. The captain of the guard, recognizable by his shoulder insignia, stood before her, his brows knotted in a disapproving frown.

'If you want to save the Khisal, this is no time to be particular,' Aurian said flatly, and appreciated the way that he accepted her words with a brusque nod. Taking the bunch of keys from the lock, he sent one of his men along the passage to open the other cells. A practical man, then. Like his prince, he seemed young for his responsibilities. There was no grey in the long black hair that was tied neatly back from his face, but his stern demeanour and the honest, level gaze of his dark eyes promised Aurian a fund of courage and common sense. She had no time to register more, for at that moment a hulking figure thrust to the front of the soldiers, elbowing them effortlessly aside.

'Bohan! Thank the gods you're all right!' Aurian reached up on tiptoe to hug him, and saw his face break into an astonished but delighted smile. Sword cuts on his body and bruises on his arms and face showed that he had sold his freedom dearly, but his strength seemed undiminished as he returned her hug with bone-cracking force.

'Someone comes!' Shia's warning thought rang clearly in Aurian's mind.

'See to him,' she told the cat. 'Quietly, if you can.'

'My pleasure!'

There was the sound of a scuffle along the passage, then silence. 'What was that?' Yazour demanded sharply.

'The Demon from the arena, dealing with one of Xiang's guards. You had better warn your men that she's on our side!'

'By the Reaper!' Yazour muttered, his eyes very wide.

The struggle in the guardroom was bloody but brief. Aurian sent Shia in first, and the cat erupted into the room in a whirlwind of teeth and claws, wreaking havoc among Xiang's

439

horrified soldiers. Aurian followed with Yazour and his men, the latter arming themselves quickly from fallen bodies, or weapons stored within the room. Then they began to work their way up through the corridors of the palace, fanning out as they went to deal mercilessly with any enemy that they encountered along the way. It was vital that no one remained alive to carry word to Xiang. At last they reached the main levels, and the long hallway that led to the audience chamber, and discovered why they had met with so little opposition so far. The corridor was bristling with guards. 'Xiang must be within,' Yazour whispered to the Mage, after a quick glance around the corner.

'Now what? We'll never get through that lot without raising the alarm,' Aurian groaned. Weary as she was, it was easy to feel discouraged. She was sickened by the bloodshed that had already occurred, and was finding the great curved scimitar with which she had armed herself difficult and awkward to handle after the straight, two-sided blades favoured by her own people. It was no easy matter to learn an entirely new technique when your life was at stake. Bohan tugged urgently at her arm, pointing back the way they had come. Aurian frowned, trying to decipher his gestures. 'You mean there's another way in?' she asked him. The mute nodded vigorously.

'Of course!' Yazour muttered. 'The kitchens. A passage leads to the back of the audience chamber, so that food can be brought there easily.'

Swiftly they made their plans. Aurian, with Bohan, Shia, and a small group of soldiers, would take the back route and storm the chamber. Yazour and his men, when they heard her signal, would mount a frontal attack on the guards at the doors. Aurian quickly assembled her party and they slipped away, Bohan leading.

In the kitchens, the terrified servants were being held by some half-dozen of the Khisu's guards. If Aurian had expected any help from them, she was quickly disabused of the notion. As soon as the fighting started, they took the opportunity to flee, keeping the widest possible distance between themselves and the tall, flame-haired warrior and her ferocious Demon. Occupied as she was with two soldiers who were bent on hacking her to pieces, the Mage could only hope they wouldn't flee towards the throne room and give the game away. Panting, she backed towards the door, defending herself as best she could with the clumsy scimitar. Then the looming figure of Bohan appeared behind her assailants, and a great hand closed around each of their necks. Shia moved in to finish them, her claws ripping through flesh and guts. 'This is fun!' she told Aurian.

'I'm glad you're enjoying yourself,' Aurian replied faintly, taking a much needed minute to catch her breath. The place looked like a charnel house, and the ridiculous, flimsy robe in which Harihn had clad her was drenched with blood. The Mage made a quick tally of corpses. Good. All the enemy dead – and two of their own, she realized sadly. She summoned her remaining men, and they followed Bohan through the low doorway that had been hidden in the shadows of an alcove at the back of the kitchen.

There was no door at the far end of the passage – the flight of steps up to the throne room ended in an archway, screened by a hanging curtain. Carefully, Aurian moved it aside, just enough to peer through a small crack. She was almost directly behind the throne, and could see Harihn nearby, held firmly between two guards and looking sick with fear. She need not have worried about being noticed, for the eyes of everyone in the room were fixed on the clear space at Xiang's feet. Anvar knelt there, bound, his eyes tightly closed, his face bloodless with terror. Over him stood a black-clad figure with an upraised sword.

'Now!' Aurian yelled. Shia sprang past her, reaching the Khisu in a single leap, her weight crushing him to the floor as her powerful jaws closed around his throat. 'Drop your weapons! If anyone moves, the Khisu dies!' Aurian shouted. She heard the sound of savage fighting outside as Yazour and his men went into action, and beckoned her own troops into the room to pick up the fallen weapons of Xiang's guards. Though she wanted to go to Anvar, she stepped up instead beside the stunned prince and bowed, catching sight as she did so of Yazour, who appeared briefly in the main doorway to signal that all was well. 'Your Highness,' Aurian said clearly. 'Today you declined the use of magic to win your throne. Now I offer it again through Mortal means. Only say the word, and you are Khisu.'

Harihn stared at her for a moment, trying to take in the sudden turn of events. She nodded affirmation and the prince, with a sudden smile, walked across to his father. Aurian followed him. Xiang's face was contorted with terror. All the cruelty of his expression seemed to have transferred itself to the face of his son, and the Mage was dismayed by what she had wrought.

'Well, my father,' Harihn said. 'How does it feel to be the victim? My mother would have enjoyed seeing you thus.'

'My son, I beg you . . .' Xiang, in his terror, had lost control of his bladder, and a dark stain began to spread across the floor. 'Please . . .'

It was plain to Aurian how much that word had cost him.

'Begging, father?' Harihn's eyes glittered. 'Oh, I like this. Beg some more.'

'My son . . . please. I'll do anything . . .'

Harihn turned away in disgust. 'No!' It was as though the word had been wrenched from the depths of his soul. Getting his voice under control with an effort, he turned to face his watchers. 'I do not want the throne,' he said flatly. 'Today I have learned all too well how power corrupts. The power of sorcery' – his gaze flicked coldly towards Aurian – 'royal power' – he glanced scornfully at his father, then across to Sara – 'and the power of one man over another.' He looked down at the crumpled scroll of Anvar's ownership that was crushed in his fist. 'Father, you may keep your throne and your life – if you swear that I and my people will be allowed to leave this land in safety. You have no need to worry – I will not be coming back. Do you agree, and will you swear to this?'

The Khisu nodded – too quickly, Aurian thought. She had seen the flicker of contempt in his eyes. 'You have my word,' he said.

'Release him,' Harihn ordered.

'Wait.' Aurian, still staggered by Harihn's refusal of the throne, placed herself within the Khisu's sight. 'Xiang,' she said, 'I have no confidence whatever that you will keep your

442

word.' His gaze slid uneasily away from hers, and she knew she had been right. Thinking quickly, the Mage assumed the most menacing expression she could manage. 'In order to guarantee the Khisal's safety, I place my curse on you, and all the people of your land.' She heard gasps of horror from behind her.

'What are you doing?' Harihn shrieked at her.

'Only this. While the Khisu keeps his vow, all shall be spared. But if he should break it, then his entire kingdom will be consumed in fire, and his people also. Crops will burn in the fields. Eyes will shrivel and flesh will melt. All shall perish in agony. Do you hear my words, Xiang?'

'I hear.' His voice dripped hatred.

'Then mark them well, lest what I say should come to pass.'

The Khisu nodded, glaring at her, but she knew that she had him now. 'Oh, and another thing,' she could not resist adding. 'I feel that you must become a better ruler in future. There will be no more cruel games, Xiang. The arena will be closed at once, and all the slaves will be freed immediately.'

'What?' Xiang roared, forgetting, in his rage, the peril of his position. At a nod from Aurian, Shia tightened her jaws a fraction, snarling. The Khisu choked, and lapsed back into sullen silence.

'I'll be watching, Xiang,' Aurian lied. 'No matter how far away I am. Remember – the curse is merely suspended. If you break your vow, it will fall upon you. Let him up, Shia,' she added aloud, for the benefit of the watchers. 'He has work to do. Get out, Xiang, and take your soldiers with you. See them off the premises, Shia.'

'You mean I don't get to kill him?' Shia's thought was petulant.

'I'm afraid not.'

'It's not fair!' The cat loosened her jaws reluctantly, her blazing eyes never leaving the Khisu's face. One of Xiang's guards, though quaking at the proximity of the Black Demon and the Outland Sorceress, went to help him rise from the wreckage of his chair. A brave man, Aurian thought.

Sara, who had remained silent while the conflict unfolded, rose to follow him, shooting a glare of venomous hatred at Aurian. But Bohan had freed Anvar from his bonds, and he

443

waylaid her, his eyes beseeching. 'Sara, wait. You don't have to go with him. You're free now. You can come with us.' His voice shook with the strain of still hoping to find her innocent in the face of all he had witnessed. Gods, can he not accept it even now? Aurian thought despairingly.

Sara turned on Anvar with a look of utter scorn. 'You fool,' she sneered. 'Do you really think I'd go with you – a mere servant – a *slave* – when I can be a queen?'

Anvar flinched as though she had struck him. 'So,' he said softly, 'I was right not to trust you. You were lying when you said you still loved me.'

Sara's laugh rang out, loud and brittle; cruelly mocking. 'And you believed me, you dolt, as I knew you would! I planned it that way, because it was expedient, and because you deserved it for abandoning me to a butchering midwife and that toad of a merchant. Come with you, indeed! You're pathetic, Anvar. Go and crawl behind the skirts of your mistress. *She* appreciates you. As for me, I'll despise you until the day I die.'

Anvar's eyes hardened to the chill ice-blue of a winter sky. 'Wait!' The word cracked out, harsh and commanding. Sara turned slowly, gaping in astonishment.

'Bad mistake, Sara.' Anvar's tone was coldly mocking. 'In your arrogance, you seem to have forgotten one important detail. Xiang no longer has an heir – and he'll be looking to you to get him another.'

Sara's face blanched to a ghastly greenish-white. All at once she began to tremble, seeming to shrink in on herself, her haughty demeanour vanished. Suddenly she bit her lip; held out her hands beseechingly. 'Anvar, I . . .'

'No, Sara – not this time. Not ever again. You got your wish, and it's up to you to deal with it.' Anvar's voice was like steel. 'Get out, Sara. Go to the king you wanted so much. Start thinking of a way to dupe him, as you duped Vannor and me – but you'd better hurry!'

Sara's face turned ugly with rage. Drawing back like a snake, she spat into his face, then turned in a swirl of golden skirts to follow Xiang. As she scurried out, Anvar sank to his knees, his face a mask of grief. Aurian had been both baffled and amazed by his exchange with the girl, but she knew that this was not the time to ask. Instead, she hurried to comfort him, her heart wrenched by the bleak emptiness in his eyes. Anvar tore himself away from her touch. 'Please,' he said wretchedly, 'leave me alone.' He turned away from her, hiding his face in his hands. Aurian retreated, respecting his mood. When he had repudiated Sara, she had almost burst with pride in him, but she knew how much it had cost him. She sat down beside him on the floor, feeling drained.

A hand fell on her shoulder. 'Aurian!' Harihn stood over her, his expression matching the chill in his voice.

'What?' she sighed, and got to her feet feeling grievously ill used. Considering that she had just saved his life, he scarcely seemed overcome with gratitude. Harihn's fists were clenched, his face scarlet with rage. 'Lying bitch! Thanks to your machinations, I've lost a throne today. You ungrateful snake! How dared you deceive me into thinking this lowly slave was your husband?'

Aurian gasped. How had he found out?

'By the Reaper, you'll suffer for this!' Harihn reached out to seize her, one hand uplifted to strike.

'Leave her alone!' Anvar stepped between them. 'She did not lie to you, Your Highness. I am her husband.'

'What!' Harihn choked. 'You mean . . . it's true?'

Aurian's astonishment was no less acute. In wondering gratitude, she sought Anvar's eyes. He put a possessive arm round her shoulders. 'Of course it's true,' he told the prince. 'Sara lied to everyone. Did you expect her to tell Xiang she had betrayed him? Furthermore, Aurian did not lose you the throne – she offered it to you, and you turned it down! I think you owe my Lady an apology – and your thanks, for saving your life.'

The prince looked utterly deflated. 'I – I beg your pardon,' he muttered, his eyes downcast. 'I should have known. The mere fact that you can speak our language as she can . . . Does this mean that you are also a sorcerer?'

Aurian gasped. So much had been happening, it had never occurred to her to wonder. Out of the corner of her eye, she saw Anvar turn pale. 'No,' he said hastily, 'and I don't know why I can speak your tongue. I think the Lady may have passed on the talent with the spell that she used to bring me back from death. But what will you do now, Highness? Aurian may have frightened your father for the time being, but we can't expect it to last!'

Aurian gave him an old-fashioned look, but he was studiously avoiding her eye. She frowned. Why had he changed the subject so quickly? Yet . . . Anvar was no Mage! Surely his explanation could be the only possible one?

Harihn was looking at her. 'Will you really smite the Khazalim with your curse, sorceress?' he blurted, fear behind his words. 'I have relinquished the throne, but these are still my people. If – if my father had refused to agree, would you have destroyed them?'

'Gods, no!' Aurian said. 'I wouldn't even know where to start. But Xiang didn't know that.' She gave him a wicked grin.

The prince looked astonished, then relief flooded his face. He burst out laughing. 'Why, you . . . You are absolutely outrageous!'

'That's what I'm always telling her,' Anvar said with a shrug, 'but what can I do?'

'Take my advice, and beat her more often. She has a habit of taking control of events that is most unbecoming in a woman!'

'That sounds like a good idea,' Anvar growled, ignoring Aurian's indignant glare. She was even more infuriated when the prince took him completely seriously.

'Very well,' he said. 'I have much to attend to, if we are to leave before nightfall. I believe I will travel north. My mother's people may take me in, if we get through the land of the Skyfolk. You will come with me, will you not? You will never cross the desert alone.'

'I think that suits us, don't you, dear?' Anvar turned to Aurian, his eyes glinting, and she realized that he was paying her out for the lie she had told him.

'Of course, dear,' she replied sweetly, restraining an urge to kick him. Inwardly, however, she was relieved. Now she had found Anvar and regained her powers, she could afford to waste no more time in these lands. But she needed Harihn's help a little longer, and was uncomfortably aware that her debt to him remained unsettled.

When Harihn had gone, Aurian turned to Anvar. 'Thank you for supporting me.'

He shrugged. 'It was the least I could do. You must have had your reasons for lying to the prince.'

'I did! Harihn had decided to make me his concubine – that's the law hereabouts for an unaccompanied woman. I was badly wounded in the arena, and he saved my life. I was helpless, without my powers, and I needed Harihn's help to find you. I was forced to lie. He left me no choice.'

Anvar scowled. 'You mean . . . I can't believe it! Did he – did that bastard . . .' He was almost choking with rage.

Aurian laid a hand on his arm. 'No,' she said gently. 'He didn't touch me, once I had told him about you. I don't believe he likes it, though.'

'Well, he had better get used to it – fast!'

Aurian could not help but smile at Anvar's fierce expression. 'Thank you, Anvar,' she said, touched by his support. 'But we must be careful. To get back north, we need Harihn's help to cross the desert. With his soldiers to back him, we're very much outnumbered.'

'Oh, gods, what a situation. But – ' suddenly Anvar looked sick. 'Does this mean that Sara was forced to – to . . .'

Anvar, I'm sorry, Aurian thought. But for his sake, she had to be brutally frank. 'You saw her today. You heard what she said. What Sara is doing is her own choice. I used Harihn to find you – she could have done that through Xiang, but she was too busy furthering her ambition. And if she'd had her way today, you would be dead by now. What sort of woman would do that to the man who loved her?'

Anvar shuddered, and his face grew stern and grim. 'That's what I thought,' he said.

28
Escape from Taibeth

As the afternoon progressed, the courtyard of Harihn's palace turned into a scene of utter chaos. The entire household was mobilizing, ready for departure. Barrels and waterskins were hauled up from cellars and outbuildings and trundled down to the river to be filled, for the prince would be crossing the desert. Light silken tents were rolled around their poles and stacked in a corner, ready to be loaded on to the mules that had been picketed in a long line down one side of the courtyard. Food for the journey was being prepared, along with fodder for the horses and pack animals. Soldiers of the prince's guard milled about the yard with their horses, adding to the general confusion.

Harihn had freed his slaves in accordance with Aurian's edict. Some would be staying behind to search for long-lost friends and families, but many had chosen to follow their prince into exile. He was moved by their loyalty, but the organization involved in crossing the desert with so many folk was a nightmare. The Khisal was constantly on the move, trying to be everywhere at once. All around, farewells were being said, freed slaves were celebrating, and people were sorting possessions, trying to make impossible choices, for everyone must travel light. A horse broke loose, panicked by the noise and confusion, and plunged across the courtyard, scattering people and goods alike.

Anvar, entering the courtyard, covered his ears against the din. This is ridiculous! he thought. To his annoyance, the prince had summoned Aurian from her chambers, cutting short her much needed rest, to help sort things out. She was talking to Harihn now, and he could hear her straining to be heard above the general racket. 'Start ferrying the soldiers and horses across the river, and get them assembled on the other side. That will clear a space, at least. Then we'll get the rest sorted out.'

Harihn nodded gratefully and went off to speak to the captain of his guard. It took a while to get the five-score troopers moving down to the river, but Aurian was right – it did clear a space. After that it was easier to apportion tasks. The courtyard was cleared of those who would not be joining the exodus, and the mules were loaded and sent, one by one, down to the ferry. Now that it was easier to count heads, Harihn looked worried. Anvar strolled across with Bohan, to hear him talking again to the Mage. 'There are some three dozen folk coming with us from my household, and horses must be provided for them. With animals needed to carry the extra food and water, that leaves us few spare mounts, and a very small margin of safety. We must get through the desert before the food and water run out, yet we dare not push too hard and risk losing horses.'

'Is there no water in the desert at all?' Aurian asked.

'There are twelve oases, and we will need them all,' Harihn replied. 'It is a journey of many days, even if we keep to the shortest route. We could not hope to carry enough water to last us right to the other side.'

Anvar approached them, shadowed by Bohan. His iron collar had been cut away and he walked taller now that it had gone, though its weight had been nothing compared with the heaviness that lay on his heart. The prince turned to him. 'And how does it feel to be free?' he asked.

Anvar heard the gibe in his voice, and knew that Harihn was deliberately taunting him with the reminder of his previous lowly station. He looked at him coldly. 'I find the change very welcome,' he said shortly, deliberately omitting Harihn's title.

'Indeed, many things have changed in a short time,' Harihn replied smoothly, but Anvar was gratified to see his mocking smile replaced by a scowl. 'In one day, you have ceased to be a slave, and I have ceased to be a prince. She is a great leveller of men, your Lady.'

'At least she won't be forced to be your concubine now,' Anvar snapped.

Harihn rounded on him, his face dark with rage. 'How dare

449

you speak to me like that! Guards – take this churl and have him flogged!'

'No!' Aurian intervened quickly. 'He meant no disrespect, Your Highness. I'm sure he'll apologize.' She glared warningly at Anvar. Their eyes locked in a clash of wills, but Anvar discovered a new, unexpected stubbornness within himself. His mouth tightened in unconscious refusal. Aurian turned her head slightly, out of the prince's line of vision, and mouthed 'Please?' She looked tired and upset, and he was suddenly ashamed, knowing that the last thing she needed today was more trouble. Anvar sighed.

'I'm sorry, Your Highness,' he muttered.

'There, that's settled,' Aurian said hurriedly. By the look on Harihn's face, it was anything but settled, but luckily they were interrupted by Yazour, who was escorting two people. The Mage's face lit up with joy as she ran to hug them. 'Eliizar! Nereni!'

'Your Highness, these people have asked to see the sor – the Lady Aurian,' the captain reported.

'Don't I know you from somewhere?' the prince asked Eliizar, who bowed low.

'I am – was – sword master of the arena, Your Highness,' he said. 'Now the Khisu has ordered the arena closed, and the city is filled with rumour and unrest. We heard that the Lady Aurian is travelling north with you. Once she offered to take us with her, so we have come to pledge ourselves to her, if she still wants us.'

'Of course I do! My dear friends, I'm so pleased to see you again! We can manage two more, surely, Harihn?' Aurian pleaded.

The prince scowled. 'You seem to be gathering a loyal entourage of your own, Lady. First my eunuch and that dangerous animal, then your mannerless husband, and now the sword master of the arena. If you remain here much longer, you may end up as Khisihn yourself.'

'I'm not remaining here, and neither are you,' Aurian retorted sharply, 'and you should be glad of an extra sword, Harihn. We're glad to have you, Eliizar, Nereni. I have never forgotten your kindness.'

450

'I have something for you,' Eliizar said. He handed her her precious staff, which had been left behind at the arena, and forgotten during her illness and her subsequent worry over Anvar.

'By all the gods!' Aurian exclaimed. 'I really am grateful to have this back, Eliizar.'

The sword master looked at Anvar. 'I see you got your husband back, too,' he said.

Nereni's eyes twinkled mischievously. 'He's far too precious to her to be a mere husband!' She turned to Anvar. 'You are a fortunate man. Do you know, she fretted herself sick about you all the time she was at the arena? How glad I am that she found you again.'

Anvar was dumbstruck. Aurian had told these people that he was her husband as well? She had actually been that worried about him? He realized what it must have cost her, with Forral so recently dead. 'I'm glad she found me too,' he said firmly, trying, without success, to catch the Mage's eye. 'And I agree with you – I am a very fortunate man.'

'It is time we were leaving,' Harihn said tightly. As he walked stiffly away, Anvar took hold of Aurian's resisting elbow and drew her into an embrasure in the courtyard wall that overlooked the stunning view of the river, the city and the dramatic cliffs opposite.

Aurian, scarlet with embarrassment, looked as though she wished the ground would swallow her up. 'Anvar, I'm sorry,' she said hastily, looking anywhere but at him.

'No need. Lady, I'm grateful – and very honoured.'

She looked at him sharply. 'Then you understand?'

'Lady Aurian, the Khisal says that we must leave now. He seems rather annoyed,' Eliizar bowed his head in apology for interrupting them.

'All right,' Aurian sighed. 'Bohan has horses for us.' Anvar wished he could have had a little more time alone with her, but there was no help for it, not now.

The prince's party were the last to be ferried across the river to join the soldiers and other members of his household. It looked like – as indeed it was – a small army, with Harihn's soldiers formed up around his retainers and the baggage-train of mules, whose burden consisted mostly of water. Of necessity, they would be eating little during the desert crossing. Yazour, a veteran of desert travel, rode forward, acknowledging Aurian with a smile as he addressed his prince. 'Your Highness, we must go now, while daylight remains. The cliff road is perilous in the dark.'

They rode up from the river crossing, past the scattering of white houses that edged the city of Taibeth. There was no one else in sight. All the inhabitants, hearing the incredible rumours which were spreading like wildfire, had gone into the city itself to find out what was happening. The land swelled in a gentle rise up from the river. At the top the road divided, the right hand fork leading to the capital, the left climbing gradually upwards towards the looming cliffs. Soon the houses thinned; the deserted fields between them were tinged with red as the sun sank. Yazour looked worried. Time was pressing.

When Aurian got her first glimpse of the cliff road, she gasped with dismay. Looking hardly wide enough even for one rider, it snaked perilously back and forth, literally carved into the soaring curtains of red stone. It was so steep that it had been cut in a series of shallow steps. In some places it actually seemed to hang out over the dizzying drop, while in others it vanished into the cliff, tunnelling through the striated columns of rock and emerging from the other side. Yazour had sent up the first contingent of soldiers, and already they looked like crawling ants against the vastness of this giant work of nature.

The captain rode up to Harihn. 'If you will lead the way, Highness . . .'

'No.'

Yazour frowned. 'But you must go up now, sire, while there is still some measure of daylight. If the Khisu should . . .'

'Yazour, there are women and children here. Should I go ahead in safety, leaving them to pick their way in darkness? These are my people. Get them up first, and this Lady. The Khisu will not attempt an ambush, if he knows what's good for him.' He glanced at Aurian.

'But, Highness . . .' the captain protested.

'Obey my orders, Yazour. Now!'

Yazour rode off, dismay written all over his face. Since he

452

had fallen in with the sorceress, the prince had grown ever more rash. Had she enchanted him? But that was nonsense. In the brief time they had fought together he had discovered respect for her. In fact, Yazour admitted, he liked her. It was simply that, at long last, Harihn was acting like a prince and a man. It would take some getting used to.

Aurian drew her horse close to Harihn's black mount. 'Well said, Highness – with one exception. I'm going to wait with you.'

'But, Lady . . .'

'Don't argue, Harihn.' She looked up once more at the precipitous road, her hands clammy on the reins of the bay horse that Harihn had given her. The thought of climbing all the way up there made her feel physically ill. 'When I go up there, the last thing I want to see is that drop. In fact, I'm not sure I can do it at all.' She made a wry face at her own irrational fear.

'Aurian!' the prince protested.

'It'll be all right.' The quiet, familiar voice at her shoulder was full of understanding. 'At least that's what you told me,' Anvar went on. 'Remember the beach?'

Aurian remembered Anvar's swimming lesson, and his terror of the water. And her so angry with him that she could have cheerfully drowned him on the spot.

'If I could do that, then you can do this,' he assured her. 'I'll be close, if you need me.'

Aurian's turn to begin the ascent came all too soon, it seemed to her, although while they waited the sun had gone down and the valley bottom was shrouded in deep purple shadow, and the red rocks of the clifftop glowed crimson with sunset light. They dismounted at the bottom of the narrow track and Yazour handed each of them a torch to light their way. The Mage took her flaming brand reluctantly. 'One hand for the torch and one to lead the horse,' she moaned. 'What on earth am I going to hold on with?'

'The path is wider than it looks, my Lady,' Yazour told her. 'Stay away from the edge and all will be well.'

Aurian gave him a sour look. 'Fine,' she said faintly.

'Don't worry, Lady,' Anvar said. 'Look – I'll go first, and

you can follow me. Just don't look down, and you'll be all right.'

Biting her lip, Aurian began her ascent. The path was fairly smooth and the torches brought the dusk down around them so that the bottom of the abyss was lost in darkness. None the less, she kept her eyes resolutely averted from the drop, fixing them on the ground at her feet and trying not to think of the plunge into empty air that waited just to her left. The real difficulty lay in turning the sharp corners where the path zigzagged. Suddenly the hindquarters of Anvar's horse vanished from sight around the bend, and there was nothing ahead of her but the vast, dark gulf below. One slip going round there . . . She stepped back, reeling, pressing her back against the comforting solidity of the cliff face, unable to move. Her horse, impatient to follow its vanished companion, nudged her with its nose, pushing her nearer to the brink and almost making her drop the torch. 'Stop that!' Aurian, shaking with shock, her heart in her mouth, smacked him hard on the nose, and the animal backed up a step, his eyes wide with astonishment.

'What's happening up there? Why the delay?' Harihn's voice came from further down the path. Aurian took a deep, steadying breath. 'Don't be feeble,' she scolded herself. 'If Anvar could overcome his fear of water, surely you can manage this!' Certainly no one could come to her aid. The path was blocked in front and behind with horses.

'It's all right,' she called back, wishing it really was. Keeping her back pressed firmly against the rock she sidled, step by shuffling step, round the corner, followed at a respectful distance by the chastened horse. Once she was round, and the solid, sloping path was before her once more, Aurian could have collapsed with relief, but there was still a long climb ahead, and she was holding up progress. Her dry mouth set in a grim line, she lifted her torch and trudged on.

It was a gruelling climb. All in all, there were nine of the terrifying bends to negotiate before they reached the top, and the higher they climbed, the more tired and balky the horses became. Aurian's back and legs began to ache until every step was torture and she was gasping for breath. The drop switched from her left side to her right, then back again, as the trail twisted back and forth, and the only time she gained a brief respite from her fear was when the road plunged into the cliff, creating blessed, solid walls on either side. Twice during the ascent she heard a blood-curdling scream from above, and men and horses plummeted past her, dangerously close; the dull wet sound of their eventual impacts leaving her sick and shaking.

'Aurian! Are you all right?'

The Mage looked dazedly around. There was level ground in front and on either side of her – she had reached the top! Gently, Anvar pried her fingers away from the torch and the horse's reins and handed both to Bohan. Then, putting an arm around her shoulders, he led her away from the edge. In the shadow of the rocks that lined the clifftop trail she clung to him, flinging her arms around his neck and burying her face in his shoulder. He held her until her breathing steadied and her trembling eased. 'There,' he said softly, his breath tickling her ear, 'I told you you could do it.' Aurian raised her head to look at him, and made a face.

Harihn stood at the brink of the cliff, looking down for the last time at the land he would have ruled. They were celebrating in the city. Fireworks were arcing into the air on comet-tails of silver sparks, to blossom with a bang into giant flowers of red, gold and green in the night sky. Their light was echoed on the ground by the flames from the burning slave-markets.

'Regrets, prince?' Aurian had come quietly up behind him, Anvar a shadow at her heels. 'If you want to return, I'm sure the people would welcome you.'

He shook his head. 'I have no stomach for a revolution. Besides, that place holds evil memories for me. My way lies onward now. Xiang will get himself a new heir, no doubt.'

'Not with this queen, he won't.'

Harihn turned abruptly to face Anvar. 'What do you mean?'

Anvar's eyes smouldered. 'I mean, Highness, that Sara – the Khisihn – is barren. She lied to your father as she lied to me. As things stand, you're still the only royal heir. You can go back one day – if you wish.'

Harihn's eyes widened. 'Are you sure?'

'Absolutely certain, Your Highness.'

'Aurian, did you know of this?'

The Mage shook her head, equally stunned by Anvar's news. The prince threw back his head and roared with laughter. 'Balls of the Reaper!' he exclaimed in malicious delight. 'What a joke on my father! I wish I could be there when he finds out.'

Anvar's thoughts had obviously been moving along the same lines. He looked sick, and Aurian finally understood the significance of his rejection of Sara. When Xiang found out that she was barren, she would be worthless to him, and her life might well be in danger. Anvar, though he had seen through her at last, felt guilty about leaving her to her fate. But does he still love her? Aurian wondered. Then she wondered why the idea bothered her so much.

The prince's caravan reassembled itself for the long trek ahead, and they set off once more. The track twisted and turned between tall rock formations that had been eroded into weird, contorted sculptures, like a frozen forest of stone. Holes of varying sizes had been worn right through some of them, and the light wind whistled and hooted eerily through these like the wailing of tortured souls, making the horses flinch and toss their heads uneasily.

After about an hour, the track appeared to end abruptly, simply dropping off into space between two tall stones, beyond which was a steep, boulder-littered slope that seemed to glitter strangely in the light of the rising moon. Below, the desert spread out. Aurian, riding at the head of the column with Harihn, Yazour and Anvar, caught her breath in sheer disbelief. 'Great Chathak!' she exclaimed in a strangled voice. 'Is that what I think it is?'

In the waxing moonlight, the desert glowed. The wind drifted skeins of glittering sand in luminous streams of mixed and muted colour; red, blue, white and green. The dune ridges caught the light and sparkled piercingly like frost on a winter's dawn. Even now, with the moon just rising, the Mage was forced to shade her eyes with her hand.

'Indeed it is,' Yazour replied to the question she had already forgotten. 'The entire desert is composed of gems and gem dust. See how bright it is? That is why we must travel by night.

In sunlight, the glare would burn out your eyes. We must camp well before daylight, for when the sun rises everyone must be safely under cover.'

He showed Aurian and Anvar how to veil their eyes with the long trailing ends of the desert headdresses they all wore, pulling the gauzy veils across their faces and attaching them to the headband at the other side. Aurian found that she could see quite clearly through the thin stuff, but it cut out the already increasing glare. The eyes of the horses and mules were bound with scarves of the same material, but Shia refused to have anything to do with such nonsense. She was still sulking at having had to bring up the rear during the cliff ascent, lest she frighten the horses. 'I don't need that man-stuff,' she told Aurian distainfully. 'I'm a cat. My eyes adjust.'

They rode out into the glimmering sea of gems, looking like wandering ghosts in their pale, veiled headdresses and flowing desert robes. The horses' feet flicked up clouds of fine gem dust, leaving behind them a trail that glittered like cold fire, and covering themselves and their riders with a cloak of scintillating light. What gems were these, that could hold such dazzling luminosity? Aurian felt a lump in her throat. Like the joyous beauty of the leaping whales, the eerie loveliness of this place was almost heartbreaking in its intensity. But it was deadly as well as beautiful, she learned from Yazour. In the proper season, great sandstorms could blow up in minutes, and the sharp edges of the windblown gems would strip a man's flesh from his bones just as quickly. Furthermore, the sea of jewels was said to attract dragons.

'Dragons!' Aurian gasped. 'There are dragons here?'

'Only in legend,' Yazour replied. 'They were reputed to dwell in the desert where they could easily sustain themselves. You know that they fed on sunlight?'

'What a tale!' Anvar scoffed. 'I'll believe it when I see it, Yazour.'

'Pray that you never get the chance,' the young man told him seriously. 'Dragons are said to be unsociable and chancy creatures; easily angered, and best left alone.'

They rode on through the night; too tired now to talk. Aurian was relieved when at last Yazour, casting an eye over the seemingly changeless horizon, advised that they should stop and camp. She was weary beyond belief. Was it only yesterday morning that she had found Anvar and brought him back from the clutches of death? So much had happened since then, seemingly without a moment's respite. When she dismounted from her horse, she felt her knees buckle beneath her, and was thankful there was nothing for her to do. Bohan was instantly at her side to relieve her of her mount, and Harihn's soldiers pitched the light, silken tents with great speed and efficiency. Even the horses and mules were picketed in shelters of their own, for no living creature could stay outside during the hours of daylight.

In the bustle of setting up camp, Aurian lost track of her friends, except for Shia, who stuck to her like a shadow. Collecting their slender ration of food and water, she went in search of Anvar. She found him sitting alone in the doorway of a small tent, a waterskin by his side, his food lying untouched as he stared blindly out at the torchlit camp. His mouth was turned down at the corners, his brooding face lined with sorrow. Aurian was about to creep away, unsure about intruding, but he turned towards her, seeming once again to sense her presence. 'You know,' he said without looking at her, 'you've never once said "I told you so".'

'I'd sooner cut my tongue out!' Aurian protested. 'Why should I want to add to your pain?'

Anvar sighed. 'No, you wouldn't. You're too fair. You warned me about Sara, but instead of listening to you I drove you away. And look what happened.'

'Anvar, I should never have left you. My damned temper! I'll never forgive myself.'

'Then that makes two of us,' Anvar said grimly. 'Why did I not see which of you could be trusted? I've done a lot of thinking, coming across the desert. Of how you defied Miathan for me at the Academy, and how kind you were when I was your servant. How you went out in the snow on Solstice Morn to get me a guitar – and what did I do?' His voice rose in self-derision. 'I said hurtful things to you – drove you away – because I was defending Sara. And what did you do? You saved me from death in the slave camp; you claimed me as your husband, while she only wanted me dead so that she could be a queen! Gods, I'm such a fool, Aurian. A blind, wretched fool!' He was shaking with anguish.

Aurian put her arms around him, comforting him as he had comforted her on the clifftop. He leaned against her shoulder as she stroked his fine, tawny-blond hair. 'You know what I would do if we were back in Nexis?' she said softly. 'I'd take you round every tavern in the city and get you more drunk than you've ever been in your life. Forral always said that that's the only medicine for a broken heart.'

The eastern horizon was beginning to lighten, and already the rising glare was enough to force them back into the tent. Aurian dropped the flap behind them, shutting out the dazzling light. Anvar grinned at her sheepishly. 'When next we reach a city, I'll take up your offer with pleasure – but I must confess that I'm not so much heartbroken as disappointed, humiliated, and plain furious with myself for being so gullible.' His mouth twisted oddly. 'I blame myself for letting you down.'

Aurian squeezed his hand. 'Don't punish yourself for that, Anvar – it's all over now. Sara was your childhood sweetheart – you loved her. You didn't know how much she had changed. Why don't you get some sleep now? Maybe things won't seem so bad once you've rested.'

He smiled ruefully. 'Looking after me again? I thought it was supposed to be the other way round.'

'Don't worry, you do your share. Now go to sleep – or else!'

'Or else you'll set that monster on me?' Anvar eyed Shia warily. She looked huge in the cramped confines of the tent.

'Don't worry about Shia. She's a good friend. She'll look after us both.' Aurian stretched out a hand to stroke Shia's sleek head, and was rewarded by drowsy purring.

'I like him,' the cat said.

'Do you?' Aurian was surprised. Shia had never volunteered such information about anyone else, even Bohan. 'I like him too.'

She turned back to Anvar, who was curled on the cushions, already asleep. Through the glittering dust that coated his face he looked drawn and vulnerable, weighed down with sorrow. On impulse, Aurian put out her hand and gently touched his cheek. And then, as it had done in the slave compound, her heart seemed to turn over within her – a pattern shifted and clicked suddenly into place. Aurian snatched her hand back as though she had been burned, aware, in that instant, that the surge – whatever it had been – was the same force that had unlocked the power of the bracelets. She sat very still for a moment, cradling her hand and waiting for her breathing to steady and her heart to stop trying to fight its way out of her breast. 'Did you feel that?' she asked Shia experimentally.

'Feel what?' The cat's answer was drowsy.

'Never mind.' Aurian tried to organize her shaky thoughts, but for some reason the only thing that would come into her mind was the image of Forral's face, tender and glowing as it had been on the day they had first made love. Grief and loneliness pierced her with a pain so acute that she gave a stifled cry. Confused and wretched, she gave in to her tears for once, and cried herself to sleep.

Some time during the long, bright day, Anvar tossed and moaned, in the grip of some nightmare. Then his seeking hand found that of the Mage, and in her sleep she clasped it tightly, and his restlessness stilled. And that was how Harihn found them at nightfall, lying close together, hand in hand. He looked at them for a long moment, frowning, until Shia opened a sleepy eye. The prince ducked swiftly and silently away, dropping the flap of the tent behind him. Since the man had gone without any attempt at harming them Shia forbore to mention his visit to Aurian.

460

29
Sewer-Rats

The old bakery had changed so much that Anvar, had he been there, would scarcely have recognized his childhood home. After Ria's death, Torl had lost heart. His thriving business in the arcade had been destroyed with the fire that killed his wife, and he had been forced to fall back on his older, smaller premises in the poverty of the workers' district. But without Ria to clean up, and without Anvar's labour, things had gone steadily from bad to worse. Despite Bern's efforts to save the business that he would inherit, the bakery was in a shabby state, its plaster crumbling and its roof sorely in need of repair. The inside was cobwebbed and filthy, and crying out for a new coat of whitewash.

No wonder we've lost our customers, Bern thought disgustedly, as he took tomorrow's loaves out of the oven. Torl, now a sullen, bitter man, no longer bothered to get up early to bake a fresh batch each day. In truth, it was scarcely worthwhile. Bern frowned at the pile of stale loaves that lay on the table beneath the window. Everyone in the district knew the conditions under which Torl's once famous bread was now made, and no one would touch it.

Just then the object of Bern's gloomy thoughts came into the bakery. The flames of the oven flared in the strong draught from the doorway, and a swirling cloud of snow followed Torl indoors, the flakes lit like sparks in the glow of his lantern. The new council, in the pay of the Magefolk, had decreed that no more money should be wasted on lamplighters. Crime flourished in the darkened streets, and people were forced to carry their own illumination.

'Rough night,' Torl grunted. 'Bloody winter!'

'Wipe your feet, dad!' Bern knew before the words were out of his mouth that it was hopeless. Torl shrugged, as he always did, and began to load the stale loaves into a sack that he had brought from the empty stable. 'I'm off to the tavern,' he muttered. 'Harkas wants these for his pigs.'

'Dad, not again!' Bern protested. 'We can't go on like this. If you brought home the money you get from Harkas, instead of drinking it, maybe we could afford to fix this place up so our bread would be fit for *people* to eat. Besides, he can't be paying you much. It's a long time since I've seen you come home tipsy, let alone drunk.'

'You mind your own business, Bern.'

'Mind my own business? This business is all I – we – have, and you're letting it go to rack and ruin!'

Torl scowled. 'What if I am? What's the point in working, while those cursed Magefolk bleed the city dry! Tithes here, taxes there ... I'd sooner burn this place down than put another penny into Magefolk coffers!'

Bern, thoroughly alarmed, strove to be conciliatory. 'Look, dad, why don't I come with you tonight? I could use a beer myself, and maybe together we could wheedle more money out of Harkas for the bread. What do you say?'

'No!' The violence of his father's reply took Bern by surprise. Torl's glance slid slyly away from his son. 'Not tonight, Bern, eh? It's filthy weather out there, and you've worked hard today. Don't drag yourself through the mud and snow just to keep me company. You have a nice rest. Come another night instead.' He was out of the door and away before his son could blink.

'What the blazes is he up to?' Bern muttered. Pausing only to bank the oven, he whisked his tattered cloak round his shoulders, lit a lantern, and left the bakery, following the prints of his father's footsteps on the snowy ground.

Torl was freezing. Carrying the sack in one hand and the lantern in the other, he was unable to pull his cloak about him, and it was flapping wildly in the icy wind. In trying to rescue it he dropped the sack, and loaves fell out to roll across the ground, so that he had to stop and pick them up. 'Bloody Vannor,' he swore. 'Don't know why I do it, now he's run out of gold.' In truth, of course, he knew perfectly well. He was aiding Vannor's rebels out of pure hatred – to get back at the accursed

Magefolk who had destroyed his family, ruined his business and wrecked his life. With that in mind, a few stale loaves and a certain amount of risk seemed a small price to pay.

Vannor had set up his headquarters within the city's intricate sewer system, in a series of tunnels built above the level of the major drains to take the runoff from heavy rains or snow-melt. Cleaner than the actual sewers, they would remain fairly dry and habitable until the thaw. The Magefolk had few supporters in this northern part of the city, so food and other necessities were smuggled down to the rebels by allies who lived above. The storm-drain beneath Torl's home was an ideal base. With his bitter hatred of the Magefolk, he could be trusted. In addition, the bakery oven was usually alight, a little of its warmth filtering down through the earth to improve conditions in the freezing drain. Karlek, formerly a siege engineer in the garrison, had broken a chimney through into the flue of the oven, so that they could have a fire without its smoke being noticed above, and of course the baker provided them with a regular supply of bread. Really, thought Torl, Vannor and his men were doing pretty well out of him.

It wasn't far to go. Torl rounded the corner of the bakery and branched off into the narrow alley that ran behind the high-walled stableyard. He paused for a brief glance all around, but no one ever came into this dead end. Putting down the sack, he bent with a grunt to lift a grating that was set into the cobbles. Taking bread and lantern with him, the baker lowered himself into the drain, reaching up to pull the cover down behind him. He was unaware that he was being watched.

Bern could hardly believe it when his father vanished into the drain. He moved quickly from his hiding place in the shadows and sped across to the grating, just in time to hear Torl's whisper echoing out of the blackness beneath it. 'It's me. Look, I need to talk with Vannor. I think my son is getting suspicious.'

Bern stiffened. Vannor? Vannor had been declared an outlaw. There were rumours all over the city that he was gathering an army against the Magefolk. It took seconds for Bern to reach the obvious conclusion – and the solution to his problems. Torl would die for treason and be out of the way for good – and there'd be a reward, of course. He could build up the business again ... Bern scrambled to his feet, and ran. Should he go to the Academy? No, the garrison was closer. They could surprise the rebels and catch Torl in the act. He'd make sure of the reward first, though. The new commander, Angos, was a vile-tempered mercenary hired by the Magefolk; the sort who'd sell his grandmother for a profit. Still, if he and his troops secured Bern's inheritance, who cared? Heedless of the snow, Bern ran faster.

'She's alive, I tell you!' Miathan's bony fists hammered with soundless violence on the thick quilt that covered his bed. His face, below the bandage that concealed the ruin of his burnt-out eyes, was twisted with frustrated rage.

Bragar stepped close to Eliseth, to whisper in her ear: 'Are you sure she didn't fry his brain as well as his eyes?'

'I heard that!' Miathan turned towards the Fire-Mage with unerring accuracy, and lifted his hand. A chill, misty vapour flowed rapidly from his fingers and pooled round Bragar's feet, coalescing into the form of a glimmering serpent that began to make its coiling way up the Mage's legs. Bragar bit down on a scream, and tried, too late, to make frantic warding gestures as the cruel head reached the level of his face. The serpent hissed, showing ice-pointed fangs that glittered with venom.

'Miathan, no!' Eliseth cried hastily. 'He didn't mean it!'

'She's right, Archmage! I – I apologize!' Bragar's voice was no more than a squeak. The serpent vanished. Miathan cackled spitefully; a laugh cut off with shocking suddenness in mid-breath. 'So what are you going to do about it?'

The Weather-Mage frowned. 'About Bragar, Archmage?'

'No, you stupid woman! About Aurian! She's coming! Coming for me; for all of us! She stalks my dreams, coming after us with death in her eyes ...'

'Archmage, how can that be?' Bragar protested. 'She drowned in Eliseth's storm. We all felt it ...'

'It wasn't strong enough!' the Archmage snapped. 'Not like when that cretin Davorshan got himself killed.'

Eliseth gasped, and he cackled again. 'Oh, I knew all about

you and Davorshan from the start. I may be blind, but I don't miss much around here, let me tell you.'

Eliseth turned on him furiously. 'That's beside the point,' she said flatly. 'Aurian is dead. What difference does it make that we barely felt her passing? It's not surprising, with the ocean between us, not to mention all the panic from her attack on you.'

'Eliseth, you're a fool,' Miathan retorted. 'Aurian is alive, and a threat to us all. If we're to keep what we've gained, she must be intercepted.' His spidery hands clawed at the crystal around his neck. 'And what about that accursed Anvar? I know he survived your blundering storm.'

'Who the blazes is Anvar?' Bragar interrupted.

Eliseth gave him a blank look. 'I've no idea.'

'He was Lady Aurian's servant.' Elewin's respectful voice came from the corner. The chief steward had been there so long, devotedly nursing his master, that they had forgotten his presence. 'My Lord Archmage never liked poor Anvar,' he continued, 'yet he was as diligent a lad as ever I – '

'Shut up!' Miathan spat. 'Yes, he was her servant, against my wishes. I want him dead, do you hear? His head on a spike! His heart ripped from his living body! His corpse hacked to pieces and trampled into the ground! I want . . .'

'Hush now, Archmage,' Eliseth murmured, handing him a cup of wine. 'Bragar and I will deal with Aurian and her servant, I promise.'

'Not Aurian, you imbecile! I want her brought to me alive. I want her . . .' Miathan licked his lips in an unsavoury manner, and lapsed into a crooning reverie. Bragar opened his mouth to protest, but Eliseth waved him silent.

'Don't worry, Archmage,' she said. 'You may leave the matter safely in our hands. Stay with him, Elewin.' Taking Bragar's hand, she hauled him firmly away from the bed.

Elewin bowed them respectfully out of the room. Then: 'More wine, Archmage?' He tugged the cup from Miathan's grasp. Slipping a twist of paper from his pocket, he poured its contents, a greenish powder, into the wine, and handed it back to Miathan. 'Is that better, Lord Archmage?'

Miathan drained the cup. 'It's good. I don't recognize the

vintage, but it's very good . . .' He slumped back against the pillows, snoring gently. Elewin took the cup from his hands and straightened, his subservience vanished. Following the Mages, he crept downstairs to Eliseth's door. Setting an ear to the panels, the steward composed himself to listen.

Eliseth's white-painted chamber was spacious and spartan, its furnishings elegant but spare and uncomfortable. Bragar squirmed uneasily on a hard wooden chair, wishing that she wouldn't insist on presenting such a chilly front to the world. He knew that the bedroom behind those doors at the far end of the room was a den of luxury; a fur-carpeted, silk-hung, perfumed temple dedicated to sensuality and lust. The thought reminded him unpleasantly that, since Eliseth had started taking an interest in Davorshan, he, Bragar, had been pointedly denied access to that inner sanctum. How glad he had been when that slimy youth had died.

'Wine?' Eliseth took goblets from a cabinet in the corner.

'Have you nothing stronger?'

The Magewoman raised her eyes to the ceiling. 'You're drinking too much, Bragar,' she snapped. 'How can I depend on you if your brains are permanently pickled?'

'Shut up and give me a drink!' Bragar snarled. You wait, he thought. Some day I'll make you pay for treating me like this. And when I'm done, you'll be begging for mercy – or begging for more! The thought, along with the glass of spirits that she grudgingly handed him, was some comfort.

'Well, what do you think?' Eliseth's voice dissolved his fantasy. 'Not that there's any point in asking you,' she added, settling herself in a chair near the fire, a glass of white wine in her hand.

'What a shame you've no one else to ask,' Bragar retorted, unable to resist needling her about Davorshan's death. He had the satisfaction of seeing her face twist with rage. 'What can I say? Miathan's brains have clearly been addled by Aurian's attack. How could she not have perished?'

Eliseth frowned. 'I'm not so sure,' she said. 'Remember how close Aurian and the Archmage used to be? He should know whether she's dead, if anyone does.'

'Rubbish! The old fool is senile, and you know it. We should put him out of his misery, and take power ourselves.'

'Bragar, you've the brains of an ox!' Eliseth snapped. 'We need the Archmage as a figurehead. He made sure of that when he spread the tale that it was his power that destroyed the Nihilim. We were able to bribe that toad Narvish on to the council as the merchants' representative, and Angos at the garrison is nothing but a thick-headed mercenary who will do whatever we say for a price, but they won't last long if Miathan is not seen to be behind them. It is only the Mortals' fear of his power, and what will happen if he withdraws it, that keeps the city in our hands!'

'If he's only a figurehead, why do we have to jump whenever he snaps his fingers?'

Eliseth took a sip of wine. 'As a rule we don't – but if there is a chance that Aurian survived, we cannot risk her returning. Miathan may want her alive, but I do not. I've been giving it some thought. We know she was at sea, and I know the strength and direction of the storm I raised. If she is anywhere, it has to be the Southern Kingdoms.'

'The south? Even if we had the people, we could not send a force in sufficient numbers to find her there,' Bragar protested. 'The southerners would take it as an invasion, and a war is the last thing we need at present. Besides, they're supposed to be hostile to the Magefolk. If that's where Aurian is, the problem will take care of itself.'

'Why rely on it, when we have other means at our disposal?' Eliseth glanced at him slyly. Bragar knew she wanted him to ask what she meant, so she could accuse him of stupidity again. Refusing to play her game, he gulped the contents of his glass and went to refill it.

'You always did have a high opinion of yourself,' he said.

'How dare you!' Eliseth rose to the bait. 'I'm the only Weather-Mage in the world. If I deal with them, the south will be lucky to have any survivors, let alone that red-headed bitch. I've seen the maps,' she went on more calmly. 'The Southern Kingdoms have huge mountain ranges and vast deserts, and even jungle, if you go far enough south. With topography like that, it's easy to produce violent weather. A sandstorm in the right place, or unseasonal blizzards in the mountains, could solve our problem. It would also soften up the southern races for conquest,' she added persuasively.

'Eliseth, you can't!' The bottle jerked in Bragar's hands, splashing brandy on the white-tiled floor. 'You'll alter the weather everywhere. It could take centuries to restore the balance.'

Eliseth shrugged. 'So what? Who cares if we lose a few thousand Mortals to storms or famine? With their numbers reduced, they'll be easier to control. We need not suffer, now we know Finbarr's preserving spell. We'll have Elewin stockpile food in the catacombs, and keep it indefinitely. It's not as though we had many mouths to feed nowadays.'

Gods, she was ruthless! Bragar was both impressed and appalled. Once he had been the instigator of their plots, but now that it was time to act instead of talk he was finding himself increasingly out of his depth. It was one thing to talk about negative magic, but having to deal with those things from the Cauldron had jarred his confidence badly. Bragar gulped his drink, remembering the horror of the Wraiths. How could Eliseth be so composed? Her slender form looked delicate and brittle as a spear of ice, yet she throve on situations that turned his blood to water. His vision of her, submissive and conquered, evaporated. He was losing this game; he knew it now. His one hope lay in going along with her, and waiting for her to overreach herself. Then, at last, it would be his turn. He decided on a change of tactics. 'Maybe you're right – ' He cut the words off, alerted by a warning prickle at the base of his neck; by the merest hint of a sound outside. Overturning his chair, he shot across the room and flung the door open.

'Bragar, what are you doing?'

The Fire-Mage peered at the empty stairway, then closed the door, shaking his head in puzzlement. 'I thought . . .'

Elewin, pressed flat to the wall round the curve of the staircase, let out the breath he had been holding in a long sigh. That had been close! For a moment he considered returning, but there was no sense in taking risks. He had heard enough, and the information must be passed on. He hurried downstairs and let himself out of the tower.

Gods! Would spring never come? This accursed winter was lingering for ever. After several hours within Miathan's warm chambers, Elewin shivered in the bitingly cold air. A new

468

sprinkling of snow had fallen while he'd been tending the Archmage, but the night skies were clear now, and the temperature had dropped sharply. The snow, frozen to a hard, brittle crust, crunched loudly beneath his boots as he crossed the courtyard, and he glanced nervously up at the lighted window of Eliseth's room. If they should hear him, and look out ... He'd never be able to explain why he was going to the library, especially at this time of night. Miathan had no need of books nowadays, he thought wryly.

Since Finbarr's death, the library had lain dark and empty. The preserving spells, which required frequent renewing, were already decaying, and as Elewin pushed open the heavy door he heard a rustling patter like wind-blown leaves as mice and cockroaches scattered for cover. The steward shook his head sadly. Finbarr would have been appalled. The irreplaceable knowledge of centuries, which he had tended with such care and skill, ending up as rat-nests! I must get someone to see to this, Elewin thought, hating the notion of Finbarr's precious volumes mouldering beneath a shroud of cobwebs and dust. It was disrespectful to the archivist's memory to let his life's work go to ruin – but in truth, there was no one to tend them. Most of the servants had fled in terror on the Night of Death, as people in the city called it, and few were willing now to come near the academy. Elewin was hard-pressed to maintain the basic necessities, let alone spare a servant to dust books.

Not daring to venture a light, the steward groped his way across the long, musty room, cursing as he bruised himself on the corner of a table, and fell over a displaced chair. If only there had been a moon to cast some light through the tall windows. If only he had Mages' sight! At last he reached the further end, recognizing by feel the recessed door that led down into the catacombs. Smiling in the darkness, he slipped an intricate key from his pocket. Eliseth and Bragar thought all the keys to the archives were safe in their keeping, and it was small wonder they wanted no one in the catacombs, considering what they had stored down there! But they did not know that Finbarr had given Anvar his own key. Elewin had found it among his scanty belongings after he fled. Entering the archives, the steward carefully locked the door again behind him.

The walls of the corridor were icy to the touch, and Elewin had trouble lighting the lantern. The flint kept slipping from his frozen fingers, forcing him to kneel and grope on the floor, cursing. How things had changed. Once he had thrashed any servant caught swearing in the academy. But that was before he'd become a spy and a traitor to the Magefolk. Their changes had forced the change in him.

Having finally managed to light the lantern, Elewin relaxed a little as its mellow glow banished the darkness, making the frigid air of the corridor seem warmer. Thank the gods! Being down here in the dark with those Wraiths was more than he could bear. Though they had been disabled, it was easy to imagine that he could hear them stirring . . . waking . . . Elewin shuddered as he began to thread his cautious way through the maze of passages and stairways beneath the Academy. When he passed the room where the Wraiths were stored, he held his breath and hurried.

The blade came whistling out of the darkness, not half an inch from his face. Elewin jumped back round the sharp bend in the corridor, almost dropping the lantern in his fright. 'It's me, you fool!' he hissed. 'What the blazes are you doing up here? You nearly took my nose off!'

'Sorry.' The small, wiry form of Parric the cavalry master appeared round the corner. He was grinning from ear to ear. 'I must be getting rusty. It was meant to be your head!'

Elewin was not amused. 'Why didn't you wait in our usual place? What if I'd been one of the Magefolk?'

Parric shrugged. 'You were late,' he complained. 'I was freezing my bollocks off down there. I had to move about to keep warm.'

'Never mind,' the steward sighed. It was clear where he was learning all his bad language nowadays. 'I have news for you. Come further down where it's safer, and we'll talk.'

'I don't know why you're so worried,' Parric grumbled. 'Who in their right mind would come down here on a night like this? I swear there's icicles growing on the end of my – '

'Parric!'

The cavalry master chuckled.

The ancient parts of the catacombs that Anvar had

discovered were little more than a series of natural caves, set low in the end of the promontory. They had been stripped of their treasures now, and the footfalls of the two men echoed loudly in the bare chambers. Since the ancient spells that guarded their contents had been broken, damp had begun to seep in from the nearby river. The dark walls were jewelled with ice crystals that splintered the lamplight, and the floor was slick and treacherous underfoot. Elewin gripped the lantern tightly to prevent it slipping from his numb grasp, and wished that Finbarr still lived. In the archivist's day these caverns had been lit by Magelight, and kept warm and dry by means of his spells.

'See? I told you. Colder than a prostitute's heart down here.' Parric pulled the remains of a broken wooden chest out of a corner and sat down, motioning for Elewin to join him. 'I don't suppose you brought some food with you? Or a bottle?' he asked hopefully.

'Didn't get the chance. Sorry, Parric. I know there aren't many comforts where you are hiding out. Still, I have some news that will warm your heart better than a bottle.' Elewin grinned, savouring the moment. 'The Lady Aurian is said to be alive!'

He hardly got the reaction he had expected. The leathery, hard-bitten little cavalry master stared at him, tears welling up in his eyes and rolling unheeded down his cheeks. Then, turning abruptly away, Parric hid his face in his hands and began to sob.

'Parric!' A startled Elewin put the lantern down, and laid an arm across the man's shoulders.

'I'm sorry,' Parric choked. He wiped his face, looking embarrassed. 'Not what you'd expect of a tough old bastard like me, is it?' He swallowed hard. 'But by the gods, I was so fond of that lass! We all loved her – her and Forral. We thought they'd both been killed – then Vannor told us she'd been carrying Forral's child . . . Elewin, it's a miracle! A bloody miracle!' He clutched at the steward's arm. 'Where is she? How is she?'

Elewin hated to dampen the man's joy. 'Don't get your hopes up, Parric. It isn't certain. But Miathan insists she's still alive, and that her servant is with her.'

'What, young Anvar? Well I'm blowed! Forral always thought that lad had some good stuff in him.'

'The bad news is that they think she's in the Southern Kingdoms, if she's anywhere.'

'What? How the blue blazes did she get down there?'

Elewin told Parric what he had overheard. 'So you see how grave the situation is,' he finished. 'If Eliseth tampers with the weather, it would not only put Aurian in danger, but it could be catastrophic for our own folk – worse than anything we've seen since the Cataclysm.'

Parric frowned. 'This changes things. I'll discuss it with Vannor, of course, but I think we'll be leaving the city now. We can't stay where we are if it thaws, and we're too close to the Academy to assemble an effective force. But when Aurian returns . . .'

'You think she'll come back?' Elewin was surprised.

'Aurian? Of course she will! It'd take more than an ocean to keep that lass from Miathan, after he killed Forral. I'll wager she's on her way back already to settle with the Archmage. And when she does we'll see a thing or two.'

'Parric! We're talking about the Magefolk,' Elewin protested. 'It won't be that easy.'

The cavalry master sobered. 'I know. That's why we need an army. Aurian can't do it alone, just as we can't, without a Mage. But together, maybe . . . Anyway, I must get back to Vannor with this news.' He hesitated, his expression thoughtful. 'Elewin, why don't you come with me? If we move elsewhere, you won't be needed here as an informant, and it's dangerous for you to stay.'

Elewin shook his head, though he was sorely tempted. 'I'd better not. If I suddenly vanish, Eliseth and Bragar will get suspicious and start searching for me, and that might put your people in danger. And if you do want to attack the Academy, you'll need someone on the inside.'

'But it could be ages before we can do that.'

'It can't be helped. I'll be all right. Besides, Miathan depends on me. To see him this way, blind and crippled . . . Oh, I know it's his own fault, but he seems so helpless.'

Parric clasped the other's arm. 'Elewin, I know this is a trial for your loyalties, and we're very grateful, but . . .'

'It's not just that. The balance of power is changing within the Academy. Be warned, Parric. Eliseth is the one to be ware of now.'

'I'll bear it in mind. Aurian always hated that bitch. Look, are you sure you won't come?'

'I cannot.'

Parric nodded. 'All right. You're a brave man, Elewin – or daft. Forral always said there wasn't much difference between the two. Farewell, my friend. Our prayers go with you. Vannor will try to get word to you from time to time.'

'Vannor? What about you?'

'Me? Personally, I have a sudden hankering to head south. It's warmer there!' The cavalry master winked, and picking up his own lantern vanished into the shadows at the back of the cave, leaving Elewin gaping in astonishment.

The sewers ran the length and breadth of the city, a democratic highway connecting the grand and lofty Academy to even the meanest of dwellings. Not the most pleasant of places to lie low, but there was a certain satisfaction in being able to move around under the very noses of the Magefolk, and it had been simplicity itself to break through the thin stone barrier into the old part of the archives. The hole was hidden in a corner, where a spur of rock formed a kink in the tunnel so that the opening was obscured by the shadow of the jutting stone. Because of his slight stature, Parric had been chosen as go-between. Holding his lantern out at arm's length, he squeezed through the hole into the narrow drain beyond. Luckily the current low population of the Academy, coupled with the cold weather, had reduced the smell, but he still tried to hold his breath. Given time, a man could get used to most things, but there were limits!

The cram ed drain continued for some distance back beneath the Academy's promontory before connecting with the main sewers. The rusted stubs of an old inspection ladder protruded, sharp and dangerous, from the wall, marking the junction. Parric hooked the lantern to his belt and pulled on leather gauntlets to protect his hands from the jagged iron before he began, very carefully, to climb. Any cuts or abrasions could be fatal down here: the chances of infection were high.

They had already lost two men; one from a poisoned rat-bite and the other from lockjaw.

The sewer was a tunnel of slick and rotting stone, with raised walkways on either side of the stinking, sluggish channel. Parric was glad that the water level was too low to reach the slanting mouth of the drain. He had sometimes done this climb with all manner of filth cascading down on him, and it was not an experience he cared to repeat. Emerging from the mouth of the drain, he made his way along the walkway to his makeshift raft. Since the stream was low, he could use it to return. When the torrent was in full spate, the journey had to be made via the slimy, crumbling walkways, with the prospect of drowning in the sewage-filled channel only a slip away. With the lantern that swung from his belt providing the only light, Parric picked up the paddle and began to make his way back through the network of tunnels that led to the rebels' hideout.

He had almost reached his destination when he heard the first harsh sounds of fighting. His heart lurched. Great Chathak, no! He steered his raft into the side, his soldier's brain already working out the odds. Who had betrayed them? No, that was for later. How long since the attack had started? How many of the enemy? They had the advantage of surprise, but they didn't know these tunnels as Parric did. Once on the walkway, he extinguished his lamp. While his eyes adjusted to the darkness he checked his throwing knives – one up each sleeve – and pulled a long dagger from his boot. He left his sword sheathed. This was close work. With a grimace, he slipped over the side and began to wade, thigh deep, up the stinking channel, gripping the edge of the walkway to keep from slipping on the sludge that coated the bottom.

Had Parric not wanted information, the guard would have died instantly. As it was, she only had time to feel a hand come out of nowhere to grip her ankle before a quick jerk pitched her headlong into the channel. Before the choking, panic-stricken warrior could flounder to her feet, Parric was on her. He hauled her up roughly, his knife against her throat. 'How many of you?' he growled. 'Answer me!'

He felt her stiffen against him. 'Great Chathak – I know that voice!' she exclaimed. 'Parric – is it really you?'

'Bloody right it is! Now answer my question!'

'Parric, it's me – Sangra! Gods forgive us, they said you were dead. Put that stupid knife away, so I can hug you!'

The emotion in her voice was too intense to be feigned, and Parric felt a surge of joy. Sangra was an old friend – a big, rowdy, raw-boned girl with assets that no fighting-vest could contain. Ah, the tumbles they had had in happier days! Grinning, Parric lowered the knife, and managed to get in a quick grope before she turned to face him.

'Now I know it's you!' There were tears and laughter in her voice as her arms went around him with a force that made his ribs creak as they hugged, oblivious of the filth that coated them both.

'Sangra, what's going on?' Parric disengaged himself reluctantly.

'The baker's son betrayed you – or Vannor, at least. We had no idea that you were down here. Parric, are any of the others with you?'

'Yes. Quite a few.'

'Gods! I've got to warn our folk. We won't fight our own.'

'That's my girl! Come on – quick!'

The troops from the garrison had Vannor's little force penned into a cul-de-sac, and the fighting was fierce. The soldiers had brought torches, but most had been extinguished in the battle, and in the half-darkness it was difficult to tell friend from foe. Sangra knew, however. She and Parric joined the mêlée from the rear and plunged into the fray. Parric, with his small stature, found it easy to worm his way through the press of fighters. His methods were straightforward. Anyone he recognized, he spared. Any stranger felt the bite of his knife. Sangra, in the meantime, was circulating, pausing to whisper to any of Forral's old troops that she came across. The change in them was immediate. Relief and joy shining on their faces, they turned their weapons on Angos's vicious mercenaries.

It was over very quickly. Vannor's rebels, freed from the pressure of the fight, were able to take the offensive, and the mercenaries found themselves under attack from both sides. Parric managed to break through to the merchant, to explain what had happened, and before very long joyous reunions were

475

taking place between the members of Forral's old band, over the bodies of the mercenary dead.

If Vannor looked bewildered to discover that his little force had doubled to some fifty-odd troops, he took it in his stride, and when Parric introduced Sangra he greeted her with the utmost courtesy, manfully ignoring the fact that she and the cavalry master were in an appalling state after their immersion in the sewer. 'If we'd known you were all down here,' Sangra apologized, 'we would have joined you. We've had an awful time since Angos brought his mercenaries in to augment our forces. But we felt we had to stay. We thought Forral would expect it, because of our oath of loyalty to the city, and because we wanted to protect the people from the worst excesses of Angos and the Magefolk.' She looked at Parric. 'What do we do? Angos is waiting with more soldiers at the mouth of the drain, and now he knows you're here, we daren't stay.'

'Go north,' a decisive voice broke in. 'It shouldn't be difficult to get out of the city. Angos can't be watching all the drains. The Nightrunners will take us in.'

Vannor grimaced. 'Dulsina, will you never stop organizing?'

The tall, dark-haired woman grinned at him. 'Not while there's breath in my body,' she said cheerfully. 'Besides, Zanna has been missing you, despite the messages we managed to send. It's about time you saw your daughter again.'

'Wait a minute!' Parric interrupted. 'You know the Nightrunners? Enough to leave your daughter with them?' The cavalry master raised his eyes imploringly. 'May the gods give me strength. Those bloody smugglers were a constant thorn in Forral's side. He drove us all to distraction trying to discover where they were hiding, and you knew all the time!'

Vannor winked. 'How do you think I managed to make my fortune?'

Parric burst out laughing. 'You villain! You were using them to trade with the southerners, for gems and silks and stuff, weren't you?'

'A man has to get ahead somehow.' The merchant shrugged. 'Besides, my criminal past is proving useful now. Come on, let's get going.'

There were few casualties among the rebels. But as they left the storm-drains, Parric discovered the body of Torl, floating face down in the sewer with a knife in his back. He sighed. Miserable as the old man had been, he'd been a good friend to the rebels. Still, it was better this way. At least he had never known that his own son had betrayed him. Or had he? On closer inspection, Parric saw that the knife was not a soldier's dagger, but a long, saw-edged domestic blade – the sort that a baker might use.

The rebels decided to use the sewers to make their way across the city, then travel downriver to Norberth, following Aurian's route. Once there, they could contact one of Yanis's agents, who would arrange a ship to take them to the smugglers' hideout. It was a nightmare journey. Vannor's band were used to negotiating the slick walkways, but the new outlaws had a difficult time of it. Every few minutes there would be a splash followed by curses as someone fell into the channel and had to be rescued. Though the troopers made light of it, Parric was concerned. He knew all too well the chances of losing some of their band to the diseases that proliferated in this place.

As they passed the drain that connected with the Academy catacombs, Parric heaved a sigh of relief. Not much further now to the outfall and blessed fresh air. He was getting twitchy, bringing up the rear as he was. His instincts, developed over many years, convinced him that they were being followed. Nonsense, he told himself. Angos couldn't track us through that maze of tunnels. But it was no good. Unable to stand it any longer, he dropped back.

'Got you!' The cloaked figure, though tall, was slimly built, and no warrior. Parric had no trouble subduing him, and at least the fellow seemed to be alone. Then, to his astonishment, a series of shrieks came from the muffled figure. Without a doubt, his captive was a woman. He was about to rip the hood aside when he heard the sound of footsteps hurrying too fast for safety on the slimy walkway, and Elewin appeared, carrying a lantern. His face broke into a smile of pure relief at the sight of Parric's captive. 'Thank the gods you've found her!' he exclaimed.

'Found who?' In the light of the lantern, Parric removed the woman's hood, and gasped. 'Lady Meiriel!'

The Magewoman spat in his face. 'Take your hands off me!'

'What's going on?' Vannor, accompanied by Sangra and Dulsina, came hurrying up. 'Parric! We thought we'd lost you.' His eyes widened at the sight of Meiriel. 'What's she doing here?'

'Mind your own business, Mortal!'

'She escaped from the Academy.' The Mage and Elewin spoke simultaneously, then turned to glare at one another.

'You say she escaped?' Vannor's eyes flicked from Elewin to Meiriel. 'Would someone care to explain?'

'It's simple,' the healer said coldly. 'I couldn't heal Miathan's eyes, so that bitch Eliseth locked me up.'

Parric pounced on her words. 'Couldn't – or wouldn't?'

Meiriel spared him a haughty glance. 'His eyes were utterly destroyed. But even if I could have healed him, I would not have done it. Not after his creatures murdered my Finbarr.' Her voice was thick with hate. 'Anyway, I managed to escape tonight. I followed Elewin, and heard what he told you, about Aurian being alive. I must find her.'

'She's alive? Why the blazes didn't you tell me?' Vannor turned on Parric.

'There wasn't time,' he protested, 'what with the fight – '

'Fight?' Now it was Elewin's turn to interrupt.

Vannor nodded. 'We've been betrayed,' he explained.

'You two must come with us,' Parric put in. 'You can't stay here now, Elewin, and it isn't safe to leave her behind.'

'Just a minute.' Vannor confronted Meiriel. 'Why do you have to find Aurian?'

'She needs my help,' the Magewoman replied. 'Miathan put a curse on the child. She's carrying a monster.'

'What!' Parric exploded. 'The bastard! I'll kill him!'

'Steady, Parric.' It took all of Vannor's strength to restrain his friend from starting back up the tunnel. 'This is not the time. We need to get away to safety before we can deal with this.'

They set off to join the other rebels at the sewer outfall; Sangra leading the way with Parric, who was still beside himself with rage and grief. Dulsina took Meiriel into her charge. As they walked, Elewin drew Vannor back, out of earshot of the others. 'Listen,' he said, 'Lady Meiriel may be telling the truth, but I'd caution you to take care. She may seem lucid now, but since Finbarr's death she has been completely deranged. You're dealing with a madwoman, Vannor. Whatever you do, don't trust her.'

30

Raven

The prince and his followers broke camp at sundown, pausing only for a few quick mouthfuls of food before setting off again across the desert. Though the moon had not yet risen, there was plenty of light. The gem dust burned and twinkled in a multiplicity of crystal hues, holding the sunset glow long after it had left the sky. Wisps of sand, drifted gently across the ground by the errant night breeze, crossed their path like roaming wildfire beneath the stars. Aurian was strangely silent and preoccupied; and Anvar, riding by her side, was marvelling at the surety with which Yazour seemed to find his way in this featureless land. Moved by boredom and curiosity, he rode forward to ask him how it was done.

Anvar caught the flash of Yazour's smile beneath his veils. 'Ah,' he said. 'It is the magic of my people. The desert is bred into our blood, over endless generations.' He laughed. 'My friend, I'm teasing. There are ways, to be sure – the lie of the land, the drift of the dunes in the prevailing wind – but mostly I navigate by the stars.'

Anvar grimaced. 'I never thought of that. I suppose it's because the stars are so different here.'

Yazour's eyebrows rose. 'The stars are different? How strange! Tell me, Anvar, are all things different in your northern home? What is it like there?'

Anvar smiled, liking this young man, and wondered where to start. Things were so different in the north that he had a topic of conversation to last the night – but he never got to reply, for at that moment his horse gave a scream of pain and lurched over, stumbling and floundering in the soft gem dust. Anvar was thrown abruptly forward, struggling to keep his balance and his hold on the reins. Yazour cursed viciously and grabbed at his bridle, steadying the plunging mare and bringing her to a halt as Anvar slid down. The animal was trembling, the tip of one hind hoof barely touching the ground. 'Blood of the Reaper! She's lame.' Yazour was examining the flinching hoof. The horror on his face went far beyond regret.

'What's wrong?' Harihn's voice came harshly from above their heads as he pulled up his stallion beside them.

Yazour looked grim. 'Anvar's mount has been hurt.'

Harihn shrugged. 'A pity,' he said coolly. 'You know what to do, in that case.'

'But, Your Highness . . .'

'See to it, Yazour.'

The warrior sighed. 'My sorrow, Anvar,' he said softly. 'If there were some other way . . .'

'What do you mean?' Anvar was alarmed by the way Yazour was looking at him. As though he were already dead . . .

'It is the desert law.' Harihn's voice was cold and remorseless. 'We have no spare horses – the last went to those friends your Aurian insisted on bringing. Because we carry so little water, we cannot allow you to delay our progress to the next oasis. The desert law states that you must be left behind.'

'What did you say?' No one had seen Aurian approach. Her hand was on the hilt of her sword. She pushed back her veils, and her eyes glinted with a fey, steely light as she advanced on Harihn. 'If you think I'll let you leave Anvar here to die, then think again, prince.'

'Lady, stay out of this. There can be no exceptions to the law.' Harihn beckoned, and a ring of soldiers materialized around the Mage, their crossbows cocked and poised. 'Will you fight my entire army for the sake of one man?' the prince asked softly.

Aurian's cold eyes blazed. 'Don't make the mistake of threatening me,' she growled. Shia, at her side, punctuated her words with a menacing snarl. The Mage pointed a finger at the prince. 'I could strike you down before those bolts had time to reach me. Would you care to reconsider?'

'Lower your weapons,' Yazour snapped. The troops, schooled to a man, obeyed their captain instantly.

'How dare you!' Harihn spat.

'He has more sense than you,' Aurian said, dismounting.

'I'm sure we can solve this problem without violence, Harihn. Anvar, let me see your horse.'

Anvar held the horse while the Mage, frowning with concentration, knelt to examine the injured hoof. 'Hmm,' she murmured softly, 'nothing to see – but what's this?'

As Anvar watched, her hands began to glow with a faint, violet-blue nimbus that extended over the foot of his mare. The Mage's concentration was so intense that it seemed to spread outwards, affecting all the watchers. No one stirred, or made the slightest sound. Just as the tension reached unbearable proportions, there was a grating sound and something slid out of the soft, sensitive sole of the hoof and into the Mage's hand. 'There,' Aurian crooned to the mare. 'That's better. Now to fix the damage.' The aura flared, then vanished. Aurian straightened, mopping her brow, as the horse set its hoof to the ground; lightly at first, then with increasing confidence.

A murmur went through the assembled soldiers. Aurian was examining something in her hand, her face suffused with rage. She held it out for Yazour's inspection. On her palm lay a small sliver of metal. 'The point of a dagger, if I'm not mistaken,' she said grimly. 'It had been driven into the hoof, and every time the mare stepped on it – the poor creature must have been in agony. Whoever did it knew that with his horse disabled Anvar would be left here to die. This was no accident – it was attempted murder!'

Yazour's face was livid. 'My apologies, Anvar, that this was allowed to happen. I swear the culprit will be found and punished. Are you all right, Lady?'

'I'm fine.' Aurian was swaying on her feet.

'Let me help you.' Yazour assisted the Mage back on to her horse, and she turned to Anvar, her expression troubled.

'Stay close,' she told him. 'Until we know who did this, we can't take any chances. I'll get Bohan to act as bodyguard.' She whirled her horse expertly on its hind legs, throwing up a luminous cloud of the scintillating dust, and was gone, calling for the eunuch as she went.

Harihn laughed scornfully. 'Bodyguard, indeed! You need a wet-nurse, Anvar. You should have remained a slave – or a eunuch. No man spends his life hiding behind a woman's skirts.'

'You . . .' Anvar leapt towards Harihn, ready to tear him from the saddle. He was brought up short by Yazour hauling on his arm.

'No, Anvar!' he said urgently. 'He wants you to attack him. If you threaten the prince, his soldiers will seize you, and not even your Lady herself could help you then.'

Anvar forced himself to breathe deeply, though he was trembling with rage. He looked Harihn straight in the eye. 'Another time,' he growled. Then, turning his back on the prince, he mounted his horse.

Harihn's comments rankled. Anvar rode beside Bohan, isolated behind a barrier of rage. As the mare's stride ate up the miles, so his anger fed upon itself. It was too much. Would he never be master of his own fate? First a servant, then a slave, and now, it seemed, less than nothing. And because he had finally acknowledged his debt to Aurian, it was humiliating that he should be forced to depend on her so much. For the gods' sake, he had promised Vannor that he would look after her! What a joke that had turned out to be. His furious thoughts chased in circles as he rode through the night.

'Anvar?'

So preoccupied was he that Anvar had missed Yazour's call to halt for the day. He looked up to see Aurian, slumped in the saddle, pulling back her veil from a face that was chalk-white. He knew that, because of her pregnancy, magic was taking a greater and greater toll on her strength, and her weariness was due to the healing of his horse. Grey guilt joined the red haze of anger in his mind. 'Lady, let me help you.' Dismounting quickly, he went to her side. At least I can fulfil a servant's tasks, he thought bitterly.

'It's all right.' Aurian slid to the ground, ignoring his outstretched hand.

Anvar gritted his teeth and seized her horse's bridle. 'I'll take care of this. You go and rest.'

'I can manage.' She tried to take the reins, but he snatched them angrily away.

'I said I'll do it!'

'What on earth's the matter?' The Mage had taken a step backwards, her eyes wide with astonishment.

'Nothing! I'm the bloody servant, aren't I? So I'll take care of the horse. It's all that people seem to think I'm fit for.'

The Mage stared at him, her lips set in a thin line, and beckoned Bohan across. 'Bohan, would you see to the horses, please? I need to talk to Anvar.'

The eunuch led the animals away. Aurian walked off with Shia at her heels, plainly expecting Anvar to follow. For some reason, that infuriated him even more.

Harihn's men had just finished setting up their tent. Aurian led Anvar aside. 'Now,' she said, 'What's wrong?'

'What's wrong?' Anvar exploded. 'Where shall I start?'

'Why not start with what made you so angry?' Her calm manner only made things worse, when he wanted a good blazing fight to work off his fury. 'All right!' he yelled. 'If you want to know, I'm sick of being rescued by you. I'm not stupid, or feeble, or incompetent. I'm a man as good as any other, but you make me less than a man.'

'But, Anvar,' Aurian protested, 'what could I do? I couldn't let you die in the slave camp. I had to use my powers again today to stop Harihn abandoning you. Would you rather . . .'

'That's just it!' Anvar jumped on her words. 'Your powers! Your accursed Magefolk powers! Well, let me tell you, Lady – I had powers too! There's Mage blood in my veins, but Miathan stole my powers and turned me into a servant.'

Anvar was so carried away by his wrath that he didn't see Aurian's stunned expression. He failed to notice that, for the first time, Miathan's silencing spell had failed. At the thought of the Archmage, the rage and resentment that he had been forced to suppress for so long, erupted beyond controlling. All Anvar could see was Miathan – Miathan, smug and gloating, hanging around his wrinkled neck the crystal that contained *his* powers, while he grovelled on the floor in agony. It was so real – so real!

Dear gods – it *was* real! Anvar's vision streaked and blurred, as though he was standing still while the world flashed past, too fast for his eyes to register. From far away, he seemed to hear Aurian's voice. 'Anvar, no!' Then the world whirled and settled, and he found himself in a dimly lit room with Miathan before him, asleep in bed, his eyes bound with a white cloth, and around his neck, twinkling softly in the lamplight, the crystal! Unable to help himself, Anvar reached out for the beautiful thing ... and there was a blinding flash of multi-coloured brilliance – a fierce, hot joyful force engulfing his body. He was in the crystal – the crystal was in him – the crystal *was* him!

Miathan gave a shriek of rage – of pain – of tearing loss. Anvar fled; the world flashed past him again in a blur of dizzy colour; but the Archmage, not old, not blind now but powerful and strong, was pursuing like a great black dragon formed from men's deepest terrors. The force of his rage was hot on Anvar's heels as he fled – where? How could he find his way back? Miathan drew nearer ... nearer ... Then suddenly a great glowing force like a spear of light shot past Anvar. It ploughed into the Archmage, knocking him back, down, away ...

'Come!' Anvar heard Aurian's voice and followed her gleaming light with relief, until, with a soundless explosion and a wrenching jolt, he found himself sprawled on the floor of the tent.

Aurian lay nearby. Her eyes flicked open, and skewered him to the spot. Anvar braced himself to meet her gaze. Anger he found there, and confusion; and worst of all, a sick, sinking fear for his safety that was entwined with the memory of an older, greater grief. It was as though her eyes were forest pools, and he could see her thoughts moving like elusive fish beneath the surface. 'What have you done?' she whispered. 'How could you do it?'

Anvar could not reply. He felt oddly elsewhere, as though a fathomless space surrounded him in place of the close silken walls of the tent. A space into which he might easily fall ... The floor seemed to ripple and melt beneath him, and he seized the Mage's hand in panic.

Aurian sat up, peering at him intently. 'Close your eyes,' she said, her tone suddenly crisp and businesslike. 'Concentrate on your body. You came back too quickly, and you aren't quite with yourself. Feel your body, Anvar. Feel your heart beating; the solid ground beneath you; the heat of the tent on your skin.' She leaned forward until her face was close to his own. Anvar looked into the green depths of her eyes; saw the long, curling

485

sweep of her lashes, the clean arch of her brows, the proud, chiselled sculpting of her high cheekbones and jutting nose. Gem dust glittered like a starfall in the slumbering fire of her hair, and he had a sudden, vivid memory of her standing on the tower stairs on a long-ago Solstice Morn, her head crowned with snowflake diamonds.

'Think of your body – not mine!' Aurian said tartly, and Anvar blushed. He had not considered that she might see his thoughts as clearly as he could see hers.

'It's all right – I feel better now.' He couldn't meet her eyes.

'Good,' she snapped, 'because you've some explaining to do.'

Just then Bohan entered, his eyes screwed up against the growing glare outside. He carried their food and water, his expression reproaching them for their forgetfulness.

'Bohan, what would we do without you?' Aurian said. The eunuch's face was alight with pleasure as he left. 'Eat,' she urged Anvar. 'Travelling out of your body uses a lot of energy.'

Anvar found he was trembling, and took a hasty bite out of a strip of dried meat. 'Is that what I did?'

Aurian sighed. 'Yes, Anvar,' she said, with laboured patience. 'That is what you did. Now in the name of all the gods will you please tell me what's going on?'

At the reminder of his narrow escape from the Archmage, Anvar froze. 'He – *he* couldn't follow us, could he?'

'No.' Aurian spoke reassuringly. 'I hit him too hard. It'll take him a while to find his body again. I wish I could have finished him, but when we are out of our bodies we're on another level of reality. A Mage can be trapped there if his body is destroyed in his absence, but he can't be killed. Anyway, forget Miathan. Let's talk about you.'

In a voice that shook with emotion, Anvar told her of Ria's death and the discovery of his powers. He went on to describe what Miathan had done to him, and ended with his escape from the kitchens and his meeting with Aurian at the garrison.

The Mage was staring at him open-mouthed. 'That's monstrous!' She struck the floor with her fist, looking utterly shaken. 'How could Miathan have done such a thing? If only I'd known. If only you could have told me.'

Anvar shrugged. 'I probably wouldn't have. I didn't trust you then. I thought you were like the others, and in league with Miathan. I know better now.' He swallowed hard.

'I'd like to know how you broke Miathan's spell.' Aurian was suddenly all practicality again. 'Also what happened when you – went off like that!'

'I can answer the second part.' And he told her what he had done.

'You got them back?' Aurian looked thunderstruck. 'No wonder Miathan was furious.' She snapped her fingers. 'Furious! Of course! Anvar, I've just worked out how you did it. In order for a spell like the one Miathan laid on you to work, you had to believe you would suffer if you said anything. Today you were so angry that it blinded you to the consequences – and your rage gave you the impetus you needed to break free.'

Anvar was appalled. 'Do you mean,' he said slowly, 'that I brought that suffering on myself all those years?'

'Of course not. Your acceptance was only part of the spell. If you had still been within Miathan's vicinity, I doubt you would ever have won free. But he is far away, and his power must have been weakened by my attack on him. That and your anger gave you the opening, and your powers drew you back to them.' She fell silent, staring at him as though he were a stranger. 'I still can't believe it, Anvar. You, a Mage.'

'Does it make that much difference?' It came out sharper than he'd intended, and Anvar realized that he was afraid, mortally afraid, that she would react as Miathan had done, and see him as some kind of monster.

'No!' Aurian's denial was swift and indignant, but then she looked away. 'Yes,' she sighed. 'I can't believe it, Anvar. You . . . *his* son . . .'

'Don't ever say that!' Anvar snarled. 'I'm not Miathan's son, and never will be. My mother was one of the Mortals he despised. You know what he did to me – to you and Forral. Do you think I could ever be like him?'

Aurian glanced away from him, shamefaced. 'Fool that I am,' she said at last. 'You're right – oh, gods, you're right! You could never be capable of Miathan's evil. You were as much a

487

victim as Forral and I.' She held out her hand to him. 'Can you ever forgive me, Anvar?'

Weak with relief, Anvar took her proffered hand. 'My own dear Lady! I don't ever want to become a Mage like Miathan, but I'm not afraid to become a Mage like you. On the contrary, I hope I will. That is – if you'd teach me?'

'Me?' Her eyes sparkled with delight.

'You must admit I'm a bit stuck for choice.'

'You . . .' Aurian burst out indignantly, and Anvar grinned. Aurian broke into peals of mirth. 'Wretch!' she growled. 'I can see this will take some getting used to. I would be proud to teach you, my friend, if you're sure you really want me.'

'Of course I do. Of all the Magefolk, you're the only one I'd ever choose.'

After that momentous day, their journey settled into a regular pattern. Anvar and Aurian continued to share a tent through the daylight hours with Shia, who guarded their privacy while the Mage began to teach Anvar how to use and control his power. Now that Aurian's pregnancy was well into its fourth month, they knew their time was short. There would be a limit to the theory she could teach him when she could not demonstrate the practice herself. Their first task was determining where Anvar's talents lay, and Aurian was amazed to discover that he too had powers that crossed the whole spectrum of magic, though his strengths and weaknesses seemed to lie in different areas from her own. While her dominant talents lay in the domains of Fire and Earth – not surprising, with her parentage – Anvar found these harder to master. But he excelled at Air-magic, and Aurian suspected that when they had more water available for manipulation he would be adept at Water-magic too. Since these two domains naturally combined to produce Weather-magic, it seemed that Eliseth might eventually find herself with some competition. But that was for the future. Anvar was a raw beginner, and he had a long way to go.

Each day, while the rest of the camp slept, Aurian would drill him mercilessly until they were both exhausted. During her time at the garrison, Parric had taught the Mage the trick of snatching valuable sleep whilst on horseback, and this too she passed on to Anvar. They spent their nightly journeys riding in a light doze, secure in the knowledge that the horses would remain with their companions. It earned them a good deal of teasing from Yazour, Eliizar, and particularly Nereni, but they soon learned to play up to the ribald speculations about their activities during the rest periods. It was safer than letting out the secret of Anvar's newfound powers.

One by one, the glittering nights and dazzling days ticked by, like bright beads strung on a thread of travel. Yazour, to his frustration, had come no nearer to finding that would-be assassin, but, perhaps due to his increased vigilance, there were no further attempts on Anvar's life. They saw little of Harihn. As the miles increased between the prince and his kingdom, he grew more aloof and shorter of temper, and most of his people were content to give him a wide berth. But at least he left Aurian and Anvar alone, and they were glad, though Aurian often wished that she could talk with him, and perhaps ease his mind. She knew how it felt to be exiled, and understood that he must be regretting his decision to relinquish his throne. She often found herself wondering what the future held for him.

Anvar, however, had his own ideas about the cause of the Khisal's fey mood. From certain veiled comments that Harihn had made, and from the way his eyes tended to linger speculatively on Aurian, and coldly on himself, Anvar began to suspect that his news about Sara's barrenness had caused a change of heart in the prince. In short, he was thinking of returning to claim his throne, and he needed Aurian's help to win it. Unaccustomed to thinking of women as having free will, he saw Anvar as the main obstacle to his plan. Though he had no actual proof, Anvar began to have a fair suspicion that Harihn had been the one who had lamed his horse. Who else could have passed Yazour's guards unchallenged? The two Magefolk were heavily outnumbered, however, and still in need of the Khisal's help to survive the desert crossing. Anvar kept his thought to himself, but as the journey continued he remained constantly on his guard; well aware that the further they went, the more likely Harihn was to make another attempt on his life.

Yazour guided them well, steering an unerring course along the ancient route that crossed the desert from oasis to oasis. Every two or three nights, a ragged outcrop of rocks would be seen in the distance, emerging from the mantle of gem dust, and the horses and mules would snort eagerly, picking up their pace as they scented water ahead. The prince and his followers would camp beside a stony basin that cradled a sweet pool formed by springs originating deep within the ridge that stretched, according to Yazour, right across the desert like a knobbly spine, most of it buried beneath the jewelled sands. Each life-giving source of water had a name, and he taught the Mages to recite them in order; something that his people learned in infancy. They encountered the first, Abala, on the third night of their trek, and this was followed by Ciphala, Biabeh, Tuvar, Yezbeh and Ecchith, which would approximately mark the halfway point of their journey. Fair Dhiammara followed, then Varizh, Efchar, Zorbeh, Orbah, and finally Aramizal.

'Wait until we reach Dhiammara!' Yazour smiled at the Mages. 'That, to my mind, is the most spectacular sight in the desert, and well worth this hard journey to see.'

'Romantic nonsense!' scoffed Eliizar, who had travelled the desert regularly in his youth. 'The fairest oasis in this waste is Aramizal, because there you begin the final step of the journey, and can see the mountains of the Winged Folk rising in the distance to mark the end of the desert.'

'Winged Folk, indeed!' Yazour scoffed. 'And you call me romantic. You might as well expect to see a dragon.'

'None the less,' Eliizar insisted, 'they exist. Their citadel is high in the inaccessible peaks, where men cannot climb.'

'How do you know it's there, then?' Yazour countered.

'It is there,' Aurian interrupted, surprising them both. 'I have it on the best authority.' She smiled, remembering her friend the Leviathan, and looked dreamily away to the north, as though trying to see across the intervening miles to the soaring lands of the Skyfolk.

Aerillia, the city of the Winged Folk, was carved out of the highest peak of the northern mountain range. The palace, an airy confection of hanging turrets and terraces, was situated on and within the topmost pinnacle, and Raven's tower room commanded a breathtaking view over the entire city. She was looking out of the window now, gazing over the snowy crags below at the lights that twinkled sharply in the clear icy air. Her shoulders were slumped in dejection, causing her great wings to droop, their glossy, iridescent black tips trailing unheeded on the floor.

'Raven?'

The princess spun round, scowling. 'Go away, mother! I refuse to marry the High Priest, and that is my final word on the matter.'

'It is not!' Grief and strain had etched new lines on Flamewing's face, but the queen's voice still carried its customary ring of authority. She paced the small circular room, her red-gold wings rustling, her expression defensive and angry. 'You will do as you're bid,' she told her daughter. 'You are a princess of the blood royal, Raven; daughter of a queen. You were brought up to recognize that you have responsibilities to your people and to the throne, one of them being that you must marry to advantage.'

'Whose advantage?' Raven cried. 'Mine? Yours? If I marry that corrupt old monster, who will really benefit? He will, and that's all! He can do nothing to help us, mother. He's deceiving you, and all our people. He has no influence with the Sky God. Have his sacrifices made any difference? All those lives – the lives of our people, that we swore to protect – wasted, and still this dread and untimely winter is upon us. And now his price for our salvation is my hand. Which coincidentally will put him in an unassailable position of power. Can you not see that he's a fraud? How can you be so dense?'

'How dare you!' The sound of the blow seemed to echo in the silence that followed. Raven staggered, horrified, her hand pressed to her face and tears in her great dark eyes. Never before had Flamewing raised her hand to her beloved daughter.

'Mother, please.' Her voice was little more than a whisper. 'You know the way of our people. We mate for life. If I wed Blacktalon, I will spend the rest of my days in misery with

491

someone I fear and loathe. Though princesses must marry suitably, never has one been asked to submit to this. I beg you, do not force me marry him. He is evil, I know it.'

Flamewing sighed. 'Child, never in our history since the Cataclysm have we suffered peril like this. Never has there been such sudden and intense cold. Nothing will grow on our terraces. All the animals are dead, or have left for warmer climes. This winter kills everything it touches. Blacktalon's intercession is our only hope. Our people are dying, Raven! I am more sorry than I can say, but I have no choice. Tomorrow you will wed Blacktalon, and that's an end to it. Now – he wishes to speak with you, and you will be civil to him. Your people need you, Raven. You were brought up a princess – act like one!' She swept quickly out of the room, as though the sight of her daughter together with the High Priest was more than she could bear.

Blacktalon's head was bald, and painted all over with arcane designs and magical symbols. His face was haggard and cruel, with its hooked nose and burning, fanatic's eyes. His wing feathers were a dull and dusty black, and his robes matched their colour exactly. His arrogance in the presence of a royal princess was so obnoxious that Raven wanted to strike him. 'I have come to make my felicitations to my bride on the eve of her wedding,' he leered. 'How lovely you look, my dear. I can hardly wait.' He reached out greedy hands to touch her, and Raven backed away hastily, drawing her dagger. 'Get away from me!' she spat. 'I'd rather die than marry you, you filthy old vulture!'

The High Priest smiled, but there was no humour in his face. 'Lovely,' he said. 'Such a little spitfire! How glad I am that you feel this way. It will make your conquest all the more enjoyable.'

'Don't count on it,' Raven retorted through gritted teeth.

'Oh, but I do, my dear. Once you are mine, a few sound thrashings will soon take the edge off your temper.'

Raven gasped. 'You would never dare!'

'I would hardly dare offer violence to the princess, no.' Blacktalon shrugged. 'How I chastise my mate, however, is my own affair – as you will discover. Pleasant dreams, my little bride. Sleep well – while you have the chance!'

492

After Blacktalon had left, Raven wasted few minutes in weeping. Time had suddenly become too precious for that, for she knew now that her only hope lay in escape. It took her about an hour of pacing back and forth behind her locked door to formulate her plans. She knew it would never occur to them that she might run away. The Winged Folk were prohibited by an ancient law from leaving their mountain kingdom. Raven had often wondered why, but no one seemed able, or willing, to tell her the answer. If anyone should leave, they were automatically condemned to death should they ever try to return, and the prohibition was so ingrained that no one from the winged race would normally even consider the notion. The very thought of what she was about to do set Raven's hands shaking so much that her preparations took twice as long as they should have done.

'I have no alternative,' Raven told herself firmly, as she put bread and meat from her uneaten supper into a small bag which tied to her belt, and fished her crossbow out from its hiding place under the bed. She braided her unruly cloud of fine dark hair and dressed in her flying clothes – a black leather kilted tunic that left her limbs free for easy movement and leather sandals with thongs that cross-tied to her knees. She decided not to bother with anything else. Raven's race was impervious to normal cold, and she hoped to move quickly away from the chill of this unnatural winter. Thrusting her dagger into her belt, she went to the window. Launching herself from the sill would cause her no problems. She had been doing it since childhood, when she had first discovered the lure of un-authorized flights. For once, she was glad that her mother had insisted that she take her share of the tedious burden of palace administration. She knew the position of every sentry in the city, and, more important, how they might be avoided.

Another of the unpredictable blizzards had blown up, and Raven flinched at the violence of the storm outside. But though it was folly, she would have to set out now, or not at all. If she should be caught, the consequences did not bear thinking about. As she climbed on to the windowsill Raven hesitated, overcome by the magnitude of the step she was about to take. If her mother had been right after all, she was betraying her entire race. Furthermore, if she left the mountains her life would be forfeit. There could be no returning. Thoughtfully, she touched the side of her face, where the imprint of her mother's hand still burned, and remembered the cruelty in Blacktalon's eyes. That was enough. Taking a deep breath, Raven leapt from the sill and spread her great dark wings, catching the air beneath them to halt her plummeting fall. Swooping round the shadowed side of the pinnacle-palace like a hunting bat, she launched herself away from her home and the lands of her people.

Flying in the teeth of the blizzard was even worse than she had imagined. Visibility was poor to nonexistent in the whirling white cloud. The strong wind gusted and eddied, buffeting her mercilessly, and on several occasions almost hurling her violently against the walls of the city's delicately wrought towers. If she'd had time to spare for thinking, Raven might have comforted herself with the thought that her escape must certainly go undetected, but it was taking every scrap of her concentration merely to stay airborne and to avoid crashing into obstacles. Her sense of direction was hopelessly confused, and she could only pray that she was keeping a level line of flight, and not going round in a circle that would eventually return her to the city – and Blacktalon.

Raven was chilled to the bone. It was an unfamiliar sensation and decidedly unpleasant, as well as frightening. Her ears and teeth ached from the wind's bite, and her wings felt stiff and slow to respond. Even her mind was becoming sluggish and confused. How long had she been flying? Why was she all alone in this lethal storm? Where had she come from, and where was she going? How much longer could her aching wings keep her aloft?

Suddenly Raven's left foot hit something hard and jagged. It was caught and wrenched, throwing her forward, off balance. She rolled helplessly head over heels in a tangle of flailing limbs and thrashing wings, bruising herself on icy rocks as she slithered to an undignified halt upside down in a snowdrift. Too battered and shaken to do anything else, she burst into tears.

'Where am I?' Raven opened her eyes. For a moment fear

obscured her thoughts, but she was not the daughter of a queen for nothing. She breathed deeply, forcing herself to be calm, and took stock of her surroundings. There was little to see. Her aching body was crammed into a narrow crevice between some rocks, and a barrier of drifted snow obscured the opening. Gradually her mind returned to the previous night, and she shuddered at her narrow escape from death. Why, she had crashed right into the mountain! Hesitantly she uncurled herself to examine her injured foot, afraid of what she might find. It was bad enough. The lacings of her sandal cut into the swollen flesh, and it was badly bruised and torn. Gritting her teeth against the pain, she melted snow in her hands to clean the abrasions. Snow might reduce the swelling, too, and she would not be helpless as long as she could fly.

Raven gasped, remembering her fall among the rocks as she had landed. Her wings . . . There was no room to move them in the crevice. With frantic haste she began to dig her way out, scooping great chunks of deep-piled snow aside with her arms. Dimly, now, she remembered crawling into the niche, instinctively seeking shelter from the storm. The way out seemed further than she recalled, but at last the final inches of the snow wall collapsed beneath her determined assault, and she burst into the open.

Using the rocks for support Raven hauled herself up, wincing as her injured foot touched the ground. It would be of little use for a while, but her wings were her chief concern. Leaning on the rocks for balance, she extended the once glossy black spans. They were stiff, but there was no pain and seemingly little damage. She'd lost some feathers; her plumage was battered and bedraggled now, but the snow had broken the worst of her fall. Taking a deep breath, she launched herself upward as best she could with one leg injured. She over-balanced and almost went sprawling, but to her relief her wings took her weight and she began to beat steadily upward. Now that her main worry had been quelled, she needed to look around her and decide what to do next.

The sky was an absolute joy after looking so long at nothing but grey clouds. Raven revelled in the soft rose, the delicate green, the translucent blues and dazzling gold of the sunset.

For a time she was too captivated by its beauty to look down, but when at last the colours faded from the sky she was astonished to find them echoed on the earth beneath. For a moment her head whirled with disorientation, but when she looked directly below her, she could see the plateau from which she had taken off. She had landed on the very last of the mountains. As its slopes descended, the snow cover thinned and eventually vanished, leaving dark tumbled rocks stretching down to a dark and sinister forest below. Beyond, the rippling sea of sunset hues extended as far as she could see. Raven caught her breath. She'd come south, then, and this was the legendary jewelled desert!

The winged girl returned to the plateau to rest. She tired easily after the night's exertions, and she needed to think – and eat. Having no experience of journeying, she attacked the contents of her bag voraciously, with no thought of where her next meal might come from. As she ate, she considered her next step. Raven had left the palace with no idea of where she might go, or how she was to live.

For the first time, she was truly afraid. What if the folk out here were like Blacktalon or worse? But the thought of the High Priest and the fate that awaited her was enough to steel her resolve. She would have to find help, however. Raven was a pampered princess, and she had sense enough to realize that she had no notion of how to survive alone. Besides, she told herself, if they threaten me, I can always fly away again. The question of where to go was easily decided. She could not return north. They would be hunting for her now. The thought of pursuit made her shudder. It was essential that she go immediately. South, away from the mountains of her birth. The sparkling sands seemed to provide enough light for her to travel by night. Taking a deep breath, Raven flexed her wings and launched into the air, heading south, across the glowing desert.

31
Dhiammara

'Behold, fair Dhiammara!'

'You're joking!' Aurian turned to Yazour in patent disbelief. By the eighteenth night of the journey, the desert's beauty had begun to pall. The gem dust got everywhere: in her hair, her throat, even inside her clothes; and because the oases they had visited were needed for vital drinking water, bathing had been forbidden. The Mage felt unspeakably filthy, and she itched. Her babe stole the nourishment from her slender rations, leaving her constantly ravenous, even though Bohan and Anvar always forced some of their food upon her. The intensive teaching sessions with Anvar had deprived them both of much needed sleep and she felt tired and short-tempered, her eyes gritty and stinging from the dazzle of the sands. She was definitely not in the mood for jokes.

Aurian slowed her horse, lifting the veil from her eyes, and squinted into the glare. Silhouetted against the moon-bright sky, the solitary mountain loomed impossibly high. Its top was oddly truncated, as if it had been lopped off by some gargantuan sword, and the sheer sides gleamed with a mirror brightness, as though polished. The structure showed no signs of weathering, and that too, in this place of scouring sand-storms, was impossible. 'That's not a natural formation!' she accused.

'I agree, though no one knows its history,' Yazour replied. 'Close up, its scale is staggering. It may look enormous now, but distance is deceptive in the desert.'

He was right, Aurian discovered. It took several hours' hard riding to reach the towering peak, and by the time they approached its sheer walls the horizon was growing pale. The mountain was immense, its size exaggerated by the fact that the land did not rise gradually towards it. The slender cone erupted cleanly from the surrounding sands, like an island from the sea. For the last miles of the ride it had been impossible to take in the entire structure, and now they had reached its foot all that could be seen was a vertical wall of darkly gleaming rock that stretched out of sight above them and for miles to either side. Yazour turned aside, parallel to the polished wall, and in a short time Aurian saw a darker shadow on the stone; a narrow opening just high enough to admit a horse.

One by one the riders led their animals through the entrance and into the cool darkness beyond, and torches, stacked to one side of the opening, were kindled and set into brackets on the walls. As the light grew, Aurian stared around her in disbelief. The cavern was huge, its ceiling lost in the shadows above. To her left, half of the floor space was taken up by two pools, the higher set on a stony shelf, its waters trickling down in a small cascade to the lower. A sloping stone ramp led to the upper pool, where the horses and mules were being taken to drink. The floor of the cavern was level rock, drifted in places with glowing gem sand that had been blown inside by the wind. This, along with the reflections from the glassy walls, served to augment the torchlight.

'This place is incredible!' Anvar, at the Mage's side, was looking around him with wide eyes.

'The lower pool is for bathing,' Yazour said. 'We keep a goodly stock of food and fuel here, so we can replenish your supplies, and today we'll feast, or so it will seem after all this rationing. We will rest here for two or three days before going on.'

'Wonderful!' Aurian smiled at him, tacitly apologizing for her recent moodiness. 'I never thought I'd get tired of riding, but right now I never want to see a horse again. I could kill for a bath, a hot meal, and a long sleep.'

'Then you shall have them.' Anvar put his arm around her and led her away to the right, where a series of small fires were being kindled close to a vent in the rock that drew the smoke away out of the cavern.

Since Anvar had regained his powers and started learning from the Mage, their relationship had altered subtly. Everyone except Bohan and Shia, who were party to the secret, accepted him as Aurian's husband, but even when the two of them were alone his old subservience had dropped away, to the point where he had been very firm about her taking extra food from himself and the eunuch. Aurian, to her surprise, had found herself not minding Anvar's new assertiveness. Since their escape from Nexis she had been forced to be the strong one, to shoulder the burden of their journey, and having someone share the responsibility had come as a relief. Although her occasional lack of patience as a teacher, coupled with their mutual tiredness, had led to some sharp words between them – Anvar, it seemed, had Magefolk stubbornness to match her own – a close and comforting friendship had developed between them that did much to ease the loneliness that was their common bond.

The Mages shared a fire with Eliizar and Nereni. While they waited for supper to cook they talked, glad of the opportunity after the enforced isolation of the desert camps. Eliizar, free of the arena and back with a military company where he belonged, seemed to have shed years during the journey. His one eye glowed with enthusiasm as he spoke of the desert he loved. Nereni, plump and smiling, was also glad to have left the arena, but was finding the journey a trial. Aurian sympathized. If she, an expert horsewoman, was wearied by the continuous riding, she hardly dared imagine what it must be like for a beginner like Nereni. Anvar, who'd had little opportunity to ride during his time at the academy except when Aurian had invented the occasional errand to give him an outing, was also feeling the strain. 'It's all right for you,' he teased Nereni, rolling an expressive eye at her rounded backside. 'At least you've got some padding between you and the saddle.' She threw a spoon at him, making him duck, and the four of them collapsed in gales of mirth. Bohan, having cared for the horses, joined them to eat, as did Shia, who had been exploring the cave.

'I don't like it,' she told Aurian. 'I see nothing, but it feels – prickly.'

The Mage, intent on Nereni's delicately spiced stew, was not paying much attention. 'Maybe you have sand in your coat,' she replied absently, and soon forgot the conversation, little

499

knowing how it would come back to haunt her later. Now that she was full of good food, she found that her eyes refused to stay open any longer. The outline of the flames seemed to dance and blur in her vision, and the quiet sounds of conversation receded.

'Here you are, sleepyhead. Do it properly.'

She blinked, brought back to herself by Anvar's voice. He was holding out a blanket. 'I wanted to bathe,' she protested, but the words were swallowed in a yawn.

'Do it tomorrow. I don't mind sleeping with a dirty woman.'

'You're just as dirty,' Aurian began indignantly, and fell silent in dismay as she grasped the import of his words. Without the tent to shelter them, they would have to play out the charade of their marriage to the full. Why hadn't it occurred to her that this awkward situation might arise?

'It's all right,' Anvar said softly, and, wrapping the blanket snugly round her shoulders, he gathered her into his arms as they lay down. The warmth of his body felt good after the cool air of the cave, and soon she was relaxing drowsily against him. It had been so long since she had felt comforting arms around her at night. As Aurian drifted into sleep, her heart ached with longing for Forral.

The fragrance that teased her into wakefulness reminded her so strongly of the arena that she opened her eyes expecting to see the white walls of her old cell. Instead she saw Anvar, holding a steaming cup. 'I have a surprise for you,' he said. 'Your friend Eliizar brought his own supply of – '

'Liafa!' Aurian beamed, reaching greedily for the cup.

'And I thought Eliizar was exaggerating when he told me how much you loved that stuff. That's the first time I've seen you smile this early in the day!'

Aurian stuck out her tongue at him. 'It's all right for some. You look as though you've been up for ages.'

Anvar grinned. 'The men – being the earliest risers – had the first turn at the pool.' All traces of the sparkling dust had gone from his skin. His hair, curled and darkened now by the water, had grown during his time in slavery, and to keep the damp strands from his face he had copied Yazour, tying the errant locks back with a thong at the nape of his neck. It suited him, Aurian thought.

'What are you staring at? Have I missed a bit?'

'Who, me? Nothing.' Aurian floundered. 'I'd forgotten what you looked like under all that dust.'

'Well, it's the women's turn now, so you'd better hurry up if you want to get rid of your own layer.'

She put down the empty cup. 'It's a pity really. I must be worth a fortune in gems right now.'

Nereni was in the pool, splashing and laughing with the other women of Harihn's household. The Mage shed her dusty clothes and stepped into the water. It was not as cold as she had expected, and while it was shallow enough for standing, there was enough depth to swim. The bottom was coated in a soft layer of gem sand, doubtless shed by generations of dusty travellers. It gleamed underfoot, reflecting the torchlight from the walls. Nereni waded over and handed her a slab of rough soap.

'Real soap! Nereni, you think of everything.'

'But of course – and just as well, for you warriors.' Her plump face dimpled. 'I must go to prepare the day meal, but I will fetch you a cloth to dry yourself, and some clean robes.'

When Nereni had gone, Aurian washed thoroughly, glad to get the dust out of her hair. Mine is growing again too, she thought. Maybe I'll get Anvar to braid it for me soon. By the time she had finished the other women had left the pool, but she lingered for a while, enjoying the peace and solitude. At last, prompted by hunger, she went to rinse beneath the little waterfall before getting out.

The Mage had no suspicion of danger until it was too late. As she placed her hand against the smooth wall where the waterfall trickled down, a strident clamour tore the air like the shrieks of a vast, unimaginable beast in torment. The rock seemed to come alive beneath her fingers, trapping her hands, her arms, sucking her body inexorably into its soft, clinging maw. Aurian, despite her struggles, was snatched into the darkness beyond. Within seconds the wall had closed behind her, blank and featureless once more.

Anvar was racing towards the pool before the first heart-stopping echoes could die away. Yazour and Eliizar were close behind, their weapons drawn. By the time they reached the edge he was floundering through the water, searching for any trace of the Mage. They joined him, Yazour diving cleanly beneath the surface, Eliizar breaststroking across the pool. Then the clamour ceased abruptly, leaving only Anvar's anguished cries: 'Aurian! *Aurian!*'

The atmosphere in the camp was tense with apprehension. The women and children huddled together in the furthest corner away from the sinister pool, guarded by armed warriors. A squad of bowmen had their weapons trained on the still waters, ready to shoot at the first sign of a ripple on the smooth surface. A grim council had gathered by the prince's fire, and Harihn looked fearfully round at the faces of the small group. 'Some beast must have taken her,' he insisted. 'What else could have done this?'

'Sire, the pool was empty,' Yazour protested. 'I had it searched thoroughly, and there is no underwater access. There was no blood, nor any remains.'

'No!' Anvar cried. The cup of hot liafa that Nereni had forced upon him spilled, soaking into the blanket she had draped around his shivering shoulders. Yazour glanced at him apologetically, and Nereni took his hand, her tear-stained face filled with pity.

'There must have been something,' Harihn insisted, with a nervous glance at the pool. 'What else could make such dreadful cries? What if it should return? Must others die to convince you?'

'There is no proof.'

'We could search again.' Eliizar and Yazour, wet and shivering in their own blankets, spoke simultaneously, but Anvar heard the doubt in their voices. Harihn shook his head and stood up.

'It is pointless. She is surely dead. Prepare to leave, Yazour. We dare not linger in this place.'

'You bastard!' Anvar flung his blanket aside and, leaping over the fire, levelled a punch at the prince. The blow, with the impetus of his body behind it, knocked Harihn sprawling. Anvar landed on top of him, hitting out blindly. 'Coward!' he screamed. He was aware of blows on his body, but his rage made him oblivious of the pain. On top of Harihn's slights and insults, his arrogance and hostility, he planned to run away and abandon Aurian to her fate. Anvar intended to pound him into the ground. He felt strong arms pulling him, dragging him off the prince. Anvar fought the new assailants in a frenzy, resisting their attempts to pin him down, until a drench of cold water hit him hard in the face. The shock brought him sharply to his senses. Eliizar and Yazour were holding him down. Nereni stood over him, a dripping bowl in her hands.

Anvar blinked water and tears from his eyes. 'I thought you were my friends,' he muttered.

'We are, Anvar,' Yazour told him sadly, 'but the prince, unfortunately, is right.' He gestured to one side, pointing at the small group of children who huddled together, weeping and terrified. 'Would you sacrifice them also?' the warrior asked softly.

'I'm not leaving her!'

'You most certainly are not!' Harihn was scowling, and Anvar noted with satisfaction that his face was beginning to bruise and swell. The prince kicked out viciously, catching him beneath the ribs, and Anvar convulsed in pain.

'Sire!' Yazour's voice rose sharply in disgust at the cowardly attack. 'He will die if you abandon him here!'

'You have your orders, Yazour. For attacking me, this churl deserves to die. Anvar will be left behind.'

'Your Highness, the man is distraught. You cannot hold him responsible for his actions at such a time.'

'I'll have him executed now, if you'd prefer.' Harihn wiped blood from the corner of his mouth, glaring venomously at Anvar, who smiled grimly.

'Any excuse, eh, Harihn? Well, at last you have what you've wanted all along – but it's too late. You may get rid of me, but you'll never have Aurian now!' Turning his head, he spat at the prince's feet.

Harihn's face was livid. 'Silence, dog!' he roared. 'Yazour, make certain that all provisions are packed or destroyed! As you slowly starve, Anvar, I will rejoice in the thought of your suffering.'

'If Anvar is to be abandoned, he will not be alone.' Eliizar's

503

voice rang out. 'I would rather stay with him than travel another mile with you!'

'And I!' Nereni strode bristling to her husband's side.

Anvar tried to protest, but he was astonished into silence by a voice that seemed to come from within his own head. 'I too will stay.' He stared in amazement as Shia's face appeared, her eyes blazing into his own. Bohan joined her, nodding his own silent support.

Harihn shrugged. 'Very well.'

'At least leave them horses, sire, and some provisions,' Yazour protested.

'No! And if I hear another word from you on the subject, you will die beside them.'

The warrior blanched. 'All this time I have served you,' he said tightly, 'and I never knew what you were. I look into your face, and I see your father.' Turning his back on the prince, he walked away to assemble his men.

The friends were guarded by a ring of bowmen while the others made their preparations for leaving. Though Anvar was desperate to continue the search for Aurian, Harihn had left orders that they were to be shot if one of them so much as stirred. While they waited, he tried in vain to persuade his companions not to sacrifice themselves, but Eliizar and Nereni were united in their indignation at such an idea, and Bohan looked hurt at the mere suggestion. Shia, though she did not speak again, snarled at him so fiercely that Anvar would have backed away if he could. She looked so savage that he wondered if he had imagined her voice in his mind. As soon as night fell outside, the prince's company departed, and the cavern seemed eerily quiet after they had gone. Anvar, without a word, got up and strode back to the pool. The others fanned out to search the cave once again.

Anvar sat, lost in wretchedness, beside the cavern entrance, his aching head buried in his hands. Reflected dawnlight gleamed through the opening. They had still found no sign of Aurian. How long had it been now? He cast his mind back over the hours since their arrival in accursed Dhiammara. They had eaten first – their laughter during that feast seemed like a distant dream now – and slept in each other's arms through the remainder of the day and part of the following night. Then Aurian had gone to bathe in the pool. Oh, Aurian! Why didn't I just let you sleep? he thought. She had been lost for the rest of that night, the following day, and another night of frantic, fruitless searching. Surely there could be no hope now?

Someone touched his shoulder, and he turned to see Nereni. 'Yazour hid some supplies for us at the back of the cave. Come and eat, Anvar. This does you no good.'

'How can you expect me to eat?' Anvar wanted to shout at her to leave him alone, but he knew that she was grieving too, and concerned for him.

She put a maternal arm around his shoulders. 'I'm sorry,' she murmured. 'I know how much you loved her.'

'You don't!' he retorted bitterly. 'I didn't know myself, until I lost her!'

Nereni went away sighing. Anvar wished that she and the others had saved themselves and gone with Harihn. For himself he didn't care. What a cruel irony! Until these last weeks, when his discovery of magic had brought them so close together, he had never admitted the depth of his feelings for Aurian, and now it was too late. It had all started long ago, on that wonderful Solstice Night when they had celebrated with Forral. But Anvar had hidden the truth from himself then.

I knew it in my heart that she was not for me, and never could be. But Aurian's love of Forral, my own hatred of the Magefolk, and then the return of Sara, all allowed me to run away from the fact that I loved her. How could I have been so blind? Self-protection, he thought ruefully. Aurian's love for Forral was unswerving while he lived, and has remained that way since his death. I knew she'd never want anyone else. And now I'll never even see her again. Never again will I feel the comfort of her friendship, the joy of her presence. She's gone.

'She is not!' The voice was Shia's.

Anvar looked up through scalding tears. 'What did you say?'

'Frame your thoughts clearly, man. You're not very good at this. But you are of the same kind as her, so I can talk to you, if I choose to. Put aside this useless grief and think. Aurian is my friend, and our minds are linked. If she were dead, I

505

would surely know. But if she lives, why can I not reach her?'

'Great gods, you're right!' Hope flared like a beacon in Anvar's breast. 'She told me that the Magefolk knew when one of their kind died. So if she were – '

'Then you would have known also,' Shia finished for him.

'But if she's beyond your reach, where is she?'

'Clear your mind, man. Listen.' Shia sat, curling her tail neatly around her paws. 'When you two were in the tent, doing things – '

'We did not!'

'Not those things, stupid.'

'Oh. You mean the magic.'

'It always gives me a most unpleasant prickly feeling in my fur.' Her tail twitched. 'I get it in this cave, too.'

'Then it wasn't a beast? You think Aurian was trapped by magic? But I've been all over that wretched pool, and never felt a thing.'

'If Aurian had felt it, would it have trapped her?' Shia asked pointedly.

'So whatever it is, it must still be there!' He scrambled to his feet and ran. Reaching the pool, he plunged in. What exactly was he looking for? Some hidden opening, perhaps? He paused, up to his waist in water, looking around wildly. It couldn't be beneath the surface – the pool had been searched from end to end. Then it came to him. Where was the obvious place to put a door? In a wall, of course. His eyes went automatically to the smooth flat surface where the waterfall trickled down.

'Anvar! What are you doing?' The others had gathered on the brink of the pool. Ignoring them, he waded across to the wall and began feeling along it with both hands.

'I've found it!' Anvar's triumphant shout was drowned in the strident shriek of the alarm. His jubilation turned to horror as the stone began to melt beneath his hands, becoming clinging and viscous, sucking him in like quicksand, drawing his head and shoulders inside. The stuff enveloped him, so that he couldn't breathe. He flailed in panic, and then his face broke through into the air, though he could see nothing in the utter darkness beyond. 'Aurian?' he called. There was no reply. But

506

his body was almost through the constricting portal. He felt a glassy surface beneath his fingers and clawed at it frantically, trying to haul himself forward. Then his feet were snatched in an iron grip. Something was pulling him back. 'No!' he howled. He was so close – he had to go on! But inch by inch he slid backwards, until his cries were drowned once more in the suffocating ooze of the portal. There was a jerk on his ankles, and he shot out into the pool on top of Bohan, who hauled him, struggling, to the water's edge.

'Imbecile!' Shia's claws were sheathed, but the swipe from her massive paw knocked him flying.

Anvar sat up groggily. 'Damn you!' he snarled at Bohan. 'I was almost through!'

'We had no choice,' Eliizar protested. 'What good would it do to have you both trapped?'

'Think!' Shia's thought was a whiplash across Anvar's mind. 'We need a way to keep the portal from closing, so we can all get in, and, more important, out again.'

'Anvar, did you see her?' Nereni asked anxiously.

'I saw nothing – it was too dark. But I called, and she didn't answer,' he told her miserably.

Eliizar frowned. 'But I examined that rock when I searched the pool, and it was quite impervious.'

Anvar stared at him. 'So it only responds to Magefolk,' he said slowly.

'Sorcerers?' Eliizar gasped. He backed away hastily, making a sign against evil. 'But you are not . . .'

'I am, Eliizar – just like Aurian.'

Nereni, though wide-eyed, was more practical than her husband. She tugged urgently at Anvar's arm. 'Can you use this sorcery to open the way for us?'

Could he? She might be right, but how? Anvar had no idea how the magic of the portal worked – he was still too much of a beginner at this kind of thing, and there had been little time for Aurian to teach him much. Then the solution came to him in a blinding flash. One of the first spells that Aurian had taught him, with the terror of the Nihilim still fresh in her mind. 'Nereni, I think I can!'

Anvar positioned himself before the featureless stone of the

507

portal. Bohan stood behind him, his massive arms locked around the Mage's waist. Eliizar and Nereni waited on the brink of the pool, not daring, to the sword master's obvious shame, to approach any closer.

'Are you ready, Bohan?' Anvar glanced back over his shoulder. The eunuch nodded, tightening his grip. 'Now!' Anvar muttered, and placed his hand upon the stone.

Again, the shrieking clamour rang out. The rock became fluid and clinging, clutching at Anvar's arm to draw him within. But this time Bohan held him firmly, fighting the pull. Anvar concentrated with all his might, trying to block out the shrill distraction of the alarm. He had to get this right. Sweat broke out on his brow. Extending his free hand, he carefully constructed Finbarr's time spell – and toppled backwards with Bohan into the water as the force that pulled at them suddenly ceased. Anvar struggled to his feet, spluttering and panting, and reached out to the stone. Bohan forestalled him, thrusting his own fist straight through and pulling it out again with ease.

'It worked!' Anvar yelled. 'Eliizar, it worked! I've taken the portal out of time! We can go through now.'

Shia bounded forward, needing no further urging, but Eliizar stood back, white-faced. 'I – I cannot!' he gasped. 'Anvar, forgive me, but sorcery . . . I cannot!'

Anvar grasped his shoulder. 'Don't worry, Eliizar – we all have our fears.' With a pang, he remembered saying the same thing to Aurian, on top of the cliff. 'I must go.' He turned back to the portal, where Bohan and Shia waited, plainly anxious to be moving. 'You and Nereni stay here, and wait for us. We'll be as quick as we can.'

'Wait!' Nereni came running, splashing through the water in her haste. 'Here.' She thrust a bundle into her hands. 'Here is a water bag, and food – the poor girl will be starving – and I put in a robe for her, and her boots – and she might need these.' She handed him Aurian's sword and staff. 'Hurry,' she urged, and reached up to kiss his cheek. 'Hurry, Anvar, and come back safe.'

It was difficult to force a way through the viscous rock without the spell of the portal to draw them. Shia, bristling with impatience, went first, with Anvar and Bohan helping her by

508

pushing from behind. Anvar followed, feeling the cat's massive jaws grasp his collar to pull him through. It was pitch dark within, even to his Mage's night vision. He turned and groped for Bohan's hand, and Shia helped him haul the eunuch through. Bohan had brought a torch, but when he kindled it the flame gave no light.

'What on earth . . .' Anvar gasped. He could see it flickering in mid-air like a pale, disembodied wraith, but that was all. It illuminated absolutely nothing.

'Magic!' Shia spat disgustedly. '*You* make some light!'

Anvar sighed. Fire-magic was not his strong point, but by dint of much concentration he managed to form a rather wobbly ball of Magelight; and fell back, screaming, as the interior chamber burst into eye-searing brilliance.

'Put it out!' Shia roared in agony. Anvar snuffed his flame, his eyes watering and blinded with crimson and green spots of dazzle. He picked himself up, only to be flattened again as the entire chamber lurched into motion with a grinding roar, rushing upward with terrifying speed.

As Anvar's vision cleared, he saw that the chamber was now illuminated by a soft glow that seemed to emanate from the walls. The walls! His mind reeled dizzily. He was within a hollowed-out gem! All around him, the gleaming facets reflected myriad images of himself, Shia and Bohan. When he moved, the images lurched and swooped, making him sick with disorientation. It was as though he, too, was part of the reflections; as though his soul, his very self, was being sucked away into the walls. Beside him, Shia whimpered unhappily. It was the first time he had ever heard the great cat show the slightest sign of fear. 'It's all right.' He tried to sound convincing. 'Lie still and close your eyes. We're being taken somewhere – maybe to the top of the mountain. It's bound to stop when we reach it.'

'For their sake, I had better not find whoever created this thing,' Shia muttered wrathfully. Her words made Anvar wonder just who the creators were. This was far beyond the power of his own Magefolk. Just who – or what – was he dealing with here? And what had they done to Aurian?

'Now, how do we get out?' As Anvar had predicted, their

strange conveyance had eventually come to a juddering, spine-wrenching halt. He looked around, confused by the images that curved into infinity on all sides. Then he saw it – a pale, glimmering blue patch of Magelight that marked the area of his preserving spell. He got to his knees and thrust an experimental hand towards it. To his relief, the spell was still in operation, and his hand passed easily through the wall of the gem.

'Let me go first.' Shia shouldered past him. 'If anyone is out there, I want to deal with them.'

They emerged on to flat bare rock that was shadowed in the half-darkness of another cavern. Looking behind him, Anvar saw a featureless wall of polished stone, with nothing but the telltale glimmer of his spell to mark the point of their exit. He prayed that the spell would last. This was the first time he had tried anything so complex without Aurian's help, and he was still uncertain of his raw, untried powers. The roof of the small cavern was low, like an inverted bowl, and the wall through which they had come swept round in a broad semicircle, its ends marked by a massive stone archway, through which the faint light came. From beyond the arch, Bohan was beckoning. Anvar hurried to join him.

Beyond the archway was a broad apron of stone, a ledge over – nothing. Anvar reeled back from the dizzy brink, swallowing hard. As far as he could see, the chasm below was endless, its sheer walls stretching away on either side and plunging down into a gut-churning nothingness, in the midst of which glowed the faint and sickly light that illuminated this massive maw in the body of the mountain. Some hundred feet away, on the opposite brink, there was another jutting tongue of rock like the one on which he stood, with a similar archway behind it. His mouth gone suddenly dry, Anvar prayed that the ledge on which he stood was more solid than its counterpart looked. Apart from the sheer impossibility of scale, Aurian, with her terror of heights, would never have managed to get across. Yet there was no sign of her anywhere. Anvar refused to countenance the obvious: that she might have plunged to her death over the precipice. But if that was unthinkable, only one alternative remained. Something must have taken her across.

Furthermore, he thought, recalling her terror on the cliff, it had taken her very much against her will. He glanced up at the low roof, where stalactites hung like dripping fangs, hoping to find some means of crossing – a rope, handholds cut into the stone, anything at all. There was nothing.

A shrill, thin screeching, like metal grating against metal, sent Anvar spinning in the direction from which the unnerving sound had come. Framed in the opposite archway was a creature that turned his blood to ice. Its bloated, spherical body was wider than a man is tall, and it moved on a weird conglomeration of jointed, angular legs – too many for Anvar to count in that frozen moment of confrontation. And not all of its limbs were used for walking. Others sprouted like hideous growths from its dully gleaming body; some ending in cruel pincers, or in deadly keen blades like curved knives, others in clumps of fingerlike manipulators that clenched and un-clenched in ceaseless motion, grasping at the air. There was no head. Clusters of brilliant lights, like eyes, were dotted at intervals around its swollen body, mounted on the ends of writhing limbs. With nightmare slowness, these twisted in the air, turning their blinding beams unerringly in the direction of Anvar and his friends.

'Dear gods preserve us!' Anvar, in blind, unthinking terror, began to back slowly away towards the sheltering archway. Beside him, Shia gave a bloodcurdling snarl.

'Scatter!' she snapped, as, swifter than thought, the hideous creature came scuttling towards them – *straight across the thin air of the chasm!*

The great cat leapt to one side and Anvar dived for the shelter of the archway. The creature paused on the stony apron, its myriad limbs clicking and rattling, its eyes swivelling, turning their beams this way and that to fix upon Bohan, who stood, paralysed by fear, on the very brink of the precipice. Once again, Anvar heard the tortured, metallic shrieking as the angular legs stirred and began to advance, step by step, towards the eunuch.

'Get him!' Shia's thought seared into Anvar's mind as she launched herself at the monstrosity, fastening her jaws around one of the slender legs. The creature's eyes swivelled towards her and several sets of limbs, their pincers clacking together, their blades whistling through the air, snapped around, only to meet on thin air as Shia darted out of reach. In its moment of distraction, Anvar dashed across to Bohan and yanked him back from the edge.

'Spread out,' he yelled. 'Surround it! Keep it confused!'

Bohan, his paralysis vanished with the hope of a plan, drew his sword and moved to one side, waving the bright blade to distract the creature. As it lumbered towards him, Shia darted in again from behind, fastening her teeth on one of the legs. The limb flipped upwards, hurling her against the side of the arch. Anvar had snatched up Aurian's sword and ran in to chop at one of the swivelling eye-stalks. There was a shower of sparks and a jarring backshock ran numbingly up his arm as metal shrieked against metal. Anvar gasped, more from surprise than pain. This was no natural beast – it was a created thing!

The break in his attention almost cost him his life. Anvar looked up in time to see one of the arced blades descending straight at his head, but Bohan moved quickly in from the other side, fastened his huge hands round one of the legs and yanked, his face crimson and contorted with exertion. Despite his phenomenal strength the creature did not budge, but the move was enough to deflect its blow at Anvar, who ducked back as the sharp edge whistled harmlessly past his face. Shia bought the eunuch time to escape by diving right beneath the curving belly of the monstrosity, swiping at the metal legs in a whirlwind of claws. It whirred and clicked, spinning violently round on the spot, but its killing limbs could not reach beneath its body. Anvar watched, horrifed, as the cat deliberately began to inch towards the edge of the precipice, the creature, reacting with mindless fury, moving with her as it tried in vain to reach its tormentor. It reached the brink – it was toppling – and suddenly it was gone, and Shia with it.

'Shia!' Heartsick, Anvar raced for the edge, and saw two sets of claws, digging for dear life into the crumbling stone at the brink.

'Help . . .'

He heard Shia's wailing cry, at the extreme of anguish, and

then Bohan was there, grasping frantically at the black paws, heedless of the yawning drop beneath. But even the eunuch's strength could not bear the weight of the cat's massive body. Slowly, he began to slip forward, his feet sliding on the stone. Anvar flung himself flat at the edge of the chasm and reached down to Shia. With a bone-cracking effort she dug the claws of her hind feet into the stone, raising herself just enough for him to grasp two handfuls of loose skin at the base of her neck. The struggle seemed to take hours. Anvar pulled until he thought his arms would snap, sick with fear that he might slide forward to his own death. But with the two men supporting her weight, Shia was able to haul herself upwards, inch by painful inch, until at last, with a heave and a great sliding rush, she was up, safely back on the ledge.

Anvar rolled away from the brink and lay panting. His arms, freed of their burden, were aching, their muscles locked. 'What a stupid thing to do!' he raged at Shia. He felt the cat's mental equivalent of a shrug.

'It worked, didn't it?' But for all her bravado, she sounded shaken.

Anvar had to smile. 'It did indeed – and it saved all our lives.'

'As you humans saved mine. My thanks to you both.'

'It's Bohan you should really be thanking.' Anvar clapped the eunuch on the shoulder, and the huge man grinned.

'It took all three of us to defeat the creature.' Shia paused, growling softly. 'If Aurian met it alone . . .'

'Oh, gods.' Anvar shuddered, thinking of her facing the fearsome metallic beast, naked and unarmed as she had been. He thrust the thought away, and got to his feet. 'I'm not giving up. We have to go on.'

'I agree – but how?' Shia looked across the yawning gulf of the cavern, her tail twitching unhappily.

'That thing managed . . .' Anvar forced himself back to the edge, trying to work out how the beast had achieved the crossing. 'There must be some way that we can't see. Shia, come over here. See if you can sense any magic at work.'

'There is!' The cat backed away from the brink of the chasm, her fur bristling. Anvar knelt beside her, feeling along the edge. Though his eyes told him nothing was there, his searching fingers encountered smooth stone that continued, as far as he could reach, out across the chasm.

'There was a bridge here all the time. An invisible bridge. We can cross.'

Bohan had gathered up their discarded bundle. Now he hesitated on the lip of the precipice, frowning. Looking questioningly at Anvar, he gestured across the chasm and made vague passes in the air with his hand. Anvar understood all too well. His own stomach was churning at the thought of crossing that dizzying drop with nothing, seemingly, beneath him but thin air. 'No, my friend,' he said ruefully, 'unfortunately I don't know how to make it visible. We're just going to have to be very careful.' Bohan shuddered.

Anvar went first, crawling out on to the invisible stone on his hands and knees. It took more courage than he had known he possessed to make that first move out into nothingness. He fought down the clutching panic that threatened to unman him with thoughts of Aurian and forced himself to inch forward, feeling for the limits of the span with hands that shook violently. He tried to call back to the others, but only a strangled squeak emerged. He cleared his throat and tried again. 'Be careful – it's very narrow and there's no rail. Move slowly – the surface is very smooth. We daren't rush this.'

Time stretched out into an endless nightmare. Anvar tried at first to keep his eyes on the opposite wall of the chasm, but it didn't help. It seemed to grow no nearer, and he found himself wondering if there was some evil magic in the bridge that kept his goal receding; trapping him endlessly suspended over the abyss until his strength gave out and he plummeted to his death. He closed his eyes and immediately felt better. He realized that he had no need of vision – the bridge was invisible anyway – and he could progress much more easily if he shut out the sight of the sickening drop beneath him. He crawled on with painful slowness, feeling blindly for the edges of the span on either side with sweating hands, the thunder of his heart loud in his ears.

'I'm across!' The feel of the stone had roughened beneath Anvar's groping hands. He could no longer find the edges of the bridge, and opened his eyes to find himself safely on the ledge at the other side. He crawled out of the others' way and collapsed gratefully, his cheek pressed to the blessed, solid rock. His body ached and trembled with tension and he was drenched in sweat, but he could have wept with relief. Bohan and Shia joined him and all three rested for a while, too overcome even to speak. Then Anvar forced them into motion once more, though the eunuch looked exhausted, and even Shia's lithe stride was unsteady. He never paused to think of the emotions that drove him beyond endurance, beyond even hope. He only knew that he had to find Aurian, or perish in this mountain as she had done.

They had expected to see another curving blank wall beyond this archway, but instead it opened out into a long narrow chamber with a high vaulted ceiling. Once again the stone had a fused, glasslike surface, as though it had been melted and recast into its present form. A weird, reddish half-light washed the chamber, seeming to come out of nowhere, and the air prickled with a high-pitched, distant humming that produced an irritating resonance in the bones of Anvar's jaw and skull. But his attention was elsewhere. Arranged along the right hand wall of the chamber was a row of tall, oval-shaped gems that glistened dully like frosted moonstones. They looked like nothing so much as the cocoons of some sinister giant insect, and Anvar, looking at them, felt disquiet stir in his breast. With Shia and Bohan following, he went to examine the nearest.

He found a single clear facet in the front of the frosted gem, like a window upon the interior. Anvar peered through, and jumped backwards with a strangled exclamation as the bony, grinning face of a human skull leered at him, seeming, due to some trick of the gem's internal structure, to leap out at him from its crystal tomb.

Shia pushed past Anvar, standing on her hind legs to look into the clear facet. 'This is what becomes of those who penetrate this place,' she growled. 'Imprisoned in crystal by the metal creature.'

Anvar suppressed a shudder. 'You don't think . . .'

'I hope not. But all the same, we must search.' Shia trotted away to the next crystal and stood upright to peer into it. Anvar, sick at heart, followed her.

One by one they investigated each cocoon in the row. Anvar

had to steel himself to look into each one, dreading what he might find. All contained bones, mostly human, but some belonging to other creatures. Some were intact, but others had been cruelly crushed and hacked by the metal beast's appendages. Some were unrecognizable, but there was one skeleton of a great cat that made Shia snarl savagely, and two of the crystals contained small, human-seeming skeletons – with a fanlike tracery of bones springing from each oddly-jointed shoulder. Winged Folk! Anvar was astounded. When they reached the last cocoon, he hesitated.

'Let me look,' Shia said. She peered into the aperture, while Anvar watched, dry-mouthed. At last she got down, her tail twitching with emotion. 'Aurian is in there.'

32
The City of the Dragonfolk

Aurian was suspended in the milky light within the gem, inaccessible through the thick crystal which sealed her tomb, frozen like a statue in alabaster, the only colour about her the brave flame of her hair. Her eyes were closed as though in sleep, her pale lips slightly parted. Anvar saw that much before tears misted his vision. He was barely aware of Bohan pulling him away from the crystal, and did not see Shia taking his place at the pane. His knees gave way and he sank to the ground, overcome with anguish.

'Wait!' Shia's voice flashed into his mind. 'She breathes!'

Anvar turned on her. 'Don't be stupid,' he shouted. 'She's dead, damn you! It's just a trick of the crystal. You saw the others – the bones.'

Shia cuffed him hard, her eyes aflame with rage. 'I saw her breathe!' she roared. 'Get her out, human!'

Slowly, Anvar picked himself up. 'If you're wrong about this . . .'

'Look for yourself. Look long and hard this time. See with your head, not your heart.'

The sight of Aurian's pale, lifeless face was a knife through Anvar's flesh, but he steeled himself to look. A minute passed, and another – he stiffened. Had he imagined it? Another minute, and he saw it again – the slightest lift of her breast, almost imperceptible, but definitely there. 'Dear gods,' he whispered. 'Shia, you're right! You're right!' Wild with joy, he hugged the great cat.

'Of course,' Shia told him smugly. 'Cats are wise, Anvar. The other remains were very old – perhaps they starved, or died from their injuries. But we still have a problem. How do we get her out?'

How indeed? An hour later, Anvar was ready to scream with

frustration. They had hacked at the crystal, battered it with the hilts of their swords, and, in Shia's case, thrown herself on it with teeth and claws. It shrugged off their efforts, remaining unscathed and utterly impervious. Anvar stepped back, panting, and scowled at the unyielding gem. 'This is no good,' he said. 'It's absolutely unbreakable, yet the creature has put her inside. It must open somehow. Shia, do you feel magic here?'

The cat had flopped to the ground, despondent. 'I feel something,' she said, 'but different, not like a spell.' She scraped the smooth stone floor with her claws, searching for the right words. 'It feels as though the crystal *is* magic, but it doesn't *do* magic, if you can understand that.'

Anvar couldn't, and he was afraid to try any of the spells from his limited repertoire lest he trigger something in his ignorance that might harm the Mage within. He ran his hands over the smooth walls of the gem, racking his brains for a way out of their difficulties, and pulled back with an oath as his fingers caught on a sharp edge. 'Bohan, did you manage to knock a piece out of this?'

The eunuch shook his head emphatically.

Sucking his bleeding fingers, Anvar investigated the place. It was high up round the side of the crystal, but he could see nothing to mar the flawless surface. Then a smear of blood led his eyes to the spot. He felt again, more carefully this time, and found a hollow: a place where a single facet was missing, its absence concealed by the internal reflections of the gem. Anvar frowned. 'There's a perfect piece missing. I wonder . . .'

'A key?' Shia was quick to follow his thought.

'If it is, we must find it, and quickly. Who knows how long Aurian can stay alive in there?' Anvar froze as a dreadful thought occurred to him. 'What if the creature had it?'

'One way to find out. Stop fearing the worst, and search.' Shia was away, quartering the chamber.

It was Bohan who finally found the missing piece, tucked behind the crystal in a niche in the wall. Anvar snatched it from his hand. It was bigger than his fist and pointed at its inner end, its smooth broad facets catching the light along their edges. Holding his breath, he reached up and pushed it into the hollow, turning it to fit. It settled into place with a click, and

518

Anvar stepped hastily back as the gem flared with a dazzling white light that sank slowly away to leave the crystal transparent, all traces of its former milkiness gone. Distorted, broken reflections of Aurian's body could be seen within; then a crack snaked down the front of the gem. It opened down its length like a hinged shell, unfolding into two hollowed segments with thick walls. Anvar rushed to catch the Mage as she slid out of the space within, and found he had hold of a demon.

The monster – the hideous spider creature – it had hold of her! Aurian struggled instinctively, striking out with fists and feet as Maya had taught her long ago. There was an oddly human-sounding grunt as she connected, and the grip on her body fell away.

'Very nice. He goes to all this trouble to rescue you, and you hit him.'

The voice in her head was reassuringly familiar. 'Shia!' Aurian rolled over and looked around dazedly, blinking in the weird red light. She barely had time to discover the presence of her three friends before Anvar seized her, half lifting her in an embrace that took her breath away.

'Oh, gods, Aurian, it's so good to see you alive!'

With her head buried in Anvar's shoulder, the Mage was unable to see his face, but his voice sounded ragged and choked. Aurian tried to answer, but her throat was too parched for speech. Anvar took one arm from around her long enough to rummage in a bundle at his side and come up with a waterskin. He supported her while she drank, rationing her, much to her annoyance, to small sips. She made a grab for the bag as he took it away.

'In a minute.' His voice was firmer now. 'You haven't drunk for about three days. You'll make yourself sick.'

'Days?' Aurian groped in vain to remember. It was hard to read Anvar's face in the dim red light, but she thought she could see the streak of a tear on his cheek. 'Was I ill? Did I dream that awful spider thing?' She groaned. 'I feel as though I've been on a three-day drinking bout with Parric.' Her mouth still felt dry, her head was throbbing, her stomach burned, and she had the same unnerving gaps in her memory that were usually the result of too much ale.

519

'I think you might want this.' Anvar fished her desert robe out of his bundle. Aurian gasped, suddenly conscious of her nudity, and the memories came flooding back of her swim, and what had happened subsequently. Anvar helped her into the robe, and gave her more water and a little flat cake of Nereni's bread, cradling her in his arms as she ate. She nibbled it slowly, feeling as though she might be sick at any minute, but once it was down it stayed down, and she began to feel better, and ready for more.

As she ate, the Mage pieced together her story for her friends. Having been captured by the portal, she had made the same accidental discovery as Anvar: that Magelight triggered the rising of the gemlike conveyance. On reaching the top, however, she had spent a long time trying to find a spell to make it descend, and return to the others. When her efforts met with no success, she had decided to leave the crystal, hoping to find some other route down. 'I got out of it in much the same way as I got in,' she went on. 'It sucked me through its wall – and that was when I met the spider thing. You've no idea what it was like.'

'We have,' Shia assured her grimly. 'We met it too.'

Aurian shuddered. 'I couldn't fight it. Did you know it was impervious to magic?'

Anvar shook his head. 'I never thought to try.'

'Just as well. It seemed to have the ability to throw the spell right back at the user – I very nearly fried myself before I found that out. Anyway, it grabbed me.' She swallowed hard, trying to keep her voice under control. Anvar hugged her closer, and she gave him a grateful smile. 'I was fighting . . . After that, I don't remember. It only seemed to be a split second before Shia was telling me I'd hit you.' She raised her hand to a lurid bruise on Anvar's cheekbone. 'I hurt you, Anvar. I'm sorry.'

'That wasn't you. That was Harihn.'

'Oh, Anvar, you haven't been fighting?' Aurian was dismayed. 'I know you don't like each other, but . . .'

'Wait until you hear the whole story.' Assisted by Shia, and with the occasional confirmatory nod from Bohan, Anvar told her what had happened. Aurian interrupted with astonished delight when she discovered that he and Shia could speak to

520

one another, and again to heap bloodcurdling curses on Harihn's head when she heard how the prince had abandoned her friends to die. When her rage had calmed enough to let her hear the rest of the tale, she shuddered to hear of their fight with the monster, and Shia's near-loss in the depths of the abyss. But when Anvar began to describe their crossing of the invisible bridge, it was too much.

'Don't tell me. I'd rather not hear about that bit, if you don't mind,' she apologized.

When Anvar had finished his tale, Aurian looked at the faces of her companions, utterly moved by their courage and loyalty. 'My dearest friends, you've been so brave . . . I don't know how to thank you . . .' She ran out of words, and brushed away a tear.

'As long as you're all right,' Anvar told her, 'you and the child.'

Aurian looked at him fondly. 'We seem to be unscathed, thanks to you three. The question is, what do we do now? We've been trapped here by that turd Harihn. If we don't find something within these tunnels to help us, we'll starve. Besides, Anvar – ' Her eyes lit up with excitement. 'Don't you realize what this place must be? The crystals, the metal creature immune to magic – it all points to one thing. We've found the lost civilization of the Dragonfolk! There must be artefacts here – knowledge, weapons, perhaps even the Sword of Fire itself – that we could use against Miathan.'

Anvar shook his head in exasperation. 'You never give up, do you? What if we find more of those spider monsters? What if there's worse?'

'After my last experience, do you think that I'm not worried about spider things?' Aurian shrugged. 'But to be honest, Anvar, I don't see any alternative. We certainly can't go back the way we came. The only way out is through.'

Though they all longed for sleep, they decided to press on at once. Food was in short supply, and despite their lack of knowledge of the mountain fastness, there was nothing to be gained by lingering. The only other exit from the long chamber was a huge arched doorway at the far end. A wide ramp sloped in a curve up a broad tunnel whose roof, pointed like the archway, was high above. Shia led the way; the Mages, by unspoken consent, following together. Bohan brought up the rear, his sword drawn. Anvar had returned Aurian's gear to her, and she was relieved to feel the familiar weight of her sword at her hip once more. She caressed the handworn hilt. Ah, my Coronach, she thought, we've been through a lot together, you and I. Her throat tightened as she remembered the day, her birthday long ago, when Forral had first given her the blade. Her hand went unconsciously to her belly. Would their child survive long enough to wield a sword?

'Aurian?' Anvar's eyes were anxious.

'I'm fine.' The Mage took a tighter grip on her staff, and tried her best to shake off her melancholy thoughts.

The disquieting red light of the chamber had been replaced by a soft amber glow that emanated from a network of shining veins that webbed the smooth, seamless stone of the passageway. The air whispered softly past their faces without moisture or mustiness, and the walls and floor bore little trace of webs or dust. The irritating hum had faded as they climbed. Aurian found herself relaxing a little. She had not realized how much the high-pitched buzz had bothered her until it was gone. 'You know,' she said to Anvar, 'this is like a spiral staircase, only there are no steps. I suppose dragons might have had difficulties with stairs. But if this corridor was built to accommodate them, they must have been even bigger than I thought.'

He nodded glumly. 'And more powerful than we thought, if they could create this place, and the metal creature. We should be careful.'

It was easy to lose track of time as the unchanging tunnel wound on and on. After a while, rooms began to appear, leading off from either side. To Aurian's frustration, some were sealed with great doors of metal or crystal that would yield to neither force nor magic. Other rooms were doorless or open, but large or small, all were completely empty, their only illumination coming from the dim stoneglow of the passage that shone through the wide entrances. Shia reported no further signs of magic.

'What kind of ridiculous place is this?' Aurian complained,

as they explored yet another abandoned chamber. 'What's the use of it all?' She felt leaden with exhaustion, and her headache had returned.

'How the blazes should I know?' Anvar snapped. He sagged against her, grinding his knuckles into bloodshot eyes. The Mage glanced sharply at his slumped form, noticing for the first time that Bohan looked similarly weary. 'How long is it since you've slept?'

He groaned. 'Days – I don't remember. Not since you went missing.'

'Anvar! Why didn't you tell me?' Taking his arm Aurian led him to the rear of the small room and sat him down, propped against the wall. 'This place is about as defensible as we can get. We'll rest here.'

They each took a small sip of water from the dwindling contents of their sack, Anvar pouring some into Aurian's cupped hands for Shia to lap. The Mage insisted on taking the first watch. 'I was doing nothing all the time you were searching for me,' she told them. 'It's only fair.' No one had the energy to argue.

'Wake me next,' Shia told her. 'We can share the watching. I need less rest than you feeble two-legged folk.'

Aurian left them asleep and sat to one side of the entrance, her sword ready to her hand. She began to count time by tapping her dagger on her palm to mark the seconds and switching hands when each minute had passed, but soon gave it up. The counting lulled her, and she found herself beginning to nod. Instead, she thought about her child. It must be about five months now, though it was hard to work out the time exactly – Magewomen were taught to suppress the monthly cycles that were such a bother for Mortals. They usually became aware of their pregnancy after the second month, and Aurian thought that was about right. She had certainly felt the child's presence once it had been pointed out to her. Not much longer before my powers vanish entirely, she thought, and what will we do then? If we ever escape from here, that is. What could have prompted Harihn to such treachery? Did I really misjudge him so badly?

The Mage wondered what was happening in Nexis. Miathan

would use the powers of the Cauldron to enslave the Mortals he despised, with Eliseth, Bragar and Davorshan as willing accomplices. What had become of her friends? Had Vannor and Parric survived? What of Maya and D'arvan, and her mother? While her powers were crippled by the bracelets, she might have been unaware of any deaths among the Magefolk. She shivered, despite the warm air of the chamber, and longed for Forral's sturdy old cloak, lost in the shipwreck. Its familiar weight on her shoulders had always been a comfort. But cloak and Forral were gone, and she was cold and alone in this dark place.

Aurian, lost in sorrowful thoughts, was startled by a cold black nose poking into her face. 'Thought so,' Shia said. 'You're almost asleep. Time I took over.'

The Mage was quick to agree. It would be a relief to escape for a while into oblivion. She crossed the chamber to where her friends slept, and lay down beside Anvar. As always he seemed to sense her presence, and turned to put an arm around her, murmuring her name in his sleep. Aurian snuggled close, and felt her burden lifting. At least I have Shia and Bohan, she thought, and especially Anvar. I never made a better decision than when I saved him from Miathan that day. What a true friend he turned out to be. Feeling comforted, she fell asleep.

The next day, if day it was, they encountered the trap. After a frugal breakfast that left them with slender rations indeed, they resumed their weary trudge, winding ever upward round the featureless stone spiral with its empty rooms until their feet dragged with exhaustion. Aurian was close to despair. Had she been wrong in her hope of finding the lost knowledge of the Dragonfolk? Did it really matter? We're doomed to die here, she thought. This mountain will be our tomb, and that will be that. Suddenly Shia, stalking ahead as usual, stopped. 'Magic!' she growled.

'You're right,' Anvar said. 'Aurian, do you see it?' A few paces in front of them there was a silver disturbance in the air, like the illusory shimmer above a stone pavement on a hot day. It stretched across the passage like a curtain, barring their way.

Danger or not, Aurian was glad that something had occurred to break the monotony of the trek. She walked forward cautiously, staff in one hand, the other held up before her, palm foremost. As she reached the roiling, silky distortion, two things happened. The shimmer vanished, and all the light in the tunnel went out. Taken by surprise, Aurian took another step forward, striking a ball of Magelight above her head. As it flared, there was a low, thundrous grinding from above, drawing her eyes upward. Her breath caught in her throat as a huge, squared-off block of the ceiling detached itself and came plummeting towards her.

To Aurian, everything happened in nightmare slow-motion. The block seemed to float downwards as she plunged forward. One foot slipped and she fell twisting, facing back in the direction from which she had come.

'Aurian!' Anvar was hurling himself forward, diving into the narrowing gap between stone and floor. The massive block plunged inexorably down . . . smashing Anvar into the floor with a jarring crunch that shuddered the walls.

'Anvar!' Aurian's shriek tore her throat. Her Magelight went out, plunging her into darkness. Her mind reeled with hideous, unbearable visions: Anvar, pulverized beneath tons of stone. She collapsed against the wall, retching, choking on sobs.

And leapt about a yard into the air as a hand touched her shoulder.

'It's me.' Anvar's strangled voice was almost lost in her squeak of fright.

'You! You can't . . . I saw . . .' Aurian found it impossible to get the words past her chattering teeth. Anvar, it seemed, was having similar difficulties as they clung together, shaking.

'Illusion,' he gasped.

Illusion? Aurian's Magelight rekindled, flaring fiery red as anger boiled up within her. She drew back, staring at Anvar's ashen face. 'You fool! You bloody idiot! I thought you were dead, damn you! How could you do such a stupid thing!' Tears of shock and rage ran down her face and she dashed them angrily away.

Anvar grabbed her shoulders, his fingers digging hard into her flesh. 'Because I'm not prepared to lose you again. I'd *rather* die, don't you understand?'

Aurian felt her anger draining away. She understood; she

525

had felt the same way about Forral. She shook her head, unwilling to accept the implications. 'Anvar . . .'

He looked away from her, biting his lip. 'Never mind. Forget it.'

'If you two have quite finished.' Shia's mental voice was a welcome distraction, but Aurian could tell from the steely tone that the cat, too, was angry at the scare they had given her. She was nowhere in sight; still hidden, presumably, behind the illusory block of stone. 'How you expect anyone to get their thoughts through such a turmoil as you have been throwing up, I have no idea,' Shia went on irritably, 'but since you've finally deigned to speak to me, have you anything constructive to suggest?'

Suddenly Aurian found herself giggling helplessly. That started Anvar off too, and they laughed together until their ribs ached and they were wheezing for breath. The little ball of Magelight, bright gold now, flickered and bobbed above Aurian's head as though it, too, was chuckling.

'*Well?*' The thunder of Shia's voice finally sobered them.

'Sorry Shia.' Aurian grinned at Anvar, speaking her thoughts aloud for Bohan's benefit. 'I suggest you walk straight through. The block is an illusion – as Anvar so conclusively proved!' She gave him a mock-fierce scowl.

Stunned silence from Shia, then: 'Could I only curse, like you humans!' Though the words came from her mind, they sounded as if they were spoken through clenched teeth. 'We're coming through!'

'No, wait!' Aurian's cry was drowned in a grating rumble from overhead. There was an anguished howl, and Bohan came hurtling through the wall of stone, Shia a black projectile at his heels. There was a deafening crash, and the Mages clutched each other as the floor of the tunnel bucked and heaved beneath them. Clouds of dust billowed up, and tiny fragments of stone stung their skin.

As the dust began to settle, Aurian was relieved to see Bohan and Shia, safe. Coughing, she stretched out a hand to the block, and touched solid stone.

'It really fell this time.' Anvar sounded shaken.

'I think I understand,' Aurian murmured thoughtfully. 'It's a time-trap, Anvar. What we saw – what we thought had hit you – ' She groped for the words. 'It wasn't an illusion. What we were seeing was the future.'

'But why? Surely if it was a trap, it might as well have fallen in the first place?'

'I'm not sure.' Aurian frowned. 'Presumably, the Dragons would recognize their own magic, so it would act as a warning to them that the trap was there, and they should get through quickly. But any strange Magefolk, like us, who come blundering in – well, if I hadn't taken that extra step forward, I would have seen the thing falling and stepped back.'

'And we would have eventually discovered the illusion,' Anvar finished for her, 'gone through, and – '

'It would have got us anyway. What a bloody devious people.' She was annoyed, and more than a little unnerved. 'What kind of power must they have had, to play tricks like that with time?'

Aurian turned to the others, and was surprised to see the eunuch rubbing his buttocks with one hand and shaking an angry fist at Shia with the other.

'Are you two all right? Bohan, what's wrong?'

Shia's voice was loaded with disgust. 'This lumbering ox wasn't moving fast enough, so I stuck my claws in his backside.'

A strangled squawk from Anvar proved that he, too, had heard the cat's words. Aurian found herself spluttering helplessly. Bohan's indignant expression and Shia's angry glare only made them worse. The Mages leaned against each other, helpless with laughter.

'But how did you know the stone was really falling this time?' Aurian asked Shia, when she had finally got her paroxysms under control. Now that they could both speak to her, the Mages had fallen into the habit of voicing their thought aloud. It made things much easier. Shia sat, primly licking a paw, though her twitching tail betrayed that she too had been shaken by their near miss.

'I didn't. But cats never take chances!'

'Really, smart-paws?' Anvar retorted. 'What about when you nearly went over the cliff fighting that spider thing?'

Shia glared at him. 'That was different!'

'Oh?'

'Something has occurred to me.' Aurian interrupted the impending fight. 'That awful howl we heard as you came through – was that you, Bohan?'

The big man looked perplexed.

'Well it certainly wasn't me,' Shia declared.

'But that means you can speak!'

Bohan opened his mouth, but nothing emerged. Aurian could see his face growing redder and redder with the exertion, and went to him quickly. 'Don't, Bohan. You'll hurt yourself. Obviously the problem isn't physical, but I'm too weary to try mind-healing just now. I promise you, though, if we get out of this place, I'll help you find your voice.'

He smiled at her, but the longing, the hope in his eyes wrung Aurian's heart. She patted his hand gently. 'Let's rest now. I think we all need some time to recover before we go on.'

This time, folly though it might have proved, no one even thought to suggest keeping watch. Careless in their weariness, unstrung by the shocks of the past hour, they slept like the dead, huddled close for comfort like lost children. When Bohan finally awakened Aurian, light had returned to the passageway, and the stone had lifted to open the tunnel behind them. The trap had been set once more.

They swallowed the meagre remnants of their food and water, but their last meal was marred by a sense of unease. Had the stone reset itself? Or, horrifying thought, had someone – or some *thing* – crept up while they slept to renew the spell?

'Nonsense,' Aurian argued. 'If anyone had been here they'd have let us know about it, you can be sure!' None the less, there was a crawling between her shoulder blades that no amount of common sense could shake off, and looking at the others' faces she knew they felt the same.

As they went on, the tunnel began to straighten, its gradient growing steeper as they climbed. There were no more rooms now, and soon the very light began to change, as gradually the glowing amber veins in the stone were replaced by a constellation of many-coloured gems that shone, like those in the desert below, with their own mysterious gleam. Soon the way was illuminated only by the flickering gemlight that surrounded them on all sides, as though they trod the starry paths of the universe itself. 'How beautiful it is,' Aurian murmured. 'I'm glad we got the chance to see this, even if – '

'Even if we die for the experience?' They were almost the first words that Anvar had spoken since they had awakened. After his outburst the previous day, a constraint had fallen between the Mages, as if both were anxious to avoid what his words had revealed. Aurian was suddenly sick of it all. Nothing's changed, she told herself. It's still Anvar. Words said in the heat of the moment – what real difference does it make? If we die, it won't matter anyway, and if we don't – well, it'll keep, and in the meantime there's no sense in ruining a good friendship over it. She took his hand.

'Don't despair,' she told him. 'Think of all the times we've almost perished since we left Nexis, yet we never did. Something will turn up, you'll see. We're too tough a team to kill, you and I.'

Anvar squeezed her hand and met her eyes at last, suddenly looking more cheerful. 'You're right,' he said, 'and we'll go through a lot more together before we're done.'

'Light! Light ahead!' They turned simultaneously towards Shia's cry.

Daylight! It filtered wanly past a sharp angle in the tunnel, dimming the star-glitter of the gems. Shia had stopped, bristling, before the bend. 'There's magic ahead,' she warned, halting their headlong rush. Aurian took a step forward, but Anvar, who had not relinquished her hand even as they ran, pulled her back towards him. 'Oh no you don't,' he growled. 'This time we go together!'

They crept forward, peering anxiously round the corner of the passage. 'Chathak's balls!' Aurian swore. The tunnel ahead of them was blocked by a large gem, resembling the impervious doorways that had defeated them lower down. The daylight twinkled through its polished facets – so near, yet, unless they could find a way to pass the obstacle, it might have been a million miles away.

'That noise is back,' Anvar said suddenly. 'Do you hear it?' Sure enough, the irritating, high-pitched hum was tickling the base of Aurian's jawbone. 'What is that?' she demanded crossly, fighting back an urge to burst into tears of sheer frustration.

'I think it's coming from the other side. Shia! Get yourself round here!'

'I hear you.' The great cat slunk round the corner with a black look for Anvar. 'There's no need to shout.'

'Sorry. Can you tell whether the magic is coming from the stone itself, or is there another trap in front of us?'

'I don't think so. It's in the crystal itself.'

'Right.' Anvar pressed forward, but Aurian caught his arm. 'Hold on there,' she told him. 'You made the rules, remember? Together, or not at all.'

Together they examined the crystal, running their hands over the smooth, hard surface. 'Just the same as the others,' Anvar said despondently. 'Unlike the one that imprisoned you, there's no key to these door-crystals. It's a dead end.'

'It can't be!' Aurian aimed a savage kick at the obstruction, howling a curse as the toe of her boot hit the unyielding gem. 'That does it!' In unthinking rage she raised her staff, unleashing a sizzling bolt at the crystal.

'Aurian, no!' Anvar, shielding his eyes, was thrown back hard against the side of the passage. Smoke curled through the corridor as the gem began to hiss and pulse with light.

'Stop!' Dimly, Aurian heard Shia's urgent cry. 'You're making it worse! The magic of the stone is growing!'

To her horror, the Mage realized that it was true. The gem was acting as the bracelets had done, leeching her powers into it to increase its own. The staff trembled in her outstretched hand as energy surged through her body and along her arm, bleeding and weakening her further by the second. No longer was she putting forth her power – the stone was pulling it from her! Her guts twisted in panic. 'Help me,' she cried. 'I can't stop it!'

Something hard cannoned into her, knocking her breathless to the ground. The staff was wrenched from her hand in a shower of sparks, breaking the deadly bond of magic. Aurian, gasping like a stranded fish, saw Bohan, fallen half on top of her, drop the smoking staff with a grimace of pain. The glare from the crystal dimmed, and the smoke began to clear.

'You and your blasted temper, Aurian!' Anvar was examining Bohan's hand.

'I know. I'm sorry, Anvar. It was a stupid thing to do. Is Bohan all right?'

'More or less.'

The eunuch echoed his words with a nod.

Anvar held out his hand to help her up. 'Aurian, we have to stop scaring each other like this.'

'It's a bargain.' Aurian scrambled to her feet, turning back to the crystal. 'All the same, I have an idea.' She remembered the bracelets sapping her power as she tried to help Anvar in the slave compound.

'Be careful!' Anvar said hastily.

'I will. I've learned my lesson. No daft fireworks this time, I promise.' She pressed her hands, then the side of her face, flat against the crystal, probing its interior with her healer's senses, feeling for the delicate lattice that was the framework and life of the stone. Since her powers had been sapped by her rash act, it took her a long time to find the weakness, the chink in its defences, that she sought. But it was there. At last, it was there! Aurian probed with her will, and pulled . . .

Ah, now the tables were turned! The Mage felt her palms tingling as power flooded back through the fault in the gem. She drew upon the stone's energy until she felt ready to burst, unable to contain so much magic. She began to wonder if she had overestimated her ability to handle the power woven into the structure of the stone. Again she felt the chill clutch of fear. If only she had taught this to Anvar, so that he could have helped her. If only she had some way to store the surplus power. But . . .

'Get back round the corner!' she yelled, straining to contain the force until they were safely away. 'Cover your eyes!' Then, flinging out a hand, the Mage hurled a mighty flare of energy at the barrier, shielding herself quickly as she did so. It exploded as it hit, the concussion impacting violently back against her shield, but her defences held, and as for the crystal – her job was done. Without the energy that held it together, the gem collapsed with a slithering whisper into a heap of fine powder at her feet. Aurian let out her breath in a huge sigh of relief.

Anvar appeared round the corner, looking pale. 'I thought we agreed not to frighten each other any more?' He spoke quietly, but there was a glint of anger in his eyes.

'Anvar, I'm sorry. I never thought . . . I didn't realize so much energy would be involved.' She brightened. 'But it worked, didn't it? And no harm done in the end.'

'No harm?' Shia spat. 'What about the harm to my nerves?'

Anvar sighed. 'I have to admit, it worked. But if you ever do anything like that again . . .'

'All right,' Aurian agreed. 'I won't. I'll teach you instead, and the next time, you can do it.'

'Humans!' Shia growled in disgust.

Together they scrambled over the pile of fine crystal dust and peered through the opening that Aurian had created. The Mage's heart sank. 'By all the gods! After all that, it doesn't even lead outside!' Throwing her staff to the ground, she sat down on the mound of dust, her head in her hands.

'Aurian, look at this!' Anvar sounded excited.

'You look at it. I've seen enough of this accursed place.'

'Don't be ridiculous.' He yanked her firmly to her feet. With a groan, Aurian picked up her staff and followed him, and stepped back quickly with a sharp oath as she saw the drop that yawned beneath her feet. They stood inside a tower – a circular chamber that stretched up and up, deceiving the eye. The walls were seamless, formed of translucent white stone and pierced in a spiral all the way up by circular windows of crystal that cast sword-thin shafts of daylight down to the floor – except that there was no floor. They stood on a ribbon of stone that clung to the walls of the tower, spiraling up into the limitless heights above. Below them was a sparkling shaft, lit by the focused beams from the windows; and at eye level, suspended seemingly on thin air above the drop, a great spherical crystal spun and scintillated, filling the air with the unnerving, penetrating hum they had heard in the corridor, and in the red-lit chamber far below.

Anvar lay on his front, hanging over the edge of the shaft in a way that made Aurian's stomach flip over. 'This is amazing! Do you want to bet that it goes right down into that chasm we crossed?'

Aurian groaned. 'Anvar, come away from there!'

'Yes, do,' Shia added, sounding far from happy. 'This place is crawling with magic.'

Anvar ignored them both. 'Of course it is! Don't you see, this is some kind of magical pump. That's why the air was so fresh on the lower levels – this makes it circulate.'

'Very clever, Anvar.' Aurian did her best, but failed to keep the despair from her voice. 'It is also, you may have noticed, a dead end. We'll have to go back down.'

Anvar scrambled up from the brink. 'I don't think so. The path' – he indicated the strip of stone on which they stood – 'this dragon stairway, if you like – it still goes upwards. I think there'll be a way out at the top.'

Aurian gazed up at the path, which curved away even higher from where they stood, and down again, at the bottomless shaft. She swallowed hard and looked at Anvar. 'I thought we weren't going to frighten each other any more?'

He grinned. 'You've already broken that promise.'

'This isn't funny!'

'I know. But it's our only way out. Look, it isn't all that narrow. It was built for dragons, you know. Come on, Aurian. I'll hold your hand. You must do it.'

'All right.' Aurian sighed. 'But, Anvar, if we get all the way to the top and there's no way out, you're going straight down that shaft head first!'

Afterwards, Aurian preferred not to recall that climb. It seemed to go on for ever as she sidled up the sloping ramp, her back pressed hard against the tower wall. They climbed until their legs were trembling with weariness, but the Mage refused to halt. 'No,' she pleaded. 'Just get it over with.' But in the end, it was clear that in their famished and exhausted state they would never make it to the top without resting. Aurian sat huddled as far away from the edge as she could, her eyes tightly closed. After a time they went on, their muscles cramped and their heads swimming, until even Aurian had forgotten the drop beneath in her preoccupation with her aching limbs. It was with a sense of disbelief that she finally saw the archway above her. She staggered into the blessed daylight.

'Be careful!' Anvar grabbed her arm, yanking her back against the side of the doorway. Aurian, reeling, fell to the ground. 'Anvar,' she gasped, 'I hate you. I absolutely hate you.'

She was awakened by a gentle hand shaking her shoulder.

533

Anvar's face was close to her own. 'I'm sorry,' he said. 'I let you sleep as long as I dared, but we must get moving while there's still daylight. Do you still hate me?'

Aurian groaned, aching all over. 'That depends. Did I really see what I think I saw?'

'I'm afraid so.'

'In that case, yes.' Moving very carefully, she peered over the edge of the platform that topped the tower. Ah, how good it was to see the sky, and the sun again after their night-time journey through the desert and the long days passed in the gloomy halls beneath the mountain. And despite her fear, the view was staggering. The tower stood at one end of an oval plain that stretched about a league – a crater scooped into the top of the mountain. The jagged walls of the peak were higher than the roof on which she perched, and shielded the vale below from the worst of the desert's blinding glare. And in the vale . . . Aurian caught her breath. There lay the lost city of the Dragonfolk!

It was arranged, not in lines and angles like a human city, but in a series of interlapping circles joined like a spider's web, all converging on a massive, conical structure like a great spire that was higher even than the tower. The sun struck fire from its pointed tip, and not surprisingly, for the edifice had been carved from a single, massive green gem. When Aurian had finished gaping, she discovered that all the buildings in the city were similarly constructed, each from a coloured jewel that blazed with coruscating light. Most were rounded and single storied with broad flat roofs where, the Mage supposed, the Dragonfolk would have basked, absorbing the sun that was their lifeblood. There were several towers, domes and minarets, all intricately carved and chased, but the highest buildings were the tower from which she looked, and the huge spire in the centre.

Anvar, it seemed, had seen the view while she slept, and was ready to be practical. 'I've seen a lot of birds down there – I suppose this is their resting-place when they cross the desert. If we can find a way to trap them we'll have food. And there must be water down there. Surely even the Dragonfolk would need that?'

'So we go down.' Aurian had already noticed the spiral path, a twin to the one on the inside of the tower, that wound down – and down and down – to the city below. 'Damn and blast them!' She struck the stone with an impotent fist, and burst into tears. 'Why couldn't they have put railings on these bloody stairways?'

'I'm sorry, love.' Anvar stroked her hair. 'But . . .'

'I know, I know.' Aurian sat up and sniffed, scrubbing at her face with the sleeve of her robe, and caught Anvar's eye, remembering an occasion long ago when he had chided her for doing just that. 'Take no notice of me, Anvar. I'm being a fool. Lead on, then – since you seem to be in charge where high places are concerned!'

It was far worse going down. The path seemed to tilt crazily beneath Aurian's feet, and there was nothing below her but thin air. The others were having similar difficulties, and the sun had long since dropped behind the high mountain walls before they neared the bottom. With the path shrouded in gloom and their attention fixed upon their feet, they barely noticed the shadow that plunged across them. Anvar, in the lead, turned to Aurian. 'What about some . . .' His face froze in horror. The Mage had no time to look behind her. Something struck her hard, wrenching her from the path. Wiry arms grasped at her, and she caught a glint of steel. She was falling – falling . . .

33
The Staff of Earth

'Aurian!' Sick with dread, Anvar hurtled down the spiral path, followed by Bohan and Shia. The ledge reached the ground on the opposite side from which the Mage had fallen, and he raced around the base of the tower, not daring to think of what he might find. He almost ran right into the fighters. A small figure, its identity obscured by the dusky shadows that flooded the bottom of the crater, was struggling with the Mage. Aurian was alive!

'Stay back!' The voice was shrill. The stranger, cloaked in deepest black, was using a handful of the Mage's hair to pull her head back. A gleaming, naked blade lay across Aurian's throat.

There was no time to wonder how Aurian had survived the fall. Anvar measured the distance between himself and the fighters, weighing the chances of a surprise attack. Not good, he thought. If I could see better . . . Magelight flashed between his fingers. He heard a yelp of shock from the stranger, and Aurian took advantage of her opponent's distraction. There was a scuffle and a grunt of pain, and the positions of the assailants were suddenly reversed. The dagger spun away, lost in the struggle, Bohan chasing after it. Aurian had her foe down and was attacking with both fists, spitting curses. Anvar, remembering the blind rage of his fight with Harihn, rushed forward to grab her arm. 'All right,' he panted. 'You've won!' But when he tried to pull the Mage to her feet, she fell away with a cry of pain. 'You're wounded?' Anvar dropped down beside her.

Aurian was swearing furiously. 'Wrenched my knee, landing,' she muttered. 'That was how she got the advantage – and because I was scared out of my wits.' She shook her head in puzzlement. 'But why did she break my fall?'

'It's a she?'

Aurian struck her own Magelight with an ease that made Anvar sigh with envy. 'You ever see a man fight like this?' Her arms and face were bloodied with long deep scratches. 'Added to that, I sacrificed a handful of hair to get out of the hold she had on me.' Aurian snorted with disgust, rubbing her scalp. Her face was grey in the Magelight, and Anvar knew that her fall must have terrified her – as it had terrified him.

'I don't know why she broke your fall, but I thank all the gods she did,' he said shakily.

Aurian's composure was crumbling, and for a moment Anvar thought she would fling herself into his arms, as she had done after their terrible ascent of the cliffs of Taibeth. But instead she took a long, shuddering breath, making a visible effort to pull herself together. 'If I start thinking about it, I'll go into screaming hysterics,' she said firmly. 'Let's take a look at our prisoner.'

Stifling an insidious feeling of disappointment, Anvar turned towards the girl, and Aurian moved her light to illuminate the huddled, weeping figure. 'Gods save us!' For the first time, Anvar got a good look at what he had mistaken for a dark cloak. 'She has wings!' Sending Shia and Bohan off to make sure there were no other Winged Folk lurking nearby, Anvar bent to examine the strange captive.

She was very small and finely made – not much over half Anvar's weight, though each of the great black wings that sprung from her back was longer than her body. The pinions were jointed, so that their upper sections rose beyond her shoulders, higher than her head, while the lower parts dropped to her feet in a graceful tapering sweep. As Anvar pulled her hands away from her bruised, tear-streaked face, she glared at Aurian with eyes that were huge and dark. 'She hit me!' The words were strangely accented, and Anvar guessed that his Magefolk ability to communicate in all tongues was in operation once more.

'What did you expect?' he told her angrily. 'You were trying to cut her throat.'

The winged girl spat at Aurian's feet. 'In my country she would die for striking a princess.'

537

Aurian groaned. 'Not royalty again!'

Raven stared at the tall, grim-faced woman who could fight like a demon, and her stomach clenched into a tight, cold knot of fear. Who were these horribly big, wingless beings? She had never seen anything like them. What were they doing in this deserted place? What would they do to her? The man with the unnerving sky-coloured eyes grabbed her arm roughly. 'Are there any more of you about?' he demanded.

Raven's mind worked quickly. 'Of course!' she snapped haughtily. 'Do you think a princess would be unescorted? Let me go, ere I call my guards to make an end of you.'

'She's lying,' the red-headed woman said.

'Tell us the truth!' The man's grip tightened, making her squirm and gasp with pain. Raven was inwardly raging, but that stern, ice-blue gaze made her quail.

'I am alone,' she confessed. She was unable to stop her tears from coming. For an instant, she thought she saw his expression soften with pity, then he looked at the woman and his face became grim once more. But it was a chance. If she could only get him on her side . . . Raven gazed up at the man with imploring eyes. 'Please, don't let her hurt me again!'

The tall woman snorted with disgust. 'Listen, you can drop that terrified-little-girl act. It's not fooling anyone. You're older than you look, I'll wager, and I've the scars to prove you're a menace.'

Raven was furious at the exposure of her ploy. 'How dare you! I am a princess of the blood royal!'

'Not here, you're not,' the woman growled. 'You're our prisoner, and in a lot of trouble. You attacked first, remember. I still owe you for pitching me off that tower.'

Well, that was true enough, Raven admitted to herself. Yet despite her attack on the woman, they hadn't actually harmed her, though they could have killed her at once. And she was so tired of being alone . . .

'Lady,' she said at last, 'I beg pardon for that. I – I saw you coming, and I was afraid . . . I thought if I surprised you . . .'

To her utter surprise, the woman grinned. 'You didn't do too badly, considering. Why did you slow my fall with your wings, though? If you had dropped me from that height, you could have killed me outright.'

Raven shrugged, making her dark, glossy feathers rustle. 'I thought if I had a hostage, the others might not hurt me.'

Just then a hulking figure emerged from the shadows. Raven gasped. And she'd thought these two were big! Behind him was a fearsome dark shape with flaming eyes. Raven was all too familiar with the savage great cats who lived on the northern side of her own mountains, and waged a constant war with her folk. She shrieked, and tried to run, but the man pulled her back to his side. 'It's all right,' he reassured her. 'Shia is a friend, and she can talk to us.'

'She says that you really are alone, but she's found a camp of sorts, with some food.' The woman chuckled. 'She's cross because Bohan here wouldn't let her eat any of it. Seriously, though, is it your camp? We're all dreadfully hungry.'

'What I have, I will share with you,' Raven offered, anxious to make some gesture of friendship. 'I caught some birds, but there was nothing to make a fire. Besides, I was never taught to cook,' she added frankly, 'so my hunger is as great as yours.'

The woman caught the man's eye and shrugged. 'Lead on – and our thanks to you,' she said.

They walked through the empty city, the tall woman limping slightly and leaning on the man's arm for support. Introductions were made, although everyone was too concerned with the thought of food to say much more than that. Raven had set up her camp in a building that consisted of a single large chamber with walls of misty blue crystal. There was no door to close, and no furnishings or signs that there had ever been any; though shelves and niches had been carved into the walls and a pile of assorted gems had been stacked along one side. The chamber's best asset was a small spring-fed pool in one corner, which absorbed the attention of the thirsty strangers for a considerable time.

Raven produced four good-sized birds that she'd caught on the wing, as she had often done at home for sport. The strangers took charge of supper with a capability that she envied. The men – Anvar and the huge Bohan – took the fowl outside to clean, while Aurian, the tall woman, scrabbled around in the pile of gems. Raven was mystified. What use would jewels be to her out here? Then her eyes nearly popped out of her head with astonishment. Aurian selected a large, flattish piece of crystal and set it in the middle of the floor. She sat down cross-legged and held her hands over the stone, her eyes narrowed with concentration. Within minutes, the gem was glowing hot and giving off a warm light that set the walls of their shelter twinkling cosily. Raven stared in utter disbelief; half afraid, half unable to believe her good fortune. 'You are Magefolk?' she whispered.

Aurian nodded briefly, still preoccupied with her task. Raven clutched at her, the words spilling out before she could stop them. She had never intended to go back, but . . . 'Will you help me? My people need you desperately!'

Aurian sighed. 'Raven, I don't know if we can. We're trapped here ourselves. But tell us about it while we eat. It must be serious if it has driven you out here alone.'

Anvar and Bohan returned with supper cleaned and plucked, and the Mages contrived to spit the birds on sword blades and wedge them in position over the fiery gem. 'Can I help you heat that thing?' Anvar asked Aurian.

She shook her head. 'I'm expending very little effort, because the crystal boosts my power. Dragon-magic has its uses.'

While they ate, Raven told her story. Her people had lived in their isolated mountain fastness for centuries, growing hardy crops in terraced valleys and tending their flocks of hill goats and ground birds. But in the last months, an unnatural, unseasonal winter had laid waste to their civilization. She told the Mages of sudden, lethal snowstorms, biting cold that had ruined the land, and the ascendancy of the evil, power-hungry High Priest. Raven shuddered as she spoke of human sacrifices; of atrocities committed in the name of salvation; of the helplessness and desperation of her mother, the queen. 'Then Blacktalon insisted on taking me as his bride,' she said. 'I knew he planned to depose Flamewing and consolidate his hold over the Skyfolk, ruling in my name.'

She described her escape from Aerillia in the storm, and the hardship and suffering of crossing the desert, flying by night from oasis to oasis, exhausted and hungry, but driven onward by fear and desperation. Tears stood in her eyes. 'I didn't want to run away. It was my only hope – I would not have survived Blacktalon's cruelty for long, but it tore my heart to go. Even at the risk of my life I would return, if I thought I could do something. Could you help us? Please? My people are dying!'

Aurian looked away, unable to meet her eyes.

Anvar both saw and sensed the Mage's distress, and knew what she must be thinking. Eliseth. Who else could have brought down this unnatural winter? The Winged Folk had fallen victim to the Magefolk's pursuit of Aurian. An uneasy silence had fallen in the chamber. Abruptly, Aurian thrust the remains of her supper aside. Without a word she hoisted herself up with her staff, and limped out of the chamber. Anvar followed her outside.

Aurian was sitting with her back against the wall of their building, shivering a little in the cool desert night, her eyes fixed blankly on the sparkling heavens. 'Go away,' she said, without turning.

'No.' Anvar sat down beside her. 'Stop blaming yourself.'

'Who else should I blame?' There was a thin edge of anger in her voice. 'All this started because Forral and I . . .'

'Don't be stupid!' Anvar snapped. 'Aurian, we've been through this. It started because Miathan turned the Cauldron to evil. It started because of the blind, arrogant prejudice of the Magefolk towards Mortals. You've suffered enough, without tearing yourself up over the Winged Folk.'

'How can you say that?' Aurian flared. 'We're all responsible.' Her eyes hardened. 'Yes, even you, Anvar. You brought Forral into Miathan's chamber that night, and forced the Archmage to release the Wraiths.'

Anvar turned suddenly cold. 'I've always wondered if you blamed me for Forral's death,' he said quietly.

Aurian remained silent, refusing to look at him. Not knowing what else to say, he went back inside with bowed head and heavy steps.

Raven looked up as he entered. 'Did I say something wrong?' she asked him anxiously. Anvar stared at her as though returning from a dream, and collected his scattered thoughts.

'No – nothing. She needs some time to think.'

Shia was not fooled. 'Should I go?'

He shook his head. 'She wants to be alone.'

The light of the crystal was dying. Anvar lay beside it, but its residual heat did nothing to pierce the bitter chill inside him. Why now? he thought. Why, after all this time, should she accuse me? But she had every right. During the months of their journey, he had thrust away the memory of his part in Forral's death, not wanting to believe it and hoping against hope that Aurian did not. Aurian . . . surely if she blamed him, she must hate him? Anvar tossed relentlessly, tormented by guilt and misery. It was hours before he finally fell asleep, but the Mage did not return.

Aurian sat long into the night gazing blindly at the stars and trying to come to terms with her guilt and confusion. Her angry, unguarded outburst to Anvar had horrified her. She hadn't meant to accuse him – the words had come from nowhere, as the thought had come into her mind. Do I really blame him? she thought. Has this been at the back of my mind all along? Suddenly she was startled out of her thoughts by a glimpse, out of the corner of her eye, of a stealthy movement in the darkness beyond her. The Mage reached quickly for her sword, and caught her breath as a figure emerged from the shadows.

'Forral!' The exclamation froze in Aurian's throat as he stepped towards her. This pale wraith was not the lusty, living man she had known and loved. His image wavered, oddly translucent and cloaked in an eye-deceiving glimmer. His ghostly face was frowning and sad. Aurian felt herself redden with shame as she heard his gruff voice in her mind.

'That wasn't very fair to Anvar, was it, love? I taught you better than to waste time doling out blame. Miathan's evil is spreading, and that's no way to deal with it!'

'I know. I'm sorry,' she whispered unhappily. The ghostly figure smiled, his expression softening into a wistful, loving look. Beckoning, he began to walk away from her. 'Forral, wait!' Aurian pulled herself up on her staff and limped hastily after him, following him into the shadows of the abandoned city.

She couldn't catch him. No matter how fast Aurian tried to hobble, Forral's shade kept the same tantalizing distance between them, though he never went out of her sight. At last he stopped, turning towards her, and she realized that they had reached the mysterious cone-shaped edifice that was the centre and focus of Dhiammara. The humming power that emanated from the structure seemed to vibrate within her very bones, but she kept her eyes fixed on the beloved figure. She limped towards him, her hand outstretched, longing to touch him once more.

'Don't!' The warning was sharp enough to halt her, though Forral's voice had been gentle. He shook his head, his expression one of deepest sorrow. 'You can't touch me, lass. I'm breaking rules as it is, coming to you like this.' He smiled ruefully. 'We were never one for rules, were we, you and I?'

'But I want to be with you!' Her voice caught on a sob.

'I know. Oh, my dearest love, how I've missed you! But I don't begrudge you your life, and that of our child. Besides, you bear a grave responsibility. The times ahead won't be easy, but I know you'll manage.' His face shone with pride for her. 'You've the courage and determination to succeed, you and young Anvar.'

Forral's words grew gradually fainter as he spoke. His shade seemed to be dissolving, drifting away from her like smoke on the wind. 'Don't leave me!' Aurian cried in anguish as his image faded.

'They're calling me back.' His voice was distant now. 'Take care of our babe, love . . . Remember . . . I love you . . . But I'm gone . . .'

'No!' Aurian flung herself forward to the space where he had stood. 'I love you too, Forral,' she whispered. Leaning her head against the cool, tingling wall of the building, she gave way to her heartache, her body shaking with sobs.

She never knew how long she wept there. But it was not long. As her tears fell on the smooth wall of green crystal, the humming began to increase in volume and pitch. The Mage, her thoughts filled with Forral, never noticed, until a door snapped open abruptly in the stone beneath her, pitching her headlong inside.

'Oh!' Aurian sat up, wiped her eyes, and looked around. She was in a wide corridor that had been carved out of the gem. Its interior glowed with a dim green light. The air was stale, and heavy with an oddly spicy scent, but it was freshening rapidly as the cold, thin air of the plateau whispered through the open portal. Once again she felt the living mind within this place; the sense of an alien power that tugged at her, urging her further within. The Mage resisted, wanting only to remain where she was, to hug the precious memory of her meeting with Forral to her as she might clutch at a dagger driven into her own breast. But the power was persistent – and Forral had told her in no uncertain terms that she had responsibilities.

'Oh, all right,' Aurian muttered ungraciously, groping on the ground for her staff. 'But you'll have to wait until I fix this wretched knee. Whatever you are, I want both legs under me when I meet you!'

The healing was surprisingly easy, and the Mage could have sworn that the mysterious power was actively helping her. Whether it was true or not, it reassured her. She stood up, and despite the growing sense of awe that this strange place engendered she crept forward into the depths of the building.

Once again the corridor wound in an ever climbing spiral. I'm getting sick of this, Aurian thought. You'd think that once in a while they might vary the design. Her smile at her own temerity faded abruptly as the passage opened into an airy, circular chamber – a dead end. The light was brighter now through the green crystal walls, and she suspected that dawn must be breaking outside. The floor of the empty hall glittered in the growing illumination, and the Mage saw that it was inlaid with a delicate mosaic of gold in an intricate whorled pattern that led both her eyes and her feet to a great sunburst shape in the centre of the room. As Aurian stepped on to it there was a sharp, deafening concussion like a clap of thunder. She recoiled, throwing up an arm to shield her eyes as a blinding beam of sunlight, focused by some hidden aperture in the domed ceiling, shot down to strike her in a blaze of gold.

'Aurian has gone!' Shia pawed roughly at Anvar, her eyes aflame. 'What happened between you last night, human?'

544

Anvar came abruptly awake. 'Gods, we have to find her. After last night, there's no telling what she'll do.'

Wan daylight shone through the crystal walls of their dwelling. Bohan was packing up the remains of their supper while Raven watched wide-eyed from a corner. 'What is happening?' she asked. 'What has become of the Mage?'

Anvar almost choked on his resentment. If she hadn't decided to saddle them with her problems . . . 'Come on, you!' he said harshly, yanking her to her feet.

When they got outside, Shia was already quartering the ground. 'Cats don't usually hunt by scent,' she told him, 'but I think I can track her. It looks as though she went into the city.'

Gradually the dazzle faded from her vision. Aurian could see once more, and could scarcely believe what her eyes were telling her. The hall of the sunburst had vanished completely, and she stood in a vast chamber that was formed entirely of gold: walls, floor and rounded ceiling. In the centre was a towering, haphazard heap of gold and gems, and on top of it – Aurian had to steel herself not to run. Couched on the jewelled pile, lit by a single ray of buttery sunlight that streamed through an opening in the apex of the dome, was a huge golden dragon.

The Mage drew her sword and backed away, looking for a means of escape. There was none. Apart from the aperture in the high ceiling, the room had no exits at all. Aurian suffered a nasty moment or two before she noticed that the dragon's eyes were closed, and that it had not moved an inch since she'd first set eyes on it. She remembered the devious time-trap. The Dragonfolk were famed for their cunning – could it be feigning sleep to lure her closer?

Nonsense, Aurian told herself firmly. Why, something that size could catch you in seconds, if it wanted to take the trouble. Squinting against the flaring golden light, she peered at the motionless creature, reluctant to go any closer, and saw at last the reason for its stillness. The bluish glimmer was difficult to see against the gilded brightness of the dragon's scales, but it was undoubtedly there. Someone had imprisoned it – taken it out of time using the same spell that Finbarr had taught her so long ago. Her Magefolk curiosity winning out, Aurian crept closer to the slumbering monster.

It was difficult not to be afraid, though she knew that the dragon was helpless. It was immense – easily big enough to fill the Great Hall of the Academy, Aurian thought. But it was beautiful, with the sun highlighting the elegant lines of its sinuous body. It lay curled like a sleeping cat, its slender, tapering tail draped across its fearsome jaws, its vast wings stretched protectively over its treasure. Those wings! Aurian was fascinated by them. They were ribbed like the wings of a bat, but between the golden struts was stretched a fragile, translucent membrane spangled with darkly-gleaming scales in a silver network of veining like the thin wire that bound the grip of her sword. The Mage recalled both Yazour and Ithalasa saying that dragons fed by absorbing the sun's energy directly through their wings. It seemed they had been right.

'Well, now what?' Her muttered words sounded obscenely loud in the stillness of the chamber. Aurian fought the conviction that she had been lured here by the mysterious power for a reason: to do the most foolhardy thing that she had ever contemplated. She had been deliberately led to this place, but whether it was for her benefit – that was another matter. Yet when she looked at the magnificent dragon, she found herself moved to unexpected sympathy. Poor thing, she thought. How long have you been trapped like that? Well, I only hope you're grateful. Backing away to what she fervently hoped was a safe distance, Aurian took the staff from her belt and began to unravel the spell.

As she did so, an intense feeling of rightness washed over the Mage – a confidence that suddenly vanished, leaving her weak-kneed, as the dragon raised its head. Huge faceted eyes of slumbering fire pinned her to the spot with an unblinking stare. The dragon opened its mouth, showing teeth like curved and gleaming swords – and Aurian's fear turned to sheer delight as the air of the chamber came alive with light and music. Whirls of pure, ever-changing colour flowed across the ceiling and walls. The air flickered and flashed with shifting tatters of rainbow. The colours danced and swirled to a music so pure, so utterly perfect that the Mage forgot her peril.

Rounded and mellifluous but strengthened with an underlying metallic edge, the fluent cascade of notes was hard and mellow as gold. As Aurian stood, lost in wonder, her powers were hard at work analysing, remembering, finding patterns. After a time, meaning began to emerge from the breathtaking display of light and sound. This was the speech of the Dragonfolk!

'I said, who awakens me?' There was an edge of irritation in the fluid fall of notes, underlaid with a plangent yearning. 'Why do you not answer? Are you the One, come at last?'

After the dragon's music, Aurian's voice sounded dull and feeble to her ears. 'I don't know,' she confessed. 'Am I?'

The dragon seemed to have no trouble understanding her. Its chuckle sent prisms of light bouncing through the chamber, making the colours tremble and dance. 'You have courage and honesty, at any rate! If you passed the first test by unsealing the temple door, there is hope, at least.'

'I opened that door?'

The creature snorted. 'Of course! This temple has been sealed for centuries; ever since the Dragonfolk quit Dhiammara. Our wise ones decided that since we departed in sorrow, after the Cataclysm, then sorrow would be the key for the One to unlock our ancient wisdom once more. Your tears were the only thing that could open that door, Wizard.' The dragon cocked its massive head, looking at her sidelong. 'I take it they were your tears?'

The Mage was taken aback. 'Well, of course they were. I was grieving for someone very dear to me, who died.'

'Grief, eh? Most appropriate.' There was smugness in the dragon's tone, and Aurian clenched her fists.

'I'm glad you think so,' she snapped. 'Personally, I don't find it particularly clever to make use of another's suffering.'

'*Who are you to question the wisdom of the Dragonfolk?*'

Aurian was flattened by the dragon's roar. The coloured lights of his speech exploded into jagged shards of white lightning that seared into her vision. The Mage picked herself up and glared at him, so angered by his bullying arrogance that she forgot to be afraid. 'Who am I?' she cried. 'I am Aurian, daughter of Geraint, Fire-Mage. My father died trying to unlock the secrets of the Dragonfolk's so-called wisdom, so don't expect me to be impressed with your powers! Spare me your games, dragon; I have no time for them. The Magefolk – Wizards, you used to call them – have turned to evil. The Cauldron has been found, and the Nihilim let loose into the world. What, in your infinite wisdom, do you suggest I do about that?'

The dragon's eyes flared bright crimson. 'Then the ancient prophecies have come true. You *must* be the One!'

'The one? Which one?' Aurian realized that she was shouting. 'I don't understand!'

'I see that the centuries have done little to moderate the infamous Wizard temper,' the dragon snapped. It rattled its wings in irritation, sending a small avalanche of gold and gems cascading musically down its sloping treasure pile. 'I speak of the Sword, you imbecile! Chierannath, Sword of Flame, whose making was preordained by the greatest of our seers, to combat the misuse of the other great weapons. You dare speak to me of loss and grief? I, who have been sundered from my people, from my friends and loved ones, to wait here, frozen in time, until the Sword should be needed. My task, ignorant one, is to identify the One for whom it was forged. And now you have come, disturbing my slumber with your questions and your puny rage!'

Aurian spoke with the calm of deep shock. 'Are you saying that the Sword – the mightiest of the great weapons – was crafted centuries before my birth specifically for me?'

'That remains to be seen.' The dragon sounded sceptical. 'I admit that when I imagined the One, I had more of an – heroic figure in mind.'

'So you'd be happier if I were some hulking, muscle-bound warrior, would you? Well, that's your problem.'

The creature's eyes flashed with a dangerous light. 'Watch your words. I will take no abuse from a puny, two-legged Wizard.'

Aurian swallowed hard, remembering the last fix in which her temper had landed her. The dragon had no right to complain about people being quick to anger. 'Very well,' she said. 'Assuming I am the One, what happens now?'

'Assuming that you are, you will complete the third test, which is to recreate the lost Staff of Earth.'

Aurian was speechless. *Recreate* the Staff? It was impossible! Doubt slid insidiously into her mind, and disappointment swamped her. He's right – I can't be the one, she thought miserably. She almost told him – almost. Instead she took a firm grip on her staff and straightened her spine, knowing that if she gave up without trying she would never be able to live with herself. The dragon was watching her intently, its curious eyes unblinking. 'Well? Do you intend to stand there gaping for ever?'

Damn you, Aurian thought. 'Am I allowed to ask questions?'

He laughed. 'Very good! I may answer three questions – but not the obvious one. Make them count, Wizard!'

The Mage remembered what she had heard of the history of the Staff. 'I was told the Staff had been lost during the Cataclysm,' she ventured. 'Was it destroyed then?'

'Yes.' That was all he said. Don't do me any favours, Aurian thought sourly.

'But,' she went on, 'you said recreate, so the powers of the staff must still exist.' In a flash of inspiration she remembered Anvar regaining his powers, and how the Archmage had stolen them in the first place. She thought of the crystal door underground that had sapped her powers, and the bracelets of Harihn's folk.

'Was that a question?' The dragon broke into her train of thought – deliberately, Aurian was sure.

'No,' she said hastily, trusting her intuition. 'This is my second question: is the crystal that holds the power of the Staff within this room?'

Starbursts of light filled the chamber. 'Yes!' the dragon sang. 'And now you must locate it.'

Aurian swore a bloodcurdling oath. Now she knew why the dragon had such an uncomfortable bed. It was a decoy and another test. Somewhere in that pile, indistinguishable from all the other gems, lay the crystal that she sought. The Mage was horrified. It'll take years to search through that lot, she thought. Think, Aurian! There must be a better way! And there was, she realized. Because by her nature she had always been drawn to her father's Fire-magic, she had had a tendency to neglect Eilin's side of her heritage. Now, at last, it would come into its own.

Grounding the heel of her staff firmly, the Mage gripped it in both hands and summoned the powers of Earth – the slow, heavy lives of the mountains and stones; the soil's fecund womb; the exuberant springing of growing things and the bright, brief lives of creatures that crawled or ran, spawning in the endless cycle of life, death, and ultimate decay from which new life would spring. By all these and more, that were the essence of its very creation, Aurian called upon the powers of the Staff of the Earth.

And the powers answered. Aurian's staff almost jerked from her hands to point at the heart of the dragon's couch. The serpent-carved wood began to hum and vibrate, and to blossom with a thick emerald light. The dragon gave a startled squawk – the most unmusical sound she had heard it make – and scrambled aside with a speed that belied its massive size as its bed began to shift and shudder, spilling in a glittering cascade across the chamber. From the centre of the pile an answering ray of green shot upwards. Aurian dropped, protecting her head, as a mighty explosion of gems and gold shot violently outwards to rattle against the walls.

In the silence that followed, the Mage discovered, to her relief, that she had kept a firm hold on her tugging staff. She stood up shakily, bruised all over from the hard-flung treasure, to find the chamber flooded with a rich green light. The dragon's head snaked out from beneath a protecting wing and she heard the rasp of air in its throat as it sucked in a huge breath. 'Upon my word,' it said, sounding awed, 'you do nothing by halves, Wizard!'

The staff pointed unnerringly to the centre of the room. There, in the space that it had cleared so vigorously for itself, a glowing green gem, about the size of Aurian's circled finger and thumb, sat in solitary splendour. The Mage approached it cautiously, narrowing her eyes against the intense emerald radiance of the stone. She halted an arm's length away, prevented from going closer by the energy that pulsed from it like a wall of green fire. Not until she had remade the Staff would that power be tamed and contained so that a Mage could wield it and survive. But how could it be done? Aurian ran her hands down her own staff, feeling Anvar's skilled and lively carvings beneath her fingers. The twin serpents that coiled around it were so lifelike that she could almost feel them move. Feel them move . . . That gave her an idea.

There was, however, one last thing to settle. Aurian turned to the dragon. 'I want to ask my third question.'

The creature seemed surprised. 'Ask, then; but I warn you, I cannot tell you how to accomplish your task.'

'That's all right. What I want to know is – if I recreate the Staff, do I get to keep it?'

The dragon threw back its head and roared – but with laughter, not the rage she had expected. 'Temeritous Wizard! No one ever beat your race for sheer gall! Yes, you may keep the Staff, for you will have earned it. But be warned – always be aware of the forces at your command, and the destruction you might wreak. Never make the mistake that the users of the Cauldron have made.'

Approaching the stone as closely as she dared, Aurian concentrated her powers; not on the gem itself, but upon her own staff. She passed her hands over the familiar surface, her fingers tingling and bathed in light as she strove, using the magic of the living Earth, to breathe life into the wood. Beneath her fingers, the serpents stirred, their carved eyes winking into sparkling awareness. Forked tongues flicking in and out, they raised their scaly heads from the staff. Aurian bent her will upon them; instructing, commanding. Holding her staff by its iron-shod heel, she held it out to touch the crystal. The serpents reached forth and took the stone, grasping it tightly between them in their fanged jaws.

An overwhelming surge of force ran up the staff, almost knocking the Mage off her feet. She swayed, holding on tightly, ablaze with the power of the stone. She felt her form expanding to embrace the room, the city, the desert . . . She encompassed the entire world – each stone, each blade of grass, every creature that drew breath – she was all of them, and they were her, and she gloried with them in the miracle of their creation! Aurian's cry of triumph rang to the very stars as she raised aloft the newly created Staff of Earth!

Shia had lost the Mage's trail. Leading the anxious

551

companions through the city, she had brought them at last to the foot of the towering green cone, and there Aurian's scent had disappeared. 'I don't understand,' she told Anvar. 'It reaches this place, then stops.'

Anvar cursed. 'Don't be ridiculous! It must be there somewhere. She can't have vanished!'

Shia glared at him. 'Would you like to try?' she said pointedly.

Anvar sighed. 'I'm sorry, Shia. I don't know what to do either. We've been all around this thing, and there isn't an entrance anywhere.' He gazed up at the steep, glassy sides. 'And she couldn't have climbed . . .'

His words were drowned by the deafening roar of an explosion. The cone blazed with a piercing viridian light; the entire edifice rocked right down to its foundations. Anvar and the others were thrown down as the earth cracked and lurched beneath their feet. A great wind seemed to come from nowhere, howling and shrieking between the city's buildings and whipping up choking clouds of dust and debris. Anvar struggled unsuccessfully to rise. 'She *is* in there!' he cried above the noise of the sudden storm. 'She must be! Great gods, what has she done this time?'

34
Earthquake!

Anvar pressed his body flat to the ground as the earth shuddered and heaved. Nearby he could see the others, all similarly flattened by the force of the tearing gale and the quaking surface beneath them. He choked on the windborne dust, and rubbed his streaming eyes to see Raven nearby. The winged girl, unable to fly in the storm, was whey-faced and weeping with terror. Even as he watched, a gust caught her beneath her wings and half-lifted her from the ground, rolling her over and over. Bohan grabbed her wrist as she slid past, his weight providing an anchor for Raven, who caught at his clothes with her free hand and clung to him, he face contorted in a silent shriek.

A hideous grating sound from above his head drew Anvar's attention upwards. Before his horrified eyes, a network of gaping cracks snaked up the tower's green sides. 'We have to get away from here!' he screamed, trying to scramble to his feet only to be thrown down again by the keening wind that snatched his words away. Shia, because of their mental link, was the only one who heard him.

'How?' The one word was harsh with fear.

The cracks were widening, and to his dismay Anvar saw that nearby buildings were suffering the same fate. The circle of destruction was spreading out from the tower to engulf not only the entire city, but the tortured bones of the mountain itself. He flung himself to one side as the ground tore apart beneath him in a widening fissure. Too late! Anvar screamed as the earth crumbled beneath him, pitching him head first into the yawning chasm whose edges were already closing back together.

Pain shot up his leg as a strong grip fastened around his ankle. Anvar lurched to a halt, dangling upside down over the closing gap. Faint as he was with terror, he hardly felt his other ankle being seized; knowing only that he was being pulled to safety as the jagged lip of the chasm gouged painfully at his stomach and ribs, ripping his thin desert robe. The grinding edges of rock snapped shut, missing his trailing fingers by inches. He felt himself being hauled roughly to his feet, and came face to face with Aurian.

'Get inside!' She shoved him towards a doorway, an aperture in the face of the green tower that had not been there before. Shia was crouched inside, her face creased in a snarl. Bohan, fighting the gale with all his strength, was tugging the winged girl towards the entrance. Anvar felt Aurian's arm around him, forcing his faltering steps up the spiral corridor that wound into the heart of the disintegrating building. With a quick glance back to see that the others were following, she dragged him forward. Choking showers of green dust fell from the crazed ceiling above, blinding them. Anvar's feet slid and stumbled as chunks of emerald erupted from the cracking floor.

Aurian suddenly halted, cursing, and he saw that the way was blocked by a cave-in. Before Anvar could blink, the Mage had raised her free hand, holding something that blazed with a dazzling green light. There was a blinding flash, an explosion of magic that knocked him clean off his feet, and the passage was clear once more. Aurian wrenched him upright, almost pulling his arm from its socket, but Anvar pulled back, frightened by the unbelievable intensity of the power he had just witnessed. 'What was that?' he shrieked.

'Staff of Earth,' Aurian replied brusquely, as if it were the most normal thing in the world. 'Come on!'

The Mage hauled the astounded Anvar along until they entered a circular chamber where a golden mosaic glinted through the fallen dust on the floor. Pulling him across the chamber at a half-run, she pushed him against the far wall. His heart lurched as he felt himself falling. He put out his arms to save himself, and his hands passed straight through the stone as his body was gripped by the viscious substance of a portal like the one in the oasis.

Once he had passed through into the darkness beyond, familiarity gave Anvar the presence of mind to scramble out of the way of the entrance, so as not to impeded the others. Shia was next – he could feel her coat, gritty with dust as she brushed past him, spitting and snarling, followed by an hysterical Raven. The winged girl was shrieking at the top of her voice and striking out blindly in terror. A flailing wingtip caught Anvar in the face as she struggled, but though he wanted to reassure her he was wheezing helplessly, unable to catch his breath, and crippled by a stitch in his side. He felt a warm, sticky trickle of blood down his ribs and belly where the skin had been torn on the edge of the chasm. Like all flesh wounds, the abrasions stung furiously, exacerbated by the sweat that drenched his body. Though he was stunned by Aurian's revelation, all he could see was the jaws of the chasm closing . . . closing . . .

Raven's struggles had ceased. Bohan was comforting her with his silent, solid presence. The chamber was becoming cramped as Aurian joined them. 'Cover your eyes!' Her voice rang through the darkness. The flash of Magelight was visible even through Anvar's closed eyelids and shielding hands, but for a dreadful moment nothing happened. He fought a stifling panic, imagining himself trapped and crushed within the collapsing tower. Suddenly, after what seemed an eternity, his stomach leapt into his throat as the chamber began to lurch unsteadily downwards in a series of shuddering jerks. 'Thank the gods! I thought we'd left it too late for a minute.' Aurian's matter-of-fact voice was like balm. With a sight of relief, Anvar let himself slip into oblivion.

'There, my friend – does that feel better?'

It did. the damp cloth was soft and cool against Anvar's face, washing away the gritty dust that clogged his eyes and mouth. He opened his eyes, and saw the plump, comforting face of Eliizar's wife. 'Aurian, he wakes,' she called.

Anvar was reassured by the cheerful ring in her voice, until he saw the Mage. Aurian had changed. She filled the whole of his consciousness, looking taller, fiercer, more vibrant and more beautiful than he had ever seen her; glowing from within with an awesome power that surrounded her like a cloak of light. Anvar swallowed hard. This was a goddess – some mighty queen of legend. This was not his Aurian.

'What happened to you?' He got the words out with difficulty, awed by her presence and fighting an urge to shrink away from her. 'You're different!'

Aurian shook her head. 'It's the same old me, I'm afraid. Do I look so dreadful?' Her smile was replaced by a fleeting frown.

'No. Not dreadful.' Somehow, her uncertainty was reassuring to Anvar. 'Magnificent.'

The Mage grimaced. 'And that's given everyone such a shock? Eliizar nearly fainted away at the sight of me.'

Anvar knew she was evading his question. 'What happened to you?' he persisted.

'Don't you remember? I found it, Anvar. The Staff of Earth!' From a fold in her robe, where its dazzling light had been concealed, Aurian produced the Staff, and Anvar quailed from the power that pulsed through its slender, glowing length. This was the source of the fire that imbued the Mage. But . . . Anvar frowned. It was Aurian's old staff, but changed. At the top, where there had been no ornamentation, the twin heads of the serpents reared up, holding between them, in their open jaws, a green gem whose incandescence could outshine the very sun. Anvar shielded his eyes, unable to look directly at the brilliant stone.

Aurian tucked the Staff back into her robe, shielding its light. 'When I learn to control it properly . . .' She spoke calmly, but her eyes blazed with savage excitement. 'At last we'll have a weapon against Miathan!'

Anvar shuddered, suddenly afraid, thinking of the earthquake that had almost killed them all, and remembering what the Archmage had done with the Cauldron. Would Aurian create such ruin in her pursuit of revenge?

Anvar noticed that Aurian's face was taut with strain. She was struggling to keep her voice light and calm as she continued, speaking too quickly to give him a chance to interrupt. 'I healed those scrapes of yours – they were full of dirt from the edge of that chasm – so you're bound to feel drained for a while. Nereni will get us something to eat, and I'm going to awaken Raven now. She was so hysterical that I put her to sleep for a while. Before she wakes I want to try to do something about language. She can understand us, but now we're back with the others there'll be problems. If I can fix it for her to understand the speech of the Khazalim, we'll all be able to communicate.'

'Can you do that?' Anvar was surprised.

'Well – I've never heard of such a thing being tried before, but I think I could manage. Remember, her people were Magefolk before they lost their powers. The understanding of languages should lie within her, if only I can free it.' Before he could speak again, Aurian was gone.

'Are you well?' Nereni sounded anxious.

Anvar had forgotten she was there. 'Just tired,' he told her. Nereni nodded. 'No wonder you were shaken,' she said. 'Down here, we thought the mountain was about to collapse.' With a worried frown, she glanced across at Eliizar, who was tending Shia and Bohan. Though they seemed little the worse for their experiences, the sword master's face was ashen.

'Anvar . . .' Nereni hesitated. 'What did happen up there? What caused the earthquake? Aurian has changed – enough to frighten Eliizar out of his wits when you came through the wall at the back of the cavern.'

So that was where they had come out. Anvar had been wondering how Aurian had brought them back. 'Weren't *you* afraid of her?' he asked, avoiding her questions.

Nereni shrugged. 'I hardly know – I was so relieved to see you all, I never thought . . .' She smiled confidingly. 'Sometimes, I think women are more practical than men – but never let Eliizar hear that I said so! Anyway, you must eat. I will prepare us some food, then perhaps you will tell me how you found that one.' She gestured at Raven, who was awake now, and conversing quietly with Aurian in, Anvar noted with surprise, the language of the Khazalim. I would never have believed she could do it, he thought, and shuddered inwardly, wondering what other powers might be now at the Mage's disposal.

After a time Aurian persuaded Raven to meet the others around the fire, and Anvar was relieved to see the winged girl responding gratefully to Nereni's mothering. While they ate, night fell across the desert outside. Aurian looked across at Anvar. 'I think the time has come to tell our friends what brought us to the south.'

557

With that, she began to give the others a brief history of Miathan's perfidy, which had brought herself and Anvar to the Southern Kingdoms. Anvar noted that she omitted all mention of Forral, and the fact that the two Mages were not wedded as they claimed, and wondered. But perhaps she was right. It did no harm, and, given the customs of these people, surely it was more convenient to keep up the charade for a little longer? Without giving anyone time to speak, she plunged on into what had happened within the mountain, and how she had come to possess the Staff of Earth.

Anvar was certain that Aurian was leaving things out of this part of her tale. They had become so close after she had saved his life in the slave camp that he instinctively knew when she was hiding something. He felt a growing sense of unease. Why had Aurian left out what had happened after they'd parted that night? What had drawn her to the emerald tower? She claimed that the door had opened when she had leaned on it. Having tried the same thing himself, he knew that to be a complete fabrication. Anvar struggled with his suspicion. What was she trying to conceal?

'Then the dragon said that I had proved that the Sword was crafted for me.' Aurian's words brought Anvar abruptly out of his worried thoughts.

'You have the Sword?'

The Mage shook her head. 'It was sent into hiding. The Dragonfolk gave it to the Phaerie to take beyond the world. If the seers were correct, they'll return it when word of this new evil reaches them. The dragon told me I must find it, and circumvent the traps set to guard it. He said that the Phaerie have an incentive to fulfil their side of the bargain, and when the Sword is returned to the world its presence should draw me to it sooner or later.'

Silence followed her words. All eyes were riveted on the Mage. Anvar tried to meet her eyes, but she bit her lip and looked away. 'What about the missing parts of the story?' he demanded. 'How did you really get into that tower? How did you know to go there in the first place? If this dragon exists, where is he now? And, more to the point, what did you do to cause the destruction of the city?'

'Are you calling me a liar?' Aurian's voice was dangerously quiet. Anvar saw hurt and disappointment on the Mage's face, and knew that he was being hard on her – unfair, perhaps – but he had to know the truth. The Staff was too powerful to risk her becoming corrupted, as Miathan had been with the Cauldron. Thinking of that, he became uncomfortably aware of the others listening to his words. Eliizar's face was rigid with fear and mistrust at all this talk of sorcery, and suddenly Anvar understood the age-old Magefolk compulsion to keep their business to themselves. This was between himself and Aurian.

'We need to talk,' he told her in a low voice, using their own language, but his words were drowned by the staccato ring of hooves on stone. Anvar turned to see the veiled and shadowy figure of a lone horseman riding through the cavern entrance, ducking low to avoid the lintel, the draught of his passage making the torches flicker and smoke.

Eliizar let out a whoop of joy. 'Yazour!'

They crowded around the young captain, all talking at once, other considerations forgotten for the moment. Yazour loosed the string of horses he had been leading, and the thirsty beasts, used to the ways of Dhiammara, made their way up the ramp to the upper pool, taking their burdens with them. Nereni persuaded everyone to stop crowding the tired man long enough for him to sit by the fire, where they all crowded around him again, their faces expectant.

Yazour took a grateful swig from the water sack and rubbed a hand over his dusty and unshaven face, looking round at them all. 'All here – including our missing Lady! I see you found the supplies, then – and who is this?' He looked wonderingly at Raven, who smiled back shyly.

Eliizar grinned, plainly much more at ease now that another warrior had returned. 'I win our wager,' he told Yazour. 'You see – the Winged Folk *do* exist!'

'Indeed they do – and if you had told me they were so pretty, Eliizar, I would have been climbing those very mountains even now in search of them!'

Raven blushed crimson, and Anvar, despite his troubles, had to smile.

'I wish I had come sooner,' Yazour was saying, 'but I had my oath of loyalty . . .' He shook his head sadly. 'It was a difficult decision to make, but I was so sickened by what the Khisal had done – well, in the end I could stand it no longer. I knew I had to come back for you. I persuaded the guard to turn a blind eye while I slipped away – I knocked the man out, to spare him Harihn's wrath when my escape was discovered – and travelled back as quickly as I could.'

'There's no chance of the prince following you?' Aurian's voice was sharp with concern.

Yazour shook his head, his face gone suddenly bleak. 'Even Harihn is not that stupid. He'll save his own hide. You see, we are in grave danger, my Lady. The weather has changed out of season, and we must leave first thing tomorrow night and cross the desert as quickly as we can. It will be a difficult crossing –we are ill equipped with what little I could bring – but we must make all haste, for our lives' sake. The sandstorms will be upon us at any time, and if we cannot reach safety before they arrive . . .'

This had to be Eliseth's work. Anvar clenched his fists. The Magefolk had absolutely no concern for the innocent lives that might be – had already been – lost in the process of Aurian's destruction. And it only served to heighten his concern over Aurian. What would *she* be capable of, now that she wielded this new power? He glanced at her as she sat, intently discussing plans with Yazour. What had happened to the trust they shared? Why had she lied?

There was no opportunity, in the excitement of Yazour's return, for Anvar to speak to the Mage, but at last, after dawn had broken, everyone lay down to rest in preparation for the journey ahead. Aurian had been avoiding him all night, and now she chose to lie down on the other side of their group beside Shia. Anvar found himself missing her presence by his side, and cursed himself for a fool. But though he wanted to stay awake in order to tackle her in private about the discrepancies in her story, his eyes refused to stay open, and before long he was fast asleep.

Some inner prompting awakened Anvar. Some vague, unconnected feeling of distress drew him out of sleep while the bright midday sunlight still reflected through the mouth of the cave. He opened his eyes and sat up, and saw that Aurian was missing. The Mage was not far away. Anvar found her seated alone by the pool, racked with sobbing, the knuckles of one hand pressed to her mouth as she wept with the brokenhearted abandon of a hurt child. Concern and pity overwhelmed him, and in that moment Anvar knew that whatever she had become, whatever she might do with her new and awesome power, he could not help but love her.

Aurian, lost in her misery, barely reacted to Anvar's presence as he sat beside her. 'Don't cry,' he murmured, not knowing how to comfort her. 'It's all right – I'm here.'

'What if you are? You think I'm a liar!' Anvar recoiled from the venom in Aurian's voce. Aware of her raw emotions, he forced himself to sound calm.

'It wouldn't be the first time I've been wrong about you. You've been proving me wrong ever since we met, I'm glad to say.' She looked at him then – a pleading look that went to his heart like a dagger. He tried to gather her into his arms, but she pushed him away.

'The dragon,' she began shakily, all in a rush, without looking at him, 'you wanted to know about the dragon. Well, he's dead. I killed him – as I destroyed the city.'

Anvar forced himself to remain silent, knowing better than to interrupt her now that she had started to speak.

Aurian was now struggling to keep her voice under control. 'The city, Anvar – it wasn't there at all. What we saw – what we experienced – was the distant past. When the Dragonfolk left Dhiammara they destroyed it, but locked it in time in the instant of its destruction, until the wielder of the Sword should come. Once that happened, the spell was freed and the city began to collapse.' Her voice choked on a sob. 'I wanted to help the dragon. I wanted to take him out of time again, but he wouldn't let me. He said he had chosen to stay behind, and now that I had come his task was done.' A tear rolled down her cheek. 'He wasn't loveable, Anvar – he was arrogant and sly and ill-tempered, but . . . Oh, he was beautiful and clever – and he spoke in music and light! He had waited so long, and for all we know he could have been the last of his kind, and it was my fault.' Aurian began to cry again, hiding her face in her hands. 'I never even asked him his name.'

'Hush.' Anvar stroked the Mage's hair. He was grieved by her grief but at the same time he felt almost lightheaded with relief. How could this woman, who could mourn the death of beauty and courage and self-sacrifice, turn to evil? 'It wasn't your fault,' he comforted her. 'You didn't choose to be the one he was waiting for. This path was set out for you; for all of us. The dragon was right, Aurian. He died centuries before our time. What you saw was a ghost, if you like – in a city of ghosts.'

With a half-articulated curse Aurian turned to stare at him, her eyes wild and wide, one hand held up before her mouth. *'How did you know about that?'*

'Whatever it is, I don't. Do you want to tell me?'

'I don't want to! You won't believe me again!'

'Look, I was wrong – '

Aurian hushed him with a brusque motion of her hand. 'This power we're dealing with – well, you were right to be concerned. The temptation to fall into evil as Miathan did is great, and we must guard each other constantly. That's why I should have told you everything. It's just that – I couldn't, before. It hurt too much. But . . .' In a low, shaking voce, she told him of her meeting with the spectre of Forral, and how it had led her to the green tower.

Anvar was speechless with dismay. Forral's ghost – haunting them – watching them . . . He shuddered, not wanting to accept this; not wanting to believe. Somehow he found his voice. 'Aurian – forgive me – but are you sure you didn't imagine this?'

'How could I, damn you? Forral led me to the tower. How else could I have found it so quickly? I knew you wouldn't believe me.'

'I do believe you – and I'm sorry I doubted you before.' He swallowed hard. 'I wish I hadn't made you tell me, that's all. It scares me, Aurian.'

'After what I said to you the night I saw Forral . . .' Aurian looked away from him, twisting at the corner of the blanket.

'That has nothing to do with it.'

'Anvar,' she interrupted him determinedly, 'I owe you an apology for that. We all played our parts in that terrible business – you, me; Forral himself, though it hurts to admit it.

562

But I truly don't hold you responsible for his death, and neither does he – I know that now. What else could you have done? You couldn't have fought the Archmage on your own. The way Forral reacted – and Miathan – that wasn't your fault. You were trying to help.'

Anvar sighed. 'I only wish I could so easily exonerate myself for what I did that night.'

'Is that why you came with me? Guilt?' Her voice was sharp.

Anvar ran his fingers distractedly through his hair, not wanting to continue, but somehow compelled to answer her question. 'At first it was – guilt and fear, to be frank. Later, after you saved me in the slave camp, I told myself it was loyalty and gratitude.' He looked into the Mage's eyes. 'But I was wrong. Now I want nothing else but to be with you; to take care of you and the child.'

'The child?' The two words contained a world of questions.

'I care about the child because I owe Forral a debt, but also because – well, I feel there's a bond between us. It's like me, the offspring of a Mage and a Mortal, not quite one thing or the other. I know how that feels, Aurian, and though it can't be the child of my body, it is the child of my heart – not least because of what I feel for its mother.'

Aurian looked at him wonderingly. 'I never knew. Somehow I never thought of it like that.'

'You don't mind?' Anvar held his breath.

She shook her head. 'How could I mind? Besides, with my powers due to leave me – well, I'm not ashamed to admit that I need you, Anvar – we both do.' At long last she smiled, and Anvar had to steel himself not to ruin their fragile bond by kissing her then and there. Instead he hugged her and ruffled her hair, trying to mask the tenderness in his voice with briskness.

'Well, now we've settled that, I suggest we get some sleep. It'll be time to set off soon.'

Anvar woke at dusk, with Aurian asleep in his arms. In her unguarded slumber the glory of the Staff had dimmed, and she looked worn and vulnerable, and all too human. Beneath the thin blanket, the slight bulge of her pregnancy could now be seen, and he felt awash with tenderness for the Mage and her unborn child. Wayward tendrils of her hair, which she had never been able to control since she'd cut it, straggled across her face, moving gently with the rhythm of her breathing. Anvar smiled, thinking of her hair when it had hung past her waist in a cascade of fiery crimson, and how he had enjoyed combing it for her the night that Forral had died. How wonderful its silken weight had felt, running through his fingers! I loved her then, he thought. I loved her, and couldn't admit it to myself. How could I, as nothing but her servant? How dare I admit it now?

She'll never love me – not with all that stands between us – the memory of the past, and the ghost of Forral shadowing our lives. If I had not gone to him that night, he might still be alive now. No matter how Aurian excuses it, how could I ever expect her to love me after that? In that moment, as he looked down at the sleeping Mage, Anvar's decision crystallized. I still owe her a debt, he thought. A debt of blood, for Forral's life. Even if it costs me my own life, that debt must be repaid – and one day, I'll find a way to do it.

Anvar reached out, as though touching her would seal his vow, and gently brushed the wayward curls from the Mage's face. To his dismay she stirred, opening her eyes, and he snatched his hand back as though he had been burned as the raw power of the Staff of Earth blazed into life within her once more. But already she was learning to control it. Even as he watched, the glory dimmed as she strove to contain it within herself.

Aurian sighed. 'Morning already?' she murmured sleepily. Anvar glanced towards the mouth of the cavern, wishing that they need not always be so driven; longing for some time alone with her. But such a luxury seemed as unattainable as the moon.

'Nightfall, I think,' he told her. 'We had better wake the others. It's time to go.'

The remainder of the journey across the desert took a score of days – some of the worst days that Aurian could remember. Ever wary of the imminence of the storms, Yazour pushed them hard, driving the companions and their horses to the limits of their endurance, and the Mage found herself envying Raven, who had flown on ahead, following the string of oases, to reach safety at the desert's edge as fast as she could. Since Yazour had been unable to bring any tents for them, the companions were forced to spend the broiling hours of daylight in the open, shaded by makeshift shelters of blankets and with their eyes, and those of the horses, bound in layers of cloth to filter the blinding glare. Since they had no pack-animals, food and water were tightly rationed, and everyone suffered badly from hunger and thirst.

Worst of all, there was the unrelenting heat. During the earlier part of their journey, there had always been the restless night breeze to cool them as they travelled, but this had ceased with the weather's unseasonal change, turning the desert into a suffocating oven. Each night the day's stored heat rose in a wave from the desert floor to engulf the riders, leaving the air turgid and stifling. The encrusted coats of the horses were dark and soaked with sweat, and their breathing, clogged by clouds of gem dust, came thick and wheezing from their labouring chests. The riders were drenched in sweat that ran stingingly into their eyes beneath their cloying veils; sweat that left their desert robes clinging clammily to their bodies as the life-giving moisture was lost to the dry desert air.

Shia, with the thick furred coat of a mountain dweller, suffered badly. At least the others were able to ride, but she was forced to lope along behind the horses on her own legs. Built for short bursts of speed, she was finding the gruelling race across the burning sands almost beyond her endurance. In addition to her dreadful weariness and thirst, her paws became raw and blistered from the friction of the hot gem dust, and before long she was leaving a track of bloody prints behind her as she ran.

Only her love of the Mage kept her going, and each day, when Aurian should have been resting to conserve her own energy, she spent herself in healing the exhausted and suffering cat; trying to lend Shia enough of her own faltering strength to continue. Anvar, who was looking increasingly worried as time went on, did his best to help, but he was no healer, and his efforts were of little practical use except that

565

they loaned the Mage an increment of strength to keep her going from day to day.

As time went on, Aurian became more and more frantic. The crossing of the desert was a race against time, and she knew she was losing. Her body was beginning to grow ungainly now with her advancing pregnancy, and already she was finding riding more uncomfortable. Even with the Staff of Earth, she knew that she was overtaxing her own fading powers, and because of this, they were failing more rapidly. Soon they would vanish completely. Whenever she thought of it, she was overwhelmed by a wave of choking panic. How could she help Shia then? How could she safeguard herself and her child, and defend her friends from the evil of the Archmage and his cohort Eliseth?

The worst of it was that, under the law of the desert, Shia ought to be abandoned. On the worst days, the cat even begged them to do it, gazing pitifully up at the two Mages with eyes that were distant and glazed, pleading with them to leave her, or put her out of her misery. Aurian would grit her teeth, forbidding Anvar with her steely glare to tell the others what Shia had said. But they were already thinking it – she could see it in Nereni's frequent tears, and in the guilty way that Eliizar and Yazour were avoiding her eyes. Even Bohan, her loyal tower of strength, was beginning to look uncomfortable, and eventually, she knew, she would have Anvar to contend with. Although he had so far refused to press her on the subject, knowing how much Shia meant to her, she knew that his concern for herself and the child were pushing him towards the unthinkable option. All that Aurian could do was to expend herself mercilessly, forcing herself with the entire strength of her indomitable will to defy them all; to keep Shia going somehow until the end of the journey.

They were still a few days from the desert edge when the worst happened, and Aurian finally succumbed to the heat and her own exhaustion. The others, having always lived in this hot climate, had been able to endure the broiling temperatures, and Anvar had built up a certain amount of resistance from his gruelling captivity in the slave camp. Aurian, however, had been cosseted; first as one of the arena's chosen, and then in the cool comfort of Harihn's palace. Even then, she might have managed, except that she was driving herself beyond the limits of endurance. Each day her suffering grew worse, until at last she was overcome by what Yazour called the heat-sickness.

Though her robes clung stickily to her body, Aurian was racked by shivers. Her head pounded, and she was dizzy and nauseated; unable to keep down any food and too weak and fevered to even attempt to heal herself. All she could do was cling desperately to the pommel of her saddle, and try to stay on her horse. By the time they reached the last oasis, Anvar had to lift her down, and she was barely aware that he did so. But as he laid her gently on the ground, the Mage was prevented from sinking into welcome oblivion by a cry that echoed in her mind – a faint, pitiful cry for help. Aurian tried to sit up, brushing feebly at Anvar's restraining hands, ignoring the pain that lanced through her head. 'Shia!' she gasped. 'Where's Shia?'

It took a great deal of determination on Anvar's part to persuade Yazour to go back and find Shia, but Aurian became so frantic that finally the warrior relented. It was an hour before he returned, with the great cat slung limply across the shoulders of his faltering and terrified horse. In the meantime, Nereni had been sponging the Mage's fevered body with cool water from the oasis, while Bohan brought her water – as much as she could keep down. Anvar had been pacing back and forth, coming to look at Aurian then striding back to peer out across the dunes, his dusty face furrowed with concern as he cursed himself for not being able to help the Mage, and also for being so worried about her that he had forgotten Shia. He helped Bohan lift the cat down from the trembling horse and laid her by Aurian's side, stroking the sleek black head now dulled and harsh with dust, hearing the faint rasp of her tortured breathing. After a moment Shia opened her eyes, their light a dim echo of its former golden glory. Her thought was as nebulous in his mind as a fading wisp of smoke. 'Goodbye.'

Anvar clasped her bleeding paws, feeling the spark of life within the great cat flicker, feeling the beating of her great heart beginning to falter. 'Goodbye, my friend,' he whispered.

'Goodbye be damned!' Aurian's voice cracked across Anvar's grief like a slap in the face. He turned to see her sitting up, her eyes smouldering grimly, her face pale but resolute. Before he could stop her, she had reached across to Shia, linking herself irrevocably with her dying friend.

Anvar caught the Mage's limp body as it slipped sideways, freed from the control of the mind that was far away in an unbreakable trance as it fought to keep Shia's soul within her failing body. Helpless and desperate, he clutched her, unable to reach her, his heart gripped by icy dread. He knew what she was attempting – had she not done the same for him in the slave camp, when she had sought his fleeing spirit and brought it safely home? But this time she was weakened, exhausted and ill. This time she had no strength for such a struggle; no strength to prevent Shia from pulling her down with her into death. And she would have no strength left to return. Frantically, he cast forth his mind as Aurian had taught him, seeking her, trying to find even a slight trace of her passing. But though he searched and searched, he knew that she was lost to him.

'Anvar!' A dim echo, the voice penetrated faintly into his consciousness, pulling him back. A hand was shaking roughly at his shoulders. To his surprise, Anvar saw the western horizon burning with the last traces of light. He'd been gone that long? Fear snagged at his breathing, but then he felt the faint movement of breath in the body that was still clutched in his cramped and aching arms; saw an answering lift of the great cat's ribs. They still lived, then – and Aurian was still fighting. Yazour let go of his shoulders, squatting before him in the open mouth of the makeshift shelter of blankets that had been rigged over himself, Shia and the Mage.

'By all the gods ever spawned, man, I've been frantic! I thought we'd lost you all!' Yazour's face betrayed a mixture of relief, concern and annoyance. 'What happened, Anvar? What can we do? Have you seen the sky? The storms will be upon us at any time.' He gestured at the western sky that was hazed and fuzzy on the horizon, and shot through with spars of lurid orange light.

Anvar's voice grated in his parched throat, but his words fell strangely calm upon his own ears. 'Aurian is linked with Shia – we can't move them. You'll have to leave us, Yazour. Take the others and go now – make a dash for safety while you still can. Save your own lives.'

'And will you come with us?' Yazour's voice was very quiet.

Anvar knew there was no hope – he could do nothing now to help the Mage and Shia. Already they were as good as dead. The sensible thing would be to go with the others, to save himself and the Staff of Earth, and take the fight back to Miathan in Aurian's name. He knew it all too well – he even knew that the Mage would want him to do so – but he looked down at Aurian's still form, and remembered his anguish in Dhiammara, when he thought she had died within the crystal of the spider creature. He remembered the terror that had pierced him when the great stone had seemed to fall in the tunnel, and how he had flung himself beneath to die with her, rather than be tortured again by her loss. The Mage's breast still rose and fell in that shallow parody of life. He knew, better than anyone, the strength of her stubborn will. How could he abandon her while yet she lived? How could he go through the years, knowing that he had left her, helpless, in the desert of a foreign land?

Anvar looked at Yazour, and shook his head. 'Don't be stupid,' he said.

35
The Well of Souls

The door was ancient, its thick weathered wood as grey and heavy as a block of stone, the time-blunted carvings on its panels obscured by the weight of years. As Anvar put a hand to it, vague shapes and intertwining patterns seemed to leap out at him, outlined in silvery Magefire – fire that leapt sizzling from his fingers, turning his hand into a blazing torch. Anvar flinched, sickened by the sight of his own bones shining darkly through the incandescent flesh, but he felt no sense of heat or pain. Soundlessly, the door swung open, and he stepped through. As he took his fingers from the panels, the fire in his hand was snuffed out, shrouding his surroundings in shadowy gloom.

Shimmering grey mist coiled around him, cutting off his vision as effectively as a curtain. Then, like a curtain, it parted to reveal a stooped figure whose form was obscured by a hooded grey cloak. The apparition held a staff in one hand, leaning on it in a way that gave the impression of great age. In its other hand a shuttered lantern cast a single, silvery ray upon the white, gleaming wet pebbles of a path. As the vision turned its head, Anvar caught the intelligent gleam of a piercing dark eye, and the fuzz of a grizzled beard within the shadows of the cowl. In that moment, the old man seemed as familiar as though Anvar had known him always, yet he could not recall having met him, or anyone like him, in his life. In fact, he realized with a shiver, he could not remember anything. He frowned. How had he come to be here? Where had he come from? As though he could hear Anvar's confused thoughts, the old man gave him an encouraging smile, and beckoned to him to follow.

At first the path led through a narrow, steep-sided cutting. Drooping trees overshadowed the way, forming a tunnel, and the high banks on each side were stacked with rounded mossy boulders and the feathery green fountains of ferns. The air was soft with clinging moisture, and musked with the scents of leaf-mould, wild garlic, and wet greenery. Anvar felt the tension in his breast beginning to relax as he took deep breaths. The damp, fragrant air was such a relief after the scorching desert . . .

The desert! Anvar stopped dead, straining to catch at the fleeting memory. He'd been in the desert . . . The old man caught his arm, with a warning shake of his head. The very tension of his body implied a desperate urgency. *Hurry*, he seemed to be saying. *No time for such thoughts.* He let go of Anvar and lengthened his stride, the faint gleam of his lantern vanishing rapidly in the misty dusk. Anvar, panic-stricken at the thought of losing his only guide in this strange, fey place, hurried to catch up.

With a suddenness that took Anvar's breath away, the narrow track opened out into a valley. The clinging murk vanished, leaving only a silken, silvery ground-mist that swirled underfoot, displaced by his soundless passage and that of his pilgrim guide. Catching a brief glimpse of the ground beneath his feet, Anvar realized that the path had vanished, and he was walking on a short, crisp carpet of turf. Above him, millions of stars speckled the velvet night, and the rounded curves of hills rose on either side, shouldering against one another and standing out as blacker humps against the star-crazed heavens. The silence wove a tangible spell around the mist-wreathed vale as Anvar, with no memory of the past or thoughts of the future, trailed after the hunched and shrouded figure with the lantern, as though this following was what he had been born to do.

The grove loomed out of the darkness as if it had materialized from a dream, holding for Anvar an eerie familiarity – but surely he had never set foot in this weird, unearthly place before. The huddle of ancient trees bowed in upon one another, as if to conceal a mystery, as though they whispered secrets to each other through the endless night. For an instant the thought of the desert flashed again into Anvar's mind. To his horror the scene before him began to ripple and

571

distort, as though he had dropped a stone into the cogent, fathomless well of the trees' meditations. He held up his hand, and found it becoming vaporous, insubstantial, the dark skeletal outlines of the trees clearly visible through the fading flesh.

The old man swung round sharply with a warning hiss – the first sound that Anvar had heard him make. His breath puffed out in a cloud before his face, spangling his bushy, greying beard with droplets that winked like stars in the light of the silver lamp. The incongruity of the sight diverted Anvar, concentrating his wayward thoughts upon this strange here-and-now; and to his relief the scene before him steadied, and his flesh became solid once more.

The old man turned back to the grove and bowed low, three times. To Anvar's surprise, a path appeared between the ancient, hoary trunks, as though the trees had accepted them and stepped back hastily to allow their passage. Anvar, awed and not a little afraid, followed his guide, passing through the archway of living wood into the heart of the grove.

In the centre of the ring of trees, cupped in a circle of soft, mounded moss, was a pool – the very womb of this magical place. Though it was overhung by protective branches, not a leaf marred its still, dark surface. Anvar followed his strange guide to the brink, looked down, and recoiled in astonishment, stepping back hastily. Instead of reflecting his own face framed by the lacework of branches above, the waters, of unguessable depth, held nothing but starry infinity. Anvar's head reeled. His heart pounded, as though trying to beat its way out of his chest. He had the utter conviction that if he should fall into those waters, he would be falling for ever.

The old man gave a long-suffering sigh. Then, to Anvar's horror, he gestured firmly at the terrifying pool and spoke at last, his voice as dry and dead as graveyard dust stirring on the chill winds of midnight. 'Never believe that death is merciless. Now comes the second part of the bargain – but remember, the third time will decide all.' With that, he vanished.

Anvar spun, looking around wildly, knowing in his heart that it was hopeless. His guide had gone. The only thing he understood was the clear edict to return to the pool. He hesitated, afraid to go near that dizzying brink. As though they had somehow sensed his reluctance, the trees began to shudder with anger as a murmurous hissing echoed through their branches, which began to twist and writhe, groping out at him like bony, threatened hands.

Hastily, Anvar returned to the pool, and the tumult of the trees died away. As he drew near to it, spars of light flashed and flared from the darkness of the glassy surface, making him flinch and shield his eyes. He approached with trepidation and knelt upon the brink, feeling more secure that way. It was as well that he had. The starry universe within the waters was spinning in a furious whirlpool of light, dragging him down into its dizzying vortex . . .

Anvar felt himself leaning perilously out over the pool, his nose almost touching that spinning surface. He was over-balancing . . . Unable to draw back from the hypnotic whirling, he dug his fingers deep into the yielding moss of the bank, pushing backwards with all the strength of his rigid arms. He blinked as a fiery speck, rare and brilliant amid the swirling whiteness, came spinning up towards him from the depths. The spark enlarged; resolved itself; took on glowing shape and form. A cry ripped from Anvar's throat. He was flung violently backwards as a figure erupted from the waters, showering him with crystal drops that burned like fire. A despairing voice called his name as Aurian struggled and thrashed in the centre of the pool, fighting with all her strength against being sucked back down into the whirling nothingness.

'Aurian!' Memory returned to Anvar in a shocking flash, and with it confusion. Where was the oasis? But there was no time to wonder. The Mage was weakening, dragged down by a great black burden larger than herself – Shia. Anvar knew somehow that if he entered the pool it would mean the end for them all. He stretched out as far as he could, leaning out to the utter limits of his reach. Aurian's wild flailings made it difficult. He missed her once – twice – although she still seemed to be wearing her desert robes, as was he, there seemed to be nothing he could get hold of. 'Your hand,' he yelled at her, praying that she would hear. 'Give me your hand!'

He saw her shift her grip on Shia; saw the whiteness of the

573

arm that she flung out towards him. He plunged perilously forward and made a wild grab, trying to fling himself back as he felt his fingers close around her wrist. The combined weights of Aurian and the cat dragged at him; he felt himself slipping . . . Anvar flattened himself against the ground and hung on with all his strength, his arm strained to breaking point. If he could have used both hands – but the other was still anchored deeply within the soft moss, the only thing that was stopping him from following the Mage into the pool. Deeply rooted as it had been, Anvar could feel it beginning to crumble beneath his fingers; beginning to tear away . . .

As the moss gave completely, plunging Anvar forward, a hand came down out of nowhere, clamping his wrist like eagle claws. Long, jagged nails bit into the thin skin, crushing tendon and bone and making him cry out in agony, but he did not relinquish his hold on the Mage. With an effortless twitch, the hand flung him clear of the pool, and Aurian and Shia with him. Though it had let go of him, Anvar could feel the imprint of the ghastly hand scorching his flesh. His skin was bloodied and torn where the nails had scored deep, crescent-shaped gouges. Biting his lip against the pain, he rolled on to his back, and his heart contracted to a ball of ice as he looked up at the scarred and ravaged face; the burnt-out sockets that had once held the terrifying gaze of the Archmage!

Miathan was robed in black, and his face was hideously disfigured. The skin around his empty eye sockets was blackened and cracked, suppurating and showing nauseating glimpses of red flesh and the white skull beneath. And set into the dark hollow of each socket was a faceted gem. The jewels burned with a glaring light, now white, now red, giving his skull-like face the soulless menace of a gigantic insect. But it was his smile, most of all, that struck terror into Anvar's heart. Aghast, speechless, Anvar was paralysed by that face, and its expression of gloating evil.

A hand grasped his shoulder. Aurian was using him to pull herself to her feet, trying to put him safely behind her. Her eyes burned silver with hatred. Anvar could feel her fear in the slight tremor of her fingers, but it did not show in her face. Shamed by her courage, he tried to rise, but the Archmage made a

574

contemptuous flicking gesture with his fingers. His crystalline eyes flared with unholy light, and a bolt of searing blackness lashed across Anvar, hurling him down again in gasping agony.

'How dare you!' Aurian stood defiantly before Miathan, and her voice thundered forward like a landslide. 'It is forbidden to use magic in the Place Between the Worlds!'

The Archmage's laughter rang out, cruelly mocking. 'Fool! You quote the Law of Gramarye at me, who taught you all you know? I dare *anything*!' His clawed and bony hand lashed out, flinging a whiplash of blackness at the Mage. She gave a cry of pain and doubled up, crumpling to the ground.

Though his eyes were gone, it was plain that the Archmage was using the arcane magic of the jewels to give him sight. The cold, hideous glitter of his empty gaze swept across Aurian and Anvar, and on his ghastly face was a contemptuous sneer. 'That's better,' he said. 'Grovel before me, where you belong!'

Aurian pulled herself to her knees and spat at Miathan's feet. 'I'll never grovel to you, you piece of filth. But one day I will kill you, you have my word on that.'

Miathan laughed again. 'Really?' he sneered. 'I doubt it – helpless as you are with Forral's brat in your belly. You'd have done better to submit to me, girl. You would have had power at my side, as much as you wanted. Instead you are nothing – a hopeless fugitive crippled by a half-Mortal abomination. Without your powers you're as helpless as a beggar woman; and like any street whore, you'll be ripe for the taking of any man who passes – including this cowardly, bastard scum!' He turned to Anvar, his voice curling with scorn. 'You will have what you wanted now, eh? Her powers have gone, Anvar, and your long wait is over. Who knows, she might even like it – she seems to enjoy defiling herself with Mortal offal such as you!'

Miathan's voice had the power to hold its victims in thrall. Anvar looked at Aurian, helpless before him, and felt his long-suppressed desire beginning to stir. He heard Aurian gasp. The fear and sudden doubt in her eyes pierced him like a sword as he realized that they had been tricked. He glared at the Archmage, his mind cleared by the scouring of his anger, which burned like an icy flame.

'I am no Mortal, Miathan,' he said evenly, 'as well you know.

I regained my powers, which you stole. And you need not put your lusts on me – the Lady knows full well which of us wants to defile her – and which will protect her! Aurian may be helpless, but if you come near her, you'll have me to reckon with.' But Miathan had the Cauldron, and Anvar's words were empty, and he knew it. Even so, he saw Aurian give him a grateful glance, tempered with a grimace at the idea of needing his protection. It was so characteristic of her that it buoyed him despite their peril.

Miathan, undisturbed by the failure of his ploy, roared with mocking laughter. 'You should have stuck to your earlier ambition of being a minstrel, boy. Already you are affording me the amusement I expected. For know this' – his voice turned suddenly hard – 'I did not save you both from the Well of Souls out of the goodness of my heart.'

'True – you don't have one!' Aurian snapped.

'Quiet!' His outflung hand sent a lash of darkness cracking hard across her face. She staggered, but refused to cry out, biting her lip against the pain.

Anvar, boiling with rage where he had been cold before, tried to launch himself at Miathan, but the Archmage froze him with a casual gesture, continuing to speak as though nothing had happened. 'I might have let you perish here, and saved myself a good deal of trouble, had I considered you a threat. But I have not finished with either of you. It would grieve me, Anvar, if your death was painless and swift, and for you, my dear' – he turned to Aurian with a chilling leer – 'I have other plans. Until we meet again in the flesh, you can entertain yourselves imagining your respective fates, but for now – farewell!'

As the Archmage spoke his final word, the scene began to waver and dissolve before Anvar's eyes. He closed them for an instant, to stop the dizzy whirling, and when he opened them again he was back at the oasis. A sickly, sulphurous light lay over the dunes, as the sun struggled to pierce the ominous banks of cloud on the horizon. I must have fallen asleep, Anvar thought. Gods, what a nightmare! But at that moment Aurian's eyes opened, and in them was horror, and a sick, sinking dread that matched his own.

Aurian was unable to explain what had taken place at the Well of Souls. Her best guess was that Anvar had fallen asleep, and his anxious spirit, freed from the fetters of the waking world, had managed to cross into death's domain to reach her. But his tale of his encounter with the Reaper of Souls, and the spectre's talk of a bargain, filled her with a vast disquiet. It seemed so familiar, somehow . . . Surely, when she had won Anvar back from death's clutches in Taibeth, the Reaper had said something similar? If only she could remember . . . And how had Miathan come to be there?

Aurian grimaced at the strip of dried meat in her hand. Her hunger was blunted by guilt for having exposed herself and Anvar to the Archmage, and by the fear that twisted her guts. Miathan had been right. Her powers, stretched past their limit when they were at their most vulnerable, had utterly vanished, leaving her defenceless. 'Damn Miathan!' she muttered. 'Why did he have to come back now, at the worst possible time?' With an oath, she flung the offending food away from her.

Anvar reached out of the shelter and retrieved the meat. Dusting it off carefully, he put it back into her hand. 'Be sensible, Aurian. You need to eat,' he told her. The Mage glared at him, on the verge of a scathing retort, but hearing the edge in his voice she subsided, and forced herself to take another bite. There were dark smudges beneath Anvar's eyes, and lines of strain on his dusty face. The confrontation with Miathan had marred the joy of their safe return – a quarrel was the last thing they needed. And to be fair, Anvar had never said a word of blame to her. It would be better if he had, she thought, instead of leaving me to blame myself. Yet – she looked at Shia, who was sleeping now, recouping her strength. The cat remembered nothing of what had taken place, though she and Aurian had both been healed of their infirmities in the Well of Souls. What else could I have done? the Mage thought. Had I not acted as I did, Shia would be dead. She prayed that the price of Shia's life would not prove too high.

'You did what you had to.' Anvar's quiet voice broke into her thoughts as though he had been reading her mind.

Aurian took his hand. 'Thank you for that. But we're in so

much trouble now, with the storm coming, and Miathan on the loose, and my powers gone . . .' She couldn't control the tremor in her voice. 'Anvar, I'm scared. Without my magic I'm so vulnerable. Now that Miathan has recovered from my attack, anything could happen.' Aurian shuddered. 'And what about the Staff? I don't think he knows that we have it, but if he should find out . . . Anvar, do you remember the shipwreck, when he possessed my body and tried to kill you?'

Anvar nodded, looking puzzled at her switch of subject.

Aurian took a deep breath, dreading what she had to say. 'What if it happens again, now that Miathan has recovered? Anvar – if he should get control of the Staff . . .'

'No!' He was ahead of her now. 'Don't say it, Aurian.'

'I must. If I – if Miathan should gain control of me, you'll have to kill me, Anvar. You'll have no choice – as I would have no other recourse if it happened to you.'

'I am not going to kill you. I won't.' Anvar's voice dropped to a horrified whisper. 'I can't.'

Aurian's heart went out to him, but she met his gaze without flinching. 'I'm sorry, love, but you must. If Miathan gets the Staff, it will be the end of everything – and better we die than let him take us. You heard what he said at the Well of Souls.'

Anvar hardly heard her last words. He knew that the endearment had slipped out without her being aware of it, but . . . He fought to keep the jubilation from his face, not wanting her to withdraw from him, as he knew she surely would. Whatever she might feel for him, she was still grieving for Forral, and would be stricken with guilt at the thought of replacing her childhood love. It's too soon – give her time, he told himself, and prayed to all the gods that the Archmage would let them have that time.

Miathan's chamber was dismal and chill. The blaze that he had left in the huge fireplace was sunk to sullen embers clogged with pale ash, and the lamps were guttered and dark. Dull light streaked through the curtains, announcing the dawn of another grim day over Nexis. The Archmage's body lay on the bed, just as he had left it, looking pale and gelid as a corpse in the dim, bleak light. His hovering consciousness shuddered, and shrank from returning to this cold, pain-racked housing, but it had to be done. Miathan braced himself and plunged downward, slipping back into his corporeal form with the ease of long practice.

Entering his body was worse than falling into an icy pool. Miathan swore vehemently, steeling himself against the pain. Since Aurian had attacked him, he had suffered agony from his burnt-out eyes, and he knew it would never leave him. With Eliseth's help, he'd discovered enough of the magic of the Dragonfolk to permit him to use crystals to give him back a form of sight, but the sharp edges of the gemstones chafed the tortured sockets, increasing his pain. Still, it was better than living blind. He cursed that mad bitch Meiriel, who had refused to heal him, and that treacherous worm Elewin, who had helped her escape . . .

Miathan reminded himself that lying here raging would bring him no nearer to his revenge. He pulled his robes around him and hauled his creaking bones from the bed, though he was shaking violently from the cold, and from reaction to the prolonged journey between the worlds, which had so depleted his energies. Leaning on his staff, the Archmage hobbled to the fire and threw on an armful of logs, deciding to let them blaze of their own accord, rather than waste the last of his strength on kindling them by magic. He filled and relit the lamps by hand, frustrated to impotent rage by the fumbling efforts of his weakened state.

By the time he had finished, the room was already cosier. The fire snapped and sizzled, dispelling the arid silence and sending tongues of orange flame over the resinous logs to brighten the dank air with the tingling scent of pine. Warm lampglow mellowed the dismal daylight, gilding the silver dish of bread and fruit on the table. The Archmage turned to the food that he kept in his quarters for his return from a journey beyond his body. He poured wine, with a stab of irritation as he noticed that the flask was almost empty. Were Elewin here, such an omission would never have occurred. But the steward was gone, he reminded himself bitterly, turning traitor as Aurian had done. Aurian! Miathan's tongue slid over his lips at the memory of her falling before him, tortured by the pain that

579

he had inflicted. When he had her back in his power he would teach her the true meaning of pain! Once he had broken her to his will he would take her – and at last, he had the means . . . smiling to himself, Miathan sent out a mental call to summon Eliseth. He hated to confide in her, but there were things she ought to know.

Eliseth was in the archives when she heard the Archmage's call. She cursed and pushed her hair back from her face with a hand that was black with dust. What did the old fool want now? Since the vermin Elewin had gone, Miathan seemed to think she had nothing better to do than run around after him. And was he grateful? Not a bit – even though she had found a cure for his blindness. Only she had thought to seek answers in the mouldering records stored beneath the library, after the escape of Meiriel and Elewin had drawn her attention to Finbarr's neglected catacombs. Bragar, of course, was too stupid to think of making use of the ancient wisdom stored there, but Eliseth had realized that any extra knowledge might give her the advantage – not only over Bragar, but over Miathan as well.

Eliseth's searches in the cold, dirty tunnels had been far from pleasant, but the results had been well worth the discomfort. While finding a way to restore Miathan's sight, she had discovered much more besides – matters of dark and arcane lore dating back to before the Cataclysm, of which the Archmage had no idea; nor was she about to enlighten him. She had found no solution to the problem of the Wraiths, but she had unearthed a great deal of information pertaining to the Cauldron, and she knew how to make better use of it than Miathan had. She only needed to find out where the old dodderer had hidden it . . . Eliseth smiled as she went to answer the Archmage's summons. His mental voice had held overtones of triumph, and she was anxious to discover what he was up to, and how it fitted in with her own plans.

She listened, incredulous, as the Archmage told her how he had sensed the presence of Aurian between the worlds, and how he had tracked her to the Well of Souls, and Anvar with her. The existence of another Mage came as a considerable shock to Eliseth. 'Aurian's servant? One of us?' she gasped. 'Did you know about this?'

'No.' Miathan shook his head, but she knew that he was lying. 'I had my suspicions,' he said. 'I knew she must be getting help from somewhere. But I hardly thought it worth mentioning – the notion seemed too far-fetched.'

'That's an understatement! How could he have been here at the Academy without us knowing? Where did he come from in the first place? Who were his parents?'

Miathan shrugged, his voice suspiciously bland. 'Who can say? He came to us as a Mortal, the son of a baker, but it seems that his true father was of a different stamp. Anvar is a bastard – a half-breed with a Mortal mother – but as to which of the Magefolk fathered him . . .' He shrugged again, the picture of innocence.

Eliseth's eyes narrowed. This is too glib, she thought. And you know too much. Well, here's a turn-up! The great Archmage, prone as the rest of us to using a Mortal for pleasure. But to be so careless as to father a child – no wonder you were upset at Aurian's pregnancy! There was no time now to consider what advantage this might bring her. She turned back to Miathan, before he could sense where her thoughts were tending. 'So where does this leave us? I don't understand you, Archmage. Why did you not kill them, and be done with it?'

Miathan's fist slammed down on the table. 'How many times have I told you – I want Aurian alive!'

Eliseth bit down on her anger. Despite what the bitch had done to him, he still wanted her. Concealing her rage, she took up the weapon of common sense. 'But with respect, Archmage, you're asking the impossible. Aurian is too far away for us to capture her, and if you wait until she comes to you – well, you said yourself that the risk was too great. And alive, will she not always be a threat to us?'

'Her intransigence will be dealt with.' The gems in Miathan's eyes flared red, betraying his anger. 'Besides,' he continued, with a chilling smile, 'Aurian's capture has already been dealt with. She and Anvar were not the only minds I encountered in the southlands. I have found one who, for his own reasons, can be easily bent to my will.'

'What?' Eliseth was dismayed. She had underestimated the

development of Miathan's new powers badly, if he could already control Mortal minds with such confidence.

'Our experiment using human sacrifices has borne fruit more quickly than I had expected,' Miathan drew her attention back to him. 'We can certainly proceed, Eliseth – but I need more power, to keep my southern pawn on a close rein. Tell Angos that more Mortals will be required tonight.'

'But, Archmage,' Eliseth protested, 'there is already unrest at these "disappearances". We must be more circumspect.'

'You have your orders! Tell Angos to proceed at once.' Miathan's faceted eyes gleamed. 'I wish I had known about this sooner. With power gained from the ritual spilling of Mortal life, nothing is beyond us. And I need that power, Eliseth. Aurian is currently in the southern desert – but when she leaves it, I have a surprise for her. She will discover then what it means to defy the Archmage!'

Eliseth stormed out of the tower on the wings of rage, sending the first terrified drudge she found to summon Angos, captain of mercenaries, to the Academy. She glared after the retreating servant, her fists clenched, her body rigid with determination. Thus far, she would obey Miathan's orders, but no further.

'Determined to bring her back, are you, Miathan?' she muttered. 'Well, *I* may have a surprise for *you*!' Striding swiftly, she crossed the courtyard to the dome in which she did her work of controlling the weather. So Aurian was in the desert? Excellent! She would never come out alive. Smiling grimly, Eliseth went to unleash the sandstorms.

36

Battle in the Wildwood

Late at night, Vannor walked with his daughter Zanna along the torchlit shingle beach in the smugglers' great cavern. Fragments of shell crunched softly beneath their feet, and the only other sound was a hushed, soothing sea-song as the waters lapped gently against the sheer walls at the rear and farther side of the cave. The companionable silence was broken by Vannor's sigh. His reunion with Antor and his daughter had been joyous, but the brief time spent here with them had flown, and tomorrow he would be leaving again.

'Cheer up, dad.' Zanna squeezed his hand, much to Vannor's chagrin. Why, he should have been consoling her! But his middle child, just turned sixteen, possessed common sense far beyond her years. She was his favourite, taking after him in all ways – including looks, unfortunately. He smiled at her, taking in her sturdy compact little body, her plain, pleasant face and her brown hair, pulled back from her face in no-nonsense braids.

'I thought you'd want to go with me,' he said.

'You should have taught me to fight, then, like the Lady Aurian,' Zanna replied. 'The maidenly arts that caught my sister a husband are wasted on me.' She sighed, betraying her true feelings. 'I wish I could come – but I'd only hold you back. Besides, I'll be of more use here.'

Vannor put his arm around her, hugging her close to his side. 'Well, you seem to have it all thought out. Do you have any plans your old dad should know about?'

Zanna smiled – a secret little smile that added a new maturity to her face. 'I have indeed – but you must promise to hear me out before you start yelling.'

'All right.' The merchant wondered what she was up to.

Zanna hesitated for a moment. 'I'm going to marry Yanis.'

583

'What? Are you out of your mind? Over my dead body will you wed some base-born outlaw . . .'

'Dad, you said you'd hear me out. You can't be choosy now,' Zanna reminded him. 'You're an outlaw too! It may not be what you want, but don't you see the sense of it? I'm not cut out to be a merchant's wife, all decorative and ladylike.' She made a wry face. 'Besides, you know how merchants go for looks. You can't afford a dowry that would tempt one to take me – and I'm needed here. Yanis has been struggling since he took over. Oh, he's brave, and full of ideas, but he doesn't know how to plan. But I do – I'm not your daughter for nothing!'

Vannor gaped at her, astonished and – reluctantly – impressed. 'But he's twice your age,' he objected.

'Not even thirty,' Zanna corrected swiftly, 'and you have no room to talk about age.'

Vannor flinched, knowing her vehement disapproval of Sara, and changed the subject hastily. 'Was this his idea?'

'Certainly not!' Zanna was all indignation. 'But Remana will help me. She thinks it's time he married . . .'

'Hold on. You mean Yanis doesn't know about this?'

Grinning, Zanna shook her head. 'No – but I don't plan to let that stop me. Dulsina says . . .'

'Dulsina again,' Vannor growled. 'I might have known she'd be in this somewhere.' He tried to quell the fond smile that was creeping over his face at the thought of his indomitable housekeeper. When he was outlawed, Dulsina had insisted on accompanying him into the sewers, where she had proceeded to organize and mother his ragtag band of rebels; learning to shoot a bow and wield a deadly knife in the process, with the same calm interest that she would have shown in trying a new recipe. Now she had come with him to join the Nightrunners, and was reorganizing the lives of his family again as though she had never left off.

Vannor shook his head. 'Dear gods!' He suddenly found himself ceasing to worry about his level-headed daughter. His sympathies swung instead towards the unsuspecting leader of the smugglers. Poor Yanis didn't stand a chance.

'Come along, dad.' Zanna tugged at his arm. 'Here comes Parric, with the others. It's time to say goodbye.'

'And that's another thing –' Vannor began, and shut his mouth abruptly. He had no right to burden his daughter with his doubts about Parric's pig-headed insistence on travelling south in search of Aurian. He should be coming with us, to the Valley, Vannor thought. Even supposing the Lady will help us, how will I set up a rebel base without his help? It's all very well to say I'll have Hargorn to help me, but the man is a soldier, not a strategist. I just don't have the military experience for this, and Parric is going off to get himself killed for nothing.

The cavalry master came out of the opening that led from his lodgings, and smiled to see Zanna with her father. He was glad the little lass had come to say farewell – he'd grown right fond of her. Why, if he'd been a few years younger . . . Parric stifled the thought. Vannor wouldn't stand for a randy soldier tumbling with his favourite daughter. Besides, her attentions were fixed elsewhere – and good luck to her. Yanis wasn't bright, but he was a handsome catch, and Parric knew whose hands would hold the reins of *that* marriage. He chuckled, wondering if she'd had the chance to break the news to her father. By the stunned look on Vannor's face, it seemed she had. Sure enough, as he approached, Zanna gave him a sly wink behind her father's back. Parric fought to keep a straight face, feeling absurdly pleased that the lass had chosen to confide in him. Even if it did imply that she saw him in a more fatherly role than he liked.

'Better get a move on.' Idris, the weatherbeaten, pinch-faced captain of the ship that was to take them south, hailed them from the deck of his vessel. 'The tide won't wait, you know.' Parric grinned and made an obscene gesture at him before turning to Vannor.

The merchant looked troubled, as he had done since the cavalry master had first broached what Vannor had called 'this crazy scheme'. Parric decided to beat him to it, for he had no time to argue the whole thing out again. 'It's all right, Vannor,' he said firmly. 'You'll manage, and I'll manage – and I'll be back as soon as I've found Aurian.'

'If you find her,' Vannor muttered doubtfully. 'You have no idea how big the Southern Kingdoms are – not to mention the hostile, warlike nature of the southerners!'

585

'But that's why Aurian needs my help.' Parric might as well not have spoken.

'Added to that, you've saddled yourself with an old man and a mad Mage,' Vannor went on, but to Parric's relief he shut his mouth hastily as the old man and the mad Mage came over the sands towards them with Sangra, who had refused to be left out of the expedition.

'Ready to go?' the warrior asked cheerfully. Parric could have kissed her, but that would wait.

'Get them aboard, love,' he told her, 'I'm just coming.' He turned back to Vannor. 'You're right about one thing – I wish we could have persuaded Elewin to stay behind. The journey here took it out of him, and he's in no fit state to go traipsing around the south.'

Vannor shrugged. 'Meiriel will be in good company – you're all mad! I don't know why Elewin is so sure that he's the only one who can take care of her – she's been lucid enough since she came with us.' Suddenly his gruff reserve broke, and he flung his arms around Parric. 'I'll miss you, you idiot,' he muttered. 'Take care of yourself – and for the sake of all the gods, come back safe.'

'Count on it.' Parric returned the hug, his own voice more emotional than usual. 'Don't worry about commanding the troops, Vannor – they know their business, and they'll keep you right. Besides, once you've found Eilin, she'll give you the help you need. I'll be back before you know it – and what's more, I'll bring that wife of yours with me.'

'I hope so, Parric – I truly hope so.'

The following evening, Vannor stood with Dulsina and Zanna on the grassy clifftop as the pallid sun set over the hills behind him. The air was chill with the unnatural winter that had lingered this year, but the view was glorious. Below and to his right was a pale sweep of crescent beach, embraced by cliffs and cradling the calm, shining sea. Some half-league distant on the opposite horn of the crescent was a green knoll, crowned by a stark and sinister standing stone. Directly below the merchant's feet, a v-shaped niche hid the beginnings of a narrow crumbling path that descended the cliff. Apart from the secret tunnel for the horses, this perilous, well guarded ledge was the only landward access to the smugglers' stronghold.

'Having second thoughts?' Yanis approached, panting from his climb up the steep path. 'You ought to,' the smuggler went on. 'Why take your folk inland, Vannor? It's safer here, and you're welcome to stay. Your children are broken-hearted that you're leaving them again.'

'That's what I've been telling him,' Dulsina put in.

The merchant sighed. 'This place is no good to us as a fighting base, Dulsina – as you very well know. All these objections are only because I wouldn't let you come.'

Dulsina shrugged, and raised an eyebrow. 'Your mistake, Vannor,' she said serenely. Vannor scowled, wishing they would leave him alone. It was bad enough parting from his children again. They were all he had, now. Nonsense, he told himself. Sara is with Aurian, and she'll be all right. And Parric had promised to bring her back. Vannor hated to admit that this was really why he had allowed the cavalry master to talk him into his crazy scheme.

'Anway, Yanis,' he picked up the thread of the conversation. 'It's my children and your people that I'm thinking of. They'll be safer if we're away from here.'

'But the Valley has an evil reputation now,' Yanis protested. 'They say the Mage Davorshan was killed there.'

'That's exactly why I'm going. Davorshan's death was no accident, I'm sure. After what happened to Aurian and Forral, the Lady will protect us – you can count on that.'

'But the risk is getting there! Angos is combing the countryside looking for you.'

'We'll be careful. And the Valley is a far better base for us – more central, and nearer the city.'

'That's what worries me,' Yanis said glumly. 'Well, I'll let you go. If we hear any news of Parric in the south, I'll try to get word to you. The gods go with you, my friend, and don't worry – I'll take care of your children.'

'Goodbye, Yanis – and my thanks for all you've done,' Vannor said, reflecting that in the case of one of his children, it might end up being the other way round.

'Take care of yourself,' Dulsina told the merchant, 'since I won't be there to do it for you,' she added tartly.

'Goodbye, Dulsina,' Vannor hugged her. 'Take care of Zanna for me, won't you?'

'As if Zanna couldn't take care of herself,' the housekeeper snorted. 'It's you idiot men I'm worried about!' With that, she left him to say his farewells to Zanna, but there was little need for words between father and daughter. They had said it all already.

'Don't you dare marry that smuggler of yours before I get back!' he teased her gruffly. 'That's a wedding I don't want to miss!'

Zanna hugged him. 'Then you'd best get a move on, dad.' She twinkled up at him through her tears. 'I don't plan to wait for ever, you know.' For a long moment they looked at each other. Zanna bit her lip, and her arms around him tightened. ' 'Bye, dad.' She whirled, and was gone.

The merchant turned away, back to his waiting rebels. Perhaps it was the confusion of the departure, but he never noticed that he was one man short.

As soon as Vannor's troop had vanished over the nearest rise, the gorse that concealed the horses' tunnel parted. Zanna emerged, followed by Dulsina, dressed in warrior's gear, and the grizzled Hargorn, carrying two packs. He looked at them and shook his head. 'The gods know why I let you talk me into this,' he sighed. 'Vannor will have my bollocks off – begging your pardon,' he added hastily, to a frigid look from Dulsina.

Zanna grinned. 'It's because you love us,' she teased him. 'Are you ready, Dulsina?'

The housekeeper smiled wryly. 'I hope my old walking muscles come back quickly,' she said doubtfully.

'With respect, ma'am, they had better,' Hargorn snorted. 'We can't afford to let you slow us up – and you'd better hurry, if we want to catch the others now. Vannor won't notice if we slip in quiet, at the back.'

'Don't worry, Hargorn. If Vannor can do it, then so can I. The man hasn't walked anywhere in years.' With a hug for Zanna, Dulsina shouldered the pack, and raised her eyes heavenwards. 'The things I do for Vannor,' she sighed.

'The things you do for love, you mean,' Zanna murmured softly, as Dulsina strode away into the dusk. Smiling, she began to pick her way back down the cliff to find Yanis.

Where in the pits of torment are we? Vannor wondered. The partings with his family and friends seemed like a long-ago dream. The rebels had been wandering for days on these bare, blighted moors that stretched from the sea to Eilin's Vale. Because they had been forced to keep to the winding valleys for concealment from the searching bands of mercenaries – far more numerous than Vannor had expected – they had soon become lost. And now they were doubly lost in this pitch-black night, for clouds had dropped to the hills, shrouding them in a thick clinging mist that brushed the merchant's face like cold cobwebs.

Vannor cursed, as he'd been cursing for days. What had the Magefolk done to the weather? By the calendar, it should be haytime going on harvest, and these hills should be basking in sunshine, swathed in the vivid green of young bracken and the cloudy purple of early heather, the sky a deep blue bowl filled with the wild, bubbling joy of the skylark's song. But spring had never come this year, let alone summer, and the land was withered and sere. People would be starving now, Vannor thought. Those who had died in the Night of the Wraiths might have been the lucky ones.

The grim, wintry weather preyed on the merchant's spirits, sapping his courage and hope. If only Parric were here, with his military skills and unquenchable spirits! *He* wouldn't have got them lost in a fog. If only they had horses, instead of having to make this slow and winding journey on foot, they could have reached the sanctuary of the Valley days ago. But there were no horses to be had. The smugglers had not enough to supply them, and most of the others had probably been eaten already, Vannor suspected. Parric had trusted him to take care of the rebels, and a fine mess he was making of it. 'I'm no good at this,' he muttered helplessly. 'Oh, Parric, why did you have to go?'

In desperation, Vannor had left his band and crept to the top of this hill, hoping to pierce the mist that lay in the valley like a deep grey river. But it was no good. Even up here, he could see nothing. 'Fional? Hargorn?' he whispered to the scouts that accompanied him. There was no reply. Confound them! Had he not warned them to stay close? Sound carried in fog, and he dared not call out to them. The hills were alive with Angos's soldiery. If they were lost there would be no chance of finding them in this murk. Angry at their stupidity and worrying about their safety, he set off down the hill to rejoin his troop.

Vannor had walked for some time before the dreadful truth dawned on him. His scouts were not lost – he was! He had reached level ground long ago, sure he was heading the right way – but there was neither sight nor sound of the rebels. Vannor's heart began to thunder, and a clammy sweat trickled between his shoulder blades. When he had been sure he was heading in the right direction, he'd been all right, but now . . . The cloying mist swirled around him, confusing him beyond all hope of finding his bearings. Vannor choked on panic. Was the ground really level beneath his feet? Was he moving in the wrong direction, and heading straight into the arms of the enemy? He fought a desperate battle with himself to keep from running blindly into the darkness; fleeing from the fear that threatened to consume him. With an effort, Vannor got hold of himself. Steady, he thought. Calm down, you fool. What would Parric have done in this situation? He wouldn't have got himself lost, for a start – but that's no comfort!

He stopped and took a swig from his water flask, wishing it contained the fiery liquor he used to keep at home. What now? He could wait until the mist cleared or dawn came, whichever happened sooner; or he could try to retrace his steps, in the hope that he would blunder into his troop. He knew the most sensible course was to stay put, but the cold was piercing and inactivity galled him, forcing his mind to futile imaginings. Was that a sound? Over there? Or that way? Was it his people? Or the enemy? Again and again he was on the verge of racing after illusory noises, though common sense told him that he risked losing himself even more completely on these vast stretches of moorland. In the end, with his nerves frayed to breaking, Vannor gave up. Better to be moving, he decided; to try to retrace his steps. At least that must surely bring him closer to his people. Turning himself carefully to face back the way he had come, Vannor set off again into the fog.

Damn and blast it! The tilt of the ground beneath his feet and the strain on his thighs were no illusion. For some time, Vannor had been wandering uphill again – a hill far steeper than the one he'd climbed before. How could it have happened? He'd been so careful! Dismayed and disgusted with himself, the merchant sat down heavily and put his head into his hands. It was no good. Maybe he could think more clearly if he rested a little.

Vannor sat up with a jerk. It was still foggy but there was a dingy grey light around him, and he could see yellowish, withered turf for a few feet around where he sat. He must have dozed. Then he heard again the faint noise that had awakened him. From somewhere on the hillside above him, the sounds of fighting carried through the fog. Fear for his troops churning in his belly, Vannor scrambled to his feet and ran, with drawn sword, up the incline.

The steep slope seemed to stretch on for ever, but the clash of battle was growing in his ears. At last, Vannor saw vague, dark shapes ahead of him. Distance was deceptive in the mist, and he was into their clutching limbs before he knew it. Trees! Thank the gods! There was only one place on this grim moor that boasted trees. He must be near the edge of the Valley. But he could hear the fighting ahead of him, its noise still undiminished. Flinging up an arm to protect his face from the tangle of springy branches, Vannor began to force his way through.

Flinging caution aside, the merchant crashed heedlessly among the undergrowth until finally he broke through into a clearing where the sound of fighting was loud ahead.

'Halt, Vannor – traitor and outlaw!' The voice was harsh. Vannor stopped, lowering the arm that obscured his vision. From the trees came a ring of unshaven, flint-eyed mercenaries, bristling with naked steel.

'Drop your sword.' The circle parted and Angos stepped forth, callous amusement on his face. 'Some rebel,' he sneered. 'You never stood a chance, you fool.' Almost of its own volition, the sword fell from Vannor's numb hand. He had failed his

591

people. Parric had been wrong to trust him. In the forest, the sounds of battle faltered and ceased. One by one, the rebels were pushed into the clearing – their numbers fewer than before, the merchant saw with a sinking heart. Their hands were bound behind them, and they were forced to kneel on the ground at swordpoint. Vannor's gaze searched the demoralized captives, picking out faces, until he saw one that turned him cold with horror. There, uncloaked and unmasked, her long black hair straggling across a bruised and filthy face, was Dulsina.

A blow from a mailed fist caught him hard across the face, sending Vannor staggering. Through swimming eyes, he saw Angos, standing over him, grinning evilly. 'The Archmage wants you and Parric for questioning. If you survive, he has a nice little public execution planned.' His cold gaze flicked over the captured rebels. 'What, no Parric? Has the little runt abandoned you? Or is he hiding elsewhere?' He shrugged. 'If you know, we'll get it out of you. If not, we'll find him, never fear. I don't think we need bother taking the rest of this scum, though. It's not even worth notching good steel on them. Archers . . .'

The mercenary's voice was drowned in a thunder of hoofbeats. Before Vannor's eyes, Angos jerked and stiffened, his chest exploding in gouts of blood as though he'd been pierced by a sword – *but there was nothing there!* His body was tossed into the air, to land in a crumpled heap several yards away. Pandemonium broke out among the mercenaries, but before they could lift a sword, or put arrow to bow, the trees around the clearing came to life. Boughs and roots writhed forward, clutching them in a deadly embrace. Thorny twigs gouged at eyes, and branches ripped soft bellies, spattering the ground with offal and gore. Then, drowning the screams of agony and the crack of breaking bones with their wild song of death, the wolves erupted into the clearing in a seething mass of grey.

It was over in seconds, though Vannor, taking in every detail of the hideous slaughter, knew that he had seen enough to furnish himself with endless months of nightmares. As the wolves finished their bloody work, the frozen calm of shock left him, and he fell to his knees, doubled over with vomiting and moaning in terror.

Vannor opened his eyes to witness what his numbed brain had been trying to tell him for several minutes. *The wolves and trees had known which people to take!* The bloody remains of Angos and his men were strewn across the clearing. Not one had survived. But in the one clear space, the bound and terrified rebels huddled together, wild-eyed and trembling – and totally unscathed! Beside them stood the biggest of the wolves; alone now, for his companions had melted away into the forest. He pricked his ears questioningly at Vannor, whined – and wagged his tail!

Shaking his head in disbelief, the merchant approached the wolf, his hand outstretched. As he closed the distance between them, the animal backed away, his tail still wagging furiously. Vannor picked up a dagger from the discarded weapons that lay about the clearing, and, having wiped it clean of blood on his cloak, he began to free the others. 'Nobody hurt the wolf,' he warned in a low voice.

'Nobody hurt it?' someone muttered incredulously. 'Nobody's going near the bloody thing!' There was a swell of nervous chuckles from among the rebels, and their courage gave Vannor the strength to take charge once more. He yanked Dulsina to her feet.

'You,' he said sternly, 'have some explaining to do!' He glared at his assembled troops. 'In fact it took a conspiracy to hide her all the time we were marching, so you all have some explaining to do!'

Everyone looked at Hargorn, and the veteran shrugged. 'Well, Parric was depending on me to keep you right, and since you were trying to set up a permanent camp without a cook and quartermaster . . .' He grinned. 'I couldn't let you make a mistake like that now, could I?'

Luckily for Hargorn and Dulsina, an urgent whine took Vannor's attention away from the miscreants. He looked around to see the wolf, still waiting patiently on the far edge of the clearing. Beyond him, the trees had somehow moved aside, leaving a clear path through the forest. The wolf turned and ran along the path, then stopped, looking back over his shoulder at

Vannor. The merchant looked at his rebels and shrugged. 'I don't know what you think, but it looks to me as though we're being welcomed.'

As the weary rebels followed the wolf towards the sanctuary of the Valley, D'arvan closed the ranks of trees behind them, concealing their passage and all signs of the carnage in the clearing. Maya was wiping her horn on the grass, cleansing Angos's blood from the sparkling weapon. She looked wistfully at the departing back of her dear old friend Hargorn, and gave a sad little whinny. D'arvan knew that she wanted to follow her former companions, and he knew how she felt. He laid a comforting arm across the unicorn's warm, gleaming back, wishing the men could see him – wishing that he could talk to them and tell them they were safe. He longed for companionship. The forest was proving a lonely place for its guardian, and it must be worse for Maya. 'Well, my love,' he said to the unicorn, 'Hellorin told us to shelter the enemies of the Archmage, and I can't think of anyone better than our old friends from the garrison. And others will come in time. It may not be much of an army yet, but at least we've made a start.'

It was dusk by the time the tree had been felled and stripped of its branches. Parric watched from the rainswept beach as it was towed to the crippled ship by rowing boats. 'Well, that's it,' Idris said. 'We'll be off now, Parric, and do our repairs as we go.' He looked heartily relieved to be leaving this desolate place.

'But surely you'll stay until the new mast is in place,' the cavalry master protested.

'Not a chance, mate. Take you to the south, Yanis said, and that was all. I'm not stopping here until the bloody Horselords come, thank you very much! From now on, you're on your own.' He spat into the sand. 'Besides, I've my crew to think about. I've never seen such storms at this time of year. No, I'm running for home, and grateful.'

'But you know these people . . .'

Idris raised his eyebrows in astonishment. 'Who told you that? We trade with the Khazalim, further south – we don't know this lot at all. Bunch of savages, or so I've heard!'

594

Parric took a deep breath, counted to ten, then, swearing a vile oath, he grabbed the smuggler captain by the throat. 'Then why the blazes didn't you take us to the Khazalim?' he grated.

Idris freed himself with a struggle and stepped back hastily, giving Parric a dirty look as he straightened his jerkin. 'Because,' he said, 'I'm not going any further south in this weather – and I'm not taking that bloody Mage another inch. She's been a pain in the arse all the way here, and she's nearly had the crew in mutiny, with her orders and complaints. Besides, her sort are bad luck – look at the storms we've had, if you doubt it. I'm sorry mate, but she's all yours – and I wish you luck with her.' With that, he got into the last boat. His men rowed away, fighting with the boiling surge of breakers, and leaving Parric fuming helplessly on the shore.

'Parric.' Sangra interrupted the cavalry master's heartfelt swearing. Taking his arm, she drew him away from the others. 'Cursing won't do you any good, love. We must get the supplies they left us under cover, and Elewin needs a fire. He's in a bad way.'

Parric nodded, knowing that she was right. During the unending misery of the storms, the old man had almost died from cold and seasickness, and Meiriel had refused to help him, haughtily insisting that it was not her business to waste her powers on Mortals.

They found an overhang – it was too shallow to be called a cave – among the rocks of the cove, and sent Meiriel and Elewin inside. Sangra began to haul the supplies into shelter, while Parric gathered driftwood. Looking at the sodden pile, he knew no Mortal could ever get it to light. And Elewin looked terrible. The steward huddled, racked with coughing, in the back of the shelter. Seeing his grey face and bloodless lips, Parric felt a pang of alarm. Remembering Aurian's talents, he suggested to the Mage that she use her magic to light the fire. Meiriel looked at him as though he were a cockroach. 'I can't do Fire-magic,' she declared. 'I'm a healer, not a Fire-Mage.'

Something snapped inside Parric. He leapt forward, seizing the Mage and twisting one arm up behind her back. With the other he drew his knife, laying the blade across the exposed white skin of her neck. 'If you're a bloody healer, then do your job,' he snapped. 'Heal Elewin now – or I'll slit your worthless throat!'

'Parric – don't move!' Sangra's quiet warning broke the tableau. The cavalry master glanced up to see several strangers blocking the entrance to the shelter. They were warriors – there was no doubt about that. Their rain-darkened hair was long on both men and women, tied back for battle in intricate braids. Though they were small of stature, there was wiry strength in their knotted muscles, witnessed by the great swords they carried. They were clad alike in jerkins and breeches of supple leather, and the men were clean-shaven. One of the women stepped forward, and spoke some words in a fluid, rolling tongue.

'That's torn it!' Parric muttered. 'I can't understand a word they say.' He felt his knife move against Meiriel's throat as the Magewoman laughed harshly.

'I can,' she shrilled triumphantly. 'She said put down your weapon, Parric. She said that we're their prisoners.'

37

Confronting the Spectre

The horse floundered, pitching Aurian forward and almost jolting her over its neck. She reacted quickly, throwing her weight back in the saddle as she pulled on the reins to help her stumbling mount regain its balance. Murmuring encouragement, she patted the neck of her weary stallion, grimacing as her hand came away coated in a layer of sweat and dust. Although the horse rallied bravely at the sound of her voice, she knew he was at the end of his strength. The Mage looked ahead, to where a line of distant mountain peaks marked the end of the desert, and cursed under her breath. They had travelled all night and dawn was breaking now, but those snow-bright pinnacles never seemed to draw any closer. Aurian wondered whether they had any hope of reaching safety before the horses dropped beneath them.

It was the third night of their journey from the final oasis and the companions had made the best speed they could, given the dreadful conditions of heat and thirst. They had been able to carry little water, and had been forced to travel at a slower pace than they would have liked, to conserve the strength of Shia and their mounts. There had been one consolation, however. The sky was covered by low, bulging swags of lurid yellow cloud that hid the sun and allowed them to travel during part of the day, although they were still forced to get under cover at midday, when the light was at its brightest. Unfortunately, Aurian thought, glancing up with a shudder at the ominous sky overhead, those clouds presaged the coming of the storms.

Almost as if the thought had spurred the treacherous elements to action, Aurian felt a breath of hot wind stir her robes. Her hands tightened unconsciously on the reins as she glanced across at Anvar. Though his face was hidden by the desert veils, she saw him tense with alarm in the growing light.

597

The wind was strengthening, driving the rolling clouds across the sky with ponderous speed and tattering their stacked towers to rags. Before the Mage's eyes, patches of clear sky began to show, forcing her to squint against the glare of the sands that brightened faster than the sunlight. Aurian bit her lip; fear like a fist clenched around her guts. It was already too windy for a shelter – thin skeins of glittering gem dust were snaking across the desert floor, threatening worse to come. 'Run!' She had no need of Anvar's warning cry. She spurred her horse forward, forcing her mount towards the safety of the desert's edge as fast as its weary legs would move.

It was not fast enough. About a league out from the edge of the desert the clouds thinned and cleared, and the blinding disc of the sun burst forth. Aurian clamped her hands over her eyes to shut out the agonizing glare as Shia's pain seared into her mind. The horses screamed, trying to rear and bolt blindly away from the source of their torment. The Mage wrestled with the reins, sightless and disorientated, trying desperately to control her maddened, plunging beast. She was pierced by terror that she must have lost Anvar, until his mount blundered into her own, almost unseating her. Wild with fear, the horses ran, keeping close to one another through herd instinct. Aurian hung on tightly, trying to keep mental contact with Shia, to guide her friend's blind flight. Through her link with the cat, she could sense Anvar doing the same, and prayed that they were fleeing in the right direction.

Then mercifully, miraculously, the white glare vanished, cut off as though it had never existed. The horses stumbled to a halt, their limbs trembling. The dazzling afterimages gradually cleared from Aurian's sight, and she saw Anvar close by, looking over his shoulder, transfixed with horror.

The hot wind tore in gusts at their clothes, whipping up stinging dust-devils of the sharp gem sand. And behind them, blowing up from the south and east and obscuring the sun, great dark clouds were rolling across the desert floor from horizon to horizon, gaining on them even as they watched. 'Sandstorm!' Aurian shrieked. 'Run!'

They ran. The horses, knowing instinctively what was behind them, put on a burst of speed that astonished the Mage.

Shia ran to one side, out of the way of the pounding hooves. With her life at stake, she could run. But how long could she keep up the gruelling pace? How long could any of them? Could they hope to outrun the wind itself?

Streamers of sand swirled around them, already beginning to tear at Aurian's robes; abrading the skin of her face as the sharp-edged dust worked its way beneath her veils. The pain acted as a spur to horses and riders, speeding their flight. Aurian caught glimpses of the way to safety ahead of her, appearing and vanishing in the far distance through the shifting curtains of sand – a steep cutting in a shallow cliff with trees growing at the top of it. Blessed, thickly planted trees; ragged and ravaged by the desert, but enough to shelter them from the force of the deadly storm. But they were too far away. As the wind ripped the shreds of her veils from her blood-streaked face and her nose and mouth filled with choking sand; even as she was forced to close her eyes on the vision of safety ahead; she knew it was too far. She could sense the gloating malice of the Weather-Mage behind the power of the storm, and she knew that Eliseth had won.

Anvar sensed, rather than saw, Aurian falter, and hauled on the reins with all his strength to pull up his crazed horse, looking wildly around for his friends. Of Shia there was no sign, and he could not touch her mind. Twisting in the saddle, he peered through shredded veils to see the Mage with her hands over her face to protect her eyes, using her knees to control the mount with the skill that was a hallmark of Parric's teaching. But this was no northern warhorse, trained to such methods, and he knew it was only a matter of time before the panic-stricken beast went berserk and pitched her off. Pain clouded his mind as gem dust scored his flesh through robes that were in ribbons, but Anvar could feel Eliseth's triumph, and it goaded him to a towering rage such as he had not felt since the night he snatched his powers from Miathan. Aurian was powerless to counter the attack – if anything could be done to defend them, it would have to come from him. Suddenly decisive, he leapt from his plunging horse and flung the reins at Aurian, forcing her to drop her scoured and bloody hands from her face in order to grab them. Ignoring her startled exclamation, he whetted his anger on the edge of his fear and, wielding it like a sword, he extended his consciousness as the Mage had taught him, flinging his power out into the face of the storm.

Peace. There was sudden, blessed stillness within the enchanted bubble of Anvar's shield, though the storm flung itself with increasing fury against the shimmering, translucent barrier that surrounded himself and his friends. He saw Aurian struggling with the frantic horses, her streaming eyes fixed on him in astonishment. The ground heaved nearby as Shia emerged, shaking gem dust from her coat in a glittering shower and sneezing violently. The cat had had the sense to lie down and bury herself, so that the sands had given her some protection from their own cutting force. That was all that Anvar had time to glimpse before Eliseth flung the focus of her power at him in frustrated fury, sensing his magic from afar.

His shield shattered from the force of her blow, and the storm was upon them once more. Grimly, Anvar closed with Eliseth, his consciousness straining to confront the core of her will. He felt her recoil in shock at the identity of her assailant, and used her hesitation to reassert his power, driving the storm away from his friends. Eliseth struck back like a viper, but this time he was expecting her, and his shield wavered but held. Their battle settled down into deadly earnest as they waged a desperate struggle, their wills locked and stalemated: Eliseth unable to pierce his shield, and Anvar forced into a position of defence, too occupied with maintaining his frail barrier to strike at her. The air around the shield crackled and hummed, glowing now red, now blue, with the stresses of the magical battle, and erupting into showers of piercing white sparks.

Anvar lost all track of time as the deadly battle continued. Though minutes or hours might have passed, it felt as though he had been locked for ever in this endless combat, and as Eliseth's malice sapped his strength he felt himself beginning to tire. He was new at this game, unused to fighting with magic, but he gritted his teeth and held on, though his face contorted with the strain and his knees were buckling beneath the relentless force of Eliseth's will. If he should falter now, they would be lost.

The hand shaking urgently at his arm was an unwelcome

break in his concentration. Anvar's shield wavered, sagging ominously inwards beneath the force of the storm. Aurian was yelling into his ear, her voice shrill with strain as she fought to attract his attention. 'Drop your shield, Anvar! Drop it and strike, while you still have the strength!'

He shook his head despairingly. 'It's too late!'

Aurian muttered a savage oath. 'Here – use this!' She thrust something into his hand. Anvar felt a tingling surge flood through his body, coursing along his veins like liquid light. The Staff of Earth! Struggling to focus its unruly new power, he dropped his shield and struck.

He had failed – he knew instantly. Air and Water, the elements of Weather-magic, were foreign to the Staff, and so its power was limited. Anvar, inexperienced as he was, used it clumsily, without the deadly precision that Aurian might have commanded. The focus of his power was weak and un-coordinated, dissipating before it reached its target to leave them exposed to attack.

'Dead and buried, Anvar! Flayed, dead, and buried without trace!' Eliseth's shrieking laughter mocked the Mage as she lashed back at him with the full force of the storm. He dropped to his knees, bleeding and choking, mauled by the gnawing teeth of the dust.

A hand – groping – catching at his sleeve ... It found Anvar's wrist, then his hand that still clutched the Staff. The hand clasped on his own, tightening his fingers round the serpent-carved wood. Then, like a benison, came the touch of Aurian's mind – not an intrusion, but a tentative questing – a touch more gentle, more intimate, than any physical caress. Though the Mage had lost her power, their minds had been linked through the power of the Staff, which he had carved, and she had imbued with magic. Ah, such closeness! Anvar knew, without question, what Aurian sought. Gladly, trustingly, he surrendered his powers to her, holding them out for her, putting them into her hands.

'Now!' Anvar never knew whether he cried the word aloud, or simply into his mind. She snatched his magic, wove it into the Staff's power, and forged it into a shield. Such was the force of her act that the sand underfoot was blasted away from

601

them, leaving them kneeling in a shallow crater as the storm's fury ceased once more.

Far away in Nexis, Eliseth staggered backwards as her magic rebounded against a solid wall of power, recoiling against her like a physical blow. The building shook as though in the grip of an earthquake and she was spun across the floor of the weather-dome, colliding with the great map table and striking her head as she fell.

'Eliseth! What's happening? I could feel the magic clear inside the Mages' Tower.' It was Bragar. He lifted the dazed Weather-Mage to her feet, his shield springing up to form a fiery wall around them both, protecting her from the vicious backlash of magic. For once, Eliseth was genuinely glad to see him.

'Aurian!' she gasped. 'She attacked me!' Bragar must not discover that she was disobeying Miathan's orders – he was too craven to join such an overt rebellion, and she needed his help.

'What? But how?' Bragar wore his usual expression of perplexity. 'The Archmage said she'd lost her powers . . .'

'He was wrong!' Eliseth was already gathering her scattered thoughts into the beginnings of a new plan. Anvar she could defeat, but he and Aurian together were too much. But if she could sunder them . . . And there was a way, she knew: one weak link in Aurian's defences that had always existed. But Eliseth was not prepared to risk exposing herself again to the power of the two renegades. Not when she had poor malleable Bragar to do it for her. Turning to the Fire-Mage, Eliseth gave him her most seductive smile. 'I'm sorry, Bragar – I didn't mean to snap. I'm so glad you've come, for only you can help me now.'

'Don't worry, Eliseth – I'll protect you,' Bragar cried. Gods, he was so simple! Chuckling inwardly, the Magewoman quickly outlined her plan.

'I'm ready,' Bragar said. The Weather-Mage looked with satisfaction at the sturdy, flaming barrier that he was maintaining with all his strength. If her ruse should fail, then she, at least, should be protected from the consequences. Sheltered safely behind the shields of Bragar's magic, Eliseth turned her will back to Aurian and began to weave an illusion, and an irresistible lure.

The minds of Aurian and Anvar were still linked through their clasped hands upon the Staff. There was comfort in their touch, and strength. Aurian, not daring to let go even for a second, used her free hand to wipe the blood and sand from her face. Beyond their shield, the storm still ravened, though its impetus had slackened now.

'We didn't finish her, did we?' Anvar's thought came into the Mage's mind as clearly as if he had spoken aloud.

'No.' Aurian replied. 'We shook her – but she'll be back.'

In wordless communion, they reviewed their options. Should they risk dropping the shield to strike at Eliseth before she could recover herself, or try to maintain it for the length of time it would take them to reach the desert's edge? It would be a long walk – their horses were gone, and would certainly be dead by now. It was Shia who settled the matter. The great cat huddled flat to the ground with her paws over her eyes, unable to function beneath the onslaught of the magic that existed within their shield. She would never make it, Aurian knew. She looked at Anvar, knowing that in that moment they reached a decision, their minds in total harmony. They would fight.

Aurian rose unsteadily to her feet, still clutching tightly to Anvar's hand that held the Staff. Once more she took up his raw power, and that of the Staff of Earth, combining them with the skilled force of her will and feeling buoyed and strengthened by the closeness of his touch. Abandoning the shield, she gathered herself . . .

And froze. Through the drifting curtains of dust, a figure came walking – the familiar, spectral shape of her lost love. Forral was calling. Spellbound by the apparition, Aurian let go of Anvar, taking her hand from the Staff and sundering their link. Unaware that she had left the others at the mercy of the storm, she moved like a sleepwalker towards the spectre of the murdered warrior. Shielding her eyes with her hands from the stinging sand and peering between her fingers through its whiplash skeins she saw him moving just beyond her reach as he had in Dhiammara; beckoning to her to follow him into the teeth of the storm. 'Forral.' The word was little more than a whisper. The Mage took a faltering step forward, then another . . .

Aurian felt, rather than saw, that Anvar had restored the shield. As the sand around her dropped and settled, he came from behind her with an inarticulate curse. A rough hand grabbed her shoulder, pulling her back, and he barged past her, blocking her view of Forral's ghostly form. 'No! You can't have her!'

'Let me go!' Aurian shrieked. 'Forral – wait!' As she struggled with Anvar, the shield faltered once more, then held, but though he was burdened by the need to keep up their only defence he still held her back.

'You had your chance!' he shouted at the spectre. 'Aurian belongs with the living! Get away from here! Leave us alone!'

'Aurian, *no!*' Shia's mental voice was filled with anguish. From the corner of her eye, the Mage saw the great cat struggling desperately to rise and falling back, defeated. But caught as she was in the lure of Eliseth's spell, even this failed to move her.

'Let go, damn you!' she spat at Anvar. She lashed out, striking him across the face. Anvar caught her wrist, so tightly that Aurian gasped with pain. The side of his face was branded with the mark of her hand and his expression was tight with misery, but his eyes burned.

'That's the second time you've hit me for saving your life. I thought we'd finished with that nonsense.'

'You don't understand!' Aurian yelled. 'I love him!'

'I don't understand?' Anvar's face was twisted into a tortured mask with the strain of fighting a battle on two fronts; maintaining his shield on the one hand, while struggling to restrain the Mage. 'Forral is dead,' he told her brutally. Aurian flinched, hating him in that moment, but his fingers were locked about her wrist, preventing her escape as he smote her with the unbearable, implacable truth. 'He's dead, you fool, but you're alive – and so is your babe. You have no right to rob it of its chance for life. This is absolutely wrong, and you know it.' Anvar looked straight into her eyes. 'I understand because I love you – and if I were in Forral's position, I'd love you too much to want to kill you and our child.'

His bluntness struck Aurian as though he had returned her blow. Unable to deny his words, she could only return hurt for hurt. 'That's what this is about, isn't it?' she retorted bitterly. 'You want me for yourself – that's all you care about. Well, I don't love you, Anvar. I hate you! Whatever happens, I'll never love you as long as I live!'

Aurian's words reverberated in the shocked silence between them. Anvar flinched as though she had dealt him a mortal blow, and then, with a curse, he let go of her wrist, almost hurling her away from him. 'Go then, if it'll make you happy. Follow your precious Forral into death. Kill your child, if it means nothing to you. Run away from your responsibilities and abandon your friends.' He turned away as if in scorn, but Aurian saw his slumped and shaking shoulders, and knew that he was weeping. She looked yearningly at the beckoning shade of Forral, but his face was suddenly eclipsed by a vision of Anvar – the hurt in his blue eyes, the ugly mark on his face where she had struck him. Aurian suddenly knew that if she followed Forral into death, she would miss that face, and Anvar's loving and loyal presence, beyond all bearing. But she loved Forral. To choose another over him would be an appalling betrayal.

Yet Aurian wavered, unable to take that last, crucial step. She knew that Anvar loved her, and if she went with Forral he would go through the same anguish as she had felt when the swordsman died. When she had saved Anvar's life in the slave compound, their very souls had touched. He had clung to her hand, then, as though she was his only anchor on life. Sara had already betrayed him – how could she do the same? Surely, after all they had been through together, she owed him more than that.

Tears flooded Aurian's face. It felt as if she was tearing out her own heart, but she straightened her shoulders and faced the shade of Forral squarely. 'I'm sorry!' she cried. 'I can't! I can't come with you!' As her anguished cry tore the air, the spirit-shape flickered and vanished.

Aurian sank down in the sand, undone by her grief, but only for a moment. She had no time to weep. Suddenly the Mage felt a new strength flooding into her – a sense of freedom and a new maturity. She had made her choice. Life over death – the future rather than the past – and whatever that future might hold, she was committed to it now. 'Get up, damn you,' she told herself firmly. 'Anvar needs you.'

Anvar had turned his back on Aurian, unable to watch her go to her own death. Though his vision was blurred with tears, he held firmly to the Staff, still using its power as a shield against Eliseth's venom. He tried not to think of what was happening behind him, knowing that he needed to concentrate on his defence against the storm, but his heart betrayed him. In his mind's eye, he saw how it would end. Aurian would penetrate his shield and walk out into the storm, embracing her death in her foolish pursuit of a vanished dream. There would be nothing left of her. The sand would strip her to the bone.

The Mage fought to master his anguish, but his will was weakening. If Aurian hated him, what was the point of continuing the battle? It would be so easy just to throw the Staff away, to drop his shield and walk after her, following her beyond this last boundary, as he had followed her for so long. As he finally abandoned all hope, the Staff fell from Anvar's fingers . . .

And was caught by a hand that seemed to come out of nowhere – a strong, capable hand, square-palmed, long-fingered, nicked with the old white scars of many battles. A hand that could bestow either death or healing.

Joy engulfed Anvar like a soundless explosion of light. Aurian's face was tearstained and grim, haggard and haunted, but she faced him squarely, her chin lifted in that old determined gesture that he knew so well. Rejoicing, Anvar put his hand on hers, and felt an answering jolt of power as their wills combined with the might of the Staff.

'Now we get the bitch!' Aurian's tight, swift grin was conspiratorial, and, through tears of relief, Anvar found himself grinning back as he offered up his powers once more. Aurian seized them, dropped the shield, and struck.

Their blow was impelled by a new strength, their wills a mighty weapon forged from shared pain and a new sense of purpose in Aurian's mind. With the power of the Staff, it was enough. As their blow struck its target, Anvar felt a distant echo of the agony that marked the death of a Mage. His shield brightened and blazed, a sure protection now against the lethal gem sand, but there was no need for it. The storm had vanished. Overhead, stars were shimmering in a clear sky that was washed in the west by the glory of sunset. Anvar looked up, amazed. Hours had passed in their struggle and the battle had lasted a whole day – but it was over at last.

Miathan had been away from his body in trance, resting for the night ahead, when he would perform further acts of sacrifice to increase his power. He would be spending a great deal of time away from his body in the weeks to come, occupying the form of his new southern pawn while he set in motion the forces that would result in Aurian's capture. Confident in his own authority, he had never realized that Eliseth might seek to thwart his plans.

The final attack on Eliseth brought the Archmage sharply back to himself, jerking him abruptly into his body as the bed began to shake beneath him. Disorientated by the sudden transition back to corporeality, he staggered to his feet, stumbling as the floor beneath him shuddered and lurched. With a deafening bang, an explosion of blinding light in the courtyard outside shattered the casements of his room, showering him with glass. His ears ringing, Miathan brushed off splinters and made his way cautiously to the window. The curtains blew wildly, shredded to smoking tatters. He brushed them aside to peer out, and gasped, aghast at the devastation. This was impossible! What had happened while he'd been out of his body?

The courtyard was choked with drifts of glittering sand, and the Archmage had to fight his way through to the blackened shell of the shattered dome. Clawing his way through the smoking rubble, he finally reached the ruined inner chamber, and saw Eliseth kneeling over a black and twisted corpse: the scarcely recognizable remains of Bragar. The stench of charred flesh filled the room, and the Archmage fought down a wave of nausea.

'Aurian,' Eliseth whispered. She was shaken but unscarred. Bragar had taken the full force of the blast, sacrificing himself in order to shield her. How had she duped the witless fool into that? Miathan wondered, then put aside all thoughts of the hapless Fire-Mage. Bragar had always been an idiot. But it was clear that Eliseth had deliberately disobeyed him, and made an attempt on Aurian's life. Shaking with rage, Miathan turned his menacing jewelled glare upon the cringing Weather-Mage. Slowly, he advanced upon her, his fists clenched at his side with rage.

'What have you done?' he snarled. '*What have you done?*'

Aurian dropped the Staff and fell to her knees, trembling with exhaustion and the aftershock of magic. Anvar sank down beside her. 'We did it,' he murmured, still unable to believe it. 'We killed her.'

Aurian nodded. 'I felt a death-pang,' she whispered. Her face was bloodless, and Anvar caught her as she began to sway. 'I'm all right,' she muttered – her automatic response – but she was trembling violently as she lifted her stricken face to look at him. 'Anvar, I . . .'

'Aurian, after what you've just been through – after all the dreadful things I said to you – don't you dare apologize to me,' Anvar scolded gently.

'But I . . .' Aurian's voice was choked off in a torrent of racking sobs.

'Ah, love.' Anvar gathered her into his arms, stroking her hair as she wept. 'My dear, brave Lady.' The magnitude of Aurian's decision filled him with awe. She had been forced into a cruel choice – an impossible choice – yet she had made it with courage; and, if he knew the Mage, with complete honesty. And having made her decision, she would stick to it. Even as he comforted her, Anvar felt a crushing weight of worry lift from his heart. Ever since the night of their escape from Nexis, when she had railed at him for saving her life, he had been haunted by the fear that she would choose that road in the end – would leave him to follow her lover into death. But now the fatal crossroad had been reached, and the crisis safely passed. Aurian had chosen life over death – had elected to stay with him, rather than follow Forral.

Though he grieved for Aurian's grief, Anvar's spirits lifted like a joyous burst of song. Oh, they had a long road ahead, to be sure. It was only a beginning – Forral had barely been dead for half a year, and Aurian would mourn him for some time to come. She would continue to fight against loving someone else with all the strength of her stubborn nature. None the less, this was one battle that Anvar intended to win – and now he possessed the strength and determination to match her own indomitable will.

Anvar smiled to himself. My dearest Lady, he thought, how much I owe you! First you made a Mage of me, and now you've turned me into a warrior too. And some day I'll pay you back, I promise – by making you happy again. Anvar tightened his arms around the weeping Mage. 'Do you know what I would do if we were back in Nexis?' he murmured. 'I'd take you around every tavern in the city and get you more drunk than you've ever been in your life!'

Aurian looked up at him gratefully, swallowing hard, struggling to find her voice. 'It's a long way back to Nexis,' she said at last.

'We'll do it,' Anvar assured her. 'And who knows – maybe we'll find you a few taverns along the way!'

'If we do, I'll definitely take you up on your offer,' Aurian said ruefully. Anvar was pleased to see the flash of her old spirit beginning to return. In her old, automatic gesture, she wiped her face on her sleeve, and he gave a mock-sigh.

'You know,' he teased, 'I don't think I'll ever break you of that revolting habit.' Aurian glared at him, on the verge of a scathing retort, and Anvar chuckled.

'Why you . . .' she snarled, but her lips began to twitch in a smile, and suddenly she threw her arms around him, hugging him hard. 'Dear Anvar,' she murmured. 'Thank you.'

Shia, forgotten in the heat of battle, crept up to them, laying her head in Aurian's lap. 'You won a brave victory, my friend. I'm glad you stayed,' Anvar heard her say.

'We both are,' he added softly.

'My friends,' Aurian whispered, and reached out to caress the cat. She looked at Shia, then at Anvar and took a deep breath. 'You know,' she said slowly, 'in spite of everything, I'm glad I stayed, too.'

Aurian's hair was wildly tangled and full of sand; her face was filthy, tearstreaked and abraded by the glittering dust; her clothes were a mass of rags – but to Anvar, as he held her in his arms, she had never been more beautiful. There was so much, in that moment, that he wanted to say to her, but that could wait for the future – the future that Aurian, whether she knew it or not, had granted him at last.

As dawn began to glimmer over the jewelled sands, Aurian looked up from her trudging feet to find that they had finally reached the end of the desert. Slowed by weariness, the Mages and Shia had walked all night, praying that they would reach safety before the sun rose. Though Aurian was footsore and tired, though her spirits were shadowed by a lingering sadness, her heart felt strangely light. I'm sorry, Forral, she thought, but I couldn't come with you, not yet. I didn't believe you when you said it would be wrong to throw my life away in grief, but you were right, my love. You were right. There is more to life than sorrow and revenge. There is friendship, and hope, and new life to follow death – and maybe, if fate is kind, I'll live to see your son take his own place in the world.

Aurian halted abruptly, reeling with astonishment. Son? she thought. How do I know it's a boy? But, she realized, she did. For certain. Stunned, she turned her thoughts inward, to feel not just a spark of life, but a mind. A tiny, unformed child-mind, but the mind of a person none the less: her son. For the first time, he knew her – recognized her – and his small, barely focused thoughts reached out to her trustingly, and with the uttermost love.

'Anvar!' Aurian shrieked. Her thoughts were awhirl with an uncontainable excitement that simply had to be shared with her dearest friend. He turned back to her, and Aurian closed the space between them as though she, like Raven, were winged. She hugged him tightly, laughing at his startled expression, her words tumbling over one another in her anxiety to communicate the good news. 'Anvar, it's a son! I felt him! He *knows* me! I – he *loves* me, Anvar!'

'You did? I mean, he is – he *does*? Oh, Aurian!' Anvar swung her around until she was giddy, his blue eyes bright, his face transfigured with joy. And suddenly, as if joining their celebration, a glad cry rang out from the rise above them, where the edge of the forest met the desert. Blinking back happy tears, Aurian looked up to see Yazour, with his arms about Eliizar and Nereni. Beside them was the vast, familiar form of Bohan, his face split in a happy grin as Shia bounded up the steep cutting to meet him. Aurian and Anvar looked at each other.

'Thank you, Anvar, for making me stay,' Aurian said softly. In answer, he smiled – that rare, wonderful smile that had always had the power to touch her heart. Aurian reached out to him, and he took her hand. Together, they went to greet their friends.

Miathan, brooding in his tower, flung his crystal away with a snarling curse, wishing that he had never decided to spy on Aurian just then. How dare she be happy! How dare she rejoice in that accursed swordsman's bastard brat! And with the other abominable half-breed, of his own conceiving! Well, he'd have his revenge on them yet. 'Let's see you rejoice, Aurian, when you give birth to that monster you're carrying,' he muttered. 'By the time I've finished with you, only the thought of death will make you rejoice!'

Still muttering darkly, the Archmage went to retrieve the crystal, which had rolled into the fireplace, chipping and scarring the marble hearth. All was not yet lost, he consoled himself. He still had a weapon or two in his armoury, and Eliseth's rebellion had not interfered too badly with his plans. His revenge would be all the sweeter for waiting – and this time, he would not fail!

HARP OF WINDS

Book Two of the Artefacts of Power

Maggie Furey

There had been four Artefacts of Power, belonging to the
four branches of the Magefolk. Now, millennia later, only
the human Mages survived, and the Artefacts were lost.
Until the coming of Aurian . . .

Child of wizards, swordmistress, the headstrong Aurian had
set her power against that of Miathan, the evil Archmage.
Whilst he possessed the Cauldron of Rebirth, Aurian had
recreated the Staff of Earth, the first of the three lost
weapons, the only defence against Miathan's plans of
conquest. Trapped in the Southern Lands, her powers reft
by pregnancy, Aurian must rely on the untried powers of
the half-blood Mage Anvar as their odyssey takes them to
the realm of the mysterious Xandim, to the peaktop city of
the Skyfolk, and to the worlds beyond. But Miathan's webs
of deceit are only just beginning to unfurl . . .

Harp of Winds is the second book in an epic tale of war and
magic which will appeal to all fans of Terry Brooks,
David Eddings and Tad Williams.

THE SWORD OF FLAME

Book Three of the Artefacts of Power

Maggie Furey

Though Aurian and her fellow Mage, Anvar, have escaped
the clutches of the dread Archmage, they have yet to lift the
curse on Aurian's child, and put an end to Miathan's evil.
Only the Sword of Flame, last and greatest of the
Artefacts of Power, can help them – but the Sword is
hidden. Meanwhile, Death awaits his third and final
meeting with the pair . . .

As the Mages set out once more, the world stands poised on
the brink of conflict. Miathan is fortifying the city of Nexis
and, in the south, the fierce Khazalim are arming for war.
The Skyfolk have abandoned their long isolation and the
Xandim prepare for their last great ride. Both the
Leviathans and the Phaerie have decisions to make which
will change their existence for ever. The future stands
balanced on a knife-edge between hope and destruction.
All await the coming of the Sword of Flame – and Aurian.

DHIAMMARA

Book Four of the Artefacts of Power

Maggie Furey

Aurian faces bitter defeat. She has failed to master the
Sword of Flame, her only defence against the forces of evil.
But she has also unleashed the deadly, unpredictable
Phaerie upon the world, and the end of that is unknowable.
And now she must journey through time itself . . .

Eliseth, the coldly ambitious Mage who has been Aurian's
nemesis since her first days in Nexis, has captured both the
Sword of Flame and Anvar, Aurian's soul-mate. Now,
Aurian and a few allies travel into an uncertain future.

Knowing she must defeat Eliseth, who controls the
Cauldron of Rebirth, without destroying the world, Aurian
is faced by many dilemmas before she finally reaches the
ancient Dragon City of Dhiammara. There, in the home of
the extinct fire lizards, a final conflict will take place, in
which Aurian must triumph or die.

In the fourth and final volume of the bestselling Artefacts of
Power series, Maggie Furey brilliantly brings together the
many threads which she has spun in her previous books.

THE HEART OF MYRIAL

Book One of The Shadowleague

Maggie Furey

The magical barriers that have held the world together for aeons are beginning to fail. But this is far more than just a natural disaster. For the boundaries have also served to keep hostile nations apart.

Catastrophe is imminent, and the only hope of salvation lies in the hands of the Shadowleague and its emissaires, in particular the Loremaster Veldan and her firedrake Kazairl. The next few days will change their future and threaten to tear the Shadowleaguer apart.

Maggie Furey's epic storytelling skills, her enthralling magical worlds and her dynamic and irresistible characters have caught the imagination of readers everywhere.

'Rich, colourful, infinitely enchanting' David Gemmell

'One of the few truly compelling fantasy sagas of recent years' *SFX*

SPIRIT OF THE STONE

Book Two of The Shadowleague

Maggie Furey

Maggie Furey's spellbinding fantasy in the magical world of
Myrial continues . . .

As the curtain Walls across Myrial continue to fail, the
threat of war grows ever greater. But the Shadowleague, the
council responsible for peace and order, is beginning to tear
itself apart. If this occurs, any hope of avoiding the
deepening crisis will be destroyed.

To prevent catastrophe Loremaster Veldan, the firedrake
Kazairl and their companions must travel down a dark and
dangerous road. One that will lead them beneath the
beleaguered city of Tiarond, deep within the mountain's
living core where the secrets of the past lie buried.

ICE MAGE

Julia Gray

'A spellbinding new storyteller' *Maggie Furey*

The remote and wild land of Tiguafaya is on the edge
of chaos. The menacing volcanoes that dominate the
landscape grumble and threaten destruction.
Repulsive fireworms, marauding pirates and ancient
dragons grow bolder every day. And the corrupt and
ineffectual government can do nothing.

The only hope for survival lies with a group of young rebels
known as the Firebrands. Led by the lovers Andrin and Ico,
and the half-mad musician Vargo, the Firebrands are
desperately fighting back. Using the once-revered but now
lost arts of magic against the overwhelming odds, they are
all that stand between Tiguafaya and total devastation.

Rich and exciting, powerful and engrossing, *Ice Mage* marks
the arrival of a thrilling new voice in fantasy adventure.

Orbit titles available by post:

☐	Harp of Winds	Maggie Furey	£6.99
☐	The Sword of Flame	Maggie Furey	£6.99
☐	Dhiammara	Maggie Furey	£6.99
☐	The Heart of Myrial	Maggie Furey	£6.99
☐	Spirit of the Stone	Maggie Furey	£6.99
☐	Ice Mage	Julia Gray	£6.99

The prices shown above are correct at time of going to press. However the publishers reserve the right to increase prices on covers from those previously advertised, without further notice.

ORBIT BOOKS
Cash Sales Department, P.O. Box 11, Falmouth, Cornwall, TR10 9EN
Tel: +44(0) 1326 569777. Fax +44 (0) 1326 569555
Email: books@barni.avel.co.uk

POST and PACKAGING:
Payments can be made as follows: cheque, postal order (payable to Orbit Books) or by credit cards. Do not send cash or currency.

U.K. Orders under £10	£1.50
U.K. Orders over £10	FREE OF CHARGE
E.E.C. & Overseas	25% of order value

Name (Block Letters) _____

Address _____

_____

Post/zip code: _____

☐ Please keep me in touch with future Orbit publications

☐ I enclose my remittance £ _____

☐ I wish to pay by Visa/Access/Mastercard/Eurocard

Card Expiry Date

_____